MAGMA HEART

MAGMA HEART

VICTOR OF TUCSON ✝ BOOK 6

PLUM PARROT

Podium

Podium

MAGMA HEART

1

ROCKFALL

Guapo's hooves echoed hollowly on the wide wooden archway of the bridge as Victor rode his spirit steed toward the center of the expanse. The river below rushed and rumbled as it coursed over the massive granite boulders that dotted its bed, and as a gust of powerful chilly wind rushed over him, Victor shuddered at the idea of falling into those white-capped waters. He urged Guapo to stop as he reached the apex, and then, with a clear view ahead, he studied the jagged enormous peaks of the Granite Gates.

Even at this distance, they were awe-inspiring. He could see how those who'd named them had thought of them as gates—at this distance, the range was like a gray wall blocking off one part of the world from another, with the two peaks directly ahead standing shoulder to shoulder, separated by a narrow canyon. He could imagine them shifting slightly and closing off the passage. Even with a few days' travel's worth of distance between him and the mountains, they were gigantic, seeming to stretch up into the sky, their sharp peaks scraping the border between sky and stars.

Beyond the bridge was a small hamlet, ringed with a high stone wall. The cobbled road continued past the walled village and turned to gray gravel as it passed between the first two peaks, smoothly rising until it wended behind the shoulder of the one on the right. It *seemed* smooth, at least, a gentle grade up to those high gray mountains, but Victor knew it was deceptive; they were still fifty miles or more from the first of the foothills, so the distance hid all the ripples in the land's contours. More than that, the two foremost gigantic mountains hid the dozens lined up behind them. His army would be marching through that gap for several days.

Borrius told him the town was called, aptly, Rockfall, and the people there were primarily employed in the imperial granite quarry at the mouth of the pass. He could see activity on the road and outside the town; it looked like wagons heading in through the gate, not out, which made sense—it would be dark in the next hour or so. Victor turned, Guapo stepping lithely, rotating, sensing his desire.

Far down the road, looking much like a row of insects in the distance, Victor's army was approaching. A column of soldiers was flanked by two narrower columns of cavalry, and behind them, like beetles following ants, were the wagons, moving through the dust stirred up by the mounted soldiers. It was an impressive sight—their numbers had swelled as they advanced over the hills and plains at the southeastern edge of the Ridonne Empire. The last count Victor had read showed that their ten cohorts were back to full strength and then some.

Borrius hadn't created a new cohort, though they had the numbers to support nearly two more. He wanted them overfull, wanted them resilient to losses. After all, if things went as expected, they'd be fighting soon. Victor was ready for it. He'd been ready for a fight ever since the Empire had tried to crush their army before their campaign even got started. The Ridonne hadn't been eager to test his wrath, though. They'd not made a peep, not shown a single imperial soldier to Victor's scouts.

Even the towns and villages they'd passed through were deserted of imperial officials. Word traveled fast, and adjudicators, soldiers, and other representatives of the Empire seemed to flee ahead of the army's arrival. Victor was fine with that. He figured the town down the road would be similarly bereft of imperials, though they'd probably slink back home after the army passed through. For all he knew, they simply doffed their imperial garb and hid among their friends and family. He turned and looked back at the mountains.

They were impressive, no doubt. Much higher, sharper, and ominous than the ones they'd skirted around the Starfall Sea. Much, much bigger than anything he'd seen around Tucson. Rellia and Borrius were nervous about passing through them—something about "wild folk" and rock trolls. Victor wasn't worried. If something terrible attacked them, he'd deal with it, and if it was just a tribe of monsters tossing rocks down on them, the army would endure. He clicked his tongue, and Guapo started forward, walking with the drum of hooves on hollow boards toward the bridge's far side.

He'd charged ahead of the army, wanting a bit of peace, some time to himself. Nobody tried to keep pace with Guapo, and the other commanders had grown accustomed to him ranging forth. While good for such a considerable force, the army's pace was mind-numbingly slow to Victor, and if it weren't for his daily sprints on the mustang, he'd probably have gone mad. Weeks of travel weren't his cup of tea, and the passage over these mountains couldn't be over soon enough as far as he was concerned.

He paused at the far side of the bridge, breathing in the fresh cool air, examining the well-traveled road and the sparse plains between the river and the hamlet. He figured they should march the army a few miles beyond the settlement and set camp for the night. They'd push on toward the pass early in the morning. "No sense lingering around the town, making everybody nervous, eh, boy?" He scratched Guapo's neck.

Looking up, he saw three figures riding out of the hamlet toward him. They rode animals that looked similar to vidanii, though they were stouter and shaggier, and their horns were thicker and swept backward in a curl, kind of like a ram's on Earth. As they grew nearer, Victor saw they were all Ardeni. They all wore mismatched armor, though some of it looked well made. The one in the middle was a bit older, a bit stockier, and carried two crescent-moon axes hanging from his belt. The others both had bows on their backs and had various weapons strapped to their saddles, from javelins to a fur-wrapped great sword.

Victor had begun to grow used to such sights—adventurers and fortune seekers coming to join the expedition. They made up a sizeable percentage of the new recruits they'd picked up along the march. The trio brought their mounts to a halt a good fifty yards from Victor, and the bigger one cleared his throat. "Well met, sir."

"Hello." Victor sat still, his hands folded on the muscular mound of Guapo's shoulders. Lifedrinker buzzed eagerly on his back, perhaps trying to urge him to leap into battle simply because three armed men stood before him. He grinned at her eagerness; he could relate.

"Are you him? Victor?" the same man asked, eyeing Victor through wide, silver-blue eyes.

"Of course he is, Thed. You ever seen another like him? Or that beast he's riding." The second speaker was on Thed's left, and he clicked his tongue, urging his sturdy mount forward a couple of steps. "We was surprised to see you come over the bridge so soon—word is your army's still a few hours out."

"I'm Victor. What can I do for you, fellas?"

"We," Thed said, nudging his mount's side with his heels, moving it forward so he was once again in the lead, "were wanting to join up with ya. We heard tell of your expedition some weeks back and rode like a banshee-chased boyii to get here ahead of you all. We made it with some time to spare; spent near a week at the tavern over yonder." He gestured back toward the walled hamlet. "Can't say I could stomach another pot of the stew the innkeep makes. What do you say, sir? Are you recruiting?"

"Well, boys," Victor said, smirking inwardly as he considered the very real possibility that these three men were more than twice his age, "we can always use some tough *pendejos* in the army. What tier are you three?" Sensing his desire, Guapo started forward so Victor could better size the men up.

"We're all Tier Four, sir; been making our fortune testing the dungeons out near the Free Cities."

"Fourth tier, huh? That's good." Victor nodded, rubbing his chin, looking farther and farther down his nose at the three men as he and his big mustang grew closer. He stopped when he was only a few feet away, and the men's faces had lost a shade of blue, growing pale as they watched him loom over them; he wasn't even in his titanic aspect. Still, he let just a fraction of his aura start to bleed out, touching the three adventurers, and watched to see if they flinched or, worse, fled. To his surprise, they held up all right, only tightening their grips on their reins and grimacing as they fought to control their mounts.

He grunted and pulled back his aura, nodding. "Good. All right, head up the road to the army. When the scouts stop you, tell them I sent you to speak to Sarl, the captain of the Glorious Ninth. You've got a lot of work to do to earn one of their armbands, but if you work hard and fight bravely, you'll find yourselves surrounded by the best soldiers in the legion."

The three men babbled their thanks, speaking over each other to profess their gratitude, and then they urged their mounts around him, cantering over the bridge in a noisy rumble. Victor grinned, always pleased to see more strong recruits joining the ranks. He'd just turned back toward the mountains when he heard a thunderous roar echoing through the air, reverberating over the wooden bridge. "Uvu," he chuckled.

A few moments later, he felt more than he heard Uvu pad over the wooden planks and then stir some gravel nearby. "Hey, Valla." He didn't turn to watch her approach.

"Getting better at noticing people coming up behind you?"

"Not hard when Uvu's scaring the shit out of some poor adventurers."

"They didn't react nearly as badly as the last ones who came along." Valla and Uvu stopped on his left side, and she smiled up at him in greeting. Victor felt his heart racing as he looked down at her, saw those big teal eyes, and basked in the brightness of her smile. She really didn't smile often, and he felt as if it made the few she threw out every day a lot more meaningful. He supposed there was a lesson in there for him—something about swearing too much, perhaps.

He wanted to tell her how beautiful she looked to him at that moment, with the reddish-orange sunset lighting her eyes and face with a sort of golden glow. He'd tried that, though, and when he was blunt about his attraction, it seemed to chase her off, make her withdraw a bit. He'd found that if he just played it cool and made himself available, she was apt to show him a little affection, hinting at the heat they'd shared the night of the battle with the imperials. She definitely wasn't ready for an open romantic relationship, but he felt as though slow and steady might win the race. He hoped. The truth was, Victor had no damn idea if he was doing things right—maybe he should be more forward. On a whim, he said, "Your eyes look pretty in this light."

"Is that any way to speak to your primus?" Her voice was scolding, but her eyes were laughing.

"Yeah, when she's got eyes like polished turquoise, and the sunset makes 'em look like they were dipped in gold . . ."

"All right, enough, Sir Legate." She chuckled and, as some color flooded her cheeks, turned toward the hamlet. "We'll push past before camping?"

"Yeah, I think that's for the best. No sense panicking the locals."

"Agreed. Imagine how it would look if we encamped outside their walls. The children would be terrified. Let's march five miles or so past the walls. The moons will be out tonight, and the soldiers are sturdy. I know you're eager to get through the pass in any case."

"Damn right. I know this is important, and the rewards will be worthwhile, at least for everyone back there." He jerked his thumb toward the army. "But I'm ready to do something else for a while. I've been talking to Khul Bach, and the old bastard still doesn't think I'm anywhere near ready to do what he wants me to do on Zaafor. I think we need to find a place to adventure when we're done here. A world that'll challenge us and where we can learn ways to push ourselves into new improvements." He frowned momentarily, reaching down to tug her chin toward him so their eyes locked. "You're coming with me, right?"

"That's my plan." She nodded gravely, pushing his arm away. Then, in a softer voice, she added, "Not sure how I'm going to explain it to Rellia . . ." She always used her mother's name when she was frustrated.

"We'll cross that one when we come to it. She's going to have her hands full anyway." He clicked his tongue, and Guapo started forward at a walk. Valla and Uvu kept pace with him. "I mean with the kingdom building and whatnot."

"Indeed, she'll be a pig in a banquet."

Victor looked at her sharply, thinking the System had broken down for a moment when he heard the word "pig" come out of her mouth. Then he remembered all the bacon and stew laden with pork he'd eaten in this world and nodded. "Trips me out that you have an animal here close enough to the one I have on my world that the System uses the same word. It's weird the System doesn't call holbyis 'sheep,' too, 'cause they're pretty damn close."

Valla didn't reply immediately, just looked at him with narrowed eyes, perhaps trying to make sense of his words. After a moment, she shook her head slightly. "The System is certainly interesting. Have you given any thought to the treasures we found after the battle? And the more potent items Edeya discovered in the valuables you had her catalog for you?"

Victor grunted, his mind turning to the list of items she was referring to. The army had scoured the fallen imperials, taking their weapons and armor and recovering more than a thousand storage containers, from rings to pouches to magical backpacks. Valla wasn't talking about the more mundane treasures—beads, jewelry, gems, various potions, lesser armor, or weapons. No, she was talking about the half dozen racial enhancement items, a conscious rapier, and a few magical artifacts that would enhance users of certain affinities.

None of those treasures were of much use to Victor. He could eat all of the racial enhancements and probably only gain one rank. He didn't want the rapier, and none of the artifacts were much good for a Spirit Caster. Edeya had cataloged a trove of wealth, and he'd taken ownership of it all; he could pass some out here and there as rewards or use the money for purchases at another time. The racial enhancements were from the field, though, found in an overturned imperial supply wagon. Could he just hand them to whomever he wanted? If Edeya had been the one to find them, he would have had her consume one immediately.

"I told you I want Edeya to have at least one."

"And I reminded you that the unit that recovered those items spread the word around camp. Soldiers are eager to see how you'll assign them."

Victor nodded, thinking it over while they rode. They were only a half mile or so from the town, and he wanted to assure the people within that the army would be passing by without any threat to their populace. "I have the lists from the captains. The ones I used to hand out medals and commendations."

"Yes, but you already did that."

"I've been thinking about this for a few days now, and I've come up with a plan. First, I don't care what anyone says; Edeya's getting one of the racial enhancements. After that, I think I'll put together a list. I'm going to write down all the treasures we have available, and I'll institute a token system." He looked at Valla, instantly knew what she was about to say, and cut her off. "Yeah, I'm ripping off the Warlord's idea. We're going to have campaign tokens, and soldiers will earn one for every battle they're in."

"That won't help if everyone has the same number of tokens . . ."

"No, hold on, let me finish. They'll also earn them by doing special tasks, like scouting in dangerous areas or training recruits. They can earn extra tokens for valor, for which they have to be nominated by a higher-ranking soldier. We can flesh out the system and add some details, but I think if we have a bunch of items for, like, one or two tokens, many soldiers will blow them early, and then it will be a race for the more frugal ones to build up enough for the better items."

"I like it." Valla didn't say more, as they were nearly in front of the gate to the little town. Victor admired the hard work that had gone into the wall— carefully chiseled stone blocks, likely cut with Energy, fit together nearly seamlessly to form a rather formidable barrier almost twenty feet high, and if the tunnel behind the gate was any indication, about half that wide. Nobody was present outside the gate or farther down the road. Victor had watched them all going inside as he and Valla approached. The gate was open, though, so he didn't think they'd terrified the populace too much—that, or they were afraid of offending him.

After they sat outside the gates for a few moments, Victor heard some commotion from the tunnel, and then a woman appeared, walking hesitantly through the tunnel and out the gate. She was clad in soft-looking yellow linens, and a white fur cap sat atop her bright green curls. She was an Ardeni and young, with little freckles dotting her nose and cheeks. She stopped by the gate and looked from Victor to Valla to Uvu, then back to Victor. "May we help you, my lord and lady?"

"We just want to assure you that we'll be passing by. The troops march-ing past your town will not seek to enter or harass any of your citizens."

Valla spoke—Victor was used to her doing so when they met strangers together.

"Will it enrage you if we close the gates until you've passed by?" The girl, for Victor didn't think she could be older than fifteen, shrank back a little as she spoke.

"That's fine." Victor shrugged. "Why'd they send you out here instead of the mayor or whoever's in charge?"

"I lost the lottery."

"What the fu—"

"*Thank* you," Valla said, speaking over Victor's outburst. "Go inside now and close your gates. We'll be gone before you've all had your supper."

"Hang on," Victor said before the girl could fully turn around. He reached into his dimensional container and fished out a small bag of beads. "Catch." He tossed them to the girl, and she deftly snatched the pouch out of the air, causing the beads to click together satisfyingly. "Don't share that with those chickenshit assholes in there."

"Thank you!" Before Victor could reply, she was gone, slipping through the gates, already swinging shut—the operator must have heard Valla's words.

"A lottery," Victor scoffed, clicking his tongue to get Guapo moving again. "Come on; let's pick out our campsite. I want to set up my house and kick my feet up for a while before Borrius starts boring me." He shook his head, laughing at his choice of words. Valla didn't join in, so he stared at her for a minute until she broke, a smile spreading her lips as her low, soft laugh joined his.

2

THE GRANITE GATES

It took the army another two days to climb into the wide pass of the Granite Gates. As they climbed the foothills, Victor saw that the wide gravel road followed a sort of natural cleft between the two nearest enormous peaks of the range. Enormous was an understatement. The mountains began to take on a kind of mythical proportion as the distance shortened. Gigantic, dark gray, very lightly treed slopes rose to staggering heights, blotting out the sky, becoming the entirety of the marchers' world.

Fanwath was a big world, and though they'd moved steadily southward for weeks, they were still in a temperate climate, and the temperature began to grow chilly as they climbed into the heights. It didn't bother Victor, and it certainly didn't affect Guapo, but he saw the breath pluming forth from the soldiers and their roladii. He saw the soldiers pulling out furs, cloaks, and hats of all sorts. The shadows grew very long, and the going was dimly lit as they progressed. Thick gray clouds filled the sky, and snow that seemed distant, remotely nestled in the peaks when they'd approached over the plains, was now visible on the nearby slopes.

Rellia's airship never managed to rejoin the army; it had needed weeks' worth of refitting and repairs, and by the time she received notice in her Far Scribe book that it was taking flight, they were only days from the pass. Victor had asked why it couldn't fly over the range or even through the very pass they were hiking, and Borrius had snorted, saying he'd understand when they got nearer the summit of the pass in a few days. Victor was starting to understand—despite the steep incline of the narrower and narrower roadway, they were nowhere near the highest point, and the winds were beginning to rip and hammer at the column.

On the third day of their ascent, Valla and Victor sat on their mounts, discussing their progress. "We're moving out of the settled lands." She tugged her heavy fur cloak tight at her throat. It was a pretty thing, made up of a dozen or more small-game furs. Each was white in some way, though dappled with differently colored fur from black to red to pale taupe. "Energy is wilder up here and south of here in the Marches."

"Yeah, I heard the briefing last night, too." Victor grinned to show he was teasing; Rellia had droned on for a while the previous night in Victor's travel home. She'd spoken about the wild nature of the Energy they were marching into, about how the System would be taking their measure, creating a suitable challenge for the army—it seemed new lands didn't come easily to the citizens of System-run worlds.

"Why do you think it does it?" He wasn't specific, but he thought Valla would infer his meaning. They were a mile or so ahead of the column, a short way behind the forward scouts, taking a small break for a bit of travel food and water.

Valla put a piece of dried fruit in her mouth, chewing slowly while she considered. She idly scratched Uvu's neck for a moment, then said, "I think the System gains something from us as we gain power. This isn't my theory; I learned it from one of the tutors Rellia hired for me before I chased him off. As we fight and die, we release Energy from those we kill. The System awards us some while it keeps a portion." She looked at him briefly, running her eyes over his frame. "Imagine the Energy stored up in your body. Not just in your Core; you can see how much is in your Core, but what about all the Energy that was put into improving your attributes? If you died, that would all be released. Whoever killed you would profit, but how much would the System leach away?"

"So it wants us to have to fight and die . . . or kill to gain these new lands. But it makes the challenge? How?"

"I don't know. Maybe monsters or savages are living in the Marches. Maybe the System will drag them from a dungeon or—" Her eyes widened. "Another world."

Victor chewed on his last bite of dried meat, washing it down with a swig of cold water. He put away his canteen. "You think the System thinks about us? I mean, do you think it's more like a force of nature or a being?"

"I don't know. It communicates with words, but they don't usually convey much emotion. Even those 'warnings' you got were sort of detached, right?" She shrugged and made a flicking motion with her finger. "It doesn't matter. We're like ants to it. Do ants try to understand the person stepping on their home?"

"I don't like being an ant." Victor looked down the road past Valla. "I can see the vanguard. Let's keep going." He turned and started forward, and the afternoon drifted by in a blur of gray rocky slopes speckled with patches of snow. The wind grew ever harsher, ever colder, and the climb grew steeper, the path narrower. By the time darkness fell, Victor was starting to worry that the larger wagons wouldn't be able to continue much farther.

The road's edge was well defined; whatever the Earth Casters had built, it had cleaved the roadway into the western, right-hand side of the pass; the shoulder grew steep and rocky, and the fall on the left became a dizzying drop—it made Victor nervous to get within ten feet of it. In the evening, he asked Rellia about it, but she assured him that her record books indicated that the road would remain wide enough, if only by a matter of inches, for her wagons to make it through. They might have to clear snow or scree from the shoulder, but that wouldn't be hard with more than six thousand soldiers ready to do the labor.

The next day, as the sky lightened from black to gray, the column started out again, eager to get through the pass. If Rellia's records were correct, they should reach the summit by nightfall, and the most challenging part of the climb would be over; the trip down was shorter—the Marches were higher in elevation than the imperial lands.

The cold wind began to sting even Victor as it delivered flecks of icy rain in its passage. Borrius called out the Wind Casters, risking the wrath of the elemental spirits in the heights by pushing the gusts to the sides, trying to clear a path for the army that wouldn't be so punishing. It paid off for most of the day, but by the afternoon, the casters grew taxed, found their efforts too little to fend off the wild winds, and the army had to buckle down and forge ahead.

Visibility was poor, so Victor summoned his Banner of the Champion, riding Guapo with the vanguard, providing a beacon for everyone to drive toward and bestowing his spirit on everyone the banner covered. Though the sun was still hours from setting, it grew very dim and gray; snow dusted the stones of the roadway, kicked up in swirling eddies by the gusts, and Victor could see the soldiers, even Valla, shivering. He noticed the sharpness of the frozen flecks of moisture on the wind, but it didn't bother him; his skin was ruddy with warmth, the magma in his chest keeping him warm despite his naked arms.

He still didn't know how to use the Breath Core, not really. He'd played around with it a bit, using his mind's eye to study the swirling, writhing ball of orange-red Energy, focusing his will upon it and trying to pull it into his pathways. It didn't move like the Energy in his other Core, though. It didn't seem to want to flow into the same pathways, and he knew there was a different trick to it, a different way to access it. He just hadn't figured it out. He'd begun to wonder if he had to do something else first. Maybe he had to build up the Core and get it out of the "seed" stage. Perhaps he had to build a different pathway, something he had no idea how to do, just as he didn't know how to cultivate the magma Energy.

He'd tried. He'd tried pulling Energy out of campfires, out of fire-attuned Energy beads, and from orbs of fire summoned by the elemental casters in the army. Nothing had worked; it seemed there was something different about cultivating Energy for a Breath Core. All that considered, Victor felt frustrated by his inability to help the army cope with the brutal inclement weather in the pass. He looked down at Valla, shivering on Uvu's back. "Hey, why won't you ride with me?" He patted Guapo's back, sliding back to show there was plenty of room. "I'll keep you warm."

She looked up at him, frost in her eyebrows, and for a second, he thought she'd accept the invitation, but she glanced over her shoulder at the first line of soldiers marching behind them, steadily driving forward into the wind, chasing Victor's banner, and shook her head. "Bad example."

"Bullshit. Come on—Uvu's fine. Let him run off and hunt himself a snack. The soldiers don't care if you ride with me." Victor leaned down, holding out his hand. Watching her eyes, he saw her will crumble. She reached up to grasp hold of him, and he tugged, almost effortlessly lifting her off Uvu's back to straddle Guapo in front of him. As the big cat yowled and ran off into the icy wind, Victor wrapped his arms around Valla, savoring the victorious moment.

"Ancestors, you're warm even in this cold." She nestled back into him, folding her arms up under her cloak. Victor reached up and pulled the front of her hood down as Guapo started plodding forward again, utterly oblivious to the weather.

"Yeah." He chuckled, once again wishing there weren't so many layers between them. Still, it felt good to hold her, and he wondered at that, at how he'd grown to think of Valla, and really only Valla, in that regard. When they'd spoken more than a month ago in Persi Gables, and Valla had called him out about his infatuation with Tes, he'd had to admit that she was right. If they were to have the same discussion today, though, he knew his response would be different. Already, Tes was kind of like a pleasant dream, a beautiful unreal near-deity whom he'd met in a strange far-off land. The whole thing was surreal to the point of feeling like a fantasy he'd conjured up.

Valla was real. She was brave, intelligent, talented, and very, very principled. "And beautiful," he muttered, wondering if she'd connect the dots and figure out his thoughts. She didn't speak, though, and he held her so close that he wasn't sure she was awake; maybe she'd dozed off. He hated that he had to move so slowly. If he and Valla were alone, they'd have crossed through the mountains in half a day, Guapo charging through the pass, ignoring the cold. "God, that would be fun!"

Victor looked over his shoulder and saw the shadowy hunched figures of the vanguard pushing forward, many with balls of glowing Energy floating near their heads. They were doing their best; it was kind of shitty of him to want to bail on them, even if it was just a fleeting impulse. He urged Guapo to slow down a little, allowing the soldiers to gain on him so his banner fell on more of them. With a determined frown, he buckled down, using his will against himself for a change, reminding himself of his responsibilities.

As the gray sky darkened and the shadows grew long and thick, Victor heard a shout from behind and slowed, turning. He felt Valla stir and realized he'd been right earlier; she'd fallen asleep in his arms. He was grinning slyly, pleased with himself, when he caught sight of Rellia and Borrius riding forward. "Hey," he called, straightening, letting his hands and arms fall to his sides. For some reason, he was self-conscious about hugging Valla close as her mother approached.

"Scouts with Far Sight spells say they see shadows moving on the slopes. We're afraid we're about to be ambushed by rock trolls or . . . something." Borrius shrugged.

"We don't think we should camp," Rellia added, her eyes drifting from Victor's face down to Valla's shrouded, hooded form. Both she and Borrius were bundled in furs, though neither looked particularly chilly—Victor had already heard about their warmth-enchanted cloaks. They weren't the only ones in the army with such garments, but the vast majority relied on good old-fashioned layers to make it through the cold.

"Yes. We'll call out for more lights and keep pushing forward. Victor, we had an idea." Borrius licked his lips, then drove ahead, "We think you should ride forward a bit more and unleash your aura. Let the denizens of this pass know what they're stalking."

"Oh?" Victor shrugged. "All right. I'll keep my banner up. Are we pushing through the whole night?"

"We think that would be best." Rellia continued to peer at Valla, and when her daughter met her gaze, she asked, "Want to join me until Uvu returns?"

"No. I've felt Victor's aura many times. I'll be fine."

"You're sure?"

"Yes. I'm finally warm—Ancestors, mother! Why didn't you warn us about the heights of this pass? I would have bought better cold weather gear."

"Is it my fault you didn't study the geography of the lands you intend to conquer?" Rellia snorted, then tugged at her reins, turning her beautiful vidanii around. Over her shoulder, she called, "We'll be close behind should trouble arise."

Borrius nodded and turned also, and Valla, with some rare humor in her voice, said, "She doesn't like that I'm riding with you."

"Tough." Victor clicked his tongue, and Guapo started forward, putting a hundred yards or so between them and the front ranks of the army's vanguard. His banner still blazed, and when Victor let go of his aura, he felt as if it brightened, as the part of his will relegated to holding his aura in check was released of its burden.

"Oof!" Valla groaned. "It's been a while. I think it's heavier now."

"Sorry."

"No. Truthfully, it's almost comforting. Something in me knows that pressure isn't meant for me."

"Hang on." Victor concentrated for a moment. Then he summoned forth a pack of pony-sized, inspiration-attuned coyotes. As they yipped and howled, pacing around in the windy, frigid island of light cast by his banner, he willed them to patrol, to climb the slopes where they could and where they couldn't, to pace the length of the army, weaving among the soldiers, spreading the influence of the inspiration Energy that bled from their silvery misty forms. He watched them pad off into the darkness, and even outside his banner's light, he could see them glowing with faint luminescence in the dark.

"Will they tell you if they find trouble?"

"Not exactly tell me, but I can feel what they're up to. I'll know if they find something."

Valla nestled back into him, and Victor continued forward, his banner banishing the darkness as they climbed. Soon he became aware of presences outside the glow, a vague feeling of animosity, and the occasional falling pebbles or stones. The impression he got from the lurkers was one of fear and flight; they weren't sticking around to watch him but were trying to get away. His coyotes' howls, yips, cries, and yapping barks echoed through the canyon, and he knew they were heartening the troops as they walked back and forth through the column.

"It's nice how the Energy you use summoning those companions of yours affects their nature."

"Yeah. I felt the inspiration had the right note for what we're trying to do. Courage would have been good, but the army isn't exactly scared right now. At least, I didn't get that impression."

"Agreed." Valla gestured to the left at the sloping rocky mountainside on the other side of the dizzying drop. "I saw a shadow off that way."

"Uh-huh. We were surrounded for a while, but most of them ran away."

"Truly?" She jerked, twisting in front of him to look up into his face, perhaps to see if he was teasing.

"Truly. You didn't feel them?"

"No, but I feel something else . . . We're no longer climbing!"

Victor immediately realized she was right; the rocky roadway had leveled off, and though the wind still blasted at them out of the heights, he thought he could see a sliver of light in the distance. "Is that one of the moons?"

"If so, it's kind of strange; doesn't it seem green?" Valla leaned forward, reaching out to grasp Guapo's mane. Victor could see she was right. The clouds and flicking gusts of frosty rain made it hard to focus, but somewhere ahead, as distant as the imagined horizon, a weird green light seemed to be glowing. "Definitely not a moon unless something in the air is tinting it oddly." Valla leaned back again, pulling her hood down.

"We'll see soon enough." Nothing attacked, though Victor felt several more entities flee his banner and aura through the night. He didn't know what they were, and they might not know what or who he was, but they knew they didn't want any part of him or his people. As the night wore on and the pass shifted into a downward slope, he chuckled, and Valla stirred, turning to look up at him again.

"What's funny?"

"What if this whole thing is that easy? What if our numbers or our levels are so daunting to the creatures of the Marches that they just kind of flee ahead of us? What if we just walk down there and can claim all the land we want?"

"A lovely thought, but don't get your hopes up. This pass is still technically part of the Ridonne Empire. Whatever the first peoples on Fanwath did to claim the lands north of here also counted for this pass. The creatures in the darkness, threatening the column, are just typical monsters similar to what you might find anywhere in the wilds of the Empire. When we emerge from these mountains, the real test will begin. Well, that's what Rellia says. I believe her, though; she's probably the most versed scholar on the subject in the Empire."

"She's wanted to do this her whole life, huh?"

"Maybe not her entire life, but most of it. Didn't she tell you about how she used to chastise her uncles about their complacency? She's wanted to conquer new lands since she learned about the Writs of Conquest."

"Yeah. She mentioned it." As they followed the road as it wound around an outcropping of solid stone, an uncommonly straight view down the pass resolved, and Victor could see the black sky was lightening, turning toward gray. He wished he could see through the mountains on the left toward the sunrise. However, the thought of sunrises faded from his mind as the path switched to the right, skirting another bend. When it straightened again, they had a view of the distant sky from a new angle, and he felt Valla stop breathing. He couldn't blame her.

"What . . ." Her voice caught in her throat. Sensing Victor's stress, Guapo slowed to a stop, his front hooves lifting up and down, pawing at the rock road. Victor hardly noticed; he was staring at the brilliant ball of sickly green light in the sky. It had to be a hundred miles away, but it hung nearly at their eye level as though a weird diseased sun had fallen from the heavens to shed its light on a small part of the world. Victor could see the contours of hills, forests, lakes, and plains under that otherworldly light, though everything was glimpsed through a haze of thin anemic fog. He tried to formulate a statement or question and was just about to give voice to his words when a System message appeared, blasting the thoughts from his mind:

*****Challenge of Conquest! Halt the invasion from the world of Dark Ember. Drive the forces of Prince Hector of Heart Rot from Fanwath and reclaim the lands they've begun to taint. Rewards: New territory, a Colony Stone, and Chests of Conquest at strategic locations.*****

3

MAKING THE ROUNDS

Borrius counseled Victor to halt the army a mile from the bottom of the pass in a particularly narrow portion where sheer rock walls climbed for thousands of feet on either side of the rough, rock-strewn roadway. They knew what was behind them, and with the massive cliffs, they didn't have to worry about their flanks, leaving the southern road sloping down into the weirdly misty valley as the only avenue by which unknown enemies might attack. As the summer sun struggled to make itself known through the thick cloud cover, Victor watched the efforts of the army to fortify their position.

"It doesn't look like they've come this far," Rellia said from beside him, sitting on the edge of a large boulder. She, along with the other commanders of the army, had ridden a short way down the road, perhaps half a mile from where it abruptly ended in the rolling hills of thick scrub and grass.

"They?" Borrius asked, still atop his barded mount.

"The forces of this Prince of Heart Rot, whatever that is. What an absurd name; why would you call your lands something so . . ."

"Gross?" Valla suggested.

"It makes me think of death magic." Lam's boots scraped on the rough stone as she moved to sit by Rellia.

"Yeah." Victor nodded. "The whole System message was like something out of a cheesy video game." He waved his hand in the air. "Yeah, yeah. I know you don't know what that is. I mean, it's like a bad fairy tale. Does that make sense?"

"Sure." Valla pointed down the slope toward the dimly lit expanse of land leading into the valley below the pass. Victor tracked where she pointed, watching as the landscape grew more and more dark, more and more covered by miasmic mists, until his eyes met the distant horizon where dark clouds roiled, utterly obscuring the land. "That's no fairy tale, though."

"This is good." Borrius turned his mount, looking upslope to where the army engineers toiled, then shifting to scan the valley. "We've got the high ground. We can see any enemy approaching. We should build something a bit more permanent here. A keep that bridges the entire pass. It's a solid foothold from which to march forth."

"If we had true fortifications here, it would alleviate us having to watch over our shoulders for the Empire. We could make the pass very costly for them to come through." Rellia idly massaged the palm of her left hand between her fingers and thumb as she spoke, her eyes distant, perhaps imagining the fortification Borrius proposed.

"There's certainly plenty of stone in these cliffs . . ."

"Are you guys forgetting something?" Victor interrupted.

"I'm with Victor," Lam said. "That System message didn't say anything about the influx of 'invaders' slowing. The longer we dillydally up here building a keep, the more enemies we may have to contend with. If we were higher in the pass, and if it was still night, we'd have that green star hanging in the sky to remind us."

As she'd suggested, Lam's words echoed Victor's thinking; as the army had descended from the heights, the clouds had begun to block their view of the green orb or portal or whatever it was. Even so, in the dark, everything had been cast in an eerie greenish glow, especially the clouds and mist in the distance. Only as the sun climbed toward noon did it begin to fade.

"We can manage both." Borrius chuckled, shaking his head. "The non-combat personnel will remain here, along with most of the Shadeni tribe. I'll leave most of the engineers and Earth Casters to work on the fortification. I propose we peel off the extra troops from the various cohorts, forming an eleventh cohort to serve as a rear guard."

"What happened to 'swelling' the cohorts to accommodate losses?" Valla knelt, picked up a smooth rock, and chucked it down the stone roadway. It flew a good distance, then clicked and clattered over the ground.

"We'll have these reserves, holding our base and ready to fill in when called for duty. We still may have more volunteers heading our way through the pass. In any event, we'll need a garrison here to receive and train them."

"All right, Borrius." Victor nodded to the old commander. "You've made a good argument, and I think it makes sense. It's clear Rellia agrees with you, so I think we can go ahead and make the order. Meanwhile, I think I'd like to ride out with the Ninth and see if I can get eyes on this enemy we're dealing with. It'd be good to size them up, don't you think?"

"The Ninth?" Lam turned to Victor. "Because they're the highest level?"

"Highest average level, and more than half of them have fought a hopeless battle already on this campaign. You know what I mean? They thought they were going to die before the Naghelli joined the fight."

"Speaking of the Naghelli . . ." Valla pointed to the cluster of dark round tents farther up the pass where the winged fighters had set up camp. They kept to themselves each night, but Victor was glad to have them in the rear— nothing would be sneaking past Kethelket and his people.

"It would be good if they'd do some scouting . . ."

"I worry about that." Rellia spoke before Victor could finish his thought. "Did they not serve a Death Caster?"

"Not happily. We've been over this, Rellia." Victor hopped down from the boulder to look at her more easily.

"Still, what if this Prince Hector tries to recruit them? What if they like his offer?"

"So we're back to not trusting them?" Valla sighed, shaking her head at her mother.

Rellia held up her hands, signaling capitulation. "I'm only trying to suggest we use caution where they are concerned. Let us not leave ourselves open to an easy betrayal." She saw Victor's scowl and pressed on. "I know we owe them much! I know they've been good, easy companions on this journey. I don't propose we sideline them; let's give them more opportunities to prove themselves. But at the same time, let's be prepared for what will happen should they act out our worst fears."

"Sure." Victor stepped away from the others, feeling the need to walk, clear his head, and speak to some different people for a change. He wanted to see Thayla and Deyni. "By all means, be cautious with them. Anyway, I'm going to go check in on the Shadeni and maybe do some axe work. I'm so close to the edge of epic, I can taste it." He turned, stalking up the slope toward the encampment, pointedly avoiding making eye contact with any of the other commanders; he didn't want to give them a chance to suck him back into another debate.

He felt a little guilty for not inviting Valla along, but he rationalized his abrupt departure by figuring she'd come after him if she wanted to. He'd spent a lot of time with her over the last few weeks, the last couple of days in particular. Hadn't he had her wrapped in his arms through the dark, frigid night? And not a word from her when they parted. Was he being unfair? Maybe, but so was she, in his mind. More brooding was forestalled as soldiers called out greetings, snapping smart salutes, pride in their leader evident on their faces. Victor forced a cheerful expression and answered back with encouragement.

"Nice-looking wall!" he said inanely to a pair of soldiers working to stack blocks from the innards of one of the massive supply wagons. They saluted, though, pleased with the praise. Earth Caster engineers would come along behind them and bond the stones more securely than concrete ever could. Despite his intention to make his way to the Shadeni section of the encampment, farther up the stony pass, he caught sight of Sarl addressing his cohort near the western canyon wall and walked that way.

". . . and that's why we have much to prove, much to live up to! Each of you who joined this cohort after the battle on the plains has a debt to pay those soldiers who died, giving you a place in this fine fighting force. Further . . . *Attention!* Legate Primus!" Sarl turned and snapped an impeccable salute when he saw Victor step up next to him.

Victor had been practicing the traditional salute the army employed. It wasn't very hard once you got the order of things. Step one: Stand up straight, make a fist, and hold it out before you. Step two: Lift your right foot. Step three: Stomp your foot next to your left and slam your fist into your chest above your heart. That was it; you just had to hold that position until the commanding officer released you or, if you were the commanding officer, for a second or two. He responded to Sarl's salute with one of his own, then said, "At ease, everyone. I need to speak to Captain Sarl."

"Dismissed!" Sarl watched his cohort disperse for a moment, then turned to Victor. "How are things, sir?"

"Victor. Call me Victor when we're alone, please, Sarl." When Sarl nodded, a small smile altering his usual dour expression, he continued, "Things look good. We're going to build a base of operations here."

"A sensible plan."

Victor looked at Sarl closely, studying his shrewd eyes. The onetime Ghelli nobleman was a clever man with a strong will. He looked shabby next to a Ghelli like Lam, but he was a skilled fencer, and he'd been through hell in his life. Victor valued his opinion. "Any thoughts on the conquest quest the System handed out?"

"I think we're in for a difficult time. The System thrives on conflict, in my experience, and I believe it's clever enough to know how to challenge even you."

"Yeah. I know there are plenty of people in the System's worlds who can whip my ass. I just hope it remembers we're on Fanwath and doesn't throw something at us that'll slaughter all these good people." Victor gestured around the bustling camp. "Anyway, we'll find out soon. I'm heading down there tomorrow, and I want the Ninth to come with."

Sarl's eyebrows arched up, and a savage grin spread on his face. Victor couldn't help noticing how his dragonfly-like wings stiffened, vibrating ever so slightly. "That's fantastic, Victor! You won't regret it!"

"Good. Have your men lined up and ready to go at dawn." By way of response, Sarl performed another sharp salute, and Victor nodded. "I've more people to speak to. See you later." As he walked away, he heard Sarl shouting orders to his lieutenants and sergeants. Something stirred in his chest as he thought about Sarl, thinking that at least one person who'd been there at the very beginning, back when he'd been a skinny kid fighting in the Wagon Wheel, was still with him. An image flashed through his mind of a face he hadn't pictured in a long while—Yrella. "God, I wish she was still alive," he said aloud to himself.

Victor rapidly blinked his eyes, banishing the thought as he lengthened his stride toward the Shadeni wagons. He didn't have to struggle to find the people he sought; Chandri, Chala, and Deyni were standing outside, near the wagon he'd left behind with Thayla. To Victor's surprise and horror, Chandri was watching as Chala and Deyni performed spear drills. Deyni was still a foot shorter than Chala, but she was fierce and quick, her movements nearly as sharp as the vicious teenager's. More startling than anything, she'd painted her face like her stepsisters.

Sharp angles of white and black paint did the job of making her look tougher than usual, but the accent of red around her lips and eyes made it all the worse. Could little Deyni be learning how to kill people already? No— Victor stopped that line of thought. She was learning to defend herself, and a damn good idea it was, too. "Hey," he called, stepping up to the trio.

"Victor!" Deyni cried, dropping her practice spear and running to wrap her arms around his waist. Victor peeled her off, then hoisted her up, hugging her into his chest and kissing the top of her head.

"You little huntress! You're learning to stab pigs?"

"Not pigs! Imperials!" she growled, baring her teeth.

"Oh, man." Victor supposed there was no helping it; the Empire had made their bed, and now they had to sleep in it. Deyni had lost friends to their assault, people she'd grown to think of as family. It would take time for them to stop thinking about the Empire or characterizing them as villains. "We've punished those responsible. Don't carry too much hate in your heart; it gives power to things like fear, and you don't want fear to grow in your Core."

"You have fear in your Core!"

"I do, and I struggle with it all the time. I much prefer my inspiration and glory. Let's try to find something like that in your spirit, all right?"

"Will you still love me if I have something else?"

"Of course, silly." Victor had been holding her against his side, on his hip, and he squeezed her close again. "Love's the best, I think. I bet you have love in your spirit."

"How do you know? Do you have love, too?"

"Maybe. I just haven't found it yet. When I first came here, all I had was rage, you know."

"I know. Old Mother taught me about it before she walked away with the spirits."

Victor continued to squeeze her as he watched the two sisters standing nearby, Chandri smiling knowingly at him and Chala leaning on her spear, looking bored. "Can I count on you three to help build our base here? We'll need clever ideas to make a place that feels like home to people used to living on the plains."

"We're settling here?" Chala asked, disgust in her voice. "I thought we'd settle the plains and forests!"

"No, *hermanita,* we're just making a base here, but it might be some time before we think it's safe for people who aren't in the army to go farther down into the Marches."

"You can count on me, Victor." Deyni reached one of her tiny hands toward his face, gently rubbing her fingertips along the rough stubble on his jawline. "Pokey," she giggled.

"All right, all right." Victor set her down and asked, "Where's your mama?"

"I want to join the legion!" Chala said, finally formulating a response.

"Uh." Victor frowned and looked at her. The truth was, she was probably the same age as many of the soldiers who'd joined back near Persi Gables. "You need to talk to Tellen about that. Even if you do, though, you'll start working here, near the base."

"Uh-uh, Chala." Chandri stepped in. "You'll be a huntress like me, and you'll help that way—with scouting and gathering food. You're not ready yet, though."

"I'm better at stealth than you are!"

"There's more to it than being sneaky, little Shadow Core! You need to have the will and discipline to make smart decisions."

"I can—"

"Hey, ladies," Victor interrupted. "I don't want to get in the middle of this. Can you point me toward Thayla?"

"She's in the wagon." Deyni pointed to the nearby conveyance.

"Of course you don't." Chandri folded her arms, scowling, then turned on her heel and started to walk away.

Victor looked at Chala, met her stormy eyes, and asked, "What's up with her?"

"I don't know. She's moody. Come on, Deyni! Let's get Wista and hunt some cliff bats."

"How's your adristii?" Victor smiled and squatted down to better look at Deyni's face. The adristii was her falcon-like pet, a raptor she'd used to hunt small game all the way from Persi Gables.

"She's good, Victor! I'm getting better and better at calling her and telling her what I want her to do."

"That's because animals can sense your good heart." Victor smiled again, reached out, and gave her little arm a squeeze.

"Will you come say hi to Wista?"

"Not right now, but yes, I will."

Deyni turned and ran to Chala, holding out her hand, and as they ran off, she called, "Just tell me when!"

Victor watched the two girls run around the side of the wagon, amazed at how quickly he'd been dismissed. Then he turned toward where Chandri had gone, seeing no trace of her; she'd slipped away between wagons, lost in the crowd of other Shadeni performing camp tasks. Maybe Thayla would know what her deal was. With that in mind, he walked around to the other side of the wagon and knocked on the door. A few seconds passed before the latch clicked and Thayla pushed it open.

"Victor! I'm glad to see you. Tellen and I were just talking, wondering how long we'd camp here."

"Yeah, I . . ."

"Come in! We're having soup, and I know you like this recipe." She backed away from the door, and Victor followed, ducking low to get through the opening but standing up straight as he stepped into the vaulted interior. The place was much smaller than he remembered but a great deal "homier," too. Woven tapestries hung on the walls, and more furniture filled the space, including several smaller beds along the wall with the two original, larger beds. Wooden folding screens separated the bed in the far corner of the room, and Victor figured that was where Tellen and Thayla slept. He got a strange feeling in the pit of his stomach thinking about that.

When he'd purchased the wagon, he'd never imagined Thayla having a family here, including a husband. He knew the feeling was stupid, the thought was selfish, but he couldn't help the emotion. Still, he swallowed it and brought forth a smile, turning to the long picnic-style table and saying, "Hey, Tellen. Man, that soup smells good! I've missed the meals I had with your people last winter."

"Come on, then. Sit down. Tell us what's happening with the army and what we'll do about those invaders and that strange green light in the sky." Tellen slapped the bench next to him, and Victor walked that way, watching Thayla as she got a bowl off the shelf and began to ladle out some of the steaming soup from her big, well-used copper pot. Another powerful wave of emotion hit him, this time nostalgia. He remembered meals shared with her on the road, in various inns, and in this very wagon. Wouldn't it have been nice just to stay with her? Why was he so intent on fighting, exploring, and adventuring?

"That's just my hunger talking," he muttered, laughing at himself. He winked at Tellen's puzzled expression and sat beside the much smaller man. "I feel like I haven't eaten in weeks, Thayla. I hope there's plenty!"

4

SCOUTING MISSION

Victor didn't sleep much the night before his "scouting mission," as Valla had been describing it. The two of them sat together at his big dining table, drinking the last of their cold bitter ale from Fainhallow. It was a relaxing time, with hardly any conversation, but it was comfortable and pleasant, and he hadn't wanted it to end. It seemed Valla felt the same way, and it was well past midnight before they'd gone to sleep. The lack of rest didn't seem to bother him much. Now he stood south of the encampment watching the soldiers muster, and his body, as always these days, felt strong, rested, and ready.

He'd been surprised that Valla hadn't joined him for breakfast, and when he'd gotten ready to leave, he'd been tempted to knock on the door to her room, but decided that if she wanted to join the scouting foray, she would; he'd never known her to oversleep. Meanwhile, the ninth cohort, or "the Glorious Ninth," as Victor, Sarl, his veterans, and pretty much everyone else called them, was forming up. They were arraying themselves in thirty rows of twenty soldiers each, their armor and weapons glinting in the dawn light.

The sun was just turning the sky gray, with brighter shades of orange and yellow to the east, pushing back some of the green glow leaking out of the dense foggy clouds near the horizon. Victor was eager to get out there, to see what that sickly fog was like, to find out what the green light in the sky was, and to test the mettle of the mysterious "invaders." With that in mind, he wondered if bringing an entire cohort of foot soldiers was wise. He wondered if he should instead use a smaller group of mounted troops. "Need more mounts in this army," he said.

"It would be helpful, indeed," a smooth tenor voice answered from behind him. Victor whirled, always annoyed when someone surprised him, a scowl darkening his expression.

"Kethelket." He tried to keep the word from sounding like an expletive, but he wasn't sure how successful he was.

"Good morning, Legate. I see you're planning an excursion."

"Yeah. Gonna see the lay of the land, so to speak."

"If it's a scouting report you're after, you might have asked me. I'd be pleased to pick a squadron of Naghelli to take a look into things. You know we're a great deal more mobile and stealthier than those soldiers, no slight intended."

"None taken. I'm still sort of formulating my plan. I'm also a lot faster than those soldiers, but if we're supposed to conquer these lands, I'd like to have a decent force along with me in case we run into an enemy outpost or something." Victor paused, considering. The truth was, Kethelket was right; his people could do this job far more easily. It all came down to trust, and Victor knew the issue was probably transparent to the Naghelli prince.

"Of course," Kethelket said.

"It's not that I don't think you all could do this on your own, but I want to ease into working with you. Do you understand what I'm saying? I'd like these soldiers to get experience not only with the territory and the enemy but with your people. Why don't you pick fifty Naghelli to join this expedition? We can have you do the forward scouting, and then you'll have this cohort to fall back to."

"I think that's wise. I'll be happy to select a squadron of Naghelli to join. I will lead them."

"Oh?"

"Yes. Like you, I'd enjoy learning to work with the rest of the army. In particular, I'd like to learn to work with you. How long do you anticipate this scouting expedition to last?" Kethelket reached up and pulled some loose strands of long white hair back, refastening his hair tie to keep them at the back of his head. It gave Victor the impression of someone getting ready to get down to work, to get his hands dirty.

"Depends on what we run into. No more than a week, but maybe as short as a day."

"Well, if we do spend some time out there, camping, as it were, I'd enjoy a chance to spar with you. I've watched you with that burly Vodkin, Polo Vosh, and I think we could learn something from each other."

"Oh yeah?" Victor grinned. "I'd love that! I feel like I'm stuck on a plateau—been feeling like I'm close to advancing for a while now but never quite get the breakthrough I need."

"Excellent! I'm sure I can help." He looked over the assembled soldiers, listening for a moment while Sarl called out orders. "Feel free to start them marching. My scouts and I will catch up. If you don't mind, I'll start getting the unit together."

"Sounds good." Before he could help himself, Victor held out a fist, and he was surprised when Kethelket reached up to knock his knuckles into his. He grinned madly, looking into the Naghelli's dark black eyes. Kethelket grinned back at him, baring white teeth with sharp canines, exposing another difference between his people and their cousins, the Ghelli. The fallen prince nodded, then turned adroitly on his heel and glided over the gravel-strewn rock roadway with unnatural grace and silence. Victor turned and tromped down the slope toward Sarl and his troops.

When he walked past the assembled soldiers, they struggled to ignore him, maintaining their attention as Sarl and his officers walked up and down their lines, inspecting their uniforms, weapons, and posture. Victor did his best not to make eye contact with them; he didn't want to get anyone in trouble by distracting them. When he reached the front of the column, Sarl approached and held out a hand. Even though Victor was currently reducing his size, the man's hand still felt small and fragile. He knew better than to judge his strength by his size, however. "Are we ready?"

"Aye, sir." Sarl knew some soldiers could hear him, so Victor understood the formality. It was good to maintain order and discipline in front of the troops.

"We can move out, but I wanted to tell you that I asked Kethelket to join us with fifty Naghelli. We'll use them as forward scouts."

"Excellent." Sarl nodded, and Victor stared into his pale eyes, wondering if he was being sincere. He didn't seem at all bothered.

He nodded firmly. "Good. I'll be riding ahead as well. Once we get down the slope and into the foothills, we'll select landmarks for rendezvous."

"Will you be alone, sir?"

Victor looked over the heads of the soldiers, suddenly a lot less cool about Valla not being there. Wouldn't she have said something if she weren't coming? What about Edeya? Shouldn't he have asked her to come along? She'd been with him a lot during the march, managing his Far Scribe book. "No, I won't be alone. I wanted to let you know you can start the soldiers marching, and I'll catch up. I've got a couple of others coming with me, mounted, so it won't be a problem."

"Very good, sir." Sarl turned to his six lieutenants and nodded, his voice suddenly much harsher and louder. "Begin the march!"

Victor moved to the side of the roadway as the order was passed down the column. He summoned Guapo and rode along the side, against the flow of troops, back toward the encampment, feeling rather foolish about his sudden change of mind. Many more people were stirring now that the sun was up. It was hard to ignore the start of the day when the troops were making so much noise down the road. Victor didn't have any trouble finding a sergeant, one from the second cohort, to holler at. "Find me Lieutenant Edeya!"

With that quest initiated, Victor hurried Guapo back to his travel home and, in the process, slapped himself in the head—wouldn't he want his travel home along with him on this scouting mission? Had he really left it sitting there just because he'd thought Valla might be sleeping in? What was he trying to prove? He hopped off Guapo and stepped inside, and he'd only taken two steps before he was hollering, "Valla! Are you up?"

"Victor?" she called almost immediately from straight ahead. He stomped up the hallway into the central living space, and there she was, leaning over a cup of steaming liquid, probably tea.

"Aren't you coming?"

"Hmm?"

"On my scouting mission!"

"Oh? You want me to come along?" She stood up, clearly feigning surprise, her voice rising comically with the question.

"Are you busting my balls right now?"

"Well, we spent four or five hours drinking together last night, and all you did was mope about Thayla and Tellen and how you missed her cooking and 'hanging out' with the Shadeni. I figured if you wanted me to come along this morning, you'd have mentioned it."

This was a side of Valla Victor hadn't seen before, at least not thoroughly on display. He stood there slack-jawed, trying to wrap his head around what she was saying. He didn't remember their conversation going that way. He remembered them sitting together, comfortably getting buzzed, hardly talking about anything at all. Had he mentioned his feelings about seeing Tellen living with Thayla in the wagon? He probably had, but it had been a passing comment in Victor's mind. "Was I that bad?"

Perhaps his lack of a retort took some of the steam out of her because Valla's expression softened. "Well, I would have liked to hear a little less about your regrets. Let's leave it at that."

"Noted. I . . . Valla, I thought we were both venting a little, then I thought we were both relaxed and happy. I think I missed some subtext or something. Well, I mean, maybe I focus on myself too much sometimes."

She sighed heavily and shook her head. "Oh, Victor! I'm not really upset. I was irritated, and, as you said, maybe we *both* were a little too focused on our feelings. Sorry if I'm being childish. When are you leaving?" She lifted her tea and gulped it down; apparently it wasn't very hot.

"The Ninth is marching. I told 'em we could catch up."

"Truly?" A look of panic entered Valla's eyes, and Victor grinned, recognizing the cause; she hated to be late.

"Don't worry. We're waiting on Edeya, too. I . . . forgot to tell her she's coming."

"Does Lam know?" Valla produced her wyrm-scale armor. It rustled and clicked as the scales rubbed together in her arms. "Help me with this."

Victor moved around the counter to grasp the heavy coat, holding it open so she could slip her arms into the long sleeves. "Nope. Think she'll be pissed?"

"She may want to come. You know how protective she is of Edeya." Valla held her armor closed and passed her hand over the seam, sealing it. "I just need to grab Midnight, and then we can go." She brushed past Victor, but not without squeezing his forearm gently, sending a tingle up his arm.

As his heart began to speed up, triggered by the tiny show of affection, Victor walked toward the foyer. "Meet you outside!" A stupid smile pulled his cheeks tight as he congratulated himself on returning to get Valla and for saying the right things—for once—when he found her. The sky was a shade brighter when he stepped outside, and he saw Edeya approaching, tromping along the stone pathway and kicking at loose stones.

Despite him giving her a racial enhancement elixir, she still looked lopsided, the wings on one side of her body cut down to stumps. He'd been bugging her to use the concoction for days, ever since they'd come into the pass, but she'd refused, afraid it would put her out of commission for too long; they didn't know precisely how strong it was or how her body would react. She was just "waiting for some downtime," she'd reply whenever he asked her about it.

"What did you need?" She glanced around, saw a few soldiers nearby, and added, "Sir?"

"We're going scouting."

"I know you are."

"No. We. Go get Thistle and meet me outside the gate."

"Oh, roots! Are you serious? I thought I'd be here a while; Lam said Borrius and Rellia want to build a fort here."

"Hurry up! I'll explain on the way. Be sure to tell Lam you're going, and don't forget the Far Scribe book!" Victor chuckled as she turned and ran, taking his words literally. He'd just summoned Guapo again when Valla came out of the home, dressed for battle with Midnight on her hip.

"Give me a ride to the gate, will you? I think Uvu is out hunting."

"Yeah, just a minute." Victor turned back to his house, touched the polished wooden railing, and sent the command to pack itself up. While it vibrated and shrank, he said, "Might be out a few days."

"It's good you're bringing Edeya. She can use the experience, and she's much better about keeping in touch with the other commanders."

"Well, it's kind of her job, right?"

"Yes . . ."

Victor snatched up the still-trembling miniature travel home and slipped it into the leather carrying case on his belt, then he hopped up on the mustang's back and reached down for Valla's hand. She jumped, and he pulled, then she slid her arms around him, leaning into his back. Victor's stupid smile returned as he urged Guapo to get moving. "How does Uvu always know when you want him? I've never seen you call him."

"He's an evolved creature, Victor. He can sense my intentions; we're sort of bonded."

"Seriously?"

"Why would I lie?" She squeezed his ribs, and Victor couldn't think of an objection. They passed through the gate and sat there for a couple of minutes under the scrutiny of the guards on the camp fortification's parapets while they waited for Uvu and Edeya. The cat got there first, and Victor swore he saw some pink stains on the pale fur around its jaws. It warbled a funny greeting, and Valla slid off Guapo to jog over to him, summoning his riding tack from her storage ring. While she got mounted, Edeya arrived, looking pleased with herself atop Thistle's proud shoulders.

She greeted Victor with, "Lam says that she'll do something terrible to you in your sleep if you let any harm come to me."

"That's . . . disturbing." He shrugged and turned to Valla, now sitting atop Uvu. "Right. Are you two sleepyheads ready to go? Can't believe how late we are!"

"That's not—" Edeya started to say.

"Are you serious?" Valla cried.

Victor laughed and whistled, and Guapo launched down the road in a clatter of sparking hooves, leaving the two outraged women behind. He could see the soldiers down the road, just now reaching the end of the stone highway. It was still strange to Victor how the Empire had come this far, exploring through the Granite Gates, creating the wide pass and solid road, only to stop at the edge of the Marches. Had they gotten a similar conquest directive from the System and lost or backed down? He doubted he'd ever know the real story unless he went to Tharcray and beat it out of someone.

He easily caught up to the column and rode around them toward the front where Sarl marched. Victor looked over the soldiers' heads and saw that Edeya and Valla were halfway to the cohort, trotting or loping, in Uvu's case, down the road. Then he saw shadows leap into the sky behind them, orange and red patterns flickering in the air. "The Naghelli are almost here."

"Perfect timing, sir."

"You think the road's end is the start of the Marches or up in the pass where we received the System quest?"

"No idea, I'm afraid." Sarl ran his gaze up toward the high mountains and then out over the hilly plains below. Victor admired that the captain marched on foot with his cohort. He knew not all of the captains did so—he'd seen Rellia's uncle, Ordus, riding a vidanii almost as fancy as hers.

"How far away do you think that greenish mist is?" Victor could see the haze hanging on the ground toward the horizon and beyond it the high bank of dark fog that everyone agreed had to be the doing of the invaders.

"We can see that fog wall because it's so tall," Sarl said, "likely fifty miles or so. The mist is much closer, maybe three miles. I can barely see it from the ground here, but I imagine it's clearer to you up on that beast of yours."

"Yeah." Victor turned as Edeya and Valla caught up, Thistle pounding the ground as he slowed. "We'll ride up and see what the story is with the mist. I don't want anyone but me going into it—at first, anyway."

"A little slower, please, Legate." Valla gave him a funny look—half grin, half narrowed eye.

"Right. Sarl, when the Naghelli get here, have Kethelket catch up to us."

"Will do, sir."

"Come on, you two." Victor clicked his tongue, Guapo started trotting, and the two women hurried after him.

"What do we do," he said to Valla as she brought Uvu up on his right, "if that mist is toxic?"

"We'll have the alchemists study it and create an elixir of resistance."

"Ahh, yeah." Victor nodded. "Magic helps everything. Still, that would be a pain in the ass."

"True. Depending on what sort of duration the resistance has and how many troops we'll need to push through to battle, it could pose quite a delay."

Victor didn't answer, contemplating the idea of having to craft thousands of vials of magical resistance potions and imagining what it would be like for the effects to wear off mid-battle. He hoped the mist wasn't like that. As they continued into the brush and hardy grass of the low hills, leaving the Empire's roadway behind, he noted how dark the soil was as their mounts kicked up the loose sod. It seemed rich and fertile. The air was temperate, not very humid, but not dry. "Nice countryside if that shit wasn't up there." He nodded forward toward the gray-green mist.

"Reminds me of the farmland south of Persi Gables," Edeya said, urging Thistle to come up on Victor's left.

Victor nodded to her, then looked over at Valla. "I was serious, by the way. I'll be the first to ride into that haze. If I feel okay, you guys can test it. First Valla, then you, Edeya. It'll give us a good gauge of its toxicity. You're still Tier Two, yeah?"

"I am, though Tier Three is calling me close after the battle with the imperials."

"Awesome." He held his hand down, palm up, and when Edeya looked up at him with raised eyebrows, he said, "Slap my palm with yours. It's called 'giving five.'"

She grinned and did as he said, slapping her small hand into his meaty palm. "Why five?"

"How many fingers do you have?"

"Ahh!" She laughed, delighted by the stupid ritual, and Victor turned to see Valla's expression. She was shaking her head, clearly struggling not to grin.

"What?"

"What's wrong with a good handshake or a firm grasp of the wrist? What's your obsession with all these hand- and knuckle-slapping rituals?"

"The troops love 'em. It's a lot faster than a handshake. I'm not saying you *shouldn't* shake hands, but sometimes you just want a quick fist bump, you know?"

"It's better than a slap on the ass," Edeya added.

"Who's slapping your ass?" Victor's voice rose with outrage.

"The delvers used to do it all the time—clap me on the shoulder, squeeze me in a stinky hug, or slap my ass! They all did it to each other! You never noticed?"

"Nah. Maybe I was too ugly."

"More likely too smelly." Valla couldn't contain her laugh as she fled, Uvu loping up the next hill. Victor and Edeya urged their mounts after her, her laugh trilling as she followed hot on Victor's heels. They'd barely crested the hill, though, when Valla pulled Uvu to a halt, holding up a hand and pointing ahead. Victor followed her gesture and saw what had brought her to a stop— some dark figures were moving through the mists ahead, and one of them was very large with baleful red eyes that glowed through the obscuring haze.

5

CONTACT

How many did you count?" Victor asked Valla, mentally urging Guapo to stop.

"I saw the big one and a few shapes behind it . . ."

"There were at least ten that I made out." Victor had watched the shadowy figures as they turned away from him, shuffling farther into the misty haze. He glanced over his shoulder and saw the army was still a ways off but noted the dark shape of Kethelket fluttering toward them. "Edeya, ride back. Tell Sarl what we found. I don't want those things to get away." He jerked his head toward the mist. "Valla, wait for Kethelket; he's almost here. If that mist is toxic, I'll warn you."

"Victor, wait—" Valla started to say, but he'd already launched himself down the hill, and Guapo's long strides left her objection behind. Twenty seconds later, the mustang's hooves were kicking up the mist, causing it to swirl and drift. It was thick and damp, and when Victor felt it clinging to his knuckles and arms, then onto his face, he took a breath, tasting the air, determined to see if there was anything for his troops to worry about.

The air was moist and carried a musty odor that reminded Victor of an old garbage bag that needed changing. It brought to mind rotting things and wet crawl spaces. Still, it fed his lungs, and he didn't cough or feel ill. If there was something dangerous about it, it wasn't immediately evident. Perhaps it was more a by-product of the invading creatures than a tool of the conquest. He urged Guapo forward, and the big horse ate up the ground, even walking.

Victor found his ability to see inside the mist limited as it closed behind him. He could make out the ground nearby and perhaps twenty feet ahead. Beyond that, things grew hazy; the shrubs, occasional clumps of stones, and sporadic small trees took on ominous appearances. Everywhere he looked, he thought he saw dark shadows lurking in wait. Victor frowned and cast Iron Berserk, savoring the power that swelled his being. As his vision tinted to red, he made room in his pathways and summoned his banner. The blazing golden sun seemed to have a physical impact on the mists, cooking them off and forcing them back.

"That's better," he rumbled, clicking his tongue. As Guapo steered around a slight stony rise, Victor reached up and loosened Lifedrinker. She was eager in his hands, and he knew what she wanted. "We might have some fun today, *chica*."

He didn't know if she would respond, but if so, she never got the chance. With strange grunts and hisses, a dozen shambling, bulky figures charged out of the mist, leaping at Victor and the mustang. They were big, bipedal, and covered with ragged cloth, strange tatters of vegetation, and mismatched patchwork armor. What flesh Victor could make out was pale, pitted with gross yellow ulcers and gaping wounds that oozed black fluid.

Victor was berserk and no slouch, so he saw the attack coming and instantly urged Guapo to dance back. It would have been a good reaction if something massive hadn't been flying at him from the top of the stone outcropping. A tremendous weight smashed into his right shoulder, bowling him over, off the horse, to tumble onto the rough ground where the other assailants piled on, grasping, clawing, and biting.

Victor roared and thrashed, grasping with his left hand, ripping any-thing he got ahold of, flinging the bulky figures off him. His right hand did even more to win him free, hacking Lifedrinker in wild arcs. Her blade almost immediately burst into smoldering orange magma-like fury, sizzling through the attackers, ripping their armor, clothing, and flesh. The weirdest thing about the attack and the creatures perpetrating it was their utter lack of vocalization—they breathed loudly and grunted. Still, they didn't growl, scream, or cry out as Victor finally fought to his feet and began to lay about him with Lifedrinker in a series of masterful cleaves, feints, and hacks.

The shambling hulks were about half his size in his titan form, and they fully occupied Victor's attention, which might be why he lost track of the bigger one, the creature that had knocked him off his horse. He was soon reminded of its presence, though, when it smashed into him from behind, knocking him forward in a stumble. Despite the attack on his blindside, Victor gathered his balance by ramming into a pair of the smaller shamblers and breaking through before turning to put all his enemies in his frontal arc.

The bigger creature—for Victor had decided these weren't exactly people—was close to his size, bulky with arms so long they dragged on the ground. It was clearly a different species from the shambling monsters; it had a yellowed bone-like carapace that covered its chest and back. Worse, its brawny, too-long, spongy gray-fleshed arms were spotted with knobby calcified growths. Despite its monstrous appearance, the thing wore black leather trousers on its stubby thick legs. Victor hadn't been able to get a good look at its face because a thick leather mask covered it, exposing nothing but apple-sized, baleful, faintly luminescent bloodshot eyes.

"Victor!" As he'd squared off with the gigantic masked brute and the remaining shamblers, Valla and Kethelket stumbled onto the scene of the ambush. She called out as soon as she saw him with Lifedrinker held ready, pacing sideways, trying to get a feel for how fast the monsters could move.

"Kill these little *pendejos*! Let me work on this big boy!" He needn't have said anything more—faster than a blink of the eye, Kethelket was dancing among the shamblers on Victor's left flank, his swords arcing with silver-blue Energy, ripping hunks off them as they shuffled to turn their attention on this new threat. Valla stayed back, but she held up her hands, and suddenly an arc of lightning, accompanied by an immediate crack of deafening thunder, smashed into one of the shamblers to Victor's right. In a whirlwind of sparking gusts, she launched herself at the creature she'd stunned with her spell, hacking one of its arms off with Midnight.

Victor saw all that, but he wasn't standing idly. As soon as Kethelket moved, he leapt forward and, Lifedrinker held high, hacked downward, determined to split the bony carapace-like armor on the hulk's chest. The bulky juggernaut flung one of its arms up, trying to intercept Victor's blow, but he was too slow; Lifedrinker, smoldering and trailing black smoke like a comet hitting the atmosphere, smashed down into that bony plate and . . . bounced off, a few chips of bone following her rebound as Victor struggled to maintain his grip. Meanwhile, the juggernaut's other arm swung up, and a fist like a wrecking ball hit Victor just under his left ribs, sending him reeling and gasping as his lungs emptied.

"Okay, okay, hang on, *chica*, I'll get you a better bite." Victor danced to the right, hopping the smoldering corpse of a shambler—one Valla had finished off with another thunderous lightning blast. He circled the colossal monster, noting that while it could swing its arms quickly, it didn't seem too quick on the uptake. It followed his movements but was always a bit behind. It was as though it had to think for a second to confirm what its bulging red eyes were telling it. At least, that's the impression Victor had as he easily outmaneuvered the creature, circling behind it to launch a blazing diagonal cleave at the leathery cap wrapped around its bulbous head.

Again, Lifedrinker sang her fury and eagerness as she ripped through the air. Again, she crashed into the target Victor had chosen, and this time her edge bit deeply, slicing the leather, spraying black fluids in a shower, and cleaving a two-inch trench through the monster's skull. The juggernaut staggered, grunting a weird whistling cry, a sound that made Victor imagine a large man trying to blow a note from a PVC pipe. Victor was a born fighter, a rage-fueled machine with a killer instinct, and he capitalized on the brute's stumble. He followed behind it, hacking left and right, aiming for any part of the monster not covered by that bony carapace.

Steaming black blood showered the battlefield, spraying the ground, the other monsters, and Victor. Lifedrinker easily bit through the gray flesh on the juggernaut's arms, hacking to the bone, biting into it, and leaving the limbs mangled and ineffectual. His rage simmered and boiled as he worked to savage the brutish creature. As he drenched himself in the hot, rancid blood, he began to laugh and roar. He worked his way around it, shredding the flesh on its arms, repeatedly cutting grooves in its skull. Finally, as he found himself at its back again, he hacked into its knee, again and again, until the thing toppled forward, causing the ground to shudder with the impact.

The juggernaut continued to writhe, flopping its ruined arms, trying to get them beneath it as though it might push itself up. Victor could see the gray flesh beneath the rim of that leather cap, and he stepped to the side, lifted Lifedrinker high, and brought her down like a guillotine blade, burying her silvery, smoldering edge halfway through that gray tree trunk of a neck. The monster bucked and thrashed, kicking its stumpy legs as Lifedrinker took her due, drawing the pulsing reddish-black Energy out of the festering flesh, helping the juggernaut realize its time in this life was over. While she feasted, Victor looked up through the eye slits of his helmet, watching the black blood drip off the metal.

Kethelket was still dancing with a couple of badly injured shamblers, and Valla was hard at work weaving between another three. Victor looked down at Lifedrinker again and saw she was nearly done, the Energy flow reduced to a thin trickle. "Come on, beautiful. Let's help Valla." He pulled the axe out and launched himself into the back of the nearest shambler, knocking it down and laying into it. In two heavy cleaves, it was dead, then he pounced on another. By the time it was motionless at his feet, Valla had finished the last of the three.

Victor turned to see Kethelket whipping his swords in an elaborate flourish, flinging the black blood from their blades just before he sheathed them. He met Victor's eyes and nodded. "Sturdy creatures. If they hit us with numbers, we'll have to fight defensively, lest we're overwhelmed."

"They were certainly more dangerous than the average imperial soldier." Valla prodded at a dead shambler with her boot.

"Huh." Victor's lack of a detailed comment was due to him staring at the juggernaut he'd slain. He walked over to it and leaned down, knocking his knuckles against its bony armor. "I couldn't cut through this shit. Is it armor, or is it growing out of him?" He heard the soft footfalls of the Naghelli as he came near, tiny next to the giant monster, and pressed his palm against the bone.

"This is a creature of death magic," Kethelket said. "I'm afraid it's been purposely grown with that bony armor. If this is an example of what the invaders are capable of, then we may indeed be in for a difficult conquest."

Valla hopped up the side of the stone outcropping, pulling herself to the top. She stood there looking southward and said, "Do you think they're aware of this? I mean, aware that we just killed some of them?"

"Belikot would know. He could feel when his creations were destroyed." Kethelket tapped his chin thoughtfully.

"I see a structure!" Valla pointed farther south into the mists.

"What kind?"

"Stone. High walls and square. It was visible for only a few seconds as the wind shifted this sickly fog."

"This was a small party. Do you think they have larger forces nearby?" Kethelket was walking among the dead shamblers, examining them. Victor glanced his way, then he noticed the Energy gathering among the corpses and braced himself—the motes boiling out of the juggernaut's corpse were purple. He saw Valla hop down from the pile of jumbled boulders, and then it hit him, and he lost himself in the euphoria of victory.

When it was over and he didn't have any System messages waiting, he felt a little disappointed, but he supposed it was to be expected. Gaining levels was, as everyone kept telling him, slower the higher one's tier. It wasn't as though he'd been in any real danger during the battle—he hadn't had to strain to win. "Maybe next time," he said, flipping Lifedrinker and snatching her out of the air by the handle. She was a big axe, but not when he was titan-sized. Thinking about it, Victor cut off his Iron Berserk and resumed his normal stature. He looked at Kethelket standing idly, perhaps reading a System message, perhaps just deep in thought.

"Hey," he said. "The army should be here soon. Kethelket, can you get your people and try to scout out that building? I think we should proceed with caution; the main purpose of this mist seems to be to hinder visibility. My banner does good work on it, but I bet there are other affinities that can burn it off; maybe even fire would work."

"I'll speak to my people. We'll have a look around."

"Any thoughts, Valla?" Victor asked, watching Kethelket flutter into the air and then streak northward. As she contemplated the question, Victor kicked at the corpse of the juggernaut again, looking for any sign of a ring or pouch—anything that might be valuable. He supposed if he were in Coloss, they'd probably harvest some of the parts. He didn't know what was worth harvesting, though, aside from maybe the dense bone carapace. How would he do it, though? He needed a knife like Tes's.

Valla said, "If you consider the fact that the area of ground apparently affected by this mist and the thicker fog farther south is hundreds, maybe thousands of square miles, and we stumbled upon this force of fifteen in the first hundred yards . . . what are the odds? What if there are units like this all over the place? What if they can communicate? What if another ten or hundred units like this are coming toward us as we speak?"

"How tough were they?" Victor asked. "I mean, really? I thought the shambling, rotting creeps were kind of weak."

"They aren't particularly dangerous one at a time, but they're incredibly resilient. Look at them; they're like constructs of dead body parts and . . . plants or fungus. Ancestors! They stink!" She'd approached one of the dead shamblers and showed Victor how the flesh was rotting on their strange pale faces. Their eyes were milky, some even rotting with ooze and pus dripping from the sockets. Victor could see strands of hair, twisted and damp, hanging down over some of the creatures' faces, but worst of all was the way gray-green creepers and clumps of moss or fungus seemed to grow in the rotten flesh.

"Yeah. Let's get back to the soldiers." Victor looked about, and as if in response to his thoughts, Guapo charged out of the mist. "Where'd you go, boy? Just hanging back watching me fight?" He pulled himself up and saw Valla looking around, a scowl creasing her brow. "No Uvu?"

"He was fighting with us at first . . . I think he chased something. He's usually better about checking back with me."

"We'll get one of the scouts to track him. Come on." Victor held his hand down, and Valla nodded, taking it. He hoisted her up behind him, and Guapo began to pound over the ground. He'd only crested the first hill when Victor saw a group of soldiers, maybe fifty strong, running down the next slope toward them. Sarl led them, and Edeya kept pace alongside, riding Thistle. When everyone had halted, Victor rode up to them and said, "They're dead, but we feel like more are probably coming. We should get the soldiers set."

"The rest of the cohort isn't far behind." Sarl gestured back the way they'd come. "What are we dealing with?"

"We killed some . . ." Victor let his words trail off as something new pricked at his ears. A distant low rumble that he almost missed at first. When he concentrated, though, he began to pick out the distinct notes—drums. He heard drums, and they were in sync, rolling through the cloying mist like distant thunder. He couldn't pinpoint exactly where they came from, other than south, but he thought there was more than one source. "I think you might have been at least partially right, Valla."

"Soldiers! Back up the hill! Form a front line! Shield wall formation!" Sarl immediately began barking orders, and the soldiers responded with alacrity, turning in an about-face and marching up the gentle slope toward the top. Victor hoped they'd be able to form up before whatever was banging those drums showed up. He hoped the soldiers were ready, and he hoped there wasn't anything much worse than what he, Kethelket, and Valla had already dealt with. "Any further commands?" Sarl asked him, breaking his train of thought.

"No. I'll be here. I'll keep my banner up, and I'll help deal with whatever comes our way. I'll be up in a minute; I want to talk to Kethelket first."

Sarl nodded and turned to follow his soldiers. "On the double!"

Victor turned back to the south, watching the mist, listening to the drums, wondering if he should just get the soldiers to start double-timing it all the way back up to the keep. What if a thousand shamblers came out of that fog? What if a hundred of the bone juggernauts did? What if the entire Glorious Ninth got wiped out because he didn't know better than to retreat when they had the chance?

"Here they come," Valla said, tugging on his shoulder and gesturing to the sky above the retreating soldiers. Victor looked and saw the Naghelli, all fifty, fluttering toward him. "What are you going to tell them?"

"Just to get us an idea of what's coming and to get a look at that structure you saw. I feel like we should maybe run. Another part of me wants to spit in my own face for thinking it. We've caught the invaders by surprise here. They might have a lot of units nearby, but for all we know, they're sending a response to the three of us. They don't know we've got more than six hundred soldiers on that hill. This might be our best chance to really sucker punch 'em."

"I'm with you. Listen to your instincts, Victor."

6

HORDES

Victor was once again enlarged by Iron Berserk, and he rode Guapo up and down the front rank of soldiers, looming over them, gigantic on his massive mustang, his great banner blazing with light that pushed back the obscuring mists. In the cohort's compact modified phalanx formation, that golden aura touched almost every one of the soldiers. The drums had grown louder, rumbling over the ground, but the troops didn't care; they were buoyed by Victor's presence, by the closeness of their shield brothers and sisters, and by the months of drilling they'd done, preparing for a battle like this.

Victor had been hollering at them to get ready, to show these "undead *pendejos*" what they could do. Now he wrapped it up by shouting, "You're the Glorious Ninth, and you have the spirits of fallen comrades watching—it's time to kick some ass!" The soldiers cheered, bashing their spears, axes, swords, and cudgels against their shields. Victor whirled Guapo, looking down the slight slope toward the sound of the drums, wondering what Keth-elket and his people were finding.

He looked to the left, at the forward corner of the formation, and saw Edeya and Valla, both mounted on Thistle. Valla wouldn't admit it, but Victor could see she was very worried about Uvu. He'd asked her, outside of Edeya's hearing, to keep an eye on the young Ghelli, to stay with her during the battle and help her break free for a retreat if need be. She'd wanted to argue, but she knew how Victor fought, knew he'd be all over the place, shoring up the shield wall and pursuing the more powerful of the enemy combatants. She caught him looking their way and offered him a kind of salute, holding Midnight high and nodding her head. Victor nodded back.

He turned back to the approaching drums, and then he saw, materializing out of the mist, a pair of Naghelli, their wings a black and glowing orange blur as they streaked toward him, covering the hundred yards or so in seconds. They landed before him, a slight woman with pale hair in tight braids and a tall, thin man, his head completely shaven smooth. They both wore close-fitting black leather armor with the signature glimmering onyx-black chainmail vests of their kind. The man spoke, his voice breathless, while the woman leaned over, her hands on her knees as she regained her wind. "Kethelket sent us to report."

"Out with it then."

"More than five hundred of those you call shamblers, a half dozen bone giants, and a great many lesser undead, more than we could count."

"Shit." Victor's curse was nearly silent; he didn't want to break the troops' morale. "How close?"

"They run, and when we set out, they were less than two miles away. They'll break through into your light in minutes. They don't move like a disciplined army. Also, Kethelket wants you to know he's taken the rest of the Naghelli to inspect the structure you glimpsed."

"We could probably use their help . . ."

The woman straightened up and spoke in a surprisingly bright contralto voice. "We're to rejoin him with orders—the approaching horde did not seem to notice us in the sky. Kethelket thinks these are . . . 'simple troops,' I believe is how he put it."

"Okay. Tell him to see what the structure is, then fall on the enemy from behind. We'll hold this ground."

"As you say," the man said, and Victor briefly wondered if he should have gotten their names. The moment passed, though, as they both crisply saluted him and then launched into the air, streaking southward toward the thicker mists.

The drums had steadily increased in volume while they spoke, and when Victor let his eyes drift down from the flying scouts, he saw the first figures break from the mists and start tearing up the slopes; they reminded him of the ghouls he had fought in the dungeon near Greatbone Mine—pale creatures, hairless and naked, long-clawed, running on all fours. They lifted their weird noseless faces to the sky and coughed out their inhuman cries through mouths lined with jagged gore-stained teeth. Their eyes were yellow in the light of his banner, and they seemed to shy from it and the sunlight that pierced the weakened mist.

Still, they charged forth in the hundreds, much smaller than the shamblers but quick and vicious-looking. When they were a mere fifty yards distant, the archers at the center of the modified phalanx unleashed hundreds of arrows at Sarl's shouted command. They streaked through the air, trailing black smoke from their blazing shafts, and when they struck home, many of the ghouls fell, tumbling over the rough ground. Victor roared his approval and summoned an enormous rage-fueled bear, placing it halfway between the army and the charging creatures. The bear roared to life, springing from a red mist of Energy and bounding into the face of the monsters.

"Hold!" Victor roared as he saw some soldiers step forward, perhaps feeling they should run to fight beside the bear. "Let my bear soften their charge!"

"Fire!" Sarl screamed, and another volley of arrows streaked into the charging ghouls with the precision only an Energy user could provide. More of them fell, and then in a flurry of coughing shrieks, dirt, and claws, they fell upon the front row of soldiers, smashing into their shields. Meanwhile, Victor's bear rampaged among them, throwing them left and right, snapping their limbs and heads off with vicious bites. Ghouls clung to its back, raking its thick hide with their claws, utterly fearless despite how the bear mauled their comrades.

Victor charged up and down the front line, smashing over the ghouls with Guapo, hacking down with his axe. Lifedrinker obliterated the monsters when she hit home, her scorching, razor-sharp blade more than a match for their leathery skin and hard bones. Meanwhile, his banner blazed, giving comfort and aid to his soldiers and seemingly causing pain and near blindness to the undead. He watched as the last of the ghouls crested the hill and the phalanx opened, the sides moving out in unison to a trumpeted command, boxing in and flanking the creatures.

Victor and his bear rampaged among the enemy while the soldiers beat them back, hacking and stabbing over the shields of the front line. Arrows and spells fell upon the horde, and Victor laughed at the slaughter, a part of him thankful to the forces of Prince Hector for their lack of discipline—it wasn't until the ghouls were nearly slaughtered that the larger part of the attacking force began to mount the hill. Sarl ordered the bugler to call for the phalanx to reform, and the wings collapsed, pressing in tight, forming that impenetrable box again. As the last of the ghouls were mopped up, mindlessly flinging themselves on the front line, Victor watched the next wave approach.

His earlier euphoria was challenged as he saw the numbers pouring out of the mist. These creatures were slower than the ghouls, but they were bigger and far more numerous—hundreds of shamblers and at least twice that number of smaller but better-equipped monsters. Despite the hundred yards between them, Victor's eyes were good, piercing the haze of the half-formed mist trying to seep into the light of his banner. He studied the smaller enemy combatants and saw they looked very much like zombies from movies he'd seen back on Earth but geared out with all sorts of armor, shields, and weapons.

They shuffled along with the shamblers, sometimes getting trampled or knocked aside by the larger undead. Their eyes were vacant, and their mouths, if they had a lower jaw, hung open. They looked almost pathetic in that regard, but Victor knew better. He could see the waves of dark Energy pulsing through their forms, and he knew they weren't just mindless, slow zombies that could be mowed down; they looked formidable.

Marching among the shamblers and zombies were at least half a dozen of the bone-plated juggernauts like those he'd faced earlier. "Five too many," he grumbled, wondering how much damage they'd do while he struggled to kill them one by one. Victor whirled to find Sarl, saw him exhorting his soldiers to tighten up their shield wall, and urged Guapo over to him. "Sarl!" he called.

"Aye, Legate!"

"You need your casters to slow the giants. The ones with the bone plates. They're hard as hell to kill, and I can't get them all at once."

"Say no more, sir!" Sarl dove into the ranks of his soldiers, pushing his way toward the center of the phalanx, where his dedicated ranged units were arrayed. Victor, trusting the captain to get the job done, turned back to the advancing enemies and watched as missiles erupted from the formation behind him. Arrows and spells showered down among the zombies and shamblers, catching them alight, freezing them, or exploding in showers of sparks or even magma. Their slow, steady march didn't stop; they didn't scream or flee. The monsters simply continued to trudge forward, ignoring their fallen, broken brethren as more and more ranged attacks fell among them.

Victor, meanwhile, eyed the six juggernauts, watching them make their inevitable progress toward the phalanx. Arrows and spells hit them to no avail; they didn't flinch, and they certainly didn't fall. He glanced over his shoulder at the soldiers; they looked good, eager even. He didn't see any dead or wounded. Either they'd had an exceptionally easy time with the ghouls, or they'd pulled their casualties back into their ranks. Victor let his eye drift further into the phalanx, looking for Sarl, wondering what he and his casters could do about the rapidly approaching juggernauts.

He'd finally picked out Sarl's red-plumed helmet when, in unison, several mages cried out, a weird note in their voices as the temperature of the air dropped by several degrees. Frost sprang into existence on the helmets of the soldiers near the center of the formation, and then with a great *whoosh*, a ball of icy swirling water erupted from a trio of casters, surging through the air, arcing high, crystallizing the thin mist as it passed, creating a sort of faux snowfall. Victor watched its progress as it hurtled down the slight slope, passing by the front rows of shamblers and zombies and then crashing into one of the bone-plated juggernauts. The creature staggered and nearly fell back, and when the splash of icy water and mist faded away, Victor could see it was frozen in place, unmoving.

"Hell yes!" He pumped his fist in the air, waving Lifedrinker. "Okay, *chica*, we need to figure out how to kill these things quicker." Victor tightened his knuckles on Lifedrinker's haft, then pushed his Sovereign Will bonus into his muscles, enhancing his strength and vitality. As the sinews of his neck and shoulders bulged and battle fury began to tint his vision red, he cast Channel Spirit, filling his right arm and Lifedrinker with his furious rage-attuned Energy.

Victor urged Guapo into a charge, and he saw another ball of icy water streak over the zombies and shamblers, bursting into the chest of yet another juggernaut. Victor veered to the left; the now frozen giant had been his intended target. He didn't have to look far to see a new goal. Not thirty yards distant, the front line of shamblers and zombies surged toward him, and just a few ranks back marched another juggernaut. It wasn't quick, but its larger stature afforded it more speed, and it was literally trampling its smaller comrades in its hurry toward the front line of Victor's soldiers. Victor leaned forward, and Guapo leapt into motion, streaking toward the enemy.

The shamblers were big, maybe big enough to stop Guapo in his tracks, so Victor aimed for gaps in their ranks, trusting the giant mustang to trample the smaller zombies despite their armor and shields. His trust was well founded; the horse crashed into the first rank, utterly flattening one zombie and then bowling aside two more as Victor's outstretched boot kicked a shambler aside. Five seconds later, they'd crashed through two more ranks, and the juggernaut was before him.

Victor couldn't have accurately guessed his speed when Guapo charged past, and he swung Lifedrinker into the juggernaut's leather-wrapped forehead, but it had to be pretty damn fast. He put everything he had into that hacking cleave, trusting that his instinct was right, that Lifedrinker could handle it, and that she wouldn't bounce off or break. He believed her haft was stronger than the juggernaut's skull. At least, he hoped so. He hoped this particular creature wasn't any tougher than the one he'd already killed.

His gamble paid off; Lifedrinker's smoldering edge sliced through the air, hardly slowing when it touched the thick leather wrapping the juggernaut's brow, splitting the bone beneath with a thunderous *crack* that echoed through the wild melee. In a steaming spray of black blood, Lifedrinker chopped through the top third of the monster's skull, slicing off a leather-wrapped bone bowl full of rancid, frothing brains. As Guapo thundered past and Victor recovered Lifedrinker's momentum in a looping swing, the juggernaut collapsed face first onto the rough, blood-spattered turf, utterly still.

Victor held Lifedrinker high, her blade smoldering and streaming black smoke into the air, and he screamed his battle lust. Despite the imminent assault on the phalanx by shamblers and zombies, many of his troops echoed his war cry, having watched him drop the giant bone-plated monstrosity. Victor whirled Guapo, hacking downward with his axe, giving the mustang some room to move. As he spun, he took in the battlefield and saw that three of the juggernauts were now frozen in place, only two more still making progress toward his army. He zeroed in on the closest one, and Guapo leapt into action.

The mustang trampled the zombies with ease, but their claws and weapons began to take a toll, leaving long gouges in the horse's flanks. Victor knew the spirit animal wasn't indestructible, knew it would have to depart this realm soon, but he hoped he could get one more good charge out of him. "Come on, *Guapito!*" He urged the horse with his will to continue the charge, trampling zombies and shouldering between shamblers. The mustang soldiered on, and Victor, too, began to amass wounds.

The shamblers' claws and the zombies' weapons cut through his sturdy leather pants, and when they met his flesh, they left shallow cuts that his Berserk Energy rapidly healed. Nevertheless, the wounds stung, and something vile was on the blades and claws, something that his body had to fight off. He began to notice the effect and felt his rage seeping away as the Energy was forced to fight harder and harder to heal him. "Dirty assholes," he growled, as with a tremendous yawp he brought Lifedrinker down on the back of the second juggernaut's skull. She split the thing's head like a dry log, showering brains to either side as it collapsed in a heap.

Victor felt Guapo fading, so he released him. As the mount dispersed in a cloud of sparkling golden mist, Victor landed on his feet and began to lay about himself with Lifedrinker, slaughtering shamblers and zombies. The zombies were surprisingly sturdy. Even though Victor was more than twice their size, some of them managed to deflect his blows. Of course, this only further enraged Victor, and he began to lose himself to the mad dance of slaughter. He swung Lifedrinker one-handed, and with his left hand, he grabbed his opponents, threw them, and swung them about, smashing them into each other and creating openings for his axe.

Simultaneously, he became aware of a low roar, like a distant river crashing over boulders, and he felt a pang from his Battle Awareness feat. Victor paused his slaughter and jerked his head toward the formation of his soldiers. Sure enough, the roar was the sound of zombies and shamblers pounding on shields, punctuated by the shouts, screams, and battle cries of the troops. Then his eyes fell on the other unfrozen juggernaut—it was carving a swath through the phalanx, already three ranks deep. Victor roared and leapt, bunching his mighty legs and exploding into the air. He arched his back, hoisted Lifedrinker in a two-handed grip, and screaming like a wyrm-scale-clad meteor, fell toward the colossal monster's back.

His aim wasn't perfect, or perhaps the monster moved, or both, but Lifedrinker's edge cut a groove through the back of the juggernaut's skull instead of completely splitting it. She slid through the bone, then her smoldering edge impacted the back of the undead monstrosity's bone carapace, and with the sound of a cannon shot, she split it.

Ayeeeeeeeeeee! she shrieked, the war cry of an avenging angel, and she *pulled* with more force than Victor had ever felt from her, burying herself into the rotten spine of the monster as it fell on its face, shaking the ground and eliciting thunderous cheers from the nearby soldiers.

"Good work, beautiful. Take what's yours." Victor released the axe and reached into his storage container, the one he'd taken from Karnice, and pulled out a massive two-handed maul. It was a hugely heavy weapon, one that Victor had examined before and determined would be a nice weapon in a pinch. Every part of the maul was made of a copper-colored metal, a single piece from which the handle and the two hammerheads were forged. The handle was grooved and rough, easy to grip, and the sides of the anvil-sized hammerhead were etched with black inlaid runes.

"Let's see what you can do, big boy." He laughed, shouldering past his troops toward the front line, where they struggled to hold back the massive shamblers. "Come on, *pendejos!*" he roared, lifting the hammer high. "Fight like you fucking *mean* it!" Then he waded between an Ardeni man with a tower shield and a wild-looking Shadeni with a silvery round shield on one arm and a short trident in her other hand. He thrust the maul forward, slamming it into the face of a shambler, knocking it back, and then he was in the fight, whipping that great hammer around like an *abuela* with a broomstick.

7

GLORY AND DEATH

Almost immediately, Victor began to regret not letting Lifedrinker drink her fill. The maul was a good weapon, probably crafted of something extremely rare or powerful, but it was nothing like his axe. Lifedrinker was alive in his hands; she *pulled* toward his targets, was weightless on his backswings, and effortlessly changed direction with just a nudge. The maul, on the other hand, felt like swinging a Volkswagen attached to a lead rod. It was ponderous, momentous, and when he heaved it to and fro, Victor had to follow through, had to move his body to accommodate the immensely dense hammerhead.

Nonetheless, the effects of all that weight and momentum were satisfying; Victor cleared great swathes of zombies and shamblers with a single swing, putting all his strength into massive, ripping cleaves that required him to take several steps to keep control. It would have been a disastrous battle if he weren't so tough, so well-armored, and so large. With each swing, as he smashed the undead aside, a dozen more rushed in behind him to claw and hack at his sides and back. The maul was a tedious weapon to redirect, and he rarely found himself able to put it between himself and an attacker. Instead, he had to focus on his ability to be mobile—he leapt, he charged, and he smashed pathways for himself, always turning, spinning, and dodging to relieve the pressure on his flanks.

Meanwhile, the soldiers in the Ninth fought like the rugged resilient terriers they were. They maintained their shield wall, pulling back dead or dying comrades and filling the gap from the next rank. They used their Energy abilities to bolster their lines, to fling fire and other elements onto the hordes of undead, and encouraged by Victor's banner and his roaring, screaming, smashing titanic form, they slowly but surely began to turn the tide of the battle. They must have been outnumbered nearly three to one at the start, but with the quick dispatch of the ghouls and the steady whittling of the zombies and shamblers, the mounds of dead, destroyed, or maimed attackers began to grow, and the numbers of those still pressing against their shields dwindled.

Things took a different turn when the undead drummers finally joined the fray. Perhaps they'd held back, lurking in the mist, using their other-worldly, gut-twisting music to bolster the attacking hordes. Maybe their Energy was running dry, and their default next action was to attack. Or, just maybe, the intelligence that drove this army against Victor and the Ninth saw that their drums weren't helping enough and urged them forward. Whatever the reason, six gigantic humanoid skeletons with purple flames dancing in the sockets of their eyes charged onto the field of combat.

The skeletal drummers carried polished bone clubs in one hand and enormous disc-like bone shields in the other. Victor knew they were the "drummers" because they came onto the battlefield smashing those clubs against their shields, creating the low concussive beat that had been the backdrop of the entire battle. This close, though, the concussions rolled up the slope, smashing through the undead and into the phalanx shield wall. The drumbeats had a physical presence—one of the giant drummers was down the hill directly in front of Victor, and when it banged out that note, the shockwave rolled into him, knocking him back several steps. It felt almost as if a wave of water had crashed over him.

The undead knocked down by the drummers' magic sprang back to their feet as if they'd been invigorated. Unfortunately, the shockwave had the opposite effect on the soldiers of the Ninth—they were knocked flat, and when they struggled to their feet, they looked dazed and disoriented. The shield wall began to crumble, the invigorated undead rushing to take advantage of the downed soldiers.

Throughout the battle, Victor had worked to kill the frozen juggernauts, and only one remained, held fast by the mages' repeated balls of icy water Energy. Victor had smashed the skulls of the other two and had been on his way to the final one when the drummers joined the fight. Seeing the effects of their sonic attacks, he made a split-second decision and used Titanic Leap to close the distance, aiming for the centermost skeletal drummer as it climbed over the corpses of its comrade zombies toward the phalanx.

He landed behind and to the left of the giant skeleton, marveled that he had to look up to see its head, and then brought the maul, whistling through the air in a two-handed overhead blow, down on the creature's spine. An ear-bleeding concussion resounded from the impact, but to Victor's shock, the skeleton stumbled forward and the enormously heavy maul rebounded—he couldn't see any damage to the bone. "No way!" he said, wondering if even Lifedrinker could cleave that bone. He'd hit the monstrosity hard enough to flatten an engine block. He might not have killed the skeleton, but he'd gotten its attention.

As it turned faster than it seemed it should be able to, the skeleton lashed out with its bone club, catching Victor in the ribs. The wyrm scales ate most of the damage, disbursing the force, but he still stumbled, though hot rage began to replace his battle euphoria. Victor needed a better weapon, and he didn't have time to hunt for Lifedrinker. Rather than dig around trying to find something else in his rings, he gripped the maul's handle tight and cast Imbue Spirit, sending his most abundant, potent Energy source into the spell pattern—fear.

Victor felt a piece of himself detach and flow with the spell's Energy into the maul. The weakness and lethargy from the loss was brief; he quickly adjusted. As the process completed, he saw the coppery, dense metal of the weapon darken. Purple-black swirls of Energy began to pulse along the haft, up to the hammer. Then they multiplied, magnifying each other, creating weird smoky discs of Energy that radiated outward from the center of the hammerhead and toward the business ends of the hammer. Victor grinned, marveling at the sudden lightness of the weapon, the sudden vibrancy of it. Why hadn't he ever tried imbuing Lifedrinker? "Because her spirit was already in there," he reminded himself.

As the skeleton staggered toward him, Victor cast Energy Charge, extending the hammer like a battering ram, and when he smashed into the undead giant, an explosion of bone fragments sprayed outward, utterly flattening the undead horde around him in a twenty-foot radius. "Fuck yes!" Victor roared, then lifted the hammer high and leapt at the next bony giant. The drummer saw him coming and lifted its shield, and Victor's enchanted maul smashed into it with a horrific *bong* that exploded over the battlefield, flattening a hundred or more shamblers and zombies—thankfully, the sound wave rolled away from Victor's impact toward the west and not the phalanx of soldiers.

The giant skeleton staggered at the blow, its shield vibrating wildly, and it pulled its arm back, giving Victor room for a perfect follow-up smash in the monster's chest. The Energy-driven hammerhead sent a wave of purple-black force through the bones, shattering them, releasing whatever Energy or spirit or malignant power drove the skeleton onward. It collapsed in a heap, and Victor whirled, looking for his next target. Panic gripped his heart as he saw the other four drummers were already assaulting the lines, pushing the soldiers back, flinging them left and right with their polished bone cudgels.

He ran toward the closest one, trying to get close enough to activate Energy Charge again, and then he heard a new sound, the susurration of rapidly flapping wings. He looked up and saw that the Naghelli had finally made a return appearance led by none other than Kethelket. They split into three groups, flying toward the farthermost skeletal drummers, and Victor took the hint—they were leaving the center one to him. When he'd closed to twenty yards, Victor cast Energy Charge, but he didn't lead with the maul; he didn't want to kill a bunch of soldiers with the explosion.

Instead, he slammed his shoulder into the giant's back, sending it flopping forward, crashing into the ground and knocking back several shield bearers who'd been bravely trying to hold it at bay. Victor hoped they'd be all right, but in his mind, they should be—no one should be out on this battlefield if they couldn't take getting knocked around a little. He stomped over to the skeleton, kicking it down as it struggled to rise, and he brought the maul down, smashing the monster into the bloody dirt. The giant's spine shattered, and Victor drove the fragments into the ground, pulverizing a handful of ribs and the creature's sternum along the way.

The soldiers nearby cheered, but Victor roared, "Don't stand around! Reform the line!" He scanned the field and saw the Naghelli were engaged with the skeletons, baiting them with rapid attacks, darting out of their reach, leading them away from the phalanx lines. Satisfied that the immediate threat was being dealt with, Victor turned to the last juggernaut and saw that it was starting to break free of its icy prison—the mages had been killed, drained of Energy, or too distracted by the collapse of the shield wall to maintain the spell. Victor tried to leap at the distant juggernaut but found his ability unresponsive.

As he struggled to figure out what was wrong, he ran toward the monster, smashing through the sparse lines of zombies and shamblers. He looked inward, wondering if the answer was at his Core, and found his hunch was correct—his Energies were dangerously low. He was about to lose his Berserk because his Rage Core was nearly empty. His fear Core was holding steady at around ten percent; had he really sent so much of it into the maul? His glory-attuned Energy was less than half, and so was his inspiration-attuned Energy—he'd been using that to power his charges. He didn't remember his Titanic Leap ability saying anything about Energy requirements, but something in his gut told him that was the problem; with his Energy so low, it wouldn't work.

Growling and gripping the maul tightly, Victor determined to finish the juggernaut before his Berserk faded. He primed his pathways with inspiration-attuned Energy, and when he was within a dozen strides, he cast Energy Charge. He tore over the ground to the side of the juggernaut, holding the maul over his left shoulder, and timed a decisive blow at the monster's chest as he streaked past. It was a perfect hit, and the enchanted maul absolutely obliterated the juggernaut's bony plate armor. The shockwave rocked the battlefield as the enormous undead creature tumbled head over heels down the slope, devoid of the Energy that had earlier animated it.

Victor was protected by the weird magic of his charge, which was probably what drained his Energy so much each time he used it; part of the Energy went into the charge, but another, sometimes more significant, part went into creating a shell to protect him from the destructive forces. Regardless, he didn't feel the concussion of his collision, but the straggling undead nearby did; they came apart in it, their rotting flesh and armor peeled off their bones. Their limbs were torn away, their necks and backs shattered, and their weapons and shields were ripped from grasping hands.

Victor felt his body contracting, felt the rage seep away from him, and he stood there leaning on the maul's handle, now long enough to come to his chin. He lifted it, found it was still easy to hoist with part of his spirit inhabiting it, and turned back to the formation of soldiers. Just as his eyes fell on them, horns sounded—the signal to charge—and the soldiers holding up the shield lines parted, allowing the third, fourth, and fifth lines to rush forth, smashing into the remaining undead, beating them back. Victor looked to the Naghelli swarming around the last of the skeletal drummers and saw that they were winning, somehow slowly draining the Energy from the giant undead, weakening the magic binding the bones.

"Victor!" Valla's distant voice made Victor jerk his head around, looking for her, wondering how he could have forgotten her for the entirety of the battle; not once had he worried about her safety or thought to seek her out. He finally laid eyes on her, waving Midnight high above her head, her other hand on Edeya's shoulder. The young Ghelli was gore-splashed, but she wore a toothy grin, and Victor jogged toward them. Along the way, he broke the connection to his Impart Spirit spell and sent the now mundane maul into his storage ring. Leaping corpses, weaving between the last of the skirmishes, he saw Edeya waving her spear above her head, trying to catch his eye.

"We did it! We won!" she cried as he drew near. Valla stood over her, fatigue clear in her expression, and Victor wondered how hard she'd had to battle to keep the young Ghelli safe. Hopefully, they'd both reap plenty of rewards for the effort. Thinking of rewards, Victor turned to scan the battlefield. Only a handful of small fights were still taking place, and it was clear most of the Ninth had survived, though an undeniable number of corpses wearing the campaign uniform littered the field.

"Another hard-fought victory for the Ninth." Valla followed his gaze, taking in the dead.

"Let's hope. I don't see any motes yet."

"Combat persists." Valla pointed to the last of the battles out on the slope. Victor was about to reply when, with a flutter of wings and shadows, Kethelket landed before them.

"We made an important discovery," he announced, forgoing niceties. Victor saw fatigue in his eyes, and blood spatters dotted his pale flesh.

"Good work on those bone drummers."

"Thank you. It costs a heavy toll in Energy, but we can weaken the death magic that binds their spirits, allowing us to damage their nigh-indestructible frames. Put that to the side, though, my lord. We must discuss the keep yonder." He pointed south into the mist where Valla had seen the stone structure.

"What about it?"

"It housed many of the creatures your army slew here on this field. When they marched past, we hid in the trees that dot the slopes near the walls. Afterward, we went inside and slew a guardian beast in the courtyard—a great rotting mound that moved with evil intent. The System then announced that we could capture the 'strategic location.' When I tried to do so, resting my hand upon a strange floating stone at the center of the courtyard, it said that a greater force must be present. I think we should go there, with this army of yours, before the invaders can rally more forces to thwart you."

Victor looked at Kethelket again, at his dark eyes and shimmering swords, at his glimmering armor and glowing wings; he seemed to know a lot about death magic and seemed highly competent. He hoped he could trust him because it was damn nice being able to rely on someone else to get shit done. He glanced at Valla, took in her slight shrug, and said, "Right. We'll get marching as soon as I speak to Sarl. Edeya, contact Lam and the others. Give them an update." He paused, looked at the gore-splashed Ghelli then at Valla, and said, "Where's Thistle?"

"He took a bad gash to his haunches, and we sent him off. He's not meant to be surrounded by undead, Victor." Valla had seen his frown and responded in kind, as though daring him to second-guess her.

"All right. Try to call him; you guys know how?"

"I know the whistle." Edeya demonstrated, holding two fingers between her lips and making a trilling call, the same one Victor had learned from Chandri.

"Good. Keep doing that, but message the base first." Victor turned toward the milling soldiers, and then he saw the golden motes starting to gather among the dead. "Sarl!" he called, walking toward the captain, getting ready for the stream of Energy that would no doubt throw everyone off task while it rewarded the victors. He'd only made it a few steps before his eyes were drawn to the thick purple motes growing out of a juggernaut corpse. He turned toward it, slapping a hand at Lifedrinker's empty harness, and hurried to retrieve her.

"Hey! Good work! Nice fighting! Gather your brothers and sisters! We march soon!" he called out to the soldiers he ran past, and then he was before the giant corpse, and he saw Lifedrinker's haft sticking out of its hunched, rotting shoulders. He reached forward, grabbed hold of her, and just as he pulled her gore-covered axe-head free, a torrent of Energy smashed into him.

*****Congratulations! You have achieved level 53 Battlemaster and gained 10 strength, 9 vitality, 4 agility, 4 dexterity, 3 will, and 3 intelligence.*****

When the euphoria faded, and he fell back to the ground, Victor couldn't fight the grin on his face or hold back his shout, "Hell yes!" He felt glorious, full of Energy, and stronger than ever. He looked at Lifedrinker and saw that she'd changed a little, too. Her blade was slightly bigger, her handle a bit thicker and longer, and more than that, he knew she was heavier. Even though she was denser, Victor had no trouble swinging her around, thanks to her spirit and the way she seemed to aid him with her movements. She ripped the air with deadly *whooshes* as he grinned, cleaving her left and right. "You're feeling good too, huh, *chica*?"

"I learned much from the dark Energy I drank from the bone-clad one we split. I grow eager to taste more of his kind; my edge itches to part their bones."

"Well, I'm sorry I didn't get to kill all these assholes with you. I wonder if you'd like to try something sometime."

"Try something?"

"How would you feel about me putting a bit of my spirit in there with you?"

"I . . . I think I'd like that, Victor. I think I'd like that very much."

8

OLD WALLS

After the battle, Sarl began to order his cohort to collect samples from the various undead, loot them for valuables, and then gather them into mounds so the Pyromancers could reduce them to ash. When Victor heard him giving the command, he approached the captain and said, "You're going to burn them all?"

"When dealing with the undead, it's usually best."

"Yeah, I guess that makes sense." Victor looked over the battlefield, taking in the piles of undead. The soldiers had been quick to gather their fallen comrades, but Victor thought he saw a Legion uniform here and there beneath the rotting, gory bodies of zombies. No doubt they'd be recovered as Sarl's orders were carried out, but Victor hated to see them, hated to think that people he'd just watched vibrantly marching forth were now cold flesh, spattered with gore, pinned beneath these vile creatures. "How many did we lose?"

Sarl inhaled slowly through his nose, frowning as he followed Victor's gaze. "Headcounts from the sergeants indicate seventy-four dead, but we've only recovered sixty-two bodies."

"I'm sure they'll turn up. I'm sorry for your losses, Sarl. Your troops fought damn well, though. I was amazed by those phalanx maneuvers."

Sarl stiffened his back at Victor's words, some pride bleeding into his stature. "Thank you, sir. I'm proud of them. We saw great gains after the battle."

"Damn right. The Ninth is going to be formidable at this rate."

"As you say, sir."

Victor watched him walk over to speak to one of his lieutenants, then turned to gaze over the field to where Edeya and Valla stood with Thistle. The vidanii had come around after the battle ended, limping from a deep gash in his left haunch. Valla had been treating the wound, rubbing some healing ointment into the cut, when Victor left to speak with Sarl. Frowning, wondering what had happened to Uvu and how he should broach the subject with Valla, he walked over to her. "How is he?"

"He'll be fine. Just a scar he can show off to Starlight," Edeya answered. She was upbeat, cheerful even. After the battle, she'd announced that she was Level Twenty-Nine, so Victor could see why—it was exciting to be on the cusp of a class refinement. Valla didn't look up, still massaging another layer of ointment into the vidanii's coarse fur, watching with a satisfied expression as the swollen red flesh around the puckered scar faded and diminished.

"Edeya, you better chug that racial advancement soon. You won't be able to advance to Tier Three without it."

"I'm well aware, sir." Edeya's toothy smile told Victor she probably couldn't think of much else.

"When we return to the base, then." Victor turned to Valla and placed a hand on her shoulder, gently squeezing. "I hate to bring it up, but . . . Uvu?"

"I can't feel him." She didn't look at him, refused to meet his gaze, as she continued her ministrations on Thistle's haunch.

"Can you usually?"

"Always." She sniffed, then looked up from her work. Her soft seafoam eyes were bloodshot as she said, "I can ride with you for now."

"Shit, Valla, I . . ."

"Nothing to be said. He's not a vidanii. He's a creature of war and conflict. I've been bracing myself for the possibility he'd get himself killed since Rellia gave him to me as a cub." Victor could see she was trying to put on a brave face, but her voice choked on the last sentence, and he knew she was hurting. He wanted to hug her, pull her close, and stroke her hair, but they were surrounded by soldiers, and Edeya was standing right there; he knew Valla wouldn't appreciate it—not at that exact moment.

"Maybe he'll come around." Edeya squeezed Valla's hand, interrupting her slow, methodical stroking of Thistle's coarse hide, trying to break the gloomy spell. "Maybe something in this mist or a different effect of the invaders' magic makes your connection to him silent."

"Maybe." Valla shrugged but offered Edeya a small smile. "Thanks for the thought."

Victor summoned Guapo, once again using glory-attuned Energy. He liked the mustang in that guise; he was showy and positive, and his brilliant eyes and the sparks of his hooves helped to drive back the gloom of the mist that kept creeping toward the army. The horse erupted from his weird sparkling golden pool of Energy and pranced about, his neck arched and his eyes flashing. "Good boy," Victor immediately said, patting his muscular shoulder. He glanced at the two women and was pleased to see some light in Valla's eyes and a broad smile on Edeya's face as they took in the proud animal.

"Let's go see what Kethelket was talking about." He swung onto the horse's back, then reached down to pull Valla up behind him. Edeya stepped into Thistle's stirrup and nodded her readiness. Before they left ahead of the army, Victor rode over to Sarl and said, "As soon as you're done here, Captain, march due southwest until you see the structure Kethelket told us about. We'll be waiting."

"Will do, sir!" Of course, he had to snap a perfect salute, which Victor had no way of returning from atop the horse. He slammed his fist into his chest, though, and gave the captain a solemn nod. Then he clicked his tongue, and Guapo leapt down the slope, weaving between the various squads of soldiers as they did their dirty work on the battlefield.

They'd already concluded that the mist, while not exactly harmless, wasn't much of a risk to soldiers. Victor couldn't notice anything when he stood in it, but some of the lower-tier soldiers complained of shortness of breath, a certain lassitude of the muscles, and a desire to get back to camp for a good sleep. Still, with the presence of stronger individuals driving them on, none seemed to be at any risk of being overcome.

Guapo and Thistle made short work of the slope, diving into the thicker mists as they thundered over the ground toward the structure Kethelket and his Naghelli were currently securing. Victor looked over at Edeya. "Doing all right?"

"Sleepy." Her eyes looked heavy, and she leaned forward toward Thistle's neck as she rode.

"Perk up, *chica*." He laughed, leaned down, grasped her shoulder, and gave her a rough jostle. "You're drinking that racial advancement the minute we get back!"

"I'm okay!" Her voice rose with outrage as she thrust his hand away, steering Thistle so he veered a few feet further from Guapo. Valla was silent through the exchange, her grip steady on Victor's ribs, and he suddenly felt ashamed for horsing around with Uvu missing. Before he could worry about it further, a dark structure loomed out of the mist ahead. He steered Guapo to the left, aiming to circle the building where, according to Kethelket, he'd find an open gate on the other side.

As they neared the corner, he felt Valla stir, and she said, "Those stones look old."

Victor eyed the building, noting the smoothly chiseled gray stone blocks and fine dark mortar lines. They'd been cut with precision and were huge; the blocks had to be three feet square. Victor followed the smooth flat wall upward with his eyes, noting crenellations about forty feet above them. Valla was right, though—the base of the stone wall was overgrown with lichen, and green-leafed vines were trying to climb the heights, though they only stretched twenty feet or so upward. It didn't look like something that had been built in recent history.

As they rounded the corner, he guessed the edifice was a square; it seemed this new side was the same length as the one they'd just ridden past. "A square, ancient keep." Valla's voice was soft and speculative.

"Does it mean something?"

"I wonder if this is part of one of the old empires from before the joining. A castle from one of the worlds that made up Fanwath. It reminds me of a story about an Onaghi empire—they were adept at manipulating earth-attuned Energy even before the System came."

"Onaghi . . ." Victor let the word trail off, his mind searching the depths of his memory for the meaning.

"There aren't many left," Edeya said, bailing him out. "They don't look like the rest of us; they float in the air and have kind of translucent skin . . ."

"Ah, yeah! The jellyfish people." Victor nodded, remembering a group of the strange folk he'd seen in Persi Gables. He turned Guapo around the next corner, and, true to his word, Kethelket waited for them before an open gate halfway along the stony wall. He stood in the swirling mists with five of his people standing in a semicircle around him, all wielding wicked, gleaming blades.

"Not sure what that is," Edeya said, responding to Victor's comment, "but Onaghi definitely aren't fish."

"Yeah, my bad." Victor only half paid attention to her; he was too busy studying the front of the keep and the area before it. Like the side and rear, it rose in a sheer wall of perfectly cut stone blocks, but above the open stone gates, long slits were carved in the wall. Victor wondered if they were meant to allow defenders to launch attacks on enemies who might try to breach those thick flat slabs. He examined the gates and noted the gigantic black metal hinges and the massive bolt affixed to the inner side; it seemed they'd be hard to break.

More than that, Victor felt the Energy in the stones around him—this was a place steeped in power, built with magical defenses that he didn't understand. He wondered why the undead had charged forth to attack him rather than try to hold on to it. As they drew near, he voiced his curiosity to Kethelket. "You didn't have to fight any defenders?"

"I didn't say that, my lord."

"Lord's a bit much, Kethelket. Call me Victor or, if you want to show respect in front of the troops, sir."

"My apologies. If I wasn't clear before, let me amend my report: Most of the defenders charged forth to attack you, but a garrison of fifty undead was left behind, along with the mound of . . . undead matter and fungi. We slaughtered them."

Victor hopped down from Guapo and held up a hand to help Valla. She took it, though he thought he saw a flicker of annoyance in her eyes as she slid down. She stepped away, down a gravel-strewn dirt track that led from the gates into the misty rolling hills, and he saw her staring searchingly into the distance. He wanted to go to her, to ask if she was looking for Uvu or if there was anything he could do, but other things were vying for his attention, things he felt a duty to address. "So, show me this stone you tried to interact with."

"Right inside, sir, at the center of the courtyard."

"Take notes, Edeya." Victor left Guapo standing where he was and started toward the opening, but first he looked at the Naghelli standing nearby and gestured toward Valla as she walked in a slow circuit around the front of the keep. "Keep an eye on her."

"I heard that." She turned to scowl at him, but he could see it wasn't a real scowl. Some lightness in her eyes gave away the fact that she appreciated his attention.

The Naghelli didn't respond, but every single one offered him a salute. Kethelket nodded to them, then gestured between the massive stone gates. "Shall we?"

"Yeah." Victor followed him through, looking up at the impressive stone slabs, noting that the insides were banded with dark metal. The oversized bolt he'd seen when riding up was one of four; three smaller ones were on the inside of the other gate. "Looks like it'd be a bitch to break this gate open."

"The warding glyphs worked into the stone are of an ancient design. I haven't seen the like; I believe this keep is from Havah."

Victor paused in the oppressive stone tunnel behind the gates, looking up at the hundreds of dark holes in the stone overhead. "Havah?"

"The world from which the Onaghi and Bogoli originate."

"Oh? The little guys who paint themselves? They came from the same world?"

"That's right. Of all the races who came to Fanwath, those two were known for their high Energy affinity and talent with using it. Well, of the races who were friendly. The Yovashi were similarly gifted."

"Yeah, I've met a Yovashi. He tried to destroy my Core." Victor turned and continued through the tunnel, imagining what it would be like if some horrible magical fire or molten metal were poured down out of those murder holes. Whether his remark had surprised Kethelket or not, he couldn't tell; the Naghelli shadowed him noiselessly without comment. When he emerged from the tunnel, Victor was surprised by the brightness of the sky. The clouds above, though pale gray, weren't obscured by any of the mist that had been ever-present outside the keep.

As he shielded his eyes, allowing them to adjust, Edeya's voice echoed out of the gate tunnel. "I can breathe again! The mist doesn't come in here?"

"Not since we killed the defenders," Kethelket said. "My people carried the corpses out and burned them. A short time after that, the mists receded beyond the walls. That's when we noticed the stone yonder." Victor jerked his gaze down from the parapets where he'd been observing the other Naghelli lurking in the shadows of the crenellations. As he surveyed the courtyard, he instantly saw what Kethelket was talking about—a cylindrical stone hovered there. It was maybe two yards high and half a dozen inches thick. It spun slowly in the air, its smooth gray surface interrupted by shimmering yellow runes. They looked like the System runes you could find on any City Stone, like the one at the center of the citadel in Coloss.

"That's from the System."

"Yes, I agree." Kethelket walked toward it. "When I tried to interact with it, the System put a message in my vision saying we needed a larger force to interact. So, we flew forth to help you slay the undead and fetch your army here."

"Ah, yeah. Do you remember what the System said when it gave us the conquest quest?"

"Chests of Conquest at strategic locations!" Edeya practically shouted.

"Exactly." Victor stepped toward the stone. He could feel the power in it; it was dense with Energy in a way that reminded him of the Warlord's cultivation chamber back in Coloss. He'd felt something similar from the City Stones he'd interacted with, but this was different; it felt more volatile, as though it had a certain raw edge to it. He felt as if it were waiting for him, and when he reached his hand toward it, the stone stopped its constant spinning, holding still while he rested his palm on its cool, lightly vibrating surface.

*****This stone is undefended, but you must have a larger force in the vicinity to interact.*****

"Still need more people here. Sarl and the Ninth will be along soon." Victor turned to examine the courtyard, noting the stone benches here and there, the piles of rotting refuse, some bones and decomposing flesh, and a large mound of decaying plant matter near a broad archway that led into a dark interior. He wrinkled his nose, wondering at the idea that the air had smelled fine to him before he'd seen the bones and refuse. "You've cleared the inside?"

"Aye. Nothing but stone remains; whatever wood was present has long rotted away. We slew the undead within and dragged them forth, but there are messes like this"—Kethelket gestured to a pile of bones and rotting flesh—"inside as well. It'll take a good deep cleaning, and we didn't think we should begin while watching for undead reinforcements."

"How many troops can be housed inside?"

"Barracks for a few hundred, and then there are finer rooms for the commanders or nobility. I'm assuming; I know little of the peoples of Havah." Kethelket shrugged, resting a foot on a stone bench and leaning an elbow on his slender leather-clad knee.

"They come!" one of the Naghelli on the wall cried out.

"The undead?" Edeya asked, hurrying forward to put Victor between her and the gate.

"No, no," Kethelket chuckled. "The soldiers."

Victor looked at Edeya and grinned, noting that she held the Far Scribe book in her arms, hugging it to her chest. "You updated the base?"

"Yes. Lam wants us to return before dark, but they're waiting to hear from you about this keep."

"We'll see." Victor moved to sit on one of the ancient stone benches, idly drumming his fingers on Lifedrinker's haft. "I wish these assholes weren't undead."

"You'd prefer a different sort of enemy?" Kethelket raised an eyebrow in amusement.

"Well, yeah. They don't carry much in the way of loot, and my ancestors have little use for their empty husks after we've slain them."

"Your ancestors?"

"He sends them treasures in the spirit realm," Edeya said. "It helps them to conquer the new worlds they walk upon."

Victor looked at Edeya in surprise. "I don't remember telling you about that."

"You talked about it for about an hour one night when we gathered in your travel home. Well, you and Valla; she went on and on about the treasures you 'burned up' back in that world you two visited."

"Is she still out there?" Victor frowned, looking toward the gate tunnel.

"I'll check on her." Edeya jogged off, still clutching the Far Scribe book, into the shadows of the intimidating keep wall.

"She's eager to please you."

"It's funny, 'cause she used to give me a pretty damn hard time." Victor sighed and shook his head, a smile touching his lips at the fond memory. "That was a different life, though. Hey—" He turned to make eye contact with Kethelket. "Do any of your people have some skill with the spear?"

"Of course. The spear is nearly unrivaled in its versatility. Before I took up the sword, I reached epic proficiency with the long spear. Why do you ask?"

"I'm trying to help Edeya. She uses a spear, but I've never seen her training with anyone. I think she could learn a lot from one of you—"

"I will train her." Kethelket spoke quickly, heading off further words from Victor. "I will consider it an honor to help a close companion of yours, Victor."

Victor stood up and held out a hand. "Thank you, Kethelket." The Naghelli prince nodded solemnly and took Victor's hand in his. As they shook, a great roar echoed through the gate tunnel, a roar that Victor recognized—it was Uvu, and he sounded distressed and angry.

9

OUTPOST

Victor ripped Lifedrinker from her harness and charged for the tunnel. As he surged through the darkened opening, he almost instinctually cast Iron Berserk, and by the time he exploded out the other side, he was hunched over, his shoulders scraping along the stone ceiling. A chaotic scene greeted him—Valla and the five Naghelli who'd been watching the gate were dancing around a frenzied Uvu and a monstrous aggressor.

The giant cat's rear haunches were both speared by barbed, harpoon-like, bony tines, and attached to those tines, long vibrating sinews stretched forth to a pulsing, sucking mound of bone-filled gelatin. The jelly-like heap shivered and pulsed. The bones within its translucent structure shifted and seemed to heave with its movements as it surged forward and back, trying to, if Victor were guessing, reel in the cat—to pull Uvu into the slurping toothless maw that kept opening and closing on the near side between the weird sinew-bound harpoons.

Valla danced forward, swinging Midnight at one of the sinews holding Uvu, but her blade bounced off. The Naghelli were fast, too fast perhaps for the mound to respond to their attacks, but their efforts were fruitless; they slashed and stabbed it, only to have the wounds they imparted instantly refilled with the clear jelly. Valla regained her momentum and went in for another strike, but then, with a sick explosion of pus-like gel, another harpoon fired out of the mound and impaled her leg. She screamed, stumbling and falling back, dropping her sword as she scrabbled at the ground, joining Uvu in his attempts to keep from being reeled in.

Victor had seen enough. With hot rage coming unbidden to fill his pathways to bursting, he focused his blood-red vision on the near side of the mound and cast Energy Charge, leading with Lifedrinker's gleaming red-hot edge. Like a smoking meteor, he ripped over the gravel and grass, and when he smashed into the mound, he buried the axe and his arms up to the elbows into its gooey flaccid body. The impalement was only an aftereffect, though—the real damage came from the concussion of his enormous body smashing into the monster. He hit it so hard, riding on a wave of powerful rage-attuned Energy, that the shockwave rippled through the thing, sending the bones inside exploding out the far side, spattering its gel-like innards and flesh over a dozen yards.

It didn't make a sound as it continued to deflate, the gel breaking apart, becoming liquid before his eyes, leaving a wet spatter of bones and rubbery sinews scattered over the stony ground. Victor jerked his eyes from the destruction to Valla and Uvu. Valla was up to one knee, her impaled thigh held out straight as she worried at the jagged ivory-colored harpoon. She kept glancing toward Uvu, but the cat was doing better now that it wasn't being pulled by those bloody impalements. He lay on the ground, stretching his neck to chew and worry at the harpoon in his left haunch.

"Be still, boy," Valla said. "We'll help you in a minute."

Victor started toward her, ready to help remove the barbed tine, but then some movement caught his eye, and he looked back at the splattered monster and noticed the fluid-like material was slowly flowing away, trickling over the gravelly ground. "Somebody burn that shit!"

"Tuvai!" Kethelket yelled, and one of the Naghelli who'd been trying to help Uvu sprang forward, a ball of flames forming between her hands. The ball grew in density and brightness until it was yellow-white, and then she flung it forth. It smoked through the air to smash into the center of the flowing pool of oozing liquid, where it burst into a carpet of brilliant flames. This time, something screamed, or maybe it just made that sound as it burned, and thick black smoke billowed into the air as the puddle ignited, almost like an oil slick had been set alight.

Victor nodded and moved over to Valla, kneeling to get a better look at the barbed harpoon. As he knelt, he ended his Iron Berserk and cast Alter Self, reducing his size further so he could better see what he was dealing with. He followed the sinewy rope away from Valla to where it ended in the smoking, burning pool. Nodding to himself, he said, "Hold still." Then he hacked Lifedrinker into the sinew near Valla's leg, where it lay on the ground.

Lifedrinker's smoldering razor edge made short work of the material, slicing through and into the ground, shattering a few gravelly clumps of granite. "Sorry, girl."

"It's okay—" Valla started to say, then she looked at his axe and into his eyes and sighed. "You were talking to her."

"Sorry to you, too." Victor gripped the barbed end of the harpoon sticking out of Valla's leg and said, "One, two . . ." Rather than say "three," he jerked and pulled the tine and the much-shortened sinew through the wound. To her credit, Valla didn't cry out, though she hissed in pain and clamped her hands on either side of the puckered hole in her leg. Hot dark blood pumped out between her fingers, and Victor dug out a healing potion, popping the wax seal and holding it to her lips. She drank it thirstily and then sighed as the magic went to work.

"Thank you. Let me help with Uvu so he doesn't bite your arm off."

Victor looked at the bloody barb he still held, frowning at the almost imperceptible edge. "This thing's sharp as hell. I wonder if your armor would've stopped it."

"I'd like to think so." Valla grunted, climbed to her feet, then moved over to the grumbling, softly growling cat. As Victor moved to help her, Kethelket barked orders at his men, having them spread out in a semicircle to watch the mists more closely. They'd gotten one barb out and were working on the other when the fire finally stopped smoldering, and Energy motes bubbled up out of the blackened sludge left on the ground. They were shimmering, purple and rich, dappled with other tiny rainbow hues, and Victor realized the monster they'd slain had been formidable indeed—it was lucky his attack had been so effective.

When the Energy streamed forth, some of it went to Victor, and tiny streams went to everyone else, including Uvu, but the Naghelli who'd burned it, Tuvai, received an enormous share, and she whooped and hollered as it lifted her into the air, limning her with bright white light. When she settled back, she looked around and proclaimed, "I've leveled! The first in a decade!"

"Congratulations!" Victor said as he yanked the second barb out of Uvu's thigh. Valla stood between him and the cat's head, an arm over the big creature's neck, but he still flinched away as Uvu roared his displeasure. "Quiet," he laughed. "Big baby! Doesn't it feel better to have that out of you?"

"He's grateful." Valla's smile had been ever present since they'd lit the gelatinous monster on fire—it was clear to everyone that she'd been sick with worry about her companion and was relieved to have him back. Victor nodded, took the barbed bone harpoon, and set it on the ground with the other two.

"Maybe my ancestors can use these." Without waiting for a comment, he cast Honor the Spirits, and in a silvery flash of ghostly fire, the three harpoons ceased to exist, disappearing in a cloud of spirit smoke that drifted out of this world and into the next.

"That was well fought." Kethelket moved closer, eyeing Uvu warily.

"Indeed, it was," another voice called out. Victor turned toward the sound to see Sarl approaching. Behind him, a long line of soldiers marched around the keep, passing through the gates to the courtyard beyond.

"You saw?"

"Aye, we heard Valla's valiant mount roaring and hurried around the corner only to find you smashing into that . . . thing. After I saw it set alight, I figured we could continue our march into yonder keep." Sarl jerked his thumb over his shoulder to the open gateway.

"Good. Help the Naghelli set up a watch rotation and get the men started cleaning out the debris and filth."

"As you say, sir." Sarl snapped a quick salute, then marched back toward the keep. Victor saw Edeya moving in the opposite direction toward him and Valla, and he paused to wait for her.

"What should I report about that . . . monster?"

"It's dangerous but apparently weak to fire. You got a good look at it?"

"Yes."

"Okay, so describe it and mention the bit about burning it. Also, concussive damage seems to break it up." Victor turned to Valla. "Can you bring him into the courtyard? I want to try interacting with that stone again now that the cohort is here."

"Yes." Valla screwed the top back onto a jar of healing salve she'd been spreading into Uvu's puncture wounds. She took hold of his reins, muddy and splattered with gore, and led the great cat toward the gateway, speaking softly and scratching him with her free hand behind the ear.

Victor turned to Edeya. "I'm sure glad he fought his way here. That mound of jelly had to weigh a thousand pounds, and he dragged it here with two harpoons through his legs."

"He's a valiant animal." Edeya nodded, though she only gave Victor half her attention; she was busily scribbling into the Far Scribe book.

"All right," Victor snorted, "come on." When he returned to the slowly rotating System Stone inside the keep, the courtyard was far more crowded.

Soldiers were gathering refuse into piles where Pyromancers set it alight, rendering it to ash. The lingering smoke tickled Victor's nose as he looked around, watching the cohort's engineers as they rapidly constructed doors to mount in the doorways and built railings to line the stone stairways that led up to the parapets. It was amazing how much faster things went when dimensional containers and magic were a factor.

Victor approached the stone and placed his hand upon its surface. Once again, it paused its rotating, and a message appeared in his vision:

*****This stone is undefended, and you have sufficient forces in the vicinity to claim this outpost. Do you wish to do so?*****

Beneath the message was a simple menu with a "yes" and a "no" option. Victor mentally selected the affirmative, and almost instantly, a breeze began to blow into the keep. The wind tickled his senses, buzzing along his pathways, and he knew it was rich with Energy; some magical working was taking place. The stone tingled under his hand, and he gently tugged but found he couldn't pull away from it. He wished he could go up to the wall to see what was happening from a greater height, but failing that, he asked, "What's happening on the wall?"

Kethelket stood nearby and shouted his question to his men, and one of them called down, "The mists recede! I can see trees and hills now! Dark creatures flee to the north! More undead!"

Another guardsman, this one a Shadeni, laughed and shouted, "They smoke in the sunlight! You should see the panic in their flight!"

"So," Edeya said, nodding, "the mist signifies their controlled lands."

"I mean, I kinda figured that, didn't you guys?" Victor looked around, and Kethelket and Valla nodded.

"I suppose if I'd thought about it . . ." Edeya stuck her pen between her teeth and chewed on the wooden end in contemplation.

Before Victor could respond, another System message appeared in his vision:

*****Congratulations! Your forces have claimed this outpost and its surrounding lands. Defend it from your enemies and continue your conquest! For your victory, your faction will be rewarded a Chest of Conquest—this only occurs the first time you claim any given territory.*****

Victor felt the weird grip on his hand fade, and as he pulled it away, a thick blue fog began to swirl out of the stones at his feet. He backed up and watched as the fog or smoke or steam—he couldn't detect any smell at all—began to swirl together, thickening and then blowing away on the weird, magical breeze. In its wake, a large wooden chest sat on the flagstones of the courtyard, the planks of which were stained the same shade of blue.

"Whoa!" Edeya cried. "I've heard of System chests, but I've never seen one!"

"I have, but only in dungeons." Kethelket stepped toward the chest, squatting to examine it better.

"Same." Victor moved to rest his hand on the top of the chest. It was warm and solid and throbbed with Energy. "Did any of you see the messages from the System as I was interacting with the stone?"

"I did not." Kethelket straightened and looked at Victor with those depthless black eyes. In his reduced state, Victor was only a couple of inches taller than the lanky Naghelli.

"No." Valla stepped up next to him, for some reason eyeing Kethelket warily.

"Nothing big; it just said we'd claimed this outpost for our faction, that we needed to defend it, and that we were being awarded this chest. Oh, and we'll only get a chest the first time we claim 'any given' territory."

"Interesting. I suppose the System wouldn't want two generals from opposing factions to take turns swapping an outpost, collecting chest after chest." Kethelket nodded as though the System were being clever, and Victor had to admit he'd had the same thought.

"Would anyone ever? I can't imagine working together with these undead monstrosities." Valla's frown had only deepened at Kethelket's words.

"I doubt every conflict the System sets up is between such polarizing factions. What if it were Shadeni fighting Ardeni?"

"I . . ." Valla closed her mouth and looked around with more understanding. "Yes, I suppose with countless worlds and even more peoples, such things might happen."

"Anyway, let's see what's in here." Victor reached for the chest's clasp, but Kethelket held up a hand.

"A moment, sir. Have you considered it may be trapped?"

"Would the System trap a reward?" Edeya's eyes bulged at the implication.

"I doubt it," Kethelket said, "but it wouldn't hurt to be sure. I have a rather talented Artificer here with me. Perhaps we can give him a moment to examine the container?"

"Yeah. Sure." Victor shrugged.

"Relekani!" Kethelket called, turning around in a slow circle, trying to lay eyes on the Naghelli in question. A shadow detached from the parapet near the keep where one of the engineers was crafting a wooden door for the upper level. He drifted down to the courtyard in a flutter of softly glowing orange and charcoal wings.

"Sir?" Relekani was a slight Naghelli, a good six inches shorter than Kethelket and with very slender limbs. He had a delicate, narrow nose and wore his white hair short and parted to the side, smoothed down with some sort of wax.

"Examine this chest. Ensure it will not harm the one who opens it."

"Ahh, of course." Relekani produced a pair of spectacles with dark amber lenses and put them on, then he held out his hands, muttering something under his breath as he carefully studied the blue container. He started in the front, staring at the clasp for a solid minute before slowly moving around it, scrutinizing every corner and edge.

"What do you guys think is in it?" Victor asked to pass the time.

"Weapons!" Edeya said with certainty.

"I don't know. It could be anything from armaments to rations to alchemical ingredients. Perhaps it's just beads—the System loves to encourage trade." Victor noticed that Valla wasn't even looking at the chest as she spoke; her eyes were on Uvu. The big cat was resting in the shadows near the gatehouse, cleaning his long sharp claws with his enormous pink tongue.

"Agreed." Kethelket nodded, eyes on Valla. "It's hard to say what the System would think was a worthy reward for this keep. I wonder if the blue color is any indication. I suppose we'll learn more as we continue with this conquest."

Victor grunted and was about to make a guess when Relekani straightened up. "I see nothing of concern."

"Good! Thanks for checking." Victor didn't wait for any further objections and stepped up to the chest, flinging the latch up and lifting the lid. More blue mist escaped the interior, and when it faded away, he peered inside. "Oh, nice!" He spoke reflexively as he saw the rack of six shimmering, pearlescent white potion bottles at the top of the chest. He felt the others crowding near to look within, so rather than explain what he'd seen, he kept looking.

He lifted the potion rack, handed it off to Valla, then picked up the next item—a bolt of dense black cloth that smoked with the dark shadowy Energy that pervaded it. Kethelket hissed in appreciation, but again, Victor handed it to Valla. She set it on the ground near the chest, and Victor heard soldiers muttering as a crowd began to gather. "Yeah," he said, glancing at Kethelket and Edeya, then around at the milling soldiers, "how about everyone stand back a bit? Valla will lay the items out as I retrieve them."

"You heard the legate!" Sarl barked from up the steps near the keep door. "Form a wide circle and show some respect!"

Victor glanced at Kethelket and saw a slight frown on his face, but nodded as the man took a few steps back. Edeya hurried to comply as well. Victor returned to the chest and lifted out the next object—a dense hunk of charcoal-black metal. He lifted it easily but could tell it was incredibly dense. It almost reminded him of his helmet, the way it pulled at his fingers as though trying to get to the ground. He handed it to Valla, and she grunted as she carried it in two hands to set on the flagstones next to the shadowy cloth.

"Is there more?" Edeya asked.

"A lot." Victor reached into the chest again and lifted out a tooled leather container. At first, he wasn't sure what it was, but as he turned it, he saw an opening on one end that was densely packed with red-fletched arrows. "Huh." He passed it to Valla. Next, he pulled out a fist-sized metallic ball densely inscribed with runes. He could feel the Energy in it—it throbbed so richly that he felt it in his knuckles. "I have no idea what this one is, but it's full of power."

"I can help to determine the use of these objects," Relekani offered.

"As can any number of Artificers with the Legion." Valla didn't frown or snap, but her words were a clear rebuke. Relekani backed up, and Victor could *feel* the frown on his face. He reached back into the chest and lifted out a gold-foil-wrapped, brick-sized object. It was light, but again, he could feel the Energy within, and when he lifted it to his nose for a sniff, his mouth began to water.

"Careful with that one," he said, handing it to Valla. She nodded and quickly set it down, careful not to allow whatever magical odor permeated the contents to waft toward her nose.

Victor looked into the chest and saw only one more object. As he retrieved it, the chest vanished in a puff of dense blue smoke. Victor waved it away with the final reward—a folded silky flag made of cream-colored fabric and emblazoned with a blood-drenched golden sun. "Huh! I guess the System likes my glorious banner."

10

❧❦❧

PIECES ON A BOARD

Victor hung the flag—or banner, he supposed—over his shoulder and looked around at the expectant faces of the soldiers gathered in the courtyard. "Well done, everyone! We've captured our first outpost and driven the enemy deeper into their conquered lands. Once again, the Legion has the exploits of the Glorious Ninth to live up to!"

The soldiers cheered his words, pumping fists and weapons in the air, slapping each other on the back, and generally creating quite a din. Edeya stepped closer to Victor and gestured at the treasures arrayed on the flagstones. "What will we do with these?"

"Right." Victor cleared his throat and held up a hand for quiet. As the raucous celebrations died down, he yelled, "We need to examine these items to find out their value, but they'll all be going into the campaign token exchange." Some of the soldiers' faces fell at that announcement, and Victor heard some grumbling, so he followed up with, "Cheer up! You all just fought a battle and won! You'll gain a token for that, and Sarl has my permission to award another sixty tokens for exceptional skill and bravery displayed during the fight!" Victor turned to Kethelket. "You too, Captain—three extra tokens for your scouts to use at your discretion."

"Thank you, Legate." Kethelket saluted, and Victor saw something like approval in his eyes. Victor hadn't called him a captain before, but it made sense; he had more than three hundred flying scouts and killers under his command.

"Edeya, you have the book. Take note of the awarded tokens, collect these treasures, and make sure the quartermaster hears of it."

"You heard the legate! Get back to work, soldiers!" Sarl barked, and then the moment was over, and the outpost was abuzz with activity again.

Edeya leaned closer and in a voice pitched low asked, "Victor, um, Legate, I know the token system is fair, and the soldiers appreciate it, but don't you think some of these items might better serve the army if they were awarded personally by you? Or, I guess, used by you?"

"Well . . ."

Valla stepped in where his words faltered. "She's right, but we can work within the system you've created. You should be sure to award yourself tokens for your various victories. You've personally destroyed many of the most dangerous combatants and dozens or hundreds of lesser creatures. Not even Kethelket and his kin come close to your impact on the battlefield."

"All right." Victor shrugged. He wasn't going to argue about what sorts of treasures he deserved, and if he claimed a prize, it didn't mean he had to use it. He could always gift it to a captain or commander if he thought they deserved it more than he did. Edeya began to gather up the treasures and scribble notes in her Far Scribe book. "Should I tell the other commanders you'll be returning?"

"Just a minute." Victor grabbed the shoulder of a passing sergeant. "Hang this over the gates, will you?" After he'd handed off the new banner, he turned back to Edeya. "Tell them we're staying here with the Ninth for the night to assess the keep and surroundings. We'll check in tomorrow." Victor turned to Kethelket. "When we depart tomorrow, will you leave some of your people here with Captain Sarl?"

"Of course. Will five suit the outpost's needs?"

"Yeah. I just want some capable scouts with good mobility here. Sarl has his captain's book, so he can keep the rest of the army updated on his situation here."

"That's right, sir." Sarl nodded, but then his eyes narrowed, and Victor could see something was bothering him.

"What is it?"

"We won't be stuck on garrison duty, will we? Just because we took the outpost?"

"No, Sarl. You'll hold it until we settle on something more permanent. I'm sure Borrius will have some ideas."

"Very good, sir."

Victor looked around the courtyard, then at the new door the engineers were installing over the entrance to the tall narrow interior keep. "I think I'll have a look around in there."

"Good idea." Valla's words said something different than her actions—her eyes were on Uvu, still licking his scarred-over wounds in the shadows near the gate.

"Talk to me. What's the deal with your cat?"

"He's . . . we aren't the same, our connection, I mean. When I lost contact with him, it was the first time in nearly a decade. Now I can feel him, but—" Valla paused, taking a deep shuddering breath and slowly shaking her head. "It's not the same."

"Maybe it needs time. Maybe whatever that *pinché* jelly monster did to cut you off will continue to fade."

Valla nodded, pressing her lips together firmly. "Yes. Yes, I'm sure that's it. I need to be patient. Let's have a look around in there."

"Legate." Kethelket, who'd been lingering, perhaps waiting for the right moment to interject, stepped up to Victor as he, flanked by Valla and Edeya, began to ascend the short flight of steps to the keep. "Would you mind if I sent some of my people out scouting? I think it would be wise to determine the extent of the lands we freed from the mist by claiming this keep. Perhaps they might set eyes on the next fortifications we need to target."

"Yeah. Of course, that's a good idea. Keep me posted, all right?"

"I will do so. If you find time before you retire, I'd still enjoy sparring a bit." Kethelket bowed this time rather than salute, and Victor noticed he almost stopped himself halfway; perhaps it was an old habit of a culture he'd left behind. As he straightened, his broad shadowy wings fluttered rapidly, and he ascended to the parapet where some of his people waited.

"It's strange, this ancient keep being here." Edeya paused near the top of the steps and looked around once again, and Victor followed her gaze. "I haven't been many places in my life, but I always thought we built up the cities and castles around the Empire long after the System joined the worlds."

"Well, you know better than that. Remember the mines? The ancient shit we dug up down there?"

"Oh, aye, that's a good point."

"I wonder how many places of power the Empire has snatched up, painted over, and claimed as their own accomplishment." Valla nodded to the engineer attaching the latches to the new doors, then passed inside. Victor followed, watching her closely. He hoped things were okay with Uvu, but he could see the strain in her shoulders and neck. His thoughts fled, though, when he saw the strange but elegant construction inside the stone keep.

A vaulted hall opened directly behind the doorway, a delicately molded circular stone stairway dominating the center of the space. Victor couldn't see any seams in the stonework of the stairs, and he wondered what sort of magic must have been used to carve or shape or join so much stone into the graceful shape. It fit in well with the rest of the entry hall—tall shapely pillars held up an arched ceiling that would seem high even to his giant alter ego. The design of the interior was, in effect, the polar opposite of the exterior. Where the building's outsides were sturdy, square, and utilitarian, the interior was a masterpiece in filigrees, spirals, shapely curves, and smooth, almost seamless joinery. "Shit, this is a lot nicer than I imagined."

"The light playing over the stonework from the high windows is a masterpiece in design. Look how the afternoon sun highlights certain carvings." Edeya pointed with one slender arm, and Victor marveled at how even now he was seeing a new side of her.

"You have a good eye." He turned to take in what she'd pointed out, noting how a circle of light fell on a stone tree, its branches heavy with meticulously carved bunches of tiny fruit.

"Aye, she does." Valla's voice was hushed, and Victor was pleased to see some of the tension leaving her posture.

"Legate, sir, you should see this," one of Sarl's lieutenants called down from over the stone banister at the top of the circular staircase.

"Coming up." Victor grunted as he mounted the steps, taking two at a time. He could hear the softer footfalls of his companions behind him as he rounded the stair and emerged on a wide landing that ran the length of the rear and two sides of the entry hall. Just as below, everything was smooth stone with arches and delicate carvings at the focal point of every viewing angle. Soldiers were scattered about sweeping, dusting, and mopping, bringing the ancient keep back to life, and the lieutenant who'd summoned Victor, a tall lanky young Ardeni with shockingly bright yellow hair, gestured to one of the arched openings leading toward the back of the keep.

"Sir, I think it's a System thing."

"Oh?"

"Aye, it has them runes, like the ones in the stone in the courtyard and in the Town and City Stones." He fidgeted slightly, taking a step back, reaching up to tug at his uniform collar.

"I'm just a man, Lieutenant. You don't have to stress out in my presence."

"Aye, sorry, sir. Begging your pardon, though, sir, you aren't just a man. We . . . me and the lads in my division, we're damn grateful to be following you into battle out here." He ducked his head several times as he stepped back, making room for the trio to pass by.

"At ease, Lieutenant," Valla said, pushing Victor's shoulder, propelling him forward past the soldier. "Do me a favor, though."

"Yes, ma'am!"

"Don't forget the soldiers in your division aren't all 'lads.' Give the ladies some credit, hmm?"

"O' course, ma'am! I'm sorry!" Again, he ducked his head several times, touching his knuckles to his forehead. Victor smirked and kept walking, torn between wanting to laugh at Valla's very valid point and feeling sorry for the soldier. "Just straight down that hallway, sir! It's the circular room at the end."

Taking the man at his word, Victor ignored the four side passages and aimed straight for the arched sunlit opening at the end of the long corridor. When he stepped through, he immediately saw what had caught the lieutenant's attention. The room was circular, about ten yards in diameter, and lining the upper third of the left-hand wall—west, if Victor's sense of direction hadn't failed him—smooth seamless glass let in the setting sun's light. That alone was noteworthy, but the center of the room was what made him catch his breath and proceed inside with great care.

"Ancient Grandfathers," Valla hissed, following him in.

"A . . . map?" Edeya breathed, close behind her.

"Sort of." Victor walked around the slightly raised platform and eyed the golden runes lining the perimeter. They shifted and pulsed inside the stone— a sure sign that this was something left for them by the System. On the plat- form itself was a miniature model of, if Victor had to guess, the area around the keep. He could see the tiny square edifice situated in a green vale. North of the building were the jagged rows of the Granite Gates and, amazingly, a tiny representation of a partially built fortress at the mouth of the pass. More importantly, the area around the keep was modeled with tiny lifelike trees and blue silky ribbons representing water and lakes.

"Is it clay?" Edeya began to reach toward the rough, realistic spikes of the mountains, but Victor snatched her wrist.

"Don't touch it. I doubt we can do any damage, but let's not risk it. I think we can learn a lot of shit from this map. Look." He gestured to the area outside the keep's influence, at the weird cloudy smoke that clung to the majority of the space. "I think this is the invaders' territory. You can just make out the land at the edges of it, though." Victor leaned forward and tried to blow at the smoke, but his breath had no effect. "Yeah. Sorry I grabbed your wrist, Edeya. I'm pretty sure we can't do anything to affect this map; it's System magic."

"Look." Valla pointed to the misty area west of the keep. "If you observe closely, you can see the trees of a forest at the edge."

"And here." Edeya pointed to the eastern edge. "Mountains."

"That's different. Look how the mountains are at the very edge of the map—I think they're part of the boundary of this 'conquest' we're all a part of. Not the forest, though." He nodded to Valla. "Those look like contested lands."

"Right." Edeya nodded. "I see why—there's a lot of map area beyond, a lot of mist. So, if you really think this is the extent of the contested lands, we've only conquered about . . ." She ran her hand above the visible part where the keep and the pass were represented, trying to calculate.

"About ten percent," Valla helped.

"Shit," Victor laughed. "I'm not complaining about conquering ten percent of the invaders' lands in one day."

"It's strange, though, isn't it?" Valla walked around the large, mostly foggy, magical map.

"What?"

"Why is the System showing us this? It's like . . ."

"Like a game." Though Valla nodded at his words, Victor knew she wasn't thinking of the same kind of game he was. "I mean, we're given a clear goal, and now we get to see the board. The System . . . it's like we're the pieces it plays with."

"Well, we know the System loves conflict." Edeya shrugged as though that was all there was to say.

"Right, because we release Energy when we kill each other." Victor spoke sarcastically, a definite edge in his voice, so he wasn't surprised by the puzzled glances the two women sent him. "Look, I'm not arguing against the idea that the System leeches some of the Energy away when we kill each other. Think about it, though; before the System came around, people used to cultivate, gather, and claim their own Energy from those they killed. Do you even know how to do that? I mean, if you killed a . . . bone juggernaut." Victor used his internal name for the undead monster out loud for the first time, but the two seemed to know what he meant." Would you know how to claim its Energy if the System didn't gather it up and send it your way?"

"No." Valla shook her head, and Edeya shrugged.

"So, like, if the System just wants Energy, why doesn't it just kill us all and take our Energy? Why do we need to fight each other so it can steal our Energy?"

"Could it?"

"Kill us? I mean, it's pretty damn powerful, right?" Victor gestured to the map. "It's everywhere." He gestured around, indicating the world at large. "It knows a hell of a lot more about everything than any of us. Nah, I'm not buying it. I think there's more to the System than it simply wanting to leech off us."

Edeya surprised him by nodding. "I agree, Victor. There's more to it. Why do we call it a 'system,' after all? We all accept the name, but . . . it must have had more meaning in the beginning, don't you think? A 'system' for what? The very name implies complexity; it also implies impartiality. You don't set up a system for things to be random or arbitrary. You don't make a system for something you want to display sentimentality or favoritism. Whatever the reason, the System is in charge of many aspects of our usage of Energy, and . . . well, I don't know where I was going with this, but I think I agree that it's got to be much more complicated than some of the detractors make out."

"Yes," Valla said, "I've listened to many debates about it. We all have our jaded viewpoints, but I think, deep down, most of us know there's more that we don't know than that we do." Valla shrugged and gestured back at the map. "But back to the original topic. What's the point of this?"

"I dunno." Victor squatted down and pressed a thumb onto the keep that represented their current location. It was like pressing onto a stone—jagged and hard and not at all movable. "Maybe to incentivize us, to keep our interest. We can see the progress we're making, and I'm guessing so can the invaders, especially if you're right, Edeya, about the System's impartiality. When they see this area we've liberated, what do you think they'll do?"

"Send another army. They likely have victory conditions just as we do," Valla said, smacking her fist into her palm.

"Edeya." Victor turned to the plucky lieutenant, still clutching her Far Scribe book. "Tell Borrius I think we're going to need reinforcements here. Tell him if he's smart, he might be able to smash another undead army between his forces and the walls of this keep."

"On it!" Edeya snapped the book open, and a magical pen appeared between her fingers. Victor watched her scribbling for a few seconds, then he started back down the corridor.

"Where are you off to?" Valla followed close behind.

"I want to talk to Kethelket. I want him to send a scout into the forest we saw at the edge of this keep's territory. I want to see if there's another keep in that direction. If we can capture it, we'll have the northern section of the 'conquest territory' locked up." Victor noticed the corridor and the beautiful hall beyond were much dimmer than when he'd first come in. "Sun must've set," he said. He saw some of Sarl's soldiers hoisting an Energy lamp up to one of the stone arches and followed the pulley line with his eye, wondering how they'd secured it to the stone, hoping they hadn't bored a hole in it. He sighed with relief when he saw the ancient ceiling was carved with elegant hooks, almost as if they'd been designed to hold just such a contraption. "And why not? They had holes for the door hinges."

"Hmm?"

"Nothing. Just kind of wondering what this place looked like when it was new."

"I imagine much like it will when we're done fix—" Valla's words were cut off by a sharp horn note blaring from the courtyard. She locked eyes with Victor. "They're here already?"

11

A BARON AND HIS RETINUE

The place was abuzz with activity when Victor, Valla, and Edeya burst into the courtyard. Soldiers were hurrying to the ramparts, and sergeants were shouting orders. Victor scanned the area for Sarl, but too many people in similar uniforms crowded the confines between the rampart walls. Finally, his eyes settled on a thicker cluster of Naghelli on the ramparts over the gate, and he figured it made sense that Sarl would be at a central location like that. He was tempted to use Titanic Leap to launch himself up there, but then he'd have to Berserk or at least take on his titanic aspect, and he wasn't ready for that yet. He wanted to see what he was dealing with.

He jogged for the nearest stairs, leapt up them two at a time, and nodded to the soldiers who rapidly cleared a path for him on the ramparts. As he turned toward the gated section of the wall facing south, he saw what had launched the mad frenzy of activity—lines of black-clad soldiers were marching over the twilit hillsides. These soldiers were different from the undead they'd faced; they were orderly and armored, moving with discipline. "Not undead?" The question came unbidden to his lips as he stepped toward the cluster of officers and Naghelli above the gate.

"We're not sure, sir." Sarl turned and nodded to Kethelket. "One of his people got close enough to see their faces. They—well, sir, they look a bit like you. I mean the coloring and size."

"Like me or like humans?"

Kethelket cleared his throat. "I've not met other humans, Victor, but my scout tells me they resemble stocky wingless Ghelli. That is to say, they aren't red or blue like our other friends here." He gestured to a pair of lieutenants, one Ardeni and one Shadeni. "Speak up, Offathi."

"Aye, sir." A slender Naghelli stepped around from behind Kethelket and looked shyly up at Victor. "They have skin a good deal paler than yours, sir, and, well, their eyes are mostly red. Brighter than Shadeni eyes. They might be a kind of undead, but I couldn't tell for certain. I didn't see any rot on them; they weren't like the zombies or . . . things we killed earlier."

"Look." Valla pointed over the crenellations toward the advancing army. A small group had detached from the main force about a mile out and continued to march forward while the bulk of the army hung back. "Do they want to talk?"

"Maybe." Victor frowned, running his eyes over the lines of soldiers, their numbers darkening the shadowy slopes of the nearby hills. "How many do you count?"

Kethelket answered before Sarl could. "Something close to a thousand."

"So, probably not the entire invading army." Victor nodded, stroking his chin. "Maybe they don't know about our forces up in the pass?"

"Perhaps, or perhaps this army was near and chose to risk a quick assault to retake the keep."

Victor looked at Sarl, then Kethelket and Valla. "Let's ride out to see what this small group coming forward has to say. Sarl, we'll let Kethelket do the talking for now. Act like you're his subordinate, as will Valla and I."

"Why?" Valla was quick to ask.

"I liked how I could observe the Ridonne when Borrius and Rellia spoke to him. Don't worry; I'll speak up when the time is right."

"Very well." Kethelket gestured toward the distant group still walking toward them over the grassy hills. "Will you ride your mounts? They seem to be on foot . . ."

"Yeah, we can walk out. Uvu is still recuperating, and I can summon Guapo if we need some speed. We'll take our time." When the others looked at him as though he had more to say, Victor added, "I mean, so we're talking closer to the keep than the enemy's army."

"Shall I come, Victor?" Edeya looked both eager and trepidatious.

"Yeah. Bring your book and look officious." As he spoke, Victor caught her glancing over her shoulder as though to see her truncated wings, and he growled, "Don't you dare worry about those. You look badass."

She narrowed her eyes, stood up straighter, and saluted. "As you say, sir!"

"Good." Victor gestured for the stairs, and the others started ahead of him. One of the lieutenants nearby cleared his throat and approached Sarl.

"Will you be bringing a guard detachment, sir?"

"I'll be quite all right with the legate, Tribune ap'Yensha, and Captain Kethelket. If they can't defend any sort of ambush, then I don't think a detachment of soldiers will tip the scales."

"Of course, sir." The lieutenant backed away, his pale blue cheeks darkening, and Victor had to give him a double take—he looked as though he were about fifteen years old. As he descended to the gate, he looked around and had to remind himself that he wasn't surrounded by people younger than he; the truth was, with Energy so prevalent in the world, nobody really looked their age. That lieutenant might very well be forty years old.

"Shit, he could be older than that," he said aloud.

"Something on your mind?" Valla rested her hand on his shoulder, squeezing lightly. "I like it when you reduce your size like this."

"I knew it was a good idea to learn that spell!" Victor winked at her, but then he shrugged and, following the others through the gate, said, "I was just thinking that I don't feel my age. I feel old. I mean, I know that's stupid, but I feel like the last year has aged the shit out of me."

"You've seen a lot. More than most people ever do—more fighting, for certain."

"Well, you've been with me for a lot of it."

"A lot more to come, too." She returned his wink, and Victor suddenly felt very damn good, far better than he had any right to feel, what with an unknown army waiting a couple of miles away.

"Keep walking," he said as Kethelket, Sarl, and Edeya paused outside the gate, waiting for him and Valla. "We'll be right behind. With our similar armor, maybe they'll think we're your guards."

"As you say." Kethelket motioned for Edeya to walk beside him. "Come, you're my aide for the moment."

Victor's plan to lure the foreign party closer didn't bear fruit; they stopped a good half mile from the keep's walls and waited. As they drew closer, Victor tried to peer through the gloom of the darkening twilight to see what they looked like. Kethelket's scout hadn't been lying; the figures were all quite imposing physically—the smallest of them had to be halfway between six and seven feet tall. Moreover, they wore glossy black plate breastplates and helmets, the tops of which were festooned with black feathered plumes.

Victor noted slung round shields on three of the seven figures, and each of them wore a sword of some sort or another, from dual short blades to one enormous man with a gigantic naked two-handed, straight-bladed sword attached to a harness on his back. "That sword must be seven feet long," Valla said, following Victor's eyes.

"Yeah. They like swords, it seems."

"Their armor shines and reflects the starlight," Edeya started to say, but Kethelket held up a closed fist, and she clamped her mouth shut. The message was clear—they were getting too close, and it wouldn't do for the enemy to hear them speaking in awe about their weapons and armor. Victor felt a little bad for the slight Ghelli; she'd no doubt heard him and Valla talking and wanted to join in, only to be chastised by the ancient Naghelli prince. Victor thought about that, about how Kethelket was supposedly from a time before the joining, from the original world where the Ghelli, Ilyathi, and Yovashi originated. Had he met anyone else on Fanwath that old?

He had so many questions he wanted to ask the man and wondered at how he'd been able to push all those thoughts to the background while they'd traveled. "Always something more important than my simple interests," he muttered, rubbing his thumb idly on Lifedrinker's haft as they walked, his scowl deepening to the point where, if he were cognizant of it, he might have worried the approaching party might think he was intent on murder. He pushed his annoyance aside as they came to a stop atop a smooth grassy hillock, just twenty yards separating Kethelket's diverse group of five from the seven uniform black-armored, pale-fleshed invaders.

"You seem to be occupying my keep," the man in the center announced by way of greeting. His voice was resonant and sharp, and he leaned forward with the vehemence of his words. He was lanky, much slighter than the giant with the massive sword, but still a formidable, imposing figure in his shiny black armor with the tall feathered plume. He wore a single blade at his hip, though it was broad and heavy and looked to have something close to a five-foot reach. Victor could feel the aura of the man, or perhaps his entire party, projected—it was heavy and full of violence. These people had fought and killed many people and were prepared to do so again.

Victor shrugged it off, though he ducked his head, playing his part, trying not to look sturdier than their "leader." Kethelket, despite his experience, cringed back a bit but managed to straighten up and scowl. His gossamer orange-lit wings spread wide, and he touched a hand to the hilt of the sword he wore at his hip and replied, "The keep just yonder?" He jerked his thumb toward the walls behind them. "No, no. I'm afraid you've been ill-informed. That's mine."

"We've deigned to give you this chance to surrender or flee; I'm not here to play games or bargain. You slew a horde of mindless chaff; don't let that bolster your ego to the point where you'll throw your lives away—those creatures were simply meant to hold these lands under the influence of my lord while I gathered my retinue and traveled here. Your trespass, while insulting, can be forgiven—you knew not whom you crossed."

"And whom is it that I have slighted?"

"Why, me—and of course, my lord."

"Must I ask again?"

"So, you truly are an ignorant victim in all of this? A simple bumpkin stumbling upon matters far above his station?" The man smirked, and some of those in his imposing retinue chuckled or tittered. For the first time, Victor realized one of the tallest, most heavily armored of his retainers was a woman. He could just make out her red-painted lips through the narrow gap in the center of her heavy helm. He'd given her a double take when a trilling laugh echoed out of that thick-armored encasement. The speaker sighed and waved his hand as though brushing off an embarrassing mistake. "I am Baron Eric Gore Lust, and I serve Prince Hector of Heart Rot."

"Such names . . ." Kethelket shook his head slowly, a note of disbelief in his voice. Victor knew the Naghelli prince was remarking about the "Gore Lust" part of the baron's name, but he couldn't help wondering about the first part—Eric. Hector and Eric were both familiar names to him, names that hearkened back to Earth, and he pondered that coincidence. More than that, if it weren't for their size and strange pale skin and red eyes, these people could very well be human.

"Such names. Now, will you depart my keep, or must I and my reavers wash the stones with your blood?"

"Well, I too serve a lord, you see. If I were to pass off this keep without a struggle, I imagine he'd be rather perturbed." Kethelket turned to Sarl. "Wouldn't you agree, Captain?"

"Oh, aye, sir. I believe our legate would be furious. Might be worse for us if we returned home having abandoned his keep."

"This is *not* his keep!" the self-styled baron growled.

"Well, what's that they say?" Sarl asked, eyeing Kethelket as he straightened the lapel on his uniform jacket. "He who holds the pie decides who will eat?"

"I've certainly heard something of the like—"

"So, you choose death?" the tall pale red-eyed man asked, interrupting Kethelket's quip.

"Choose it? No, sir. I believe we'll put up a fight."

"And your men?" the baron growled. "Will they stay and fight with your head on a pike out here?"

"Are we not going to honor the standard terms of parley?"

"Why should we? Our kind has little concern for the respect of the quick-blooded."

"Quick?" Kethelket peered more closely at the baron. "Are you undead, sir?"

"We are immortal." As he answered, the eight-foot giant with the massive sword reached up and grasped the hilt, taking a step forward. "Hold, Porter. We'll not yet water this grass." The baron held up a finger, as though urging everyone to pause and pay attention, then looked at Kethelket, eyeing him more closely, taking in his swords and luminescent wings. "I have another option, sirrah."

"By all means! I'd love to hear all of my options."

"You have a sharp tongue; are your blades as bold? Let us settle this like gentlemen. A simple duel here on this hill; should you slay me, my men will leave for the nonce. If I kill you, your men will have one hour to take flight." After he spoke, the man who'd named himself Gore Lust let his eyes drift over Edeya's slight form, then to Sarl, and finally to Victor and Valla, still lingering behind the other three. "What say you, soldiers? Do you wish to die tonight, or would you appreciate your leader settling this score here and now?"

Kethelket grinned and turned to regard his companions. "Yes, do any of you have something to say in this matter?"

Victor stepped forward and nodded. "I do." He regarded the self-styled baron. "So, you're saying you want to duel the leader of our little army here?"

"That's right, young man. Should I win, you have my word that your people will have a full hour to depart these lands. I won't promise you'll remain safe after that. I can promise that if you don't linger near my keep, I personally will not give chase."

"And if our leader wins?"

"My army here will depart."

"Depart this world?" Victor pressed, noticing some of the baron's retinue had begun to fan out, shifting their hands to weapons.

"Oh . . . well, I can't guarantee that. Prince Hector, you see, is a rather demanding lord. He may insist on fealty from my thralls."

"No, Lord," the giant said. "My allegiance would be to your lady back on Dark Ember."

"Ah, Porter. Ever loyal to my blood. This is a moot point, good reaver—I will not lose. Still, you should know Lady Charisma will be unable to draw you home past the prince's lines. He'll have first claim."

Victor watched the exchange, trying to make sense of all the words but gaining far more understanding in the expressions of the few invaders wearing open-faced helms—they didn't like the idea of serving Prince Hector directly. They were loyal to this man and his "lady." He found it interesting and a bit heartening; some infighting among his enemies was good in his book. He didn't like the idea of all these soldiers returning to serve the prince, but he couldn't pass up the opportunity to cut the head off this particular snake. He leaned forward, knuckles white on Lifedrinker's haft. "Okay, I'll accept."

"You?" The baron took a step back and eyed Victor more carefully, then glanced at Kethelket and back to Victor with confusion in his eyes. "You're this one's champion? I hardly think a lanky young man with a crude weapon will serve as an appropriate opponent for me. Do you not fight your own battles, sirrah?" He scowled at Kethelket, who'd stepped back beside Sarl.

"Oh, I do indeed, *sirrah*. Sadly, this isn't my fight; you said you wanted to fight our leader."

"This one? You all bow to this man?"

"Oh, aye, he's the strongest of us." Valla stepped to the side, edging in front of Sarl and Edeya, putting herself between them and the other invaders who'd slowly been forming a semicircle around their leader.

"Truly?"

"Truly," Victor growled, and he cut the connection to his Alter Self spell. His body swelled with power, surging with mass and Energy as his true, nigh-eight-foot form took shape. Simultaneously, he released his hold on his aura, letting the full murderous fear-fueled fury of his being roll out in a heavy wave that fell like a lead blanket of scorching hatred around him, so palpable that it rippled in the air, like shimmering heat on a blistering day in the desert. "Draw your blade, Eric." His voice rumbled from his belly, thick with intent so evident that images of corpses and splashes of blood flashed through the minds of all who heard him.

The baron's retinue balked, stepping back, even the giant stumbling in his involuntary haste to escape the cone of Victor's gaze. Eric's jaw had slackened, and his eyes widened, but, to his credit, he held his ground, and his hand found his sword. "So, it will be a contest after all." He turned to his six retainers. "You all heard my wishes. I made an offer, and this man has accepted. We will dance the blood waltz on this hill, and you all will witness my victory."

"Stand back," Victor growled, and though he addressed nobody in particular, everyone scrambled to obey, creating a loose circle around him and Eric. Edeya and Sarl, in particular, stumbled in their haste to put a bit of distance between themselves and the two fighters; they might have felt his aura before, but never with such baleful fury behind it. Something about the baron's haughty attitude and desire to fight an opponent he'd seen as weaker than himself had angered Victor; no, pissed him off was a better way to describe his feelings. He wanted to teach the asshole a lesson about coming to his world and thinking he could walk all over everyone.

If he'd been more aware of his inner dialogue and motivations, Victor might have been surprised to note that he was thinking of Fanwath as his world, his home. Later, he might reflect on this moment and wonder at that change, but for the moment, he had eyes and thoughts only for Eric Gore Lust and the shimmering smoky blade he drew forth from his scabbard. It was a deadly-looking weapon, moving in flickers and jumps as Eric stroked it through the air, and Victor knew it was alive and that it wanted to taste his blood. The thought brought a savage grin to his face as he unslung Lifedrinker. "Time to drink, *chica*."

12

A WALTZ OF BLOOD

Victor and Eric circled each other. Victor held Lifedrinker light and ready to strike, crosswise before him, while Eric deftly stroked the air as if testing it with his broad blade of black smoke. Victor definitely had a reach advantage on the smaller man, but he wanted to test him, wanted to see what sort of style he would fight with. Was he about to face another lightning-fast opponent, or was the darkly armored stranger a brawler, a man of brutal strength? His sword was certainly dangerous looking, but could he use it? Were his skills a match for his braggadocious mouth?

Full dark had set in, but plenty of light lit the grassy hilltop. The sisters were bright in the sky, and in the distance, the southern horizon was limned with sickly green light. "I can see your eyes strain to follow my movements in the dim lighting," the baron said, though he couldn't have seen such—Victor's eyes were good, and he saw him clearly enough. "Karl, a light for my opponent to see by, if you would."

"I don't . . ." Victor began to protest but then shook his head, growling; he didn't need to take the bait, didn't need to be distracted. Even so, a member of the baron's retinue summoned a shimmering globe of reddish-yellow Energy, sending it aloft, throwing everyone's shadows into sudden movement. It was with that unexpected flare and the flicker of shadows that Eric made his first move. He grunted, almost noiselessly, more a heavy breath than a vocalization, and lunged forward, driving the point of his long broad sword straight at Victor's belly.

Victor moved with grace and precision, stepping lightly to the right and hacking Lifedrinker down and to the left, sweeping the dark smoke-clad blade to the side with a clang and shower of bright red sparks. "So, there's metal under all that smoke." Victor grinned and lunged forward in a follow-up, pressing the attack, sweeping his axe in careful, precise cleaves and jabs, using his long arms and height to keep the baron on his back foot as he struggled to bring his long, apparently heavy, blade between himself and Lifedrinker's biting edge. Victor was bolstering his agility and strength with Sovereign Will, and he seemed to be more than a match for the red-eyed invader. He danced around him, repeatedly slipping his guard, smashing and dragging Lifedrinker's edge against that polished black-enameled armor.

He wasn't one to show all his cards at the start of a fight, and thus far, he'd done nothing but use his prodigious attributes and skill with an axe to press the baron, pushing him into an increasingly erratic, defensive struggle as he backpedaled. He almost stepped outside the circle of onlookers, but his giant follower, Porter, blocked his path, allowing his shoulder to bump into his chest. As Victor pressed forward, Porter nudged the baron back into the circle and said, "How long will you toy with the man?"

"Toy? He presses me more than you do when we spar!"

"Come, Baron, it's not kind to play with your food," the big red-lipped woman said through the narrow gap in her helm.

Victor heard all of this, of course, but he wasn't one to let banter distract him in a fight. He was on the verge of sealing the deal, casting Energy Charge or something similar to end this annoying man's defensive retreat, when the baron began to exude thick hot red Energy that was very familiar to Victor. He'd felt something similar when he'd killed ap'Horrin in his secret oubliette and again when he'd fought the Ridonne. He'd come to recognize the heat and taste of it—a blood affinity.

The surge was massive, a level of Energy that Victor had come to expect only from himself or from enemies he found too dangerous to tangle with, such as the Warlord or his War Captains back in Coloss. The sensation triggered a burst of adrenaline in him, an instinctual need to act, to interrupt whatever was happening. Without a second thought, he cast Energy Charge, fueling it with rage, and, in a flash of red light, he ripped over the grass, sending dirt and debris into the air in his wake, and smashed into the tall armored baron.

As always, the impact he delivered was devastating, but it wasn't exactly the effect he'd hoped for. Victor had planned to smash the baron, send him sprawling, and interrupt whatever he was trying to do. Unfortunately, Eric's spell was in progress; he was sheathed in his hot red, hungry, blood-attuned Energy, and the forces generated by Victor's impact rolled off him, shattering the night with a tremendous *boom* that shook the ground, spraying grass, soil, and rocks outward in a stinging, tearing shockwave. Everyone save Victor and the baron were knocked back and sent sprawling. For his part, Victor was protected by his spell's nature; the very Energy that propelled him shielded him from the impact.

When the dust settled and Victor was able to take stock of his situation, he found that he stood in a shallow crater, nothing but dirt under his feet. Before him, the baron loomed, much changed. He glowered down at Victor through red eyes set deep in a twisted gray, snouted countenance. Enormous fangs hung over thick black lips that twitched into a semblance of a smile that was half snarl due to the very nature of that face.

More shocking than the change in his countenance was the transformation of the baron's form. His mass had increased by half, though the alterations extended beyond size. The baron's shoulders in their dark armor were like cast-iron stoves; his arms were long, knuckles close to the ground, his once massive sword like a toy in the grip of his right claw. He leaned forward, lifting that dark flickering smoke-bladed sword high, and snarled, "Let's finish this little dance; me and my kin are thirsty." Then he brought the blade down like a falling star, straight at Victor's neck.

Perhaps worse than the baron's new size, strength, and speed was the dark wave of something Victor felt a kindred connection to that seemed to radiate from the man—terror. If he'd had an ordinary will, something akin to what Valla, Rellia, and others of their tier had built up, Victor would likely have fallen to his knees at the touch of that dark aura. Even with his prodigious will, he might have met his fate in that moment, but another factor came into play. Victor was no stranger to fear, and as the baron's dark Energy washed over him, it felt almost familiar, almost natural. He didn't so much as flinch, and he brought Lifedrinker up, catching that falling sword on the top of her axe-head.

Despite his quick parry attempt, the baron's strength felt as if it had multiplied tenfold. Victor thought to drive the blade up, step under the arc of the swing, and deliver a terrible hack to the baron's chest. That idea flew out the window when his opponent exerted his new might, continuing to drive the blade down despite Victor's efforts to deflect it with his axe. The dark, smoky sword screeched as the edge rubbed against Lifedrinker's steel, and Victor growled, driving with all his strength. His efforts fell short, though, and the baron relentlessly gained ground. Soon, the edge was touching his shoulder, heating the scales of his vest as it tried to cut through the formidable armor.

They hung there for a moment, Victor and his armor struggling against the baron's inexorable force, and then the wicked blade parted one of his scales, and the faintest touch of its edge reached Victor's flesh. Pain erupted in his shoulder, and Victor cried out, kicking reflexively with his right foot at the baron's knee, breaking free of the contest, launching himself backward to roll over one shoulder and back to his feet, axe ready. The baron hadn't chased him, though; he stood there leering, as his long bright-red tongue slipped out between his lips and tasted Victor's blood from the edge of his evil sword.

"*Pendejo*," Victor growled, reaching up to rub at his shoulder, warily pacing to his left, eyeing the monstrous man for any hint of attack. At the periphery of his vision, he was aware of movement and the sounds accompanying it—his companions and the baron's retinue had regained their feet and were gathering around the area blasted by Victor's collision with the baron.

"Rich blood, sirrah," the baron-creature growled in a hissing, clicking voice that seemed to emanate from somewhere in its throat.

"You like that?" Victor smirked, continuing to circle the creature, contemplating his next move. In a way, it was amusing how his enemy felt entirely at ease in his supremacy. He was clearly stronger and faster than Victor now, and Victor had to admit he was beginning to enjoy the not-so-subtle game he was playing. How long could he fight the monster before he had to play one of his cards? Should he Berserk? Cast Inspiration of the Quinametzin? Summon one of his totems? Conjure his banner? He shook his head at all the ideas—he'd do what felt right in the moment, but for now, he wanted to see if he could cut the bastard as he was.

Victor stalked forward, feinted to his left, and looped Lifedrinker in a downward hack at the monstrous man's knee. The baron was much faster than before his transformation, though, and he dodged back, returning the blow with one of his own. His blade flicked out and caught Victor just above the ear. He hardly felt it; his juggernaut helm absorbed the impact and sent the weapon skittering along the top of his crown. Meanwhile, the baron was wide open, and Victor used one of the many tricks he'd learned in his sparring sessions to capture his momentum and reverse the trajectory of his cleave. Lifedrinker raked along the dark plate at the baron's thigh, scraping off a thick pile of enamel and sinking into the joint near his knee.

The baron hiss-screamed as she bit into his flesh and erupted in a frenzy of hacks with his sword. Victor ducked a shoulder, taking the blows on his scale hauberk and helmet as he was pummeled backward, forced to pull Life-drinker away before she could begin to drink. The baron's powerful blows smashed into him, crunching against his armor, marring the scales but not quite cutting through. "Fool! Do you not see you are beaten? Relent, and let me finish you with dignity."

"What are you?" Victor asked, breaking his rule about not talking during a fight. He was curious and couldn't help himself.

"What am I? A lord of blood, an immortal master of death, a drinker of knaves and weaklings. You impress me with your boldness, however. Perhaps another fate will suit you, hmm? Would you like to join my blood reavers?" At his words, angry snarls and bitter curses erupted from the circle—Victor could see the baron's lieutenants weren't keen on sharing their privileged status.

"Perhaps. What would it entail?" While he spoke, Victor let his eyes drift past the baron, searching for his comrades. The "reavers" had survived his explosive impact with the baron just fine, but how about his friends? Some of them were less sturdy. He saw Valla immediately, standing tall in her wyrm-scale armor, Midnight Hope resting, naked, on her shoulder. Next to her was Edeya, and as he circled the baron, he saw Sarl and Kethelket—all were fine.

"Let me work my blood magic upon you. Let me plant the seed of blood-lust in your soul. Let it consume the life in your flesh and replace it with something far more potent!" The baron seemed to believe Victor was interested. Perhaps what he was offering was something appealing to the people of his homeworld, but Victor wasn't intrigued. Still, he toyed with the man.

"And my companions?"

"Take them as your first thralls! They will serve well in our army!"

"Lord!" one of his retainers—Victor couldn't see which—cried, outraged.

"Are you, like, being literal?" Victor asked, half playing around and half curious. "Do you drink blood? I mean, are you a vampire?"

"Vampyr!" the baron crowed, his guttural voice rolling the r and enunciating the second syllable with a distinctive "y" sound. "So, you've heard of my kind?"

Victor frowned; this was all starting to feel too weird to him. He supposed he shouldn't be surprised—he'd fought ghouls and zombies, why not vampires of one sort or another? Still, the familiar names and the oddly human-like appearance of the baron before his transformation into a hulking monster were starting to feel like too much. He'd had enough of messing around. "Sure, but I have to ask, why would I want to do what you suggest? What would I get out of it?"

"Are you daft? Perhaps I've offered my gift prematurely. Do you not see the power that awaits?" The baron stood tall, spreading his arms wide, demonstrating his immense reach and the robust frame that lurked beneath his thick armor. "In my vampyr form, I am ten times the man I was!"

"Not really a man, though, right?" Victor smirked, carelessly tossing Lifedrinker from one hand to the other and back again. "To be honest, it looks like a bit of a downgrade."

"Enough! I grow weary of this banter. I shall feast on your blood, and if my rage is sufficiently cooled, I may restrict myself to our earlier bargain and give these morsels a chance to flee." He ran his long pointy tongue over his lips, lingering on his left fang, allowing it to curl wetly around the protruding tooth. Then his eyes began to burn more balefully, more brightly in the deep hollows of his protruding brow, and Victor felt another surge of that hot, coppery Energy. This time, he acted even more quickly, but rather than charge the man, he reached into his own Core and pulled forth a torrent of rage-attuned Energy, pushing it into the pattern for Iron Berserk.

As power exploded through his pathways, flooding his every cell, engorging them, expanding them, Victor roared, holding Lifedrinker aloft. His body flared with the potent baleful Energy in his Core, and the ground shifted under his feet, tiny fissures erupting in clouds of freshly exposed soil. Eric the vampyr was no longer looming over him. No, it was with wide eyes and a flinching flourish that he finished his spell and sent a spray of hot needle-shaped bloody rain from his outstretched hand toward Victor. His attack fell somewhat flat, however. Rather than engulfing a large human, pouring into every crevice and nook of his armor, it splattered against a titan-sized chest, losing its terrible inertia and dribbling ineffectually to the ground.

Victor lunged, suddenly much, much faster and stronger than before. The baron wasn't ready; perhaps he was still in shock from Victor's sudden change in stature. Victor smashed a shoulder into the huge armored man, sending him stumbling, but he wasn't done. He pressed his advantage and hacked Lifedrinker one-handed into the man, smashing against his armored shoulder and his helmet, and into the arm he lifted to defend himself.

Victor felt more potent than ever, hungrier, and more lustful for battle than he could remember, even with the Ridonne. He wanted to see this fool's insides on the outside, and he wasn't even sure why. Perhaps it was his pathetic use of terror in an attempt to cow him. Perhaps it was his almost lackadaisical threat against Valla and the others. He didn't know, but he was seeing red like he hadn't in a very long time. As he hacked, his grunts of effort became a growl, and Lifedrinker screamed, whistling through the air, her axe-head ablaze, throwing black smoke in her wake, sparking with the impacts and throwing hunks of rent armor into the darkness like a smith pounding out an ingot on an anvil.

The vampyr was silent, desperately trying to turn intact pieces of his armor into those blows, swinging his sword in turn, trading blow for blow. Victor felt the sword smash into his armor and slash over his bare arms, slicing like a caustic razor into his flesh, but it only served to anger him further. Each wound the baron inflicted sprayed hot blood, and then it was closed, his flesh knitting together, closing those clean, precise cuts with hardly a scar. Meanwhile, Lifedrinker's smoldering silver blade grew hotter and brighter with each smashing impact, and Victor could hear her screaming her fury in his mind. A tiny fragment of his consciousness wondered if others could hear her too or if her battle song was for him alone.

One thing was sure, Victor thought, as he and the baron beat on each other—the vampyr was a sturdy, sturdy bastard. Victor was pounding him with such force that the blows rang out like gunshots, *boom, boom, boom*, and though the baron's armor was battered, dented, and torn, few of Victor's blows got through to the flesh. When he did manage to cut his opponent's thick gray hide, it, like Victor's flesh, seemed to have the power to regenerate. This furious, brutal exchange went on for a handful of seconds, and then the baron regained his balance, digging metal spikes protruding from the toes of his boots into the soil and driving forward, shouldering into Victor's midriff and careening past him.

Something feral was in his big red eyes, something insane about how he leered as he spun and greedily licked the blade of his sword. "Gods be good, but you've a rich taste!" he groaned, a weird orgasmic note in his voice.

"Come," Victor growled and opened his pathways wide, channeling a thick river of glory-attuned Energy into them, pouring it into his Banner of the Champion. Suddenly, the light cast by the baron's retainer was banished by his banner's glorious pulsing sun. Blazing golden light bathed the hilltop, driving back the shadows and exposing every rend, dent, scrape, and muddy smear on the baron's armor. Eric shrank back from the glow, shielding his eyes, and suddenly Victor understood why his follower had earlier provided the illumination—some quality in it was comfortable for the undead crea-tures of the night. His golden bloody sun, though, seemed to offend them on a cellular level. In fact, Victor could swear he saw smoke rising from the seams in the baron's armor.

"Kill him!" the vampyr shrieked. "Kill them all!"

13

CONTESTED GROUND

At the baron's words, Victor pounced. His already smoldering rage flared like coals under a bellows, and in his blood-red vision, he could focus on only one thing: the cowardly liar with the smoking, bleeding flesh before him. In the light of his banner, much of the baron's supernatural vitality seemed to have fled, and when Victor fell upon him, he smashed his knee into his chin, sending him flopping back into the torn earth of the hilltop. He drove forward, crushing his prodigious bulk onto the baron's midriff and hacking Lifedrinker at the vampyr's neck with all his might. She was furious, her rage an echo of his own, and when her smoldering blade met the bent chipped gorget at the baron's throat, she bit clean through.

Lifedrinker knew what to do at that point, and she jerked in Victor's hand, pulling deeper and deeper into the pale gray flesh while the baron bucked and screamed, trying to throw Victor off. Victor held onto his axe, pushing, aiding her in her desire to dig deeper and draw the Energy from his foe, but just as she'd sunk halfway through the sinewy neck, a massive form crashed into him, knocking him loose. Victor kept his grip on Lifedrinker, and as she pulled free of the baron's neck, great gobs of black viscous jelly-like blood flew forth in her wake. The baron screamed and thrashed, rolling about, reaching up to squeeze his wounded neck in an odd caricature of a man choking himself.

Victor saw the baron's throes as he slid on his back, another bulky vampyr driving him forward with thick arms around his waist. The creature was bigger than Eric. If Victor were guessing, he'd say it was Porter, the loyal giant. He was large, but Victor could tell from the force of his grasp that he was weaker than the baron, far weaker than he. Perhaps it was the light of his banner affecting the monster, but Victor had no trouble pulling on the creature's bulky neck, driving him down and to the side, and pushing him off. As he did so, he smashed Lifedrinker several times at the gap where the vampyr's shoulder armor met the plates covering his arm. She tore through the thin links of the joint, sliced the gray flesh, and burned through the sinews and cartilage.

When Victor stood up, he held Porter's arm in one hand and Lifedrinker in the other. The huge vampyr screamed in outrage, thick near-black blood pumping from his ripped shoulder as he scrabbled backward. Victor ignored him, scanning for the—hopefully—mortally wounded baron. He saw his friends fighting a defensive retreat down the hill's northern slope, the other five vampyrs pressing them with a brutal offensive. Victor wanted to help them, but he saw movement to the south, a dark form slithering downslope over the grass, and he pounced, unable to stifle his lust for a bloody victory and hoping his companions could hold out just a little longer.

He crashed to the ground just feet from the crawling form of the vampyr, and his banner's light exposed the baron, no longer huge and gray and monstrous, but man-sized, bloody, and screaming with pain as Victor's light burned his flesh. Victor felt the urgency of the situation and knew he was putting his friends—Valla!—at risk, so he was quick and efficient as he fell upon the wounded vampyr. He smashed Lifedrinker through an already bent and jagged backplate and buried her through the creature's spine, halting his writhing retreat.

"Bastard! Spare me, and I will plead your case with Prince Hector." A gurgle of black blood chased Eric's words as he vomited onto the grass.

"Shut up." Victor yanked Lifedrinker free, then grasped the man by the collar of his battered breastplate, flipping him onto his back. He lifted the axe high, aiming it at the side of Eric's neck where she'd already started the work he was about to finish.

"You can't stand against him, against the others . . ." the baron began to wheeze, but his words were cut short as Lifedrinker separated his head from his shoulders. Victor didn't gloat or savor the glory of the kill. He snatched the body into one of his storage rings and turned, charging back toward Valla and the others. Where he'd left Porter, he saw only a black stain on the grass. He raced past it, scanning the northern downslope, and he didn't have to look far. His friends were surrounded, beleaguered, losing . . .

Victor screamed with fury as he saw the giant woman, the one with the helm that hid all but her blood-red lips, lifting Edeya into the air, swinging her by one frail-looking ankle, smashing her with a wet thump into the ground. Victor's Core emptied itself of rage, flooding his pathways, his muscles, and his brain with its hot fury. He cast Energy Charge, and as he streaked over the last twenty yards to the enormous woman, he lifted Lifedrinker high, bringing her down at the point of impact. Like a guided missile, she impacted the big woman at the crook of her neck and left shoulder. Lifedrinker screamed, and her voice was echoed by the ripping metal of the vampyr's armor as she split the giant woman in twain, from shoulder to hip.

Hot blood showered the battlefield, and Victor roared his frustration, fury, and horror as an echo from his past floated through his mind, overlaying the battlefield—Yrella, dead, limp, the life gone from her eyes, as Victor watched on the sidelines. With desperation in his heart, Victor summoned his great bear, pumping the spell pattern with the mix of Energies needed to form courage. A cacophonous roar sounded, echoing over the hillside as the great bear burst into being. He was a mighty, wonderful creature with blonde-brown fur, enormous gleaming teeth and claws, and eyes that shone with red-gold reassurance.

In the light of his banner, Victor saw the bear fall upon one of the three vampyrs pressing Valla, crushing him to the ground and savaging him. The great creature engulfed his entire head with his jaws and began to rip and jerk his neck like a terrier with a rat. Victor prayed Valla could hold her own for a moment, hoped Sarl and Kethelket could double-team the other vampyr, and then he knelt by his broken, battered friend. Edeya was still. One of her arms was bent awkwardly, a shard of bloody bone piercing the flesh. Her face was a mottled mess of bruises and cuts, and as Victor pulled her battered lips apart to try to administer a potion, he saw that most of her front teeth were broken or missing.

"*¡Que horrible, chica!*" he cried, the rage fleeing his body as horror and fear replaced it. Had he lost her? Was Edeya dead? He tipped the potion between her bloody lips into her swollen mouth. The thick silver-blue liquid shimmered and sparked as it flowed over her torn bloody gums, and he saw the cuts pull together, her flesh knitting. He took it as a good sign; would it heal a corpse? Relief began to wash over him as more of her swollen bruises faded, and the cuts on her cheeks and forehead stopped bleeding and scabbed over. He could hear the sounds of combat fading away to his left and, no longer afraid that his delay had inadvertently killed one of his oldest friends, Victor looked up.

His bear had ripped the head from the vampyr and was lumbering toward Valla, bearing down on one of the two she was defending against. Part of Victor wanted to leap up and run to her defense, but another part was stunned, admiring her grace as she slipped between their swords, lashing out with Midnight, giving far worse than she got. When his golden bear crashed into the tall vampyr on Valla's left, smashing him to the ground with a roar, Valla switched gears, taking the offensive, and rapidly slashing and stabbing her last remaining opponent, beating her down until she got a clean opportunity for an overhead cleave, ripping Midnight through the woman's neck.

Victor scanned for Sarl and Kethelket and saw them fighting farther north, off to his right. They had one of the transformed vampyrs between them, huge and monstrous. They stabbed and slashed it, Kethelket applying three devastating wounds for every one of Sarl's, but the creature kept healing, lashing out and screaming its fury. Victor grunted, standing up with Edeya still in his arms, and began to trudge toward them. He was no longer Berserk, but his banner still hung in the air behind him. With one more glance toward Valla and his bear, ensuring they would defeat their two opponents, he summoned Guapo.

He gently laid Edeya over the stallion's shoulders, then hopped up behind her. As he trotted toward Sarl and Kethelket, he wondered why some vampyrs had transformed and others hadn't. Were they not all able to do it? He didn't bother hopping down from Guapo as he came close to the furious battle the two captains were waging against the huge creature. He watched, smiling grimly, as it screamed and began to smoke in the light of his banner, and then Sarl and Kethelket cut it to pieces. Just like the baron, this vampyr couldn't seem to heal with his banner's light shining upon it.

In moments, the fight was over, and Kethelket removed the head from the smoldering bleeding creature. Victor nodded to him and then pointed to the keep where a unit of soldiers was charging through the gates, rushing toward the scene. "Get back. I'll get Valla."

"Aye. Is . . . is she alive?" Sarl pointed at Edeya, frowning as his dragonfly wings twitched in agitation.

"Yeah. Hurt bad but alive." Victor whirled Guapo and galloped up the hill toward Valla. When he arrived, he found his bear lying in the bloody grass near another headless vampyr and Valla strolling toward him, wiping Midnight with an oiled swatch of leather.

"Is she . . ."

"Alive, but another healing potion might not hurt. Let's get back to the keep." He held down his hand, and Valla took it, hauling herself up behind him.

She wrapped her arms around his waist and said, "They're coming."

"The soldiers? Yeah, they saw us fighting."

"No, the other army. Look. Listen." She pointed to the north, and Victor saw it—a darker shadow rolling over the night-clad landscape. They were still a mile out, but it seemed as if the vampyr's entire army was charging. He clicked his tongue, and Guapo broke into a canter, smoothly running over the grassy hills toward the keep. Victor yelled at Sarl and Kethelket to hurry as he rode past, but he didn't slow; he wanted to get Edeya inside, check her out, and maybe give her another potion. He needn't have worried, in any case. Before they reached the gate, the air brightened, and he turned to see a braided ribbon of thick purple-gold Energy flowing toward the three of them atop Guapo.

"Ah, shit," he had time to say before it hit him. Guapo had the good sense to stop his forward movement as Victor and his passengers were seized by a paroxysm of Energy and euphoria. He howled inadvertently as he flung his arms wide, absorbing the lion's share of the river of Energy. Still, quite a bit flowed into Valla and Edeya, and he saw his diminutive friend's bent arm straighten and her eyes pop open before the wave of victory blinded him momentarily. When he came back to himself, the System had words for him:

*****Congratulations! You have achieved level 54 Battlemaster and gained 10 strength, 9 vitality, 4 agility, 4 dexterity, 3 will, and 3 intelligence.*****

*****Congratulations! You have learned the skill Titanic Leap, Improved.*****

*****Titanic Leap, Improved: Whenever your form reflects the aspect of your titanic bloodline, you will find that you are able to leap quickly and powerfully, covering distances seemingly impossible, even considering your tremendous size and power. Foes who wish to contain you will find their efforts stymied by your ability to burst free from most mundane bindings.*****

"Victor, are you there?" Edeya said tremulously, her high scratchy voice lisping oddly. She was still face down on Guapo's shoulders in front of him, so he put a hand on her shoulder, giving it a gentle squeeze.

"I'm here, *chica.*"

"I . . . I almost leveled, but the System said I need to advance my race."

"As you should." Valla leaned to the side, peering around Victor's shoulder at the young Ghelli. "You need to regrow some teeth along with those wings."

Edeya gasped, and as she gently bounced with Guapo's plodding steps, she slapped a hand to her mouth, probing for damage. "I don't remember anything after we . . ." She got quiet for a minute, then said, "That big one, she stuck her sword in my side, then she grabbed me. . . . That's the last thing I can remember."

Victor steered Guapo through the gates and shouted down to the lieutenants standing there, waiting for news, "Get ready! They're charging, but I don't know if they'll try to scale the walls or if they can fucking fly or something. Be ready for anything; Captain Sarl will be here in a few seconds." He and Valla hopped down, then he reached up and helped Edeya slide off Guapo's high shoulders. "It's good you don't remember." He gently pinched her chin between his thumb and forefinger, turning her to look him in the eyes. "We need to toughen you up some more, or I'll need to start making Valla do all my Far Scribing."

"That wouldn't be my preference, Edeya, so please, go advance your race."

"Here?" Edeya lisped, holding a hand in front of her mouth as her cheeks bloomed red.

"Yeah. We're not going to lose this keep. Not if I can help it, and if we do have to retreat and you're still out of it, I'll carry you myself. Go find a quiet room, lock the door, and do it." She hesitated, looking at the gate, at the walls, then back to Victor. He could see she wanted to protest, so he grabbed her shoulders and turned her toward the keep, giving her a gentle shove. "Now. It's an order."

"I don't think she realizes how close she was." Valla watched Edeya's slight figure climbing the steps to the keep's door.

"I thought I'd lost her. I thought I'd let another friend die."

"Let?"

"Yeah. I chased that fucking baron and killed him instead of running to help you guys."

"I'm glad you finished him. What scum! How could he betray the sanctity of parley like that?" Victor looked at Valla, surprised by her vehemence.

"That's what you're pissed about?"

"Among other things. Still, they're all dead. They paid the price for their treachery."

"Not all." Victor sighed, shaking his head. "The biggest one, Porter? I took an arm from him, but he got away while I was finishing the baron."

"Damn." Valla frowned and turned back to the gate. "I was hoping that army would be leaderless."

"Well, regardless of that dude getting away, I'm sure they left someone in charge of those troops. Someone must have ordered them to charge."

"True." Valla snapped her fingers. "The Far Scribe book! I mean Edeya's!" She turned and jogged after the Ghelli as Victor connected the dots—she wanted to see if Borrius had replied. She wanted to know if he was coming to flank their attackers.

"Come on, old man. We're serving them up to you on a platter." Victor turned to a stairway and stomped up to the parapet, intent on watching the enemies charge. He'd just reached the top when Sarl and Kethelket came through the gate. Victor had to admire the Naghelli for staying afoot, keeping Sarl company as they hurried back to the walls. He walked around the wall, toward the front, then stomped up the short steps to the higher section just above the gatehouse. From that vantage, he could see the southern hills clearly and the enemy forces flowing down their slopes.

None of the "reavers" were mounted, but they certainly moved quickly, somehow maintaining orderly lines as they ran. They seemed to glide effortlessly over the ground, holding a speed that was something close to a standard mounted roladii. As they drew near, despite the dark, Victor could make out their individual shapes. He saw that every one of them wore shiny black-enameled armor similar to the baron and his retinue. They ran in rows of fifty or so, each line capped with a standard-bearer. It was hard to see the colors in the weird green illumination of the sky and the pale light of the moons, but it seemed the banners were deep red, stitched with a black fist under a crescent moon. He wondered if the symbol represented the now-dead baron or Prince Hector.

Victor could hear Sarl and his lieutenants shouting orders in the courtyard, and he saw soldiers running about madly, unloading and carrying munitions to archers lining up on the southern parapet. He pushed forward, making room for a row of them behind him, noting the humming Energy in their bows, primed to fire with the magic of their class abilities. Even with the losses the Ninth had suffered earlier that day, nearly six hundred defenders were in the keep. Did these thousand attackers think they could take the castle with such a garrison? Were they suicidal? He remembered Porter's words to the baron, remembered how he'd seemed fiercely loyal. Perhaps he *was* suicidal. Perhaps the troops he was leading didn't know what they faced.

"He responded!" Valla's voice called from his left. He turned and looked at her, running toward him with Edeya's Far Scribe book clutched under one arm.

"Borrius?"

"Yes! He's sent the fifth cohort, fully mounted. They're swinging out to the east and will flank the attackers."

"Shit. These guys don't know what they're in for if they attack the keep." As he spoke, Victor watched the charging enemy come to a sudden halt. No horns blew, no drums sounded, but they all stopped running at nearly the same instant—an awesome exemplar of unit cohesion. They paused for a few seconds, and then, as though they'd heard every word Valla had just said, they turned to their right, the east, and began to run in that direction, every single one of them.

"Are they . . ." Valla trailed off, so Victor finished for her.

"Charging our reinforcements." He turned, pushed his way to the parapet on the courtyard side, and shouted down, "Sarl! We have to get out there, or the fifth cohort is going to be wiped out!"

14

FOR THE LOVE OF BATTLE

Are you mad? We have no mounts! We'll be caught flat-footed, outnumbered, fools for their feint!" Sarl's face betrayed the conflict he felt, standing up to Victor, a man to whom he owed so much.

"They aren't feinting, Sarl! They must have scouts or magic or . . . something! They must know that the fifth cohort is coming around from the east. They'll crush them, just as you fear they'll do to us! If we can catch them from behind, though . . ." Victor looked around at the lieutenants, at Valla and Kethelket, then back to Sarl. He hated how his voice sounded pleading. He was the boss here, right? He supposed the problem was that part of him feared Sarl was right. He wasn't totally sure it was the right move to charge.

"But we can't catch them." Sarl sighed, his voice losing its edge, clearly troubled by the idea that another cohort was going to die out there without his troops' aid.

"We can catch up, though!" Victor felt his frustration mounting and heard the rumble in his voice as his rage began to seep into his pathways. "They'll smash into the Fifth, probably do some damage, but we can get there in time to make a difference, to turn the tide."

"And if we march forth," Kethelket interjected, "gain some distance from the keep, and they turn to charge us? You saw how fast they run! We don't know how close the Fifth is. They could be an hour or two distant."

Victor stood straight, squared his shoulders, and looked at the dark sky.

He inhaled deeply through his nose, and with his exhalation, he sent his doubts and frustrations into the air. While everyone watched him, waiting for his next words, he cleared his mind and listened to his instincts. Everything in him said to summon Guapo and charge after the black-plated pale warriors—the late Baron Eric's reavers. With a calm steady voice, he said, "Valla, you will ride with me. Bring the command Far Scribe book. Captain Yarsha isn't responding to the messages we've sent to the Fifth; perhaps they're already fighting and she can't check her book, but you have yours, right, Sarl?"

"Yes, sir."

"I will ride after the invaders, ensure they aren't laying a trap for you, and Valla will send word via the Far Scribe book. When you see the command to march, you will double-time it onto the field, and you will smash into the reavers. Get your troops ready to move." Victor turned to the gate, hardly registering Sarl's salute or the troubled look in his eyes—if Victor had to guess, the captain was worried that he'd burned a bridge with him by challenging his command in front of his soldiers. Victor was too stressed to think about it; it was a problem for a more peaceful night. He reached into his Core, pulling forth a ribbon of glory-attuned Energy, and summoned Guapo.

As the great mustang burst into being, leaping out of the shimmering golden pool of Energy, Victor reached into his ring and pulled out the corpse of Baron Eric Gore Lust. The dead vampyr still gripped the smoky evil deadly-potent sword as it flopped onto the hard-packed gravel outside the gate. Valla and the others who'd been following behind gasped at the sudden reminder of what Victor had slain earlier that night.

"What are you . . ." Valla started to ask, but Victor was already acting, building the pattern for Honor the Spirits. The big, oddly bloodless corpse, clad in battered dark plate, and the wicked, probably living sword, flaring with bright white flames, elicited gasps and curses from the officers and soldiers nearby. The flames lingered longer than usual, surging as they consumed the man and the sword. The baron's body was gone before the sword, almost as though it fought against the workings of the spell, but Victor's spirit magic was strong, and with a final burst of brilliant white flames, it winked out of existence, and nothing but ghostly smoke remained.

Victor swung atop Guapo and held out a hand, hoisting Valla up behind him, then he turned to Sarl. "Get them lined up and ready to march." Guapo didn't need him to kick his heels or flick any reins; he knew what Victor wanted, and he delivered, bursting into motion, streaking over the dark rolling hills, leaving a trail of golden sparks where his hooves struck the ground.

Victor had ridden Guapo flat out a few times, and he knew what he could do. Still, it brought a surge of adrenaline into his blood as the wind screamed past his face and the moonlit countryside became a blur.

Valla squeezed her arms around his waist, burying her face in his back. Victor would have worried about her, wondering if she was afraid or angry, but he couldn't think of anything other than the idea that he had soldiers out there who needed him. He hadn't felt any pangs from his Battlemaster feat, but something told him he had to get out there, had to make a difference; those troops were coming to help him—how could he leave them to hang?

The wild ride through the dark proved mercifully short. After just a few minutes, they mounted a sizeable grassy hilltop with a solitary tree at its crest, and on the other side, all of Victor's questions and concerns came into focus. At his urging, Guapo slid to a halt, tearing up a deep furrow of sod, and Victor looked down into a wide grassy meadow upon which hell was breaking loose. On the far side, perhaps three or five miles distant, he saw the fifth cohort, beset by massive wolf-like creatures in the hundreds. Nearer, still charging toward the fight, were the black-plated reavers. In a minute or less, they'd pile into the fight, and the Fifth would surely be destroyed.

"Get off," he grunted.

"Victor—"

"Get down and tell Sarl to hurry." His voice had become a growl.

"Will there be any Fifth left to save by the time—"

"Now, Valla!" Victor reached behind himself to nudge her with one big hand, pushing her to the side until she relented and slid off Guapo's back. "Wait here for the Ninth."

"Victor! I know I won't stop you from acting, but promise me you aren't going down there to die! Think about why you aren't taking me with you!" Valla's words were pleading and had taken a desperate edge. They gave him pause, and he looked down at her, into her beautiful eyes, and he resolved to talk to her about his feelings again, really talk to her, not just play around with hints and hugs.

"I'm not planning to die, Valla, but I have to slow those *pendejos* down." She nodded, taking the small victory, and with those final words, Victor summoned his banner and, almost simultaneously, cast Iron Berserk. As the brilliant light of his banner's sun burst into being, illuminating the hilltop like a fallen star, he exploded with furious Energy, and Guapo grew with him. Victor urged the mustang forward and, responding to an instinct that ran deep in his blood, roared into the night, "Ancestors! Watch me fight these mother*fuckers!*"

Sized as he was to accommodate Victor's titanic form, Guapo devoured the distance between the hilltop and the charging reavers. As they tore over the grassy meadow, Victor pulled Lifedrinker free of her harness and held her high, ready to lay about himself with her smoldering blade. "Come on, boy!" he urged, willing the great mustang to run even faster. As they thundered over the ground, everything became a blur, everything except the rear ranks of the reavers, the center of Victor's focus. In seconds, they were upon them, and then Guapo was trampling through them like a draft horse running through a schoolyard.

The reavers screamed and flailed as the mustang smashed through them, crushing them to the ground and sending many more flying left and right, all while Victor's banner seemed to ignite their exposed pale flesh. In the chaos, Victor could see smoke billowing out of helmets and the seams of dark armor, and he knew these reavers suffered even more than their late baron in his glorious light. He howled and roared, mad with wild battle lust as Guapo trampled through rank after rank. He cleaved left and right with his axe until he and his mount finally burst through the far side of the reavers' formation.

The mustang had suffered many gashes and cuts in his passage, but he was snorting, prancing, neck arched in a proud display of resilience as he whirled and paced in front of the host of reavers, he and Victor the only obstacle between them and the beleaguered fifth cohort. Even so, the reavers had slowed their mad charge and taken pause to examine this new threat. Victor could see dozens of broken forms lying in Guapo's wake—victims of the mighty mustang's hooves and Victor's vicious axe blows.

The idea that he was facing down nearly a thousand enemies filled him with mad battle lust, a hunger for glory that dwarfed anything he'd ever felt. Victor wanted to leap off Guapo's back and wade into the host, wanted to feel their bones and flesh breaking under the blade of his axe, and wanted to bathe in their blood and howl with their screams of defeat. Part of him was rational, though—part of him knew he would kill many of them, but that eventually, he'd run out of Energy, and they'd overwhelm him. As Guapo pranced in front of the army, up and down their front rank, as his banner bathed them in its light, forcing them to shrink back and shield their eyes, that lucid part of his mind urged him to shout, "I've killed your leaders. Will you be next?"

If he'd been hoping to send them running, he was disappointed—his words seemed to enrage them. Whatever bond they'd had with the baron was still there, or at least their loyalty to his faction had survived his death. Victor could feel them gathering their Energy, could see many of them, dozens, hundreds, exploding with growth, taking on vampyr forms like the baron and some of his retinue had done. He saw weapons bursting into flames or limned with other kinds of Energy, from frost and lightning to acid. Some of those who shrank from his banner's light straightened up, shimmering with magical defenses, perhaps banking on killing Victor before their Energy ran out.

Victor saw that his shout hadn't cowed the horde, and his heart sang with the news—it was time to get bloody. He slid off Guapo's back and slapped a massive hand on the mustang's shoulder. "Good boy. You did enough. Go recover in the spirit plane, and I'll call you again soon." The horse, part of Victor's spirit, nudged him with its muzzle, perhaps unwilling to leave him, but Victor chuckled and severed his connection, sighing deeply as the horse dispersed in a shimmering fog of golden Energy.

Victor turned to the horde of reavers and saw that the transformed creatures were starting to rush toward him, pushing past their smaller brethren. He could feel the gathering Energy of spells and knew the momentary standoff was nearly over. Soon he'd be surrounded, and though he was much larger and more powerful than these lesser vampyrs, he knew he couldn't hold off a thousand of them for long. As he hefted Lifedrinker in his fists, channeling rage-fueled Energy into his arms and into her, he grinned. "Hope you're hurrying, Sarl." The reavers and vampyrs screamed in a cacophonous frenzy and charged him.

Rather than meet the elite of their number as they shoved to the front ranks of the host, Victor bunched his legs and launched himself into the air, soaring over the first several ranks. Missiles of fire and ice, lightning and magma, acid and metal tore through the air at him. Many struck home, but he shrugged them off. His mass, his durability, his armor, and his magical belt did much to mitigate the attacks. The damage that got through was quickly mended by his incredible ability to regenerate while Berserk. When he landed at the center of the armored reavers, none of whom were even half his size, he flattened one outright, and then he began madly hacking at the screaming horde.

Lifedrinker was ablaze with her own fury; her silvery blade was magma orange, and black smoke roiled in her wake. She split the reavers' enameled plate like porcelain. She burned their flesh and shattered their bones, and with each wide cleave Victor made, she left broken, writhing, screaming reavers lying and flailing on the ground. Victor felt impacts on his back, against his impossibly dense helmet, and from every other angle. He began to amass wounds on his legs and arms, and though he was seeing red and focused on slaughter, a corner of his mind suggested he seek more armoring if he meant to battle this way in the future.

The stray thought brought wild laughter out of him, and as blood showered up from a terrible cleave he laid into a reaver's chest, Victor wondered if there would be a future for him. Despite the broken mounds of enemies, despite the mist of their blood hanging thick in the air, the host of enemies stretched away from him in every direction. He was alone, and as fast as he could kill them, they kept coming. They, too, were wild with the desire to kill. They'd seen his devilish work, seen how he'd destroyed their comrades and boasted about killing their lord, and whatever else might be true about these invaders, they weren't cowards.

At some point, Victor summoned his mighty bear, fueling it with fear-attuned Energy, and the powerful beast gave him some respite, clearing one of his flanks, so he turned his back to the monstrous black bear with its indigo eyes. He listened to its roars and responded in kind, the two of them drowning out the din of the hundreds of reavers as they fought. When he'd summoned the totem, Victor had seen how his fear-attuned Energy was more prevalent in his Core than the others, so he decided to use it, throwing out waves of black terror with Project Energy. The effect varied, causing some reavers to flee, others to stand stunned, and others only to grimace in discomfort.

The transformed vampyrs were the least affected, and though Victor killed them in the dozens, they were the ones to leave the deepest, most painful wounds on Victor's flanks as they fought through their allies to get at him. He took spear stabs, axe wounds, crushing blows, and gashes everywhere he wasn't covered by Tes's amazing wyrm-scale armor. If not for that armor and his helmet, Victor knew the fight would have ended far sooner.

He did all he could to prolong his fight. He used Energy Charge to make space for himself, smashing through several ranks of reavers, crashing into a vampyr or large reaver with a devastating explosion of Energy, giving himself a brief break before more unwounded enemies filled the gaps. He used Titanic Leap to much the same effect; when he felt he had too many powerful enemies nearby, he'd jump away, smash into a distant section of the reaver horde, and work on those laggards for a while, slaughtering them while their stronger comrades worked through the ranks to get at him again.

So the incredible wild battle dragged on. Victor couldn't possibly count the number of reavers he slew, couldn't count the number of wounds he'd healed from. He knew he'd have a new patchwork of pale scars on his body if he managed to survive, but he was starting to believe that wouldn't be a concern—his Energy was running low. He could feel his rage waning along with the rest of his affinities; he'd been trying to spread their usage, and he'd done a good job, but they were all drawing down, and he knew it was soon going to be over when his Titanic Leap would no longer activate.

In his blood-red vision, things seemed darker, and he wondered if it was a result of him losing so much blood; was he starting to fade? Then, it clicked when he saw that the reavers and vampyrs nearby weren't smoking and that their wounds were mending before his eyes—his banner had faded. Victor thought about trying to choke down a heart, an arachnid one from Zaafor, perhaps, or—he laughed madly at the idea—the Ridonne heart he'd ripped out not long ago. As his deep, insane laugh rumbled out of his blood-soaked face, some of the reavers in front of him shrank back, triggering more laughter from the titanic berserker.

"What fucking *fun!*" he roared, and then he forgot about his Energy, he forgot about his Core and his spells, and he began to dance in earnest. He felt Lifedrinker's joy in battle echoing his own, and the two of them began to move with a new kind of grace and rhythm. He moved with speed and power that was a pile of thermite burning next to the wax candles of the reavers. He wove between them, smooth and easy, ducking hacks and stabs and carrying with him a shard of death and destruction, leaving bloody bits and broken armor in his wake.

As the last of his rage burned up in his pathways and his vision returned to normal, Victor found himself surrounded by vampyrs that were more massive than he and reavers he could no longer shove aside or fling about, but he didn't care. His laughter rang out as he continued his dance. In his joy of battle, he almost appreciated the wounds that no longer near-instantly healed. He relished the bloody, painful work of fighting, and he savored each hard-fought victory. Still, the injuries began to mount, his vigor began to fade, and he knew it was nearly his time to join Old Mother on the spirit plane.

"Good!" he screamed, proud of his efforts—surely Sarl and his foot soldiers were nearly there. Surely they'd come in time to mop up this army of reavers and join with the fifth cohort. They'd see what he'd done. They'd tell stories of his last battle. Valla would be sad, but she'd be free. She'd live a great life, and maybe Victor would meet her in the next one. A huge vampyr smashed a spiked mace into his stomach, puncturing his vest with one of its long barbs, and it growled savagely as Victor's wind was knocked out.

"He fades! Kill him!" it screeched. Of course, those words brought more laughter from Victor; hadn't they *been* trying to kill him?

"Come on, you fucking *pendejos*!" He whirled, rolling his shoulder to the left, jerking the mace from the vampyr's grip, and then, with the weapon still hanging from his midriff, he continued his bloody dance between a pair of reavers. Lifedrinker took the head from one, and he kicked the other down to the torn bloody sod. He whirled in a circle, swinging his wonderful axe in a wide arc, and the reavers and vampyrs hung back; they knew he was dying, but they also knew he had what it would take to bring more of them with him. "Come on! You *pinché* ratfuckers!" he screamed. "*Abuela! Ancestors!*" Tears sprang into his eyes at the thought of his grandmother among the rest of his ancestors. "I'm coming to you!"

Is your bloody work over? I don't think so, child of the Quinametzin. I am Chantico, brave son, and I lend you my strength and my fire. Stand tall among these undead fiends. Teach them what it means to corner a titan!

15

ANCESTOR'S FIRE

Kethelket gestured to the hillside bordering the western side of the vale, directing his thirty brothers and sisters to land next to the lone armored woman. He recognized the shimmering scales and knew it was Valla. He wasn't surprised to see her with sword in hand, staring into the narrow valley where her—their—leader was streaking over the grass on that magnificent mount of his. How fast it was! Even airborne, on wings and magic, he and his squadron couldn't match its pace. The mad giant was charging directly toward the rear ranks of the reaver army, more than a thousand strong, and beyond them, Kethelket could see what had prevented the fifth cohort from responding to messages; they were beset by enormous hounds.

"It's madness," Rincella cried from his right as they descended toward Valla.

"Aye, a mad scene, indeed." Valla looked up at the sound of their voices, and he called down, "Do I need to send word to Captain Sarl?"

She watched him and his folk land lightly on the grass, shaking her head. "I spoke to him through the book. He marches. How long will it take?"

"If they double-time? Over these hills, maintaining some semblance of order? Half an hour? Three quarters?" Kethelket shrugged. He wasn't an expert on foot soldier speeds.

"That's what I feared, and look." Valla pointed as Victor's incredible charge neared the enemy ranks. Kethelket held his breath, wondering if the madman would veer at the last instant, taunting the enemies, trying to get them to slow or chase him. He heard Valla's intake of breath as she, too, braced, watching the distant figure and the trail of sparks his horse threw up in its wake.

"Gods!" she cried as he smashed right into the charging reavers, trampling through them. The explosive impact took a heartbeat to reach them, and in that gap, Kethelket looked at Valla, wondering where she'd taken the strange habit of invoking gods. Then the sounds of crashing metal, screaming men and women, and the thunderous roars of the mad titan echoed up the slope to them, and those wandering thoughts were chased from Kethelket's mind as he watched the incredible giant mount smash through the entire formation of reavers.

Gasps, cheers, curses, and various other exclamations broke out among the Naghelli flanking him and Valla. "I yearn to join him, but we'd be slain. There are too many; we'd be swarmed." His words weren't only for Valla; he knew some of his kin would want to join the titan in his madness. "His size gives him mobility among their host that we could not match."

"I know," Valla said, "but I won't stand here and watch him die. I hope he's in control of his rage. He's seemed so much better lately, but tonight . . . tonight he seemed different."

"My lord," one of Kethelket's men said, forgetting that he was no longer a true prince, "will we not at least join the cavalry on the far side of the vale? There we may make a difference against those giant hounds."

"Good question, Givahn. Yes. Go. Rincella, you will lead these thirty to aid the fifth cohort. I will stay with Tribune ap'Yensha."

The dark Naghelli lifted her fist to her heart and leapt into the air, her shadowy wings with their amber markings streaking into the sky as the rest of the thirty flew after her. Kethelket watched them, trusting they'd be wise enough to avoid death among their soil-bound comrades. Quick strikes, feints, and retreats were the order of the night—Rincella knew as much.

"You don't have to stay with me."

"No, but I will." Kethelket followed Valla's gaze to the giant, now riding his bloodied prancing mount to and fro before the line of reavers who'd come to a halt and were cringing in the light of his enormous blazing banner. "You wish you were with him."

"Of course!" Valla spat the words, and Kethelket's suspicions that she saw more in Victor than a leader began to deepen.

"He can break free. His size and speed—"

"I know." Valla sighed in frustration, turning to look back toward the west, perhaps trying to spy some sign of Sarl's troops.

"On a positive note, it seemed the fifth cohort was holding its own against those giant hounds. With my squad of Naghelli aiding them, they may prevail while Victor delays these reavers. Ancestors!" His outburst came as Victor slid from his mount, sending it away, and then charged into the thick of the reaver army with explosive force. More sounds of smashing metal and screaming soldiers echoed over the hillsides. "Did he actually dismiss his mount?"

"It doesn't surprise me." Valla now sounded resigned, though her eyes darted about, following Victor's movements, and her breaths were slow, each one held until her body forced her to exhale and take a new one. Kethelket watched the giant and realized he didn't seem so gigantic anymore; many of the reavers, hundreds of them, had exploded with their own growth, taking on vampyric forms like the baron and his kin they'd met earlier in the night. "Shit!" Valla cried, using one of the strange legate's favorite curses. "Some of those vampyrs are nearly his size!"

"He's far mightier than they, however." Kethelket tried to sound reassuring, but she was correct; there were so many of the creatures. How could he hope to win? He attempted to answer his own question. "They can't match his explosive power and speed, his ability to leap great distances. He merely bides his time, tormenting and slaying many of them. Without question, he'll fight free before he succumbs to their numbers, and hopefully he'll have delayed them long enough for Sarl to come."

"Yes." Valla looked up at him, gratitude in her eyes; she knew he was trying to reassure her. "If I didn't think it would be a distraction, if I didn't think I'd be overrun in minutes, I'd charge down there."

"As would I, Lady Valla. If there were but a hundred for me to slay, I would try it." Kethelket rested his hand on the pommel of his off-hand blade, Gevel, and listened to the hunger in her song as it trilled through the bones of his palm. She wanted to fight, but then she always wanted to fight. Valla didn't respond, and Kethelket allowed his mouth to rest while his eyes followed the mad, beautiful dance of destruction the titanic legate wove among the reavers. At this distance, it was hard to see details, but he could see the orange streak of his massive axe as it ripped, smashed, and tore among the reavers and the dark mist that clouded the air in its wake—smoke and blood.

Victor smashed through row upon row of the reavers, never standing still long enough for them to pile on. Still, it was clear he took wounds, and Kethelket couldn't imagine the kind of Energy he had coursing through his pathways to mend him so quickly. Aside from his rapid healing, he was unfathomably sturdy. Kethelket saw spears, driven by large powerful men, strike the giant's legs and fail to penetrate enough to find purchase, falling away or shattering under the sweeps of Victor's axe.

"He's like an iron colossus."

"He's a true titan while berserk; his bloodline is rich. Still, he bleeds, Kethelket, and the spells he weaves to bolster himself take a toll. He's been fighting too long, been cut so many times. If not for his armor—"

"Such armor. Yours is the same?"

"Not the same, but crafted by the same artisan."

"Wonderful stuff. Might I know the name of—"

"Not now, sir." Valla's words were clipped, her eyes narrowed as she stared at the battle below, and Kethelket felt a fool for trying to make small talk about armor while such a great man battled for his life. In the hope of redeeming himself, he launched into the air and turned to the west, scanning the hillsides. Sure enough, perhaps a mile distant, he saw the lights of the ninth cohort, the Glorious Ninth, as Victor had styled them.

He quickly descended, announcing as he did, "I see the Ninth—only a mile distant."

"A mile over shrub-covered hillsides. Ten minutes, maybe? An eternity for Victor. Ancestors damn it! Why doesn't he break free? Look at how he slows . . ." Her voice rose in a near-panic. "Oh no! His banner!" Kethelket saw what she meant—the blazing light of Victor's glorious banner had winked out. Valla jerked her sword up, pulling its point from the sod, and began to jog down the hill. Kethelket hurried after her and grabbed her by the shoulder, darting back as she reflexively lashed out at him. "Unhand me!"

"Lady! Hold! Use your reason—would Victor want you to charge now? Would you even be able to get near him? Hundreds of reavers stand between us and him! Surely he has a plan! Surely he doesn't want to die this night."

"He . . ." Valla stopped pulling, some of the anger fading from her eyes, bright moisture pooling there to take its place. "He's not so easy to predict! Something comes over him when he's fighting—he loves it. His heart, his spirit, there's so much conflict there! Rage, fear, glory, inspiration! It's what he is, he's . . . I can't see him running, damn it!"

"He still battles, despite the banner's fading, by all the dead and the spirits that claw at the gates, look! He's no longer a giant, yet he fights on!" Kethelket pointed, and Valla, perhaps accepting that she couldn't get to Victor in time to make a difference, joined him in his appreciation of Victor's prowess. He was remarkable; the skill he showed among that host of enemies was the seed of a legend being born. Kethelket might fight so beautifully against a single foe, a dance of skill and grace with his two living blades, but he couldn't hope to move that way among a horde of clamoring armored enemies. He'd be overrun, unable to find or create the gaps to move about like Victor did.

"He's gotten so good with that axe," Valla said, echoing his thoughts. "He's making fools of them. Look how he ducks and weaves—I taught him that one!"

"I pray he'll win free so I may yet spar with him." Kethelket's voice was hushed, watching how Victor, just a dark shadow at this distance in the moonlight, moved among the reavers and vampyrs, large and small, his glowing axe hacking limbs off, smashing skulls, and ripping in wide arcs, spraying steaming blood in misting clouds. "He truly is like a dancer . . ."

Every so often, Victor would explode with light and speed, ripping through more of the reavers, thunderously colliding with an enemy, and driving the hordes back with the concussion of his impact. Now, after just such a move, Victor paused, leaning on his axe, and in the bright green-tinted moonlight, Kethelket could see his shoulders heaving up and down with his inhalations—the man was exhausted. He knew if he were closer, he'd see that he was covered with wounds, that he was dark with blood, and that he must be near the end.

He glanced at Valla, saw tears streaking her cheeks, and turned to the west to see that the Ninth was close, cresting a hilltop only a quarter of a mile distant. "I will go to him. I'll try to pull him free, fly off with him!" Valla's eyes focused on him, and she nodded emphatically, something like desperate hope springing to life in them. Kethelket leapt into the air, streaking toward the army and the lone heroic warrior at their center. He'd only covered half the distance when it seemed that Victor burst into flames.

Is your bloody work over? I don't think so, child of the Quinametzin. I am Chantico, brave son, and I lend you my strength and my fire. Stand tall among these undead fiends. Teach them what it means to corner a titan!

At his ancestor's words, Victor's eyes began to smolder with deep yellow-orange flames, and his vision took on a bright yellow tint. He felt a warmth in his belly, an echo of the fire in his chest where his Breath Core smoldered. At first, it was an echo, but as the reavers closed in, overcoming their fear of Lifedrinker's edge, ready to finish him, the fire in his belly grew hot, turned into an inferno, and then exploded through his body.

His pathways blazed with the Energy, and Victor arched his back, screaming his enthusiasm for the fire, welcoming it as it invigorated his tired muscles and fueled his body's healing. Victor's dozens—hundreds—of wounds were cauterized on the spot, sealed beneath hot new flesh, and though the fiery Energy wasn't compatible with his Core, and he struggled to bend it to his will, to push it into his spell patterns, Victor could feel his Breath Core yearning for it, could feel it pulsing and throbbing, aching to absorb that hot Energy.

Had his ancestor known that he had an affinity for magma, for fire? Had she known about his Breath Core? Had she gifted him this Energy for that use or simply to heal and revitalize him? Victor began to dance again, moving with grace and power, slipping blows, hacking limbs, and weaving between his many, many foes. All the while, he felt that fire burning, felt his Breath Core yearning, and he wished he knew how to bring them together. Could he solve the puzzle before he was overwhelmed? Did it matter? He'd slain so many! Surely his ancestors were proud. Surely he'd left his mark on this world. Sarl must be close—the fifth cohort would be saved, and Rellia would have her foothold in these lands.

Valla . . . Valla would be proud of him, though she'd be angry at first. He was angry that he wouldn't hold her again, and that thought made Victor turn more of his attention to his pathways, to his Breath Core. "What's the fucking deal?" he growled, shouldering aside a massive vampyr and hacking down with Lifedrinker, carving a groove through its femur as he danced around it and spun, cleaving in an arc, driving back several reavers. Even with half his attention pointed inward, he and Lifedrinker were making fools of these *pendejos.*

He'd looked at his pathways so many times that he didn't need to look now to know how they traversed his body. They rose from his Core to his head and out to his arms and hands. They went down from his Core to his legs and his feet. They branched into little tributaries that touched different parts of his body—his heart, his lungs, his . . . Victor paused, and he felt as though a spark had ignited in his brain. His lungs . . . his *Breath* Core. Victor exerted his will, gathering all the Energy in his pathways and pushing it, driving it into the pathways that went to his lungs, driving it harder and harder until he forced new openings as he had in his hands.

He was a man, a titan, and he was used to doing *things* with his hands. He directed his magic with his hands, and he pulled it in through his hands. Humans and titans didn't naturally have a Breath Core; they didn't naturally pull or push their magic with their lungs. "Time to change that!" Victor roared as he split the head of yet another reaver. Lifedrinker screamed with fury and pleasure, excited to still be fighting, proud of Victor for finding a second wind. Victor pushed the fiery magic in his pathways into his lungs, and then, with a deep inhalation, he willed it to flow into his Breath Core.

He'd never felt anything like what happened next. It was, for lack of a more eloquent analogy, orgasmic. Pure pleasure radiated through his being as his Breath Core swelled, as it split a shell Victor didn't know had held it, and it expanded, flaring like a miniature fiery sun, sending heat through his body. Victor felt his chest swell as he inhaled, felt his breath ignite, and savored the feeling. It was as if all his life he'd been breathing something dead and lifeless, and now he had a living, dancing, raging wind in his lungs, and it wanted *out*.

Whatever fiery magic his ancestor had sent into him, Victor knew it was potent beyond his means, something epic and magnificent, something not meant for the world of Fanwath. The gift brought tears to his eyes as he realized what he'd received, as he tasted the life the flames had filled him with. He spread his arms wide, expanding his chest as he strained to fill himself with as much air as possible, savoring the pleasure as his Core continued to ignite it, as he swelled with the potent flames of his ancestor. His inaction encouraged the reavers and vampyrs, and they began to creep close, weapons and claws raised. Then Victor exhaled, and the world burst into flames.

Fire streamed out of Victor's mouth like water from a fire hose. It cooked the flesh off the reavers before him in a thirty-foot cone, blackened their bones, and reduced them to ash. Victor wasn't done—he turned in a circle, blowing that terrible, wonderful, awful yellow-white fire in a circular cone, utterly destroying hundreds of reavers and vampyrs. He wasn't sure if it was the potency of the fire his ancestor had given him or a particular weakness for fire, but his enemies crumbled before his efforts, and the ones outside his cone, who only felt the *heat* of his flames, fell back, scrabbling to get away from him.

By the time he'd turned full circle and the awesome fire had fled his Breath Core, Victor stood at the center of an enormous black circle of smoldering corpses. The reaver host was in disarray as they fought over each other to put more distance between themselves and the one who'd breathed the fury of a sun onto the battlefield. Victor lifted Lifedrinker high, and he roared his enthusiastic thanks, praising his ancestors with an ululating, howling scream. The reavers were broken, their will to fight demolished by the display of destruction, and that's how the Glorious Ninth found them as they charged down the slope and smashed into them with Valla and Kethelket at the center of their front rank.

16

MASTERS OF THE AXE

Lesh'ro'zellan sat by his solitary campfire, and he contemplated. Campfire was a generous term for the handful of smoldering coals and hot rocks. He sat upon a partially petrified log, more stone than wood, and he gently caressed the smooth polished handle of Belagog, his cudgel. His mind was in turmoil, his usual drive blunted, his heart and soul torn, and his contempt and hatred of the System soared to new heights. Things had been going well until earlier that night. He'd been set to isolate and slay Victor, had been ready to call him out and challenge his honor, sure the warrior would take the bait. That had been before Lesh saw him breathe fire that would give even a full-blooded dragon pause.

"A Breath Core! A *mighty* Breath Core. And the System wants me to slay him? For what?" Lesh spat into the coals, watched his saliva sizzle, and tried to contemplate his options. It had taken him more than a month to catch up to Victor's army. He'd stalked them—no small feat with those shadowy flying scouts—for further weeks, and then, when they'd finally crossed that damnable frozen pass, he'd used every trick in his bag to slip by their encampment to follow the titan-blood farther into these new lands.

It had been a surprise when the System offered him the conquest quest. Still, it explained why Victor had come to these lands with his army. Lesh hunkered down over his coals, adjusting his mottled gar viper cloak, peering out through the voluminous hood at the sickly mists that fought to cover the tiny island of warmth his coals created. Without the cloak, he'd have been spotted several times by the titan's scouts, but it hid him well, and thus far, he'd managed to avoid slaying any of the soldiers that followed the giant warrior.

After he'd witnessed the epic battle between Victor and an entire army of undead, Lesh hadn't felt right about piling on. He hadn't thought it would be an honorable way to gain victory. Only a fool would presume that Lesh would jump upon a beleaguered rival, only a fool who didn't understand Lesh's pride, his honor, and his determination to be the best. Could he claim such if he had to fight his enemy when he was near death, surrounded by a horde of enemies? No. If anything, Lesh had been tempted to aid the berserker. He'd been tempted to try to fight to the center of those undead warriors, hoist the battered human, and fight free, giving him a chance to recover—before Lesh challenged him, of course.

That was putting aside the feelings that had begun to roil in Lesh's chest as he watched Victor battle, though. He'd never seen such a contest, such a desperate battle that seemed so hopeless yet dragged on, one new surprise after another. He'd never seen someone, not even his mentor, Thov'kinal'rovessi, fight so artfully, so gracefully while surrounded by so many enemies. It was clear that Victor was made for war, made for the battlefield. He'd never looked afraid, never seemed discouraged or weary, even when he'd been drenched in his own blood and covered with wounds, one arm hanging limply by his side, the axe warrior had worn a grin, his eyes shining with excitement—eagerness. Then he'd breathed fire, such fire, that when it ended, Lesh had been surprised to find himself kneeling, mouth agape in awe.

"And the System wants me to kill this man?" He snorted, reached down, and poked at the coals with one long black claw, shifting away some ash to expose the red heat. "No. Not yet, at least. I think I'll watch this man for a while longer. I think I might try to puzzle out why you want him dead. Do you hear me, System?" Lesh spat again, hawking up phlegm from deep in his throat. He doubted the gods-damned System listened to him—doubted it would spare him a thought until he'd done its bidding. Still, it felt good to voice his disdain, his bitterness. Watching his mucus bubble on the coals, a new thought occurred to him. "Do you want him dead, or do you want *me* dead?"

Victor stood at the center of his blasted wasteland, the remains of corpses and molten armor steaming and smoking in a wide circle around him as the Glorious Ninth smashed into the remnants of the reaver army. He was tired; the breath attack he'd pulled off had been exhilarating, incredible, but it had pulled all of his ancestor's Energy out of him, leaving him standing at the epicenter with just his slowly replenishing Core to sustain him. He could still fight, but hadn't he done his share? He chuckled at the idea, lifting Lifedrinker to rest on his shoulder while he watched Sarl's troops use their discipline and fresh reserves of Energy to dominate the battlefield.

He wasn't surprised when, amid the screaming fighters, crashing weapons and shields, and explosions of Energy, he saw Valla dancing through the combat toward him. She ran on gusts of wind that sparkled with bursts of lightning, and soon she was before him, concern in her eyes as she looked him up and down. They stood in an area of relative calm; the remaining reavers seemed to want to avoid the place he'd burned to ash, and the Ninth was driving them farther west, away from the scene of his one-man war. "Are you all right?"

In answer, Victor smiled and shrugged, pleased that most of his wounds had been mended by his ancestor's fire. "Thanks to my ancestor."

"You're an asshole!" Valla growled, and Victor, probably angering her further, couldn't help laughing.

"I'm rubbing off on you!"

"You were going to fight to the death!" Valla didn't look amused, standing before him, lightning dancing behind her eyes, Midnight naked in her hands, held ready, almost as if she meant to swing the dark blade at him.

"I don't know about that . . . I had some hope that my ancestors might step in. You heard me call out to them when I charged."

"Some hope," Valla growled and leaned close to him, her face livid beneath the eyeholes of her helmet. "And if they chose not to aid you? If you died on this field, you were okay with that? No thought of retreat? No thought of me?"

"I thought of you. You were in my mind the whole time." Victor frowned. What more could he say but the truth?

"I was?"

"Yeah, of course. I was . . ." Victor sighed and turned, looking to where the Ninth was driving the reavers, farther and farther westward, toward the fifth cohort. He couldn't see it from where he stood, but he hoped the Naghelli and the cavalry had been able to hold their own against the giant wolves. He hoped they'd come together and smash the remains of the reavers. He looked back at Valla; the noise of combat had lessened, and they were, surprisingly, quite alone. "I was full of regret." He reached a hand, caked in dried blood, to her chin and tilted her face toward him. Her eyes were brimming with tears—relief, frustration, anger, fear? Victor didn't know, but he thought they were beautiful. He leaned toward her and softly said, "I wished I'd at least kissed you."

To his relief and immeasurable delight, she didn't pull away, didn't say anything. He touched his lips—probably disgusting to her, covered in blood and gore—to hers. It was a simple gesture, a soft pressure, nothing overly amorous, but it meant everything to Victor. Her lips were soft and warm, and she pressed them into his, and when he pulled back, she leaned toward him, eyes hungry. When he continued to straighten, though, she smiled with a corner of her mouth and said, "If you think that gets you out of trouble, think again."

"Nah. What would I do with myself if I was out of trouble? I wouldn't know how to act." He looked inward to his Core, saw that he'd regenerated nearly a fourth of his Energy, and said, "Come on, let's go help them finish this. I think I have enough in me to summon my banner again."

Victor called Guapo using inspiration-attuned Energy, and the mustang burst into being from a simmering white-gold mist. He was beautiful, with brilliant blazing eyes, a tawny coat, and a long flowing white mane. Victor hopped onto his back and pulled Valla up behind him. Then as they charged toward the ongoing battle, he summoned his banner. If they'd been winning before, driving the reavers across the meadow, when the soldiers felt Victor's presence and the effect of the sun blazing over his shoulder, they truly began to slaughter the exhausted reavers and vampyrs.

Victor rode wherever he saw clusters of the huge gray vampyrs still putting up a fight, and when his banner's light touched them, the soldiers of the Glorious Ninth bore them down, hacked them to pieces, and continued on to the next. Soon the two cohorts came together, and Victor got his first good look at the pony-sized wolves that had been holding the cavalry in check. Their corpses littered the field, yet those that survived fought on mindlessly, rage in their eyes, and Victor saw that they too were undead; bones showed through their ragged fur, and the flesh as often as not was missing from their snouts, leaving their fangs exposed in perpetual snarls.

Once Sarl's troops provided some relief and took the pressure off their flank, the Fifth began to put their mounts to use, breaking free, whirling, and charging into the enemy's exposed flanks. In just minutes, a strange calm fell over the blood-soaked meadow until, in the relative silence of soldiers catching their breath and the coughing wheezes of the dying, cheers began to break out, and the men and women of Fanwath celebrated another hard-fought victory.

Sarl and Yarsha, the captain of the fifth cohort, began to bark orders, and their lieutenants passed them around, and soon the field was busy with squads combing the piles of bodies for survivors and collecting their dead comrades. Other units began to pile the undead, stripping them of weapons, jewelry, and pieces of armor—many of the reavers still wore plate that was largely intact, and there wasn't any denying its fine craftsmanship. With the soldiers performing after-combat activities, the System must have decided the battle was over because a sea of golden Energy motes began gathering in the little valley, and the soldiers' cheering started again.

Victor, still sitting atop Guapo, his banner blazing at the center of the bloody field, felt Valla's arms tighten around his waist, and she said, "I think I should hold onto you; maybe some of the ocean of Energy coming your way will bleed into me."

"Ha! If the System would let me, I'd be happy to share."

"I know you would." She squeezed him harder, and Victor felt a different kind of warmth ignite in his chest, right next to his Breath Core. He savored the feeling for a few moments, but then a cascade of Energy unlike anything he'd felt before washed over him, and he was made insensate, lost to the world, as rivers of golden light poured into him from all corners of the battle-field, lifting him into the air like a rising star, blazing in the night. Victor's consciousness departed his physical form for a while, a sensation not unlike when he'd advanced his race and had visions of his ancestral past.

This was different, though; he didn't have the feeling that he was traveling anywhere, be it through space or time. Instead, he felt as if he were hovering between places, on the edge of universes or planes of existence. He felt presences nearby, beings he could barely comprehend as such and whom he could not fully fathom. In a way, it felt as though he was being looked at, studied, and perhaps judged. He didn't feel threatened—just as he couldn't fully grasp those entities, he felt they couldn't entirely interact with him. He was being glimpsed through a veil, and in his titanic pride, bursting with Energy as he was, he shrugged and willed them to know that he didn't give a shit.

Victor had the immediate impression that some of the entities departed. He felt more strongly the ones that lingered, and in the less crowded space, he became aware that they were struggling with one another, a contest of wills nearly beyond his comprehension. As he hung there, suspended in that weird in-between, nothing but angles of light and strange swirling patterns to occupy his mind, the entities around him winked out, one by one, until he felt the looming presence of only one being. As if through a great tunnel, echoing and vibrating with the passage, a voice came to him. Despite its odd reverberating nature, it was masculine and powerful, and it said, "I am Golgothaz, and I am pleased with your axe dance, young warrior."

Victor opened his mouth and tried to respond, to at least say thank you, but he couldn't form the words.

The voice came to him again. "Do not try to speak; you haven't the will to make your voice heard in this place. I can read your intent: You desire to give me thanks. Instead, I will thank you—when we masters of the axe felt your contest and your breakthrough, we watched your dance, and it was entertaining. Great spans of time often pass betwixt the occasions when I might consider myself entertained. I will give you my blessing, a mark upon your soul. It will help you to shape a destiny of true mastery with your weapon. Good hunting, young warrior!"

As the voice faded, Victor saw a point of light pierce the strange fabric of the place he hung in, and then it lanced forth, searing into Victor's chest. It was painful but nothing close to the worst thing he'd ever felt, and as the burning sensation began to fade, so too did the limbo he hung in. Bright lights filled his vision, and Victor found himself lying on his back in the bloody grass of the battlefield, hundreds of soldiers encircling him, watching with rapt attention as he struggled to sit up. Valla was nearby, and she spoke, but her words didn't register—Victor's attention was on the System messages that filled his vision:

*****Congratulations! You have achieved level 55 Battlemaster and gained 10 strength, 9 vitality, 4 agility, 4 dexterity, 3 will, and 3 intelligence.*****

*****Congratulations! Your mastery of the axe has advanced to Epic.*****

*****Congratulations! Your Breath Core has evolved beyond the seed stage. It is now an active Core.*****

*****Congratulations! Your Breath Core has advanced to Base 5.*****

*****Congratulations! You have gained a new Class feat: Battlefield Presence.*****

*****Battlefield Presence: Your Battlemaster Class has allowed you to expand your presence on the battlefield. Any aura, bolstering, or debilitating effect that you radiate will affect an area twice as large as normal.*****

As he finished reading the messages, a slow smile spreading on his face, Victor became aware of the cheering of the soldiers surrounding him. They were chanting, stomping their feet, and smashing weapons against shields as they thundered, "Victor! Victor! Victor!"

Victor leapt to his feet and saw that Sarl, Kethelket, and Captain Yarsha stood nearby. Of course, right next to him was Valla, and she wore a bit of a frown, probably annoyed that he'd ignored whatever she'd been trying to say to him when he snapped out of his trance. He reached down to rest a hand on her shoulder, then he snatched Lifedrinker out of her harness and held her high. Of course, the axe was happy to put on a show, bursting into furious yellow-orange heat, igniting the air around her blade, and sending black smoke into the night. The soldiers' cheers grew louder and more frenzied.

Victor turned slowly, making eye contact with as many soldiers as he could, then he brought the axe down next to his side, and the cheering died down. The soldiers wanted to hear him, and Victor couldn't deny them. He felt terrific, fully replenished by the post-battle Energy, his high affinity allowing his body to make instant use of it, healing his wounds, banishing his fatigue, and replenishing his Core. More than that, he was exuberant about his gains, about having his ancestors act through him, and most of all about being alive with Valla by his side.

"That was a hell of a battle!" he roared. He probably could have said anything—announced he loved warm tortillas or that cold beer was best, and the troops would have gone mad with more cheering. In any case, they screamed their bloodlust and their pride, and Victor basked in it, fed off it, and nearly cast Iron Berserk and summoned his banner, but he saw the fatigue on the officers' faces, and he felt Valla reach up to grip his thumb with her cold fingers, and he knew not everyone was as fresh and full of joy as he.

Victor lifted Lifedrinker and brought her down, and again, the soldiers ceased their raucous cheering. "I'm proud of you, soldiers! We've surely put a dent in the invaders' armies. That said, we need to get back to the keep we captured. We need to secure this land, and we need to make plans for how we'll keep up this momentum. Listen to your captains, your lieutenants, and your sergeants."

He turned, figuring he'd summon Guapo and ride back to the keep with Valla, but some brave soldier shouted, "We love you, Legate!" Victor turned, trying to find the speaker, but he couldn't make him out. He saw many eager faces meeting his gaze, many soldiers who looked ready to claim ownership of the words, so he sighed and smiled.

"Do you think I'd face down a thousand reavers for men and women I didn't care about? You're my soldiers, and I'm here to fight with you every inch of the way to that bastard green star! I'll never leave any of you hanging. If I'm the only backup I can bring, then damn it, I'll be there." The soldiers erupted in cheering again, and Victor gave up trying to calm them. They'd settle down when he wasn't around. He summoned Guapo, and after the glorious mustang burst out of his puddle of sparkling Energy, he mounted and reached down a hand for Valla.

"Where will you go?" Sarl asked, shouting to be heard over the din.

"Meet you at the keep!" Guapo began to walk, and the soldiers made way for him, those close by reaching out to run their fingers over the great stallion's silky coat as he passed.

"You need a bath," Valla said as they finally broke free of the clamoring soldiers and Victor urged the mustang into a trot.

Victor twisted in the saddle and looked into her eyes. "Yeah. I'll set my house up in the courtyard and take one. Maybe you should join me." She looked down, and if the light were a bit brighter, he might have seen her pale blue skin darkening. She didn't say no, though, so Victor's grin broadened, and Guapo began to gallop.

17

A FULL LIFE

When Victor and Valla dismounted from Guapo, she ran over to Uvu, who uncharacteristically was still lying in the same spot near the courtyard gates where Victor had last seen him. He patted Guapo's shoulder and sent the spirit totem back to his realm, then stood there, pondering Valla and her giant cat. Could he do anything to help the creature?

Sarl had left fifty soldiers to hold the fort—a risky number, but he'd obviously not wanted to arrive short-handed to help Victor and the fifth cohort. The watch commander, a young Shadeni lieutenant, had greeted Victor and Valla at the gates, and after asking about the battle's outcome had returned to patrolling the ramparts. Now Victor stood alone, trying to decide if he should set up his travel home or speak to Valla. He'd been on such a high when they rode back toward the keep, rich with the endorphins of post-battle Energy, victory, and the hope of amorous activities—at last!—with Valla. Things weren't so clear now.

His feet crunched on the gravel-strewn cobbles as he approached her and the big cat. He saw dark smears in her hair where it had come loose from her helmet and soaked up blood that splashed her way during combat. Her armor, however, glimmered in the moonlight, shiny and fresh looking, the enchantments having mended the damage and cleaned away the gory residue of battle. She knelt beside Uvu, who lay on his side, a listless look in his saucer-sized eyes as he made odd cat grumbles. "He's no better?"

"Something ails him. Something clouds my connection to him." She looked up at him, and he saw her eyes brimming with unshed tears. Her voice was thick with emotion, and Victor could hear the strain in it; her earlier relief at his survival and the army's victory had fled before a renewed concern for Uvu.

"There's nothing stuck in his wounds? I mean, under the scars, a bit of the creature's harpoons, maybe?"

"Nothing I can feel. I used an expensive healing salve; I've seen it pull broken arrows from a soldier's ribs."

"Huh. If it's not physical . . ." Victor knelt beside her, Uvu's forelegs between them. He held out a hand toward the big cat's nose, and the beast lifted his head, snuffled at it for a moment, then dropped his chin to the ground and closed his eyes, apparently comfortable enough with Victor's presence. "Let me see here." Victor thought about when Thayla had been infected, overtaken really, by Belikot's spirit. He remembered how he'd been able to force that spirit out of her and back into the skull where he'd locked it away. Could Uvu have a similar affliction of his spirit?

He leaned forward and rested his hand, palm down, on Uvu's side. As the cat inhaled and exhaled and Victor felt his ribs moving up and down, he closed his eyes and turned his mind inward toward his pathways and his Cores. He could see them both now, his Cores. The multicolored constellation of his primary Core outshone his fiery Breath Core, but it was there, smoldering comfortingly, a single orb north of his Spirit Core, in his weird mental sense of direction. His pathways ran between them and outward, like highways ready for the powerful traffic of his Energy. He traced the one that led out through his arm and hand to the opening, where it met with Uvu's flesh.

As he'd done with Thayla, Victor sent a trickle of Energy through that pathway, some inspiration, because of all his Energies, he felt it was the most benign. He let it pour forth from his hand, tracing over Uvu's flesh, seeking an opening into the cat's pathways. Did animals have them? Victor didn't know, but he assumed they must. Hadn't Valla told him that Uvu was an "evolved" creature? Did they not use Energy like people? Before he could doubt himself further, his probing Energy found an opening. He should have guessed where it was—in Uvu's mouth. Thinking about it, he didn't doubt the cat had openings in his paws, too, but it didn't matter; Victor had found what he needed.

He sent his Energy gently probing into that opening, into the wide straight pathway that led from Uvu's mouth toward his Core. He wondered at the ease with which he did so; Uvu didn't resist at all. Could he? Victor would think so, would assume the cat's will, in his own body, should have been difficult to overcome. Had he recognized a friendly touch? Was his will too taxed? As Victor's inspiration-attuned Energy progressed, his mind's eye became aware of everything it touched. He saw Uvu's Energy pathway; he saw how wide and simple it was, not convoluted and twisting like his own. It was a highway straight to his Core, which Victor could see like a smoldering campfire in the distance, a dim light down a dark road. "What kind of Energy is that, *hermano*?"

He heard Valla say something, but her words didn't register. Victor was too focused and too intrigued by what he was seeing. He let his Energy progress, probing toward that distant Core, exploring the pathway, illuminating it. Victor felt no traces of Uvu's Energy. Shouldn't there be some in there? Victor's pathways were never totally empty. As his consciousness pressed on, he soon began to realize that Uvu's Core wasn't exactly smoldering, as he'd first thought. He'd seen the sensation of flickering or pulsing, but the closer he got, the more he realized that it was the result of something moving about the Core, something dark and gray, something translucent that let the light of Uvu's Energy through, but not clearly.

"Ah, I see what that fucking thing did!" he hissed as he pushed his Energy farther, nearly at the cat's Core now.

"What is it?" Valla asked, her voice loud and clear, impossible for Victor to ignore.

Before he got too engrossed with what he knew he had to do, Victor answered her, "There's something around Uvu's Core. Give me a minute to fight with it." That said, Victor released his hold on his own Core; he let the trickle of Energy he'd sent into the cat swell into a torrent, and he pushed it forth with all the strength and determination of his prodigious will. His body began to glow with a white-gold aura, and then Uvu's did as well. He knew why the cat hadn't resisted his initial intrusion; he couldn't. His Core was bound up, his will utterly spent in an effort to keep that gray . . . shit from thoroughly corrupting him.

Victor drove his inspiration-attuned Energy like a spear into the weird sickly membrane around Uvu's Core, and it recoiled. It thrashed and lashed out, but it was like a puppy trying to maul a grizzly bear. Victor wrapped it up and bore down on it with his will, twisting his Energy like a boa constrictor around that gray blob, crushing it into oblivion. Uvu's Core immediately brightened, though it was obviously worn down. It pulsed with pure golden Energy, and Victor could feel the cat's spirit start to recover and probe at his Energy. He began to pull away, back into himself, still holding onto that compressed blob of gray corruption.

Victor wondered what he should do with it when he dragged it back into himself. Then he had a thought. He tugged it through his pathways and pressed it toward the new opening he'd made leading to his lungs. When it was through, Victor inhaled deeply and pulled that corruption right into his smoldering Breath Core. He felt it flare as the magma-attuned Energy ignited it. He felt the urge to cough as soon as that bright flare faded. As he hacked, he lost his concentration and resumed his normal perspective of the world through his eyes. Some black smoke hung in the air, and more joined it as he continued to cough out the burnt corruption.

Uvu stood up suddenly, arched his long back in a tremendous stretch, and then began to lick Victor's face. Victor laughed and pushed at the cat's big head, still sputtering, still trying to take a breath that didn't tickle his lungs. "Thanks for the kisses!"

"Victor! You healed him?" Valla practically tackled him as she threw her arms around his neck and squeezed him into a hug. She was standing, he was still kneeling, and Uvu was purring loudly as he tried to get in on the affection, rubbing his long body on them both as he pressed into them, walking in a circle, looping his tail around Victor's and Valla's necks. Victor was still sputtering, trying not to cough on Valla as her hug transitioned to gentle kisses on his cheek, then his forehead. "Thank you, thank you, thank you," she kept saying between each kiss.

Victor wasn't someone who'd complain about affection, not from a woman and not from a giant cat. He laughed, waving away the cloud of lingering smoke, and then he stood, hoisting Valla up with him, holding her pressed tight to his chest as she continued to shower him with kisses, tears streaming freely down her cheeks. Uvu chuffed and yawned, making big cat sounds as he continued to circle Victor, pressing his big body into him. Pretty much anyone else would have been knocked over by the cat's enthusiastic affection, but Victor stood tall, hugging Valla close, and let the pony-sized monster cat show his gratitude.

He came to realize they'd drawn a small crowd; the garrison troops had turned their attention toward the inner courtyard, and many were staring, smiling, and laughing. They could recognize an occasion of joy when it was in front of them, and they were happy to join in. The mood in the keep was good enough already, what with Victor's news of the Ninth's second victory of the day. The happy legate and his tribune primus were just icing on the cake.

After a long moment of celebration, Victor finally set Valla down and gave Uvu a big friendly shove. "Okay, big guy. That's enough. You're welcome."

"You've earned a true friend this night, Victor." Valla leaned into him, grasping one of his hands with both of hers.

"I thought you were already my friend . . ."

She shoved him playfully. "Always joking around." She turned to the center of the courtyard. "Where's your house?"

"Ah, yeah." Victor's smile broadened, and he took his home off his belt, walked toward a particularly empty corner of the courtyard, and placed it on the flagstones. He activated it, and as it rumbled and jumped, expanding to its full size, he stood with Valla and watched Uvu as he worked on cleaning himself in earnest. "He seems happy."

"Of course! You healed him! I can feel him just as before. What was wrong with him, Victor?"

"Something was wrapped around his Core. Something . . . vile." It was a word Victor wasn't sure he'd ever used, but it fit. "I burned it in my Breath Core." He chuckled.

"The smoke?"

"Yeah."

"I wanted to ask, how did you find your breath? I mean, how did you do what you did in the battle? Such flames; I've never seen anything like it, not even from a fourth-tier Pyromancer."

"It wasn't me. I mean, the breathing of the fire, that was me, but the fire was from my ancestor." Victor searched his memory, the name coming to him easily. "Chantico."

"Chantico? Was it a woman?"

"Yeah."

"She saved you, I think. You were . . ." Valla grew quiet and then gestured to the house, now fully enlarged, sitting quietly in the courtyard. "Let's speak within." She tugged his hand, and following behind her, Victor cast Shape Self, reducing his size to something more like he'd been when they first met. Valla led him straight to the stairs toward his bedroom, and Victor felt his stomach start to flutter, a nervousness like nothing he'd experienced in a very long time. As they walked through the long hallway that led off to branching empty rooms, Valla continued, her voice small. "You were going to die, weren't you?"

"I don't know. I didn't want to. I was going to fight until I couldn't anymore. I think I'd come to accept that I might die."

"I know I already said this on the battlefield, but, well, maybe I didn't say this—Victor, I don't want you to die. I don't want you to be okay with dying!" She still wasn't looking at him. She walked before him, still holding his hand, but he could tell she was having a hard time finding the words to match what she was feeling.

He tried to help her out. "I thought about you a lot while I was fighting. I thought about you with regret, angry at myself for not acting on my feelings more. I know I've told you how I feel about you, but, well, I let you think you weren't the most important woman to me. I let you believe I was stuck on Tes."

"Weren't you?" Valla had stopped before his door, and now her back was to it, and she looked up into his eyes.

"I think I was confused. Like you were."

"I wasn't—"

"Yes, you were," he said, leaning toward her, one hand on the door next to her head, his eyes inches from hers. "You were confused about yourself. You were comparing yourself to Tes, and for some reason, you were coming up short in that comparison. Valla, you're every bit as incredible as she is. She's had more time to gain levels, to learn things, but you—shit, I bet you're twice the woman she was at your age."

"Truly?" She looked up at him, her big turquoise-green eyes staring into his soul as she delicately bit at her lower lip, and Victor felt his heart jump in his chest.

"Yeah. Truly." He leaned closer and stopped, his lips a hair's breadth from hers, and waited. Valla inhaled through her nose and then pressed her lips to his, and this time, their kiss was far deeper, more passionate. Victor felt as if he couldn't get enough. He savored her warm soft skin, her hot breath, and the tender gentle way her hands grasped the backs of his arms, holding him close as they stood locked together.

Victor wasn't exactly experienced in love. His one "serious" girlfriend back on Earth had been a girl he texted and hung out with now and then—nothing like the women he'd met on Fanwath. His feelings back then were different; they were kid feelings. Even his affection for Chandri felt small and shallow compared to what he felt here with Valla. When he thought about shallow feelings, he couldn't help thinking of Teil, but he couldn't find any regret; she'd needed him, and he hadn't suffered for their night together. Still, what he felt with Valla was different; he knew her so well, her quirks, her dreams, her fears. She'd been with him through thick and thin. She'd watched him nearly die half a dozen times, and she'd always been there to support him. He swore, in that moment, while they kissed, he could feel her spirit.

Victor felt as though his heart would pound out of his chest, as if he were high on something better than anything he'd ever tried, even better than the euphoria following a System-granted Energy rush. He could certainly feel Valla's Energy, hot and vibrant, electric under her skin, tickling his flesh. He let his hand slide down the door to the handle. He pulled it open, then he pushed her through, still trying to kiss her while they stumbled into his room. Valla pushed him off, then ran a hand over the front of her hauberk, slipping out of the armor and letting it fall to the hardwood floor with a clatter. She was panting, breathless, as she started pulling off the rest of her clothes. Victor did the same, proving he'd had more practice with rapid clothing changes by getting naked several seconds before she did.

They never made it into the bathtub, at least not at first. They didn't even make it to the bed; they fell to the floor on a plush gold and crimson rug that had come with Victor's travel home. Valla wrapped her legs around him, and they shared every part of themselves. Though they were both breathless and eager, hungry for each other, Victor tried to take things slow, and again, he reflected on how different the experience was for him. It meant so much more to him than the other sex he'd had that he couldn't find a valid comparison. Nothing he'd ever done came close to the mixture of physical and emotional release he went through that night.

For her part, Valla seemed just as happy, just as engrossed by their amorous activities. After they'd exhausted themselves there on the floor, they'd bathed, but then Valla started things up again, and they wound up in his bed together. Sometime later, they lay together, and though the room was dark and Victor was on his back, staring at the ceiling, his mind wandering through a replay of their activities, he knew Valla was staring at him. He cleared his throat and asked, "Are you regretting anything?"

"Me?" Her hand snaked under the thin linen sheet, and she rested a cool soft palm against his chest, over his heart. "I regret nothing."

"Do . . ." Victor struggled, trying to coax out his thoughts into words. "Don't you regret waiting this long?"

"What? No. That's like asking if I wish I'd eaten a meal before it was cooked."

Victor rolled to his side, trying to find her eyes in the near total dark. Almost without thinking, he summoned a tiny Globe of Insight and let it float toward the ceiling, casting their bed in its dim pale light. He smiled as she shifted to look him in the eyes better. "Are you comparing me to a meal?"

"A big hearty stomach-filling meal, aye." She grinned and leaned toward him, then her eyes widened, and she touched his chest. "What's this?"

"Hmm?" Victor looked down at his pectoral and saw what she pointed at. It looked almost like one of the many dozens of pale scars on his body, but it was darker and had a definite pattern, like a crescent moon with a straight line descending from the bottom point. "Huh. A weird scar?"

"It looks almost like an axe . . ."

"Ah! Golgothaz!"

"Excuse you!"

"No! It's a name, a being who spoke to me when I finished the battle. I guess when my axe skill advanced to epic—"

"Epic?" Valla's eyes widened.

"Yeah! Some beings were interested in my fight, and one of them, well, I think he chased the others away, and then he said he was giving me his mark." Victor rubbed a finger over the scar. "This must be it."

Valla flopped onto her back and got quiet, and Victor wondered if something was bothering her. "Something I said?"

"Something I let myself forget for a little while."

"What?"

She sighed and turned back to him. "You're born to fight. Every time you push yourself to the breaking point, you come out stronger. Like a piece of rare metal being worked over and over, heated and cooled. You're not going to stop, are you?" She stretched out her pale blue fingers to trace his jawline as she spoke, and Victor reached out to her, resting a hand on her hip.

"Here come the regrets?"

"No." She smiled. "This is you, and it's nothing new. I have to accept that you're going to be pushing the edge. You're not a small man." She chuckled. "I don't mean physically. You have large *goals,* and you're not meant for small things. I like that about you, Victor, despite the risks. Besides, if you or I die in this life seeking and tasting glory, then we'll meet again in the next one, yes? Isn't it better to live a life like that—a full one of our own choosing, of our design, out from under the thumbs of those who would control us?" Victor knew who sat heavy in her mind with those words—Rellia, the Empire, the responsibilities thrust on her since she'd been strong enough to hold a sword.

"Damn right." Victor leaned toward her and kissed her forehead. "This life or the next."

18

MAKING TIME

Victor wasn't sure what time he and Valla finally fell asleep. If the soldiers returned, they didn't bother him, and when he slept, Valla's soft hair tickling his nose, sharing the same pillow, he'd really slept, deep and untroubled. When he woke, Valla was awake, but she was sitting in bed beside him, writing in one of her Far Scribe books. She smiled at him, raising one feathery seafoam eyebrow. "Must have been tired."

"Well, I had a big day. Had to slay a monster, and before that, I fought a whole army . . ."

"A monster? Slay?" She reached out and snatched his ear between her thumb and forefinger, giving it a tweak.

"Just a euphemism." He laughed.

She smiled and let go. "You have a good vocabulary when you want to. It seems to me that sometimes you curse and roar just because you think it's what we expect of you."

"Is this you trying to change me? Is it happening already?" Victor grinned, his white teeth bared as he shifted to look at her better, a mischievous arch to his eyebrow.

"Oh no." She held up a hand. "Don't start, not this morning. Rellia and Borrius are on their way, Lam too."

Victor groaned, shifted to his back, and arched into his pillow, stretching his spine and sucking in a deep yawn. "I figured it was too much to hope we'd have more than a night to forget about this campaign." When he turned back to Valla, he let his mouth get away from him. "I like that you're cool hanging out naked with the lights on."

Valla was sitting up, pillows piled behind her, and she looked down at her breasts, then narrowed her eyes at Victor. "You expect me to get dressed while in bed?"

"Nah, course not. Some women would, though. Wear something, I mean."

"Would they?" Again, that eyebrow shot up. "Know the sleeping habits of many women, do you?"

"Uh, no . . ."

"Just how many women have you spent time with? In bed?"

"Oh, wow!" Victor looked at his wrist. "Sheesh! Look at the time! I promised Kethelket some sparring, and I should probably check in with Sarl." He shifted his legs to the side of the bed and started to stand up.

"I'm teasing! You don't have to flee!"

He looked back at her, and as he took in the sight of her there, pale blue skin against white sheets, he silently thanked God and his ancestors for his luck. "Nah, I know you're messing with me, but we should get out there, don't you agree? I keep thinking of this campaign like a fight, and one thing I know about fighting—when you've got your enemy on his back foot, you should push the attack."

Valla's book disappeared into one of her rings, and she stood up, nodding. "You want to find the next keep and attack."

"*Exactamente.*" Victor started pulling clean clothes out of his ring and dressing. When he looked up, he saw Valla was also dressed and already shrugging into her scale armor. "That was fast."

"As you said, there's much to do." She smiled then, scales clinking, stepped over to him and pointed her face up. Victor didn't need an invitation; he kissed her softly, and she pulled away. "Come, let's check on Edeya."

"Right!" They stopped by the kitchen for a glass of cold water, magically dispensed from a dimensional container that held a massive reservoir. The container was built into the ground beneath the basement level, and next to it was an identical one holding hot water. Victor had learned of these little features after purchasing the home, and sometimes he wondered what other little secrets the place held. As they drank their water, he perused the cold cabinet, or fridge, as he liked to call it, bothering Borrius to no end. "Nothing great in here unless you want me to cook up some bacon and eggs."

"I'm in the mood for something sweet, and I have some pastries in my ring from Gelica."

"Gelica? Those are old as hell."

"The ring preserves them!" She scowled at him as she produced a woven basket lined with a pale linen cloth and stuffed with frosting-covered pastries. Victor's mouth began to water as he smelled the warm sugary dough. "You don't want one?"

"Yeah, I want one," Victor grumbled sheepishly.

He was halfway through his second helping when a voice called out from near the front of his home, "Victor! Are you up?" He recognized Lam at once. Only a handful of people had access to enter his home unaccompanied, and she was one.

"In the kitchen," he called, covering his mouth to keep from spraying bits of pastry. He heard her boots before he saw her, and then she came into view, walking around the long empty table to the kitchen counter that separated the dining and cooking spaces.

She sat in front of the counter. "Where's Edeya?"

"In the keep." Valla leaned forward and pushed the basket of pastries toward her. "She consumed her racial advancement reward yesterday."

"Really? Here?" Lam delicately plucked a pastry from the basket. "No milk?"

"In the fridge." Victor's voice was muffled because he'd stuffed the second half of his pastry into his mouth.

"The fridge? Oh, right." Lam walked over to the cold cabinet and fished out a bottle of milk.

"We thought she needed to do it; she almost died again in a skirmish on the field, and Victor wanted her to level; she's nearly thirty."

"Well, I'm glad someone finally pushed her to it. She's been dragging her feet long enough. Did she . . . suffer much?"

"From the injury?" Valla asked.

Victor shrugged. "She got beat to hell and knocked out. She didn't remember much of the fight."

"And you? You seem different." Lam looked Victor up and down, then her eyes drifted to Valla. "You too. What did I miss?"

"Victor leveled and gained some abilities last night. He, well, didn't anyone give you a summary of the battle?"

"Not exactly. I heard you beat another army to the east. Caught 'em between the Ninth and the Fifth, if I'm guessing, yeah?"

"Sort of." Victor shrugged.

"Victor held off an army of a thousand reavers—undead heavy fighters with some ability to transform into more deadly monsters. They were close to pouncing on the fifth cohort while they dealt with an army of hounds."

"More like wolves." Victor leaned his elbows on the table, watching Lam eat.

"Well, they seemed like boyii hounds, but the size of roladii. I guess they weren't colorful, and I didn't see any with more than one tail . . . Does that sound like wolves?"

"Yeah . . ." Victor frowned at Valla. "You've never seen a wolf?"

"They don't come to this part of the world," Lam interjected, obviously trying to move the side discussion along.

"Anyway," Valla continued, "Victor rode his steed down among the reavers and fought them until Sarl could arrive with the Ninth."

"The Glorious Ninth." Victor smiled, pleased with the moniker he'd given Sarl's cohort.

"You fought off a thousand heavy troops?" Lam gave Victor another appraising look.

"I had help from my ancestors and probably would have died anyway if not for the Ninth arriving."

"That's a discussion for another time." Valla frowned at him, and he figured she didn't like being reminded that he'd been ready to fight to the death. Victor had been trying to downplay his heroics, but he'd gone a while without putting his foot in his mouth, so he just shrugged and picked up another pastry.

"So, you destroyed three armies yesterday?" Lam pulled a stool out from beside the counter and sat down. "I don't know if I should be annoyed or pleased. On the one hand, I'm glad we're making headway in this conquest, but on the other . . . I'd like to get some of the action!"

"Victor improved his axe skill to epic!"

"Probably not helping . . ." Victor mumbled as Lam turned wide eyes his way.

"Polo Vosh was decades between advanced and epic, if I'm not mistaken."

"Well, he didn't have an axe like Lifedrinker. I think she's taught me as much as anyone I've trained with." Victor rested his hand on the warm gleaming metal of Lifedrinker's bearded blade.

"I certainly chose the right man to give that weapon to."

"You gave him Lifedrinker?" Valla joined Victor, leaning forward over the counter, resting on her elbows, and letting her gaze travel between Lam and Victor. "Why haven't I heard that story?"

"I never thought . . ."

"The axe wasn't awake back then. I thought I was giving Victor a decent blade, an old weapon I no longer used. He was the one who woke her up, so I take none of the credit."

"Victor, your she-wolves speak about me?"

"That's right, beautiful." Victor smiled at the expressions he received from Lam and Valla. "Not you guys! She wanted to know if you were talking about her." He almost told them what the axe had called them but decided he didn't feel like having his skin flayed off. He shrugged and turned back to the earlier topic. "I wasn't exaggerating when I mentioned how much I've learned from her. When we get into a really good fight, it's like she and I move together as one. Like a dance almost, but bigger. Shit, I can't think of the right words."

"Well, if that's helped you advance so quickly, you are a lucky man." Lam took a drink of her milk and contemplated the remains of the pastry in her hand.

"I am lucky. No argument from me." Victor glanced at Valla, and they shared a knowing smile. Then he asked, "Where are Rellia and Borrius?"

"En route. They march with the army. We're leaving the Shadeni and the reserve cohort Borrius made from surplus troops. All eight cohorts will be here within the hour to join the Ninth and the Fifth. Talk to me about your losses."

"Let's get Sarl in on this; he'll have more concrete info. Valla and I were . . . out of it last night."

"Oh?" Lam raised an eyebrow and narrowed her eyes as she looked between the two of them but said no more.

Victor shrugged and led the way out of his house, unwilling to expound on the subject. They were met with a flurry of activity when they stepped into the courtyard. Soldiers were sparring in loose circles, others were cleaning, and still more were carrying items to and fro—sacks, barrels, boards, even furniture. Victor flagged down a passing sergeant. "Where's Captain Sarl?" Several soldiers passed by in a group, interrupting the man's answer, and Victor reflected on the fact that the keep was overfull—it was meant to house a force smaller than a single cohort, not two.

"He's outside the gate, sir."

"Fetch him, please. We'll be in the . . . map room on the second floor." Victor turned away from him and said to Lam, "You gotta see this." He led the way into the keep, up the spiral stairs, and down the long hallway to the weird round room with its raised dais depicting, in three dimensions, the contested lands of the Untamed Marches.

"Wonderful!" Lam said, walking around it, her dragonfly wings twitching and fluttering with excitement. "So, the unobscured lands are the ones we hold."

"Right." Valla pointed to the little model of the keep. "That's us. Up the road there, that's the pass. Victor, look!" She pointed to the grassy hilly area east of the keep. "Wasn't more of this obscured yesterday? I think we opened up more land when we beat those armies last night."

"Makes sense." Victor stepped around the dais and pointed to the foggy area west of the keep. "See those trees there? You can just make them out on the edge of the fog. I think it's a forest, and I'm betting Hector's forces have another stronghold in there. If we take it, we'll have the northern edge of the Marches under our control. Then we can start pushing south."

He'd just finished speaking when Sarl and Kethelket came into the room. "Legate!" Sarl saluted. "I'm glad you're well. Quite the heroics you pulled off last night."

"I was stunned, Victor. Sir." Kethelket, too, saluted. "I was determined to try to fly you out of that melee. I was on my way in when you burst out with those . . . incomparable flames."

"It's true." Valla smiled at Kethelket. "He was on his way into that madness. It was when you paused, your Berserk gone, your banner . . ." She trailed off, shaking her head. "Let's not dwell on it. Sarl, can you report on the losses for the ninth and fifth cohorts?"

"Of course. The Fifth suffered heavy losses at first but rallied and soon took control of their fight with the great wolves—that's what the Naghelli have been calling them. They lost, in total, a hundred and twelve soldiers. "We fared better. The reavers and vampyrs were demoralized when we smashed into them. Only seventeen losses, sir."

"The Ninth grow harder and harder," Kethelket said, grinning at Sarl.

"And what about your troops, Captain?" Victor asked the lanky Naghelli.

"They are ready for action, sir. I wondered if you wanted to put together a scouting force to prepare for the next offensive."

"I do. We'll wait for Borrius and Rellia, but I have some ideas. Speaking of . . . sometimes my head is clearer after some exercise. Kethelket, while Lam grills Sarl and Valla, how about we get in some weapon practice?"

"It would be my pleasure, sir."

"Right." Victor nodded and turned to the doorway, refusing to look directly at Lam or Valla, fearing the daggers that might be lurking in their eyes. "We'll be in the courtyard!" he called over his shoulder. "Don't worry, we'll stop as soon as the other commanders arrive."

To his surprise, Lam called back, "Thank you, Victor. I'll try to get up to speed so I can help brief Borrius."

"Huh. How about that." Feeling decidedly braver, he turned to get a final look at Valla. She stood tall and serene, arms folded on her glimmering wyrm-scale armor, watching him depart. He saw amusement in her eyes, though, so he winked, then hurried ahead of Kethelket to the stairway, down, and out of the keep.

"You seem well, my lord. My apologies—sir." Kethelket hurried to walk beside him, and Victor looked over at the man; they weren't too different in height, with his size reduced as it was.

"I am well, Kethelket. I had the most epic battle of my life last night. I was blessed by my ancestors. I broke through to epic with my axe, and, well, things are just going well for me. Hope I didn't just jinx things by talking about everything like that . . ."

"Jinx? As in curse? Excuse my bluntness, sir, but that's nonsense. It's important to acknowledge our blessings. Welcome them in, share them; in a world of war and despair, good tidings should be welcomed by all."

"Huh." Victor eyed the ancient warrior and gave him a nod. The more he spoke to Kethelket, the more he liked the man. He wasn't what he'd imagined when he'd learned about the Naghelli and when Vellia had told him about the leader of her "faction." He'd pictured him as old-looking and stodgy, not fierce and eager to engage with the enemy. He led him to a relatively quiet corner of the courtyard, an area behind Victor's travel home in the rear northwest corner. Standing, facing each other, he asked, "Do you remember a lot about the world, I mean yours, before it was joined to Fanwath?"

"I remember much," Kethelket said. What I don't remember is the joining; the System either made us dream or forget, but one day, we were fighting our own small fights, and the next, we were part of something far greater. It was world shattering. I mean, personally. Our small wars became large ones. My servitude to Belikot saw me embroiled in a massive conflict with peoples from all four worlds. Oh, how I regretted the bargain I'd struck with that man!"

Victor contemplated his words, unslinging Lifedrinker and limbering up his shoulders. "Are there many like you? I don't think I've met anyone else who was alive before the joining."

"You'll find many in Tharcray. There are others around the world, though, if you take the time to look for them."

"Were the Ridonne from the old worlds?"

"Oh, yes. How do you think they gained the upper hand so quickly? The Shadeni and Ardeni outnumbered the civilized peoples from the other worlds by a factor of four. The Ridonne were the strongest among them, other than the Vessi, but they'd been at war for centuries before the joining, and the Vessi were all but gone by the time the System brought us together."

"The Vessi . . . an Ardeni bloodline, yeah? Supposedly as strong as the Ridonne? Did you ever meet one?"

"Aye, I did, Victor! You're full of questions today!" Kethelket's words were friendly, and though his large strange black eyes were hard to read, Victor thought he saw kindness in them.

"I've wanted to talk more for a while now. I always feel so driven, though, worried about expectations of me. I'm going to start putting a change to that. I need to make time for life while I'm living it, you know?"

"Indeed, but you also have the right intensity when it comes to winning battles; you seem to know when to push an enemy, and you have an instinct for finishing things."

"A killer's instinct?" Victor raised an eyebrow.

"That's a good way to put it." Kethelket nodded. "Shall we see how you fare against Gevel and Uthac?" He drew his two dark metal blades, and they danced with flickering, swirling blue-yellow Energy.

"They're both awake?"

"Aye, have been since before the joining."

"Yeah, let's dance, but hang on! I was curious—what did the Vessi look like?"

Kethelket let his blades hang down, and he looked up at the sky, somewhere beyond Victor's head, his eyes going distant. "They were every bit as impressive as the Ridonne, Victor. Where the Ridonne are golden and red, the Vessi were blue and silver." His voice grew soft with remembered wonder. "Beautiful, fast, taller than other Ardeni, with silver-feathered wings that cut the air so fast I couldn't begin to follow. My wings are better now than they were then, but I still am no match for their soaring glory . . ."

"Sounds awesome." Victor grinned and lifted Lifedrinker. "All right, come on!"

19

PARAGONS AND BATTLE PLANS

Victor soon realized he'd been missing out when it came to weapons practice; he'd had access to Kethelket ever since the battle on the plains with the Ridonne, and he'd squandered that time. The Naghelli prince was a dervish with his blades, easily outclassing Victor's other sparring partners. He was faster, more versatile, and somehow just as strong as Polo. With Midnight, Valla's skill level was described as "epic," but Kethelket soon showed Victor that she had much to learn. He had a way of moving those twin blades of his, one always seeking an opening while the other parried or redirected Victor's attacks.

The man was clearly at an epic level with the sword, and had Victor not recently had a breakthrough of his own, he figured Kethelket would have had to hold back considerably. As it was, though, Victor found himself stretching himself to new heights, finding the rhythm of combat that rarely came to him during a practice session. Usually, he had to be dancing the killing dance, the all-out full-contact frenzy of combat that came to him when the stakes were high, and he was pushed to his limits on the battlefield. With Kethelket as his partner, Victor began to find that rhythm and began to feel the changes in himself since his skill had broken through to the epic tier.

As he wove Lifedrinker in and out of clashes with the Naghelli, using her size and power and his near-absurd ability to move her about in lightning-fast cleaves that cut the air in *whooshes* and *snaps*, he began to enter a battle trance that excluded the rest of the world. Kethelket seemed similarly engrossed, his face serene, his body flowing with his movements, his swords like extensions of his arms. He and Victor were similar in size and reach, and though they both knew the match would be different if Victor released his Shape Self spell and let himself stretch to his full potential, that wasn't the point—they were trying to work on their weapon skill, and having Victor dominate the contest with size and overwhelming power wouldn't serve either of them in that regard.

A Globe of Insight hung over them, feeding their creativity, pushing their already brilliant weapon work to the limit, and as they clashed, soldiers began to gather, their faces slack-jawed in wonderment to see the skills on display. Later, sergeants and lieutenants would report that many soldiers had breakthroughs of their own simply by observing the two masters at work. While Victor and Kethelket danced, moving about their corner of the yard, pushing, retreating, circling, all the while weaving their weapons in an elaborate contest of feints, parries, slashes, thrusts, and cleaves, something extraordinary began to happen.

At first, Victor didn't realize it was happening, but eventually he became aware of his cuts extending beyond the physical dimensions of his blade. Lifedrinker was mindful of the friendly nature of their bout, so she hadn't burst into smoldering orange heat; her silvery edge was cool in the air as she cleaved the wind, but something new was happening. Her blade was limned with a shimmering, ghostlike edge that extended outward a hand's breadth from her metal and even farther from the top and bottom. That blade of force cut the air like a laser, creating tiny concussions in her wake as the air hurried to fill in the gaps she sliced.

Kethelket's eyes widened as he realized what was happening, and Victor's axe became harder and harder to counter. He seemed to begin to struggle to get his swords into position fast enough to match the blurring speed of Lifedrinker's ghost edge, and when he did, his parries were rebuffed, and he had to hustle to move with the force to compensate for the extra speed and power of Victor's attacks. To his credit, he maintained his defensive dance for several long minutes before his constant giving of ground began to wear him down. He finally backpedaled out of the "circle" of their contest and with a flourishing salute said, "I yield."

Victor, a huge smile plastered to his face, was almost startled at the end of their dance. Lifedrinker hummed in his hands, light as a feather, eager to keep going, but he brought her around in a weaving cut, slicing the air between himself and Kethelket, then let her hang from one hand as he said, chest heaving with the healthy exertion of their efforts, "What a match! Thank you, Kethelket!"

Before Kethelket could respond, the soldiers who'd gathered in the courtyard, both on the flagstones and up on the parapets, began to clap and cheer, whistling and shouting their excitement. As the noise died down, Kethelket stepped closer to Victor and said, "You were manifesting a paragon."

"A what?"

"The Paragon of the Axe. The essential spirit of it. It was projecting forth from your fabulous weapon there." He nodded to Lifedrinker, still hanging from his hand. "I could feel Gevel and Uthac strain to deflect it; I fear that had you been intent on harm, you may have shattered one or both of them. Certainly, you could have done some damage." Kethelket spun both of his swords in his wrists, then held them up, scrutinizing their blades. "They're fine, however. I thank you."

"I didn't even know . . ."

"Few can manifest a paragon of a weapon at will. I, well, what I know is only through the lips of old masters; I've seen the Paragon of the Sword a time or two, but not in my own hands. My first master, Inderiga, brought it forth during her duel with Queen Aledra. I was just a boy, but the memory is burned in my mind." Kethelket shook his head and smiled at Victor. "A time long gone, my friend. Thank you for this wonderful exercise; I feel I've gained some ground in my mastery of the sword for the first time in a long, long while."

"Are you kidding me?" Victor's voice was light with the pleasure of good rich fun. "I've never had such a good match. I've only felt that . . . I don't know what to call it. Trance? I've only felt that *connected* to the axe, to my fighting, a couple of times, and that was when everything was on the line, like I was near death. I have a feat, Desperate Grace, that sometimes kicks in, and in our match just now, I felt even faster and smoother than it makes me. Shit, I don't think I've ever seen that paragon before. That's the right word? Paragon?"

"Yes!" Kethelket looked around, taking in the crowd of observing, listening soldiers. He raised his voice so others might hear, "You all witnessed something rare today! Your legate manifested the Paragon of the Axe. Mark this moment well in your minds; you'll be telling your grandchildren about it!" If he hadn't had enough cheering directed his way, those words pushed Victor's love for attention to the limit, and he cleared his throat, chuckling and shaking his head a bit sheepishly.

"All right, everyone. Show's over. Get back to your duties." The soldiers began to disperse, but Victor knew there weren't really all that many "duties" to get to; the outpost was overcrowded with troops, and two-thirds of them were free of active obligations. Thinking of obligations, he realized he'd lost track of time while sparring. Glancing at the sky, searching for the sun's position, he wondered what time it was. He looked back to Kethelket. "Wonder if Borrius is close."

"Aye, the army approaches." Victor had begun to turn toward the gate, but he gave Kethelket a second glance, narrowing his eyes.

"How can you tell?"

Kethelket pointed to the parapets where a pair of his Naghelli stood talking quietly. "I saw Cheksi arrive. She's part of the main group of my people, one of those I'd left in the pass."

Victor nodded and reached up to connect Lifedrinker to her harness. "Speaking of your people, I've hardly seen Vellia. Is she well?"

"Aye." Kethelket nodded, stroking his chin. "Well, but busy. I've given her most of the responsibility for governing our people. She's constantly dealing with disagreements and making decisions I'd rather not be troubled with."

Victor chuckled. "Smart." He led the way over to the stoop outside his travel home, and the two sat there, drinking water from containers they each produced from their storage rings, and waited for the madness of the main army to arrive. The opposite of Victor's expectations came to bear, however, as a messenger arrived, calling the fifth cohort out of the keep and out to the field where the army was setting up an encampment. As half the soldiers in the garrison filed out, things became a lot calmer in the courtyard; that is, until Borrius and Rellia arrived with their retainers.

When Victor saw Darro, he remembered Edeya and wondered how the young Ghelli was doing. With luck, the racial advancement was a potent one, and she'd be out for a while yet, perhaps days more. Still, he wanted to look in on her and resolved to do so after he'd spoken to the commanders about his plan. Lam, Valla, and Sarl came out of the keep to greet Rellia and Borrius and arrived at the front of Victor's home at nearly the same time. "Greetings," Borrius called from the saddle of his vidanii, sliding down to allow one of the staffers to lead it away.

"Borrius, it's good to see you." Victor stood from the step, and Kethelket followed on his heels. He took a minute to shake hands with Borrius and Rellia. Then he gestured to the jade travel home. "Shall we?"

"Don't you want to show them the map in the keep?" Valla stepped forward and pulled her mother into a brief hug. Rellia responded warmly, a look of surprise on her face; such affection wasn't something Victor had often seen between them.

"I do, I do," Victor said, "but it's easy enough to describe for now. We have a lot to discuss, and that room isn't exactly comfortable. Let's go sit around my table; I bet Tribune Borrius could use a drink after that ride."

"Indeed!" Borrius nodded enthusiastically. The ride down from the pass to the outpost keep was a short, easy one, but the older man was happy to behave as though he'd had to battle for every inch of land between the two places.

Soon enough, the commanders of the army were sitting around Victor's table, and Victor had included Kethelket in that number, though he only held the rank of captain. He'd grown to value the man's opinion and experience, and Kethelket held a unique position as the leader of an entire culture. Additionally, he had invited Sarl because he had the firmest grip on the logistics of the previous night's battles and the garrison of the outpost.

He began the meeting by describing, for Rellia and Borrius, the previous day's encounters with the undead. The retelling of their fight with Baron Eric and his reavers took a while; Borrius and Rellia had many questions and interrupted the account several times. After that, Victor tried to hurry through the fight with the reaver army as they attempted to crush the fifth cohort, aiding the animalistic great wolf army.

Borrius, of course, wouldn't allow the story to unfold without interruptions. "So they were using their superior mobility to turn our maneuver against us! They wanted to slay the Fifth and then perhaps catch the Ninth outside the keep, destroying them as well?"

"I believe that was their hope, aye," Sarl said. "I'm embarrassed to say I was so fearful of such a maneuver that I argued with our legate about whether we should rush to the aid of the Fifth."

"Nothing to be ashamed of!" Borrius growled, slapping a hand on the table. "Every good legate needs clever commanders who aren't afraid to speak up! Your reasoning was sound, but it seems none of us quite understood Victor's ability to catch, and single-handedly distract and delay, an entire army."

"Delay, sure, but not beat. I owe the Ninth and the Naghelli for my life."

"Well said." Rellia nodded to Victor.

Victor could see Sarl start to open his mouth, perhaps to object, to try to expound on Victor's exploits, but he spoke first. "So, now you're mostly up to speed. We beat three of the invaders' armies yesterday: the undead horde, the reavers, and the great wolf 'cavalry.' I believe we caught Prince Hector unprepared. It seems he's had little resistance here in the Marches, and his armies are spread out, holding various 'points of conquest.' I want to move quickly to the next. I want to keep our momentum."

"And you know this how?" Borrius frowned, sipping his chilled wine.

"I don't know it, exactly, but I have a feeling. My every instinct is saying to keep pushing, to keep him on his back foot until we knock his ass down."

"This isn't a duel, Victor." Borrius shook his head. "You can't treat a general with many armies at his disposal the same way you would a brawler in the arena." Kethelket snorted, and Borrius turned to him. "Something to say, *Prince?*" His use of the title came out as a sneer, and Victor frowned at the older man; he hadn't acted so petty in the past. Was he angry about something? He wondered if the one-time legate was upset that he'd missed all the action so far.

"I do." Kethelket cleared his throat and shifted in his seat. Victor thought it looked as if he wanted to stand up. He settled for leaning forward, gripping the tabletop with both hands as he glared from Borrius to Rellia to Lam and then back to Borrius. "This man beside me led us to victory not once but four times yesterday. He fought a great monster that called itself a vampyr, and then he, against the arguments of myself and Captain Sarl, rushed to save the fifth cohort. He nearly died and wouldn't have come nearly so close to defeat had we rushed forth with our troops as soon as he suggested it. Instead, we chose caution." Victor liked how he was saying "we" in support of Sarl, even though he'd flown out with his Naghelli almost immediately.

Kethelket paused for a moment, then he continued. "His instincts were spot on. He knew the Fifth was in trouble. He knew the right move was an aggressive response. He's a natural-born fighter, sure, but he's also a natural leader. If he says the right move now is to push our advantage, to drive on to the next target, I will be there with my people."

Victor saw Rellia nodding and knew he had her vote, but clever as she was, she didn't speak up. She looked at Borrius and waited, perhaps hoping, perhaps betting that he'd read the room, see the tide changing, and row with it rather than against it. Victor knew he could bulldoze the situation, especially with Rellia's support, but he followed her lead, holding his tongue, waiting to see if Borrius would come to the correct conclusion. If the old commander came to see things his way, he'd be a lot more helpful than if Victor had to cow him by flexing his rank.

Borrius looked at Kethelket for a long moment, then sighed and shrugged. "I, too, would have held the army in place, just as Sarl argued. It was the right, conservative move, one that any Legion commander would make. Being baited out of the keep and then potentially turned on by the larger, more mobile force could have been disastrous. I appreciate that Victor, our legate primus, didn't force Sarl to march immediately but compromised, offering the solution of scouting out the situation. Still, it cost him dearly, and nearly cost us our champion. Perhaps a bit more trust in our leader's instincts is in order. I've been wrong to rely on my imperial training several times on this campaign."

"So?" Lam asked after a pregnant pause in the conversation. "What's your order, Victor?"

"I'll take the Naghelli and the Ninth to the west, into that forest, and we'll take the conquest point there. I'm sure there is one. Meanwhile, Borrius and Rellia will lead the bulk of the army straight south where, if I'm not wrong, Prince Hector is going to be amassing more of his armies in a plan to come here to crush us. I'll strike first, and when he sees that we've conquered yet another territory, he'll either split his force or hurry northward, hoping to recapture this outpost while we're occupied to the west. You'll fall upon his forces from a fortified ambush."

"So we won't march all the way south but lie in wait?" Rellia clarified.

"Right. You'll find a good choke point near the edge of the land we've conquered and lie in wait."

"You're certain you can conquer another outpost with just the Ninth?" Borrius asked, though his head was nodding, his eyes distant, perhaps picturing an imaginary map.

"The Ninth and the Naghelli." Victor amended.

"Might I suggest leaving some of my people with Borrius to act as scouts? They are able to hide and have excellent mobility."

"Thank you, Kethelket, that won't be—" Borrius started to say, but Victor cut him off.

"Borrius, if you have to cut down a tree, would you turn down the use of a saw just because you held your favorite hammer?"

"I . . . no, Legate." He turned to Kethelket and nodded. "Some of your people would be well received by my captains."

"All right." Victor turned to Kethelket. "Can you send some troops out scouting now? Try to find a good ambush site to the south and begin scouting out the forest that lies in the mist to the west. I'd like to leave as soon as possible. Sarl, how quickly can the ninth be ready?"

"We'll be ready in a day, sir. Thanks to the Far Scribe books, Borrius and Rellia brought reservists to fill our ranks, and we're at full strength; I just need to integrate the new troops with their units."

"Sounds good. If you study the map in the keep—we'll adjourn soon, and you all can check it out—you'll see that the contested area is about ten times the size of what we control here on the northern edge. There's no way Hector will be able to gather all his forces or a significant number of them from the various areas he's holding within a day. Not without using portals or something, but I don't think he can do that. The baron we killed, the leader of the reavers, suggested that the mindless undead horde was here 'holding' these lands for him while he gathered his forces from their homeworld."

"Which would imply some travel time was required." Rellia nodded.

"I'd like to come with you this time, Victor." Lam leaned forward earnestly, and Victor could see that old hunger in her eyes, that look he'd seen so many times back in the mines. It sparked a similar one in him, a desire for exploration, growth, and glory. Perhaps Lam was more like him than he'd ever noticed before.

"Of course, Lam. We'll go into that forest and mess up some undead *pendejos*."

20

GHOSTLY GUARDIANS

Victor grunted as he lifted his helm to his head. He stood outside the gates, Guapo huffing out plumes of hot breath in the chilly morning air. The idea of his spirit horse breathing hot air brought a lot of questions to his mind, but he was distracted from the thought as Valla came bounding into view, riding atop a very spirited Uvu. The big cat was full of energy, a definite spring in his loping passage, and lots of grumbling, groaning, big-cat noises emerging from his broad chest as she directed him over to Victor.

"He wanted to chase every animal he heard! It feels like when I first started training him!" Valla's flushed cheeks and big smile let Victor know she wasn't upset with the cat's enthusiasm. Rather, she was thrilled by his exuberance.

"So, he's feeling good, huh?" Victor swung himself up onto Guapo's back. They were going to ride out, just the two of them, while Lam, Sarl, and Edeya marched with the Ninth. Kethelket and two hundred of his Naghelli were already gone, leaving before sunrise to scout the edges of the forest to the west.

"He is! Speaking of exuberance, did you see Edeya yet?"

"Nah, she was in the bath when I went to check on her. Lam said I'd see her soon enough, so I packed up and headed out to find you. Looks like, as usual, you found me first."

"I was with her when she woke." Valla leaned forward, resting her elbows on the front of her cat's soft, burgundy-stained leather saddle, and stroked his furry shoulder. As he began to rumble a definitive purr, she said, "You heard she gained five ranks, yes?"

"Yeah, I heard. Lam said she's showing signs of a bloodline, too—Cobalt Wing? Is that right?"

"Yes. I've never seen one, but I think they're rather revered among the Ghelli. Instead of the yellow Energy motes like Lam's wings give off, Ghelli with the Cobalt Wing bloodline have distinctive blue wings and give off azure motes."

"Is that the only difference?" Victor clicked his tongue, and Guapo started moving, trotting away from the keep, away from the sunrise.

"No!" Valla laughed as Uvu pounced into motion, swerving so much toward Guapo that Victor thought they'd collide. The cat chuffed and pulled away, just coming close enough for his furry side to rub against Victor's leg. "It's more than the color of their wings; it also changes their Core! Edeya is gaining an affinity for water, though she says it's not as strong as her pure Energy affinity yet. However, if she keeps advancing her race, she should be a formidable elementalist someday."

"Huh, that's cool."

"Cool." Valla shook her head and snorted.

"Hey, that word did a lot of heavy lifting in my old life."

"I can tell!" Valla laughed, but then, as a bit of silence grew between them, and they rode without speaking for a few minutes, she spoke up. "Are you worried about our . . . disparity?"

"Huh?" Victor frowned at her.

"Every time you do just about anything, you grow in power. I heard about your 'sparring' session with Kethelket. You displayed some sort of paragon? I never knew such a thing was possible." Victor started to try to explain, but she hurriedly kept speaking. "It's not just that; you fought off an army the other night, an army of foes any one or two of which would have given me a difficult battle. I'm not weak, Victor. I'm strong, maybe stronger than nearly anyone else in our army, save Kethelket. I think I could beat Polo, my mother . . ." She trailed off, sighing and shaking her head. "I've lost my train of thought. I think what I'm trying to say is—"

"You think I'm going to leave you behind."

"Not intentionally!" She was quick to protest, but Victor could see the worry behind her words.

"Like how, then? You think I'll just kind of become so powerful that I'll ascend into a new realm or some shit?" Victor was, perhaps irrationally, irritated by the turn of conversation. Things had been going so well between them lately that he couldn't help but feel she was inventing a problem where there wasn't one.

"No, you Urghat-brain!" she growled, and Victor barked a short laugh; she'd never called him that one.

"Urghat? I think I fought some of those in the pits way back in the day."

"Don't change the subject! I'm not saying you'll 'ascend' or anything like that. I'm saying that you're going to keep facing challenges that I'm not ready for. You're going to look at me and think about how risky things are for me, and then you'll want to leave me behind. 'For my safety,' you'll say. 'I'll return when it's safe,' you'll say, and before we know it, you'll spend more time away than with me, all the while growing more powerful, creating a larger and larger disparity between us."

"Holy shit, Valla! Take a breath. Tell me something; were you feeling too happy? Did guilt have something to do with this? Did you speak to Rellia? Did she warn you about our 'disparity'? I'm asking because things were going great this morning when we woke up together and—"

"What if she did?" Valla asked, frowning, eyes stormy. Her voice was a little muted, though, and Victor could tell he'd made her think.

"You know she's got ulterior motives, right? She doesn't want you to leave her. If—when—we conquer these lands, she's going to have governing to do. She raised you to be her right-hand woman. I think she knows I'm not planning to stick around, much as I love some of the people here. I fully intend to return, to visit, to share what I gain in my explorations of the larger universe, but I have bigger plans than the Untamed Marches. You do, too! Don't lose sight of that."

"I know. But—"

"But she was convincing. I get it. You're worried about our disparity? Then get stronger! Shit, you never thought you could do what Tes showed you, improving your affinity, learning to use your affinities together, fighting with ranged abilities. What level are you now?"

"Fifty-Eight."

"Fuck yeah! Two more and you get a new class. You think you won't see huge gains after all you did in Coloss? Everything we've done since? You're going to get an awesome class. Oh, what about your race? Have you ever told me what rank you've gotten it to?"

"I'm at Improved Five."

"That's enough for you to get Level Sixty, right?"

"I think so." She'd lost some of her steam and looked contemplative as she answered his questions.

"Let's get it up to advanced, anyway, just to be safe. I'll share my tokens with you; I'm pretty damn sure one of those conquest awards was a racial advancement. My mouth started watering when I smelled it."

"Aye, mine too! But, Victor, you should use it."

"That's the first of many. It feels like the System is treating this conquest like a game or a contest, and if I know anything, things are going to get harder, and that means bigger rewards. I'll get something like that advancement cake or even better. Believe it." He laughed and reached into his storage container, pulling out a blood-soaked white linen towel. He held it in his hand, hefting the weighty contents. "I still have this to eat, too."

"Ancestors!" Valla wrinkled her nose. "Is that . . ."

"That huge Ridonne's heart. I got it out of him before he shrank again." Victor stowed it away again and shrugged. "Looking forward to seeing what that one does."

"What if it's not good? Could you absorb a negative trait?"

Victor snorted and shook his head. "A Quinametzin absorbs the strength of his foes by eating their hearts, not their sickness or weakness."

"Always? Can you be so sure?"

"I know it like you know how to breathe. When I had my vision, I was inside my ancestor's mind; I *was* him! I knew what he knew, and he *knew* this. You understand?"

"Aye." Valla smiled and nodded, locking eyes with him as though to convey her trust in his words. "I haven't had a vision like that."

"Yeah, well, things are changing for you, Valla. You're on the road to some great shit, and just because I'm leading the way a little right now, you're with me; you're taking every step I'm taking. Let's get you to sixty, get you a racial advancement or two, and see how things are shaping up, hmm? I mean, with Midnight, your sword skill is already epic, yeah?"

"That's true. If I can push my true rank to epic, I wonder if Midnight can carry me to legendary."

"That would be fucking badass!" Victor yelled his enthusiasm, and his voice echoed through the grassy hills. Valla laughed and looked around, perhaps wondering if they were as alone as they seemed. Victor wasn't worried; the Naghelli had already scouted this way, and they had an army coming behind them. If some undead wanted to challenge him in broad daylight, it would be their funeral.

They rode for a while in relative silence, just a comment about the country-side here and there. The landscape was pretty, almost idyllic. Victor came from a country where green wasn't so common, and what green there was existed on tough, hardy trees and bushes. He'd experienced massive grasslands, extensive forests, and even the twilight plains of the spirit plane since then. Still, this landscape reminded him of what he'd always imagined fantasy worlds to be like. They passed through rolling green hills dotted here and there with clumps of trees, some of which bore fruit that resembled apples or pears.

The influence of the undead seemed to have wholly fled the lands, and the greenery seemed no worse for its previous presence. While he watched the trees and grass pass by, noting that the blue tint was much fainter here than in the lands north of the pass where he'd done most of his adventuring, Victor's mind drifted toward his sparring bout with Kethelket and the paragon he'd somehow brought into being through Lifedrinker. He'd seen it, like a ghostly overlay on Lifedrinker, but he'd been so absorbed by the perfection of his movements, his oneness with his axe, and the dance they performed with Kethelket and his swords that it hadn't registered in the moment.

Looking back, though, Victor wondered what that paragon had been doing for him. What exactly was it? Was there an actual spirit out there, some essence of all axes? That's what Kethelket seemed to think, but it seemed so wild to Victor. Axes weren't even alive, in general, so how could they have a spirit? Was the paragon more like an idea? "Or an ideal," he muttered.

"Hmm?" Valla looked up at him.

"Just trying to think through this idea of a paragon. Kethelket said he'd seen an old master summon the Paragon of the Sword, so I know it's not just axes. Is there a paragon for everything?"

"I don't know. For perhaps the first time, I know even less than you on the subject." She chuckled. "Let me know if you figure it out."

"I think maybe that something needs to have a lot of devotion and energy put into it to create a paragon. People, me included, have spent a lot of time, big parts of their lives, working to master the axe. I think that kind of energy and effort helps the paragon to come into being. I doubt there's a Paragon of the Fork."

"Some people devote a lot of energy and practice to the art of eating . . ." Valla chuckled, but Victor had to concede she had a point. Were there people who made the use of the fork an art? He doubted it, but he had to wonder.

"It's got to be more than that. Maybe it has something to do with the mortal intent of the axe or the sword, the lives they take. The different arts and styles clashing, perhaps. You might love to eat and practice with that fork, but will you ever clash with another eater? If so, it doesn't happen with the bloody results brought forth by the clash of weapon wielders."

"One would hope." Again, Valla chuckled, and Victor looked at her with a smile of his own.

"Glad to see your mood has improved. It's almost like with distance from Rellia comes an increase in good humor."

"Look!" Valla pointed, conveniently spotting a reason to change the topic. Victor followed her finger with his eyes and saw what had gotten her attention. They were riding down a long sloping hillside, and not too far ahead, perhaps three miles, a dark line of mist began to cloud the horizon.

"Here we go." Victor loosened Lifedrinker in her harness despite the sunny sky and the fact that the Naghelli were already scouting the area ahead of them.

"Should we wait for the Ninth?"

"Nah, let's see if Kethelket left a scout behind to fill us in."

"Right." Valla urged Uvu forward, and Victor let Guapo keep pace, though he had to exert his will to get the mustang to settle as he began to snort and lunge, lengthening his stride; the big horse didn't like to have another mount leading the way. In minutes, they were kicking up wisps of foggy mist as it gradually enveloped them. They slowed, and after another couple minutes of walking, large, wide-boled trees with high broad canopies began to blot out the sun, further darkening the foggy area. Everything grew quiet; even Guapo's big hooves were muted as they crunched down on soggy dead leaves and damp earth.

The branches were high, hanging over even Victor's head, and the ground between the big knobby trunks was free of undergrowth; if not for the mist, they would have had an easy passage between them. As it was, their visibility was low, and they had to keep their mounts moving slowly lest they ride into a trunk or get separated by the need to maneuver around the trees. After just a few minutes, Victor was wondering if they should stop and light a fire or something. Then Valla spoke up, and he slapped himself on the head. "Why not summon your banner?"

"I'm an idiot!" He laughed and channeled his Energy into his pathway, summoning the glorious Banner of the Champion. It blazed to life, palpable heat radiating from its sparkling, pulsing, blood-drenched sun. The mist recoiled like a living thing, falling back from the circle of light the banner cast, and Valla laughed, a sound Victor had come to love, though he heard it all too infrequently.

"It's like the light of your banner burns it off."

"Well, if it's created by the same Energy that powers the undead, that's not surprising. My banner has a way of messing those dudes up."

"We should hold here, no? If we get too deep in these woods, the army will have the same trouble finding us as we were having before you summoned the banner."

"Yeah. I suppose the Naghelli can find us . . ." Victor let his words trail off as several dark shadows with glowing ochre wings drifted into the light of his banner, seeming to fall down from the heights.

"My lord," one of them said, offering a salute. "We saw your banner and made haste to report. Kethelket has eyes on the next fortification."

Victor almost corrected the man, explaining that he wasn't a "lord," whatever qualified someone for that title, but thought he'd spend his time better asking about Kethelket. "What's the story? How far is the keep? What kind of defenders?"

The Naghelli looked left and right at his compatriots, his eyes wide with something like apprehension, perhaps dreading what he had to say. He sighed, straightened his back, and opened his mothlike wings wide, maybe to give himself confidence. "The keep is not more than three leagues further west. We've slain dozens of undead in these woods, but something else lurks on the parapets, my lord. We saw figures cloaked in mist and shadow but oddly illuminated. Kethelket sent two of our number to try to subdue one, a single guardian on the southeastern corner. My brothers fought valiantly, but it was plain to see that their weapons could not touch the being. We watched, aghast, as invisible knives slashed them, their blood pulled from them in great fonts. Their bloodless corpses hang above the gates."

The Naghelli scout bowed, folded his wings, and stepped back, waiting for Victor's response to the news. "Ghosts?" Victor asked, looking from the dour-faced scout to Valla. She wore a puzzled, pensive expression and narrowed her eyes at his question.

"Ghosts?" she asked. "Like haunting spirits?"

"Exactly. If they're spirits, but they're hurting people here outside the spirit plane . . . Is that possible? Does that happen?"

"I don't know. I didn't think so. You can't interact with this world when you spirit walk, can you?"

"Forgive me, my lord, but Prince Kethelket said we need not despair. He said that you would know what to do, that you were a master of the spirit, and that if anyone could face these beings, it would be you. Did he speak true?"

This question came from one of the other scouts, a woman whom Victor recognized; she'd been one of the scouts who'd first spotted the reaver army.

"Well, I'll be honest." Victor took a moment to look each of the five Naghelli scouts in the eye. "I don't know what those things are, but if that's how they're doing what they're doing—avoiding the weapons of your brothers by lurking on the spirit plane, then, yeah, I know what to do about 'em. I'll go into the spirit plane, and I'll fuck their shit up."

21

A GHOSTLY GAMBIT

You can't do it here!" Valla gestured around the forest, at the mists pushing against the light of his banner as if it were some kind of palpable barrier.

"I'm not going all the way back to the keep. Besides, the Ninth will be here soon, and you know Borrius and the others are expecting us to take this keep sooner rather than later. They can't keep up an ambush position forever. Who knows when some undead scout or scrying magic will reveal them? We need to capitalize on the invaders' urgency, their need to get back what we've taken." He saw she wasn't happy, looking into his eyes with doubt in hers. "I've got you and all these Naghelli to watch over me. I'll summon my coyotes, too."

As Valla frowned and folded her arms over her chest, Kethelket spoke up. "Will your banner persist while your spirit walks?"

"I don't know. Maybe not. My totems can think for themselves, but the banner . . ." Victor searched for the right words. "It kind of needs me to concentrate on keeping it around."

"Aye. I have a spell or two that require concentration." He nodded and turned to Valla. "My kin have slain any undead within a mile of this location. The mists don't bother us much; our eyes see through most of the obscuring magics. We'll see that nothing bothers Victor."

"Are you sure?" Valla wasn't speaking to Kethelket; her eyes were boring into Victor's. He reached out, resting a hand on her shoulder, running a thumb gently along her neck, brushing the soft stray hairs hanging down beneath the rim of her shiny helmet. Kethelket pointedly turned away, ostensibly to observe the positions of his scouts.

"I'm sure, Valla. We talked about this. Something in me feels the challenge these ghostly assholes are presenting. They took Kethelket's men and hung them from the keep's walls. I can't turn away from that." His words were soft, meant for Valla, but he saw Kethelket's shoulders stiffen. He hoped he hadn't offended the man. Valla's helm had a nose guard and angular slits for her eyes, making them look perpetually angry, but her mouth was exposed, and a soft smile curled her lips as she shook her head in resignation. Victor wanted to kiss those lips but knew their helms would clash long before his mouth could find hers.

"There's no way you and Uvu would let anything happen to me anyway." Victor loosened Lifedrinker from her harness, holding her in both hands crossways over his lap as he sat down on the damp mulch, back to a huge tree. He concentrated briefly, summoning his coyotes with a surge of inspiration-attuned Energy. "Good boys," he said and wondered if they were all boys. They were aspects of his spirit, so he assumed they were, but he'd never made the effort to examine them all that closely. A chuckle escaped him at the random thought.

"Something's funny?"

"Nah, just thinking about my coyotes." Victor watched them as they took shape from the white-gold mist his spell called into being. They yipped and whined, pacing around, sniffing at the Naghelli, and taking up positions in a loose circle around Victor and the tree he leaned against.

"Fascinating creatures." Kethelket knelt next to the closest coyote and stared at it, his dark depthless eyes peering into its bright shining ones. "Like large boyii hounds, but those sounds they make; it's like they speak to one another."

"They're bigger than normal coyotes. I put a lot of Energy into their summoning."

"It's the same ability that allows you to create that steed of yours and the great bear?"

"Yeah."

"Amazing. I've never heard of a Spirit Caster with such talent. It puts our contest of weapons in a different light. How would I fare should you unleash these loyal guardians while we matched blades?" He shook his head, sighing as he stood up, making the rhetorical nature of his question evident.

Victor replied nonetheless, "Don't sell yourself short. You've got some abilities you held back while we sparred."

"Thank you." He bowed briefly and then turned to face the mists, drawing his blades, ready to take up his guard. Victor admired that he didn't try to push the comparison of their abilities further. He could have protested, pointing out that Victor could go berserk or turn his banner or spirit affinities against him. Instead, he took the compliment and let the matter drop.

He turned to Valla and smiled again. "All right. I'm heading out. See you soon." He closed his eyes and began to form the pattern for his Spirit Walk spell, but he'd only just started to pull some Energy into it when he felt Valla's hot breath on his lips, then she pressed her mouth hungrily against his, and he kissed her for a long moment. When she finally pulled back and he opened his eyes, he saw she'd taken her helmet off in a rush, her teal hair hanging loose and wild.

"Hurry back," she said, then she stood, pressed her helmet back onto her head, and whipped Midnight out of her sheath. Victor smiled and closed his eyes again. He had a warm spot in his chest as he cast his Spirit Walk.

When he stood up, he still clutched Lifedrinker, but she was different—her dark polished haft was brighter than ever with the starry motes that lurked within, and her blade shone with ghostly light. If Victor were guessing, he'd say it was her spirit, more evident in this realm than in the land of the living. He looked around, heartened to have her close, and saw that the twilit spirit plane was darker, more foreboding, and more ominous than in other places he'd walked. The trees had persisted across planes, and their great dark canopies blocked out the brilliant star field usually visible on Victor's spirit walks, and adding to that gloom was the mist that had also somehow persisted in this realm.

"Fucking Death Casters." Victor's words were a growl as he stared into the fog, twisting his hands on Lifedrinker's haft. "All right, *chica*, let's go find out what these ghosts are made of."

"I hunger for your foes, Victor! When will you share your spirit with me?"

"Oh, yeah, well." Victor was caught by surprise by her sharp, lilting, but vehement words. "It's been a busy few days. Maybe we can try it here, huh? Let's see what we're up against first."

She didn't respond with words, but he felt her emotion, transferred through the axe's haft, straight to his heart—eager anticipation, acceptance, trust.

Victor turned toward the west, wondering how stealthy he should try to be. He'd never tried to sneak around on the spirit plane before. He walked boldly, probably too boldly, and never feared what he'd encounter. Did he need to worry about scaring the ghosts off? They were defending a location; if they ran off, wasn't that a win for him? Was he worried that he might draw too many of them? Victor couldn't find any sense of caution in his heart. He was on Fanwath; the spirits knew him there. Who were these invaders to come into the spirit plane where he'd hugged Old Mother goodbye and act as though they owned the place?

Victor growled, twisting his hands on Lifedrinker's haft again, and then he did what he wanted to do: He cast Iron Berserk and summoned his glorious banner. As he exploded in size and his banner's light burst around him, he lifted Lifedrinker into the air and screamed his challenge into the shadowy twilit forest. His voice echoed through the trees, leaves fell, and the mist rolled away from his light, seeming to retreat from his roar. Victor began to stomp through the forest.

He held Lifedrinker in his right hand, her ghostly edge bright in the darkness. His eyes smoldered with the red heat of his rage affinity as he prowled forward, the mist pulling back before his light and very slowly, almost reluctantly falling back in behind him as he passed through the woods. Victor's long strides were quick to deliver him to the keep. He hadn't gotten a good description of the place from Kethelket, so he couldn't compare its appearance on the spirit plane to what his Naghelli friends had seen. However, he imagined it must be vastly different because he couldn't believe they wouldn't have described it if they'd seen anything like what his eyes beheld.

Bus-sized black stones stood vertically at the base of the round walls. Atop them ran a ring of horizontal stones of the same size, then another row of vertically aligned blocks, and so on. The circular keep rose a thousand feet into the starry sky of the spirit plane. Victor stood at the edge of the trees, looking out over the faintly luminescent grassy clearing at the massive keep and wondering how he was supposed to assault the ghosts within. Growling, he stalked into the open and began to walk in a wide circle around the walls, looking for a gate. "If I can't find a *pinché* gate, I'm going to climb that son of a bitch."

As he walked through the wavy knee-high grass, he heard a faint whistling and looked up toward it, only to see a dozen bright bolts of Energy rippling through the air toward him. He broke into a jog and watched over his shoulder as the magical missiles struck the grassy turf, sending up ghostly white flames that did no harm to the environment. He didn't think the bolts would be so harmless if they touched him; they gave off a chill he could feel in the bones of his spirit body. He picked up his pace as he heard more whistling in the air, and he wondered how long it would take the shooters to figure out they had to lead him a little in order to pelt him with those spells.

Rather than take chances, as he scanned the walls for a gateway, he began to zig and zag, cutting left and right, and even leaping periodically. The keep was enormous, at least here on the spirit plane, and it took him several minutes to make his way halfway around it, even as he jogged and leapt. When he'd seen no sign of a gate or doorway after covering more than half the perimeter, Victor's frustration began to mount. He glanced at the wall, squinting in the dim, silvery light, trying to determine how hard it would be to climb. "Doesn't look that bad," he grumbled. He felt a pulse of encouragement from Lifedrinker, and that was all he needed.

With a burst of speed, he sprinted toward the wall, bunched his massive powerful legs, and launched himself with a Titanic Leap toward the wall. He timed his jump well; Victor had just hit the apex when the wall came within grasping range. "Sorry, beautiful!" he cried as he aimed Lifedrinker for a seam in the giant black stones. Her silvery head burst into molten glory as she smoked through the air and buried her blade between the monolithic stones in a shower of sharp black chips.

Of course, being an axe, her wedge shape was perfect to lodge her firmly in place, and Victor held onto her handle as his body smashed into the hard stones. Hanging there, Lifedrinker's blade creaking and the stones cracking further, tiny crumbles falling down the wall, he wondered what his plan was. The gap between stones was too thin to jam his fingers between. How would he climb it? When he looked away, up and down the wall, he found his answer. The stones, side by side, were nearly seamlessly lined up. Lifedrinker could find the gap, but his fingers couldn't. The tiers, though, one atop the other, were offset by half a foot or so; the tall circular keep grew ever so slightly narrower with each level.

Victor grunted and wriggled Lifedrinker's haft until she slipped free, and he fell—two feet to the tiny ledge atop the tier below him. He hooked Lifedrinker into her harness as he pressed his body against the wall, arms spread wide. His toes in their boots worked heroically, holding him there, fifty feet or more above the ground. Victor craned his neck to look up, gauging the next ledge's height, then he bent his knees and exploded upward. He didn't activate Titanic Leap, but he still soared up enough to grasp the next ledge with his fingertips. Grunting, he pulled himself up. The only tricky part was leaning forward so he didn't topple as he got his feet underneath him.

Victor looked side to side. The curved wall of the keep stretched away in either direction, disappearing in the fog. Then he craned his neck and looked up toward the top of the towering, impossibly high wall. Again the smooth obsidian wall disappeared in thick fog. It hadn't seemed foggy from the ground, and he wondered if some sort of twisted enchantment was at work, messing with his perspective. "Huh." He rolled his neck side to side, eliciting loud pops, then he jumped up to the next ledge. "Let's see how high this fucker is."

Valla watched Victor's still form. He seemed serene, untroubled, sitting there against the tree. His eyes were closed, but his dark brow was unfurrowed, his hands at ease on Lifedrinker in his lap. When he'd first gone into the spirit plane, she'd felt the surge of Energy, then a short time later, a much greater surge, and she knew he was casting spells in that other realm, a place that was a complete mystery to her. She couldn't quite understand how Victor could be here yet travel about in that other place.

She'd known of people with Spirit Cores, Spirit Casters everyone called them, but she'd always thought they did things like make love potions, help troubled children, or cause problems—berserkers, Fear Casters, and the like. She'd never known about spirit walks. In a way, it gave her comfort; if Victor's spirit was on the loose, moving about in some parallel world, didn't that mean there was proof that further lives were possible? She'd begun to believe so, and she knew Victor did. She'd tried to show him as much when she'd said they'd find happiness together in the next life, if not this one. She found the idea romantic and, judging by his amorous response, so did Victor.

"I knew he was a powerful Spirit Caster." Kethelket's voice broke her from her musing, and she, perhaps a little guiltily, jerked her gaze away from Victor's face. "But I had no real idea, I think. I shouldn't be surprised. Belikot was formidable on the spirit plane, a dangerous man indeed with his knowledge of breaching the veil and dominating the spirits he pulled through. Still, Victor slew him, so I shouldn't be surprised that he's willing to rush forth and do battle with those 'ghosts,' as he termed them. A fitting name, I think." He squatted, resting his elbows on his knees as he stared at Victor.

"Why?" Valla found the ancient Naghelli fascinating. He had something interesting to say about nearly any topic, and his skill with those swords was inspiring; she could see he knew things she didn't, even with Midnight in her hands. She wasn't surprised he'd achieved the epic rank.

"Ghost. It's a word we use to describe one who moves without sound, unseen, a killer who can send your spirit out of this world with a silent touch. It was a title given out by our queen in the old world. Only a handful ever walked the face of Kthella at any given time."

"Kthella? The Ghelli home world?"

"Aye, and we Naghelli, don't forget."

"Of course." Valla nodded. She knew as much, of course, but she hadn't heard the name of that particular homeworld in a long, long while—not since she'd studied with the myriad tutors Rellia had saddled with her, perhaps. "So, you think those spirits, the ones who killed your men, are like those ghosts? I think it makes sense." Valla looked at Victor again, her heart swelling and fluttering in her chest as she stared at his strong brow, angular nose, and sharp jawline. As she thought of her youth and all that came with it, she realized she felt like that again, like when she was a girl, sent off to the Legion, spending time with young men who weren't in some way related to Rellia for the first time. Victor had woken something in her heart that she'd let go dormant, and it frightened her.

"He's a master of spirits. Even his banner is doom to the undead. We're lucky to have him in the battle."

"Yes." Valla watched as Kethelket stood and turned, scanning the forest in a slow circle. His soldiers were all around them, hidden in the trees, behind trunks, and even in the fog. They were silent, efficient fighters, and she knew most of them were many times her age, with experience she could only begin to comprehend. Knowing that, her chest swelled with pride a little, knowing she was a match for any of them, save maybe Kethelket. Victor was right; she'd vastly improved in the time she'd known him. Of course, Tes was the main reason, but she'd never have met Tes if she hadn't been following him.

"I'll go speak with Sarl, check on his cohort, and see that they're ready to charge."

"Good." Valla nodded and watched him move off to the east, where the Ninth was encamped near the edge of the fog. Too many of Sarl's troops were affected by the strange malaise the mist caused for him to have them stand ready, idle, in the forest. Instead, he'd set them in a ready position close by, prepared to charge when the word came down. She let her mind wander, trying to picture how things would go. Victor would find and kill or at least get an understanding of the spirit guardians on the walls of the keep. He'd return, and then they'd attack? She wasn't sure how things would go at that point. Perhaps he'd find he couldn't affect the "ghosts," even from the spirit plane.

"Beware!" Kethelket cried, interrupting her reverie, charging toward her from around a trio of trees grown so close together that their canopies were intertwined. At almost the same time, Victor's ghostly coyotes broke into yips and howls and grew restless, coming closer to Victor and pacing in little circles, eyes focused outward, watching the mists.

"My scouts are engaged. Undead have come in great numbers; they swarm this way. I sent word to Sarl, but in this darkness and the mist . . ." Valla didn't need him to finish the thought—they were on their own, at least for a while.

Valla whipped Midnight out of her sheath and put her back to Victor, standing between two coyotes. "Which direction?" she called.

She heard Kethelket's swords ring as he pulled them free. She glanced at him and watched as he put his back to her on the other side of Victor. "All."

22

A FATED MEETING

The climb to the top of the keep's wall was brutal, but whatever had been bombarding him on the ground stopped, so Victor was thankful for small mercies. He wondered if perhaps the defenders so high up couldn't see him clinging to the shadows of the black stone monoliths, especially now that the mist seemed to have made a reappearance, crowding the light of his banner, making it difficult to judge his progress. In any direction beyond fifty yards or so, all he saw was gray. Still, he climbed, leaping from one narrow ledge to the next, devouring the heights with superhuman endurance, strength, and agility.

He'd been climbing for several minutes, perhaps longer, when he felt some agitation from his coyotes. Something was happening around his body, but Victor refused to leave, to retreat to the material plane, as one of Valla's books called the realm of the living. He'd come too far to give up now. Distances were strange on the spirit plane; Victor had always found them to be shorter so long as he knew where he was going, a person or place he wanted to reach. He was beginning to understand that things could work in the opposite manner. Something the Death Casters, perhaps Prince Hector himself, had done to this place made it difficult to find the top of the keep's wall. It wasn't this high in reality, but here, in the land of spirits, it seemed to stretch endlessly.

"So," he grunted, leaping to the next ledge, "is it a matter of wills? Is their desire to keep me away stronger than mine to end this climb?" He growled, stoking his rage, allowing his vision to tint red as he pulled himself up. "Bullshit." This time, before he leapt further, he stared at the wall before him, not the ledge he aimed to climb. He focused on the wall and firmly planted his desired destination in his mind, the wall's top, and visualized it under his feet. Focusing on that image, he stretched his hands up, fingers ready to grab the top of the wall, and jumped. This time, he felt it, the familiar blur of passage, the sensation he usually felt when he was "walking" toward Old Mother on the many occasions when they'd met in this realm.

When his fingers found purchase and his knees bumped against the hard stone, Victor opened his eyes and pulled, a savage grin of triumph baring his teeth as he pulled a leg over the crenellation to stand atop a dark stone parapet. He yanked Lifedrinker from her harness and stalked toward a weird flickering red-and-black shadow to his right. One of the guardians, if he had to guess, was standing with smoky hands atop the stone wall, leaning down in a posture that made Victor think it was searching for something. Was it looking for him? Victor didn't have to wait long to find out. As the circle of his banner's light fell on the shadow, it screamed and turned to him with wide open, blood-red eyes.

The smoky shadows blasted away from it as though the light was a gale-force wind, and the ghost, as Victor had come to think of the keep's defend-ers, summoned a shadowy spear and charged. Victor met the spear haft with Lifedrinker's shimmering moonlight blade, cleaving through it like a twig, then he brought her up in a loop, arcing to the diminutive spirit's armpit, and she lopped its right arm off in a spray of weird luminescent black-red blood. The ghost was the size of an average human with weird gray-tinted, faintly translucent skin, and when Victor maimed it, its mouth stretched into a noiseless howl of agony.

The ghost tumbled back, stumbling in its haste to avoid another cleave. Victor's moves with Lifedrinker were machine-like in their perfect execu-tion, though, and he compensated for the ghost's movement, slipping the axe through its shadowy black leather armor, disemboweling it as it fell. Shiny slippery entrails fell forth onto the black stones. They were silver, red, and cloaked in smoky shadows, and the ghost thrashed, bucking in silent agony as the smoky red Energy spilled out onto the stones. It grew paler and more translucent, and then the spirit was gone. Nothing but a slippery mess of weird Energy remained on the stones.

"Not so tough, are they, *chica?*"

"Simple pawns with weak Energy. Let us seek their master!"

"Not a bad idea," Victor growled, stalking toward the inner rampart and peering left and right, then down, wondering where the rest of the defenders were. His vision was limited to the circle of his banner's light, however, and he couldn't quite make out the stones of the inner courtyard. He thought he could see a gap in the parapet near the edge of his light. "Maybe some stairs there." He was tempted to jump down, come what may, but decided he'd check the perimeter a bit further first.

Victor started around the corner, moving along the walkway, aiming for the gap he'd seen, but then a horde of silently screaming ghosts burst into the light of his banner, black smoke flowing off them as if it was caught in a stiff wind. He tried to take stock, to count the enemies coming toward him, but it wasn't easy with them bunched into a crowd, obscured by the smoke as they were. He thought there must be more than twenty.

Victor took advantage of his much greater size, reach, and strength, stepping toward the throng and cleaving Lifedrinker in a wide powerful arc, shearing through their weapons, armor, and ghostly bodies, breaking their charge. He stomped forward and used Project Spirit to send a wave of sickly yellow, twisted, inspiration-attuned Energy through the crowd. His cleave and the wave of anti-inspiration broke their momentum, and the survivors stumbled back, only to have Victor dance among them, weaving a deadly Lifedrinker through them as if they were practice dummies.

"Pathetic!" he roared, ripping them apart, and then another crowd of the ghosts came from the other direction, and he was forced to increase the ferocity of his deadly dance, kicking, hacking, whirling, cleaving, grabbing, throwing, and utterly destroying the spirit-like assailants. To their credit, though he broke their momentum, smashed their comrades, and dashed their ghostly blood in a thick mist, they never fled. Pack after pack came at him, and Victor felt his movements forming a rhythm, his cleaves and chops the percussion for the roars, howls, and screams he and Lifedrinker let loose.

When he stood heaving for breath, Lifedrinker's metal head blazing with ghostly light, engorged on the bloody Energy of his foes, the keep's high, black stone wall was drenched in the weird luminescent blood-like remnants of his enemies, and the mist stretching away from his banner's light seemed thinner. Many minutes had passed while he wove his dance of destruction, and he could feel the rage in his Core ebbing low. Victor let his Berserk fade, wanting to give his Core a chance to recover. As his size reduced and the slick ghostly blood slowly misted away, he stalked toward the gap in the now much taller-seeming parapet. He could see it clearly. His banner was still burning brightly; only half his glory-attuned Energy had been spent.

Valla wrenched Midnight, trying to pull her from the ghoul's skull, grunting with the effort as the bones clung to the blade and the creature's undead body flopped along the ground. A shambler, as Victor called the giant plant-and-corpse monstrosities, lurched toward her, and she ducked a shoulder, trying to present her armor to its claws as it raked at her while she struggled to free her blade.

They were surrounded, overwhelmed, the Naghelli outnumbered ten to one and falling back into an ever-tighter circle around Victor. Still, the undead broke through, and Victor's coyotes, Kethelket, and Valla struggled to keep them from charging past to attack his freakishly serene body. In the distance, she could hear the horns of the Ninth, and she hoped it meant Sarl was pushing his soldiers into the mist, into the rear or flank of the undead horde. She didn't know what position they held relative to the monsters; all she knew was that they were beset from every direction, and they were losing ground.

The shambler knocked her back, and she fell to the damp mulch, using the momentum to give another yank to Midnight, pulling her free from the ghoul's corpse. She jumped up, only to see two of Victor's great coyotes pull the shambler to the ground, grabbing its arms and loose bits, yanking them apart with frenzied jerks of their necks.

Valla took the short respite to look around. The Naghelli were fast and deadly with their weapons, their coordination the polar opposite of the undead horde's fanatical, mindless charge. She could see them fighting shoulder to shoulder in the nearby mist, moving like orange-lit shadows, slashing, stabbing, and hacking at the endless wave of monsters that pushed at their thin line. How long could they hold? Would the Ninth be enough? It seemed thousands of undead beset them, and Sarl commanded a mere six hundred. They needed Victor's banner, its light, and its bolstering effect. Should she wake him? *Could* she wake him?

Victor started down the steps, noting the lack of any sort of Energy award from the hundred or so ghosts he'd just slain. He wondered if the System deemed his combat still ongoing or if the Energy wasn't coming to him on this plane. He supposed it was possible the ghosts hadn't been worth any; maybe he hadn't even really killed them. The fog continued to retreat as he pushed forward with his banner, and when he reached the base of the steps, he could see a wide circle of black flagstones leading away into the courtyard. He felt something ahead, something malevolent and powerful, a different sort of presence than the weak ghosts who'd thought to challenge him. Was it their leader?

"I feel it, my champion! Let us go! Let us fight what awaits! Don't you wish to taste its blood?"

"Easy, *chica.* Of course I do. Give me a minute to breathe, though. Let me get my rage back." Victor looked inside himself, at his Core, and saw his fear and inspiration were full, his glory above half, and his rage slowly building, stoking itself from the ever-full furnace of his spirit. His Core was different from those like Valla's; it fed on emotions, not elements or other forces that existed in the world. He could be in the vacuum of space, and his Core would recover, building up its power from the feelings that roiled within Victor's spirit. Could other cultivators say the same? He honestly didn't know, but the important point remained—he was recovering even in this strange place controlled by death.

As he stood there at the bottom of the steps, gazing into the fog at the edge of his light, a voice came to him, whispering sibilantly on the wind, "Why delay? Come to me, warrior. Come and let me behold you, who have slain my guardians. Let me feel the fury of that mighty spirit." The voice was decidedly feminine and seductive. Victor knew that, had he a weaker will, he would have felt a powerful pull, an urge to obey and walk into the mist, releasing Lifedrinker to clatter upon the stones. His will wasn't weak, though; he could detect the pull, ignore it, and grasp Lifedrinker's haft even more tightly, twisting it between his hands as he stood there, watching his Rage Core grow ever brighter.

He was feeling good, almost ready to charge forward, when a pang struck him, a pain in his heart that told him one of his guardians had fallen; one of his coyotes had succumbed and returned to the spirit plane. "They're fighting, and it must be bad."

"Let us make haste, then! Slay the presence before us, and we will return to our corporeal bodies and lay waste to whatever threatens our mate!"

"Our . . ." Victor let the thought drop; there was too much to unpack at that moment. Instead, he took Lifedrinker's advice and began to stalk forward, revealing more and more of the courtyard as his banner's light burned off the mist. The stones he trod upon were black and smooth, enormous like the ones on the walls. His boots clicked upon them, echoing oddly in the foggy space. He'd traversed a dozen yards when he heard the voice again.

"Good, come to me, angry one. Let me help you find peace in that throbbing heart of yours." The words came to him as a husky, feminine whisper, and it sent shivers along Victor's spine as if the lips that uttered the words were just an inch from his ears. He swore he could feel the cold breath of the speaker on his flesh, and, despite his will, his love for Valla, and his simmering rage, he could feel his pulse quicken at the touch.

"I'm coming," he growled, stalking forward toward the presence he could feel but couldn't see. Lifedrinker vibrated in his palms, grounding him, and Victor opened his pathways, pulling some rage into them, letting it smolder through him, limning his body in waves of red flickering light and tinting his vision crimson. As the mists continued to part before his banner, he finally saw her, the author of the whispers. She was a woman, ghostly in complexion, her flesh luminescent and faintly translucent. She was tall, lithe, and utterly naked, swaying back and forth on long legs, moving to a rhythm or tune Victor couldn't hear.

Her eyes were a piercing bright cobalt blue that seemed backlit by the Energy within the woman's frame. Her hair, long and black, drifted behind her in the nonexistent breeze, reminiscent of how hair floated when a person was submerged in water. Victor tried to ignore her naked form, but his traitor eyes wouldn't avoid a darting glance down, taking in the woman's pale bare chest and the dark triangle between her legs. When he jerked his head back to her face, she smiled seductively, spreading cherry-red lips to reveal white teeth that, like her eyes, seemed too bright. "Why so grumpy, warrior? Come, wouldn't it be better to talk and take comfort in my hospitality? You've slain my watchers; surely you owe me the courtesy of a conversation."

Victor stalked forward, Lifedrinker held crossways before him, her comforting buzz a reminder of who and where he was, something he needed as the woman's mesmerizing gaze locked with his. He found himself looking her in the eye; she was nearly as tall as he in his non-Quinametzin form, and he frowned at the realization. Was she so tall before? Wouldn't he have noticed something like that? "A spirit then," he growled.

"Aren't we all, in this place?"

Victor had to admit she had a point. Even Old Mother had looked young when she spirit walked. He knew very well that he could manipulate his appearance on the spirit plane if he tried hard enough. He'd simply never felt the need. "Where's your body?" he asked before he realized the words were forming on his lips.

"Nearby. Does it matter? Tell me, angry one. Why do you come to my keep? Why do you attack my guardians? Now you stand before me, full of rage, murder in your eyes, and I have to ask, again, why?"

"This keep, these lands, they aren't yours. You're part of an invading army, and you've slain men of mine."

"Have I?" She frowned, an expression that looked decidedly like a pout on her beautiful face. Victor, forced to stare into her eyes lest he look upon her nakedness, found they were pulsing ever-so-softly with pale blue light. "Who were they?"

"The Naghelli. Two men who came bravely to scout your keep, to have a look at the ghostly guardians atop its walls. Not only did your ghosts slay them, but you hung them from the walls. You shouldn't have done that." Victor's final sentence was a growl, and he began to pump his pathways with rage again. His red flickering aura surged intensely, casting a red glow that reflected from the polished black flagstones.

"I shouldn't make an example of assassins that came out of the darkness to attack one of my guardians? I thought to forestall further violence. I hoped their display above my gates would deter further invasion!" She'd come closer as she spoke, and Victor was stunned to see her cool pale fingertips resting on his wrist, just above his fist where it gripped Lifedrinker's haft. "Wouldn't you like to put that brutal weapon down? Sit with me and see what I've done with this special place. I've built it up here on the spirit plane, and there are wonders to behold within these walls. Can't you feel them?"

Victor loosened his grip on Lifedrinker as he looked into her eyes. He wanted to stare into them, to plumb their depths, and to learn more about this mysterious, amazing woman. "What's your name?" he asked, letting his rage recede, pulling back his aura and holding it close.

"I'm Victoria. And you, angry one? What do I call you?"

"Seriously? I'm Victor . . ."

"A fated meeting!" Her expression brightened, her eyes lit up, and Victor found himself letting go of Lifedrinker with his left hand, letting her fall to his side, loosely held in his right. "We were meant to come together here, Victor! Can't you feel it? I think we could learn much from each other. Such strength flows through you, and now that your rage has ebbed and you've let go of that brutal aura, I can see there's a great deal more to you . . ." She'd come close, just inches separating them, and Victor smiled into her face, his hot breath mingling with her cool, quick exhalations. She tilted her chin, staring into his eyes, and Victor felt that she wanted him to kiss her. He could feel her *willing* him to do it.

Victor brought his left hand up, brushed her wild black opalescent hair away from her cheek, and then let his fingers settle against her neck, the side of his hand resting lightly on her shoulder. "You're beautiful, and I bet there is something interesting about you, but—" Quick as a viper snatching up a rodent, he wrapped his fingers around her pale, slender throat. "I don't like Death Casters trying to mess with my mind!" He growled, tightening his grip and flooding his pathways with rage again. He lifted Lifedrinker, and her edge burst into ghostly orange flames as she howled her fury.

23

A RISKY BARGAIN

Valla looked to her Core, saw her Energy was dwindling, and cut short her plan to launch another lightning strike into the pack of ghouls that harried one of Victor's coyotes. The brave white-gold hounds were beset, as were she and Kethelket. If she looked farther than the small circle they made around Victor, she knew the other Naghelli and likely the Ninth were also overwhelmed; there were just too many of the damnable undead pouring out of the fog-shrouded forest.

She was tired, her body sore and battered, her helmet dented and smeared with gore, and her arm like a lead weight. If not for the magic of her blade, if not for Midnight's desire to fight, she didn't think she'd be able to swing the sword with any effect. Desperately, she stole a glance at Victor, still sitting with his back to the tree, oblivious to the battle despite the ghoul corpse atop his lap—Kethelket had beheaded it at the last instant—and the splashes of gore that marred his fierce countenance. "Wake up, Victor!" she cried for the dozenth time, and then she lowered her shoulder, allowing her wyrm-scale armor to block the slashing claws of yet another ghoul.

Victoria's beautiful ice-blue eyes sprang open with shock, and her mouth twisted in fury as she burst into mist, leaving nothing but damp air between Victor's fingers. Lifedrinker cleaved the cloud, but nothing came of it save a swirl of steamy moisture, and the axe screamed her frustration. A trilling laugh echoed around the courtyard, and Victor spun in a circle, scanning the area illuminated by his banner and seeing nothing. "So vicious!" Victoria's mocking, laughing voice echoed without a source. "What a will! Were you even tempted?"

"Come out here and let me show you." Victor released his aura, letting it fall around him like a blanket of murderous intent. He, in fact, had *not* been tempted by the ghostly woman's words or her beauty. When he felt her will pushing against him the entire time she spoke, it turned a part of him critical, and he'd seen through her façade; she was a Death Caster, and her attempts to bend his will to hers were a low and dirty kind of magic, a prettier version of the control collars the slavers in the mines used. Victor wasn't having it. Her laughter echoed again, but Victor thought he heard the original note in the air above him this time. She was flying, perhaps.

It made sense, he supposed, that a Death Caster who'd taken on a spectral form would be able to fly. He thought about berserking and leaping into the air, hacking Lifedrinker about when he next heard her voice. He discarded the idea. Iron Berserk was a marvelous ability, but it wouldn't serve him here. He needed something a bit more versatile, a bit more unexpected. She'd seen and tasted his rage. She'd felt his will. Perhaps it was time to give her a taste of fear. Before he could talk himself out of it, Victor formed the pattern for Aspect of Terror, channeling his fear-attuned Energy into it.

As always happened, black shadows exploded into being around Victor and began to wrap around his rapidly changing form. He grunted and screamed, a sound that started deep in his gut, rumbling with bass, and ended with a high shriek—a sound no human throat could make. As his cries and shrieks echoed around the courtyard, Victor felt his body changing, elongating, shifting, and hardening as it absorbed his mass, his weapons, and his armor. His vision changed as the colors faded away; everything turned gray, and the misty fog summoned by the Death Caster no longer troubled him; his hungry eyes saw through it, spotting bright flaring spirits here and there, but none that shone as brightly as the one that hung in the air a hundred yards overhead.

When Victor's baleful yellow-red eyes settled on the brilliant spirit, clearly staring right at it, it seemed to realize he could see it. It began to fly in a slow lazy circle, perhaps thinking he'd caught a glimpse and that it could lose him in the fog. It was wrong. Victor's hunger surged, his Core cried out for Energy, and he tracked that spirit with his deadly hunter's vision. As it settled, hovering near the top of a round tower, a structure Victor hadn't been able to see before, he took a step toward it, and his hard razor-sharp talons clicked on the obsidian stones.

"What have you done to yourself?" a feminine voice asked his mind, but Victor had no patience for words. He shook his long head, clicking his razor beak angrily, then he focused on that bright spirit, on the Energy within it, and he leapt into the air, his great black-feathered, shadow-clad wings snapping with a *crack* that echoed off the courtyard walls. Victor hadn't cast Iron Berserk prior to taking on the Aspect of Terror, and his pathways were utterly flooded with fear-attuned Energy. The shadowy steam streaking off his feathered form was rife with it, tainting the air, radiating outward, giving everything within sight of his terrible aspect a taste.

More than the sight of him, the sounds he made carried the palpable fear in his nature through the spirit plane. Any spirit not belonging to the Death Caster who'd claimed that keep and its environs fled at the sound. Victor was dimly aware of the lesser spirits' flight; he could see their bright forms streaking away through the twilight realm. However, the prize, the brilliant one he'd seen flying above him, was the center of his focus, and its radiant Energy kept his attention. Victor wanted to breathe his fear into that being, wanted it to feel it, to experience it, and to send it back to him. He would feast on one so bright.

He screamed his hunger as he streaked through the misty air, a gigantic vulture-like hunched form of black feathers, razored talons, and glowering red eyes. The radiant spirit erupted with blue Energy, launching a beam of the stuff directly at him. It hit Victor in the chest, turned his feathers to ice, blasted them off, and froze the leathery black skin beneath, peeling it back and frosting the ivory-hard white bones beneath. It hurt, an icy fire that spread to his very marrow, but Victor was beyond caring about pain. Pain was a matter of concern for lesser things, things that didn't hunt in the dark and feed on the terror they inspired. He shrieked and snapped his wings all the harder, hurtling toward the startled spirit.

Completely absorbed by his Aspect of Terror, Victor didn't think to cast spells, channel Energy, or project it; he had one plan—grasp onto the spirit, drive it to the ground, and consume the fear he would pull forth. It was a simple plan, but sometimes simplicity was what a situation called for. The spirit flitted indecisively left then right, perhaps surprised at his ability to shrug off its attack. When it finally chose a direction and began to flee, it was too late; Victor was upon it, his great dark talons gripping the faintly translucent pale flesh between its shoulder blades, and, as he'd planned, he cracked his enormous black wings and dove for the unforgiving black flagstones, planning to use the spirit as a landing perch.

His quarry screamed, thrashed, and with a surge of Energy, attempted to apparate, intending to burst into ghostly mist and flee again, but Victor was wise to it, and his hungry talons, formed from his Energy-drinking axe, pulled the spell out of the spirit's pathways, foiling her attempt to flee. He crashed to the hard flagstones, and his talons burst through the shimmering flesh and bones to gouge the stone, leaving an enormous bloody smear as he came to rest atop his prey. The spirit screamed and cried, thrashing its limbs weakly. Victor felt the fear and terror truly begin to flow from the being, great waves of it that washed over him, adding to the frenetic edge of his hunger.

His ability to impart fear was unchecked now, the spirit unable to fight him off, and its deep wells of Energy began to convert, rolling out in those heavy, satisfying waves of fear-attuned Energy that Victor's Core greedily drew in. Despite his hunger and the glorious feeding frenzy he undertook, Victor never truly lost himself; his Born of Terror feat wouldn't let him, not to mention his prodigious will. That said, he didn't really want to control himself, and he gave in to his hunger for a long while, pulling until only a trickle of Energy still drizzled forth from the pale, dull spirit. He was contemplating pulling that last bit into his Core when the spirit shivered violently and coughed out a hoarse plea, "Stop! Please! I can save your army!"

The words struck a chord in Victor, and he climbed out of the shadowy corner of his mind, pulled back on the Aspect of Terror, pushed his way into the driver's seat, so to speak, and took some control. He shifted away from the spirit carefully, methodically extricating one talon after another from its dull gray form. The satisfaction of his feast began to fade as he came more and more into himself and slowly severed the connection to his spell, grunting with discomfort as his body, wrapped in writhing shadows, returned to its usual form. When the dark cloak of shadowy tendrils faded, he found himself straddling Victoria's blood-drenched body, a bloody Lifedrinker held crossways over her naked chest.

She shivered and trembled, pale as snow. All her luminescent blood lay pooled around them, shimmering on the black flagstones. Only a tiny spark of light still hung behind her sky-blue irises. She coughed weakly and whispered, "I'm sorry I underestimated you. I'm sorry I tried to control you. Please don't kill me. A horde, a true undead horde, is attacking the army you brought here."

"And?" Victor growled, leaning forward, staring into her nearly dead eyes.

"And they are winning; your troops are outnumbered fifty to one."

"Fifty thousand?" Victor couldn't help the surprise in his voice.

"Yes! Mindless, but fearless and tough. They will overwhelm your forces before you can rally them and fight free. Spare me, and I'll issue a command for the horde to be still. It will buy you a reprieve."

"Fifty thousand . . . and you're in the keep?"

"I am! I was here with my spectral guards, whom you slew."

"Call the horde off and open the gates. We'll come inside."

"Impossible! Prince Hector will—"

"Nah, no deal. I'll kill you now and take my chances." Victor lifted Life-drinker, and the woman flinched and took a slow, shuddering breath.

"Very well. Very well. Perhaps you're strong enough to break the tether he has upon me. If you can do that, then I can aid you. I'm close to death, though! Let me leave this place so I can seek healing. I can only grant you a short reprieve from the horde; when Hector sees what I've done, he'll retake control."

"How short?"

"Minutes!"

"Listen." Victor stood up and glowered down at the once beautiful figure. "I found you once on this plane, but I can find you on the other, too. Don't make me hunt you down. Get your gates open and wait for my army."

"You have my word." She coughed the words, chasing them with flecks of luminescent blood, and Victor found he believed her. He didn't trust her, not even a little, but he believed she'd complete this bargain, at least. He pulled back his aura, released the almost unconscious hold he'd pressed on her with his will, and then she was gone in a puff of pale mist. He took one last look around the black stone courtyard, then he cut the ties to his Spirit Walk spell.

Victor's eyes sprang open, and he was greeted by chaos. Undead corpses lay piled around him, his four remaining coyotes snarled and howled, whin-ing with angst as they wove between ghouls, biting at their legs, pulling out tendons, dragging them away from him. Valla, drenched in gore and blood but still bound in lightning and wind, hacked Midnight in a two-handed grip, grunting with the effort to hold the ghouls, zombies, and shamblers at bay. Other forms writhed in mortal combat nearby, Naghelli, no doubt.

Victor surged to his feet, cast Iron Berserk, and summoned his banner. Many of the Naghelli had invoked orbs of light, but they paled in compari-son to the light that poured out from the bloody sun on his standard. The undead shrank back, cringing, their flesh steaming, and Valla turned with wide, relieved eyes to see Victor towering over the piled corpses at the center of their circle. From his new height, Victor could make out Kethelket and

Uvu fighting a cluster of shamblers further afield. He filled his lungs and bellowed, "Follow me! We need to join up with the Ninth!" Then he strode to the east, toward the edge of the fog-filled forest, hacking Lifedrinker in wide *whooshing* arcs as the Naghelli, his coyotes, and even Uvu fell in behind him.

His banner had broken the enthusiasm of the undead creatures' charge, winning his guardians a bit of a respite as they followed him through the trees. Victor could hear the Ninth fighting and knew they weren't far. He hoped to get to them before Victoria called off the undead; he wanted to lead them through the fog to the keep. Part of him questioned the sanity of his decision to bring the army farther into the forest, to put them into the keep while nearly fifty thousand undead lurked outside. Part of him thought they should break free, charge over their claimed lands to the keep they already held, to the support of the rest of the army.

Victor didn't like that idea, however. If Prince Hector had such a huge force here, in this territory, it stood to reason that other parts of his lands weren't so heavily guarded. If Victor could find a way to occupy this horde, even destroy it, then Borrius and Rellia could push harder into the next territory. He drove forward, hacking, kicking, even throwing undead out of his path, carving the way for those who had so steadfastly defended him. He still couldn't quite believe that they'd been fighting so vigorously around him and he hadn't noticed a thing. The idea that Valla and the Naghelli had been bleeding, maybe dying for him, caused a twinge of guilt, but he shook it off. Hadn't he bled for them? Hadn't he been willing to die to defend his troops?

When they burst through the tree line, Victor found the Ninth in a defensive phalanx, surrounded by a sea of undead. Thankfully, this horde lacked the giants they'd faced earlier—no bone colossi or gigantic skeletal drummers stood out in the massive army, and the Ninth seemed to be holding their own, able to keep the immense horde of undead at bay with their Energy-bolstered shield wall. Victor didn't know how many of the monsters surrounded them; it would take hours to count them all, even if they stood still. In that thrashing, surging throng, all he could do was estimate.

The Ninth had roughly six hundred soldiers, and he could see them clearly at the center of the horde. If he were guessing, he would say there were easily ten times as many undead heaving and pressing against those shields. Where was the rest of the horde Victoria had warned him about? Were they still in the forest, still coming this way? Victor looked left and right over his shoulders and saw the Naghelli, blood-soaked though they were, ready to follow his lead. Victor was proud of them, proud of Valla, who stood stoically to his right. They didn't know a reprieve was coming, didn't know Victoria had promised to call off the horde. For all they knew, they were about to charge into a hopeless battle to try to help the Ninth.

His banner kept the undead off them, the ones behind in the forest, but he could still see clusters of them breaking from the trees further away, rushing over the plains to join the thronging horde pressing against the Ninth's shields. "Listen!" Victor roared. "This looks hopeless, but it's not! These undead will break away soon, and then we'll have minutes to make our next move. Stay by my side, and we'll get through this!"

The Naghelli responded with cheers, weapons smashing on shields, and feet stomping the ground. Kethelket, standing to Victor's left, whipped his twin blades in an elaborate flourish and said, "On your lead, my lord!"

Victor didn't want to waste the time or breath correcting him. Instead, he ensured his boost from Sovereign Will was on his strength and vitality, then he held Lifedrinker high, and he began lumbering over the muddy torn-up grass toward the rear ranks of that enormous undead army. His four coyotes loped beside him, and he contemplated sending them home and calling for his bear, but they'd fought so hard to keep him alive that he didn't want to take this from them. No, they deserved to join him in this charge. "Come on, *muchachos!*"

When he was just a dozen yards from the thrashing, bucking horde, Victor cast Energy Charge and ripped over the ground to smash into them. Dozens of zombies flew away from his impact like pins before a bowling ball. Turf exploded into the air, and blood, rotten flesh, and bones showered down in a rain of destruction. Victor didn't slow. Rather, he capitalized on the momentum, using his enormous size and strength to push his way among the undead, cleaving their smoking, smoldering flesh apart with a red-hot Lifedrinker.

His banner did more damage than any cleave of an axe. As its illumination fell on a vast area of the battlefield, the undead lost their focus, cringing away from it, physically affected by the fiery light. It seemed to cook at the bindings of death magic that held them on this plane, held them together. They writhed and screamed their silent screams as they fought with one another to get out of it. Victor drove forward, the Naghelli, Valla, his coyotes, and Uvu at his back, slaughtering the few that escaped his cleaves, pushing through the ocean of undead, and carving a pathway through it.

As he grew nearer and his banner's light fell on the Ninth, cheers erupted over the sounds of battle, and Victor roared his encouragement as he drove ever closer. The undead were weak and mindless, and he began to wonder if they might be able to win even without Victoria's help. At one point, when he was a mere fifty yards from the front lines of the phalanx, he looked over his shoulder to see thousands of undead pressing toward him over the plains, hanging back just far enough to avoid his banner's light. He grunted and reassessed his idea that they might survive out there—when he ran low on Energy, things would get ugly.

As if she were somehow reading his mind, Victoria waited until Victor began to feel some doubt in his assessment of her word. He began to wonder if something had gone wrong and she'd failed to issue the command to the horde—however that was done—to fall back. Had she died, after all, from the damage he'd done to her spirit form? As that doubt took shape, and Victor pressed his way through the last few hundred zombies and ghouls between him and the Ninth, something happened. A bell toll sounded like a great clarion gong that rang through the air on reverberating waves of magic.

The undead, already creepily silent in their aggression, grew still, lowering their arms and swaying in place like horrible, rotting corpses somehow put to rest in a standing position. In the stunned silence of the living combatants, Victor shouted, "Glorious Ninth! With me! To the west, into the forest! We're going to take the keep while these *pendejos* sleep! Come on!"

24

GOOD HABITS

Victor didn't wait for the soldiers to respond or for any of their leaders, Sarl included, to rush forward with questions that might delay their movements. He didn't know exactly how long Victoria's command to halt the undead would last, but she'd said minutes, and they were several miles from the keep. They had to move. "Let's go! Let's go!" he roared, turning and stomping back the way he and the Naghelli had come. He could hear Sarl's sergeants shouting commands, could hear the Ninth moving forward, hacking and bashing their way through the strangely dormant undead that still surrounded them.

Victor wondered how much of a dent they could make in the horde if they went wild with slaughter. How many could they slay before Prince Hector gave them the command to resume their attack? "Can't risk it," he grunted. There might have been twenty thousand undead on the field, but that meant another thirty thousand lurked in the woods, still making their way to the fight. The undead were sturdy and not so easy to dispatch for a typical soldier. It would take a long time to kill them all, and Victor didn't think they'd be halfway done before they reanimated and fought back.

"What's going on?" Valla asked, jogging to keep up with his long strides. Now that they didn't have to fight through the undead as they progressed, Victor wasn't surprised she'd taken the chance to get some answers.

"I fought with the commander in the keep. I beat her, and she swore to halt the undead long enough for us to get free."

"In exchange for?"

"For not killing her."

Valla muttered something under her breath. Victor grinned as he realized she'd cursed. "Let me guess—she was beautiful with soulful eyes and a pout that tore at your heart . . ."

"I was in my nightmare form. It was hard to stop feasting, but she managed to say something about my army—you—being surrounded. I pulled back at those words." Victor didn't enjoy talking about "feasting" on a sentient being, but he knew it would straighten out Valla's perception of events.

"I'm sorry. I was being petty."

"Nah, don't apologize. She did try to seduce me at first. She tried to twist me to her will, but mine was stronger. Besides," Victor said more softly as he leaned down from his towering height, "all I had to do was think about you."

Valla's answering smile swelled his heart, and Victor almost canceled his Iron Berserk so he could more easily hold her hand and run beside her. He held off, though—no telling what heroics might be needed before his army was safe behind walls. Thinking of the army, he turned and walked backward for a moment, looking between the trees to see the Ninth rushing behind the Naghelli, a loose column of soldiers. They held their shields and weapons ready, eyes wide as they looked at the piles of vanquished undead and the shifting, listless hordes that still lingered farther from the trail of destruction Victor had wrought. "Keep moving! No slowing!" Victor roared, then he turned and continued to trudge forward.

"The keep will open to us?" Kethelket asked, hurrying to jog beside Valla.

"It better," Victor growled. He gave the Naghelli captain another look and added, "I have a bargain with the lady inside. She swore to open it to us."

"And if she betrays her word? We'll be smashed between this horde and the walls."

"If it comes to that, I'll open those fucking gates. Believe it." At his words, Kethelket looked up and locked eyes with Victor, nodding gravely. He believed him. The confidence made Victor feel glad and proud but also nervous; what if he couldn't deliver? Shaking his head, he turned his attention back to the present. They were traversing the scene of Valla's and the Naghelli's stand, where they'd defended Victor's insensate body. The corpses of the undead were so thickly piled that it seemed like an impromptu fortification around the loose circle of slaughter.

Victor pushed through the area, past the tree where he'd sat, then he sent his four shimmering white-gold coyotes ahead, ranging toward the keep, seeking the best path. He didn't wait for their report, though, continuing between trees, working his way in a generally westerly direction. All the while they walked between trees, they passed by clusters of undead, and Victor didn't hesitate to smash and decapitate them as he strode by. He could hear the wet *thunks* of others' weapons doing the same and knew the Naghelli and the Ninth would carve a bloody path through the dormant horde. The idea that though they might kill a thousand, they were hardly denting the undead army was a little daunting.

"I see Lam," Valla said at one point. Victor turned and scanned back over the column, and sure enough, he saw Lam's shimmering golden Energy hammer smash apart another cluster of idle undead.

"I'd forgotten she was with the Ninth. Do you see Edeya?"

"No . . ." Valla's voice was pensive, and Victor knew she was worried. He slowed further and concentrated, looking back. After a while, near the rear of the column, a flicker of bright blue movement caught his eye, and staring, he made out Edeya's slim form striding among the rear troops. Her wings were back; they were larger than before, and they glittered with sparkling blue Energy.

"I see her! Near the rear of the column." Victor pointed, and Valla sighed with relief.

Following the wordless messages from his coyotes, Victor wound his way past standing trees, clusters of zombies and shamblers, and other obstacles like great fallen trees, lichen-filled ravines, and tumbled boulders; the forest wasn't anything close to parklike, and though his banner burned away the fog, the going wasn't easy. They'd only been traveling for about twenty minutes when the zombies began to stir. Thankfully, the undead were far less dense in this part of the woods, but Victor and the army had passed by thousands and left tens of thousands behind. As the creatures woke, they began to noiselessly make their way toward the column as if they somehow could feel their presence.

"Let's go!" Victor roared. "Double-time! Run for the keep!" Though he ordered the soldiers to run, Victor continued to walk, urging them to rush past him as he tried to benefit as many as possible with the light of his banner. When he felt that he was in the middle of the troops and they were surging around him, jogging with their shields up, he started forward again, pleased to note that Valla rode beside him, once again in Uvu's saddle. Clashes sounded from the edges of their column, and Victor knew the undead were closing in again. Still, if they kept moving forward, he knew they could outpace the bulk of the horde. He hoped. What if a great many undead sat outside the walls, waiting? Had he led the Ninth to their doom?

His doubts were unfounded. When they broke out of the trees into the clearing around the keep, only a hundred yards of gravel-strewn dirt and patchy grass separated the troops from the high black walls. Mist still clung to the area, thick in the air near the keep, but as Victor started forward over the cleared land, his banner's light drove it back, and he saw the gates standing open, the corpses of two Naghelli hanging above them. He frowned at the sight and stood still, waiting to take up the rearguard, letting the rest of the soldiers pass him by.

The keep was impressive, though nothing like the spirit plane version. The wall was circular, carved from obsidian-colored stones, but there the resemblance ended. The parapet was only thirty feet high, maybe forty, and the gates were made from iron-banded wood. No towering walls disappeared into the clouds, and no monolithic stones made up the walls—the black blocks that formed the keep were more the size of overlarge bricks. Still, the keep was large. The walls were probably a quarter mile in circumference, and the tall, round towers that rose behind them were impressive. There wouldn't be any trouble fitting the Ninth and their Naghelli comrades into the fortification.

As the last soldiers rushed past him, Victor turned and watched the tree line as their undead pursuers began to break through into the light of his banner. They shied back, parting as they rushed forward, working around the banner's glow along the edges of the clearing as though they meant to go around him to keep up their pursuit. Victor chuckled and turned, walking with long, heavy strides toward the rear lines of the soldiers as they pressed forward into the keep.

The gates were probably twenty feet high, and when Victor stood before them, he took a moment to reach up with Lifedrinker to slice the cords holding the dead Naghelli against the stones. He carefully cradled their lifeless pale bodies, strangely light and limp, in his arms as he stepped into the tunnel behind the gate. The passage was long with high ceilings and lined with various defensive measures—murder holes for arrows, flanged wide-mouthed brass openings that looked perfectly suited for spraying oil, and large ballista tips protruding by the dozens. Victor was grateful Victoria hadn't yet betrayed him; he'd hate to be walking through that tunnel observing the damage done to the troops he'd sent through before him.

When he stepped into the courtyard, he noted again its similarities and differences from the spirit plane version. Smooth black stones lined the ground and the inner walls, but again everything was smaller. He could see the ramparts easily. The steps leading up to the keep with its round towers were just a few dozen yards beyond the gate, and standing atop them was a tall woman clad in black gossamer. Lam, Sarl, and Kethelket stood before the steps, the soldiers arrayed in rows, filling the courtyard. Still sitting atop Uvu, Valla waited just beyond the inner gates and nodded to Victor as he stepped through.

Victor wanted to address the woman and reassure his troops before someone did something violent, but first, he looked at the nearest sergeant and said, "Take some soldiers and get that gate closed. The undead are coming."

"Sir!" She saluted him sharply and then addressed the line of bloodied soldiers she was standing with. "Come on, Green Squad!"

Victor watched them hurry into the tunnel behind him, then he gently laid the corpses of the dead Naghelli on the black stones to the side of the gateway. Straightening, he turned and strode forward down the central aisle between the ranks of soldiers. Valla rode beside him, keeping pace atop Uvu. The soldiers stood up straighter as he passed. Whether it was pride or the bolstering effect of his banner, Victor didn't know. Voices muttering echoed over the stone flags, and Victor knew the soldiers wanted to know what was happening. Who was this black-clad woman, why were they in the keep, and what would they do about the horde of undead closing around them?

Victor stopped behind Lam and the others and looked up the steps, making eye contact with the woman—Victoria. She looked similar to how he'd seen her on the spirit plane, but not exactly the same. She was tall and pale and had blue eyes and long hair, but she didn't glow with ethereal light here. On this plane, her eyes were like pale ice, not cold stars. Her skin wasn't like polished ivory; it was a white, almost sickly pallor, and her lips weren't plump and red. They were thin, pressed together in something like a grimace as she obviously struggled to stand before them. She swayed slightly and gripped her side with one long-fingered hand, clearly in some discomfort.

"Lord Victor. I've kept my part of the bargain. Will you keep yours?" Her voice rang through the courtyard, high and clear, and the soldiers grew quiet as they realized they were about to be privy to important talks.

"My part?" Victor's voice rumbled, rolling over the stone, bass notes echoing off the hard black walls.

"You agreed not to kill me, and to help me free myself from Prince Hector."

"I'll give you a chance." Victor reached down and jostled Kethelket, getting the Naghelli's attention. "Choose three of your best. Three with the highest will. Take this woman to a room in the keep and hold her until I have a chance to come speak with her." Victor turned back to Victoria. "You are not to speak a word to anyone—not until we've spoken further. Your guardians will report to me immediately if you utter so much as a syllable. Is that clear?"

"It is clear, Lord." She attempted to curtsy and nearly collapsed. Sarl moved to climb the steps, intent on aiding her, but Victor shot out a long arm and held him by the shoulder.

"Careful, Sarl. She's not one to be underestimated." Victor stepped forward, mounting the steps three at a time, and when he loomed over Victoria, he held out his left hand, palm up. "All of your rings, jewels, and dimensional containers. Don't test me by trying to be sneaky."

If possible, she blanched further, but she started to comply, pulling several rings off her left hand. "Lord, some of these are precious to me. Heirlooms. Will you grant me a chance to bargain for their return?"

"I'll keep them safe for now." He stood waiting as she deposited ring after ring into his enormous palm, then she untied her silky lace sash and unwound it from her waist. She rolled it into a neat ball and pressed it to his palm.

"A container," she sighed. Victor had to hand it to her; he wouldn't have thought the sash held a dimensional space.

"Where's the System Stone?"

"You intend to claim . . . of course you do." She looked at him, her ice-chip eyes staring into his warm golden brown ones, and when she spoke, he noted the yellowed nature of her teeth. They looked almost like old ivory, and he wondered if she was undead. He supposed it was likely; hadn't everyone else they'd met from the invading army been undead? "It's in the great hall beyond the doors here. Lord Victor, if you claim this keep while I'm here, I don't know what will happen to me."

Victor turned to see Kethelket standing behind him with three darkly cowled Naghelli. Had they put those cowls on as some sort of protection? As a means to intimidate their charge? Victor didn't know, but he liked it. "Take her." He stepped past them, ignoring Victoria's pleas to speak further, and when he stopped before Sarl, Victor cut his connection to his Iron Berserk, reducing his size to something a little more comfortable for his captain to speak to. "Get your soldiers on the walls. Find out everything you can about this keep's defenses. We have a horde to kill."

"Aye, sir!" Sarl turned and began barking orders to his lieutenants.

Victor looked at Valla and Lam. "Let's get a dialogue going with Borrius. I think our plan has changed, but it might be even better now." He nodded to a less crowded area of the courtyard, a corner to the left of the steps leading up. He walked over, and they followed. He noted a pensive expression on Valla's face.

She gripped his arm. "Do you want to try to claim this place first?"

"Let's talk to Borrius first; it might be wise to time that with his assault. Hector is going to know it when I claim this keep. He'll surely react. Let's be certain the main army's in a position to take advantage of that."

"Of course." Valla nodded curtly, and Victor paused to really look at her. She was covered in gore—well, all but her hauberk, which had already cleaned and polished itself. She'd taken her helmet off in the courtyard, and he could see how her hair was soaked with sweat, how thick layers of grime covered her jawline where her sweat had dried with dust and blood over and over again. She'd been through hell while he was on the spirit plane.

"I'm sorry I took so long." He spoke softly, and Lam cleared her throat, moving a few steps away. She waved an arm and called Edeya closer, and they moved off, speaking in low tones.

"You did your best. It sounds like she was quite cunning." Valla tightened her grip on his forearm, pulling his attention back to her.

"She was, but most of the time I was gone was because I was an idiot and didn't remember how to move about on the spirit plane."

"An idiot?" Valla raised an eyebrow. "Do you know that no one else in this entire army could have done what you did?" Again, she squeezed his forearm, and he loathed the idea of her ever taking that hand away. At that moment, he wished she could hold his arm forever, however impractical. "Will she aid us, do you think?"

"I think so. Maybe not willingly, but she seems to have a healthy sense of self-preservation. Speaking of that." Victor turned back to the keep where the Naghelli had taken Victoria. "I think I should speak to her sooner rather than later. She's dangerous." Victor realized he was still clutching the Death Caster's rings and sash in his left hand, so he raised his voice and said, "Hey, Edeya."

The two Ghelli, one with golden wings and one with blue, turned away from their quiet conversation and walked toward him. "Yes, Legate?"

"Your, uh, wings look cool."

Edeya's eyes opened wider, and she smiled. For someone who'd just been embroiled in a massive battle with the undead, Victor thought she looked damn good. She'd gotten taller, filled out a little, and her cheeks were glowing vibrantly. Her wings were broader and much more robust looking. He wondered if she could fly at all. Standing next to Lam, he could see she still had a ways to go to reach her stature, but she was definitely not the frail-looking wispy girl he'd become friends with. "Cool?"

"Yeah. Now quit trying to think of a way to make fun of me and come take these rings and stuff. Keep them separate from your other things, okay? We need to go through them carefully."

"Yes, sir!" Edeya winked at him and smartly saluted, then took the bundle of Victoria's belongings from him. "Lam and I are going to explore the keep a bit. Will that be all right?"

"Yeah. Let me know if you two find anything like that weird map in the other one."

"That's the idea." Lam grinned, and they walked back up the steps and into the open double doors.

Victor continued to stare at the doorway, his mind drifting toward the strange undead woman he had to interrogate. Valla shifted beside him. "I should go with you."

"Do you want to?"

"I think so."

Victor knew there was more to her desire than simply wanting to be present or to hear what Victoria had to say. He couldn't blame her. He'd feel the same in her shoes. "God, so much is happening. I need to slow down and take a beat, get some advice. Shit! When's the last time I spoke to Khul Bach?"

"You spoke to him regularly while we traveled, but I haven't seen you do so since we came into the Marches. In your defense, you've been busy, one fight leading to the next."

"Yeah, I know," Victor said as he shook his head, "but it's just that I always feel like this—like things are running away from me. Like I'm running behind a horse, trying to grab the reins, trying to steer it away from one disaster or another. Remind me to take a minute to talk to him and, shit, to look at the Far Scribe book I share with my cousin."

"I will. For now, though, shall we contact Borrius?" She produced the command book from her storage ring.

"Yeah. Do you mind writing?"

"Not at all." She smiled at him, and Victor could tell she was trying to help him relax. She was always like that. Always so damn supportive and cool. He remembered the first time he'd come to realize that, back in Coloss, when she'd followed him over to the arena. He remembered how surprised he was when she didn't try to talk him out of enrolling in the fights. He'd grown so used to others like Thayla, Lam, and Rellia trying to direct his actions. Valla never did that. Did she? He couldn't think of an instance. As he cleared his mind and tried to think of the best way to voice his intentions to Borrius, Victor resolved to let Valla know how much he appreciated her. He'd said as much recently, but he wanted to show her again. He wanted to make a habit of it.

25

TIES THAT NO LONGER BIND

W hat it boils down to"—Victor sighed, closing the Far Scribe "command book" he shared with Rellia, Borrius, and Lam—"is that we need more information. I think I need to speak to Victoria."

"Isn't it odd?" Valla asked. "Her name? I've never heard one like it before I met you." They sat together in his library. Victor had set up his travel home inside the courtyard, much as he had in the first keep they'd conquered. They still hadn't "conquered" this keep, but for all intents and purposes, the Ninth and the Naghelli were in control despite the fact that a massive horde of undead surrounded them.

"It's definitely a name you could hear in my homeworld, same with Eric and Hector." Victor looked at Valla, watching how she pressed her lips together and clenched her fist. She was stressed, and he wasn't sure he should add any more detail, but he also wanted to be honest with her. "She said our meeting was 'fated' when she learned my name. I think she's full of shit, that she was just struggling with things to say to keep me from killing her. Still, it's weird that our names are so similar. I want to get some answers from her. Are you ready?"

"Of course." Valla stood, her chair clattering on the hardwood as it slid back.

"You okay?"

"I think I'd like a little more time between near-death experiences, but other than that, I'm fine."

"Yeah . . ." Victor let his response trail off as she turned to walk toward the front door. He sighed, straightened his clean shirt—they'd taken a few minutes to wash up and change clothes—and ran a hand in front of his wyrmscale vest, sealing it shut. That done, he followed after her. She was waiting for him in the courtyard, looking up at the walls, watching the activity there. The soldiers were thick on the parapets, and it looked as though they were taking shots at the undead outside.

Before they'd gone into his house to communicate with Borrius and Rellia, Victor had watched from the parapets as the undead horde stopped and gathered outside of easy bow-shot range. They were so thick and tightly pressed together that a few zombies would inevitably stumble out of the formation—if you could call it that—and meander a bit closer. The soldiers were making a sport of trying to kill them from range. He didn't mind, and it seemed Sarl didn't either. It kept the troops entertained, and if they killed a few of the undead in the process, well, that meant fewer enemies to deal with down the road.

"Still at it?"

"Yes. I wonder if we shouldn't get more serious about it." Valla reached up, resting one slender-fingered hand at her throat, gently fidgeting with the choker Victor had given her. She was clearly deep in thought, picturing something, but she shook it off and looked up at him. "Should we put together some larger attacks?"

"Yeah. Definitely. Not yet, though. Let's get some information out of Victoria. Come on." Victor turned to the steps leading into the keep, and when he'd reached the top, he looked at the sergeant on duty and asked, "Where are they holding the . . . lady who was here?"

"Inside, sir. Second level—the western tower. Guards are posted outside the door."

"Thanks." Victor stepped inside. He'd only looked around the keep briefly before going into his travel home, but it was a very utilitarian, if impressively designed, structure. The smooth black stones of the exterior continued inside, rising to arched ceilings illuminated by windows and lamps, all glassed with blue and red stained crystal. The tinted lighting made the shadows strange and mysterious and gave the dark stone more depth. Just beyond the door was a great hall, and at its center was a hovering, slowly rotating stone just like the one in the other keep. Victor figured he'd need to interact with it to officially "claim" the keep.

Borrius and Rellia had agreed that he should wait. They were at odds, though, on what they should be doing in the meantime. Borrius wanted to hold his position. He'd found a valley just south of the other keep where he'd set up a massive ambush, hoping to catch Hector's troops as they rushed to retake the first keep. Rellia thought they should scout out the next territory to the south, get into position, and attack when Victor claimed this place. They'd all agreed to hold off on a decision until Victor had interrogated Victoria.

He climbed the stairs leading to the second level and followed the directions of posted guards to the hallway leading to the tower stairs. Two Naghelli stood outside the doors, darkly cowled, their faces so shadowed that Victor couldn't see their eyes. His earlier curiosity came to the fore, and he asked, "Are those cowls significant?"

"Aye, my lord," said the one on the left in a lilting soprano, startling him with its clarity. "They're heavily warded to protect us against Mind Energy."

"Do you all have them?"

"No, my lord," said the other guard. "A few of us have the Mage Hunter Class, and as such were outfitted with gear to help us in our profession."

"Outfitted by?"

"Belikot, my lord," said the first guard, her voice hushed, likely still nervous about uttering her old master's name aloud. Victor frowned, not pleased to be reminded that some of his best troops were once the bloodthirsty servants of a madman bent on world domination. He contemplated telling the two Naghelli to stop calling him "lord" but decided he had bigger fish to fry. Part of him also, he might admit with some guilt, wanted them to harbor as much respect and deference toward him as possible; he thought it might hinder thoughts of rebellion from forming in their minds.

"The prisoner is above?"

"Aye, my lord, with three guards."

Victor gestured to the door, and the female guard hurried to pull it open for him. It swung silently on hinges that fit into the stonework as though grown from it. He started through but paused and looked at the solid hardwood door and the hinges again. "Were the doors here already, or did our engineers make them?"

"They were here, my lord."

Victor nodded and started up the narrow steps, winding his way to the top with Valla's boots clicking on the stones behind him. They'd passed a couple of doorways when Valla spoke up. "You didn't stop them calling you lord."

"You noticed?" Victor glanced back at her with a crooked smile. "Can you guess why?"

"You . . . want their respect."

"Yeah, but not for egotistical reasons."

"No, I didn't mean that. Some of our fear, the other commanders, has rubbed off on you. You have doubts about the Naghelli and want them to fear betraying you."

"You can read me like a book, huh?"

"I think I'm learning to know you fairly well." Her voice carried a hint of amusement, and Victor wondered if a double entendre was mixed in there.

He changed the subject. "You noticed this keep seems newer than the other?"

"It seems that way, but it could be just as old with better preservation magic."

"Oh. Good point." Victor stepped onto a broad landing at the top of the stairs, and when he looked to his left, he saw two more cowled Naghelli. He stepped toward them. "Where's your third?"

"Within, my lord. One of us has eyes on the prisoner at all times."

"Good." Victor nodded to the door. "Any problems? I'm going in."

"No problems, my lord. She's not uttered a word." He turned to the tower, twisted a large silver key in the latch, and began to open the door.

"The key was here?"

"Aye. In the door."

"Huh." Victor stepped into the room, squinting against the bright light. The room was circular and clearly occupied the entire top of the tower. Pale blue stained glass panels, bonded with strips of melted silver, filled alcoves in every wall, and the sunlight coming in was thus tinted and seemed to draw out hints of blue in the dark stones of the floor and vaulted ceiling. The only furniture in the room was a plush straight-backed wooden chair at the center where Victoria sat. A Naghelli, who'd been standing in front of the door, turned to bow as Victor and Valla stepped into the room.

"You can wait outside." Victor nodded to the guard.

"Aye, my lord." The slight figure hurried past him, and Victor caught a whiff of something like cinnamon on the air stirred by her passage. Every time he started to think he was getting to know the peoples of this world along with their customs, he found more unanswered questions. He pushed the thought aside and regarded Victoria. She sat with a straight back, her dark multilayered silky dress and skirts hiding most of her body; only her pale neck, face, and hands were exposed to the light. She tracked his movement with her pale blue eyes, never once glancing at Valla, who also stepped into the room, closing the door with a satisfying well-oiled *click* behind her.

"I'm glad you didn't try to influence my soldiers." When she didn't reply but only watched him unblinking, Victor added, "You may speak."

"I'm not a fool, nor do I wish my existence to end this day. You brought me to the brink of true death, and I'll not soon forget the feeling."

"Hmm." Victor stood in front of Victoria, rubbing at the rough stubble on his chin, staring at her while Valla walked in a slow circle around the room, looking out the windows, then back at the woman, then up at Victor. She never said anything, but he knew she was thinking, taking things in.

"Hmm?" Victoria dared to echo after a few moments of silence.

"I was thinking about that term—true death. What do you mean, exactly? Are you undead?"

"No sense hiding it, is there? I'm sure you have Death Casters in your army who will be able to confirm your suspicions. Where I come from, if you're not undead, you're a slave, a meal, or fodder for the army. If we're honest, even if you're undead, you're likely one of those things anyway."

"Where you come from?" Victor arched an eyebrow, trying to imagine a world like the one she described. It wasn't that hard for him; hadn't he seen movies and played games with similar premises? He supposed it would be horrible in person, but hearing about its reality was just as abstract as those fictions.

"Dark Ember." She winced as she spoke, and then gasping, she said, "If you want me to tell you more, Lord Victor, you'll need to sever my connection to Prince Hector. I'll die if I try to tell you anything of consequence."

Victor looked at Valla and raised an eyebrow. It took her a moment to realize he was waiting for her to say something; she'd been staring at Victoria's face. "I don't know." Her eyes said she wished she could help more, but she had no experience with this sort of magic. Victor had an idea; he'd dealt with a tether tying Belikot to his phylactery and to Thayla. Still, he wasn't exactly sure how he was supposed to help Victoria.

"What do I need to do?"

"You'll need . . ." Again, she winced and coughed, and dark flecks of nearly black blood touched her faded pink lips. She looked up at the ceiling, avoiding Victor's gaze, and said, through a throat that sounded strained and constricted, "If someone were to attempt to sever a tether of control between a Death Caster and his thrall, he or she would need to open their inner eye to the Energy. When they found the thread stretching away, they would need to focus their will upon it and break it with a knife of their own Energy." She squeezed her eyes shut and looked down, trembling, and Victor saw heavy dark droplets leaking from the corners of her eyes, leaving long red tracks on her chalk-white cheeks. Was she weeping blood?

"Watch me," he said to Valla, then he turned his mind inward, focusing himself by looking at his Core. His four orbs of Energy pulsed and throbbed, full of power and potential, and he found it easy to calm his breathing and steady himself as he observed them. That done, he followed his pathways out of his body, taking the short route through his lungs and marveling at the smoldering magma in his Breath Core as his mind's eye traveled past. Then his "inner" eye was seeing outward, and he regarded Victoria before him, a thin wavering pale-blue ribbon stretching from the top of her head to the north-facing window.

The ribbon fluttered as though caught in a breeze. Every so often, he could see a flash of brighter blue Energy traversing it, and he wondered what that was—just a bit of Energy that refreshed the spell from time to time? Information from Prince Hector to his thrall? The other way around? Could he see what Victor was doing? Victor didn't like that idea. He took two strides to close the distance, then he reached out with his hand, cupping the ethereal ribbon. He couldn't feel it with his flesh, but he felt the tingle of the cold Energy as it penetrated it, touching the pathways beneath.

Without a second thought, Victor yanked a heavy tendril of inspiration-attuned Energy out of his Core and pulled it through his pathways to his hand. He wasn't sure how to form the flowing Energy into a knife, but he had another idea. Focusing his will, he bent the bright pulsing rope of his Energy around the pale shimmering blue ribbon of the tether, and he drew it tight. Victoria gasped and began to seize, shaking and shuddering. "Hold her," he growled as he focused his will, tightening his inspiration-attuned Energy, aiming to strangle and sever the tether.

"She's frothing at the mouth!" Valla cried, but Victor couldn't look down to see her struggles. He was too focused, straining with everything he had to constrict his rope of Energy around the tether. He grew frustrated and angry as it resisted him, and he released his nearly ever-present hold on his aura, growling with his frustration as he bore down on his efforts. Still the tether resisted him, and Victor, worried that his captive would die or be damaged beyond healing, reached into his Core and pulled out thick bands of his other three Energy types, stretching them out through his pathways where he wound them around the tether next to his original strand.

The baleful red rope of rage, the dread-inducing coil of fear, and the glimmering, sparkling ribbon of glory joined his inspiration-attuned Energy, and Victor pulled them all tight with a grunt and a headache-inducing effort of will. A keening wail burst from Victoria, and Valla cried out as she fought to hold the undead woman still. Victor focused on his task, watching as the tether went from pale to dark blue to black and then crumbled into motes of ash, utterly destroyed. He sighed heavily and let his Core retract his Energy. When he opened his eyes, he found Valla sitting on the polished black stone floor with Victoria lying insensate in her lap.

"Is she . . ."

"Not dead. Well, not totally dead." Valla frowned, and Victor could tell she wanted to drop the woman, to stand up and maybe wash her hands. Victoria's chin and throat were drenched in dark blood, as were her cheeks and ears; she'd been bleeding profusely, it seemed.

"Do healing potions work on the undead?" Victor asked.

"I don't know." Valla gingerly laid her palm over Victoria's brow, one of the few places unstained by her blood. "She's cold, but I can feel her breathing. Why do the undead breathe?"

"Good question."

With a soft groan and a wheezing cough, Victoria opened her bloodshot eyes and struggled to sit on her own. Valla helped her, pushing her off her lap so she sat legs sprawled out with her dark dress covering them in front of her. After a few minutes of wheezing breathing, she cleared her throat and said, "There are undead, and then there are undead, Lord Victor. My body still breathes and flows with blood, though more sluggishly than yours."

"Did I free you?"

"Yes, but far more slowly and torturously than I'd hoped. Why didn't you simply sever the tether? You strangled it to death! All the while, Hector tried to pull my spirit through it."

"Be grateful, witch!" Valla growled, and Victoria jerked to look over her shoulder at her.

"My apologies, Lady." She put a hand on the cushioned chair, struggling to stand up, but her arm was too shaky, and she fell back to the ground. "I should, indeed, be grateful. Not I nor any of Prince Hector's barons could have severed that tether."

"Here." Victor held out a hand, and when she took it in her cold fingers, he pulled her to her feet. "Sit down." He nodded to the chair. Valla hopped up before Victor could offer her a hand. "Well? Can you answer all of my questions now?"

"All that I know the answers to, aye." She wiped at the blood around her mouth with the back of her long black sleeve. "Would a bath be possible? Perhaps when you're done with my questions?"

"If we don't decide to execute you." Valla stood behind Victoria, and for the first time in a while, Victor noticed her catlike canines as she growled the threat. She'd leaned close and spoken into Victoria's right ear.

"Ah . . ." Victoria's eyes widened, and she looked from Victor toward Valla, but the Sword Dancer had noiselessly stepped back and was on her other side. Victoria looked back to Victor and nodded. "Of course. I might say, I do hope you'll find mercy in your hearts . . ."

"Let's not get bogged down with emotion right now." Victor squatted before the undead woman and began his questioning. "Tell me what these lands were like when Prince Hector's army arrived. Were there any defenders? Natives, I mean? People living in these keeps?"

26

INFORMATION

There were beasts and monsters; at least, that's how Prince Hector characterized them. I wasn't with his vanguard—I didn't see the initial settlement. I was allowed through the portal nearly six months after his conquest began. That's why I'm here, on the edge of his territory and not in Heart Sorrow."

"Heart Sorrow?" Valla asked from behind the pale woman.

"His capital in the new world. The city—well, town, really—beneath the veil star."

"Veil star?" This time, it was Victor who prodded.

"The green light in the sky?" Victoria widened her bloodshot eyes, surprised, it seemed, by her captors' ignorance. "It's a ritual creation of death-attuned Energy. Prince Hector uses it to weaken the veil, the barrier between the spirit plane and a number of other planes where the undead thrive."

"And that has the effect of . . . ?" Valla leaned close to Victoria from behind, speaking into her ear.

"It makes Death Casters' spells more effective and easier. It allows Prince Hector to bolster his forces with beings he pulls through the veil. It, well, it weakens the living, supplanting the natural Energy that suffuses an area with death-attuned Energy. Many such stars hang in the skies of Dark Ember."

"Are all undead Death Casters?" Victor dug around in his ring for a chair and produced a plain wooden one with wicker slats. When he set it down and slowly lowered his frame atop it, the slats creaked with the strain.

"All undead have some death affinity. Some have stronger affinities that they focus on, though."

"Like blood?" Valla asked, still pacing behind their prisoner.

"Exactly." Once again, Victoria tried to twist her head to look at Valla as she answered, but like a cat, Valla had silently stepped away. "Will you kill me?" She turned back to Victor.

"I'm not in the habit of killing in cold blood, but there are some crimes we'll need you to answer for. The more helpful you are now, the more it might aid your case." He surprised himself with the answer. He wasn't sure where it came from but supposed it was true. She had killed the two Naghelli who'd flown into the keep, but it could be argued that they were in the wrong—invading her territory, attacking the ghost. Still, she didn't have to hang them from the walls. That was going to be hard to get the troops to forget.

On a more personal level, she'd tried to . . . do something to Victor on the spirit plane. Again, though, they'd been at war. Could he forgive it? He'd given her worse than he'd gotten in their little scuffle. The truth was, he wasn't sure what he'd do with the undead woman. Was her very nature a large enough crime to warrant destruction? Were undead ever peaceful? He had too many questions, but at the moment, he needed answers to more pressing concerns. "What tier are you? What about Prince Hector?"

"Tier?"

"If the word confuses you, then tell us your level, witch." Valla, Victor thought, was doing a fantastic job of playing bad cop. Every time she spoke, Victoria flinched.

"I . . ." She licked at her dry pink lips, and Victor was almost surprised to see her tongue provide some moisture. Did the undead create saliva? Apparently this one did. "Forgive my hesitation. It's not something one speaks of on Dark Ember. Still—" She held up a hand when Victor scowled. "You have me at a disadvantage. I am Level Fifty-Nine, and Prince Hector is significantly stronger than I."

"You don't know his level?" Victor's scowl deepened.

"I do not, though many have speculated that he's above seventy." At her words, Victor looked past Victoria's shoulder to Valla, and she raised her eyebrows but shrugged. He knew what she was thinking—Victor had faced worse on Zaafor.

"You're doing well, Victoria." Victor shifted, leaning back slightly, and his chair creaked in protest. "Do you want something to drink? Do you? Drink, I mean."

"I . . . yes, I do. Might I have a touch of wine? I'm exceedingly nervous, and my mouth is dry. The ordeal of severing the tether has . . ." She stopped speaking as Valla stepped around to face her, producing a silver cup and a dark bottle of wine. She held the cup out, Victoria took it, and Valla carefully poured it full of the wine. "Thank you." Valla didn't smile or respond. She put the bottle away, sending it into one of her rings, and then she walked behind Victoria again.

Victor watched as his prisoner carefully sipped at the dark liquid. "How many troops does Hector have? I was surprised to hear that there are fifty thousand undead around this keep."

Victoria swallowed and exhaled softly, closing her eyes as though savoring the beverage. "That wine is exquisite, Lady . . ." She trailed off, perhaps hoping Valla would respond. When she didn't, she answered Victor's question. "The undead in the forest around this keep are mindless chaff. They are the bulk of the lesser undead that Hector commands, though there are some thousands here and there, adding to the numbers of his more potent forces. As I'm sure you know by now, there are five perimeter keeps like this one. A baron or baroness holds each." She gestured to herself. "And each has an army, though some, like myself, have only a few loyal guards. Well, *had*."

"And past the perimeter keeps toward Hector?" Valla leaned close again, startling Victoria with her words.

"The Gateway Citadels. They guard the causeway leading to Hector's fortress under the veil star."

"And we can't just go around the citadels?"

"It would be difficult. Hector's foothold sits atop a mountain. Well, a dormant volcano, really. As I told you, I wasn't here when he first arrived, so I don't know if he built it into what it is or if the System deliberately placed his portal there, but sheer cliffs protect him on all sides. The citadels guard the only road leading up."

"So, why is the undead horde here?" Victor was trying not to get bogged down in details that wouldn't be pertinent for a while; they'd deal with the citadels when the time was right. It was enough for him to know they were there for now; he'd let his subconscious stew on the issue for a while.

"This forest and the lands to the east, which you just took from the reavers, are the northernmost border of Hector's new domain. I believe he was gathering forces to push through the mountains."

"You believe?"

"Hector does not confide in me. The only person who might know his full plans is his consort, Catalina."

"Catalina?" Victor sat up, grunted, and rubbed at his head. Each question this woman answered led to five more in his head. "Are you guys from Earth?"

"Earth . . ." Victoria's eyes grew wide, and she stared into nothing for a moment, then she refocused, looking directly at Victor. "Not we, but those who settled Dark Ember."

Victor lifted his focus over Victoria's head, meeting Valla's gaze. She looked surprised, but she nodded, encouraging him to continue that line of questioning. "How long? How long ago did they 'settle' Dark Ember?"

"The Ebon Circle came to and conquered Dark Ember twelve hundred years ago." She sipped her wine as Victor stared at her, silently doing math in his head, trying to imagine some powerful Death Casters leaving Earth in the eighth or ninth century. "How do you know of Earth?"

"You don't think it's odd that my name is similar to yours?"

"But Earth was dead, devoid of Energy . . . It's why the founders fled!"

"Well, that might be, but people still live there."

"You're not that old?" Valla leaned close as she asked her question, once again startling Victoria.

"Me? I'm no founder. I've yet to see my first century. No, the rulers of Dark Ember weren't invited by the System to this little conquest. The portal repels those beyond a certain threshold of power."

Valla looked interested but shook her head and stepped back, meeting Victor's eyes. "We need to focus." She gestured to the windows, and though it was vague, Victor knew what she meant. They were surrounded by undead, had Borrius and Rellia waiting for information, and needed to make a deci-sion about their next move. He stood from the chair, stretched his back, and paced in a small circle behind the poor overtaxed piece of furniture.

"Problem is, I've got a million questions. How sensitive are Hector's forces to light? Is it just my banner? Certain types of Energy? Are the other barons any stronger than Eric was? Are—"

"*Was?*" Victoria interrupted. "Eric is dead?"

Victor held up his hand and continued his train of thought. "How many more invaders are coming? How many undead can Hector create, pulling them through the 'veil'? Doesn't he need bodies for them?" He saw Victoria inhale, saw her preparing to speak, but he cut her off. "Don't answer yet. I've got a dozen more questions, but we really need to focus on one thing: What will Hector do if I claim this keep?"

"He'll assume I'm dead now that you've cut the tether—dead or being tortured." She licked her lips, noticeably stained by the wine. "He may be acting already. He knows his horde is alive—he can feel his thralls, all of them, to one degree or another. He'll assume they're holding your army here in the keep, preventing you from marching forth. Even without you claiming this keep, I would wager that he's already sent forces to reclaim the one meant for Eric. He's likely sending one of his stronger barons here as well. He knows his horde, the mindless undead outside these walls, cannot breach these walls. He'll send someone with siege units. Someone like Karl the Crimson."

"Valla, come with me for a minute." Victor walked to the door and opened it. He looked at the trio of cowled Naghelli standing on the landing outside. "Watch her. I'll be right back." Then he walked down the stairs a ways, putting some distance between himself and the tower. When he turned, he found Valla right behind him, still moving with near-silent steps. "We need to make some preparations here, but, more importantly, we need Borrius to hold fast in his ambush position. I hadn't thought about Hector knowing we were trapped here."

"Are we?" Valla frowned.

"Trapped? I mean, not you and me. Not the Naghelli, but the Ninth? I think so, Valla; there are fifty thousand undead surrounding this place by now. We have to think of a way to destroy them, or the Ninth won't be able to leave."

Valla nodded and pulled the command book out of her storage. "What should I tell them?"

"Tell them to hold their position, to crush the army on its way to the keep." Victor shook his head and rubbed his chin. "We need to think of different names for these keeps. I'm not feeling particularly creative, but we'll call the first one Old Keep and this one Black Keep for now."

Valla raised an eyebrow, and her mouth twisted into a half smile. Victor knew she wanted to tease him, but she didn't, and he was grateful. "Very well. They're to destroy the army coming to reclaim Old Keep and then come to help us?"

"No. Then they're to push south and take whatever keep those forces came from."

That got a reaction out of Valla. She lowered the book, still unopened, and looked at him with something like alarm. "We're going to take on fifty thousand enemies? Plus whatever monstrosities this Karl the Crimson is bringing?"

"We can't risk getting our whole army bogged down with this horde. We need to deal with it. As long as we're holding this keep and fighting them, then it's like we've tied one of Hector's hands behind his back. We've already beaten three of his armies. If Borrius and Rellia can kill the army coming to take back Old Keep, then take the next . . . he's going to get desperate. Desperate enemies make mistakes."

Valla nodded, and her expression told Victor she was trusting him, and it stressed him out more than if she'd argued. What if he was wrong? What if Karl the Crimson came here and smashed the walls, allowing that enormous army to swarm into the keep? The best he could hope for in such a scenario was for a small percentage of them to flee. Victor forced his face to remain neutral, to project confidence as he said, "I'm going to get some more answers from her." He jerked his head up the steps. "Can you communicate with the other commanders? Can you fill in Lam, Sarl, and Kethelket on what we've learned? Get Edeya to help you if you want."

"I will . . ." She paused, her mouth slightly open, and glanced up the steps. When she looked back at him, she smiled and continued, "I want to caution you about her ability to manipulate you, but I don't think she's your type. Something about cold dead skin doesn't seem like it would attract you . . ."

Victor chuckled and reached out, pulling Valla into a hug. He was three steps down from her, so she pressed nicely into his chest as he said, "She's definitely not going to manipulate me that way, don't worry. It wouldn't matter if she were fully alive and beautiful; she doesn't hold a candle to you."

Valla pushed out of his hug, her hands on his chest, then she reached up and grabbed the sides of his neck, tugging. Her fingers always felt cool to him, probably because he had a Core of magma inside his chest. He leaned into her pull, and she kissed him softly and briefly. Then without another word, she was gone, slipping silently down the steps, not even her wyrm-scale armor betraying her passage. Victor turned and trudged back up to the tower door.

Inside, after the guard had left and closed the door, Victor carefully sat down in the chair again. Victoria stared at him, eyes full of concern. They were very expressive, those eyes. Her flesh was pale, but dark rings circled their hollows, and the pale irises had layers and depths that Victor could look into for a long while, guessing at the thoughts inside her head. He didn't have time for that, though, so he asked, "Why shouldn't I kill you?"

"I can see the oceans of blood you've shed in your gaze, Lord. I can see that my death would be just a feather atop a pile of lead. Still, I think it would come to weigh on you—I mean you no harm. I'm free of my bond to Prince Hector, and I *want* to live. Trust that, if nothing else. I will not act in a way that will make me a threat to you simply because I know you will then have a reason to slay me. Keep me bound in this tower if you like. When you win this war, you can banish me."

"And if I lose?"

"Then Prince Hector will likely kill me. He won't trust that I didn't aid you. I *have* aided you, have I not?"

"I've dealt with undead and Death Casters in the past, but it was always with an axe in my hand." Victor rested a hand on Lifedrinker's haft in illustration. "Tell me, can the undead live peacefully among the living?"

Victoria chewed at the dry flesh of her lower lip nervously, and her eyes darted up to Lifedrinker's haft and then back to Victor's face. "In truth? Not easily, Lord. We must cultivate death-attuned Energy. It's difficult to do so in a thriving environment among living things. In worlds where the undead don't dominate, we keep to ourselves in places of death. Of course, Prince Hector has other ideas for this realm; that veil star is the first of many he intends to call into being. He means to turn this world into one much like Dark Ember—a place where the living are held in pens or kept as pets and used . . ."

"I get it. You don't have to sell me on the idea that I need to stop Hector. Tell me how you're going to avoid his fate. Won't you wither away in this tower if I claim these lands and we don't bring you near any sources of death Energy?"

"I have many reserves, Lord. I will be fine if I stay here and don't use my Energy. It will sustain me for years. As I said, you can decide where to send me when you've won. I have suggestions—"

"Tell me about this Karl guy." Again, Victor interrupted her. He wasn't sure if he was impatient, angry, or just trying to keep her off balance. Whatever the reason, it seemed to be working; for a woman who was at least partially dead, she seemed incredibly stressed.

"Karl is a brute! He's a colossus of a man with gargantuan constructs of flesh and bone for soldiers."

"Big like Eric or big like me?"

"More like you, Lord. He's worked for centuries modifying his mortal vessel. He's a Carnemancer—a certain type of Death Caster who uses death Energy to control and mold the undead. He himself is undead, and he's done much work on his form." Her lips twisted in distaste, and Victor chuckled at her double standard.

"You think you're better?"

"I am! My phantoms serve me in their natural forms, growing more powerful through their cooperation with me. I don't enslave them and warp them and—"

"Enough." Victor shook his head and stood up, depositing his chair into storage. "Same rules as before—no talking unless it's to me. I'll be back to speak to you soon enough." She nodded, and Victor stepped out of the room. After reiterating his expectations to the guards, he started down toward the courtyard. He had to meet with Sarl and the others; they had a siege to prepare for.

27

OLD FRIENDS AND MORE PLANS

A fire?" Edeya frowned, peering beyond the parapet over the rough ground to the distant milling throng of the undead.

"Yeah, a real horror of a forest fire. Something you'd never wish to see happen, except for maybe if your forest was full of zombies and shit." Victor leaned against the smooth black stones on one elbow and looked at Edeya with a wry smile. "What do you think?" He'd been standing on the ramparts, watching the undead for hours. Valla had gone off to write in the command book, hoping for an update from Rellia or Borrius. Sarl was busy with his lieutenants, Kethelket was scouting with a few of his Naghelli, and Lam was sleeping—catching up on a few nights of inadequate sleep, as she'd put it. Edeya, though, had been keeping him company.

"I . . . I think it sounds too easy. Do you think they'll burn?"

"I don't know, but I'm betting if we send the Naghelli south, over the horde to the edge of the forest, then have them light it up, fan it with some magical winds . . ." Victor pantomimed flames burning with his fingers wriggling in the air and then blew on them. "Whoosh! I bet we can cut down the number of undead outside our walls."

"But the forest . . ."

"I mean, fires happen, right? It sucks, but the forest will recover. Don't some trees need fires to make their seeds sprout?"

Edeya's blue dragonfly wings vibrated rapidly for a second, shedding thousands of little motes of light, and she blushed. "Sorry! I'm still getting used to how expressive my wings have become!" Victor just grinned at her, and she continued speaking rapidly. "It's true; a forest will recover from a fire. A *normal* fire. I hope whatever flames the Naghelli Pyromancers can summon won't prove too destructive."

"Let's put it this way—that forest is never going to recover if Prince Hector wins. It'll become a dreary, dying, horrible place."

"A fair point, Legate." Edeya smiled, and Victor marveled at how good she looked. He'd never have recognized her if she had shown up looking like this back in the mines—her wings were twice the size of the runty things she'd had before. She was a good deal taller and far more filled out; her forearms, protruding from her rolled-up uniform sleeves, were wiry with muscle.

"Have you had a chance to practice with Kethelket?" Victor asked.

"Huh?"

"Oh, never mind. I guess he's been pretty busy, and so have you. I asked him to work on your spear skills with you."

"You asked . . ." Edeya's eyebrows turned down, and her newly blue eyes turned stormy. "You asked a Naghelli to teach me to use the spear?"

"Not teach you to use—"

"Do you know how insulting that is to a Ghelli?" Her voice had grown shrill with outrage.

"No, I guess—"

"I will *not* take lessons from *Prince* Kethelket!" Her eyes sparked with blue Energy, and Edeya turned on her heel and stomped away.

"What the hell?" The abrupt display of fury completely took Victor aback. Hadn't Edeya been one of the more reasonable ones when it came to accepting the Naghelli? What was the deal with her eyes flashing with Energy? Was it something to do with her new bloodline? The more Victor thought about it, the more he felt that was the answer to the puzzling outburst. He considered how his Quinametzin bloodline sometimes rose up in him and made him say something or act a certain way. Maybe some Cobalt Wing ancestor of Edeya's had a real problem with Naghelli, and she was unconsciously channeling her. "Or him." Victor shrugged.

He looked out over the clearing toward the forest again, watching the shifting, aimless, uncountable thousands of undead. How long did they have before some baron of Hector's showed up and took charge of the horde? How long before these undead were pouring through a shattered wall, flooding the keep with their bodies, overwhelming the Ninth? They needed to do something. He had half a mind to jump out there and start going to town with Lifedrinker, killing as many as he could before his Energy ran low and he had to retreat. Wouldn't that work? If he killed a few hundred or even thousands of them at a time? The answer was that it depended on how much time they had.

"Yeah," he grunted, starting for the stairs, nodding to the soldiers he walked past, "time to quit wasting time." A young woman with bright yellow hair saluted him with wide eyes, clearly having heard what he said. Victor winked at her and hopped down the steps, five at a time. "Sarl!" he yelled.

"Sir!" Sarl replied, startling him; he'd been standing near the base of the stairs.

"Can you get ahold of Kethelket? It's time to do something about this horde."

"He's within the keep, sir. Something about updating the maps in the command book."

"Can you grab him and Valla? Also, get Lam—wake her if you need to. We'll meet in my house in fifteen minutes."

Sarl didn't waste time with words. He slammed his fist to his chest and then hurried to the keep. The two lieutenants he'd been speaking to looked around with blank expressions, clearly wondering what to do now that Victor had interrupted whatever they'd been up to with Sarl. He nodded to them. "Go on, then. Practice with your weapons if you don't know what else to do." He strode across the courtyard and into his house, only to almost smash face-first into Edeya. She'd been heading for the exit when he stepped in.

"Victor, I—"

"You okay?"

"I'm sorry! I don't know what came over me! I got filled with such anger when you mentioned the . . . you know."

"You can't say it?"

"I don't want to! Something in me really, really doesn't like them."

"It's your bloodline, I'm guessing. Did you have a vision when you advanced?"

"Yes! An amazing experience! I walked in the Blue Deep when the world was new. I—"

"Hold up!" Victor held up a hand, chuckling. "I want to hear about your vision, but come sit with me. The others will be here soon, and we might be interrupted, but I want you to know that I get it. My bloodline changed me a little, too." He laughed and walked past her to the long table, where he pulled out the chair at the right end and sat down. "Sit down."

"Thank you." Edeya was stiffly formal as she pulled out the chair and folded her hands before her on the tabletop. Victor knew she was trying to make up for her outburst.

"Relax, all right? I'm not upset. Sometimes my Quinametzin ancestry influences how I respond to certain things, especially when I feel like someone is challenging me. I'm sure your Cobalt Wing ancestor has a good reason to hate the Naghelli, but you can take control of those emotions. They don't have to control you. It's a matter of practice and, well, I guess will."

"My will is one of my lower attributes, but Lam thinks I should start to focus on it now that I have a new affinity."

"Yeah, I agree with Lam. Everyone could benefit from more will. You know it comes in handy in many ways, right? It helps you to resist mental influences, it helps you to affect others with your magic, it helps your Energy pool to grow, but even more, it helps it to recover more quickly. I could go on, but did you know will is my primary attribute? It's higher than my strength and even my vitality."

"No." Edeya's eyes were wide, and she leaned forward with genuine interest. "I never would have guessed that, but looking back, it makes a kind of sense. You never broke, no matter the hell you went through. When you disappeared into the depths with Thayla, I thought I'd seen the last of you."

"Yeah. Well, I'm trying to make the point that you don't have to let your bloodline dictate your actions or feelings. You can push back if you want to, and I think in the case of Kethelket, you should try. He has a lot to teach someone like you—hell, anyone, really. He's very skilled with weapons. You know he was alive before the joining, right?"

"Yes, I knew that." She frowned, and he saw her fingers tightening where she held them clasped. "I guess I never *really* thought about the implications, though. I didn't know he was a spear fighter."

"He learned the spear before the sword."

"I will try to hold my feelings in check, Victor." She nodded curtly, and Victor knew she was struggling to maintain her composure. He decided to let the matter drop for the moment.

"All right. I don't want to keep bugging you, so I'll drop it. You know, Edeya, I'm still Victor—the one you met in the mines. I have nice armor and I've gained a bunch of levels, but I'm not really much older or wiser or anything. I'm still screwing up constantly. Don't worry about yelling at me, okay?"

Edeya smiled, and it was the same expression he remembered despite the many changes that had occurred in her. "You've changed more than you think.

You're a hero—a literal hero. You've saved so many people and performed some feats that people all over the Empire are talking about. You might feel the same in here"—she rapped her knuckles on his armored chest—"but you're not. You've learned a lot."

"Well," Victor said, coughing into the back of his hand to hide a brief surge of emotion, "I appreciate you saying that. I'm glad I still have you to talk to. You know, of all the people in this army, even Thayla, only one person has known me longer than you have."

"That's kind of sad. Who? Lam?"

"Uh, well, I guess technically Lam has known *about* me at least as long as you, but you *knew* me first. Right? Anyway, I was talking about Sarl. I met him when I was new in the world."

"So . . ."

"So, you're important to me. Remember that! Now, have you had a chance to look at Victoria's things?"

"You're important to me too, Victor. Don't worry, I won't forget what a strange idiotic boy you used to be." She laughed and punched him on the shoulder. "About the undead lady's things—only briefly. I was afraid to do more than a cursory examination. The containers are still bonded to her, and I didn't know if you intended to return any of the objects."

"What kinds of things did she have?"

"Two storage rings. That lacy sash was also a storage device. Let's see: a mundane if pretty bracelet, three other magical rings, and a very Energy-dense amulet that frightened me. I didn't try to investigate it."

"Let me see it."

Edeya opened a large leather satchel she wore attached to her belt and dug around for a moment, then she deposited a silver pendant attached to a long fine-linked silver chain on the table. She placed it face up, and Victor could see it was carved with the likeness of a youthful woman, complete with fine details like individual strands of hair looping down over the sharp jawline. Her eyes were just as detailed, and the irises were tiny, perfectly cut red gemstones. "Damn." He picked it up and ran his thumb over the carving, marveling at the craftsmanship and wanting to confirm that it wasn't some trick of the light, that it wasn't, in fact, a portrait.

"Do you feel it?" Edeya asked.

"Nothing in particular. I mean, other than the tiny carved details."

"I felt something stir within. It almost seemed alive when I touched it."

"Well." Victor frowned. "Do you want me to take it? I can ask her about it."

"I can keep it with the other things." Edeya held out her hand, and Victor handed the amulet over. He was about to ask her to let him see one of the storage rings when he heard footsteps approaching from the foyer.

"Tell you what," he said, standing up to greet the others, "I'll bring you with me when I go talk to her later. We can give her the plain bracelet and try to go over some of that stuff. Cool?"

Edeya smirked. "Cool."

"Now you're getting it!"

"You have a plan?" Lam's voice rang out as she strode into the room. "I was looking for you, Edeya."

"Oh . . ."

"She was helping me with the plan," Victor said.

"A plan?" This time, it was Kethelket who spoke up as he entered the room. Right on his heels were Valla and Sarl.

"You're all here—good. Sit down, everyone." Victor gestured to the empty seats, then he led by example, pulling his chair up, grinding its feet over the wooden floor.

"Please tell me you aren't going to try to fight the whole horde all alone." Valla ran her fingertips over the nape of his neck as she passed, sending an electric shiver down his spine. She grinned at him as she sat in the chair to his right.

"Not exactly." Victor waited for everyone to sit down and give him their attention. "We're going to start a forest fire, a real motherfucking inferno of one."

"Mother . . ." Kethelket shook his head, eyes wide with disgust.

"Not literally! Relax, listen. Kethelket, how many Pyromancers are among your people here?"

"I'm not exactly sure, but at least . . ." He looked up at the ceiling, and Victor could see his fingers moving as he silently counted. "Thirty. At least thirty of my two hundred have fire affinities. Some much stronger than others."

"And you have a similar amount with air affinities?"

"I'd say so, yes." Victor could see him connecting the dots in his head, putting together what Victor was going to ask of him. "There may be some problems with this plan."

"Yeah, I figured I might not have thought of everything."

"You want the Naghelli to fly past the undead and light the forest afire?" Sarl nodded enthusiastically. "I like it. They seem to burn well, the undead."

"The mist is thick in the woods, and it seems to hinder flames. My casters were mentioning it after the battles the other day, but . . ." Kethelket stood and paced about while Victor watched, waiting for him to finish his statement. "We may be able to mix some potent alchemical accelerants. Yes. I believe Vussa and Holn have what we'd need. May I speak to my people?"

Sarl also stood. "I have an alchemist with four assistants in my cohort. I'm sure they can help."

"Well, shit, I didn't have to explain much at all. Okay, go try to make a plan. Keep one thing in mind for your logistics: When you're ready, I'm going to ride out and try to get the undead to chase me on Guapo. I'll lead them deeper into the woods." At his words, Lam, Valla, and Edeya all groaned. "What?"

"I was simply waiting to see how this plan would involve you risking your life. When you mentioned the Naghelli, I was hopeful that you'd decided to let some others carry part of the burden for a while." Valla sighed heavily after speaking, and Victor saw Lam nodding along with her.

"You don't think I should do that? They can't catch Guapo . . ."

"Can Guapo truly charge through tens of thousands of undead?" Edeya held her face straight, but Victor could hear the laughter in her words.

"Well, I'm sure he could get through a lot, and then I can leap and hack, and, well, you guys know I'm pretty resistant to fire, right?"

"Forgive my dissension." Kethelket had been nearly out of the room when Victor spoke up, but now he walked back to the table. "But I feel you should be at the keep in case this other baron you mentioned shows up. He may already be en route, and the fire may not deter him, not if he's as strong as your prisoner indicated."

"Well, I guess . . ."

"Additionally," Kethelket continued, "I have some plans to lure the undead farther into the woods. My people are quite adept at baiting foes."

"All right, all right." Victor waved a hand toward the door. "Don't let me slow you down. Let's make this happen." He turned back to the table as they left. "Any word from Borrius?"

"They're lying in wait, but the scouts Kethelket left with them report an army approaching. They only counted two thousand, and Borrius is frothing at the mouth with anticipation."

"That's what I'd hoped. I bet Hector thinks the main army is here. He either split his forces or sent the only nearby army he had to try to take Old Keep. I bet it's option number two. I think Borrius and Rellia will be able to push south and claim another territory with hardly any resistance."

"You really think this forest fire idea is going to work?" Victor could always trust Lam to speak her mind.

"I feel confident that it will at least partially work. We'll still have fighting to do here, especially if this Karl the Crimson asshole is on his way. Which"—he paused and summoned a bloody rag from his dimensional container—"brings me to my next question. Do you guys think I should eat this now or save it?"

"Oh, roots! Is that a heart?" Edeya recoiled; she knew about Victor's strange ancestral habit, but she'd never seen him in the act.

"I'm not gonna eat it here, relax." Victor sent the organ back into his ring. "I'd like to be in my titan form first anyway."

"Will it leave you insensate? Is it like a racial advancement?" Lam didn't seem bothered at all.

"I've eaten a couple of potent hearts, and both times I lost myself to some kind of vision, but only briefly."

"Is that heart more or less potent?" Lam looked from Victor to Valla as though she'd keep him honest.

"I think it's less potent. A lot of tough *pendejos* had to work to bring the wyrm down, and our very strong friend killed the night brute prince."

"I've never heard—" Edeya started to say, but Lam interrupted her.

"Then eat it. You might as well have every advantage."

"I agree, Victor." Valla reached over and put her cool soft palm atop his knuckles. Edeya's eyes nearly shot out of her head as she looked from Valla to Victor and back again. She opened her mouth, but Lam punched her in the shoulder, and she closed it.

Victor stood up, accidentally knocking his chair over behind him, and nodded to the three women. "Right. It's settled then. I'll eat this thing right away. That corpse-crafting dude could be here at any moment."

28

WRONG PLACE

Victor was alone in his travel home, sitting on the floor of one of the empty rooms in the basement. He had several tasks to accomplish, and for the first time in a while, he'd told everyone to get on without him. He'd given Kethelket his objective, and the Naghelli prince was working with the alchemists to create fire bombs that would hopefully significantly reduce the number of undead lurking in the forest. Valla, Lam, and Sarl were coordinating the defensive preparations in the keep while Edeya kept a close eye on the command book. If Victor planned to get anything done before things started to boil over, now was probably that moment.

"Let's see what you've got to say, old man." Victor touched the pink gemstone on his bracer and sent some Energy into it. He was used to the weird aspect of the ancestor crystal's realm now, but it still took his attention enough, with its sharp, angular planes and lights, odd refractions and shadows, that when Khul Bach spoke, it startled him.

"I see much has changed since you last visited. That nascent Core in your chest has ignited into a smolder."

"Hello, sir." Victor shifted so that he was more directly facing the giant Degh spirit. "Yes, I had a breakthrough with some Energy gifted to me by my Quinametzin ancestor."

"Excellent! So, you've learned to cultivate the Core?"

"I think so. I had to create a pathway opening into my lungs, and when

I pull Energy into them, I can harvest it into my Breath Core. I haven't had much time to experiment, but it seems to work."

"Good! This will increase your power, young titan! Imagine your strength with two powerful Cores to draw upon! I've known the great wyrms had a second Core; the learned among the Degh have studied them for millennia, though we never thought we could claim one for ourselves. A shame that you cannot share with us your ability to grow stronger from the consumption of your foes! I wonder if it's something that can come about naturally. If my kin were taught to consume the hearts of the vanquished . . ."

"I don't know, Khul Bach. Maybe? I understand my gift and know how it works, but not its origin. If I ever learn more in a vision of my ancestors or through communion with them, I'll let you know." Victor didn't see the harm in the promise—he doubted he'd ever learn the secret of how the Quinametzin got their uncanny ability to gain strength from eating hearts. He didn't know, but it could be a matter of belief or faith. It could be a matter of DNA. Whatever the reason, the Quinametzin were strong and grew stronger with each enemy they vanquished. The same could be said about any cultivator, but the Quinametzin, with their heart eating, took it to another level.

"That is good. The more you learn, the stronger you become, and the better it will go for my people when you return to Zaafor. Do you come to me for advice or simply to visit?"

"I was wondering if you knew anything about paragons. I apparently manifested the Paragon of the Axe recently." Victor rested his hand on Lifedrinker's haft while he spoke, and she vibrated eagerly against his flesh.

"Excellent! This is something that many of those who break through to the higher tiers of weapon skill are able to do. Not all, but many. It's a matter of talent, focus, and will. Not all warriors can exhibit all three, at least not so early as you. In the legendary tier, it becomes more commonplace."

"Are many on Zaafor at that level?" Victor was surprised by how the giant took the news in stride. He'd fought some talented people on Zaafor and never seen evidence of a paragon. If anyone in Coloss would have been able, he'd have thought it would be Karnice. Had he? Victor tried to remember the times when Karnice grew annoyed with him in the arena and beat him down. Had he displayed the Paragon of the Spear and Victor hadn't noticed? Had he assumed it was some kind of Energy ability? He remembered Karnice manifesting a great red doppelganger that wielded spears in all four arms . . .

"Not many," Khul Bach said, "but enough that the phenomenon is well known."

"Does it do anything?"

"Ha!" Khul Bach slapped his knee. "Of course! A paragon manifests in a reflection of your spirit. It can make your weapon larger, faster, and sharper. It can mirror your weapon and give you two cutting edges—assuming we're talking about the axe. I've heard stories of an archer manifesting the Paragon of the Arrow, and when she took her shot, nine mirrored arrows would join hers to devastate her target."

"Where do they come from?"

"The paragons?" Victor nodded, and Khul Bach rubbed his chin. "I believe they're like spirits, great spirits that move on a different plane. They gather Energy from the dedication and focus of those who practice their craft. When they feel a practitioner has reached a certain level of art, they visit them with boons."

"You *believe*?" Victor frowned.

"Aye, young titan. I don't know. I wasn't given a secret manual of the universe with all of its secrets laid bare. No, I must learn from experience and make my own hypotheses about such matters. Are my answers not wise enough for you?"

"No, I didn't mean that . . ."

Khul Bach waved Victor's objection away. "How goes your conquest of these young fertile lands?"

"I think well, so far. We caught the invaders with their pants down. We've slain a few thousand of their troops, but I'm currently surrounded by a massive army. I'm not too stressed yet, though, because our main force is free and wreaking havoc while my smaller army keeps Hector's attention."

"Clever. A stiff thorn in his heel to distract him from the blade coming toward his neck? Is Hector the name of the enemy commander?"

"Yeah." Victor shook his head. Had it really been since before the Granite Gates that he'd spoken to Khul Bach? "He's some kind of powerful Death Caster. We're fighting a lot of undead."

"Ah. Death Casters are anathema to the living. Be wary of their wiles."

"I will. Hey, speaking of that, I captured one of his barons, and she's giving me intel. Do you think it's safe to bargain with her? I mean, all I intend to offer her is her life—I'll let her flee after we've won. In exchange, she's giving me information about Hector and his armies."

"So long as you guard your will when you're with her. Death Casters are dangerous in their own right, but many, for whatever reason, also have an affinity for mind Energy. Still, they suffer from the same primary desire most mortals do—the urge to keep living. If she'll trade information about this enemy army in exchange for her continued existence, it seems a triumph to me." He paused and frowned. "I doubt this enemy lord is eager for her to share all of her secrets with you. Be sure to guard her well . . ."

"Shit." Victor stood, suddenly stressed. How safe was Victoria in that tower? He'd placed three guards to watch her, but were they strong enough to *protect* her? Victor hadn't claimed the keep yet—would it even be difficult for some winged assailant to enter that tower? "Thank you, Khul Bach. I think I should check on her."

"Until we speak again." Khul Bach's words faded to a soft echo as Victor severed the connection of Energy to the bracer on his wrist, and the natural world snapped into focus. Despite knowing that he was probably overreacting, Victor stood up and jogged all the way out of his house, into the keep, and up the steps to the tower where Victoria was being held.

He was relieved to see the two Naghelli guards outside the door. "Any problems?"

"No, my lord," the woman on the left replied, and Victor thought her voice was familiar.

"Have you been on duty here since I first spoke to the prisoner?"

"Aye." Instead of calling him lord this time, she snapped a salute with her answer.

"Don't you need a break? Some sleep?"

"Of course, my lord. We take turns resting out here. I hope it's not against protocol . . ."

"No, only that I think it's a shitty duty. I could understand it for a short time, but there's no reason you three should give up your freedom to watch this woman. It could be months before I move her. I'll mention it to Kethelket and see that you have some guards to switch off with so you can get time to yourselves each day."

"Thank you, my lord. Going in?" She reached for the key in the door. Victor nodded, and she turned the key, pulling the door open. He braced himself; some small part of him was convinced that Victoria and the guard inside the room had been slain. His fears were unfounded, however. The guard stood by the windows watching Victoria from the side, and she sat with her hands folded in her lap. Victor wondered how uncomfortable she must be after hours and hours in that chair. Did the guards let her walk around to stretch? He stepped into the room, and the inside guard moved out, closing the door quietly behind him.

"Am I mistaken, or do you look relieved, Lord Victor?"

"I . . . had a sudden thought that it wouldn't be so hard for a talented assassin to reach you here."

"That may be, but you have not hobbled me. I'm far from defenseless. The guards you've placed with me seem quite capable as well." She smiled, exposing her strange teeth, more fit for an old skull than a youthful woman's face.

"Well, that's good. Still, I'm wondering if this is the best place for you. I think my travel home might serve better. It's, um, a kind of dimensional container. I think it might be harder for Hector or assassins to find you there."

"An extraplanar dwelling? Yes, Hector would not be able to sense my presence there easily."

"If I move the home, I'll have to take you out, but for now . . ." Victor nodded and called out, "Guards!"

The door crashed open, and the three Naghelli suddenly stood around Victoria with naked swords inches from her flesh. Victor had nearly forgotten how fast they could move with that strange shadow magic they all seemed to share. "My lord?" the slight guard he'd spoken to earlier asked.

"Sorry! Nothing's wrong, but we need to move her. We'll hold her in my travel home, but you'll still guard her, just as before. I'll lead the way. Follow me, Victoria, and please don't make eye contact with anyone we pass by."

"As you say, Lord Victor." Victoria waited until the Naghelli stepped back and sheathed their shining blades, then she stood and nodded her readiness. Victor turned and led the way back to his home, Victoria right behind him and the Naghelli keeping pace, shadowing them from various angles. They drew many stares from the soldiers in the keep, but Victor didn't say anything. He figured the sooner they passed by, the sooner the soldiers would get back to their duties.

He knew better than to expect to make it through the courtyard without drawing attention from Valla and Lam, so he wasn't surprised when they both, leaving Sarl to continue a meeting with his lieutenants, walked toward him from the gatehouse. "You're taking her somewhere?" Lam asked, frowning, but Valla just folded her arms, waiting for Victor's response.

"Just into my travel home. I suddenly grew concerned about an assassin. My home is warded and"—Victor glanced at Victoria—"extraplanar. We'll continue to guard her there."

"Ah!" Lam nodded, looking up to the top of the round tower where Victoria had previously been held. "Not a bad idea—if Hector has killers who can fly . . ."

"Not only fly but teleport short distances." Victoria spread her lips in that uncanny smile again. "I can, for instance." Victor whirled on her, Lifedrinker suddenly in his fist, but she held up a pale hand. "I am not keen on seeing true death anytime soon, Lord. I know you can track me down, so I will not flee. I've already promised you as much."

"Right," Victor grumbled. "Come on, then." A few minutes later, Victoria was seated in the same cushioned chair—one of the guards had brought it along in a storage device—in the center of one of the empty rooms in the home's lower level. "Comfortable?"

"The tower had better lighting . . ."

"Really? Banter already?"

"I'm sorry, Lord." Victoria looked down, and Victor suddenly felt like a bully. She was undead, probably three or four times his age, likely responsible for all kinds of atrocities back in her world, but she'd been cooperative with him.

"Just remember that we're not friends, all right? What else do you need? A better light? A bed? You can't be comfortable in that chair all the time."

"I have some things in one of my rings that would make this room much more tolerable for me." She looked up at him with a hopeful expression.

"We'll go over your belongings a bit later. I have to take care of something first, and, as you know, we're in the middle of a war. Your things are safe, though, and we'll do it soon. Understood?"

"Thank you!"

"All right." Victor turned and stepped outside, holding the door open for one of the guards to take his place. Once he'd closed it, he pointed to another empty room across the hall. "I'll be in there."

"As you say, Lord."

Victor sighed, stepped into the empty room, and was about to close its door when Valla appeared, silently descending from the stairs. He waited so she could step inside with him, then he pulled the door shut. "I was just about to, you know, eat that heart."

"I'm sorry! I came down because it seemed you'd become distracted with your prisoner, and I was curious what she might be saying. Should I leave?"

"Depends. You want to see me munch down on a raw heart?" Victor chuckled, then moved to the center of the room and sat down in a cross-legged position.

"It's not something I haven't seen before." Valla shrugged and sat down on the bare wooden floor beside the door. "Nothing dangerous will happen?"

"Uh." Victor frowned, looking at her. Hadn't he burst into flames when he ate the elder wyrm's heart? When he ate the night brute prince's heart, hadn't the room filled with tendrils of terror-attuned Energy? "That's not a sure thing. I don't really know how strong this heart is, compared to . . . other hearts. I think maybe you should wait outside."

"I think I'll be fine." She looked him in the eyes and smiled. "You wouldn't hurt me."

"No. It's not that, Valla. Sometimes the Energy I'm absorbing does things outside my body. When I ate the wyrm heart, I torched a huge area of the battlefield."

Valla sighed and stood up. With a scowl of scrutiny, she looked around the room, studying the close walls and low ceiling. "Is this a safe place, then? If you do too much damage in here, you could cause the home to collapse."

"Shit! Seriously?"

"I think it would take a lot—this home is designed to self-repair, and the material is very strong and dense. The . . . jade; I've forgotten the name."

"Ha, me too. Anyway, I guess I shouldn't risk it. I'll go back to the tower where we were holding Victoria. That way, if I explode, it will be above the rest of the keep." He laughed, but Valla wasn't smiling. "Do you want to come? I mean, it should be safe to wait a few steps down." Victor stood up and walked through the door as Valla opened it.

"I think I'll return to work with Lam and Sarl on the siege preparations. Sorry if I've disturbed your plans."

Victor put an arm over her shoulders—he was in a reduced size—and led her to the stairs. "Not at all, Valla. You might have just saved all of our lives!" He winked at the two Naghelli guards as they walked by.

"Perhaps!" She shook her head, and Victor couldn't tell if she was amused or dismayed. When they returned to the courtyard, she shrugged out from under his arm and said, "Please be careful, will you?"

"I will." He leaned down, and she kissed him softly, and then he hurried back into the keep, up the stairs, and into the now empty room at the top. He closed the door and sat in the center, looking around at the stained glass windows, admiring the play of colored light on the shiny black stones. "Well, she was right—the lighting in here is a lot better."

Victor severed the connection to his Shape Self spell, groaning with relief as his full power and potential returned, and his mass rapidly increased. "Right. Let's see here," he muttered as he formed the Iron Berserk pattern and cast the spell. His vision tinted red, his muscles and bones filled with roiling hot Energy, and he expanded again. Victor lifted his arms, a grunt that turned into a roar escaping his throat as he stretched, and his muscles erupted with power. Cords like iron stood out on his forearms and around his neck, and his wyrm-scale shirt grew to its natural size—Tes had crafted it for a true titan.

"Yes!" he grunted, enjoying the surge of power. Victor reached into his storage ring and pulled out the Ridonne Heart. He unfolded the bloody cloth and tossed it aside, feasting his eyes on the still-warm, bloody organ. His mouth began to salivate, and Victor took a bite, ripping a third of the flesh off and chomping on it. The rich coppery juices sluiced around in his throat, and when he swallowed them, Victor groaned with pleasure. He felt the power of the flesh almost immediately. It was hot and rich and began to roil in his gut as his Quinametzin body and soul began to consume it, along with its Energy and, Victor suddenly realized, a shard of spirit still clinging to the heart.

He felt that spirit, the bit of the Ridonne ancestor to whom the heart belonged, recoiling and fighting him, and suddenly Victor made another connection—that bastard was still alive somewhere. He growled and took another chomp of the heart, then focused his will on that spirit, squeezing it in his gut, holding tight. "You're not getting away, *pendejo*," he growled, droplets of hot blood running down his chin and onto his chest as he ground the meat of the heart in his mighty molars and swallowed down the chunks. He was reaching up with the last bite when the window before him shimmered brightly and exploded into colorful yellow and orange motes. A moment later, in a burst of crackling red electricity, a black-robed and cowled individual took shape before him.

"Wrong place," Victor grunted, then stuffed the last bit of the Ridonne's heart into his mouth.

29

WHAT YOU WISH FOR

Victor tried to focus on the strange hooded intruder, but he had a fiery battle taking place in his gut and with his spirit. He grunted as he sat there, crunching down on the remains of the heart, smashing the meat between his teeth, and then swallowing it. The being who'd appeared before him took a step back, brushing against the stone sill of the window. The hooded head glanced rapidly left and right, taking in the strange scene at the top of the tower. "Who are you?" The voice that echoed oddly out of the hood was definitively masculine, and as that dark cowl shifted to look more directly into Victor's eyes, some of the light coming through the windows penetrated those shadows to reveal smoldering orange eyes set within deep black sockets.

Victor didn't answer. He wasn't sure he could. He'd swallowed the last of the heart, and now he was truly battling the fragment of spirit the Ridonne had left behind. The only explanation Victor could muster was that it must have been tied to the heart's flesh. Now that he'd consumed it, the fragment of spirit was trying to flee this plane of existence, to rip through the fabric of time and space and rejoin the greater whole, which apparently was alive and well elsewhere in the universe. He growled and bore down with his will, surrounding the fragment with his Energy, calling on the instincts of his primogenitors to handle this strange situation.

This bit of spirit, this remnant of his foe, was what his bloodline would use to garner strength from the defeated Ridonne. Victor was too busy to think about it, but some part of him realized that this must be what happened when he pulled the hearts from his foes. Some instinctual magic in that ritual bound a bit of the departing spirit to the flesh, and when he pulled it forth and consumed it, the Energy or essence or some other intangible quality of the defeated enemy became his. He was determined to take his due from the Ridonne.

"I asked who you are, giant!" the hooded figure repeated, stepping closer, perhaps noting Victor's internal struggle and growing bolder, seeing his pre-occupation. Again, Victor ignored him, and the hooded figure stepped closer still. He would be a tall man with broad shoulders, but next to Victor's hulking form, he looked tiny. Victor sat, legs crossed, but still the hooded man had to look up to meet his gaze. He stared into Victor's eyes, but Victor was gazing inward, and it was evident he wasn't giving the hooded intruder any attention. "What goes on in there, giant? I can feel the Energies roiling within you. Have you consumed a racial advancement? Are you insensate? What a fortuitous occasion!"

Crackling red Energy began to spark around the intruder's black-gloved fingers, dancing and buzzing along those long digits and then arcing between his two hands. The energy created a red lattice of electricity that sparked and ignited something in the air, sending puffs of black smoke up to the domed ceiling of the tower. Just as a corner of Victor's mind became aware of the intruder's words and the bright red sparks flashing in his eyes, he finally managed to fully surround the Ridonne's spirit fragment with layers of his Energy, bearing down on it, smashing it, letting his bloodline work its mysterious magic, ripping it to shreds, and pulling it into himself on a cellular level.

A weird disembodied howl of agony broke through the fabric of reality and reverberated through the air, echoing through Victor's mind and apparently that of the intruder. His red sparking magic faded as he stumbled back and grasped his head, pushing his cowl back in the process. Victor had been fighting the battle of wills; he'd been prepared for the burst of Energy and whatever might come with it, so the howl didn't bother him much. He surged to his feet and inhaled deeply, swelling with the power of the heart now that he'd broken apart the Ridonne's still-living spirit fragment. Even large as he was, the tower's domed ceiling was spacious, and he lifted his arms wide and roared his triumph.

His outburst was so loud that, had one of the windows not been broken to serve as an outlet, he likely would have shattered more of the stained glass. The intruder was still staggering, gripping his ebon hairless head, but Victor didn't have attention to spare him. He was preoccupied with the rivers of hot red Energy surging through his pathways and into his Core, where he converted it to affinities that suited him. As the power pulsed through him, he began to notice a subtle change in his essence. He felt it tickling his bones and pulsing out through him into the weird extra dimension where he always observed his Core, his pathways, and his aura. Along with the sensation, an otherworldly scene took shape in his mind's eye.

Stazzo-dak stood tall under the red glower of the Vizashath sun. He cut an impressive figure—the height of two grown Shadeni, one standing atop the other, burnished red-gold flesh, crimson-feathered wings that shimmered with the ruby light of his Energy, and a crown of ebon horns that were the envy of his peers. He shouldn't feel nervous, he reminded himself. He was a proud archon of his people. Steeling himself, he looked out over the assembled forces. Before him stretched rank upon rank of gold- and crimson-clad soldiers. They stood on the field that spanned from the orange grass before his podium to the extent of his vision. As he turned left to right, letting his gaze glide over their burnished helms, he saw that their ranks extended to every horizon.

Half a million soldiers, half a million natives of Ridonne stood before him, ready to march against the Thivaan at his bidding. Stazzo-dak relaxed his will and allowed his Aura of Command to roll out, touching the soldiers nearest his platform, perhaps ten thousand of them, a drop in the great sea of conscripts, but enough to spread his influence. He felt their attention focus. He felt his aura bending them to his state of mind. When he lifted his voice to address them, it mattered not what he'd say; his aura had done most of his work for him.

"Listen well, soldiers!" he began . . .

Victor blinked rapidly, the weird vision fading from his mind to be replaced by his reality. He immediately became aware of a deep burning pain in his leg, and when he looked down, he saw the robed intruder standing there, stabbing a spear of crackling red Energy into his thigh. He grunted and brought his fist, larger than the intruder's head, down to swat him away. As his knuckles cracked into the man's shoulder and neck, he felt bones break. The intruder tumbled back to smash into the stone wall, his head shattering a pane of blue stained glass. The spear of Energy winked out of existence, and Victor felt immediate relief as his Berserk healing closed the wound.

The intruder groaned, and Victor stepped toward him, but the man burst into crackling red lightning and disappeared with a *zwap*. Nothing but black smoke hung in the space where he'd been, and Victor whirled, scanning the room. No sign of the intruder remained. He stepped over to the window the strange cowled man had come through and peered out. Shouts echoed up to him from the courtyard below, and Victor saw a flurry of activity. The window was too small for him to fit through, or he might have flung himself out when he saw what was happening.

The intruder was on the ground, each hand clutching a long red-lightning whip that snaked out to snap and rip at the soldiers surrounding him. Victor vacillated for a couple of seconds on what he should do. Should he drop his Berserk and jump out the window in his natural state? Would he survive the fall without injuries? No, he decided, he'd run for the courtyard. He'd just begun to turn when he saw Valla step forward into the square, Midnight in her hands, blue lightning and wind wrapping her like a crackling miniature tornado as she streaked toward the assassin.

Victor turned and ran for the door, yanking so hard on the little knob that he wrenched it from its hinges. He leapt down the steps, a flight at a time, and reached the bottom in seconds. Soldiers ran for the main doors of the keep, cries of alarm in their throats. To them, it must seem the keep was under attack. Maybe it was, Victor reasoned; just because he'd only seen the one invader didn't mean there weren't more. He leapt from the balcony to the front entry hall and stormed for the door, trying not to stomp or knock down any of his soldiers.

When he burst out, he found hundreds of soldiers standing in a circle, crowding the courtyard and lining the parapets. At their center, Valla and the whip-wielding invader were fighting. Victor wanted to scream at the soldiers to get in there and help her, but then he saw how they held their weapons and shields up, making a circle, and he wondered if this was Valla's wish. Had she warned them off, wanting to do battle with the invader alone? His suspicion solidified as he saw Kethelket and Lam standing near the gatehouse, on the inner ring of observing soldiers, watching Valla's struggle with intent worried expressions. They wouldn't hold back unless she'd told them to.

Victor stood at the top of the steps outside the keep and did battle with himself, turning the full force of his will against his urge to leap over the assembled fighters and interfere, smashing the intruder to a pulp. Instead, he let his rage simmer in his pathways, and he watched the woman he'd professed his love for, truly watched her in a way he hadn't in a long time.

Valla's style with her sword differed significantly from Kethelket's. She wielded Midnight in an alternating two-handed and one-handed grip. She moved with speed and fluidity, which made her fight look more like a dance. Kethelket knew a million counters, combinations, and gambits, but Valla's grace made you forget you were watching someone in a fight. It made you want to drop everything and learn to move like her. Despite the invisibly fast cracks of the invader's red-lightning whips, she always seemed to be elsewhere when they snapped on empty air. She surged with the speed of the wind, her sword like a moonbeam arcing out of a gusting breeze.

At first, the intruder matched her, winking out of existence in quick bursts of bright crackling red lightning, only to appear behind or to the side of her. From his new position, he would snap his long buzzing whips, but Valla was too quick, too aware, too graceful to be caught. Midnight might parry a whip, or she might flash away in a burst of speed before it snapped. In either case, she was unscathed, and Victor could see she was taking a toll on the intruder. Each time he teleported, he covered less distance. Each time he snapped that whip, his smoldering orange eyes telegraphed the strain.

Victor found himself clutching his fists, his knuckles white with the effort as he watched, every part of him trembling to interfere, but he knew how that would look to the soldiers and how it would infuriate Valla. She was winning, and he needed to bide his time and watch, much as he had during her duel in Coloss. At least here, she wasn't fighting a rigged match. "She's kicking his ass!"

"Aye, my lord!" a nearby Naghelli said.

"What a fighter!" another soldier cried, making Victor glance away from the fight to look at the watching troops. They were riveted by the contest, eyes tracking every move, mouths opening and closing in silent reactions, clearly stunned and impressed by the prowess of their tribune primus. More than ever, Victor realized he couldn't interfere. This invader's assassination attempt had turned into a duel, whether he liked it or not, and the soldiers would be demoralized if he involved himself.

The more he watched, though, the less Victor worried. Valla still seemed fresh and graceful, unscathed, while the intruder's face continued to betray his strain. His lightning whips were shorter, and he swung them less frequently. He'd stopped teleporting and was fighting in a constant circular backpedal, using the reach of his whips to keep Valla at bay. After several seconds of that, his whips disappeared with a crackling sizzle, and suddenly a single six-foot spear of lightning appeared in his hands. It was obvious, to Victor at least, that he'd summoned a less Energy-intensive weapon.

Valla smiled and paused, whipping Midnight in an elaborate flourish as she bowed. Was she signaling something? Victor decided he really needed to read up on dueling etiquette. The stranger only scowled at her gesture and hefted his big crackling spear. Valla streaked forward and, in a series of feints and slashes that Victor struggled to follow, she knocked the spear aside, hacked the assassin's left leg off at the knee, and glided past him. Midnight arced up, and Valla pivoted, bringing the sword down on the back of the intruder's neck. In the silence that followed the brilliant attack, the intruder's bald ebon head struck the stones of the courtyard with a hollow *thunk* that brought to mind a melon rolling off a kitchen counter.

"Jesus," Victor invoked, for once sincere in his holy appeal. He snatched Lifedrinker from her harness and lifted her high, screaming, "Valla!"

The soldiers were quick to take up the cry, and soon they were chanting and stomping their feet. "Valla! Valla! Valla!"

Valla whipped Midnight in another flourish, sending droplets of black blood spattering to disappear against the equally dark courtyard stones, then she sheathed the magical blade. She turned a slow circle, and when her eyes fell on Victor, her lips twitched in a small smile as she bowed. Suddenly, motes of purple Energy began to bubble up from the intruder's corpse. When hundreds of them had burst into existence, they flowed together and surged into Valla, lifting her into the air, arms wide, face lost in the ecstasy of Energy euphoria. The soldiers' cheers grew louder as though they were lifting her up, and Victor's heart pounded as the warmth of pride poured through him.

It was a different sensation, that pride. He wasn't proud of himself; he wasn't stoking the flames of his glory affinity. He was proud of Valla, and if he hadn't already been so fond of her, he would have found himself smitten at that moment. He wondered how many soldiers were silently proclaiming their love for his girlfriend. He chuckled as that term entered his mind. Girlfriend. Victor shook his head at the notion; it seemed too juvenile for what he felt. Watching Valla absorb her Energy, Victor finally noticed a System message in the corner of his vision. He'd been so intent on catching the intruder and watching Valla that he'd completely disregarded it. With a brief concentration, he brought it to the fore:

*****Congratulations! You have gained a new feat: Aura of Command.*****

*****Aura of Command: The right to rule runs in your blood. Those exposed to your aura become aware of your nature and, should their will prove weaker than yours, they will be more amenable to your commands.*****

Victor frowned as he read the description. Was that the secret of the Ridonne? Had they gained their power by pushing their will upon the people of Fanwath? He didn't like the sound of it and was a little disturbed to know it was now a part of him. Was it something he could control? Would he be forced to keep his aura in check now if he didn't want to influence the people around him unfairly? Victor's frown deepened as he remembered his conversation with Valla about gaining something he didn't want from the Ridonne. He'd scoffed at her, and now he found he very well may have done just that.

Victor let his Iron Berserk drop, and as his size came more in line with the people around him, he sat down on the step. He watched as Valla came back to herself, listened to her celebrate with the soldiers around her, and hated that he wasn't able to stop stewing about the feat he'd gained from the Ridonne heart. He was dimly aware of the soldiers' excited chatter, of the slaps on his shoulders and back as the bolder ones congratulated him on Valla's success as though he had something to do with it. He heard Sarl shouting for order, Kethelket calling his Naghelli to him, and then he felt Valla's cool hand on his wrist as she sat beside him.

"Thank you for letting me have that fight." Her voice was soft, and despite her victory, she sounded trepidatious. When Victor realized that, he was able to snap out of his funk long enough to look at her and see the concern in her eyes.

"Hey." He forced a smile. "I was so proud of you. What a fighter you've become!"

"But you seem upset."

"It's not about you, though. I loved watching you fight, and . . ." He sighed and let his words fade. "Don't worry about me, Valla. I ate that Ridonne's heart and it wasn't the experience I'd hoped, that's all."

"Do you want to talk about it?" She added her other hand to the one on his wrist and squeezed gently with them both. Victor loved her touch; he loved her attention, but he felt gross and dirty, and something in him didn't want anyone to be kind to him just then. He cleared his throat and stood up.

"Not right now. I think Kethelket's getting ready to try to burn the forest down. Let's see how things are going." He paused a moment, then added, "And we should check out that guy you killed." He didn't look her in the eyes, and he forced a hollow smile to his lips as he started down the steps. He'd have to come to grips with the new feat somehow, but he didn't want to dwell on it at the moment; shit was about to get crazy around Black Keep.

30

❧

CORRESPONDENCE

Victor hefted the lead-stoppered blue jar in his hand, watching the thick liquid sluggishly slosh around inside. "It just starts burning when broken?"

"That's right." Kethelket grinned as Victor handed it back. "Once the containment runes are broken, the alchemical mixture will ignite. We have ten for each of my Naghelli. As you'd planned, we'll try to lure the undead further into the forest, then we'll fly past them, into the thicker trees, and start bombarding."

"Good." Victor did the math as he looked over Kethelket's winged troops massing on the battlement, lining up to receive their bombs. He had two hundred here at Black Keep, having left some back at the pass and still more with Borrius and Rellia. "Two thousand firebombs ought to do the trick!"

Sarl spoke up. "I'd have had my doubts, considering this mist, but the alchemical agent is meant to cling to surfaces and burns very hotly. We tested it on a section of grass, and the mist retreated before the heat."

"That's great. Be sure to award your alchemists with an extra campaign token." Victor turned back to Kethelket. "No sign of giant mutant undead monstrosities coming this way?"

"My scouts have not reported back yet for this hour, but, as of the last, no."

"Right. Well, let's get this show on the road." Victor watched as the alchemists and their assistants continued to make their way down the line of waiting Naghelli, handing out their explosive jars. After a minute, he cleared his throat and raised his voice. "Naghelli! I'd like to speak to you briefly before you depart!" The conversations died down, and soon the only sound was the clink of glass as the crates of bombs were slowly emptied.

Victor continued, "When you joined the conquest expedition, there were many among us who had their doubts about your intentions. In my mind, you've already proven yourselves, but after your heroics in the last few days, none can doubt the sincerity of your bravery! Here we are, asking you to risk your lives again, flying into this shitty, clinging, death-stinking mist to confront a monstrous host, and it's not without risk! If you somehow get knocked out of the sky, you'll face a thousand times your number of undead out there. If that happens, I want you to retreat and try to regroup. If it's chaos and you can't find your brothers and sisters, then make your way north, out of the mist."

Everyone had grown even more quiet and still at his words, and Victor didn't want them to feel demoralized by his doom-laced words. "Listen! That's a worst-case scenario. If all goes well, you'll fly out, throw your bombs, and fly back. We appreciate the risk you're taking, and we know that each of you represents one of the very last of your kind. Don't sell your lives cheaply!" Victor didn't know where some of the phrasing of his words was coming from; it wasn't the way he usually spoke, but he supposed he'd heard people speak that way before, and his brain was just better at pulling stuff out of the recesses of his memory than it used to be. That said, he didn't want to end on a dour note, so he lifted Lifedrinker and screamed, "Now get out there and torch some *pinché* undead!"

His words brought a cheer out of the darkly clad flyers, and many of them lifted firebombs in their hands as they cheered, which made Victor more than a little nervous. Still, he laughed and cheered and then watched as Kethelket took command of his troops, ordering them into the air. They split in the misty twilit sky into two lines of flying shadows, each circling the keep in opposite directions. Victor knew they were planning to use ranged attacks to draw the undead into a chase, trying to lure the ones in the open clearing around the keep into the forest before flying farther out and lighting their fires.

They'd only been at Black Keep for a little over a day, but he was both nervous and optimistic about the timing of their attack. On the one hand, he worried the invaders' heavy reinforcements they'd been anticipating would arrive at any moment, and on the other, he hoped they were close—maybe they'd be caught in the fire, too.

"They'll be all right," Valla said, though Victor felt her words were meant to reassure herself just as much as him.

"Yeah, I mean, the undead out there don't have ranged attacks to speak of . . ."

"Unless something worse lurks farther into the woods." Edeya shrugged, and Victor nodded, pleased to see that she was speaking up more and more, even with other commanders present. If it were up to him, she'd see a promotion soon.

Valla leaned forward, peering into the dim light, and then turned to Lam. "Wouldn't the scouts have seen them? We've had Naghelli flying out there all day."

Lam nodded. "I think so. I've also flown out a couple of times and seen no sign of anything other than this mindless horde." She pointed. "Look! They've started to draw them." Victor followed her gesture to see sparks and flashes in the darkness, and he knew the Naghelli were throwing spells down at the horde.

"Can't really see much through the fog." The flickers and flashes grew in intensity and number, and then they seemed to fade, and Victor knew the Naghelli were moving farther into the woods. He'd been tempted to claim the keep, hoping it would cause the obscuring haze of death magic to withdraw as it had around Old Keep, but they'd been afraid it would tip their hand to Prince Hector. So much had been happening, and things were going well, he'd decided to hold that card for later. Thinking of things going well, he turned to Edeya. "Any further word from Borrius and Rellia?" The main army had earlier reported a decisive victory over yet another of Hector's undead armies; their ambush had gone off flawlessly.

Edeya pulled out her command book and skimmed the most recent entries. "They've burned the corpses on pyres and are marching on a keep that their Naghelli scouts have located six leagues to the south. Borrius says it's similar in size and fortifications to Old Keep, though it's clearly of different origin."

Victor cracked his knuckles and clenched his jaw, trying to think of something he should be doing. Valla must have read his mind because she said, "I know it's hard to leave matters in the hands of others, but right now you're doing what you must. We're still likely to be attacked here, so we must wait a while to see how this fire gambit will play out."

"Yeah, I know." Victor glanced at Valla and met her eyes, noting some dirt or ash or something smudged on her chin. His instinct was to reach out and brush it off, but he knew that would probably irritate her, especially with Lam and the others standing nearby. Instead, he said, "You've all been working hard with no rest. Let's grab a minute while we can. If the firebombs work, we'll know soon enough."

"Victor? Um, Legate?" Edeya said, holding up a different Far Scribe book, a thinner, narrower one. "You asked me to keep an eye on this, and I noticed a new message from your, uh, cousin, is it?"

"Seriously?" Victor had only given the book to Edeya the day before and hadn't had any new correspondence from Olivia then.

"Yes! I checked before coming up here to watch the send-off, and there it was."

"Right. Well, I'm off to check on the troops." Sarl saluted and marched away, but Lam and Valla didn't seem to have any such intention. Victor sighed and held out his hand, resigned to having an audience watch him read the message. Edeya handed him the book, and he flipped to the last written-in page:

Victor,

I hope this message finds you in good health and that your military campaign is having some success. I'd be dishonest if I didn't say I know you've already had a run-in with the imperial forces. Word has traveled, even all the way out here to the "frontier," as the Ridonne citizens call our corner of the wilds. I know you've been hoping for an update about ap'Gravin and the magic he used to summon you, but I'll rip the bandage off and let you know that I haven't learned anything. Ap'Gravin has fled, and though I intend to track him down, I've been preoccupied with matters closer to home.

First Landing has gone through a bit of a political upheaval recently, and I've been needed here to help maintain some stability as power has shifted away from some of the original council members. You see, there was a bit of a scandal, but I won't bore you with all the details. Suffice it to say that things are looking better, and I think the human colony is in good hands. We're going to be moving away from the simple council leadership model, and as we expand, we will be establishing a parliamentary system with executive, legislative, and judicial branches. This is important because we're looking to set First Landing up as a free city outside the control of the Ridonne Empire.

I don't want to get lost in the details here; I know you're probably busy, but I wanted you to know that I've made contact with a member of Rellia ap'Yensha's clan through Fainhallow Academy and that I'll be able to use one of her family portals to visit when you get things settled. Once I'm there, I'll give you a portal stone that will link First Landing to your settlement, if that's still amenable to you.

The link will be purely for travel and convenience; we are not trying to lay claim to your lands in any way, though should you desire it, I'm sure the argument could be made for adding whatever settlement you establish as a member state.

I've been using your story as an example to the people here, trying to educate them on the dangers of complacency. Even after the troubles we've encountered, many of the citizens of First Landing aren't convinced that the pursuit of personal strength is all that important. Many live as though they're still on Earth, seeking to establish themselves financially or politically or, worse, to live a simple peaceful life raising their children. As much as I admire such an idyllic pursuit, I don't think the human species is yet in a position to stop and smell the roses, so to speak. There are great powers out there, and I don't mean just the Ridonne Empire.

To that end, I was hoping there might come a time when you could visit and give a talk or lead a public square discussion or something of the sort. You could talk about your time in other worlds, highlighting the ease of travel between planets for the powerful and also the dangers those powerful beings represent. As I said, I know you're busy, but perhaps you'd consider this request when things have settled down. I think it would be good for you to set your eyes on the human colony here, in any case; I know you have people in this world you care about, but won't it be good to eat some familiar foods, hear some familiar music, and perhaps make some connections here among people who share so much heritage with you?

I'm sorry this letter brought you no answers but only requests. I'm sorry that ap'Gravin is a cowardly worm who fled, perhaps completely off-world, when he caught wind of his son's transgressions. I'm determined to find answers for you, though, and I'm a woman who has a way of making things happen. I'll check this book daily in hopes of hearing from you. I look forward to getting to know you better, cousin.

In much anticipation,
Olivia Bennet

"Huh," Victor said, reverting back to his old vernacular.

"Well?" To his surprise, it was Edeya who prompted him, though Lam and Valla also watched his face intently.

"Oh, well, nothing much. She didn't get any answers for me, and she wants me to visit." He shrugged. "I wasn't expecting much anyway." He snapped the book closed and handed it to Edeya.

"Aren't you going to write back?" Valla reached for the book.

"Maybe, but I'm kind of busy. You know, in the middle of a war." He gestured into the disturbingly quiet fog-filled night.

"You seem upset," Edeya said, handing the book to Valla. "Are you sure there wasn't anything—"

"I'm fine," Victor growled, then he snatched the book from Valla. "I'll be in my house. Come and get me if something happens." He turned and walked, not waiting for an answer, and anyone looking at his face would see that he knew he was being a jerk. He almost stopped and apologized, but he didn't. He stomped down the steps, over the courtyard, and into his house. He pointedly didn't think about anything until he'd gone into his library and sat down in one of the comfortable chairs. Sitting there, staring at the book-cases, only about ten percent full of books, he frowned and tried to figure out why he was feeling pissed off.

He supposed it would be easy to say he was mad that ap'Gravin was in the wind and, along with him, any further answers about how Victor had been summoned—if he'd been brought through time intentionally, by accident, or at all. What if he was from a different universe? The stupid idea had been tickling the back of his mind lately, but he had no idea if such a thing was possible. He'd heard people use "universes" in the plural sense, but he didn't know if they were using the term generically to mean the vastness of the cur-rent universe combined with different planes of existence and all the things in between.

Still, he'd found himself fantasizing that his *abuela* was alive and well in a different universe with a slightly different timeline than this one. At other times, he was at peace with the idea that his *abuela* had moved on and even thought of her living among his other ancestors. The truth was, Victor had no idea how such things worked, and he knew it. Sitting there alone, stewing in his bad mood, he began to realize that a part of him had believed his new "cousin" would come through with some answers. He'd offloaded some of the weight of his worries and, worse, his hopes on her, and now he was pissed off that she'd failed. He knew it was irrational. He knew she'd said she wasn't giving up, but he couldn't help how he felt. Could he?

"Yeah, I can," he sighed. He could do better; he knew what was bother-ing him, and he knew it wasn't something he or, more importantly, Olivia could control. With an audible groan, he summoned a pen from his ring and opened the book:

Olivia,

I don't blame you for not being able to get answers. I also don't expect you to. Don't do anything foolish or dangerous trying to figure out something that likely was an accident. Ap'Gravin isn't some kind of mysterious magical genius. He hired Boaegh to try to build up his own power and probably didn't pay any attention to what that evil bastard was doing. I'll get my answers someday, but I doubt they'll come from that little prick.

You're right about the worlds being full of dangerous things and people, but they're also full of wonder and mystery. It's good that you're trying to get the people from Earth to accept their new reality and see beyond whatever little lives they're building there in First Landing, but you should also know that plenty of natives do just that. I'm sure you've seen the simple people living in the village around Fainhallow. Not everyone is suited for adventure and power, and if someone doesn't feel the drive or calling, you can't force it.

I wouldn't wish my experiences on anyone, to be honest. It's a miracle of lucky coincidences that I'm even alive to write this. Well, that's not true—you mentioned that I've met people I care about, but that's a massive understatement. I wouldn't be alive if I didn't have these people to care about and to care about me. Olivia, personal connections are essential, especially for someone who's an emotional wreck like me. You know, we really don't know a lot about each other, having only met once, so why don't I write a little about myself? Maybe you can do the same, and next time we meet, we might feel like real cousins who actually know each other.

You see, an important thing I learned right away when I got summoned to this world was that I'm a very emotional person. I am so emotional that my Core and the affinities I have are based on emotions. They call it a Spirit Core, but what I've learned is that our spirits are built up of our aspects, our virtues and vices, our experiences, and our feelings about those experiences. I had a lot of rage in my heart when I first got here, and I might have become something a lot worse if I hadn't been shown compassion and love by some of the first people I met . . .

Victor wrote for a long time, losing himself in his story and finding some genuine therapy in the act of writing about his experiences in the Wagon Wheel. He finished writing about how Yund had betrayed him, selling him to ap'Horrin, and decided to call it good for the time being. He signed the letter, asking Olivia to get back to him soon, and snapped the book closed, feeling as if he'd dropped a heavy weight, one which had sat on his shoulder for a long, long time. Was that all it took to feel better about something, to write about it?

He was still sitting in that comfortable chair in his library when he heard the front door open and close, and then Valla quietly stepped into the room. She had a funny expression, and Victor figured it had something to do with her being mad at him, mixed with feeling sorry for him, mixed with not knowing if she should interrupt him. He headed things off by saying, "I'm really sorry I was an asshole earlier. I wrote a bunch of stuff to Olivia, and I hope you'll read it, too. It's stuff I never talk about."

Her expression brightened, and she said, "Really? I think I'd like that. Can I see it later, though? I think your plan is working, Victor. The darkness is gone, and the night is aglow with orange light bleeding through the fog. I think the forest is truly burning."

Victor stood up, something unwinding in his chest. At some level, he'd been afraid his forest fire plan would fail. "Yes!" He started toward her, slipping his Far Scribe book into a storage ring. He'd just pulled her into a hug when the door opened and slammed again. A moment later, Lam stormed into the room.

"Valla, check your Far Scribe book! The legion's under attack! Also, Kethelket is here; some of his people are missing. He's enraged, Victor. He's raving about betrayal!"

31

⧓

ALLIES IN NEED

Victor sprang out of the chair and started for the foyer at Lam's words, brushing past her. His mind raced, trying to make sense of what she'd said. As he hurried toward the front door, he gave voice to his questions. "What do you mean? What betrayal?"

Lam and Valla were right behind him, and Lam said, "Not sure! I came to get you immediately. He's talking to Sarl." Victor's mind continued to spin, dark scenarios playing out—had Kethelket's people betrayed him? Had he failed to root out all of Belikot's loyalists? Was Prince Hector about to gain some new followers with intimate knowledge of Victor's military structure, positions, and capabilities?

Victor stepped out of his house, planning to jog up to the ramparts, but found himself face-to-face with Kethelket. "I need to speak to her!" he growled by way of greeting. His face was streaked with blood, soot, and grime, and his dark depthless eyes looked unusually strained.

"Who?" Victor asked.

"The undead witch. She lied, and my people died as a result!" Victor noticed that one of Kethelket's longswords was naked in his hand, blade pointed down beside his leg. "I need answers!"

"Whoa! Tell me what happened first, Captain." Victor hoped the use of his honorary title would ground the man, but Kethelket only scowled further.

"There were no giant abominations, no heavy reinforcements coming this way. Instead, we faced great winged monstrosities in their hundreds.

Thousands! They came upon us from the south as we lit our flames. We saw the moon and the green star fade from view as their wings darkened the night sky, and then they were upon us. My people, Victor! The last of our kind! Less than half of us got free!" While he spoke, Victor gazed upward, scanning the parapets, wondering where this horde of flying monstrosities was; why weren't they attacking the keep?

"Where are they?"

"That's your question? My people die, we become extinct before your eyes, and you seek to verify my tale?"

"No, Kethelket!" Victor growled, the man's fury sparking a similar emotion to life in Victor's heart. "I'm trying to determine if we need to brace for an attack!"

"As we broke free, those of us who could, they fell back, flying south, away from the burning forest. They clutched my kin, paralyzed, in their talons!"

"Valla, Lam, get in touch with Borrius and Rellia. I'll need an update when I come out. Kethelket, come with me." Victor waited a moment to lock eyes with Valla, to see her nod in understanding, then he stepped into his house. With Kethelket striding beside him, he hurried downstairs to the room where Victoria was being held.

"Stand aside," Kethelket growled as they approached the door to her room, and his men hurried out of their way. Victor pulled the door open and stepped inside. He'd been half expecting Victoria to be gone, dead, or something equally vexing, but he found her sitting on her chair, a look of surprise evident as he and Kethelket strode into the room. He saw Kethelket lift his sword, blue flickers of Energy dancing over the dark metal, but Victor held out an arm, barring the man from pressing too close to his prisoner.

"Victoria," he said, hoping to get ahead of Kethelket's burgeoning outburst. "Tell us about Hector's flying troops."

"His flying . . ."

"Gray, hairless, yellow eyes, wings that make Victor's arm span seem small!" Kethelket growled, lifting the point of his sword and gesticulating with it as though to punctuate his words. Victor had never seen the man, usually so calm and cool with his advice, agitated like that.

To her credit, Victoria didn't flinch before Kethelket's rage. She didn't shrink back from his sword point. She looked Victor in the eye and said, "You describe creatures belonging to Baron Dunstan. He's a creature similar to Eric Gore Lust. A type of vampyr, though he dubs his creatures, his followers, wampyr—in their monstrous form, they have wings and can fly.

He holds the keep south of here, south of this forest on the shores of the Silver Sea."

"Silver Sea?" Suddenly, Victor felt stupid. Why hadn't he made Victoria draw a map depicting what she could of the Marches?

"A great body of water that borders the western edge of these lands." She turned to Kethelket and said, "You'd be able to see it, flying out over the forest, if not for the fog Hector has summoned to obscure and poison his lands."

"Why did you not warn us of these flying fiends? Why did you spin tales of hulking monstrosities bound to the ground?" A note of desperation hung in Kethelket's words, and Victor knew the man was strained to the breaking point. What must it be like to know that you were in charge of the remnants of an entire species? What must it be like to know that each time you flew out to do the bidding of a giant stranger, you risked extinction? As he examined his use of the Naghelli in that light, Victor felt shame, even though Kethelket and his kin had insisted they wanted to help.

"I wasn't trying to hide anything! I answered the questions Victor asked of me! I thought it most likely Hector would send his heavy champion, Karl the Crimson, to face his might." Though she answered Kethelket's question, her pale blue eyes locked with Victor's.

"Why did he take my people alive? Are they doomed?" Kethelket had lowered his sword, and his voice had lost much of its angry edge, though a note of desperation still clung to his words.

"He's a fiend, sir." Victoria looked Kethelket in the eyes, and Victor saw his rage continue to cool as the ancient Naghelli saw the genuine sympathy in her expression. "He will torment and torture them. He'll turn as many as he can into followers and feed upon the rest."

"How many of these 'wampyrs' are there?" Victor growled.

"I'm not sure. I'm sorry, but I never set foot in Dunstan's lands, not here and not back on Dark Ember. Hundreds? I doubt it can be much more than a thousand; otherwise he'd be too hard for Hector to control. He's a very powerful creature. Much stronger than Eric or me. He holds the largest of the outer keeps, a great double-walled castle that backs up to a cliff beside the sea. He bragged at great length the last time Hector called us to a council, describing great winding tunnels and sea caverns that open up in its depths."

"Then I must go." Kethelket turned, sliding his sword into its sheath and moving toward the door.

"Hold, Kethelket." Victor put a hand on his shoulder. "I'm coming with you."

Victoria peered at Victor, narrowing her eyes. "If he took your people, there's a chance they may yet live, though for how long, I don't know. Do you have time to march an army to his keep? It's thirty leagues or more from here, and the terrain isn't easy—forests and hills before you can descend toward the sea."

"I can make it fast. The army will remain here." Victor had never told Victoria about his strategies before. She didn't know that he only commanded a small part of their overall army here in Black Keep. She didn't know that Borrius and Rellia were elsewhere, hopefully winning another conflict with the bulk of the legion. He didn't intend to change that, just on the off chance that she might have some way of communicating with Hector or his people, just in case she might yet betray him.

"I can help you! I have magic tailored for such a challenge, Victor! Let me prove myself to you!" She saw his eyes narrow with doubt, saw that he was about to shut her down, and desperately pressed on. "I can hide you from his wampyrs. I can get you past his wards without alarming him! We can get to your people without his entire army learning of your presence and putting themselves in your way or, worse, slaughtering the prisoners before you can reach them."

The last point struck a note, and Victor glanced at Kethelket, hoping the older man would have an opinion. He frowned and nodded. "I have confidence in my ability to get past his guards, but I'm not sure I could find my people without raising an alarm. If she can do as she claims, perhaps . . ."

"I can move quickly, too! I can take on an incorporeal form and fly beside your friend here."

"You can?"

"Yes! Please, Victor, let me help you! Let me earn some bit of trust from you and your people. I do you no service languishing imprisoned. Let me help you against Prince Hector with more than simple information. I'm doomed if he wins this war, so let me aid in his destruction!"

Victor frowned and rubbed at his chin. He could feel Kethelket's agitation; the man wanted to be moving, and he couldn't blame him. His people were in grave danger, and every second they lingered here deliberating put them at further risk. If he trusted this woman, this undead creature, to help him, then he was risking her betrayal. And so what if she betrayed him? Was he so worried about her that he'd refuse a chance to save a hundred or more of Kethelket's people? "All right. Walk with us, and do not use your Energy until you've cleared it with me. Every time." He stared at her until she nodded.

"Understood."

Victor left the room, glanced at the guards, and said, "You can return to normal duty for now." With Kethelket and the Death Caster in tow, he walked out of his home, only to find Edeya, Valla, Lam, and Sarl waiting for him right outside. The sky was aglow with orange light, the fog in the air strangely illuminated, amplifying the glow of the fires raging through the forest surrounding the keep. When Valla laid eyes on Victoria, she hissed and drew Midnight. "Easy." Victor jerked a thumb at Victoria in her layered, gauzy black dress and robes. "She's going to help me and Kethelket rescue his people and, I suppose, kill another of Hector's barons."

"What?" Victoria and Valla both asked. Valla frowned and glared at the undead woman, and Victor turned to her with a raised eyebrow. Victoria stammered, "You didn't mention killing Dunstan!"

"Yeah. We'll capture the keep once we get Kethelket's people free." Victor shrugged as though it made perfect sense. Kethelket nodded, locking his dark eyes on Victor's; he was in agreement.

"Why infiltrate an enemy keep if you don't intend to do the most damage possible?" Kethelket grinned savagely, perhaps savoring the idea of some payback.

"He's very strong, Victor." Victoria clenched her pale long-fingered hands before her, clearly feeling some regrets.

"I'll come as well," Valla said, surprising no one.

"I have to get through those flames, Valla." Victor gestured to the orange sky. "I'll probably have to dismount and do some leaping; you know I'm not as sensitive to heat and fire as . . . others are." She knew he meant her, and she opened her mouth, prepared to argue, but he could see she was struggling to find the words to convince him.

"Perhaps I could cloak myself in winds and hurry through . . ."

"Those forests blaze with a terrible fury," Kethelket said, "not just a narrow band of flame, but miles of inferno. I could try to carry you past them." He folded his arms and looked past Valla into the courtyard where some of his people sat, drinking water and recovering from their ordeal. "I could order a pair of my people to transport you via a harness . . ."

"No. No, it's fine. I must accept that I can't always rush into battle with Victor. What shall the rest of us do while you're gone?"

"I can probably fly past the flames," Lam interjected.

"So could I," Edeya was quick to add.

Lam frowned at her. "I think not, Edeya! Your new wings are strong, but you've never flown more than a few hundred yards."

"Relax, you guys!" Victor growled, his agitation rising with every second he delayed his departure. "I need you all to stay with the army. There's a chance that not all the undead will die in this fire. There's a chance yet another army is coming to attack this keep. I want you to hold it, but don't claim it yet. Hector has to be wondering why we don't; he may assume we don't have enough people here to do so and send others to take control, in which case we'll need strong people here to help the Ninth battle them off. They may have a champion or two—hell, they might send that big asshole Victoria already warned us about. Valla, Lam, it'll be on you guys to defeat or hold him off until we finish our mission."

He looked at Kethelket, saw the agreement in his eyes, and continued, "We need to go. Every second we stand around, the captured Naghelli are more at risk." He looked at Victoria and then Kethelket. "You two fly. Now. I'll meet you due south of here, beyond the forest. I think you'll see me coming." Kethelket didn't wait for further instruction. He leapt into the air with a blur of black wings, flickering with the ochre light of his Energy.

Victoria said, "Cover your ears. For your protection." When Victor and the others did so, she took a deep breath and shrieked in a weird horrible multivoiced cry that echoed off the courtyard walls, then white misty Energy burst out of her, washing the color out of her flesh and giving it a strange translucent nature. She looked like a ghost. Without moving her lips, she spoke in a strange disembodied echoing voice, "I will await you beyond the flames. Thank you for your trust." Then she streaked into the air, quickly catching Kethelket and matching his pace.

"Roots!" Edeya said, watching her luminous black-clothed form streak into the glowing orange sky.

"I hope you didn't make a mistake . . ." Lam said softly, but Victor didn't feel like justifying himself. He turned to Sarl.

"Command your soldiers well, Captain. Don't lose this keep." Sarl saluted without a word, his expression serious and dour. Victor turned to Lam, Valla, and Edeya. "I'm counting on you three. Keep in touch with Borrius and Rellia. . . . Shit! Any word from them?"

Edeya brightened, and she spoke excitedly. "Yes! They had just captured the fortress south of Old Keep when another army arrived, perhaps meaning to add to the garrison there. The forces he described sounded a lot like the army we first met when you were scouting—shamblers, ghouls, giant skeleton drummers. They hurled themselves mindlessly at the walls, and the legion destroyed them."

"Borrius wants to keep pushing. He's sent scouts out looking for the next objective," Valla added.

"Okay. Okay, you guys. I'm sorry I have to leave right now, but I think this might pay off. I think we'll be in a great position if I can keep this Dunstan guy busy or kill him. That'll mean we have control of four of the five perimeter keeps, and a lot of Hector's troops will be dead—or I guess more dead. Destroyed. After the fire's gone and you've assessed things here, go ahead and claim the keep, Valla."

"I'll record any awards." Edeya held up her logbook. Victor had almost forgotten about that. The System would give them another chest when they claimed Black Keep. "Did Rellia claim the other keep? The one they just took?"

"Yes. They're calling it Rust Keep on account of it having an outer wall made from some kind of iron alloy. The bottom half of it is stained orange with rust." Lam shrugged. "Not a very pretty or creative name, but it's in keeping with the names you've chosen so far."

"They aren't permanent! Just for keeping track . . ." Victor shook his head, dismissing the topic. "I need to get going." He began to reach into himself, preparing to sever his connection to the Alter Self spell, allowing himself to expand to normal proportions and power, but Valla rushed forward and grabbed him into a hug. Victor hugged her back and winked over her head at Edeya and Lam, who both smiled and turned away, leaning close to whisper. Sarl saluted again and walked across the courtyard, calling for his lieutenants. Victor appreciated the courtesy, but he didn't care. He wasn't trying to hide his feelings for Valla anymore.

"Hush," he said, despite her silence. He put his hands on the sides of her face and tilted her head away from his chest so he could look into her eyes. "We'll be back together soon. As much as you might worry about me, you know I'm worried about you, all right? Stay safe, and don't do anything crazy. This is just a keep. Hold it if you can, but don't give your life for it."

Her brows creased, her eyes narrowed, and she said, voice firm, "I won't abandon any soldiers here. You know that."

"Yeah, I know." Victor hugged her again, happy she hadn't asked him to promise anything. "I've gotta go." He let go and kissed her softly once, then he opened the floodgates of his Core and cast Iron Berserk. As he surged in size and power, he summoned Guapo. The glorious mustang burst out of a pool of shimmering golden Energy, whinnied loudly, and rose up on his hind legs, pawing the air with his front hooves. "That's my boy." Victor laughed.

"He's something." Valla chuckled, and though she tried to make it nonchalant, Victor saw her wipe the back of her hand at the corner of her eye. He reached down with his gigantic hand and gently took her tiny palm between his thumb and fingertips, giving it a soft squeeze. She sniffed, nodded, and smiled at him, then he turned and sprang atop his stallion. As Guapo's hooves thundered over the black stones, he roared, "Open the gate!"

32

FROM FIRE TO SEA

As Victor and Guapo tore through the smoke-filled forest surrounding the keep, he truly began to appreciate how much his body had changed since he'd left Earth. It was one thing to say he was stronger or bigger or that he was sturdier and healed faster, but some of the more subtle changes weren't so glaring. They weren't things he noticed every day. Sure, he'd accepted the fact that the more he evolved, the more his body became dependent on Energy and the less sustenance it required from other sources, but he hadn't realized just how little he needed to *breathe*. That night, charging through dense rolling waves of hot smoke, he came to realize that he could take a deep breath and not think about breathing again for a very long time indeed.

He leaned forward, hugging close to Guapo's neck, and let the mustang do what he did best—run. With Guapo doing most of the work, even navigating through the forest, Victor's mind began to wander toward the changes that had occurred in his body as he'd advanced his race. Could he even call himself human anymore? He shook his head; he'd been down that road before. He was Victor, and that was the important thing. If his *abuela* saw him today, she'd know him. Thinking of the changes he'd gone through, he began to wonder what was in store. His race was at the seventh stage of "advanced." What would happen when he broke into epic? Was there something beyond epic? Did the System categorize "race" in the same way it did classes?

The undead were everywhere in the forest, but they wandered in the smoke, listless, only lashing out at Guapo if he came close. Even then, they seemed disoriented, and Guapo was huge and fast, and more often than not knocked the undead down before they could make contact with claws or rusty weapons. Victor was no expert on fires or the undead, but he had a feeling most of these slow dumb zombies, shamblers, and even ghouls would burn that night.

Guapo leapt over a fallen tree, crashing through smoldering underbrush, and Victor noticed that the smoke had a different quality now. It was hot and bitter, thick to the point that it burned even his advanced eyes. The air itself was stifling, and though it wasn't much of a concern for him, he began to wonder how resilient Guapo was. The mustang was a creature of spirit, of *his* spirit, and he'd seen him trample hundreds of undead, suffering many gashes and stabs, certainly more than a normal horse could handle. Would he be able to keep charging through these smoldering woods? What about when they came to the fire itself?

The thought of Guapo running into the flames, bravely pushing forward while he slowly burned, turned Victor's stomach, and he decided that when they got to the worst part of the fire, he'd send Guapo home to the spirit plane and make his own way through. That time came sooner than he'd expected. The orange glow in the sky had steadily grown brighter, the smoke had steadily grown thicker and hotter, and now Victor could hear it, a great roar that brought forth images of ancient locomotives or landslides or something equally massive and destructive. He'd never been in the proximity of a fire like this, and he found himself awestruck by its size and power.

He climbed off Guapo as they crested a slight rise in the forest. Down the slope, he saw the advancing line of fire, like a living, hungry monster, surging through the woods. A ravenous orange wave that consumed the trees, the undead, and anything else that hadn't fled; it was insatiable, relentless. Victor couldn't see what was beyond the wall of flames or tell how deep the furnace extended. All he saw was smoke and ash and embers. "See you soon, *Guapito*." He hopped off the mustang's back and sent him home in a cloud of sparkling Energy motes. Then, perhaps to bolster his confidence, he summoned his Banner of the Champion and charged toward those flames.

Victor's massive legs ate the slope in just a few bounds, and then he was careening into the face of the towering inferno. Fire didn't evoke fear in him the way it might most people, not since his ordeal with Boaegh, not since he'd nearly died from his magical fireballs and been burned from the inside out by the cleansing, scalding, final breath of the firedrake. More than that, Victor had a Magma Core in his chest and an affinity for fire-based

Energies. Combined with his titanic constitution and berserk healing ability, these made him quite confident that he could pass through this fire largely unharmed.

As he ran into the whipping, furious flames, smashing past staggering, smoldering undead, Victor bunched his great thighs and, using his Titanic Leap ability, launched himself upward and forward. He exploded through the smoky roaring fire, smashed tree branches that had yet to ignite, and then he was over the bulk of the smoke, and he could see and breathe clearly for a few seconds until he began to descend. He fell back down into the whirling cinder-filled clouds, squinting his eyes against the sting, and landed with a crash that shook the ground. He slid through hot ash, blackened tree branches, and the still smoldering corpses of the undead by the hundreds.

Victor smashed his way forward, bunched his legs, and did it again. It took him five leaps to make it through the worst of the forest fire, and then he was running through a smoky blackened wasteland. Trees still stood in the forest, though they were bare of leaves and soot-covered. The undergrowth was gone, and nothing remained of the undead who'd been in the area save their smoking bodies. Victor summoned Guapo again and swung himself onto his back. The two of them continued their mad dash to the south.

While they raced through the burned forest, Victor took stock of himself. His skin was soot-stained, and his eyes stung from the smoke, but he was otherwise unmarred by the flames he'd passed through. Even his leather pants had survived, and he supposed the material, being resilient in itself and enchanted for self-repair, had been the right choice for this endeavor. Lifedrinker was, of course, fine. She'd drained an ancient magma wyrm of his Energy and had a strong molten heart; he could probably toss her in a volcano, and she'd come out all right.

With Guapo's speed and the forest clear of many obstacles thanks to the fire, it didn't take too long to break free of the trees, and soon Victor found himself charging over moonlit grassy plains, the fire just an orange glow on the northern horizon, almost like a false sunrise. He'd been streaking over the grassland, Guapo's hooves leaving a bright trail of sparkling Energy, for a few minutes when he felt a presence nearby and slowed. He looked up to see Kethelket's orange and black wings blurring with effort as he streaked toward him. Keeping pace with the Naghelli prince was Victoria, a faintly luminous spectral figure that effortlessly flowed on the breeze.

When they landed next to Guapo, two tiny figures compared to the enormous titan-sized mustang, Victor could see that Kethelket was exhausted.

He held down a hand and said, "Come on. Ride with me on Guapo for now. Recover your strength."

"Aye." Kethelket took his hand and pulled himself up, surprising Victor with his lightness; even Valla was heavier than the tall thin Naghelli. "It's for the best."

"Victoria," Victor said as he turned to the spectral woman, "you lead the way." And so they ran, racing over the plains and hills, Victoria setting a pace that strained even Guapo's significant reserves of speed. If they passed within sight of enemy patrols or other creatures that might have been a threat, Victor never knew it. Enlarged as he was, riding a gigantic mustang faster than any creature native to Fanwath could run, they didn't linger in any area long enough to warrant caution. Besides, in Victor's mind, they didn't have time for caution; Kethelket's people could be dying or suffering with each second they delayed.

Even considering all that, Victoria had other ideas, and she led Victor ever downslope, into ravines and gullies, alongside rivers and streams that no doubt wended their way toward the Silver Sea she'd spoken of. Using those hillsides and narrow canyons as cover and as a means of descent, there was little chance anyone could see them from a distance, even with Guapo's showy, sparkling progress in the night.

Guapo had no trouble racing through shallow waters, running on the uneven stones of the streambeds that would have tripped or broken the legs of a natural horse. His uncanny ability to balance and run over the ground without disturbing the soil seemed to know few limits, and so they made incredible time as the Death Caster flew ahead with Victor and Kethelket close behind on the spirit steed's steady back. The moons were still out, and the sun had yet to brighten the eastern horizon when they charged out of a tree-choked gulley onto gravel-strewn sand that stretched for half a mile to the shores of a beautiful placid body of water.

The invaders must have named it the Silver Sea because they'd first found it at night, for it reflected the light of the Sisters with a pale, shining luminescence that truly brought to mind the luster of the precious metal. "Is there something in the water to make it shine so?" Kethelket asked, echoing Victor's curiosity.

"No idea, but it's something else, isn't it?" Victor scanned the water, wondering if he could see the far shore, but no hint of it touched the horizon. Looking from right to left along the sandy shoreline, he saw hills and copses, inlets and rocky outcroppings, and far to his left, backing up to a steep stony cliffside, a great looming keep with a massive curtain wall surrounding a smaller, closer inner wall. "Shit! We're here."

"We are," Victoria said, gliding down to the sand and looking up at Victor and Kethelket. "We should walk now, and I will work my magic to hide you from the eyes of Dunstan's watchers."

"All right." Victor and Kethelket slid from Guapo's back, and then Victor sent the steed back to the spirit plane. During their mad run toward the sea, Victor had let his Berserk drop, not wanting to arrive without any rage in his Core. Now, he considered casting it again but decided to wait; they would rely on stealth for the time being. When the sparkling lights from Guapo's dismissal had faded, he saw that Victoria had taken on her more corporeal form, and her black gowns blended into the night so thoroughly that her hands and face looked almost bodiless, floating in the night.

"May I work my magics, Victor?"

He stared into her pale eyes for a moment, then nodded. "Go ahead." Suddenly, the air felt ten degrees colder, and he saw his breath begin to plume forth as pale mist seemed to pour out of Victoria's hands. It hung in a cloud around her, then expanded to wrap around him and Kethelket. Victor thought he'd be blinded by the dense mist, but as soon as it engulfed him, he found he could see through it, and the world was tinted with a strange pale-yellow luminescence.

"My mist will hide us; those who look upon it will see a thin haze in the air, nothing more." Victoria's voice was clear and echoed strangely as she continued, "It will also enhance your senses; you should be able to see and hear more clearly within it."

"A clever working," Kethelket said, nodding his approval.

"Come on." Victor gestured toward the keep. "We need to hurry."

"Of course." Victoria started forward, gliding gracefully over the rocky beach toward the keep. "Dunstan is powerful, but his abilities are more inclined toward destruction than subterfuge. I don't believe he'll have defenses against my magic. We may be able to walk right through the gate."

"Nah." Victor shook his head. "Don't risk it. Find a quiet place on the wall, and we'll scale it. Well, I'll scale it; you two can fly."

"I'll lower a rope." Kethelket clapped a hand on Victor's shoulder.

"I cannot maintain my mist and my banshee form."

"Then I'll carry you up." Victor jerked a thumb toward his back. "I won't even feel your weight."

"As you say." She didn't look happy, perhaps feeling Victor was being overly cautious and not trusting her magic to hide them as they walked through the gate, but Victor didn't care. He wasn't here to win Victoria's approval; he had people to rescue, and he'd avoid the guards until he couldn't, and then he'd start killing. With those thoughts in his mind, he turned to Kethelket.

"If we get caught and shit starts to go sideways, I want you and Victoria to find your people. I'll keep these vampyrs busy."

Kethelket looked at him gravely, then nodded. "Once I free them, we'll come to your aid."

"How many of your kin were taken?" Victoria glanced over her shoulder, almost flinching, as she looked toward Victor, perhaps afraid she'd overstepped.

"More than a hundred."

"With so many, they're likely being held together. I don't know Dunstan's policies when it comes to dealing with prisoners, but he'll likely want to choose several for his own . . . needs. These creatures are nocturnal, and though they are strong flyers, I can't imagine they got here much ahead of us, considering they had to carry prisoners. With dawn nearing, I'm hopeful your people will be held until night falls again."

"I thank you for the added hope." Kethelket's words were calm, but Victor could see his right hand gripping the hilt of one of his swords. His knuckles were strained, and Victor could hear the leather of the hilt squeaking under the pressure. He was angry or stressed or both. Of course he was, Victor silently chided himself.

"If you get your people free and I'm fighting, just get the fuck out of there, Kethelket. I can get away if I have to, but there's no sense getting more of your people killed. They have us ten to one."

"Dunstan is a powerful man, Victor. He has several underlings who rivaled Eric Gore Lust." Victoria glanced at him again, perhaps gauging her odds of escaping the keep alive.

Victor kept walking, staring at the fast-approaching curtain wall, and thought about her words, about Kethelket and his people, and then about the greater campaign. What was he hoping to achieve in there? A rescue? No, he decided, it was more than that. "I'm not planning to leave that place until this Dunstan guy is dead."

Kethelket jerked his head to stare at him, locking his dark eyes on Victor's for a moment, but he didn't say anything. He didn't object, but he didn't encourage him either. Victoria kept walking, and Victor could feel the tension thickening the air as she fought back some kind of retort or objection; she knew it wasn't her place. Was she afraid he'd keep her with him until he was satisfied with his slaughter, or, worse, was overwhelmed and killed? That made him wonder what his intentions for her were. Did he expect her to fight against such wildly lopsided odds?

"Relax, Victoria. You'll stay with Kethelket and go with him as he fights free of the keep with his people."

"I . . ." She started, perhaps to object, but Kethelket spoke before she could formulate her response.

"If I leave you to battle this keep full of monsters, Valla will slay me herself."

"Well," Victor sighed, "you need to make her understand; I'm not trying to kill myself. This is a keep with tunnels and caves under it. It's not a battlefield where hundreds of enemies can face me at once; I intend to move and kill as I go, never allowing myself to be surrounded. Besides, listen: We'll use stealth as much as possible and hopefully free your people before any fighting starts. Then I'm going to blitz my way to this Dunstan asshole and deal with him. Before you object, think about how you're going to get your people out. You'll need the distraction."

"Dunstan's people will suffer greatly with his demise. If you have a hope of winning, that's how you must do it: slay him early to weaken his many thralls."

"Victor." Kethelket stopped walking and turned to him. "I yield to your leadership, but I must argue this point. There are more than a hundred of my people in there. If we free them, that means odds of only ten to one, as you said earlier. If you slay their leader and weaken the other vampyrs, shouldn't we stay and try to kill them all? Shouldn't we capture this keep? You hinted as much before you left Black Keep."

"Well, yeah, but as I traveled here with you two, I started to think about how precious the few remaining Naghelli lives are. Even if we win, but you lose half of your people, is it worth it?" Before Kethelket could respond or object, he shook his head and said, "No. It's not. Listen, Kethelket. You will get your people out of that keep, and after I've killed Dunstan and you see the effect it has on his people, we can reassess. You can reassess." Victor looked at Victoria. "Do you know how much it will affect his 'thralls' when he dies?"

"I do not. I know he has a stronger connection to them than Eric did to his. They're, as I said, a different bloodline of vampyr. I don't know their origin or history or anything that might be of use, only that Dunstan calls his thralls wampyr and refers to them as his children."

"Okay." Victor looked at the high curved gray-stone curtain wall and cracked his knuckles. He knew what he was going to do, and it didn't matter what anyone said. Even if Valla were standing right there, his plan would be the same. He had a goal in mind, and there wasn't going to be any turning him away from it. "It's settled then. Stealth by any means until the Naghelli are free, then I'll make my way to where Dunstan is and kill him. You guys will get free and wait to see what happens between me and the wampyr lord." He couldn't help the grin that exposed his teeth, shining in the moonlight. Had he really just announced that he was going into a big dark castle to kill a vampire lord? Who was he, Van Helsing?

33

RESCUE

Victor carefully descended the inner courtyard steps, warily avoiding clomping or scuffing his boots on the stones. Victoria's obscuring mist had worked like a charm so far, clinging to the three of them, hiding them from the watchful eyes of Dunstan's posted guards. Kethelket had flittered up to the top of each wall, lowering a rope for Victor to climb while Victoria clung to his back, a process Victor hadn't much enjoyed.

Victoria's flesh was cold, and despite the heat his body radiated, it never warmed. She'd held on to him, her chilly, oddly rigid arms around his neck, and not made a sound as he climbed, but he'd savored the moment she let go, allowing the cleansing air to touch his skin where she'd held him. If he'd had doubts about her status as an undead creature, they were banished after that.

The courtyard was enormous and filled with barrels, wagons, coaches, and myriad odds and ends. It was a trivial matter to walk carefully around the clutter, avoiding the handful of guards walking about, and make their way to a side passage that led into an area that once must have been kitchens. The ovens were cold, the pantries bare, and Victor was reminded that Dunstan and his people, his thralls or "children," didn't take sustenance like normal, fully alive people. It was probably to their advantage; not a soul lingered in those big dusty kitchens and dining halls, and they found an easily accessible stairway leading down.

None of them knew where they were going, but Victoria knew Dunstan and his people had discovered hidden depths to the keep. She'd heard him boasting about their expansive darkness, hidden away from the sun, the ideal place for people of his ilk to rest during the day. Victor didn't know much, but one thing he knew was that when you were searching for "hidden depths," it was probably best to go down. So, they descended every stairway they could find, and soon they were walking through damp dripping stone tunnels. Those tunnels were constructed of rough-hewn blocks, but the mortar was looser and patchy, with occasional stretches of natural stone lining one side or the other.

Once they'd passed beyond the courtyard and descended their first flight of steps, they hadn't encountered any of Dunstan's people, no vampyrs or wampyrs or whatever they wanted to be called, no people whatsoever. Victor was beginning to wonder if they'd entered some unused portion of the underground, a set of tunnels and rooms to which the invaders hadn't yet spread. That doubt nagged at him for a while but was banished when they passed through a dripping, ancient stone arch into a massive vaulted cavern, and Victoria softly hissed, "There!" and pointed to the ceiling.

Sure enough, straight out of a horror movie, Victor saw dozens of naked, gray-skinned, monstrous humanoids hanging from the great calcified wooden beams that held up the vaulted ceiling. They were large, probably nine feet tall, and hung upside down with leathery vein-filled wings folded about their forms. Their hairless gray heads protruded with long pointed ears and ugly noseless faces lost in slumber. Victor scanned the chamber and saw another high arch on the other side. He motioned toward it, and Victoria nodded, leading the way.

She and Kethelket were noiseless and probably would have been even without her obscuring mist, but Victor had to concentrate, watching where he set his large booted feet, careful to step lightly. Even so, with her magic aiding them, they passed through the room without disturbing the sleeping creatures, and when they'd progressed into the next damp tunnel a short distance, Victor asked in a rough whisper, "Are they always like that? They don't change shape like Eric's vampyrs?"

"His oldest thralls, aye. The younger ones need to exert Energy to transform."

Victor considered Victoria's words and then nodded. "I guess we're on the right track. Hold here for a moment." Victor concentrated, and channeling some fear-attuned Energy, he summoned his coyotes. Being a part of him, they knew he was hunting, stalking something, so they emerged from the cloud of roiling shadows silently, padding around the trio with noses lowered, sniffing, silently circling them. "We'll wait here a minute and let my *hermanos* prowl around and see if they can find Kethelket's people. No reason to spend all day going down the wrong tunnels."

Without direction, responding to Victor's will, the coyotes drew near Kethelket, sniffing him carefully, then darting away down the tunnel, silent, black, cloaked in shadows, and invisible to Victor's eye after just a few steps into the darkness, even with Victoria's magical mist enhancing his vision. "You don't fear they'll alert Dunstan's thralls?" Kethelket stared into the darkness of the tunnel intently, perhaps readying himself to react to an alarm or outcry.

"They're sneakier than we are." Victor grinned at Kethelket. "Even you." He could sense his spirit companions, as usual, and though he couldn't see through their eyes, he knew he'd feel it when they found something. Confident in that knowledge, he leaned his armored shoulder against the damp stone wall and waited.

"Your companions, are they spirit shaping?" Victoria stepped close, speaking softly.

"Yeah."

"As a Death Caster, I've always found Spirit Cores fascinating. Few Spirit Casters I've met, though, had much power at all. There's some prejudice among my kind about them; at least on Dark Ember, they're looked at as primitive." She hurriedly held up her hands and continued, "I know how that sounds, but I'm not casting aspersions; I'm simply noting that we were clearly misinformed."

"Speaking of casting," Victor replied, choosing to ignore her fishing expedition, "if we come upon Kethelket's people and have to kill some guards, can you use this mist of yours to keep the noise down?"

"I can, but Dunstan will feel it when his thralls die."

Kethelket frowned, locking eyes with Victor. "I suppose there's a limit to the stealthy part of this endeavor."

"Unless you two know a way to silence and incapacitate the guards without killing them."

"Were they not undead, I could." Victoria's words were almost a sigh.

"Can undead be rendered unconscious from a blow to the head?" Kethelket directed his question to Victoria.

"Not easily, not these wampyrs. Perhaps with the sunlight from Victor's banner, though I fear it will also banish my mist, which would thwart my ability to mute the sounds of conflict." As she spoke, Victor got a sense of

excited success from one of his coyotes, and he knew they'd found the missing Naghelli. Rather than tell Kethelket and Victoria, he concentrated his
will upon his companions and tried to impress upon them what he wanted.
He pictured the hanging wampyrs, then tried to direct the coyotes to find the
biggest, greatest creature like that. When he felt that they understood and
sensed that they were on the hunt once again, he turned to Kethelket.

"It doesn't matter. When we break your people out, I'll head for Dunstan,
and I'll make a pretty big scene about it. You all should be able to fight free;
I'll leave one of my coyotes to guide you."

Kethelket looked him in the eye, saw his conviction, and slowly nodded.
"Once we're out, we'll make an assessment. I won't risk all of my people, but
if we can aid you, we will."

"That's all I could ask for."

"Assuming we find your people alive . . ." Victoria said, perhaps before
she could consider the impact of her words. Kethelket growled and whirled
to face her, reaching a hand toward the blade at his belt. Victor forestalled his
angry retort, though, by putting a hand on his shoulder and speaking.

"My coyotes found them. I'm not sure how many, but definitely your
people."

"Why are we standing here?"

"Patience. They're learning the layout of these tunnels so they can guide
us where we need to go."

Kethelket nodded. "You mean after we rescue them."

"Exactly." They stood in silence a few minutes longer, and then Victor
felt a wave of excitement from his dark coyotes; they'd found his quarry. He
could feel them struggling to remain quiet, to remember to sneak back to him
rather than yipping and howling, surrounding their prey, and calling him to
them. He couldn't have blamed them if they'd done it; they were smart, clever
helpers, but they had a nature of their own, and he was asking them to behave
very much outside of it. Still, he exerted his will, calling them back to him,
reminding them of their need to be silent, and they contained themselves,
gliding through the dark damp tunnels and caves, clinging to the shadows as
though they were a part of them.

A few minutes later, Victoria gasped softly and pointed into the darkness;
several sets of dark smoky purple eyes were bobbing toward them up out of
the recesses. "It's time," Victor said, loosening Lifedrinker from her harness,
grinning savagely as she hummed in his hands. He stalked into the darkness,
and his coyotes turned to lead the way. They silently descended, turning at

junction after junction, and he congratulated himself a few times on having the forethought to send them out hunting; he might have been hours exploring all of the branching passages, and each minute they spent down there was another minute they might be exposed too soon.

They passed half a dozen vaulted chambers like the one where they'd first seen the wampyrs hanging from the supports, sleeping away the day, and, all told, probably passed by another hundred of the creatures. Knowing that the ones perpetually in that monstrous form were Dunstan's oldest, strongest thralls, he had to wonder where the more junior members of his army were. Did they sleep up in the keep in regular barracks? If so, it might make his job easier. He reasoned it would take them more time to get down to join the fight against him than it would take him to get to wherever his coyotes had found Dunstan.

As he contemplated, planning in his mind how he'd fight his way to Dunstan, visualizing his moves, the abilities he'd use, and picturing how he'd most quickly dispatch any wampyrs that got in his way, his coyotes stopped before a tall narrow opening with arched curved blocks holding up the boulder-like lintel. They paced in a small circle, and Victor knew they wanted to yip and cry, wanted to signal that the object of the hunt was there. He stepped forward, holding out his left palm reassuringly. He looked to Victoria and Kethelket and nodded. Approaching the archway, he realized it was much wider than it had seemed; it was just so tall that it seemed narrow.

He couldn't see any light in the space beyond, but within Victoria's magical mist, he could see rows of iron cages lining the far wall of an enormous natural cavern. High stone-block arches held up a rough cavernous ceiling from which water fell in steady drips down to pools dotting the uneven cavern floor. Victor could see the huddled forms of dozens of Naghelli within the cages, and he breathed out a sigh, releasing some pent-up stress; it looked like most of Kethelket's people still lived.

At first, he thought they might be unguarded. He couldn't see any wampyrs hanging from the ceiling, and the lack of light or furniture made him wonder if any non-monstrous guard would be present, but then he saw a faint flicker of silvery light from the left side of the cavern. Peering that way, he could just make out a small archway. He pointed, and Kethelket nodded, whispering, "A guard room?"

Victor nodded again, then gestured for his two companions to follow him. He crept into the cavern, stealthy and silent within Victoria's mist, and when they rounded a heap of broken crates and stood only a dozen feet or so from the first of the iron cages, Victor could see into the distant archway. Two men sat at a small table with a tiny silvery orb of light hanging above their heads. They were playing a board game that looked almost like chess. Victor looked at Kethelket and Victoria and pointed at the cages, then he pointed at himself and then to the guards. When Kethelket nodded, Victor stalked forward.

He was still a dozen feet from the archway when he cast Iron Berserk. He strained to contain his usual roar as he surged in size and power, and his vision tinted red. He must have succeeded, or Victoria's mist was still working to hide and silence him, because the guards never looked up. When he was just five feet from the archway, Victor channeled fear-attuned Energy into Lifedrinker, imparting her with dark, roiling, shadowy power. Then, almost simultaneously, Victor summoned his Banner of the Champion and cast Energy Charge, streaking toward the two guards and hacking Lifedrinker in a broad, forward cleave.

The two guards might have been able to put up a bit of a fight had they seen Victor coming, but he took them entirely by surprise. If Lifedrinker's razor-sharp gleaming edge hadn't separated their heads from their bodies, Victor's impact would surely have rendered them insensate. When he struck the guard on the left, such a concussion resulted that both men's bodies crunched into the far wall with wet, bone-grinding impacts, leaving little doubt that they were destroyed. Victor whirled, red fury tinting his gaze, and stomped back into the large chamber with the cages.

He saw Kethelket breaking locks with a gleaming chisel and hammer, saw the Naghelli silently crowding the doors, and then he took in Victoria; she was standing near the archway, weaving a cloud of writhing mist that filled the opening, perhaps hoping to buy them some time by damping down the noise of their activities. Victor whistled for his coyotes and they slunk out of the shadows, crowding close. He stared at one of them, letting his will be known, and it yipped and whined but hurried over to Kethelket's side.

"That one will guide you out." He looked from Kethelket to the men and women in the cages. "I'm glad you all are alive! Follow my coyote and listen to your captain." They answered him with muted cheers and thanks, and when he turned his hulking form and started for the exit, he heard some of them asking Kethelket where he was going. He didn't linger to hear the answer. As he stepped into Victoria's mist, he said, "Don't betray me. Listen to Kethelket. He'll honor our bargain if something happens to me."

"As you say." She ducked her head, refusing to meet his gaze. Was he so terrifying in his berserk state? Perhaps it brought back memories of the ordeal she'd faced on the spirit plane with him. When he saw her mist burning away, he realized it wasn't fear that made her look away; it was the burning heat of his banner's bloody sun. With a rumbling growl in his throat, he strode into the dark passageway, banishing the shadows as he progressed. His coyotes yipped and barked as they followed him, somehow knowing the time for stealth was past. No, it was time for Victor to make some noise. He gestured ahead with his left hand, letting his pack know he wanted to find the big wampyr leader, and they surged past him, trotting up the sloping tunnel.

He'd barely followed them to the next junction when he felt their alarm, and then he saw the roiling, hulking shadows of a pack of wampyrs. Had they felt their lesser compatriots' deaths? Victor had been expecting as much, so he didn't react with alarm. Instead, he lifted Lifedrinker and ran forward, letting loose a terrible roar that shook the dripping water loose from the stones, showering everyone in the tunnel with a fine mist. He laughed as the light of his banner refracted in the damp haze, making an incongruous rainbow in the middle of the corridor between Victor and the wampyrs.

He felt as if he'd been stuck in traffic, forced to drive five miles an hour, stopping and starting for the last hour, and now he had an open freeway ahead. He stomped the accelerator. Roaring and laughing, he charged among the big leathery-skinned gray figures. He hacked Lifedrinker left and right, and as soon as she sliced the first wing, she burst into molten white-hot glory, adding her screams of battle lust to his grunts and roars. The wampyrs weren't silent either, hissing, screeching, crying out as their claws raked his arms or slid off his armor. They yowled in pain and tried to retreat as he delivered vicious mortal wounds, hacking into them like a butcher making scraps.

"You're not going anywhere!" he roared, using his bulk to keep them from surrounding him, forcing them to face him one or two at a time and utterly dominating them. These wampyrs were probably as tough as the monstrous vampyrs he'd fought out on the plains, but he was fresh, and he wasn't facing them in the hundreds, surrounded, bloodied, and beleaguered. He worked his way through the pack like a terrier let loose in a rat den, and in minutes, he was standing at the far end of a bloody corpse-littered stretch of corridor, heaving and panting, blood dripping from every inch of his person.

His coyotes came out of the shadows, hazy purple eyes focused on him, yipping in a way that almost sounded like laughter as he urged them to continue on, to find the object of their hunt. He chased after them, winding through the tunnels, howling, laughing, and roaring alternately as he progressed. He was mad with battle lust, but only because he'd allowed himself to be. He'd decided early on that he would put on a show, savage his way through these corridors, drawing the wampyrs into a chase that would leave Kethelket and his kin in peace, allowing them to find their way out with as little resistance as possible.

It seemed his plan was working because he could hear the sounds of pursuit, and it didn't sound like a small number. He could hear their claws scrabbling over stone in the gaps between his roars. He could hear their outraged cursing in sibilant hisses, and he knew they were frustrated by his speed and unerring sense of direction, thanks to his coyotes. His companions guided him through the maze and away from the larger packs of enemies. When he came upon one or two wampyrs, Victor's axe fell with bloody crunching hacks, severing limbs, cleaving bodies, and spraying hot black blood on the stones. He never lingered long enough for the bulk of his pursuers to catch up and slow him.

Because they helped him avoid the larger packs and because they could tell their quarry was on the move, his coyotes didn't lead him on a direct course to where they'd seen the wampyr lord. They followed their noses, yipping, braying, and howling their way through the subterranean maze. Along the way, Victor probably killed several dozen wampyrs, and he knew he could probably clear the place out if his Energy would hold out that long. As it was, he knew he needed to find Dunstan sooner rather than later, lest his rage run low. He needn't have been concerned; just as he began to allow such worries to find root in his mind, he burst into an enormous cavern and immediately caught sight of his quarry.

Dunstan stood before a massive throne-like stone chair at the far end of the cavern. Perhaps cavern was the wrong word to describe the space, Victor revised, noting the high massive wooden beams holding up the stone ceiling, the thin, ancient red carpets laid out over the marble-slab flooring, and the furnishings—tables, chairs, benches, and candelabra in their hundreds—scattered about the space.

Victor slowed and took everything in, sauntering forward, his coyotes yapping nervously as they walked around him in a loose circle. Dunstan was a big wampyr, twice the size of the ones Victor had faced thus far, with enormous wings that were more black than gray. Like his brethren, he was naked save for a thick, gleaming obsidian crown that sat atop his ugly bat-like head. He had baleful red eyes, and as they watched Victor approach, he spoke in a deep guttural voice, wet with loose consonants and the promise of violence. "So you come into my home bold and full of fury? You dare? I'll bathe in your blood and spend the next hundred years hunting everyone you've ever known. They'll be my playthings for millennia."

Victor continued forward, trying to decide whether he'd break his rule about shit-talking. He'd gotten halfway into the large chamber when he heard his pursuers catch up and start to file in. He'd figured they'd do so, but he had plenty of ideas to deal with the superior numbers, not least of which was charging back into the tunnel and forcing them to funnel into him in smaller packs. He just wasn't sure if he'd start the fight with the big bastard first. Dunstan made his decision easier when he growled, "Stand back, children. Watch your lord slay this great buffoon."

34

A DUEL IN THE DEPTHS

Victor's Quinametzin heart surged with fury at the wampyr's words—a challenge and an insult. Did this ugly gray monstrosity think it could stand before him so brazenly? Did it believe itself a match for his fury? Victor glared around, Lifedrinker on his shoulder, and as blood dripped from his armor, his knuckles, and his elbows, making little pools on the marble, he smiled a toothy, fierce smile that said more about murder than amusement. His aura was fully untethered, lying heavy around him, sharing space with the smoldering heat of the bloody sun on his banner. The wampyr lord's "children" could feel it; they shrank back from him, hugging the edges of the great chamber in their hundreds.

"Well, then? Come to me, *meal*." Dunstan's voice was thick with lust as he turned to his enormous throne-like chair and snatched up a great jagged sword that looked to be carved from rose-colored stone. Despite its strange material, the blade looked sharp and heavy, and the tiny part of Victor's mind that wasn't hot with bloodlust didn't relish having it strike him. He took a step toward the monstrous figure, but Dunstan had other ideas, cracking his vast veiny wings and streaking toward him, sword held high.

Victor was no novice when it came to a brawl and certainly not where the axe was concerned. The great wampyr was fast, but Victor was a match for him, and he sidestepped, ducked a shoulder, put his thick juggernaut helm in the path of that stony sword, and hacked Lifedrinker down in a brutal chop, aimed at where he could predict Dunstan's leg would land. The gambit paid off perfectly, or it would have if Lifedrinker had been able to do more than scratch the wampyr's thick wrinkled gray flesh.

The sword rang like a gong as it smashed into the crown of his helm. Lifedrinker rebounded from the creature's knee, and Victor danced behind the monstrosity, ducking under a wide wing. As he passed behind Dunstan, he tried to drag Lifedrinker along the veiny gray membrane of that wing, and again she failed to penetrate it. She was fully ablaze, engorged with his dark fear-attuned Energy, yet she wailed in frustration as she fruitlessly slid along that dense pliable flesh.

"You bring a toy to fight with me?" Dunstan laughed and whirled, whipping his huge cleaver-like stone sword in a wide arc. Victor backstepped and brought Lifedrinker up in a parry, aiming to knock the blade away with the flat top of her axe-head. He was just a fraction of a second too slow, and though she slid along his sword, he didn't have the right angle or momentum to stop that ripping edge, and it bit into his shoulder. For once, Victor wasn't happy to have only a vest of wyrm-scale armor. The cold razor edge of that stone sword parted his flesh like a scalpel with an anvil behind it, cutting him to the bone and then some.

Victor stumbled back, pain lancing through his shoulder as his arm went numb, and he nearly lost his grip on Lifedrinker. Growling in frustration, he circled the wampyr, watching as the monster ran a long pointy tongue over the edge of his sword and chortled wetly. Victor held his axe in two hands, using his left to support most of the weight while he waited for his Berserk healing to knit his muscles and tendons together. His failure to harm the creature with two good hits combined with the blow to his shoulder had sobered him, turning his feral grin into a frown of concentration.

More than the injury and Lifedrinker's ineffectual cuts, Victor's serious state of mind frustrated him. He inwardly railed at himself—why wasn't he getting pissed? Why was he being so cautious? Just beat the fucker down! Still, despite his harsh self-talk, he circled and listened to the jeers and taunts of the gathered wampyrs. He had half a mind to turn his back on Dunstan, ignoring the giant wampyr while he waded through his "children" and gave Lifedrinker another bath in their blood. He knew better, though; if he took his eyes off that stone cleaver, he'd wind up losing his head.

Dunstan cracked his wings and charged forward again, and Victor met his flurry of blows with parries and dodges, ducking slashes and cleaves, catching them on his helm or knocking them aside. When they separated, he had no new wounds, but neither did Dunstan, and the wampyr didn't look tired. He looked as if he was just getting started. As the creature lifted his hacking sword high, preparing another charge, no doubt, Victor beat him to it, launching forward with a rage-attuned Energy Charge. He smashed into the enormous creature's chest, Lifedrinker leading the way.

Victor had crashed into some big creatures before using that spell. Each time, his own magic sustained and protected him while he either sent the enemy sprawling or they somehow shielded themselves. This time was different. Dunstan didn't shield himself, but neither did he fly backward from the concussion. He flapped his wings and stepped back, but that was the extent of the damage. Victor, for once, had met his match in bulk and strength. The wampyr was built like a diesel engine, solid, unyielding, and just as ugly.

While red rippling Energy clouded the air in the wake of their crash, Dunstan lifted a hook-nailed foot and kicked Victor in the thigh, dragging his toe claws savagely downward. They ripped through his pants and his flesh, leaving burning tracks that instantly began to bubble and turn black with putrescence. The foul creature had used some disease-ridden Energy to corrupt Victor's flesh. Victor stumbled, agony opening his pathways wide, making room for more rage as he compensated for the knot of fear he felt forming in his gut. Had he bitten off more than he could chew?

Lifedrinker bucked and vibrated in his hand, yearning to fly forth and strike the demonic wampyr, but Victor held her tight; she'd only get herself knocked away, out of his reach, unable to help him further. *Help me . . .* The thought struck a match of inspiration alight in his head, and Victor began to chuckle, annoyed and amused at himself for waiting, once again, for near disaster to think of or, worse, remember what he should have done all along.

"You laugh, meat?"

"Yeah." Victor could already feel his robust vitality and Berserk regeneration battling the corruption in his leg. He could feel the dark putrescence running down his leg as his body pushed it out, the flesh in his muscles knitting. "Did you call her a toy? My axe?"

Dunstan backed off a step, whipping his stone sword in great, whooshing arcs before himself. "That pitiful blade cannot harm me. I wonder, how long can you maintain this state? This berserk nature? I've fought your kind before—simple-minded rage casters. The berserker rage is certainly intoxicating, but it doesn't last. You're a big man, but you're no wampyr. I'll wear you down, and then we'll sup on that rich blood, me and my kin. Worse, I'll pay your kind back tenfold for the children you've slain tonight. Take those words to heart, fool; do they not bring despair?"

Victor flexed his thigh, feeling it respond without pain, then he lifted Lifedrinker and said, softly, for her alone, "Okay, *chica*, let's kill this fucker. I'll give you a boost." Then Victor cast Imbue Spirit, powering the spell with inspiration-attuned Energy. He sent a shard of his spirit into Lifedrinker, and she instantly reacted, flaring with white, heatless flames. Victor swung her left and right, and her cries of fury and hunger rang through the chamber, bodiless but savage and fierce. A wave of nausea and fatigue struck him as his power poured into Lifedrinker, but he quickly compensated, and then he changed his Sovereign Will boost from strength and vitality to dexterity and agility; it was time for Lifedrinker to work, and that meant he needed to land some more hits.

Victor watched as Dunstan observed his axe coated in ghostly flames. Then, as the great wampyr took in a deep breath, perhaps ready to shout something or release a spell, Victor used some of his abundant fear-attuned Energy and cast Energy Charge. This time, he aimed to the side, and as he ripped over the hard marble floor, he swung Lifedrinker with all his enhanced speed and accuracy, aiming for the giant creature's chest. Dunstan was fast, though, and he managed to get his huge stone sword between Lifedrinker and his flesh. It was a move that may have saved him a mortal injury, but it cost him dearly.

Lifedrinker, tempered by Victor's spirit, imbued with his very soul, his power, his potential, rang like a chime as she impacted that enormous rose-colored blade, and she bit clean through the stone, parting it like a chisel through sandstone. Dunstan roared in fury as he fell back, avoiding Victor's follow-through, clutching the stump of his sword, shortened by two thirds. Victor, as always, knew when to press an advantage, and he darted forward, weaving Lifedrinker through feints, hacks, thrusts, and cleaves as only a true aficionado of the axe might do. Dunstan, meanwhile, was hobbled, unable to use his broken sword effectively. He might have tried to get a new weapon from some storage container, but Victor's incessant pressure wouldn't allow it.

Lifedrinker began to take a toll, carving away his thick gray flesh and exposing the rotten, thick sludge that passed for Dunstan's blood. Victor roared and laughed, reveling in his foe's distress. "That's right, *chica*! Carve that fucker like a turkey!" He drove the great wampyr back toward his throne, and as he exposed more and more of the meat beneath the creature's flesh, his banner began to take its toll, sizzling the creature's blood, muscle, and bone with the hot glittering yellow light of its bloody sun. Dunstan roared in frustration, gnashing his teeth, hissing, and swinging that truncated blade in futile attempts to stop Lifedrinker's graceful weaving cleaves.

Victor pushed forward, the dance of death upon him. He was in tune with Lifedrinker, aware of her blade, her handle, every hair's breadth of her steel and wood. He could feel her life force, and she could feel his; they were joined in battle, and nothing Dunstan could do, no trick of Energy, no feat of strength or speed could save him from that slashing, weaving, flaming axe. The heat of her molten core was transformed, adding to the ghostly fire of Victor's inspiration Energy. Each cut she made left a gaping blackened wound that refused to heal, not only because of Victor's banner but because of the melding of Victor's and Lifedrinker's spirits within the axe.

Defeated, broken, cowering, Dunstan groveled and scurried, trying to avoid Victor's cuts with the bulk of his stone throne. When he finally realized there was no salvation, he cried out, "Slay this fool! Extinguish his light!" The frenzied susurration of rushing gray-skinned creatures and flapping hairless wings distracted Victor and made him glance away for just a moment, and that was all Dunstan needed. He depressed some hidden catch on his throne, causing a hidden clockwork mechanism to rotate it, revealing a deep black hole down which the elder wampyr dropped, and then his children, in their hundreds, were upon Victor.

Kethelket looked at his haggard, bloodied people. They were gathered upon the banks of the Silver Sea, the dark brooding fortress of Baron Dunstan the wampyr several miles away. The sun was still high in the sky, else they'd no doubt have been pursued further. The corpses of Dunstan's thralls, the ones who'd chased them this far, littered the rocky beach. Further upslope toward the keep were dozens more of their corpses—the brave fools who'd tried to keep the Naghelli from fleeing forth.

He silently counted his kin, coming up with ninety-three. He turned to Offathi. "Well? What was your count?"

"Ninety-four, Lord."

"Ninety . . . oh, you counted me?"

"Aye, Lord." She ducked her head, and Kethelket noted the bloody claw marks on her cheeks, the ripped and battered nature of her armor. Most of his people had been stripped of their dimensional containers. Most of them had damaged or missing armor. Most of them were using weapons he'd passed out from his own containers or taken from dead enemies. He wanted to take the fight to the wampyrs and their thralls. He wanted to slay them all and loot the keep, taking the price of his dead kinfolk in dark tainted blood. But looking at their faces, the bloody wounds, and the abused state of their equipment, he knew it would cost them dearly to do so.

Even with Victor possibly distracting the worst of the wampyrs, perhaps even killing the lord of the keep, hundreds of fresh, well-armed troops were within those walls. He had no doubt that his people could take a heavy toll, perhaps killing them all, but he'd lose too many. No, he couldn't do that, not when these ragged men and women represented nearly a third of all the Naghelli left in the world.

"Will he live?" At her voice, Kethelket whirled to face Victoria. He'd almost forgotten the strange undead witch was there.

"He's a survivor."

"So you think he will?"

"I wouldn't bet against him." Kethelket frowned, wishing there was some way he could tell how Victor was doing, some way he could sense him.

"I cannot feel him. He's too deep," Victoria said, uncannily guessing what he'd been thinking.

"Well, witch, what will you do?"

"I will follow you and await my release." She smoothed the black lace bodice on her incongruous flowing gown. Her hands were pale as new snow, even more devoid of color than his own flesh. At least his skin flushed with exertion; hers was always the same, flat white punctuated by dark veins here and there. She was an odd creature, sure, but she'd shown some honor this day, and if things went badly for Victor, Kethelket would uphold her bargain.

He nodded to her then called out, "Fanasti?"

"Aye, Lord?" The tall scout, sporting a new eyepatch, pushed his way through the huddled Naghelli to stand before him.

"Can you still work your Far Sight magic?"

"Aye, even one-eyed, I can see farther than any of you!" He managed a brave smile despite his obvious discomfort.

"Good. Study those thralls on the parapets yonder. Tell me if you see anything amiss with them."

Fanasti nodded and turned, holding his two hands in front of his face and concentrating. A moment later, the air between his palms shimmered and turned opaque, taking on an almost liquid nature. As he watched through the strange air, he said, "I see a hundred or more on the walls. They patrol with heightened alertness. Many stand atop the gatehouse, watching us as I watch them. They don't seem upset more than they ought to be, considering our escape and their comrades' corpses littering the trail of our passage."

Kethelket turned back to Victoria. "You're sure they'll react when Dunstan dies?"

"Aye. I'm not sure how severely it will affect them, but they'll feel it. I'd be surprised if they didn't wail with mad hysterics when it happens."

Kethelket looked to the sun, then back to the keep. His people were tired, and they weren't as fast as the wampyr on a good day. They needed a head start if he wanted them to find safety back at Black Keep. Was he betting against Victor if he left now? "No." He shook his head. "I have to think of my people first."

"Pardon, my lord?" Offathi asked. She was probably the only person in this group of Naghelli who would question his mutterings, feisty scout that she was.

He put his hand on Fanasti's shoulder. "You can stop watching. Spread the word. We fly soon." Then he turned to Offathi. "I was saying we need to leave."

"What about Lord Victor?" Her frown was profound, and he could see the tremor along her jaw. She wanted to scream or cry or argue, and she was battling with the impulse. To his surprise, it was Victoria who came to his aid.

"Lord Victor fights to give your people a chance at freedom, at life. If you go back to the keep or linger here too long, any sacrifice he makes, any heroic efforts, will have been wasted."

Kethelket nodded. "She speaks true. Victor bade me assess my people and the defense of the keep and decide what to do. I have decided to get you all back to Black Keep and to rally the Ninth to come here to finish off these ghoul-faced, blood-sucking batmen." He raised his voice as he spoke, noting that many of his people were gathering close, trying to hear.

"But Victor . . ."

"We cannot flee!"

"No!"

"I will fight until my fingers cannot hold . . ."

The protests took many shapes, and the faces of his people, fierce and fiery, gave him pride, but Kethelket raised his voice and shouted them down. "Silence! We will return to Black Keep, and the Ninth will venture forth to give Victor aid. If Lord Victor wishes to leave this place, do any of you think some wampyr vermin will stop him?" That brought silence to their lips as the Naghelli survivors looked at one another, waiting to see if anyone had a different answer. Kethelket knew what they all thought, however. "No!" he shouted. "If Lord Victor wishes to leave without killing every undead creature in that keep, then he will do so. He will break free and rejoin us. For now, though, we fly. We fly to safety because that's what he's bought for you, for us."

Kethelket turned and nodded to Victoria, then he spread his wings, and with a surge of primal shadow-attuned Energy, he launched himself into the air. He didn't look back. He didn't need to; he could hear his people following him. They may have been exhausted, but they would make haste, and old ancestors willing, the Ninth would be free to march forth and finish the hard work Victor had started in that keep.

35

INTO THE DARKNESS

Victor roared with fury and dove toward the opening at the base of the throne, but it slid closed as he hurtled through the air. He smashed a shoulder into the huge stone seat, and he felt it give, but nearly imperceptibly so. Victor was just contemplating pulling his gigantic hammer from his storage ring when the first of the wampyrs slammed into him, screaming in a strange mixture of fury, fear, and pain as it found the courage to brave his banner's light and strike a blow for its fleeing lord.

Victor whirled, fury incarnate, and hacked Lifedrinker's razor edge through its throat, sending a fountain of hot black blood spraying forth. Then the horde was upon him, and despite his superior size, strength, and skill, he found himself losing ground, being pushed away from the dais upon which the throne sat. Victor growled curses in fury and pain—he was fast, and Lifedrinker, enhanced by his spirit, cut the lesser wampyrs like a scythe through grass, but he was overwhelmed as they clawed over each other, pressing him from every angle, like swarming ants upon a grasshopper.

As their clawed hands grasped and grabbed, pulling at his arms, his helmet, his armor, even his legs and ankles, Victor felt a strange panic, almost like claustrophobia, grip him as he found himself unable to swing Lifedrinker. The wampyrs behind him had taken hold of her haft and were using her length for leverage to pull his arm back. They screamed in agony as the ghostly flames burned their evil flesh, but still they held on, yanking, howling, and gnashing. Victor had had enough; he bunched his legs, instinc-tually channeling his Energy to break free with a Titanic Leap. He exploded upward, wampyrs clinging to his every limb, and nearly smashed into the high vaulted ceiling.

His helmet brushed one of the colossal support beams, then he began to descend. He'd shed many of the clinging creatures, but some still held on tight—not tight enough, however. Victor found he was able to swing Life-drinker again, so he did, smashing her edge through the skull of a wampyr holding tight to his left leg. The creature fell away in a shower of black steam-ing blood and brain matter. Victor's feet hit the marble floor, and he charged for the tunnel entrance. A wampyr on his back bit and clawed at his neck and arms, trying to get past the rim of his helmet, finding purchase in the flesh not covered by his wyrm-scale vest.

Victor roared in pain and mad frustration, reaching a hand over his shoul-der to grasp the creature's bat-like ear, yanking it hard as he ran. He felt flesh tear and heard the monster scream, and then it was off his back and falling behind him. When he reached the archway leading to the tunnel from which he'd come, Victor whirled and faced the throng of wampyrs chasing after him. He was insane with fury at this point, completely letting go of reason, letting his rage consume him. He had no intention of allowing Dunstan to get away, had no intention to flee these creatures. If a slaughter was what the wampyr lord had ordered, Victor would deliver it.

The first wampyr to leap into the tunnel with him met Lifedrinker's edge and was split from its right shoulder to its left hip, falling in two bloody squelching halves at his feet. Victor roared into the mist of blood, and the charging creatures slowed, realizing they couldn't overwhelm him as easily now that they couldn't surround him. Victor didn't pause, didn't think; he squatted down, smashed a fist into the open chest cavity of the wampyr that he'd just split, and yanked out its hot black heart. In a calm, relaxed setting, Victor might have balked at what his Quinametzin alter ego was doing, but his titanic rageful self didn't flinch. He'd eaten worse—arachnid hearts, night brute hearts; this was nothing, just a snack.

He tossed the steaming morsel into his mouth and bit down with his strong jaws. The heat of the blood seemed to intensify as he swallowed, and he felt it explode with Energy in his gut as his Quinametzin bloodline did its thing, capturing some essence from the slain wampyr and sending it into him. Victor felt his nearly depleted rage-attuned Energy surge with renewed power as the heart's Energy flowed into his Core. As his vision darkened to deep crimson, tunneling on the edges so his only focus was before him, the creatures keeping him from his prey, Victor let loose.

He cast Energy Charge with fear-attuned Energy, streaking to the front of their pack, punching Lifedrinker's smoking axe-head through the central wampyr's chest, and blasting a dozen of the creatures back into each other, breaking bones, cracking skulls, and rupturing flesh with the thunderous impact. Then he began to lay about himself with Lifedrinker, moving like a graceful executioner among the condemned, hacking limbs, cleaving skulls, and smashing bones. All the while, he continued to roar and scream his fury. Soon the air of that underground hall was thick with a hot, humid mist; blood and piss and fear filled the air.

Whenever the wampyrs began to crowd around him, using their numbers to overwhelm him, Victor would charge or leap away, regrouping in the tunnel and slaughtering those who came after him. When the creatures grew too wary to pursue, he'd charge them instead, starting the cycle anew. Twice more, Victor ate the hearts of his foes, and each time, he felt his Core swell with the Energy, not only refueling him but expanding, pushing toward advancement. The idea of it made him laugh all the more, reveling in the slaughter and the fact that while he wore the awful creatures down, he grew more powerful.

To their credit, the monstrous wampyrs never gave up, never fled. Perhaps they couldn't—the only exits to the great hall that Victor could see were the tunnel in which he stood and the closed throne. His banner's light kept them from regenerating and likely reduced their strength and potency. Something about the light shed by his bloody sun was too real for them, too like the sun outside, and it burned their exposed wounds, sizzled their blood, and stole the confidence from their movements.

When the attacks stopped coming, and Victor stood in the tunnel mouth surrounded by piles of corpses and pools of blood, it was almost a surprise to him. He'd gotten into a rhythm of death, a dance of destruction, and nearly lost track of his purpose beyond fighting and slaying. He stood, a gore-covered giant, chest heaving, axe dripping and sizzling with the blood of his vanquished enemies. After a moment, when it registered that he'd won, that the fight was over, he strode toward the throne, but not before the System decided the lull in his fighting was enough, that it was time to award him the Energy he'd won.

Gigantic pools of it, gleaming golden in the dark, began to form above the mounds of corpses, and soon they flowed together and streamed toward

Victor, joined by thinner streams from the corridors above where he'd fought his way to face Dunstan. The shimmering purple and gold Energy told Victor these creatures weren't much higher than Tier Five. Still, altogether, the Energy he'd won from them was enough to lift him into an insensate paroxysm of euphoria. He arched his back and yawped like the titan he was, and his victory sound echoed through the chamber and into the corridors above.

*****Congratulations! You have achieved level 56 Battlemaster and gained 10 strength, 9 vitality, 4 agility, 4 dexterity, 3 will, and 3 intelligence.*****

*****Congratulations! Your Core has leveled: Advanced 6.*****

Victor's fury hadn't survived the flood of euphoria, and when he finally fell back to the floor, refreshed and renewed, he was no longer berserk. He stood and took stock. It seemed the wampyrs who'd been willing to fight were all dead; no sounds of pursuit or reinforcement came from the tunnel. The room was silent save for the occasional drip of blood from one surface or another into puddles on the floor. Victor looked at the throne and frowned. Though his rage had faded, his determination to chase Dunstan had not.

Lifedrinker still smoked with the fire of inspiration, flickering with white flames ignited by the shard of his spirit he'd sent into her. "Are you good, *chica?*"

The axe didn't answer him with words, but he felt overwhelming confidence and affection as the haft vibrated eagerly in his hand. Victor smiled and then looked at the mounds of dead wampyrs. He could spend some time searching their hairless naked mangled corpses for loot, but instead, he figured he could earn some points with his ancestors. He walked around the room, casting Honor the Spirits on each pile. As they burst into ghostly fire, he gathered the lone corpses scattered here and there and sent that pile to the spirits as well. After burning the last mound of bodies, he held Lifedrinker before himself and pronounced, "This fight was for you, Chantico. Thank you for saving me and granting me your flames!

"Now let's see about this *pinché* throne." Victor was about to summon his maul from storage, but then he saw the bloody smears near the rear corner of the throne where Dunstan had been scrabbling with his mangled arm. He studied the marks and the stonework and then reached out to press on a loop of stone with a hairline gap around it. It pressed down with a soft grinding click, and then the throne rumbled and slid to the side, revealing the dark hole down which Dunstan had leapt.

"Okay, *chica*, what am I supposed to do here? Jump in there? That fucker can fly; what if it's a mile deep?" Victor summoned a Globe of Insight, sending the ghostly light down through the hole. All he saw was the orb in a void of blackness. He sent it farther and again only saw the orb, even as it grew small. "That's one big damn hole or cave or something." He looked at Lifedrinker, studying her ghostly flickering flames. "I'm going to take my spirit back for now. Time to change things up a little." Lifedrinker pulsed with emotion, sending it into Victor through his hands, where they held her.

The emotion was so raw and direct that Victor momentarily felt it was his own. He felt as if someone he loved was leaving, as if his heart was breaking, as if he'd be left all alone, and he found himself on one knee before the open hole in the ground, blinking back tears. "Jesus, *chica*! It's not that bad! I'll be right here, like always."

"Not the same!" Her words came to his mind in a rushed whisper, tinged with despair. *"I've never felt so close to you before. This is more, Victor! Please don't leave me long."*

"I won't. You know I fight a lot. I'll share my spirit with you again." Reluctant acceptance came to him through the axe, and Victor breathed a long shaky sigh. He carefully severed the connection of Energy to the spell, and he felt his spirit come back into him, expanding his potential and adding to his attributes and Energy. He wiped his forehead, breathing a deep shaky breath, unable to lose the feeling that something about him was different. Had his spirit changed while it was with Lifedrinker? Had he changed from the connection they'd shared?

He found himself cradling the axe, still kneeling by the hole, and shook his head, standing up and growling as he tried to refocus his mind, remembering why he was there. "Time to find this *pendejo*. Okay, buddy, if you want to hide in a deep dark hole, maybe I should give you a reason to fear the dark." He knew that Dunstan had fled into the depths, weakened and horribly wounded, but the wampyr had the ability to regenerate. Could he have fully healed in the time Victor was fighting his thralls? Victor could have, he knew that, especially with the aid of healing potions. Surely the wampyr lord had healing potions . . .

"Oh well. I'll find him. Then if I need to, I'll beat him down again." Victor reached into his Core, pulled out a thick ribbon of fear-attuned Energy, and cast Aspect of Terror. As the shadows poured forth, cloaking his body in their cold embrace, he groaned and growled, accustomed to but not loving the feeling of his body changing, stretching, twisting into something terrible. Perhaps it was his mind growing used to the effect, or maybe it had something to do with the strength of his Core and his powerful will, but the metamorphosis seemed faster, less jarring, and though his sense of himself, of Victor, fled to a corner of his mind, he still felt aware, in control, as the shadows fell away to gather at his taloned feet.

The world had grown colorless, just a field of grayscale angles and shapes. As he'd changed, his Banner of the Champion had faded, and Victor knew, on a basic level, that his glory-attuned Energy couldn't share his pathways with his fear-attuned Energy; they were incompatible. He thought about that, about how his inspiration Energy was probably the same, as his Aspect of Terror stalked around the hole, turning to glare around, noting the absence of life, of Energy in that big vaulted chamber. There was nothing there to feed his hunger, nothing there to share his fear. No, what he sought was down below, through that dark opening. Without another thought, he dropped through.

The space he fell into was gargantuan—a vast underground cavern in which a city might be erected. Victor didn't fall; he spread his black-feathered wings and banked, gliding in a wide circle as he scanned the gray expanse. He saw signs of life, little glimmering spirits among the stones and boulders so far below. He saw them in the heights, near tunnel mouths and adjoining caverns. They were pitiful little things, hardly worth the effort to chase down. No, he sought something more; the foe that had fled him was down here, and it had a rich spirit, something worthy of his time.

Ever widening his spiral, he glided, peering into the darkness with his smoky purple-black eyes. No shadow could obscure his quarry; the blooming glow of spirits was the only color in his world, the only brightness. He knew that when he saw the object of his hunt, it would be like a star rising in a black sky. So vast was the cavern that he could only see two sides of it, even from his high spiraling flight. He began to bank away from the walls, into the darkness, farther toward the distant reaches of the enormous space, hoping to find the extremities.

Hunger gripped him, twisting his mind and making him consider desperate ideas. Should he leave this place? Could he fight his way to the surface where he might find more spirits to feast upon? He'd only been wearing the Aspect of Terror for a dozen minutes, yet it was already twisting his intention. Yes, there was a feast for him down here, but it was hiding, and how enriching could one spirit be? Shouldn't he seek more fruitful pastures? Couldn't he find a city nearby? Something like the one he'd glimpsed back when he'd been new to the aspect? Surely there must be better hunting grounds than . . .

Victor was saved from further debate with his terror-born self by the rushing flap of great leathery wings and Dunstan's savage roar as he tore through the air, driving a yard of steel, the tip of a great pike, through Victor's side, forcing him down, twisting and bleeding, toward the rocky ground. He didn't feel pain, not in that shape, not as a manifestation of terror. What would be the point of that? No, he felt the spear, knew it was piercing his shadowy flesh, but he didn't care. All that mattered was his loss of control. Dunstan was much larger than he, and his wings were powerful. Soon he'd crash into that ground, and he'd be trapped by that glimmering dark-metal pike.

In the corner of his mind, Victor reached into his Core and summoned forth a thick rope of rage-attuned Energy, letting it loose in his pathways as he invoked his Iron Berserk. Suddenly, the Aspect of Terror opened its razor-edged beak and screeched with fury, a shriek that elongated and rose in volume as his mass surged, doubling in an instant. He twisted, wrenching the pike sideways, ignoring the pain as he furiously lashed out with his talons, grasping Dunstan's shoulders and squeezing, driving their long, dagger tips into his skin, griding down into the bones.

The wampyr lord roared in agony, twisting the pike, still piercing Victor's shadowy torso. They tumbled together, falling rapidly, but the Aspect of Terror was in control now, and it cracked open its great wings, taking charge of their descent. Now it was Dunstan falling backward toward the ground, with Victor's nightmarish form on top, wings spread wide. Still, when they impacted the ground, despite his back and head smashing into the hard stony surface, Dunstan held onto the pike, and the leverage it afforded him, poking through Victor's body, sent them tumbling apart.

When the dust settled, Victor lay twenty paces from the downed wampyr, the pike still jutting from his guts. He grasped it with a bloody talon and yanked it free, allowing his shadowy flesh to swirl and close over the gaping holes. Dunstan was already on his feet, a tremendous spiked mace in one hand. "Quite the transformation. A more suitable guise, indeed. I felt the loss of my children, fiend. Trust that your kin will suffer for an eternity to pay for the passage of their souls. Come then, you'll not fare so well down here in the shadows of my seat of power."

The Aspect of Terror studied the brilliant flaring spirit. Such colors! It pulsed from yellow to ochre to crimson, always bright, always alluring. It was speaking, saying some words that didn't register, but it didn't matter—here was a feast worthy of his efforts! He lifted his razored beak and shrieked, sending out a wave of fear-attuned Energy, watching to see how it would affect this spirit. Would it take root and begin the process of converting its Energy into something he could consume?

Dunstan stepped back from the screech, holding the mace high, ready to strike the monstrous nightmare should it leap for him. He reached up to touch the puncture wounds on his shoulder with his free hand. He smiled as his fingers felt his flesh knitting closed. His eyes flashed with crimson light as he began to summon Energy. The creature snapped its wings, leaping for him, claws extended. Dunstan whipped his spiked mace as fast as a thunderbolt, deep red-black Energy enhancing the weapon. It smashed into the nightmare's side, but the creature completely ignored the attack, falling on him with slashing, stabbing talons and beak.

The Aspect of Terror ripped and clawed, ignoring the crushing, puncturing blows Dunstan delivered to its side, ignoring the blasts of dark burning Energy that rolled out of the wampyr. Victor's Berserk Energy, his nightmarish form, was durable beyond Dunstan's ability to harm him. For each crushing blow that bent or broke his bones, shadows poured forth, weaving around the damage, knitting him together. His very flesh was shadow, and as Dunstan damaged it, more flowed to fill the gaps.

Meanwhile, he ripped and tore, but that shimmering, glowing spirit never broke, never bled forth, never flowed into him, shaped into fear. Dunstan was resilient, and the Aspect of Terror couldn't rip him enough to pull him apart, couldn't break his will, not in that dark place. Deep in the corner of his mind where he'd retreated, where he'd gone to allow the aspect to do what it did best, Victor became aware of its frustration. Dunstan healed too quickly and was too strong without the light of his banner weakening him.

Victor knew he was the one really in control, knew he could banish the Aspect of Terror with a thought, but he also knew he was in a gigantic dark space. If he couldn't fly, Dunstan could flee. If he dropped the aspect, he feared the wampyr would escape. Instead, he considered an alternative. With a desperately fervent focus of his will, he urged the aspect to look to his chest, to his lungs, to feel the fire burning there. He urged it to use those roiling flames.

36

THE VOICES IN OUR MINDS

Valla stood atop the parapet and watched as the world burned. When Victor had come up with the idea to burn the trees, to start a fire that would hopefully kill the undead hordes hiding in that foggy forest, she'd tried to visualize what it would be like. She'd never seen a forest fire, never seen one of the brush fires that sometimes brought refugees into Gelica from the northern plains. She'd smelled the smoke in the air and seen the sun turn into a hazy red-orange globe in the sky, but she'd never been close enough to see the flames. She'd never seen the night sky light up with such an evil amber glow.

"I didn't realize how big it would be . . ." she muttered, mostly to herself, but Edeya heard her.

"It's like we unleashed a monster, something a hundred times worse than the undead lurking in those trees." Apparently the young Ghelli was also struggling to come to grips with what they'd done. The flames hadn't yet reached the trees directly bordering the extensive clearing around the keep, but they couldn't be far off. Valla could hear the fire, a low incessant rumbling roar. If you didn't focus on it, you could almost forget it was there, a testament to the adaptability of the mind, almost like living near a loud river or waterfall.

"Hard to believe that low rumble is the sound of the fire. Imagine! If you broke down those noises, you'd hear crackling flames, cracking and popping wood, falling branches and trees, thrashing, burning undead. Stampeding animals!" She turned to Edeya, looking into her bright blue eyes, her pale face highlighted by the beautiful blue shimmering lights of her new wings. "The flames will reach us soon. Sarl has his Wind Casters ready to funnel the smoke away while it passes."

"Good for us, but what of all the creatures that made this forest their home?"

Valla frowned. "As Victor said, if we don't beat these undead invaders, this forest would soon be dead or twisted, the animals worse off. At least they can flee the flames."

"True. However, many creatures have perished already. Did you see the stampede a couple of hours ago? I've never seen so many woodland animals together!"

"I was corresponding with Rellia, but Sarl told me about it." Valla gripped the smooth black stones of the parapet and, still staring out into the glowing orange smoke, quietly asked, "Do you think they've made it yet?"

"Victor?" When Valla's only response was a quick nod, Edeya clasped her slender hand around her wrist. "I'm sure they have. You've seen how fast that great spirit mount can run!"

"I hate that he took that woman with him."

"I know! She . . . gives me a bad feeling. I suppose it's primarily because she's one of them." Edeya gestured toward the forest, and Valla knew she meant the undead. "Still, I worry that she's taking advantage of Victor's big stupid heart." She laughed to soften the words, and Valla chuckled along with her.

"He certainly suffers from that affliction. Too much heart." Her smile fell away, and she looked upward, blinking rapidly. "Of course, that's what I love about him, too."

"I know. I *know*!" Edeya squeezed her wrist again, and Valla cleared her throat, glancing up and down the parapet, confirming that the soldiers on watch weren't staring at her.

"Well, that's enough misty-eyed nonsense. Those flames will be here soon, and with their passage, we'll learn how effective they were at culling the undead."

At the urging pressure of Victor's will, his nightmarish alter ego, struggling in a slashing, gnashing, grappling match with the huge wampyr, took note of the warmth in his otherwise cold hard chest. Now that he was aware, that fire within vied for his attention, almost outshining the brilliant crimson-orange-yellow spirit with which he fought. The heat tickled there, almost like an itch, like a pressure that wanted to release. Yes, that was it; it wanted out. It wanted to vent forth!

Gripping Dunstan with his talons, slashing at him with his razor beak, the Aspect of Terror flapped his wings, fighting against Dunstan's near-equal strength as the huge wampyr gripped and clawed at his shadowy flesh and pushed and pulled with his own wings. The two wrestled and rolled, smashing into stones and sliding over the enormous cavern's floor. They tore through great fungi mounds, slid through brackish muddy water, and scattered ancient bones left over from some vast predator's meal. They screamed and shrieked and cried out with fury and pain, though the latter came only from the wampyr; the Aspect of Terror felt no pain, only hunger.

As they battered and struggled, Victor's nightmare form exuded fear, pushing it out in cloudy purple-black waves. His roiling shadows sought to wrap around the wampyr, tried to enter his wounds and twist his spirit. Dunstan was powerful, though, and his will resisted him. The nightmare's frustration mounted, and he continued to ponder the fire in his chest, seeking a way to send it forth. Victor, tiny in that dark corner of his mind, was aware of his hungry nightmare form's frustration, and he tried to guide it. He willed it to breathe, to open its Energy pathway and exhale.

With a triumphant shriek, the Aspect of Terror finally made the connection. With a minute shift of his will, the Energy pathway to his lungs opened, the roiling flames of its Breath Core drained into his lungs, and he opened his mouth to let them pour forth. Dunstan instantly released his hold on Victor's terror-born aspect. His monstrous face twisted in agony and surprise as those hot liquid flames bathed his chest and neck, pouring down over his torso and splashing onto his arms, face, and legs. He thrashed desperately, trying to get free, but the nightmare held him, claws bone-deep in his shoulders and thighs.

As Dunstan thrashed and his flesh burned away, his magical healing halted by the fire, Victor's monstrous archon of fear began to taste the echo of that dark emotion in Dunstan's heart. Finally, he'd overcome the wampyr's prodigious will. That bright spirit began to bleed out in dark purple-black waves, and he took it in. Dunstan moaned and writhed, but he grew ever weaker as his spirit dimmed and Victor's Core expanded with his feeding frenzy. Victor felt it, knew what was happening, and let go of any control he'd been fighting to maintain; his alter ego had earned his reward.

Sometime later, he opened his eyes to utter darkness. He lay flat on his back on a hard surface, and the only sounds he could make out were faint drips of water, distant rustles like a paper blown by a breeze, and occasional scrabbling scratches that evoked images of mice or rats in his mind. The last thing he remembered was being a passenger to his Aspect of Terror, watching and helping as it sought to kill Dunstan. He remembered the glorious release of his Breath Core and the subsequent feasting on Dunstan's spirit, but then he'd let go, exhausted by his struggles with the aspect's will.

It was a strange thing to think about. The aspect was him. The will he'd been struggling against was his own. What part of him was putting up that fight? What part of him was "Victor," and what part was the aspect? He knew objectively that the part of him that was ruled by fear, that hungered for its release, took over when he transformed, but that was just his Energy. No, he corrected himself; it was a part of his spirit, of who he was, and it was strong. He supposed "Victor," when it came to those struggles, was the rest of him, the other facets of his nature.

Shaking his head at his waking musings, Victor pushed himself to a sitting position, immediately noting that he clutched Lifedrinker's haft in one hand. "*Como estas,* beautiful?" The axe didn't answer him with words, but she vibrated comfortingly in his hand—she was fine. "Let's get some light on this subject!" Victor built the pattern for Globe of Insight and pushed a huge amount of Energy into it. Like a flare igniting, a brilliant ball of white-gold light exploded into being above his head. Victor willed it to rise and watched as his surroundings were revealed.

He knew immediately that he was still in the great cavern beneath Dunstan's castle. He could tell from the hunks of rock, the pools of water, the mounds of fungi. Even in the brilliant light of his orb, he couldn't see the walls, couldn't see the distant ceiling. "Where is that *pendejo*?" Victor frowned, realizing he had no System messages waiting for him. Even so, he'd only recently leveled. There was a good chance he hadn't gained anything tangible from the death of the wampyr lord—the System wouldn't tell him if he'd improved skills or levels unless they'd crested the next threshold.

He scanned the ground nearby, saw scattered bones, smears, and smudges of mud and blood, and knew he'd been fighting the wampyr nearby. Had he sacrificed his body to his ancestors? No, the aspect wouldn't do that, and Victor would remember if he had. He turned in a slow circle, looking for clues, and then he saw, on the other side of a shallow brackish pool, smears of silty clay and blood, almost as if something had been dragged through the water and out the other side. "Or like something dragged itself," he grunted, striding forward, willing his globe to follow.

He splashed through the shallow pool, only sinking to his ankles in the thin sediment at the bottom, and when he emerged on the other side, he stood stock still, closed his eyes, and listened. He heard dripping water nearby and in the distance. He heard the soft flutter of tiny wings, the scuttle of little clawed feet, and then, almost too soft to notice, the faint panting breaths and scuffing rustle of flesh dragging over stone. Victor opened his eyes and walked toward the sound. He rounded a large boulder, skirted a monstrous mushroom, and saw his pitiful quarry.

Dunstan's body was withered and frail. One wing was gone, burned to a blackened stump; his torso was similarly charred, and both of his arms were more like something you'd see on a rotting corpse than a vital, powerful vampiric creature. Through his blackened charred flesh, Victor could see the white of bones, and he knew his enemy must be on death's door. "Leaving?" he asked, striding forward, Lifedrinker in a loose two-handed grip.

Dunstan grunted and hissed, twisting to peer back at him through a face half burned to the skull. Only one eye reflected the glow of his light as he coughed in a wheezing voice, "Leave me."

"Is that a request?"

"Mercy, devil!"

"Oh? *I'm* the devil? Wasn't it you who threatened everyone I knew, said you'd make their lives an eternity of suffering?" Victor wasn't a cold-blooded killer. No, he liked to think he only enjoyed fighting and killing when his blood was hot. Nonetheless, he couldn't find any mercy in his heart for the twisted, ignoble monster crawling before him. He had questions he'd like to ask, information he'd like to gather from this man, this thing, but he couldn't stomach the idea of bargaining with the fiend. Though he didn't feel any qualms about finishing him off, he couldn't bring himself to embrace the idea of torture, either.

"I'll help you against Hector!"

Just as Victor had surmised, he was bargaining already. Could he take his information with false promises? Say he'd let him live, get what he wanted, and then kill him? He felt that was taking things beyond justice and into territory that might feed the darker parts of his soul. Instead, he tried honesty. "I'm going to end your suffering, Dunstan. I will not allow you to recover, and I will not bargain with you. Is there anything you'd like to tell me before the end?" As he mentioned allowing Dunstan to recover, Victor wondered what that would entail. Did he need blood like the vampires in the stories on Earth? Did he simply need time? Rather than risk it, he summoned his

Banner of the Champion and watched as its glittering yellow light joined that of his globe, and Dunstan cried out, recoiling and curling into a fetal position.

"Devil!" he croaked. "Kill me, then! Know that I'll curse you to hell and back. If I don't kill you in this life, I—" His words stopped short as Lifedrinker's smoking edge severed his thick blackened neck. Victor watched the wampyr's misshapen head roll away, then he kicked the giant charred corpse with his boot, flipping it onto its back. He lifted Lifedrinker and chopped at the blackened flesh over the ribs, hacking again and again until she split through those lifeless bones. The corpse was less resilient than in life, and soon he'd made a large opening.

"Thank you, *chica*." He carefully wiped Lifedrinker's edge on his sturdy leather pants and slung her into her harness. "Come here, bastard." He grabbed the edges of the wampyr's ribs and pulled, straining to widen the opening. When the dead bones still resisted him, he remembered his Sovereign Will bonus and switched it from dexterity to strength. As his muscles swelled and he felt a surge of vigor, he yanked and pulled on those bones, eliciting wet crunches and cracks as the cartilage and bone cracked and tore. When the hole was big enough, he plunged his fist into the opening and dug until he wrapped his fingers around the huge stiff muscle of the creature's heart.

Victor tugged and jerked, but the damn thing wouldn't come loose. In frustration, he let his rage loose into his pathways, and as his vision reddened and his anger began to mount, he gave in and cast Iron Berserk. His fist was still closed around the heart, and as he exploded with size, mass, and power, he roared and yanked, ripping the heart out of the creature with a triumphant bellow. Bits of flesh, blood, and bone showered down as he beheld the glistening prize in his fist. His chest heaved with the effort, and his mouth began to salivate at the sight.

A soft crackling sound distracted him enough to look away from the heart. Looking down, he saw that the wampyr's corpse was slowly blackening further, and as the flesh fell off, the bones had become like blackened coals with orange embers burning their way out from the inside. The creature was burning to ash before his eyes! Even in his rageful state, Victor wasn't dumb, and when he felt the heart growing hot in his hand, he understood what was happening—his trophy would burn up and join the rest of the wampyr as it dissolved. Without a second thought, he opened his titanic jaws and bit the organ in half, choking it down as quickly as he could before stuffing the other half in.

Beneath his rage, Victor felt satisfaction; even in death, Dunstan had tried to cheat him of his due, but he'd acted quickly and decisively. He wanted to laugh, roar, and taunt Dunstan's departing spirit, but his mouth was full, and he could feel the flesh trying to ignite despite his efforts. It was hot, as if he'd gulped a ladle of boiling soup, but he didn't care. He was flame-touched and a child of the Quinametzin. Hot flesh wouldn't dissuade him. Victor chomped the rest of the meaty, bitter heart and swallowed it down. As it ignited in his belly, he lifted his head and roared into the enormous cavern. Echoes responded—titans roaring back to him—and he smiled at the sound as he fell to his knees, then tilted backward as darkness took him.

In the light of dawn, Valla looked out again over the castle's ramparts. She saw nothing but a blackened, twisted wasteland that surrounded the keep. She walked the parapets, looking in every direction for signs of the undead, for signs of other enemies, and most of all for signs of Victor. The fires had come an hour after sunset and burned with the fury of mythical hells—walls of flame that rose hundreds of feet into the air, higher than the tallest trees surrounding the keep. If there hadn't been half a mile of damp misty grass between the forest and the keep, she wasn't sure even the Pyromancers and Wind Casters could have saved them. They might have cooked to death inside the stone walls.

As it was, the casters of the Ninth had been taxed, working for hours to funnel the smoke and heat away from the keep while the wall of fire slowly burned its way past them. Valla couldn't see any undead moving on the scorched fields around the keep, and nothing moved in the blackened forest. She wasn't surprised; she didn't know how anything could live through that. Had Victor even made it through? She'd seen him leap and knew he was resistant to fire, but even so, she had a new worry now that she'd seen the fire's ferocity.

She stopped her tour on the north side of the keep, looking to where the fire had gone, wondering if it had reached the edge of the trees. Had it consumed all the fuel, starved itself, and ended its brief violent reign of terror? That's where she stood, hands gripping the black stone parapet with white knuckles, her tension bleeding into her every move, when a soft flutter behind her and a sparkle of blue light told her Edeya had found her. "Did Sarl give you the news?" she asked as she settled onto the stone beside her.

"No!" Valla cried. "Tell me!"

"They rescued the Naghelli, almost all of them. Kethelket is bring-ing them here, but he says Victor stayed. He ordered Kethelket to get the Naghelli out while he created a distraction and tried to kill Dunstan."

"Why are they coming here? We're only hearing this now?" Valla practi-cally shrieked.

"I asked the same. Ronaga, one of Kethelket's lieutenants, let me read the message. His people were badly injured, missing their armor and weapons. They were fleeing pursuit, and he knew we couldn't leave until the fire passed anyway, so he didn't write immediately. He didn't want to leave, Valla, but Victor told Kethelket not to let his people die trying to help him. He says—"

"Damn him!" Valla interrupted, and didn't know if she was angry at Keth-elket or Victor. She turned and reached for her sword hilt, trusting in the spirit within the blade to calm her. She'd yet to awaken it, to hear its con-scious thoughts, but she swore she could feel things from it. As she'd hoped, the cool, vibrant Energy within the hilt helped to ground her. "Go on."

"He says that his people need to recover, but he wants to join you and the Ninth in taking Dunstan's keep. He says that the keep's defenders are weakened whether Victor wins or not. He says it may not be too late to help Victor." Edeya stopped speaking and watched Valla's face. When Valla's emo-tions and thoughts spun out of control and she struggled to find a response, Edeya said, "Let's claim this keep right now and march! Leave a hundred soldiers to hold it with Kethelket's wounded people."

Edeya's words were like a slap in the face, snapping her out of it. Of course! They needed to march! Victor might be in trouble, might need her help. Despite her conscious thought, a tiny voice in the back of her mind said, "Or he might be dead." She scowled, squelching that dissenting fragment of her mind, and started jogging for the nearest stairway. "Let's go! I'll meet you by the System Stone!"

37

OUT OF DARKNESS

Victor floated in a dark timeless void, his meandering thoughts the only clue to his continued existence. His physical presence was gone; his inner self, the place where his aura and Cores existed, was gone. He drifted free, weightless, bodiless, a clump of thoughts held together by his conscious perusal of them. He looked at his youth, at his frustrations with identity, at his fear of being abandoned. He studied his teen years, his anger, his violence, and his desperate grasp at control and belonging in competitive sports. He reviewed his time on Fanwath and Zaafor and studied his growth, the relationships he'd made, and the control he'd gained over his raw emotions.

Victor, if he were able to mark time, would have noted the disparate length of time he spent watching, savoring, and rewatching the parts of his life with those he held affection for. He remembered Yrella, poor, kind, luckless Yrella. He watched himself grow close to Edeya, saw himself lose his mind trying to protect her from the vile bastards who ran the mine. He saw himself befriending Thayla and then growing to love and respect her. Yrella and Edeya had been enough, but when Victor saw Thayla, he felt his heart would burst, and that's when he remembered who he was and believed he still existed, still lived.

Still, the void lingered, and his mind continued on, reviewing his relationships. He saw Chandri, felt his infatuation with her again, felt a sting and warm glow in his shoulder, and that sensation nearly pulled him out of the void he lingered in; he had a body, he just couldn't see it, couldn't feel it. His heart was fit to burst, but then he relived his time with Oynalla, Old Mother, and a stinging, itching sensation reminded him that he had eyes and that they were weeping. His mind drifted on, and he remembered Valla. He saw her as he'd first met her, standing in the antechamber to Rellia's quarters—prim, polite, stiff as a board. Again, his heart swelled to bursting as he relived his relationship with her.

He remembered getting to know her on the ride to Persi Gables, how she'd gone against Rellia to aid him in his quest for knowledge and vengeance. He watched as they were trapped on Zaafor and how they grew closer and closer, despite Tes, or perhaps because of their mutual affection for her. Tes! Victor hadn't thought of her in a while, but he did now, and his affection and love-swollen heart panged with a nostalgia his young spirit wasn't used to. What could have been? What might be?

"Gods be good, lad; your tethers pull hard! I almost lost hold of you!" The voice shattered his reminiscence, pulling him back to the dark void, to the nothingness in which he drifted. He recognized it, a gruff, deep, manly voice—Golgothaz. He tried to respond, but, as before, he hadn't the means with which to form words. "Don't fight to speak. Just listen! I took an interest in you and told you I'd give you my mark, and I did. Through that connection, I felt a struggle within you, and now I've pulled you here to provide a warning. Hear me well: the spirit you've consumed and tried to integrate into yourself will indeed grant you a boon, but it comes at a great cost. Gain the unnatural resistance to death of your foe at the expense of your vital force. If that isn't something you desire, I suggest you fight it; battle the change, crush the spirit, and absorb only its Energy."

Victor's mind spun. Vital force? Did Golgothaz mean that literally, as in the attribute, vitality? Or did he mean vital as in life? Was Dunstan's heart making him undead as he drifted in the strange timeless void? Again, he wished he could speak, to question the powerful entity, but his drifting had taken on a different nature; he experienced the sensation of falling despite the lack of gravity or even a body, and Golgothaz's final words came to him as though from a great distance. "You've been warned. Choose as you will."

Suddenly, Victor was back in his body, fully cognizant of his flesh, his heart, his Core, his spirit, and his pathways. He could feel the burning, acidic touch of the heart's strange brand of Energy as it worked to corrupt his cells, to change them into something more resilient, more dense, and capable of holding Energy, but thanks to Golgothaz's warning, he recognized the cost; his body would become more immediately powerful at the expense of his vital living force. What other costs would he have to bear? Would his unfeeling flesh affect his spirit? His heart? Would he lose the depths of his emotions? How different would a Victor numb to his passions be? Would he even be Victor?

These thoughts rushed at him, conclusions he leapt to by following logic that may have been faulty but was surely grounded in anecdotal evidence. Victor was a man of passion and warmth, a man who loved deeply and rode raging rivers of anger like a mythical steed. He knew one thing for certain: he would never trade his life, his potential, his current dreams, and his goals for an undead existence, even if it strengthened him in the short term. Hadn't he just beat the shit out of thousands of undead? Perhaps he'd not met their greatest exemplars, but there was no way he wanted to join that team.

With that conviction, Victor gathered his will. He turned his gaze inward and pulled on his indomitable aura for strength. He reached out beyond his pathways and pulled it in, using it to lead the charge against the foreign Energy he'd consumed, driving it out of his pathways, ripping it from the cells it had invaded, corralling it into his Core where he wound his furious hot rage-attuned Energy around it, then layered his other Energies, one after the other, around that cold blue-black ball of death-attuned Energy that had exploded out of the heart. Within that ball of Energy, at the very center, a shard of Dunstan's spirit burned like a white-hot coal, pulsing and flexing, resisting his efforts to break it down.

Victor growled, clenching his teeth as sweat exploded from his pores. His face turned bright red, and the veins in his eyes burst, turning the scleras crimson. He pressed his mountainous will down on the ball of Energies, exerting such a psychic pressure that he felt certain its collapse would cause an implosion that might be his undoing. Still, he focused and squeezed, pouring more and more of his Energy into the ball, and finally, with a release that felt like death, the fragment of Dunstan's spirit broke apart and bled into the death-attuned Energy. Without the wampyr lord's spirit providing resistance, his other Energies crushed the death affinity out of the ball, converting it to roiling, pure golden Energy that he carefully fed into his four affinities.

Victor sighed, releasing his hold on his Core, relaxing his aura, and letting himself breathe. When he opened his eyes, he saw nothing but darkness, but bright against that black landscape was a System message:

*****Congratulations! Your Core has leveled: Advanced 8.*****

"No 'unnatural resistance to death,' but two Core levels. I'll take it." He sighed heavily, sat up, and cast Globe of Inspiration. He still sat in the depths of the massive cavern beneath Dunstan's castle. Not far away was a vaguely humanoid-shaped pile of ash, and he knew it was the wampyr's remains. The idea that he had almost joined the ranks of the undead sent an involuntary shiver up the nape of his neck, and he said, "Fucking hell. Thanks, Golgothaz."

Thinking about it, though, he wondered why he hadn't had any trouble consuming the lesser wampyr hearts. Were the shards of their spirits too weak to begin the process? Had they simply collapsed under the weight of his will? One thing was sure: Dunstan's will had been prodigious. He'd fought off his Aspect of Terror for a long, long time, only succumbing when he'd been nearly cooked to death. His shard had put up a hell of a fight, too, not wanting to be broken down to pure Energy. "Note to self: Don't eat powerful undead hearts."

Victor stood up and walked over to the pile of ashes. He dragged his boots through them, sifting for anything the creature might have left behind. He was about to give up, finding nothing but rocks and fungi beneath the remains, but then a tinkling clink of metal caught his ear, and he reached down to snag a large silver key with four sets of teeth. It hung from a finely crafted, jewel-studded chain. Victor held the key and its lovely chain up in the bright light of his orb. "I wonder what you're meant to open," he said to it aloud. He stored the key away, then he sent more Energy into his light, growing it to floodlight proportions and sending it as high as he could with his will.

In the brighter light, he could just make out the extremities of the cavern in front of him and on his left. Looking up, he saw the distant ceiling, but scrutinizing it, he didn't see the hole he'd fallen through right away. He turned toward what he thought was the center of the enormous space and started walking, scanning his surroundings for clues and constantly looking up, trying to see the hole that would be his exit back to the keep above. It only took him a few minutes. The opening was small, a square shadow among other shadows, but Victor had good eyes, and his light touched the ceiling just enough to highlight its contours.

"How the hell am I supposed to . . ." Victor let his words trail off as he contemplated how he could get up to that distant opening. It had to be a thousand feet high. Could he leap that far? He didn't think so. He supposed he could summon his Aspect of Terror, but he was loath to. He hated the feeling of being locked away in a corner of his mind while the aspect did its thing. Worse, he knew the aspect would be focused on finding spirits it could absorb. Would he be able to steer it up to that hole, into Dunstan's underground throne room where nothing lived?

Victor growled in frustration and, on a whim, extinguished his Globe of Inspiration. In the pitch black that resulted, he slowly turned in a circle, staring into the depths of gloom, wondering if he might have missed something, some clue to navigate the buried recesses of the ancient cavern system. He knew from experience in the Greatbone Mine that the depths of Fanwath could be very deep indeed. He was already a tremendous distance beneath the surface, but if he tried to explore, he could find himself going into places from which egress might become nearly impossible. Still, something in his chest didn't want to allow the aspect loose, didn't want to fight that battle of wills again so soon.

He was about to give up, a half-baked idea of stacking boulders into a platform from which to leap forming in his mind, when he saw a faint flicker of yellow light. It was well beyond the opening above, high in the cavern wall but not nearly as high as the ceiling. Grunting with surprise and renewed hope, he started toward it. He didn't resummon his globe, fearing it would make his surroundings so bright that he wouldn't be able to navigate to the faint, distant light. Instead, he worked his way through the darkness by feel, walking slowly and carefully, trusting his incredible senses and instincts to help steer him around obstacles.

After a while, he realized he wasn't just "instinctively" walking around boulders, fungi patches, and pools. There might not be any light to speak of, but the shadows where objects existed had a different depth to them. It wasn't something he could readily see, or at least consciously point out, with his eyes, but he felt them. That said, he made good time over the cavern floor, and the tiny spot of light gradually grew more prominent and easier to see. It stretched into a circle, and then, as the minutes dragged on, and he felt he'd been walking more than an hour, he could clearly make out an ovoid tunnel opening, something like a hundred feet up the cavern wall.

He could remember seeing many tunnels in the walls when he'd been a passenger to the Aspect of Terror, but he didn't remember seeing light in any of them. What was this place so deep under the keep's grounds that was illuminated? When he made his way through the wampyr lair, it had been clear that they didn't value light. Why would they illuminate this buried passage?

He might not feel confident about leaping a thousand feet into the air, but he knew he could make it to that tunnel. Rather than cast Iron Berserk, Victor formed the pattern for Titanic Aspect. He didn't feel like getting pissed off again so soon after his ordeals with the wampyr. His body enlarged, he felt his perspective change, and then he squatted low and exploded into the air, hurtling toward that glowing opening in the darkness. The cool air rushed past him, whistling in his ears, and then he landed on hard, dusty stone, sliding several yards into a well-lit passage.

The mystery of the light's source was immediately cleared up. An ancient-looking glow lamp hung from the stone ceiling, and Victor could see in its illumination that the dusty corridor had been crafted, or at least refined; it wasn't a natural tunnel. The floor was solid stone, but gray granite blocks made up the walls. They were thick with rusty-orange mold, and Victor could smell a strange sulfurous odor in the air as he walked, kicking up little clouds of dust with his boots.

Despite his titanic size, the ceiling of the passageway was several feet overhead, and he didn't feel cramped by the walls. Whoever had crafted those stone walls had built something impressive. He didn't feel nervous, didn't feel watched, but he still reached up and loosened Lifedrinker in her harness, pulling her down into his hands. She was a comforting presence, and holding her reminded him of their last interaction, the one where she'd practically begged him to leave a fragment of his spirit with her. How was he going to deal with that? His approach to a T-junction chased the quandary from his mind as he slowly advanced.

When he reached the junction, he looked left and right and contemplated the choice. The tunnels looked identical, save a very slight downward grade in the one on the left. "What the hell am I doing? Dummy!" He laughed, shook his head at his behavior, and summoned his coyotes with inspiration-attuned Energy. They came into the world from a cloud of white-gold mist, yipping and crying, walking close to him, rubbing his legs as they circled. "All right, *muchachos*, find me the way out of this place."

As they yipped and barked, charging into the branching tunnels, he sat under the faint yellow glow of the ancient crystal-and-brass glow lamp and took a long deep breath. He didn't want to lean against the weird orange mold or fungi, or whatever it was called, so he sat in the middle of the floor and pulled a still-warm loaf of bread and a tall copper bottle of water from his storage ring. Five minutes later, he was munching on slices of bread spread with butter and jam and taking long satisfying gulps of water from the bottle. "Damn, that's good. Thirsty work messing up all those *vampiros*."

He got the impression from the feelings his pack sent his way that they were traversing a lot of ground and not finding much. Sometimes, he'd sense that one of the coyotes was chasing something small, probably a rat, but never that they felt any threat or alarm. It took an hour before he finally felt a surge of excitement and a sense of success from one of the pack; the faithful companion had found a way up and out. Victor stood up and turned right, instinctively knowing the coyote who'd signaled success could be found in that direction.

He only walked up that passage for ten minutes or so before it started to slope upward gradually. He continued, and slowly, one by one, his coyotes found their way back to him. The last one to rejoin the pack was the one he'd been waiting for, and when it saw him, it turned and started trotting ahead. Victor broke into a jog, following it through ancient dusty tunnels, turning again and again, gradually working his way up and up through the bedrock beneath the mountain on which the wampyrs' keep had been built.

Eventually, he came to an ancient stone stairway and noted the different nature of the mold clinging to the stones and the damp, seeping water that shimmered in the still-present glow lamps. He wondered how old those lamps must be, silently praising the long-gone individual who'd crafted them. With his pack at his heels, he climbed those steps, two at a time; his titanic aspect had long since faded. After a hundred steps or so, he came to the rotten, partially petrified timbers of an ancient iron-strapped door. He tried to open it, but it was swollen, wedged to the stone by moisture and moldy growths.

Victor smashed a boot into the ancient rusty latch, and the door broke apart, fragments flying off into the dark room beyond. "No more ancient lamps?" As his coyotes, panting, yipping, and crying, rushed past him into the new area, Victor summoned his Globe of Inspiration. The light revealed an ancient stone room, and Victor could see large gaps in the walls, through which, he was quite certain, stars flickered. He stepped through, turned left, and saw an archway beyond which he could see the light of the Sisters glimmering on silvery waves as they crashed with a distant roar on a beach.

Victor hurried out and stood on the crumbling landing of a long-forgotten stairway. Behind him rose a similarly crumbled tower, and to his right, half a mile along the slopes of a tall granite cliff face, Dunstan's keep rose against the mountainside. "Huh. Well, *chica*, let's go see how those wampyrs feel about me killing their *padre*."

38

❈

DIFFERENT KINDS OF FREEDOM

Victor patted Guapo's shoulder as he approached the big curtain wall. He wasn't trying to hide or sneak into the keep this second time. He'd killed anything in there that was a threat to him, and he was tired of skulking around in shadows. He'd cast Iron Berserk and summoned his banner, and now he sat atop a glory-attuned mustang, the center of a blazing circle of daylight in the middle of the night. He wasn't sure how much time had passed since he first entered the keep with Kethelket and Victoria. It felt like a dozen hours to him, but it could have been longer—he'd lost track of time when in his Aspect of Terror and also when he ate the wampyr's heart.

The strange thing was that he didn't see any defenders atop the wall, nor were there any lights to speak of. Hadn't he noticed lamps when they'd snuck in? Dunstan's non-monstrous followers seemed to require illumination to see. This time, the keep was dark and quiet and felt utterly deserted. Victor rode straight up to the gate, and when no challenge, no arrows, no magical bolts came his way, he sat there for a moment and watched. The gate was impressive—thirty feet high and twenty wide, constructed of massive thick planks of some kind of hardwood. He could see the bolts in the wood that must hold the crossbeams on the other side in place.

Victor figured that given time, he could break through that gate, but he wouldn't waste the effort. If he had to force his way into the keep, he'd just leap up to the parapets. After studying the weathered stone of the wall for a while, hoping to catch sight of any movement within, he grew impatient and shouted, "Open the gate!" It was a long shot, he knew, but still, he figured if they weren't actively trying to defend, maybe the soldiers within were broken or fled, and some forgotten servant or thrall might do as he asked. He was just getting ready to dismount and leap up to the ramparts when he heard clacking and creaking as someone turned a windlass in the gatehouse.

The gates shuddered and shook as the bar was slowly lifted. "*¿Interesante, verdad, chico?*" Victor patted Guapo again as he waited and watched the left-hand gate haltingly swing open. He could hear grunting and muffled curses, and he saw a pale hand gripping the wooden edge, so he knew someone was there, working to grant him entrance. He still didn't feel any threat, so he sat relaxed, Lifedrinker still in her harness, and waited until the gate was pulled wide and a man stepped out from behind it into the light of his banner. He squinted and shielded his eyes, but his pale flesh didn't burn or smoke.

He wore a black tunic over black leggings and carried a sword sheathed at his waist. When he slowly lowered his hand, exposing his face, Victor was surprised to see a very normal, if pale, human man looking up at him. "Hail, Lord. We beg your mercy."

"We?"

"We that survived the death of Lord Dunstan."

"Explain." Victor nudged Guapo forward, and the massive mustang's hooves danced with sparks as he pranced toward the gate, each step a bass drumbeat on the gravel roadway. The man stumbled back but caught himself as Victor slowed, stopping inside the entrance, making it clear that he wasn't going anywhere.

"Some of us were newly taken by Lord . . ." He shook his head, and Victor saw him grimace. "By Dunstan. We hadn't taken much of the wampyr nature from him yet, so when he died, we reverted to our old selves. Well, our old selves in addition to memories of a waking nightmare. Most of Dunstan's people burned to ash when he died. There's just a hundred or so of us inside."

"Gather everyone. Bring them to the courtyard. If you deal with me honestly, there will be mercy."

"Thank you, Lord!" The man bowed and turned to hurry through the gate tunnel, but he stopped and turned. "Lord, do you mean the inner courtyard or the bailey here between the walls?"

"Inner."

Victor watched him hurry away, running up the slightly sloping cobbled roadway that led from the curtain wall to the inner keep gates. He took his time following, contemplating the man's words. Dunstan's grip on the wampyrs had been so thorough that when he died, so did they? What did they get in that bargain? Eternal "life"? A faster route to power than gaining their own levels and skills? Perhaps it wasn't a gift. If he believed the man who'd just spoken to him, it was more of a curse. It sounded as though he hadn't come into Dunstan's service willingly. Whatever the case, it highlighted another difference between the wampyr and vampyr factions of the invading army.

As he allowed Guapo to walk toward the open inner gateway, he looked left and right, taking in the bailey grounds. The whole space between the walls was cobbled, and he saw ballistae and barrels lining the inner parapets. Barricades stood on the bailey ground, and he could imagine archers using them to slow attackers who'd breached the curtain wall. It was a strong keep, and he figured the right defenders could hold off quite an army from within. Scanning around, he tried to see remnants of the defenders who'd supposedly spontaneously combusted at Dunstan's death, but the air was damp with mist, and he could smell rain. So close to the sea, he wouldn't be surprised if they'd been washed away.

Even taking his time, Guapo's steps were huge, and soon he *clip-clopped* his way through the inner gatehouse and came into the courtyard where, in rows of twenty, more than a hundred men and women, dressed much like the first man he'd seen, knelt on the hard cobbles, heads down, waiting for him. He sat atop Guapo, looking down at them, running his eyes over the rows, staring at each of them for a second or two, wondering what he might see. None looked up to meet his gaze. None gave off any whiff of power or Energy use. He thought he saw several of them trembling, from fear or weakness, he didn't know.

"Who spoke to me at the gate?"

A figure in the front row straightened and looked up, meeting his gaze. "I did, Lord."

"Your name?"

"Smythe, Lord. Perry Smythe." His voice was steady, and he looked earnest, his brown eyes unflinching when Victor gazed into them.

"Perry, what would you have me do with a bunch of one-time enemies? Undead creatures who sought to slay me and mine?"

"Lord, we aren't undead. If we were, well, it's 'cause that bastard took us from the villages on his lands and made us so."

"On Dark Ember?"

"Aye. We were serfs on his lands; the vampiric lords and ladies keep us for food and to fill their armies."

"And entertainment," a woman said from somewhere in the middle of the group.

Victor frowned and contemplated the group. He believed them, but could he trust them? "What happened to the belongings of the ones who burned up?"

"Most of their things burned with 'em, Lord, but we found some weapons and jewels in the ashes."

Victor took a deep breath through his nose and sighed heavily. "Listen. I'll give you all a chance to earn some trust. Bring everything you looted from the dead and from this place and pile it before my horse. Let's keep this orderly—one by one, left to right, row by row." Victor watched as they did just as he'd commanded. The one-time wampyr thralls stood and began to deposit knives, swords, maces, axes, spears, and jewelry of all sorts, but mostly rings, in neat piles in front of Guapo. He maintained his banner and watched them as they approached, looking into their eyes, trying to read if any were harboring hidden animosity or faking their tolerance of the fiery sun hanging behind him.

In the end, all he felt was pity for the wan, thin, desperate men and women. The piles of jewelry were impressive, and Victor wondered if these poor survivors had thought themselves rich and free until he'd shown up. When they finished, he asked Perry, "Did you loot the dead in the tunnels beneath the keep?"

"Aye, Lord."

Victor pulled out the huge silver key from storage and held it up by its chain. "Do you know what this opens?"

"Aye, Lord," he said again, "that's the key to the silver door atop yonder tower." He pointed to the big round tower that rose near the rear of the keep. There weren't any windows near the top, and its roof was made of some kind of dark unreflective metal. Lead?

"Okay, Perry, let me ask you again: What would you have me do with you all, undead or not?"

Again, a woman spoke up before Perry could answer, "We want free-dom!" Murmurs of agreement vied with shushes and pleas for mercy from the kneeling crowd. Victor frowned and contemplated the people. If what they claimed was true, then they certainly deserved pity and probably the mercy they asked for. They'd taken up arms for Dunstan but hadn't been part of the winged wampyr horde that had kidnapped Kethelket's people. Could he blame them, anyway? Apparently Dunstan had taken them and infected them with his brand of vampirism against their will, and somewhat recently, if he were understanding things correctly. That was why they hadn't burned to ash.

Even taking all that at face value, their demands for freedom were a bit much. All the men and women in the legion and supporting it were here, fighting for their own lands, their own freedom. Should it just be given to these people? Shouldn't they help? He thought about it some more, watching the crowd, knowing he held their lives in his hands. "I'll grant you the mercy of not holding you responsible for the actions of Dunstan and his wampyrs. I'll also grant you your freedom, but if you're hoping to settle in these lands, you'll need to aid our cause. If you don't want to do that, if you don't want to fight against Hector's undead invasion, then you'll need to march your asses north through the pass, and you can try to find your freedom in the Ridonne Empire."

As he spoke, many of the kneeling black-clad former wampyr thralls looked up, their pale faces staring toward him atop his gigantic steed, and Victor saw hope and relief in their eyes. He knew what they were feeling; he'd felt it too when the nobility of Fanwath had enslaved him and sent him into the mines, and then he'd had a glimmer of hope sparked to life in his heart with just a touch of kindness from Captain Lam. "Stand up," he growled. As they complied, rising to stand in ranks before him, he continued, "If you mean to stick with me and put the undead assholes invading this land to the torch, then stay put. If you want to head out and try to make your fortune beyond the mountains to the north, then walk out this gate and wait for me. I'll write you a letter so the people guarding the pass will let you through."

He watched as the people slowly looked around at each other, none speaking, none moving. After a few minutes, when they'd ceased their looking around, and every one of them still stood before him, he said, "You're sure? None of you want to leave?"

The same woman spoke up again, her voice strident, "Lord, there are different kinds of freedom, and my heart won't feel truly free 'til I've seen that green star extinguished and know the portal to Dark Ember is closed." The crowd shouted their agreement, some of them raising fists in the air, and for the first time, Victor saw fire in their eyes, perhaps fanned to life from the hope he'd given them.

"That's how you all feel?" Victor slid off Guapo's back and, with a firm pat to his haunch, sent the mount back to the spirit plane. He stood before the assembled defectors, towering over them in his titanic form, his banner blazing behind him. When none of them objected to the woman's words, Victor nodded, loosening Lifedrinker from her harness and holding her before him. "If you want to stay with me, you'll need to swear an oath. I want each of you to stand before me, tell me your name, and swear that you'll stay loyal to our cause. Swear that you'll fight against the invaders from Dark Ember. More, I want you to swear to learn about the customs of this world and work to fit in."

The woman was the first to step to the front, and the man who'd first spoken to him, Perry Smythe, lined up behind her, then everyone else jostled to get into line. The woman was slender but tall, and her long wavy red hair was pulled back and tied into braids with leather cords. She took a knee before him and looked up, tiny next to his bulk but pale eyes fierce as she said, "Lord, I am Agnes, and I swear to help you and your army to push the invaders out. I swear, on the bones of my mother, Sigrid, that I will stay loyal to you and learn the ways of this new world."

"Well said, Agnes. I accept you and swear to treat you fairly and fight with you against our mutual enemies." Victor saw tears spring into the woman's eyes as he said the words, and when she stood and moved back into line, they were streaming freely down her cheeks. So began a very emotional experience for Victor and the survivors of Dunstan's vampirism. One after another, the former thralls knelt before him, swore their loyalty, and heard his pledge in return. Many of them wept openly, and Victor struggled to keep his own eyes dry, imagining the roller coaster of emotions these people were feeling, the struggles they'd gone through.

As he'd thought earlier, he had some common ground with them, had known the feeling of a yoke around his neck. He also knew what it felt like to be free and to feel the bond of loyalty when he'd thought he was alone. He didn't know what these people had planned when their lord died, didn't know if they were expecting to be recaptured or killed, or if they had some hope that they might break free and find a way to live with their newfound freedom. He hoped they didn't see his arrival as that of simply a new lord they had to serve. That was why he'd offered them the chance to leave, to find their way outside these lands. To him, their unanimous decision to stay meant a lot; they could have, just as easily, all decided to leave.

When the last one swore to him, Victor nodded to his newly assembled allies and severed the connection to his Iron Berserk spell, reducing himself down from mythic proportions. "Thank you, everyone. One thing you'll need to know, though, is that I value your word, and I consider you my brothers and sisters in battle now, but the people of Fanwath aren't so quick to trust. They have customs that are hard to shake. Everyone in our army has bound themselves with a System contract, agreeing to pretty much the same thing you all just swore to me. When I assign you to a new captain, you'll need to do the same."

"How long will we be so bound to the captain, Lord?"

"Only until this campaign ends. Once we've driven the invaders out, the contract expires, but I'll always hold you to the oath we just swore to each other. Does anyone have an objection?" Silence met his question, so Victor nodded, swinging Lifedrinker back up and into her harness. "Someone show me the System Stone in this keep. I mean to claim it."

Agnes pointed to the keep's darkly stained wooden doors, which stood open, and said, "In the great hall, just past those doors and through the next."

Victor strode forward, down the ranks of his new soldiers, and heard them fall into line behind him. When he glanced over his shoulder, he saw two single-file lines, remarkable in their orderly formation. He climbed the steps, passed through the door, and saw a faintly illuminated pair of doors straight ahead in the dim, unlit shadows of the grand foyer. He walked toward them and pulled the handle of the one on the right. It swung open with a squeak of unoiled hinges, and then he saw Dunstan's former great hall, or, at least, the one he hadn't used, the one not buried in twisting catacombs full of ugly vampiric monsters.

The hall of the Sea Keep, as Victor was starting to call the place mentally, was vast. It wasn't remarkable for much more than that, however. The ceilings were massively vaulted with at least twenty two-hundred-foot beams spanning the length of it, holding up the great weight of the stones above. It spread out from left to right, rectangular in shape, with a grand stone fireplace at either end. No furniture adorned the ample space, but floating at the center, directly in front of the door where Victor stood, was another System Stone, just like the ones he'd seen in the other keeps.

Victor walked forward, the former thralls at his heels, and placed his hand on the slowly rotating stone. It stopped its movement immediately, and he saw a familiar message before his eyes:

*****This stone is undefended, and you have sufficient forces in the vicinity to claim this outpost. Do you wish to do so?*****

"Good," Victor muttered, glad to see the System had recognized these people as his "forces." He mentally affirmed his decision to claim the outpost, and, just as before, an Energy-rich breeze began to blow through the keep, seemingly coming out of nowhere or perhaps from the stone itself. It gently blew over his flesh, tickling it with an electric touch, and he heard the people around him sighing and laughing, perhaps feeling Energy untainted by a death affinity for the first time.

Though no lights came to life in the hall, his banner brilliantly lit it, and the stones, the wood, and the very air seemed to feel lighter, less oppressive. He knew that if he went outside, the darkness wouldn't be so dark, the mist and fog in the air would be gone, and he and his new followers would be able to breathe easier.

*****Congratulations! Your forces have claimed this outpost and its surrounding lands. Defend it from your enemies and continue your conquest! For your victory, your faction will be rewarded a Chest of Conquest—this only occurs the first time you claim any given territory.*****

Cheers broke out around him as the System's message appeared, and Victor smiled, glad his new allies were sharing in the victory. His hand suddenly fell away from the stone, released as the process of claiming the outpost ended. Smoke began to gather at his feet, and he knew what it was: the Chest of Conquest was about to take form. Something was different, however. He remembered blue smoke at Old Keep, but this smoke was purple and sparkled with silvery lights.

39

TREASURES AND MYSTERIES

As the chest took form, Victor looked around at the men and women who'd just joined his cause. "Perry, can you take some soldiers and secure the gate?"

"Aye, right away, Lord." Perry called out several names and led a small group toward the courtyard. Victor nodded, looking around the crowd.

"Agnes, will you put together a list of troops for me? Everyone's names, their level, and their particular talents? It'll help me get your people placed with the proper units when the army arrives. Oh, and go ahead and pick out an assistant or two—we'll need to catalog all the weapons and other loot you found on the dead wampyrs."

"I can do that."

Victor noticed her eyes linger on the chest by his feet, and he shook his head. "This one's for me. I went through quite a bloodbath to earn this chest." He spoke loudly, looking around the crowd, meeting the eyes of any who would dare. He wasn't ashamed of claiming this prize, and if anyone objected, he'd love to hear their arguments. None did, however. In fact, most of the one-time thralls nodded enthusiastically to his declaration.

"Lord Victor?" Agnes spoke up, interrupting his perusal of the room and the expressions on the soldiers' faces.

"Yeah?"

"Do you have an extra bit of paper and a writing utensil?" She looked almost embarrassed, and Victor felt stupid. These people had been little more than slaves before Dunstan had died, and then he'd come along and demanded they give up all the loot they'd scavenged.

He produced a notebook and an enchanted pen from one of his storage rings and handed it over. "Of course." He almost asked her if she knew how to read and write, trying to imagine the kind of village she'd come from, a place where normal humans were allowed to live and have families but were treated as livestock to the wampyrs. He caught himself, though, deciding to trust that she'd say so if she couldn't. Even so, he couldn't help asking a tangential question. "You all had access to Energy, to cultivation and whatnot back on Dark Ember, right? I mean, back in your villages before Dunstan took you."

"We did, to a degree, though Dunstan's sheriffs saw to it that none of us grew powerful enough to pose a threat."

"Well, that's over now. At least for you all."

"It is, but the thirst for vengeance burns in my throat. I hope you won't send us far from the front, into some training camp or on garrison duty." Victor could hear the ferocity in her words, saw the spark in her eyes, and knew she spoke the truth. It resonated in his chest, echoed the fury he'd once felt when he'd wanted to rip the arms off every baton-wielding mine employee.

"Don't worry about that. If I have my way, you'll be joining up with the Glorious Ninth—my army's best cohort, and you'll see plenty of action with them."

Agnes nodded and smashed a fist to her chest before turning and calling out the names of her chosen helpers, striding out of the hall. Many of the others had already left, returning to the courtyard, perhaps to go up on the walls and witness the withdrawal of the sickly fog. The ones who'd remained were likely hoping to see something of the treasure he would pull from the chest, and Victor, too, was interested to see what he'd earned. He briefly considered setting aside whatever he got for the "campaign store," but decided he'd been selfless enough; it was time to take his due. He'd claim what he wanted and give the rest to the quartermaster for the store.

He bent to lift the hinged lid of the dark metallic chest, watching as more sparkling purple smoke escaped from the interior. It was odorless, that smoke, and when Victor waved it away, not a hint of it remained. It had simply dispersed into nothingness, much like the smoke left behind by his spirit fire when it consumed the sacrifices he made to his ancestors. Peering into the open container, Victor saw only four items. An ornately carved silver spyglass sat beside a shimmering opalescent potion bottle, and next to that were two gold-foil-wrapped, apple-shaped objects.

"Hmm," Victor said, reaching into the chest to retrieve the spyglass. It was small in his hand, only six inches long, but every square millimeter was delicately carved in whorls and tiny images, from flowers to stars to weird angular runes that, despite his System Language Integration skill, meant nothing to Victor. It was heavy for its size, and even from a distance, Victor could see the weird flickers of Energy and color within the lens.

He held the small end to his eye and pointed it at one of the former thralls at the other end of the great hall. The blurry image clarified almost instantly as the magical lens focused, and then the close-up view of the soldier changed slightly as a pale green halo took shape around her head. "Huh." Victor pulled the spyglass away from his eye and then chose a new target, aiming his view at a burly man near the exit. Just as before, the glass focused quickly, and a soft pale green halo appeared around his head. Victor pocketed the little scope, intent on experimenting with it further, then turned back to the chest.

He picked up the opalescent potion and, to his relief, found a handwritten label stuck to the bottom of the little bottle. "Vanderstahl's Regenerative Tonic," he softly read, raising an eyebrow. He'd of course learned about potions that could regenerate lost limbs and worse while he'd been in Coloss, and he wondered if this was just such an item. He nodded, pleased to have something like that to fall back on, and tucked it away in a storage ring. Next, he reached down and plucked up one of the foil-covered fruits.

The feel and heft served to confirm his theory; it felt just like an apple. He needn't have wondered, however. Just as with the potion, he found a label affixed to the gold foil on the bottom of the fruit, reading, "Apple of Evolution." The fruit had no odor, and he couldn't sense any Energy within it, though he reasoned that could be because of the foil—it might be magical, designed to keep the fruit's potency intact. He tucked them both into his ring, already making plans for what he'd do with them; he might have decided this chest's rewards were his to claim, but that didn't mean he couldn't share.

While he'd been studying the final contents, he'd expected the chest to disappear, but it was still there when he glanced down. Wondering what he'd missed, he peered back inside to see the lining at the bottom hadn't been just part of the container—it was another banner. When he lifted it out, the chest broke apart into purple shimmering smoke and was gone. Victor hung the banner, exactly like the one he'd gotten at Old Keep, over his shoulder and walked outside. It wasn't lost on him that he had an entourage of a dozen or so soldiers who seemed intent on following him around.

In the courtyard, he found Agnes and three others sitting around the pile of weapons and other loot, sorting them by type and apparent quality. Looking up on the ramparts, he saw Perry and a dozen or more other soldiers walking about, keeping watch. The skies were cloudy, though brighter, the unnatural fog having fled the keep's environs. Victor took a good long deep breath and nodded. He held out the banner in one big fist and said, "Someone take this and put it over the outer gates so my allies don't mistakenly attack us."

"Aye, Lord!" one of his hangers-on said, stepping forward to grab the big silky cloth. Victor watched him hurry out of the courtyard, running through the bailey toward the curtain wall, and then he let his gaze drift up to the big tower. "All right, let's go see what this key will reveal." He was talking to himself, mostly, or maybe Lifedrinker, but he realized the soldiers following him around thought he was speaking to them—several muttered their agreement, and they turned to the keep, hurrying to open the door for him.

Victor paused to look over the group of men and women. There were nine of them gathered near the door, watching, waiting for him to move or say something. He wasn't sure how he felt about having an entourage escorting him around the new keep, but he didn't know if he should even make a big deal about it. Maybe they were just bored. There wasn't a lot going on while they waited for word from, well, anyone.

He'd hoped to find Kethelket outside when he emerged, but he hadn't been surprised not to. He must have taken his people to rejoin the rest of their forces. Still, he'd hoped for some sign or signal from him, Valla, or even Rellia and Borrius. "Should have kept one of the command books for myself." He looked up, noting the puzzled looks on those nearby, and asked, "How many days ago did I kill Dunstan?"

"Five days, Lord."

"Five, sir!"

"Five days and nights have passed . . ." The third to answer trailed off as they all hurried to be the one to give him the news. Five days was a lot more than he'd thought, but he wasn't too surprised. How many times had he passed out, had visions, and lost days or even weeks as his mind and body processed whatever weird thing he'd done to it? The news made Kethelket's absence even more understandable.

"Right. I'll be surprised if my people aren't nearby, perhaps already watching the keep. Hopefully, we'll get word when they see my banner on display. For now, I need you folks to help keep watch for them. Be sure to explain that I'm in the keep and that I'll come to speak to them if any appear. Be aware that some can fly and may approach from the air. Don't respond with violence! Spread the word." Several of the group nodded and hurried off, but Victor wasn't satisfied. "I only need one of you to stay with me. Someone who knows the way to the tower so I'm not wandering around this keep."

"I will!" a young woman announced, glaring at the others until they nodded and began to shuffle off, a few with unhappy grumbles. Victor chuckled and examined his guide. She was an interesting-looking character. The sides of her head were shorn down to a black stubble, and the top hung in braids woven through with carved wooden and bone loops, if he wasn't mistaken. Her pale face was marked by dozens of deep, raised, red scars, and the hollows of her dark eyes were shaded by black paint. She looked fierce and sturdy, tall and broad-shouldered.

"What's your name?"

"Nia, Lord."

"All right, Nia. Lead me to the tower, please." At his words, she turned and began to hurry through the keep. She led him up two flights of stairs, down several long corridors, and then through a heavy polished door into another steep winding stairway. Victor could tell they were in the tower by the nature of the curved walls and by peering through the occasional window. "Did Dunstan have this glass installed, or was it here?"

"I believe it was here, Lord."

"You don't have to say 'lord' whenever you speak to me. I'd rather you didn't."

"Very well." She climbed steadily without tiring, and as they passed the first door on a short landing, she pointed to it. "Nothing much in there. Some old scraps of furniture."

"Okay. You know the keep well?"

"Aye, from our time here as thralls and from the last few days scrounging for food and valuables."

"Food . . . what did you have to eat when you were thralls?"

"Lord, please forgive me, but I'd rather not dwell on my time under the curse. It's a nightmare I'd soon put behind me, but to answer your question, we ate but sparingly; our bodies were changing, and we hungered for only one thing—the blood Dunstan's wampyrs doled out to us."

"Yeah, that's shitty. We'll get your bellies full of warm, good food soon." He followed her up several more levels and then asked, "Do you have any idea what's behind the door?"

"Likely something unholy. Dunstan kept it well guarded, and it resisted all our attempts to break it open. The door's metal is magically warded and infused; we pounded and pried at it, but it mended itself faster than we could damage it. Some of the lads were thinking of chipping away the stone walls to get inside, but our explorations through the keep and catacombs kept us distracted." She looked over her shoulder, her dark shadowed eyes briefly locking with his. "Then you came along."

"Do you resent me?"

"Resent? The one who freed us? The one who saved our very souls? Not in a million lifetimes, Lord."

"What level are you, Nia? Forgive my bluntness."

"I'm Level Twenty-Four. I have the damned blood affinity of my former master, but I'll be using it for healing. I swear on the graves of my mother and my baby sister, taken by the fiend that was my father."

"Your father . . ."

"Aye. He was taken by Dunstan when I was a girl of twelve. He came back to visit us in Brook Hollow, the village where we lived when I was fifteen, and on that visit, he flew into a rage . . ." Her voice grew quiet, her words trailing off.

"Forget it. I'm sorry I asked; I didn't mean to open up old wounds."

"Thank you, Lor . . . thank you."

Victor let his mind wander down dark roads, imagining the lives of the people, the ordinary humans on Dark Ember, and their horrific existence. Despite his efforts to avoid it, despite consciously trying to keep the thought from forming, he found a part of himself beginning to wonder if he'd be satisfied with simply killing Prince Hector and driving the invaders out of Fanwath. He scowled, shaking his head. Hadn't Victoria told him that Hector was a minor lord in the grand scheme of Dark Ember? Hadn't she said the old ones, the truly powerful undying masters of that world, had been in power for hundreds of years, that they'd been ancient even before fleeing Earth? "Talk about biting off more than I can chew . . ."

"I'm sorry?"

"Nothing, Nia. Well, not nothing, but nothing I can really contemplate right now." As he spoke, they rounded the final curve of the stairs, and there before him was an ornate rune-inscribed silver door with a big four-pronged keyhole at its center. "Well, well. What's hiding behind such a fancy door, I wonder?"

Nia moved to the side, taking up a position against the stone wall to the left of the door. Victor produced the heavy silver key and stepped forward to insert it into the weird slot. It sank home with a satisfyingly smooth series of clicks, almost as if a magnet had pulled it in. He slowly rotated the key, each quarter-turn eliciting a resounding click in the silver door. When he'd spun it through a full rotation, the door pulled away from the frame with a hiss of moist warm air. "Whoa, airtight." Victor held an arm over his nose, troubled by the strange musty ripe air. It didn't quite smell like decay or death, but it didn't smell fresh.

Before he opened the door further, he listened, waiting to see what might reveal itself. The only sound to come to his ears was a faint ticking as the door's metal began to contract, perhaps adjusting to the much cooler ambient temperature outside the interior room. Victor put a hand on Lifedrinker's haft and pulled the door open with the other. When the steam wafted out of his eyes and he focused on the weird, red-lit interior, he almost ripped her free from her harness and cast Iron Berserk.

The room was oval in shape and completely lined with the same rune-inscribed silver as the door he'd just opened. It was like a vault almost, making Victor realize the former thralls never would have been able to break into it by chipping away the stone walls outside. A globe of red-veined crystal hung from the center of the domed ceiling, pulsing with crimson light, and beneath it was a silver chair. What had startled Victor and almost sent him into a violent rage was the naked shriveled body of a man on the metal chair. He wore nothing save the same black stone crown that Victor had seen on the horrible wampyr, Dunstan.

Victor might have thought the wampyr had cheated death somehow, reconstituted himself in this chamber, if not for the gaping hole in the body's chest where a heart should have been. Had Victor stopped the creature from resurrecting itself by eating its heart? If not the consumption of the flesh, had his destruction of part of its spirit disrupted the weird magic? Victor turned to Nia. "You know anything about this?" He moved to the side, making room for her so she could gaze within, and watched as her eyes widened in horror and a hand flew to her mouth. Her surprise seemed genuine.

"There were rumors, whispers that Dunstan was immortal, more than . . . usual for his kind. It's certainly true that he was very old, though not as ancient as the great masters of Dark Ember."

Victor jerked his chin at the metal door and the room beyond. "Was this silver chamber here when you all arrived?"

"I don't think so, Lord. I was a lowly thrall, however—I know not what Dunstan brought from Dark Ember. I was set to watch the battlements almost from the moment we arrived. I do recall seeing the windows of this tower being filled in with stone, though."

"Okay. Do me a favor and go to the stairs. Holler if you hear anyone coming." Victor gestured around the curve of the tower to where the landing was. Nia hurried to fulfill his request, and he turned back to the door. He'd had a strange wave of paranoia when he thought about investigating the chamber, a spine-tingling wave of claustrophobia at the idea that someone might swing that silver door shut on him. With that in mind, he moved around to the front of the door and tried to remove the key, but it wouldn't slide free in the open position.

Growling, Victor summoned his great bear totem with inspiration-attuned Energy. The monstrous creature stepped out of a cloud of shimmering white-gold mist, a deep rumble of greeting in his throat. A yelp from the other side of him, near the stairs, told Victor that Nia had noticed his massive companion, so he called out, "Don't worry; he's here to watch my back, too."

"As you say, Lord." Nia's voice came to him from beyond the bulk of his friend.

"Okay, *hermano*, you sit in front of that door and don't let anyone close it on me, *comprende?*"

The bear huffed, pressing his enormous forehead down and into Victor's shoulder, then he stepped back and ponderously lay down before the door. There was no way anyone was going to swing that thing shut without making a hell of a scene trying to move his companion. Nodding, Victor steeled himself and stepped into the weird round chamber, ready to try to figure out the mystery of the humanoid corpse wearing Dunstan's crown.

40

A NEED FOR CLARITY

The air in the spherical chamber was moist and warm, and Victor hated breathing it into his lungs. Nonetheless, he walked in and let his gaze drift over the rune-inscribed walls, floors, and ceiling. With nothing else to focus on, he stepped toward the body in the silver chair and the crystal globe suspended above it. Victor had seen plenty of undead, and though they often looked much like a corpse, much like the body before him, they always had some sort of aura, an Energy that gave their deathly aspect some palpable vitality. This body was inert, of that he was certain.

Was it Dunstan? Victor found himself asking the question repeatedly as he took in the frail withered form. He supposed it could be. This is what the man might have looked like sans his transformation into a wampyr. How would he ever know? Even if he could test DNA, he didn't have a sample from the previous monster before it was reduced to ash and left buried in the depths of the catacombs. "The crown," he muttered. It was the only real clue he had—that and the hole where the corpse's heart should be. Why would nothing but the key to this chamber remain in the ashes of the wampyr? The crown hadn't been there; it was here.

With dread sending a chill down his spine, he lifted a hand toward the weird, crudely inscribed stone circle. The artifact certainly didn't match the aesthetic of the silver sphere. Its stone material was one thing, but its sharp, angular runes were also at odds with the elaborate, fanciful text scribed on every square inch of the sphere. When his flesh touched the stone, his mind flashed with images of Dunstan's wampyr form wearing it, looming large with lustful red eyes. He couldn't tell if it was just his memory jumping to recollections of his battle or if the crown really projected them.

It was cold to the touch but thrummed with Energy, a powerful artifact indeed. "But what do you do?" Victor whispered, running his fingertips along the rough sharp runes. Was it alive? Did a spirit dwell within? Did he dare try to bond with it? Victor had undoubtedly done some impulsive things in his day, but the idea seemed like madness, even to him; there was no hurry here, no reason he had to make a breakthrough with this strange ancient-seeming artifact. No, he decided, it was better to wait and have someone with more knowledge evaluate the thing first. In any case, he was careful with it. He lifted it from the desiccated scalp, leaving behind imprinted gray flesh and wisps of white, dead hair.

Victor found a leather strap in one of his rings and tied it around the heavy crown, hooking it to his belt so it dangled near his hip. On the off chance that it was alive, he didn't want to risk damaging the spirit within by putting it into a dimensional container. Victor studied the naked withered corpse for another moment, then gripped it by the shoulder and dragged it off the metal chair. He took it to the doorway and threw it out of the room to crumple against the stone wall beyond. He didn't know what this silver room was for, but he wouldn't leave that thing in there. He had a vague notion that the sphere was meant to reanimate the dead wampyr somehow, and he didn't want to leave any possibility that it might have some crazy potential to bring Dunstan's spirit back to the body and restore him with vigor.

He studied the room carefully one more time, and, not seeing anything else of note, he backed out and swung the door shut. He grabbed the key and twisted it counterclockwise to relock the door, and when it had completed its full circuit, Victor felt some give as though he could continue twisting it. "Hmm," he muttered and turned the key further to the left, eliciting one more click. The silver metal flashed brightly with Energy, and then the key was yanked out of his hand as the door, and the room to which it was attached, began to shrink rapidly. It was so fast and flared so brightly that when Victor's vision cleared, he was stunned to see the key, still attached to the jeweled chain, sitting in the center of the original stone-walled room of the tower.

Stepping toward it, Victor saw, upon closer inspection, that the key no longer ended in its original four prongs but had a small round, silver ball attached to it at that end—the room. The key remained the same size, but the whole room had shrunk down to the size of a large marble. Victor picked it up and looked over his shoulder at his big bear totem, apparently asleep with its gigantic head on its front paws. Shrugging, he hung the chain and key over his head and stuffed them down inside his armor, another object he'd need someone with the proper talents to identify.

"Lord Victor!" Nia's voice came to him from beyond his giant sleeping companion.

"Yeah?" He waved a hand at his bear, releasing the creature from this realm.

As he strode through the mist left behind, Nia called out again, unaware that he was mere steps from her, "Some of your people are at the gate!"

"That's good! Do me a favor and burn this corpse while I go see who it is." When Victor mounted the steps, he saw another soldier leaning forward, hands on knees, trying to regain his breath. "Did you sprint all the way up here?"

"Aye, Lord."

"Thanks!" Victor waved as he bounded down the steps, leaving Nia and the other soldier watching him with wide eyes. He was in the courtyard in less than a minute, jogging toward the inner gate, then across the bailey to the big curtain wall. He hollered, "Open up!" as he drew near. He slowed as he entered the gatehouse tunnel, standing under hundreds of tons of stone and the murder holes above his head. Somewhere within, he heard the windlass creak, and then the massive gate bar lifted up and away from the gates. As soon as it was clear, Victor grabbed the handle and pulled the right half open.

He'd barely pulled it halfway before an armor-clad woman with a shiny helm and bright teal eyes smashed into him, hugging him with a ferocity that made Victor laugh as he stumbled back against the wall. "I missed you too!"

"Idiot! For days, we've been marching, and for days, I've been dreading what I'd find. You couldn't send word?"

"Edeya has my book!"

"What about these soldiers you conscripted?"

"I only just got here! I've been unconscious for most of that time!" Victor's laugh had faded, and he spoke soothingly, still squeezing Valla close. "I'm sorry, okay, but I'm glad you're here. Come on, let's go inside, and I'll fill you in." He'd been leaning slightly down, speaking into the side of Valla's helm, and when he looked up, he saw Kethelket, Lam, and Edeya waiting in the gateway. "Hi, everyone! It's great to see you all. You especially, Kethelket; I wasn't sure you'd made it out, but I had a feeling you had." He smiled down at

Valla again, then turned and motioned for everyone to follow him. "It's good that you all didn't attack. I mean, I'm glad you waited at the gate and didn't kill any of our new soldiers."

"Well, your banner was flying, and we could tell you'd claimed the keep, so it would have been madness to assault it without checking what had happened." Valla entwined her fingers in his while she spoke, and they led the way through the gatehouse.

As they walked, Kethelket spoke, raising his voice to be heard from behind Edeya and Lam, "Victor, we fought our way free quickly, my kin and I. I want you to know that most of my rescued brothers and sisters wanted to rush to your aid, but I wouldn't allow it. They were wounded, stripped of their gear, and many foes were left between us and you. Taking stock, I remembered your words and felt it prudent to bring them to safety. Tell me, though, how came you to the soldiers patrolling the walls above?"

"It's a long story." Victor slowed in the bailey so that Kethelket could walk beside him. "Let me see if I can give you a brief version—I killed Dunstan deep underground after a pretty good fight. Due to some impulsiveness on my part, I ended up losing consciousness for a handful of days. When I found my way out of the depths and back to the keep, all the wampyrs were dead, even those I hadn't killed with my axe. Dunstan's true followers died when he died. Some of his soldiers, more thralls than true believers, who hadn't yet grown into fully undead creatures, regained their humanity. I mean, they returned to their true selves, their living bodies, and healthy spirits." Victor guided the others through the inner gatehouse.

"I gave them the option to flee to the north, seeking their freedom in the lands beyond the pass, or to join us in the destruction of these undead invaders. Not a single one of them opted to flee, and they all swore loyalty to me." He glanced over his shoulder at the faces of the others, expecting objections, but they were surprisingly calm and introspective. "Kethelket, the survivors gathered all the treasure and gear they could find from the dead wampyrs. I bet your people's things are among them."

"Thank you." He nodded, but his eyes were distant. "I'm pleased that you've given these people a chance to redeem themselves. I know what it means to serve an evil master."

Victor frowned, wondering how far he should go with the thought that had struck him. Should he voice it? Too late to pull it back, his mouth started almost of its own accord. "That's good, Kethelket, but keep in mind that these people were raised like cattle, enslaved by the vampiric asshole who owned the lands where they lived. They didn't want to join his army, and they definitely didn't want his 'gift.' I wish I could do more for them than give them a chance to kill more of the monsters from their homeworld, but it's the best I could do."

"Understood, Victor. Sir." The tone in his voice almost made Victor regret his words, but he felt it was an important distinction. These people had no redeeming to do; they had vengeance to seek. He felt Valla's hand tighten on his and let the matter drop. He had Kethelket's support, and that's what mattered.

"Anyway, I claimed the keep, and I took the treasures the System doled out. After I have them identified, if I don't need them, I'll either put them in the campaign store or gift them to people."

"Well deserved." Lam clapped him on the shoulder as they stepped into the courtyard. Many of the former thralls were present, watching to see the leaders of the army they'd be joining, perhaps wondering if someone would talk Victor out of his decision to welcome them. He hated the idea that they had to worry about their future, that they didn't feel secure in their place.

"Edeya, I have work for you."

"I'm ready!" She stepped forward, and Victor was once again struck by the beautiful changes in her appearance due to her new bloodline. Her wings were dazzling, and she just seemed so much more . . . everything—confident, powerful, capable. It all added up to a weight of presence that just hadn't been there before.

"First, where's Sarl?"

"With the Ninth, ready to rush to our rescue should we need it."

"Lam, can you go ahead and give him the all clear? Have him get his soldiers in here, and let's set up some duty rotations."

"Well." Lam looked around, sighing heavily, perhaps annoyed that she'd been the one selected to play messenger girl. "On my way. Save a drink for me; I want to hear about your battles!"

"I'll wait for you!" Victor laughed, watching her turn and launch herself into the sky. "Edeya, come over here. I want you to meet Agnes." Victor walked over to where Agnes still sat with her two assistants, going through equipment and jewels, many of which must have been dimensional containers. Valla and Kethelket kept pace, clearly interested in what he'd have Edeya do. "Edeya, this is Agnes, and she's been cataloging not only these items but also the soldiers who swore fealty to me. I want you to look at her notes and help with the process. Can you do that for me?"

"Of course, sir."

"Thank you." Victor made eye contact with Agnes and added, "Edeya is a very old friend as well as a high-ranking lieutenant in our army. Understood?"

"Aye, Lord." Agnes stood up straight, eyes on Edeya, waiting for her to come forward and take charge of the process. Victor nodded and led Kethelket and Valla away from the group, leaving them to their work. When they stood relatively alone near the stairs leading into the keep, he turned to Valla. "Is it too much to hope that you brought my travel home?"

"I did. After we claimed Black Keep, we marched, and I brought it with us, not knowing if we'd return."

"You claimed it? Good! What about Borrius and Rellia?"

"They've claimed Rust Keep and are now besieging the southernmost outpost. They're calling it High Keep because it sits high in a pass that controls access to the south beyond these contested lands. The legion has it surrounded, having left garrisons in Old Keep and Rust Keep, but are waiting on word of you and the Ninth before committing to an attack. Additionally, they have eyes on the two citadels that guard access to Hector's base of operations—the walled town that sits atop the mountain beneath the green star."

"Damn! They've been busy. So we've locked down four of the five outposts? Any word from the pass? Are our people doing well? Any word from the Empire?"

"Let's expand your house and go within before we speak further. Briefly, though, our people in the northern pass are well. I believe Edeya has correspondence for you from Thayla." Valla dug around in her belt pouch and pulled out the little jade rectangle of his travel home. "I'm glad you gave me permissions with this."

"Yeah, me too, but I guess it would've been safe in Black Keep. You all left a garrison?" Victor moved farther toward the corner of the courtyard, looking for a good spot to set the house down.

"Of course! Kethelket left nearly a hundred of his people, those who needed rest, and Sarl left fifty of his soldiers behind."

Victor grunted, setting the jade down and activating it. As it thumped and jumped around, he backed up. "It's good I got us another hundred soldiers here, then."

Valla opened her mouth to say something but seemed to change her mind, looking around the courtyard. "Let's get inside," she said instead, nodding to Victor's fully expanded travel home.

"Right." He stepped up to the door and pulled it open. Pausing, he glanced back toward the gate to see if the Ninth was making its way inside yet but didn't see any activity. Victor was a little worried about how the troops would respond to the new recruits, but he could trust Sarl to maintain order, couldn't he? Growling with annoyance, he said, "Hang on a minute." He looked down at Valla and met her eyes. "Are you wanting to get me inside so you can try to talk me out of adding these folks to our army?"

"Not exactly, but couldn't we discuss—"

"Nah, this isn't going to work like this. I need to talk to everyone. I think there's a need for some clarity about these people. Kethelket, will you please fly out and meet Sarl and Lam? I'd like the cohort assembled in the bailey. I have words for everyone."

Kethelket looked at Victor, his dark eyes narrowing as understanding clicked in his mind. "Of course, Victor. Consider it done." With that, he spread his wings; they fluttered, and he streaked up and over the inner wall.

"What's going on, Victor?" Valla's voice was hushed, subdued.

"I love you, Valla, but the prejudices and traditions of Fanwath rub me the wrong way sometimes. I need to make a few things very clear to the soldiers and officers about our new soldiers and about how things will be going forward."

Valla stepped back, her mouth closed, lips in a straight line, and Victor could tell she felt rebuked. It wasn't what he'd wanted, but he didn't want to go into the privacy of his house and have her start in on him about how he couldn't trust all of the former thralls. He didn't want to hear it because he wouldn't agree but also because he wanted to have a sliver of fantasy in his mind that she wouldn't do that. "As you say. I'll take my place with the troops." She turned stiffly and began to walk away, but Victor took another step and reached down to grab her hand.

"I feel like you missed the first part of what I said. I love you, Valla. Come on, stand by my side and hear my words. I'll listen to you afterward if you have objections, okay? I promise."

She glanced up at him and quickly glanced down, perhaps not wanting him to see the moisture in her eyes. She nodded, though, and squeezed his hand back, so he took the win. Striding to the center of the inner courtyard, Victor raised his voice and shouted, "Perry, Nia, Agnes, and every other survivor of Dunstan and his wampyrs, get down here and line up!" As the former thralls nearby scurried to obey his command, Victor walked up to Edeya. "Put that stuff on hold a minute. We need to have a bit of a briefing out in the bailey. Would you mind going to stand with Lam and Sarl?"

"On my way, sir!" Edeya winked at him, letting him know her old self was still in there, as she fluttered her new wings and lifted into the air, showering him and Valla with beautiful blue motes of Energy. Victor turned to see most of the new soldiers already forming ranks in the courtyard, many of them watching Edeya fly away with wonder in their eyes. He imagined such a sight wasn't something they might witness in a dark undead world.

"Listen up, soldiers!" Victor said, turning and holding Valla's hand aloft. "This is Valla ap'Yensha, the tribune primus of our army, and if that doesn't mean much to you, you need to be aware that she's the third highest-ranking officer in the entire legion." The former thralls weren't disciplined in the way that ordinary soldiers were—they'd been controlled by fear and magic their entire lives. Still, they stood still and straight, gazing at Valla with wonder and admiration plain in their eyes, and Victor felt Valla tighten her grip when she looked into their faces.

She gave his hand one more squeeze, then let go and, lifting her voice to be heard, she said, "I'm very pleased to meet you all, and I'm pleased that you're joining our cause. I have much to learn about your kind and each of you, but you can believe that if your legate primus here"—she nodded to Victor—"has vouched for you, then everyone in this army will respect you."

Victor felt his grin growing wide as she spoke. "That's right. Now, form a single-file line and follow me into the bailey. Your brothers and sisters at arms need to meet you, and I have some words of introduction for all to hear."

41

POSTMORTEM

Victor stood before the ranks of the ninth cohort, running his eyes up and down their rows. They were tough-looking men and women. Every single one of them, from the smallest, slightest Ghelli to the biggest, most muscular Shadeni, looked as if they could handle themselves. They each bore scars and carried experience in their eyes. Many wore ribbons and medals on their chests. Some wore awards from previous campaigns in the Imperial Legion, but most only displayed what they'd earned during the campaign, and in this cohort, almost everyone had won accolades.

About half of them had earned multiple medals for the battle with the Ridonne. During the weeks of travel from Persi Gables to the Untamed Marches, the legion quartermaster, with his many assistants, had been hard at work creating more medals and ribbons to be handed out after further skirmishes and battles. Sarl's lieutenants had been busy awarding them for the cohort's many victories against the undead. Victor saw silver battle commemorations, red-ribboned medals for valor, blue for sustaining injuries, and gold medals for exceptional prowess, usually measured in enemies killed. The Glorious Ninth were the most decorated men and women in the legion, of that Victor was sure, even not having seen all that Rellia and Borrius had taken the rest of the army through in the last week.

While the cohort stood at attention, quiet, ready to hear his words, Victor turned his gaze over his shoulder to see the black-clad men and women who'd survived their existence as thralls under Dunstan. It was a much smaller group, about a sixth as many as were lined up facing them, but they were solid, serious-looking people. Of course, they were all human, so they had a size advantage on the Ardeni and Ghelli and certainly on the occasional goat-like Cadwalli and the diminutive Bogoli. Victor thought about that briefly while he let his eyes run along their number—these were the first non-undead humans he'd run into other than his cousin, Olivia.

How strange! It was weird to lay eyes on so many men and women who didn't have red or blue skin, who didn't have brightly colored eyes or hair or horns or wings, or any of the other myriad oddities that he'd grown accustomed to in his time on Fanwath. It was plain that these people's ancestors had come from Earth. They, too, stared back at him quietly, waiting for him to speak. He locked eyes with Perry for a moment and offered a brief nod before turning back to the cohort. He looked to the left, glancing over to Sarl and the heavily cowled figure beside him—Victoria. He was glad she hadn't tried to flee; he had questions for her. Beside them were Edeya, Kethelket, Lam, and now Valla, as she finished walking over and turned, standing shoulder to shoulder with Lam. Suddenly, he felt nervous.

Victor frowned, reminding himself of who he was. He was the man who'd delved into the dark twisting depths below this very keep. He'd descended into the nest of wampyrs and single-handedly slain most of their number. Then he'd battled, deep underground, their evil lord and freed this keep and the people behind him. He was Victor, the man who'd faced down a thousand reavers and bought time for these other men and women to arrive on the field, saving the fifth cohort. He was the man who'd led these people to victory against the Ridonne, slaying their champion from another world or dimension. He had no need to be nervous; these soldiers loved him. Many had said as much. They'd listen to him, and his words would be well received. He was sure of it.

Victor reached into his Core and opened his pathways to a flood of inspiration-attuned Energy, using it to cast Inspiration of the Quinametzin. As the white-gold Energy spread through him and radiated out, touching every soldier assembled in the bailey, he saw eyes light up, smiles widen, and understanding flash across their faces—it was obvious why they were there; it was time for Victor to explain who the men and women lined up behind him were. "Brave, tireless Ninth!" he began, speaking in a loud, clear voice.

He wasn't titan-sized. He was just Victor, a man larger than life with or without his titanic aspect. He stood before them, decked out in his shimmering magical wyrm-scale armor and his massive intimidating Helm of the Kethian Juggernaut. With the bright light of inspiration running through his mind, Victor knew it didn't matter what size he made himself; these soldiers respected him. They'd seen him put himself on the line for them again and again. They not only would listen to him, but they wanted to. They wanted to please him. He suddenly realized that this wouldn't be difficult at all; his nervous energy was from his fear, and it had no place here.

Everyone stood quietly, so still that a distant observer might think they were statues. Victor nodded and continued, "Thank you for rushing to this keep, ready to come to my aid. As you can see, Dunstan is dead. His ugly undead wampyrs are dead, and the keep is ours." He paused a moment as some of the more exuberant soldiers began to whoop and cheer. He smiled, nodded, then lifted a hand, and they grew quiet. "When I killed the foul creature that ruled in this keep, some of his thralls were set free from his control." He turned and held out a hand as though presenting the humans lined up behind him.

"I know it's easy to be suspicious of them. These are men and women who, not long ago, might have been forced to fight against you. I think it's important that you all understand the hell they've been through. On the world of Dark Ember, where Hector and his undead servants come from, people like these"—again he gestured to the one-time thralls—"are allowed to live small lives in villages. They're controlled by bullies, not unlike the Ridonne, but a thousand times worse. Whenever the vampiric lords want fresh meat or soldiers for their armies, they come to the village and take them. They don't offer riches and power; they don't convince them to sign up. They simply take them, infect them with the dark magic of their vampiric bloodline, and force them to become monsters like those you and I have been fighting.

"It seems the curse takes time to grow roots in a person's soul, to really grab hold and twist their spirits into undead things. These men and women behind me were the lucky few who weren't fully consumed by it. Whether consciously or with some instinct for survival, they'd been fighting against it. When Dunstan died, his magic fled their blood, and they became normal living people again. More than that, they have a thirst for vengeance in their blood! They remember the vile things Dunstan and his kind have done to them and to their families and loved ones. They want justice! I offered them freedom. I offered them the chance to flee this war. Every single one of them chose to stay and fight. They want to see that green star snuffed out! They want to feel the undead break beneath the blows of their weapons!"

Again, Victor paused, looking left to right, up and down the ranks, meeting many eyes, looking for dissension. He didn't find any. "Can I count on you, Glorious Ninth? Can I count on you to take these new soldiers under your wing? Will you teach them the ways of our legion? Will you help them fill your ranks? You won't find fiercer companions! Nia, come here." Victor turned and watched as the tall scarred woman stepped forward stiffly, her broad shoulders pulled back. Her eyes were nervous, but Victor saw the spark in them, the same light that had made him want to ensure his people would treat her and her kind fairly. "Nia, how many loved ones have the wampyr and their kind taken from you?"

"All, Lord. More than I like to think about to count."

"What does it mean to you to join the Ninth here?"

"Everything, Lord!" She spoke with breathless passion, eyes bright, springing with tears as she looked upon the assembled soldiers, her desire to be one of them so plain, so desperate, that it was palpable.

"Thank you, Nia." Victor turned back to the line of black-clad former thralls. "Let me see your fists in the air if you have a score to settle with Lord Hector!" He watched as they each lifted their fists, scowling fiercely, perhaps thinking of one lost family member or another, perhaps remembering being treated as cattle. Victor nodded and turned back to the cohort. "Well? Can I count on you?"

"*Yes!*" they thundered, slamming their fists to their chests in a vigorous salute.

"Captain Sarl." Victor locked gazes with him until he stepped forward and saluted.

"Legate, sir!"

"Get your lieutenants together and work these new soldiers into your unit rosters. Take their oaths of service and assign each of them a partner, someone who will be there to guide them through the many customs and routines of our legion."

"Yes, sir! Lieutenants! Step forward!"

Victor nodded, then lifted his voice again. "Thank you, Ninth! I'm counting on you to make this work. I'm counting on you to help these men and women find the justice they seek."

"That was a good thing you did, if a bit awkward for your recruits." Lam pulled out a chair at the table and sat down, smiling across at Victor and Valla. Edeya and Kethelket took seats on either side of her.

"Awkward?" Victor nodded. "Yeah, I don't know how I envisioned it in my head, but I suppose putting them all on the spot like that, on display, I guess, was a little rough. Still, I wanted the army to know how I felt. I didn't want there to be any doubt that if they held grudges or conspired against the former thralls, they'd be acting against my wishes." He turned to Sarl, the last of them still standing, leaning on the chair to Valla's left. "Did I put you in a bad spot, Captain?"

"Not at all. I need the bodies. If you trust them, then I trust them. Besides, they're signing the same contract the rest of us did."

"Good. That's the attitude I was hoping for." Victor glanced around, noting the silence from everyone else, especially feeling it from Valla. He knew she'd meant to argue caution with the new troops, but he'd put her in an impossible position to do so with his public display of acceptance. Now, he supposed, they would all wait and find out if he'd been short-sighted. It was fine with him. As Sarl said, the former thralls were all signing a contract, and he believed their sincerity when it came to their desire to fight their former masters. "Enough about them. Where's Victoria?"

Sarl gestured toward the front door. "She's waiting for you to call her in. I told her we had strategy to discuss and you'd call for her when you were ready."

"Good. Edeya, any word from Rellia and Borrius?"

"Yes! They're thrilled to hear of your success here. They still hold High Keep under siege. Borrius is reviewing strategic options but has some ideas. Rellia fears that if you bring the ninth cohort to support them, we'll make it easy for Hector to make a counterstrike against one of the outposts we've secured. Borrius is in agreement and even thinks we should perhaps start putting pressure on one of the citadels, relieving them of the worry of undead reinforcements coming to High Keep."

"What about the 'baron' there? Isn't he some gargantuan flesh-shaping guy, the one Victoria thought might come to Black Keep to attack us?"

"Yes, they've had sightings and encounters with his constructs. So far, Polo Vosh and Rellia have risen to the occasion. It seems the legion outnumbers Karl the Crimson's forces handily, and though he has some powerful units, he's loath to send them out, not after he lost many in his first engagement."

"It's not just Polo and Rellia," Lam interjected. "There are hundreds of tier-four and higher individuals with the legion. Even considering their average level is lower than the Ninth's, they've had little difficulty wiping out the undead chaff. Only a few of this Karl fellow's units are a significant threat, and, so far, the legion has had the numbers to neutralize them with ease, usually with the help of well-planned control magic."

"Aye," Edeya nodded. "It seems they're quite weak against certain elemental magics."

"So, we leave them to wrap up that siege and move against one of the citadels. How are they situated with regard to the plateau where Hector's base is?" Victor took out a blank piece of parchment and began to draw the contested lands between the mountains and the Silver Sea. On the northern edge, he drew a square and labeled it Old Keep. Then he shaded in a forest southwest of it and drew Black Keep in the center. Mentally tracing the path he'd taken on Guapo, he drew in the square for the Sea Keep, and then on the eastern edge, he made a square for Rust Keep. To the south, before the second row of mountains, he made a square for High Keep. Finally, at the center, he drew a representation of a big flat-topped mountain and labeled it Hector.

"The citadels are here and here," Edeya said, leaning forward and pointing to the northern side of the plateau. "They're near each other, connected via an enormous, vaulted span. Either can send troops to support the other."

"And they guard the only road up the plateau," Lam added.

"That's inconvenient for us, but it also limits Hector; he can't easily send troops out unless they go down that road." Valla leaned forward and pointed. "If we're besieging them or even making feints and ambushes around those citadels, Borrius and Rellia will be free to finish with High Keep."

"Guys . . ." Victor took a deep breath and shook his head. "Maybe it's because I haven't laid eyes on it, but I have a hard time believing some undead invader with powerful magic would be stuck using roads. Can't he have his minions carve a path down the side of the mountain elsewhere? Come to think of it, can't we carve a path up?"

"Certainly." Kethelket nodded but kept speaking, "But I've had scouts observe the place, and it's not what you might be picturing. It's more a tremendous mountain with sheer rock walls and cliffs that rise to a concave mountain top. I can see why people are calling it a plateau—the area on the top is significant. However, there were similar peaks on Kthella before the worlds were joined. I think those who describe it as a dormant volcano are more correct." He stood and began to pace as he continued to speak. "I'm not saying your point doesn't stand, but it would be a massive undertaking to create a new roadway of any significance down or up the side of that peak. If I'm not mistaken, Borrius has stationed scouts to observe the slopes; we'll be well warned if Hector begins work upon a new egress from his base."

"You're not mistaken." Edeya tapped the command book, indicating she had the reports available to read.

"Okay." Victor sat back and folded his arms before his chest. "How long will it take to get the Ninth into a position to harass those citadels?"

Sarl cleared his throat to respond. "It took us five days to get here from Black Keep, but Victor, the soldiers are exhausted. We double-timed it and only slept in four-hour shifts. I recommend the opposite as we move toward the citadels. We should travel slowly with plenty of time for rest and drills at the end of each day's march. We still need to integrate your recruits. Considering the distance, linearly, is a bit smaller than the march to Black Keep, I'd estimate a seven-day journey."

"We should be able to do that," Lam chimed in. "We must have bought ourselves some downtime, destroying so many of the invaders' armies. Consider the horde that burned to ash in the forest. Consider that four of Hector's five barons have fallen. If he's raising an army of undead to try to take back some territory, he can't possibly do so faster than that. Kethelket?"

"I agree. I know a thing or two about Death Casters, and even if this Hector is twice what Belikot was, it would take months to raise a significant force, something that could truly challenge the legion. However, that doesn't consider the forces he has available at the citadels or in his base. It doesn't take into account more troops he might pull through the portal. Even so, I think seven days is an appropriate pace. What's the alternative? Pushing the Ninth to the point of breaking? As tough as they are, they're mortal and require rest."

"Okay. So, numbers-wise, we've got how many troops?" Victor looked at Sarl for the answer.

"We have a hundred or so Naghelli, the ones who didn't stay behind at Black Keep. We have five hundred and sixty-two soldiers in the Ninth, not counting the hundred-plus recruits you just got for us."

"Victor," Edeya spoke up, hot on Sarl's heels.

"Yeah?"

"There are more than a cohort's worth of soldiers at the pass. Thayla wrote to you in the book, and that was one of the things she mentioned. You should read her message, by the way—some of it was more personal."

Victor mentally made a note to read the message. "Does that include the Shadeni tribe?"

"No! Borrius left behind many of the extra troops who'd been swelling the cohorts on the march, and there's been a steady influx of fortune seekers coming over the pass."

Victor looked to his right, locking eyes with Valla. "Thoughts?"

"We should call for reinforcements. We should bolster the Ninth to a double cohort. Have six hundred of the highest-level soldiers at the pass meet us at the citadels."

"I like the sound of that. Sarl?"

"It would be easy to double up unit numbers. I could keep the same command structure in place."

"Kind of the beauty of the legion structure," Lam added. "Cohorts are often bolstered like that, depending on the assignment."

Victor nodded, looking at Edeya. "The troops at the pass have been drilling? They know the commands?"

"Yes, of course. Most of them were drilling with the legion all the way here during the march."

"Right. Okay, I'll leave that to you, Sarl and Lam. Coordinate the meet-up. Now, I have one more request, Sarl. When it comes time to leave behind a hundred soldiers to garrison this keep, take volunteers. I'd like those who are the most weary, those who could use a break from the constant fighting, to stay here. I promised the former thralls that they'd be brought to the front line, that they'd get a chance at spilling some undead blood."

"Understood."

"Okay. I want hourly watch rotations this afternoon and tonight so that no one has to be on duty for long. Let's let the soldiers relax and celebrate a little; they deserve it." Victor smiled at the people around the table and added, "You all deserve it. I'm so lucky to have such dependable, competent friends leading this army."

"Here, here!" Lam laughed, pounding a fist on the table.

"Well said!" Kethelket nodded, inhaling deeply through his nose and sitting up straighter.

Valla reached under the table and grasped Victor's hand, squeezing it tightly. Her cool fingers against his hot flesh brought to mind another matter, and he added, "When you march tomorrow, Valla and I will stay behind."

"What?" Edeya was the first to respond, eyes wide, voice rising with a tinge of panic.

"Relax!" He laughed. "I don't mean permanently. We're going to use these." Victor fished the two Apples of Evolution out of his ring and set them on the table. "I received these when I claimed the keep, and I'm . . . claiming them. Valla will, of course, object"—he chuckled and winked at her—"but she deserves one. I'm eating the other because I have to keep advancing, too, regardless of my current strength. We don't know what Hector or his closest subordinates will be like. I have to be strong."

"What are they?" Sarl leaned close, looking at the foil-wrapped fruit.

"Apples of Evolution, whatever that is. I'm assuming racial advancements."

"Victor, I . . ."

"Didn't I already say you'd object? Overruled." Victor squeezed her hand.

"He's right, Valla." Lam reached over the table and took Valla's other hand. "You're too selfless, and you're often in the thick of things with Victor. I've even pushed my race to advanced. What are you? Still in the improved ranks, yeah?"

"I, too, am at the advanced stage." Kethelket nodded.

"Well, I . . ." Sarl chuckled and shook his head.

"You need to spend some of the campaign tokens you've earned, buddy." Victor laughed. He smiled and nodded at Valla as she bit back further objections. "Okay, it's settled then. We'll eat these apples here, then haul ass on Guapo to rejoin you all. Oh!" He paused and snapped his fingers, reaching back into his dimensional storage container. He retrieved the silver rune-etched spyglass and held it up. "Before we end the meeting, help me figure out what this thing does."

42

❈

RELATIONSHIPS

After their meeting, when everyone had had their fill of talk and drink and things going forward were settled, Victor walked his command staff to the front door to say goodnight. On the way, as they passed by the short hallway leading to his library, Edeya tugged Victor's sleeve and asked, "Could I speak to you for a minute? It's about the message from Thayla."

Valla had been walking beside him, and she squeezed his hand briefly before stepping forward. "I'll show the others out."

"All right. Night, all!" Victor called, smiling stupidly—Valla had produced a bottle of brandy she'd been hanging onto from Coloss, and Victor had enjoyed it a bit too much. He followed Edeya into the library and on a whim lifted the little spyglass, focusing it on her. A green halo limned her body almost immediately as the glass magically clarified the image. They'd figured out the little artifact's purpose, or at least one of them, while sitting around the table. It seemed to indicate the strength of the people observed through it, relative to the viewer, with a crude, if effective, color system.

When Victor had studied the soldiers outside, almost all had been green, like Edeya, but he'd gotten some more clues when he'd looked at Valla, Lam, and Kethelket. They'd all been shades of blue. The real breakthrough had come when he'd handed the spyglass to Valla, and she'd seen him as deep crimson, Lam and Kethelket as pale yellow, Edeya as pale blue, and Sarl as green.

Victor was shaken from his thoughts of the spyglass when he walked into the big map table, stumbled, and nearly dropped the little scope. "Are you okay?" Edeya laughed.

"Heh, fine." He shook his head, grinning, and slipped the spyglass back into his storage ring. Edeya produced a thick Far Scribe book and held it close to her chest, hugging her arms around it. She seemed nervous to him, as if she was struggling to find the right words. "Spit it out, *chica.*" He knew calling her that would break the tension.

"Back to that, are we?" She laughed, then set the book down on the big table. "Well, I wanted to let you read this message from Thayla. There are two Far Scribe books at the pass that they're using to stay in touch with the legion—this one that I carry and another that Lieutenant Darro carries for Rellia and Borrius." Edeya flipped the book to one of the most recent entries, and Victor saw some paragraphs of Thayla's sharp-angled handwriting addressed to him. Edeya pointed to a note at the bottom of the page. "Edeya, please pull the next page from the book and give it to Victor so he can write back when he has a minute."

"Oh, I see." Victor nodded, his buzz fading as he began to worry about what the hell Thayla had written to make Edeya so nervous.

"Yeah, she even wrote on the top of the page." Edeya pointed to the next page where, neatly printed on the top, were the words *This Page for Victor's Use.* Without further ado, Edeya ripped the page out along with the previous page where Thayla's message was written.

"They'll still work?"

"Oh yes. These two pages will still reflect the words written on them with the ones in the copy back at the pass." Edeya smiled, then gripped Victor by the back of the arm, squeezing gently. "If we don't talk before we march, be careful, and don't take too long to catch up to us, okay? I'm nervous about what awaits us as we move toward the center of all this corruption."

"Yeah, all right. Don't worry; I don't plan to take my time." He watched her leave, and as she got to the doorway, he added, "Thanks, Edeya." She smiled again, nodded, and left, her shimmering azure wings drifting through the dim hallway like fairy dust. Victor sighed and picked up the two pages, shuffling them so Thayla's letter was on top. He'd just turned his eyes to the first line when Valla spoke up from the doorway.

"Anything to worry about?"

Victor held up the pages. "I don't think so, just a letter from Thayla. Haven't read it yet."

"Ah, that's right. Edeya mentioned it earlier. Well, I'll leave you to concentrate on that. I'm headed to bed. See you soon?"

"Oh yeah. I won't be up much longer." Victor's eyes were still on the page, and when he looked up to see if Valla had more to say, she was already gone. Was she upset? He didn't think so. "Let's see here." He straightened out the page and began to read:

Victor,

We hear much of your campaign here in Northpass, as they're starting to call the little village between the walls the engineers and Earth Casters are building. I know this book isn't for our private use, so I'll trust Edeya to stop reading here and pass this note along to you. Things sound promising with regard to the campaign, and you should know that things are good here, too. I won't bore you with all the details, as I'm sure Edeya gets reports from the legion personnel in this same book, and you've no doubt heard it all from her already. Things are exciting, though! We've all enjoyed watching the construction process, learning to hunt the slopes south of the pass, and observing the reserve forces here drilling on the new parade grounds outside the walls. What a strange name for a bunch of gravel fields! It must have something to do with imperial traditions, don't you think?

Deyni is well! She's become quite a huntress with that bird of hers! She and Chala go out every morning, and they've impressed everyone with their contribution to the food stores. It's not me or Deyni that I write to you about, however. I'm worried about Chandri, and I'm not sure what to do. Tellen isn't any help—he's too hands-off with those girls, and I've come into their lives too late to change any of that. He says she'll figure things out, and she probably will. That said, I've made the perhaps foolish decision to add to your no doubt immense pile of worries. Chandri has grown bitter and angry. When I confronted her about her attitude, she made an offhand comment about things being her fault, her "choice to live a small, stupid life."

When I pressed her, she fought with me, saying things women say to each other when their anger gets ahold of them. I know she didn't mean them, so I won't bother repeating her words here, but your name came up more than once. I think that when you left in the winter, when you said goodbye, Chandri figured it would be the last she'd see of you. I don't think she ever imagined she'd be embroiled in a campaign like this, that she'd ever see you leading an army, dragging her people along with it. She'd never imagined spending so much time in your proximity, and if she did, that she'd be such a footnote, someone whom you passed by now and then and said hello to. I think she imagined she was more than that to you.

She knew you'd be moving on to bigger things, but she thought it would happen far from her. She feels snubbed, Victor. She thought she held an important place in your heart. It may not seem logical, but she was ready to have you fade out of her life, but she wasn't prepared for it to happen while she could still observe you.

What can you do? I have no idea. Talk to her? I know you care about her, despite what she might think. I know you're very, very busy, but I'm sure you'll find a way to make things right with her. I just wasn't sure you knew things needed making right. I hope this news doesn't distract you too much. I hope you'll have great success and hopefully have a chance to rest soon, a chance to visit those of us who aren't on the front lines.

With much love,

Thayla

"Oh, what the hell?" Victor groaned as he lowered the page and stood from the edge of the table. He walked over to the big comfortable chair he favored and collapsed into it. "If it's not one thing, it's another." He reached over his shoulder and pulled Lifedrinker loose from her harness. At first, he was just trying to get comfortable, but he realized he also wanted the comfort she usually provided. He pressed the cool metal of her axe-head to his forehead and sighed. "Well, beautiful, once again, I'm dealing with some damn drama I seem to have created simply by being myself."

He wasn't sure what he'd expected from Lifedrinker. Usually when he complained about things like that, she provided some clarity in the form of a simple desire to fight something. He didn't always agree with her urge for combat, but it always made him feel better to see a different perspective, a different focus on priorities. One thing was sure: Lifedrinker never made him feel bad, always supported him, and was usually quick to point out how he was in the right and those who disagreed shouldn't have crossed him. Of course, on this occasion, Lifedrinker decided to complicate things instead of providing clarity. Rather than love, unquestioning support, and a desire for battle, she sent waves of uncertainty, doubt, and even resentment through their bond.

"Victor, why do you forsake me? You promised to share your spirit again soon, and I've ached for it!"

An image flashed through Victor's mind. A great silver-furred wolf, alone, howling into the dark, waiting for a response and hearing nothing but silence as the howl echoed away. He frowned and held the axe at arm's length, staring at it. "Seriously? It hasn't been very long! You know I love you, *chica*!

I'm . . . conflicted, though. What exactly am I doing with you when I join my spirit to yours? Is it . . . am I being faithful to Valla? I know people teased me about it, about us, I mean, but I never thought of you like that before. It wasn't something possible, you know? You were an axe; I was a man. If our spirits can get together, though . . . what does that even mean?"

Lifedrinker was an axe of few words, and rather than answer his question, she pulsed hot emotion out of the haft into his hands. Her feelings were clear; she didn't care about anything other than her love for him. She didn't care what he said or did with anyone else so long as they were together. Images of him standing tall, swinging her through battle after battle, killing monsters, creatures, and men and women in the hundreds flashed through his mind. Along with those images flowed Lifedrinker's feelings of raw, palpable excitement, pride, hunger for conflict, and, under it all, a deep, unwavering devotion to Victor.

Victor shook his head and balled up his fist, gently thumping it against his forehead as he squeezed his eyes in frustration. "God, you're so good, Lifedrinker, so straightforward and true. You don't lie. You don't play games. Are you too good for me? Do I even deserve you?" He sighed and sat up, shaking his head. "Still, you must know how I'm different than you, right? I love to fight, true, but I also enjoy other things in life. You know I'm not always focused on you or what we do together, right? You know how I feel about Valla. You know I care about other people and other things. I want people who enjoy peace to have it. That's why I'm here, in these lands, fighting these undead *pendejos*."

Victor paused, unsure what he was getting at, where his thoughts were going. "I think what I'm trying to say is that I understand what you want and how you feel, but you have to understand that my life and my desires are a little more complicated. You have to understand that I'm a little concerned about what it means to you and me when I connect our spirits like that. If I'm not doing it to win a fight, am I just doing it to be closer to you, to show my love and affection? If so, is that disloyal to Valla? Because you've got to understand something, *chica*—I enjoyed it, too. I felt different somehow when I pulled my spirit back, and it was *good*."

"If it's good, it's good!"

The words were so clear and so simple that Victor had to laugh. Still chuckling, he turned Lifedrinker crossways over his lap, holding her haft with both hands, admiring the weird depthless nature of her living-wood haft with its tiny motes of light winking at him from the dark grains and whorls. "Let me think about things a little more, okay? Hell, let me talk to Valla." Reluctant acceptance came to him through the dense, warm wood. "*Gracias, amor mío.*"

Victor rubbed his temples and pressed his eyes shut briefly, trying to wrap his head around everything. He'd hoped to get some comfort from Lifedrinker, but now he had another thing to worry about. With a grunt, he stood up, re-slung his axe, and moved over to the table, summoning a pen from his storage ring. He took the blank page on which he was supposed to write a response, smoothed it out with his hand, and got to work, trying not to let his frustration bleed into his words.

Thayla,

Thanks for the message. I appreciate you looking out for me concerning Chandri's feelings—it's certainly not something you had to do, but I recognize that you're looking out for her as much, or maybe more, than me. I promise I'll have a good long heart-to-heart with her when I get back. Problem is, I don't know when that'll be. Things haven't really slowed down here, and we're trying to capitalize on our momentum. Realistically, it'll be weeks, at least, before I can get back up there. In the meantime, maybe you can let Chandri know that I'm awfully sorry for not . . . Scratch that! If you do that, she'll realize you messaged me about her, and she'll probably get even angrier. How about this: next time you're all together, let her, Deyni, and everyone know that I asked about them and that I'm looking forward to spending time with them all. I promise I'll try to make things right.

No matter what, it was nice to hear from you, Thayla. It's nice to be reminded of what I'm fighting for.

Love,

Victor

Victor sighed and folded the pages in half, sending them into his storage ring. Feeling a little lighter for having at least responded to Thayla, he made his way downstairs and into his room. The lights were dim, hardly on, but he saw Valla curled up under the blanket, breathing peacefully in her sleep. He started to undress, hanging his armor and Lifedrinker on a rack of wooden pegs near the door. He'd just sat down on a bench to pull his boots off when he heard the sheets rustle, and Valla sleepily spoke up. "Coming to bed?"

"Yeah."

There must have been something in his voice because she asked, "Want to talk about it?"

"I don't think my current troubles are anything you want to hear about, to be honest." He chuckled a little ruefully and tugged at his boot.

More rustling of sheets signaled Valla sitting up against the pillows as he started on his second boot. "I always want to hear about your troubles. How else can I be any help?"

"Well . . ." Victor's nervous chuckle returned as he dropped his boot and decided to be honest. "I guess you could say I'm having some women troubles."

"Excuse me? I think I'd know about that. Something to do with Thayla? I thought you and she were—"

"Nah." Victor stood and pulled his shirt off. "It's not like that. She's fine; she wrote to me about Chandri."

"Chandri? Did you and she? Victor, really?"

"No, it's not like that! We were close, is all, back when I was staying with the clan. I mean, we almost were something, but it was just a couple of flirting kisses, and then she . . . God, Valla! You don't want to hear all this!"

"Well, hold on!" Suddenly, her voice wasn't sleepy at all. "You said 'women,' not 'woman.' Is there another former lover I need to . . ."

"Oh my God, Valla! For one thing, Chandri wasn't a 'former lover.' Anyway, the other 'woman' is Lifedrinker." Victor glanced at the axe hanging by the door, feeling a surge of guilt for talking about her like that.

"*Lifedrinker?*" Valla leaned forward, the sheets falling away from her, revealing a sheer silky white nightgown that Victor hadn't seen her wear before. Did that mean something? He slapped his head, groaning.

"I'm an idiot. Our first night back together, and I'm coming to bed late, moaning about problems with other women. It's not what it sounds like, Valla. I'm just worried about their feelings. You know me."

She sighed and leaned back, letting her furrowed brow relax. "Yes, Victor, I know you. Your heart is too big, but of course that's what I love about you. So, let's start with the woman in the room with us. What's wrong with Lifedrinker?"

Victor unbuckled his pants and let them drop to the ground, then he walked over to the bed and sat on the side of it, nudging Valla's legs over to make room. "Well, you remember my Imbue Spirit spell? The one I used on you and Barn when we fought the night brutes?"

"Yes, you shared your courage with us."

"Right. Well, it was more than my courage. It was a piece of my spirit. I guess, in that case, it was a piece that reflected my courage because that's the

Energy I used when I cast it. Anyway, that's beside the point. Recently, I cast that spell on Lifedrinker, sending part of my spirit into her. It empowered her, allowing her to damage Dunstan, for instance, when she couldn't before."

"Mmhmm. What's the problem with that?"

"The problem came when I called my spirit back into me, and Lifedrinker got depressed! She loves having my spirit with her. It brings us closer together, and, well, I hate to deny her, but I also feel guilty. What exactly are we sharing when I do that?"

"You feel . . . guilty?" Valla frowned at him, narrowing her eyes again. "Why?"

"Because I love you, and I'd never do something to hurt you. I wouldn't . . . well, shit, I wouldn't cheat on you. When I share my spirit with Lifedrinker, we're *close*, Valla. How is that okay?" Victor spoke from his heart and wasn't trying to hide anything. Valla must have recognized that because he could see the sympathy in her eyes. She didn't get angry as he'd feared she might. Instead, she reached out to grasp one of his big hands in her slender, cool fingers, gently squeezing it.

"You're an idiot."

The words were familiar to Victor, but he was used to hearing them from people like Thayla and Edeya. Hearing them from Valla brought an instant bark of laughter out of him. "Am I?"

"Yes! Do you love Lifedrinker in the same way you love me?"

"No!"

"Then why would you feel guilty about being close to her? You *should* feel close to her! You've been through quite a lot together, haven't you?" When Victor nodded, she pressed on, "You're allowed to love people other than me, you know. Do you feel sexually attracted to her?"

"Valla! No!"

"Well, I had to ask because you're being very strange! You don't feel guilty about loving Thayla, do you? Don't deny it; I know you love her!"

"No, I don't feel guilty 'cause we both know we aren't going anywhere in that . . . direction."

"Well, I think you and Lifedrinker know you won't become mates, right?"

"Yeah." Victor sighed, chuckling nervously. Was he being honest? He could speak for himself, but what did he know of Lifedrinker's true feelings? Hadn't she spoken possessively of Valla before? Was that something he should mention? "I can't really speak for her; she's not the same as us, you know? Some of her memories are ancient and come from the heartwood in her haft. I'm saying she might view a relationship differently than you and I."

"I care about what's in here." Valla held her palm to Victor's chest, over his heart. "If you can make her life better, this spirit who's done so much with and for you, don't you think you should? Share your spirit with her when she wants. I love her too, you know? If she hadn't been there for you, loving and caring for you, you'd have died on more than one occasion. Am I wrong?"

"No." Victor couldn't say anything else; he was too fraught with emotion. He squeezed his eyes shut, images of battles where he'd almost died running through his mind. From the "boss" of the dungeon Lifedrinker had drained to his duel with Rellia, where she'd gifted him her own life Energy, to half a dozen other close battles where she'd made the difference between a loss and a win—where she'd been the difference between life and death. He felt Valla pull on his wrist, and he fell forward into her arms.

She stroked his head, rubbing her fingers through the stiff shorter hair on the sides of his head. "Shh," she said, leaning forward to kiss his forehead. "Did anyone ever tell you not to worry quite so much about everyone else's feelings?"

"Yeah," he mumbled, "Lifedrinker."

43

BLOODLINES

Victor and Valla watched the Glorious Ninth march away from the keep, a long column of armor-clad individuals wending its way east and north along the beach toward a gap in the hills where they'd turn toward the center of the contested lands. Victor let his gaze drift that way, proud of the clear air and bright sun in the vicinity; he'd been responsible for removing the sickly haze, allowing him to see the heavy curtain of mist that hung in the eastern sky so clearly. It was distant, days and days of travel away, but it was there. Even in the morning sunlight, he could make out the faint green glow of the Death Caster's "veil star."

"They'll be all right." Valla had mistaken Victor's angry scowl for one of concern.

"Yeah. I just want to get these undead assholes out of here. It stresses me out to think he's got an open portal there, but we don't know what kinds of limitations he has on calling more troops through."

"Limitations?"

"Remember what Victoria said? I mean about the portal repelling those beyond a certain threshold of power."

"Oh yes, I remember." Valla frowned, watching the distant column of marching soldiers. "I hope Lam keeps a close eye on that woman."

"Lam and Kethelket will both watch her. Kethelket won't let her surprise him."

Valla turned to lean an elbow on the parapet, looking more fully at Victor. "Did you suspect there are other limitations?"

"I suspect, but I don't know. The System seems to have rules for this invasion. Hector already has far more troops than we do. Well, he did before the forest fire and our recent victories. Still, if he had the resources back home, would he be allowed to send out the call to bring another fifty thousand troops through? It doesn't seem that would be fair, so would the System deny their passage through its portal? Of course, the System might consider us as part of Fanwath as a whole. It might think we could gather more troops if we tried our hand at diplomacy, begging the Ridonne or the Free Cities for aid."

"Or it might just consider the number of us who have the quest it issued in the pass . . ."

"Well, that's what I'm getting at. We just don't know. Hector might have already pulled through all the troops he has access to. We might be about to wrap this whole thing up." Victor shrugged.

"I can see it's the frustration of not knowing that's bothering you. I suppose all we can do is find out, and that starts with you and me eating those apples." She stepped close to him and gazed over the parapet at the waves crashing against the beach. She leaned her head against his arm and entwined her fingers with his. "Are you ready?"

Victor squeezed her hand and nodded, though she couldn't see the gesture. "Yeah, let's get this over with." He led the way off the parapets, returning the salutes of the guards stationed on the wall. When they'd crossed the bailey into the inner courtyard, he saw Uvu reclining on the cobbles outside his travel home and felt a surge of fondness for the big cat. He was lying on his side, soaking in the sunlight, his head just at the foot of the steps leading up to the house. Victor wondered if, in his mind, he was guarding their home. "Good boy!" He squatted to scratch the lazy cat's ear, eliciting a twitch and a partial yawn.

"He's enjoying the sun." Valla, too, paused to give the cat some affection, hugging him around the neck before following Victor up the steps and into the house. He turned and, pressing his finger to one of the runes next to the door, activated it with a trickle of Energy, securing the magical locks. A few minutes later, he and Valla were in his bedroom, kicking off their shoes, hanging up their armor and weapons, and then reclining on the bed, propped up by pillows, side by side.

"Hope these apples work fast. I mean, I hope they have a big effect, but we don't lose weeks in the process." Victor produced the two gold-wrapped fruits, handing one to Valla.

Valla lifted it, weighing it in one hand. "Do you remember the racial advancement rewards for sale in the Warlord's token store?"

"Yeah, of course."

"Remember how he sold them in tiers—advanced, epic, legendary?"

"Oh, yeah. You're wondering what tier these might fall under, huh?" Victor regarded the apple as Valla nodded. "Well, I guess we don't get to know. If they're only 'improved' or whatever, then it won't affect me as much as it does you."

"Well, I hope they're potent, as you said. Then we'll both make good strides."

As he thought about her words, Victor nodded and stood up, moving to the foot of the bed. "I think I'll lie on the floor. There's no way my Alter Self spell will last through this process, and if this process does add a lot to my Quinametzin bloodline, I might grow even more. Don't want to break the bed . . ."

"Okay, but I wasn't trying to hint at that." Valla began to run one of her sharp nails along the gold foil's seam. "Ready?"

Victor grunted as he lay on the rug at the foot of the bed. "Ready." He couldn't see Valla any longer, but he heard her sharp inhalation and slight gasp. Peeling the foil from his own apple, he soon understood her reaction. It smelled amazing, bringing to mind every food Victor had ever loved—hot pancakes dripping with syrup, fresh hot tortillas with his *abuela's* homemade refries, albondigas sprinkled with fresh cilantro and lime juice; the images kept flashing through his mind with every tiny whiff of the apple's potent vapors.

"Eat it quickly!" Valla called. "Its essence escapes with each second!" That was the last he heard from her before the telltale sound of teeth crunching into an apple came to him. Victor couldn't argue, so he took a huge bite, ripping through almost half the apple with his powerful jaw and teeth. Of course, the smells only amplified with the fruit's juice exploding in his mouth, and Victor almost lost himself in an ecstasy of pleasant tastes. It was sweet but also carried hidden depths of flavor, things his mind couldn't immediately wrap around. He thought he tasted vanilla, and he'd try to focus on that flavor only to be swept away by something altogether different, like hints of rosemary or cinnamon.

Soon, he couldn't focus on the flavors any longer because, as he swallowed down the second half of the apple, he became aware of the roiling ball of Energies in his stomach. He knew it was more than one type immediately.

He recognized the pure natural Energy, the hot, metallic touch of a blood attunement, and the many biting flavors of elemental Energies. He was sure there were others. He even felt hints of spirit attunements—the cloying cold fingers of fear, the hot fangs of rage, and something warm and pure that he couldn't pin down. As he tried to examine those forces, turning his mind's eye inward, wondering what the magical fruit was doing, they began propagating through his pathways and into his body, touching every cell. Victor's awareness began to slip away, no matter how he scrabbled to hold on, to watch the process.

Ichtaca sat upon his carved bone stool and looked into the red sweating face of the youngster. "Mecati, can you hear me?" The girl shivered and shook, her brow furrowing and relaxing at odd intervals. She was deep in a fever dream, the poison coursing through her blood. Was what the father said possible? A poisoned barb shot from the bow of a fey creature? The puckered, oozing wound looked plausible, but why hadn't he brought the offending dart? It didn't matter; whether he lied or told the truth, the solution was the same—this was Mecati's time to earn her place among the Quinametzin. Whatever the source of the toxin, her fortitude must prevail against it.

Ichtaca took the cloth from the bowl of cold spring water and twisted most of the water out. Then he laid it upon her brow and tried again, speaking forcefully into her ear, letting his prodigious aura press against her. "Mecati, open your eyes."

The girl's eyes snapped open, glossy with fever, red veins standing out. She was still, though, observing, taking in her surroundings. "Healer?" Her use of his status was a good sign; she recognized him.

"It's time to fight now, Mecati. You can't let your body, strong as it is, do all the work. Turn your mind inward. Quinametzin need not fall prey to things as mundane as a toxin. It's an invader in your system, and you can drive it out."

The girl's eyes darted from him to the window and back again, then she licked her dry peeling lips. "How?" Her voice was hoarse, the breath pushing the word past her lips thready and weak. If she didn't master the poison that rampaged through her veins, she'd be dead soon.

"How do you see your Core? How do you force your essence to bend to your will? The same way, Mecati! You are Quinametzin, and we do not suffer poison!" Her dark brows drew together as his words woke something in her, breaking through the fear and weakness, stirring her Quinametzin pride. "Good! You are above these things, are you not? Do you suffer as the small people do? Do you cry from hunger or whimper in fear of the dark?"

"No!" This time, though her voice cracked, Mecati spoke clearly.

"A Quinametzin worships no other. We do not seek salvation or guidance. We do not bend our knees. We do not tolerate invaders on our lands or in our bodies! Are you Quinametzin?"

Mecati's teeth ground together, her lips pulled back in a fierce grimace as she scrunched her eyes tight, clearly struggling to do what he'd asked, to look inward, through her pathways and into her body, into her blood where the offending toxin must now lurk. Could she do it? Could she peer into herself in such a way? Could she use her will to drive her essence against the invading poison?

"You are one of the mighty, Mecati! You are one of the great ones, the rulers of these lands! Will you tolerate that poison in your blood?" Ichtaca slid off his stool and crawled onto the wooden cot, straddling the girl, placing his tattooed, fetish-bedecked hands on either side of her neck, pressing his hot, powerful flesh against hers. How far should he go to help her? Not far, he decided. This was a test for the girl, a rite of passage. He shouldn't interfere much. Just a touch of essence to aid her weakened Core. He let the barest trickle bleed forth into her, and she began to tremble, no, vibrate! Her heels bounced up and down on the cot, her body convulsed and thrashed as her head bounced upon the pillow her mother had brought.

Despite her convulsions, Mecati's brows stayed furrowed; her bared teeth maintained their grimacing snarl, and Ichtaca felt the heat from her body begin to radiate like a forge. "Good!" he growled, squeezing her shoulders in encouragement as he stood up. She'd found the path, and she was doing what she must. If he knew medicine, and he did, she'd soon be free of the toxin. She'd be exhausted but stronger for the ordeal. More importantly, she'd proven her worthiness to walk among her people. Ichtaca nodded firmly, then turned for the door; it was time to give the young Quinametzin's parents the good news.

Valla drifted into nothingness. Though she opened her eyes wide and looked from left to right, up and down, she saw naught but blackness. Why did she have the sensation of drifting? Was it because she couldn't feel anything beneath her? Nothing was under her feet, nothing beneath her back. When she moved her arms, she felt nothing. Could she even be sure she moved them? That thought brought brief panic, but she forced herself to calm. She must be dreaming or having some sort of vision. Hadn't Victor described something of the sort?

She'd advanced her race several times but never experienced anything as he'd described. She'd never had a fruit like what she'd just eaten, however. It had been labeled as providing some sort of "evolution." Was that hinting at a bloodline? Was she about to have a vision as Victor did when he'd learned of his Quinametzin heritage? Hope sprang into her heart, though she wasn't sure she even had a heart. Was she breathing? Again, panic ran through her consciousness, but realizing it, she reasoned that she was at least thinking and feeling emotions. Would that happen if she didn't exist any longer? Somehow, her consciousness was apart from her body, but that was all right. "Nothing to panic about," she tried to speak, but she wasn't sure it worked.

As she drifted and lost track of time, she let her mind run through all those things that weighed heavily upon her but which she rarely felt she had the time to ponder. Of course, Victor was foremost in her thoughts. She thought of their closeness and their intimacy, and warmth infused her floating consciousness. Then she thought of her fears—of losing him to death or simply due to falling behind, forgotten as he took on quest after quest where she wouldn't be strong enough to follow. What did it say about her that she feared the latter more than the former?

Unable to think of a resolution, she let her mind drift to other worries. What about her mother? What about Rellia, the woman who'd adopted her, raised her, and spent so much of her life forging her into an aide and successor? How would Rellia handle it if she left Fanwath to adventure with Victor? Would she break down? Would she grow bitter and distant? Would she and the others they left be overrun and killed by the Ridonne?

In despair at the idea and her lack of solutions, Valla turned her mind to other things, wondering if there couldn't possibly be something pleasant to think about. Of course, her mind had other plans and began to consider the campaign and question whether her thoughts of leaving with Victor weren't premature. How closely had Victor come to death already? How nearly had he died against the reavers? What wasn't he telling her about his clash with Dunstan? Why had it taken him almost a week to climb from the depths to claim the keep?

Flailing, trying to escape the negative worrisome thoughts, Valla tried to force herself to think of anything else, and had she been able, she would have sighed with relief when her thoughts settled on Midnight Hope, her sword. What a wonderful weapon! She was sure she was making headway with bringing her to consciousness. She'd begun to feel emotions from the weapon—anger, excitement, hunger. The blade loved to fight and loved to be held by Valla. She would have laughed at that thought; it reminded her of Victor's troubles with Lifedrinker. If only he knew how she could relate. Her sword was a jealous blade, always eager to be held and disappointed when Valla sheathed her.

"I've been listening to you, Valla."

The voice seemed to come from nowhere and everywhere at the same time. Valla was just grateful for a change in the empty nothingness. "You have?" Again, she formed the words and spoke as she would at any other time, but she couldn't feel her mouth, her lungs, or her ears. Did the words take shape?

"Yes. You're a kind and strong woman, and I'm impressed by you."

"Who are you?"

"I'm a fragment of your lineage, a tiny bit of your ancestry, a progenitor that has faded to near nothingness in the dilution of your bloodlines."

"The dilution . . ."

"Many are the peoples who make up your history, Valla. My time was long and long ago. I faded in your ancestors' blood even before my people began to die out among the larger population. Still, I was there, near the beginning, an ancient spark that traveled through history to bring you into existence."

"You're my ancestor? Who are you, though?"

"So little of me still exists. Heranya was my name, and I rode the winds around the Tarcris Peaks."

"Tarcris? That was in the old world, on Alurath? I've never met someone with that name; is it Ardeni?"

"Alurath, aye. Ardeni, nay, Valla. I was Ordeni with the Rihven bloodline."

"I had Ordeni ancestors?"

"At least one! As you drifted here, I searched your thoughts for my people, but they're gone, aren't they?"

"They were small in number when the worlds were joined. They were the first to come together to build a new civilization. I wasn't alive, but it's taught that the Yovashi, a species from another world, called down pieces of the moon to destroy their city, all but wiping them out."

"As I feared. I saw glimpses of your world, and not a single Ordeni face graced the crowds in your memories. I feel great sorrow, Valla, this fragment of me that lives in you. Will you help to revive the memory of my—our—people? Will you take up the mantle of an entire species and carry it forth into the worlds?"

"I . . ." Valla could feel the sadness lacing the words of her ancestor, and she struggled with the impulse to immediately agree. "Will I have your bloodline, too? Can you tell me about it?"

"In your memories, I saw many Shadeni and Ardeni but only one Ridonne. Do the Vessi and Ridonne no longer wage war?"

"The Vessi are dead. The Ridonne have wiped their bloodline clean from the world. I've only seen one Ridonne because they rule from high places and don't mingle with those they deem lesser."

"What a tragedy! The worst of us lives on, then. No Vessi and no Rihven—a fallen world."

"It's not that bad . . ."

"Forgive me, Valla, daughter. Little of me lives on in you, but it's enough for me to feel—enough for sorrow and rage to war for space in my fragmented heart. You've consumed something potent, daughter, something that wants to wake a bloodline. You have more and newer contenders. You could spurn me, and something else will wake in the place of your Rihven heritage, but I beg you to embrace me!"

Again, Valla grappled with emotion and the impulse to say yes. Her ancestor hadn't answered her question, hadn't told her what a Rihven was. Still, she'd given her a hint—the Ordeni had been the strongest Energy users from Alurath, driven to extinction by the jealousy of the Yovashi, though they'd been few in number before that. Had their Rihven bloodline been the cause? Had they been brought low because of the Ridonne's obsession with exterminating the Vessi and apparently the Rihven? Valla stopped deliberating and answered her progenitor with her heart, "I will embrace the Rihven bloodline."

44

REST AND REFLECTION

As his vision faded and Victor suddenly felt himself in his own body again, he snapped his eyes open, only to be bombarded with System messages. He inhaled deeply and blinked his eyes a few times, trying to push past the strange disorientation he felt, lying on the floor, looking up to see, beyond the obscuring, opaque System windows, a cloud of something like smoke or steam. Figuring he'd reorient in a few seconds, he turned his attention to the messages:

Congratulations! You have refined your bloodline to the epic stages! As a result, for all species-related considerations, you are effectively Quinametzin. You stand as the embodiment of your ancient progenitors and will continue to inherit their talents and further reflect their nature as you delve into the secrets buried in your ancestry. Stand tall, Quinametzin, for you are a titan!

Congratulations! You have gained a new Bloodline feat: Epic Quinametzin.

Epic Quinametzin: As a result of breaking through to the epic levels of your bloodline, all of your attributes have permanently increased by 50 points.

Congratulations! Your feat, Titanic Constitution, has been refined to Greater Titanic Constitution.

***Greater Titanic Constitution: Your titanic bloodline has enriched and fortified the microscopic structures of your body, from your blood to

your bones to the hairs on your head. Your body is capable of sustaining legendary levels of Energy, with the potential for tremendous physical attributes. Henceforth, you will automatically receive 5 bonus points in vitality each time you gain a level. Moreover, your battles against invasive Energies and infections have fortified you, making your resistance to such incursions unrivaled in the natural world.***

"Holy shit." Victor had to blink his eyes several times and reread the description of his new feats before it really sank in. He'd just gained nearly ten levels' worth of attribute points. Were Quinametzin really so much more robust than humans? His prideful instinct was to say, "Of course!" Still, he had to remember that he'd apparently reached the epic level on his racial advancement stat; an "epic" human might receive a similar boost. He chuckled and shook his head, somehow doubting it. Before he could become distracted by anything else, he looked at his status page for the first time in a while:

Name:	Victor Sandoval			
Race:	Quinametzin Bloodline: Epic 1			
Class:	Battlemaster: Epic			
Level:	56			
Breath Core:	Elder Class: Base 5			
Core:	Spirit Class: Advanced 8			
Breath Core Affinity:	Magma: 9		Breath Core Energy:	500/500
Energy Affinity:	Fear 9.4, Rage 9.1, Glory 8.6, Inspiration 7.4, Unattuned 3.1		Energy:	21412/21412
Strength:	330	Vitality:	439 (483)	
Dexterity:	174	Agility:	197	
Intelligence:	160	Will:	541	
Points Available:	0			

Titles & Feats:	Titanic Rage, Ancestral Bond, Flame-Touched, Greater Titanic Constitution, Titanic Presence, Desperate Grace, Challenger, Elder Magic, Born of Terror, Battlefield Awareness, Battlefield Presence, Aura of Command, Epic Quinametzin

"Holy shit!" he said again, this time more vehemently. His Energy levels had massively increased with the fifty points added to his intelligence and will. Aside from that, his other attributes looked much healthier to his eye. Six months ago, he would have been overjoyed to see his secondary physical attributes so high; they were on par with what his strength and vitality had been back then. He almost lost track of himself lying there, daydreaming about his next sparring match with Kethelket, wondering how much quicker he'd be.

Victor let his eyes drift over the various line items he'd taken for granted in the past, and something stood out to him. His race was listed as "Quinametzin Bloodline." There was no mention of "human." "*Que intere-sante*," he muttered, again thinking of himself six months ago and chuckling. He would have been freaked out by that fact, but now he didn't care. He was Quinametzin. Surely they were plenty compatible with humans, or else he wouldn't exist.

One other thing got him thinking as he looked over his status sheet—his Breath Core Energy was clearly influenced by his Breath Core level, but not by his intelligence and will as his normal Energy stat was. Did no attribute affect his Breath Core? Was he missing some other stat that creatures born with such an ability had? It would be something he'd have to investigate, but he knew he wouldn't find answers to that question on Fanwath. Putting the thoughts aside, Victor sat up and regarded his surroundings.

His early impression that the room was clouded with a haze of fog hadn't been a hallucination. A faint mist of blue-gray steam hung in the air, hot and moist in his nostrils as he breathed deeply. Victor had a hard time concentrating on the anomaly because he couldn't get over the lightning-charged strength, vitality, and overall wellness that pervaded his body. He felt incredible. Holding his big powerful hands in front of him, he stared as he squeezed them into fists, released the pressure, and squeezed again. It felt as if he could crush rocks with those hands.

He stood up and found himself engulfed in the weird steam, and then his head bumped into the generous nine-foot ceiling. "Ha!" A wild chuckle escaped him as he considered his new stature. It wouldn't do for the indoors, he decided, not until he'd built himself a home fit for a titan. He reached into his Core, teased out a bit of Energy, and cast Alter Self, reducing himself to something closer to what he'd once been—a tall, powerfully built human. The spell formed effortlessly, and his body absorbed the potent Energies much more easily than before. He felt he could have reduced himself a lot more if he wanted. Hadn't Tes said something about his then-advanced bloodline allowing the spell to work? It seemed it worked even better now.

As his height lowered and he came out of the steam cloud lingering near the ceiling, Victor immediately noticed its source—Valla lay cocooned in writhing coils of the thick stuff. He couldn't see her clearly, only occasionally catching a glimpse of her face or feet as the steam roiled. Was this what it was like when someone underwent a sizeable racial advancement? The apples must have been potent to give him three full ranks and take him into the epic tier. How greatly must they be affecting Valla? She'd only been in the improved ranks.

She didn't seem to be suffering or in any kind of trouble; her body was still as the steam did whatever it was doing. Victor began to wonder how long he'd been out and how much longer Valla would be. He reached into his storage ring to pull out the Far Scribe sheets he and Edeya had exchanged before the ninth cohort marched. Sure enough, he had several updates from her, each written a day apart. "So, assuming she's writing an update each day, I was out of it for four."

He skimmed through the messages, pleased to find that the Ninth had been having an uneventful march thus far. They'd been traveling at half-time, taking long rests between marches for drills and rest. The new troops were fitting in well, learning the tactics and camp procedures quickly. Edeya described them as fierce and eager to fight their former overlords. Most importantly, according to the last message, they weren't yet halfway to the citadels that guarded the road up to the poison-shrouded mountain where Hector held his seat of power.

Victor looked again at Valla, wondering if he should do anything. Should he sit nearby, or could he venture out of the house to check on the keep and the soldiers standing guard? If the apple were affecting her anything like the racial advancement he'd consumed inside the dungeon near Greatbone Mine, she could be out for days or weeks. He was tempted to lean close, to wave away the steam surrounding her face, but he feared such interference might cause some sort of problem. No, he decided, best to leave her to the process. He'd go outside and check on her frequently.

With that decided, Victor put on his armor and picked up Lifedrinker, shrugging into her leather harness. He hurried out of the house, eager to stretch his legs, get a breath of fresh air, and bask in some sunlight. When he stepped out into the courtyard, he squinted into the bright sky, gauging the sun to be nearing its zenith but not there yet. "Morning still." He smiled, turning his face upward, soaking in the heat. The sunlight was warm, but this close to the sea, the air had a bit of cool dampness to it, and he stretched his lungs, pulling in a prodigious breath. "Damn, that feels good."

Some soldiers performing day-to-day chores, dumping feed out of a flat-bed wagon the Ninth had left behind into a handcart, looked up at the sound of his voice. They dropped their shovels and snapped to attention. Victor smiled hugely and returned the salute. "Come here, men." His voice boomed out, echoing off the stone walls and cobbles, and the two hurried over. Victor saw more soldiers move into view on the parapets, responding to the sound of his unintentional hollering. "Give me an update. How long was I out?"

"It's the fourth day, sir!" The Ardeni had to crane his blue face and bright green eyes upward to look Victor in the face.

"Mmhmm, good. That's what I thought. Well, what's the update? How's the keep?"

"Shall I get Lieutenant ap'Fanin?"

"Is that who Sarl left in charge?"

"Aye, sir!"

"All right, get him. I'll stretch my legs and walk out to look at the sea. Send him after me." As the Ardeni and his silent partner hurried away, Victor strode for the courtyard gate. It was wide open, so he walked through and into the bailey, glancing to his left at the sound of clashing weapons and shields. A dozen soldiers were practicing under the shouted instruction of a sergeant Victor recognized but whose name he'd forgotten. He waved as he continued toward the curtain wall and the exterior gate. "This is a good keep." He rested a hand on Lifedrinker's haft as he spoke, and she immediately responded.

"I've missed you! You feel different, stronger. Will you share your spirit with me? Your she-wolf said she cared not!"

"Now?" Victor laughed, strolling into the corridor under the gatehouse. "Why not?" Victor pulled her from his harness and gathered up some glory-attuned Energy. He cast the spell, sending a portion of his prideful spirit into Lifedrinker. "See how you like that!" Her reaction was instantaneous. Her blade shimmered and sparkled, motes of golden sizzling Energy dripping from her gleaming edge. A burst of emotion came through his grip on her haft—excitement, pleasure, and of course pride. Whether she was proud of him for sharing his spirit or proud of herself for convincing him to do so, he had no clue. For all he knew, it was just his spirit bringing out her own cockiness.

The gate was closed, but a guard was stationed beside it. From the center of the trap-lined tunnel, Victor shouted, "Open up!" The guard yanked on a chain, causing a bell to ring up above, and moments later, the windlass began to turn, lifting the great bar holding the gates closed. "Thanks." The guard snapped a fierce salute. Victor nodded, then stepped outside. He stood in the shade of the tall curtain wall and gazed down the rocky slope to the beach and the cresting silvery waves of the sea. "Hell yeah. I like this keep."

The ocean was loud, crashing and crashing as the wind-tossed waves hit the shore. He watched them, admiring their relentless power as he walked down the slope a short way. A rocky overhang made a direct approach to the keep impossible, forcing the gravel roadway to wend its way down to the beach like a snake. Victor didn't want to go down, though, so he stood on the rocky ledge, and holding the buzzing Lifedrinker on his shoulder, he stared out over the water, savoring the fresh air, the warm sun, and the glorious view. He felt more alive than he ever had, more ready for anything. He wanted to venture forth into that wild, wide world. He wanted to find new things and conquer new places. He wanted to . . .

"Ahem, excuse me, sir."

Victor turned to see the young Ardeni Lieutenant ap'Fanin standing at attention behind him. "Relax. Thanks for coming out to speak with me. I wanted to see something other than stone walls."

"My pleasure, sir. I, too, grow weary of the confines of yonder keep."

"Mmhmm. So, tell me, how have the last few days gone?"

"Uneventfully, sir. We've spent our shifts keeping watch, cleaning, and drilling. So far, we've not laid eyes on anything more threatening than a flock of erebii, and they weren't a problem for anyone save poor Delia, whom they shat upon as they flew past."

"Erebii? Those are the big white and brown birds?"

"Aye, sir."

"Heh, well, my condolences to Delia." Victor smiled, gazing back at the keep, imagining the soldiers standing watch on the walls when the birds flew overhead, scurrying to escape their indiscriminate bombardment. "Well, I'm going to be here a while longer, I figure. Tribune Primus ap'Yensha isn't yet ready to leave. Anything you all need help with? Could I help with some sparring? I think it would be good for the troops to practice teamwork against a larger opponent."

"I think that would prove invaluable, sir." The man spoke firmly and nodded to add weight to his words.

"What's your first name, Lieutenant?"

"Rano, sir."

"Care if I call you that?"

"I'd be honored!"

"Good! All right, Rano, how many troops are at the keep? A hundred?"

"One hundred and one, sir."

"Okay, have you broken them into squads?"

"Aye, sir! We have ten squads."

Victor looked away from the keep, back to the ocean, wondering why there wasn't a dock. Who built this keep, anyway? Judging by the old watchtower he'd used to escape the underground, it had been on these lands for a while. Were they remnants from an old world before the joining, as others suspected? Wouldn't there have been a village by the sea? Had the sea come from one world, the keep, and these lands from another? The idea that the System had somehow squashed four worlds together to make Fanwath still boggled his mind. When Rano sniffed and moved his arm to push some hair out of his eyes, blown there by the breeze coming off the water, Victor turned back to him. "Right. Well, go make a schedule. I'll work with two squads daily—one in the morning and one after lunch."

"Right away, sir." He saluted, and Victor copied the gesture, then watched him jog back to the keep.

"That's a good idea, isn't it, *chica*? Those guys might face a big bastard wampyr or something on the battlefield. They should get some practice fighting a guy like me." The truth was, he itched to get some practice in, to cast Iron Berserk and let his Energy swell his frame. He wanted to do a lot more than spar, but he'd settle for that over nothing. With one last look at the water and a few more thoughts of adventure and exploration, he returned to the keep, resigning himself to finish what he'd started before he entertained thoughts like that. He had to get rid of these *pinché* undead, which meant he needed to stick around for a while longer.

The next few days fell into a relaxing routine for Victor. He spent the evenings and nights with Valla, watching her, marveling at the weird

Energy-dense steam that seemed to perpetually issue from her, completely swathing her body like a billowy cocoon. She didn't stir, or if she did, he couldn't see it through the thick clouds. He slept on the floor, quite content on the rug, and when he woke in the mornings, seeing no change in her, he'd go outside and spar with one of the units, encouraging them to use their skills and abilities to gang up on him.

For the first hour of those practice sessions, he'd keep himself hobbled, sized down the way he liked to be when indoors. After everyone was warmed up, he'd release his hold on his form, cast Iron Berserk, and let the soldiers go all out. He still held back, and Lifedrinker recognized that they were "playing," in her words. She didn't burst into flames, and it almost felt as though she helped him to pull back or angle her edge away when he slipped someone's guard too easily. Still, the soldiers were battered and tired at the end of each session, and Victor felt relaxed, his stress driven away by the good fun of helping others learn something. It didn't hurt that he also cast Globe of Inspiration and Inspiration of the Quinametzin, and many soldiers reported skill gains at the end of each session.

At noon, he'd check on Valla, eat a hearty meal with the soldiers in the keep, then start a new session with a second unit. After that, Victor would spend time cultivating, trying to work on his outdated cultivation drill, incorporating what Khul Bach had taught him. He knew his drill was pathetic for his power level, but he'd been cheating to improve his Core by eating hearts, an ability people like the Warlord would be and had been quite willing to murder and commit atrocities to learn.

He met with Khul Bach twice during those three days and had long conversations about the nature of titans, what Victor should be working on, and how he'd made good progress toward his goal of being strong enough to return to face the Warlord one day. Khul Bach, as usual, didn't like to talk for long, acting as though every second Victor spent in there speaking to him was a second he could be out trying to improve himself. It was after the second meeting, on the third day, when the soldiers on the parapets raised an alarm. Victor was in his home at the time, so he didn't hear it, but eventually, Rano dispatched one of his sergeants to pound on his door.

When Victor heard the pounding and hurried upstairs to open the door, the Shadeni woman, a soldier he recognized from an earlier sparring bout, spoke breathlessly. "An army approaches, sir! Hundreds of foot soldiers and half a dozen giants! We can't see them clearly in the dark, but the giants have eyes that glow with red flames!"

"Hello, Ileya. Is your arm still sore?"

Her eyes widened when he spoke her name, and she answered him, anxiety thick in her voice, "My arm? Yes, sir, but I've put some salve on it. I'll be fine. What of the army?"

"The army? Hmm. Seems like they think they're going to score an easy win here, what with only a small force left behind to guard this big keep. I'm afraid they've made a big mistake, though." Victor grinned, his chest swelling as his Quinametzin pride opened his pathways, letting his Energy seep into them, his will to hold his aura in check slipping just a bit. "Yeah, a big fucking mistake."

45

A CLASH OF GIANTS

Victor stood on the parapet, flanked by Lieutenant ap'Fanin, or Rano, and several of his sergeants. The beauty of the Sea Keep was the one-sided approach any attacking army would have to take, assuming they couldn't fly. The sheer cliff behind the keep butted up against a great rocky mountain range that stretched east for dozens of miles before giving way to more rolling hills and plains. Meanwhile, the front of the keep had limited exposure due to the rocky slope leading down to the shore. Only a narrow winding gravel-strewn road gave access to the sliver of hard stony ground before the curtain wall. Victor caught his first glimpse of the incoming army down that winding stretch of road.

"How do they know we have a light garrison?" one of the sergeants asked, squinting as he peered into the moonlit shadows.

"They must have spies, observers. Who knows what manner of undead creatures might lurk up on yonder slopes." Rano jerked a thumb to the right, toward the high rocky peaks leading away to the east.

"Yeah." Victor nodded. "They counted our guards, watched the light activity in the courtyard, and figured we were easy pickings. I just wonder where these guys came from." He peered down at the army, his Quinametzin eyes easily piercing the shadows. To him, the darkness was tinged in strange orange and red tones, the pale light of the moon enhanced by his epic-level physiology. However it worked, Victor had a clear view of the shambling undead creatures and the hulking monstrosities marching in their midst. "Looks like around eight hundred undead and six of those giants."

Rano turned to look up at him. "You don't think they're from the other keep? The southern one?"

"I dunno. Maybe. Maybe they were outside when Borrius and Rellia surrounded it. It could be that this force was on its way to help one of the other keeps, even this one, and whoever commands it saw an opportunity. We don't know how Hector communicates with his generals. Maybe he gave the order."

"Can this wall resist those giants?" a sergeant to his left asked.

"For a while, maybe. They're about twenty feet tall, and I don't know if you all can see this, but they're kind of built like gorillas. Ugly deformed hairless gorillas, but what I mean is their oversized arms are practically dragging on the ground while they walk. I bet they pack quite a punch."

"Gorillas?" Rano turned to lift an eyebrow at Victor.

"Doesn't matter. I'm just saying they look like they were built to smash stuff." Victor watched the army for a minute more, judging they were only about a mile distant, halfway up the winding road. "If we're going to do something before they hit the wall, we better decide now. Any ideas?"

"If it were just the undead, we could hold them at the wall, I'm sure." Rano sounded stressed, almost as if he'd done something wrong. Victor could guess what he was thinking.

"You're wondering if you should've built some defensive measures on the road, prepared more for a circumstance like this."

"Aye. We spent too much time drilling and cleaning. We should've been out there digging trenches, laying traps, building barricades."

"Eh, we don't have time to play what-if. What are we going to do about those giants?" Victor had an idea of what he'd do, but he was hoping to get some more ideas before he charged out there and tried to carry the battle on his shoulders.

A feminine voice piped up from off to Rano's right. "What if we don't close the outer gate?"

Victor leaned forward to see around the lieutenant and one of his burlier Shadeni sergeants to lay eyes on the speaker. She was a thin pale-haired Ghelli with tiny wings, reminding him of Edeya before she'd gone through her racial enhancement. "I'm listening."

"If we don't close the outer gate, they'll funnel toward it. Why smash the wall when there's a big opening? Let them drive through, use the murder holes and whatnot, while you wait in the bailey for any giants that come out.

We have ballistae on the inner wall to help with them, too. Obviously, we'll keep the inner gates closed."

Rano nodded. "I like the idea of turning the bailey into a killing ground."

"Huh," Victor said. "Not bad. I'll stand at the gatehouse tunnel and smash any that come through. We'll need men on this wall in case they try to use ladders or something to swarm over. If we get overrun, you can use the wall to retreat to the inner courtyard, yeah?"

"Aye, sir!" Rano turned and began to give his orders. Victor turned away, focusing again on the approaching army. Were all those giants the same? Who was leading this force? Did they come without a general? Were they just an extra patrolling force Hector had called to action? He was beginning to think so, watching as the army neared the last bend in the road. He was getting ready to hop down to the courtyard to get into position, but then he noticed that one of the giants was hanging back while the other five plowed forward to the front of the pack of undead. "Are you the boss? Okay, *pendejo*, we'll see what you guys are made of."

When he turned away, he found all the sergeants were busy ordering the hundred defenders into position. About two-thirds of the soldiers looked ready to defend the curtain wall from climbers or whatever the army tried to send up the wall. He turned to look over the bailey to the inner wall and saw fire teams near each of the six ballistae. He knew other defenders were inside the gatehouse, ready to rain hell down on the undead that came through the tunnel. Victor pulled Lifedrinker from her harness, still gleaming and dripping with golden, glory-attuned Energy. He'd left his Imbue Spirit in effect and didn't plan to cancel it anytime soon. "This'll be interesting, beautiful."

"I yearn to cleave their flesh! I hunger for it! Let all witness our might as we lay your enemies low!"

Victor chuckled, then severed his Alter Self spell, expanding to his natural size, nearly ten feet tall. He placed a hand on the parapet and hopped over the wall, landing on the cobbles with a thud that shook dust from the stones. He strode to the inner gate and stood at the opening as the soldiers inside raised the portcullis. The tunnel leading through the curtain wall was big but not big enough for those giants to get through easily. He could still walk through it, but they'd have to stoop. He'd have a similar problem if he berserked.

Over the last few days, while drilling with the troops, he had discovered a few things about himself. First, he'd learned that, as the System had informed him, he was considered a Quinametzin now. He knew that because his Titanic Leap worked without Iron Berserk or Titanic Aspect. Another thing was that, just as he'd grown in his natural state, he was larger when he cast Iron Berserk, something like eighteen feet tall and God knew how many pounds. Finally, he'd begun to notice changes in himself, in his personality. At first, it didn't register with him, probably because he was himself, and it's always a little hard to look at oneself objectively. Still, he'd begun to notice a certain pridefulness that made the old Victor seem mild.

This revelation might have been troubling to him once upon a time, but, likely due to the changes in him, he couldn't find it in himself to feel upset. So he was changing, wasn't that good and proper? Shouldn't one evolve as one grows in power? Should he still act like a lost kid from Tucson? No, he'd moved well past that stage in his life. He was a warrior, a titan! He was Quinametzin, and those who challenged him should learn the folly of their ways . . . "Heh, there I go again." Victor chuckled, catching himself in the midst of his inner monologue.

Standing before the gatehouse tunnel, he looked up at the parapets and shouted to Rano, "What are they doing?"

"They've stopped at the end of the road! It looks like they're forming ranks—the giants are in the front. Well, five of them!"

"Well? Start shooting! That's only two hundred yards!" That was one of the things Victor appreciated about the Sea Keep; there wasn't enough room atop the rocky shelf for a proper army to assemble out of harm's way. The outer ballistae could easily reach the edge, and many of the soldiers had abilities and spells that could accurately launch missiles at that range.

"Sorry, sir! I thought we might wait to hear their intentions!"

"Hell no! They marched onto our land with undead soldiers. Fuck them up!"

Rano's voice rose to new heights as he screamed the order up and down the line, "Fire! Fire! Unleash your ancestors' fury! Burn the dogs!" He went on and on, and because of the distance of the enemy force and the discipline of the soldiers atop the wall, his words rang clearly through the bailey. Victor smiled at his colorful enthusiasm and nodded, twisting his fist on Lifedrinker's haft. He listened to the thump of the ballistae and the cranking of their windlasses as they were reloaded. He watched the sky brighten with flashes of color as the elementalists threw their fire and lightning at the incoming undead.

Soldiers began to yell and cheer, buoyed by their small victories, as the undead began to fall. For a moment, he regretted hopping down from the battlements so soon, thinking he should have watched the attack for a while, but then he considered the magical nature of his enemies and the idea that they might spy him standing up there. No, it was better to wait there, out of sight, and give them a titan-sized welcome as they came through the tunnel. Still, he was curious. "Rano!" he bellowed. "Do the ballistae hurt the giants?"

"I . . . I think so, sir! They still come, though blood leaks from their misshapen forms!" Victor watched through the dark tunnel, waiting, getting ready. He wanted them committed, wanted them in the tunnel before he exposed himself. The shouts and screams of his soldiers grew more frenetic, the flashes of magical Energy more strobe-like, and Victor felt his breathing quicken, his heart begin to thump. He wasn't nervous; he was excited. Thunder and flashes were frequent now, the casters with shorter-ranged spells unleashing all they had. When a cacophonous peal of thunder rolled over the courtyard, shaking the stones, Victor almost cheered, impressed by whichever soldier had cast such a spell. His enthusiasm dimmed, though, when he realized it wasn't friendly magic.

A new kind of darkness obscured the moons, throwing more shadows around the courtyard, and then a frigid stinging rain began to fall, bringing forth screams of pain from the garrison troops. Victor felt it, cold and burning on his flesh, but he shrugged it off. It would take more than that to hurt him. Still, the soldiers suffered and needed his support. "Time for action, *chica*," he growled, then he cast Banner of the Champion and Iron Berserk, and suddenly the entire bailey was awash with brilliant golden light. Victor stood so tall that his massive banner hung in the air, visible over the parapets.

Lifedrinker, despite the growth she'd gone through in the last months, was once again a hatchet in his massive hand, and Victor held her high, ready to bring her down on the first fools to push through that tunnel. Despite his bolstering light, the soldiers were suffering, screaming in the burning rain, and Victor bellowed, "Get inside the gatehouse, or fall back to the inner courtyard! Take cover!" His voice was booming, breaking through the screams, the crashing thunder, and the sounds of the undead horde as they streamed for the open gateway. He saw the soldiers hurry to obey, many going into the enormous gatehouse before him. Many others ran, panicked, with shields over their heads, for the far ends of the curtain wall, aiming for the heavy metal doors that would admit them into the higher inner keep walls.

Victor wasn't worried. So what if some of the undead climbed the wall unmolested? Where would they go? Into the bailey with him! He laughed at the thought, and before he grew too busy with fighting, he looked at his current physical ability scores.

Strength:	330 (1377)	Vitality:	439 (596)
Dexterity:	74 (313)	Agility:	197 (355)

His laugh grew louder at what he saw, a throaty chuckle that rumbled out of his chest. Even giving ten percent of his power to Lifedrinker, his attributes were monstrous. His strength and vitality were boosted by Sovereign Will; his strength, dexterity, and agility were increased by Iron Berserk. On top of all that, his Titanic Rage feat further enhanced his strength. His physical attributes were far beyond what his level might indicate, and he could feel it. In his mind, he could drop his axe and smash his way through that wall with his bare hands.

As his red-tinged eyes took in the first of the giants struggling to get through the tunnel, he held Lifedrinker high, waiting off to the side. Arrows pumped into the hulking shape as it lurched, hunched over, stumbling and jiggling toward Victor. As hot oil doused the form, sloshing over the creature and sloughing off great swaths of cooked flesh, he began to wonder if the poor bastard would get through to him. Another throaty chuckle escaped him as he began to stoke the flames of fury in his pathways, pumping it into his arms with Channel Spirit but leaving it out of Lifedrinker; she was glorious as she was, and he didn't want to distract her with more fury.

He itched to charge into the tunnel, to ruin the giant stumbling its way through, but he didn't want to stand under those arrows, oil, and other projectiles being lobbed by those in the gatehouse. He waited, grinding his teeth in anticipation, and then the first giant came out of the tunnel, lifting its misshapen knobby head in a bellow of victory, raising its giant pink club-like arms high in the air. Victor brought Lifedrinker down in a vicious hack, her brilliant gold-lit blade ripping through the thing's shoulder, removing one of those big arms with a thunk and a thunderous crack as she tore through the bone.

Victor laughed and lifted one mighty boot, kicking the reeling giant in the hip and sending it sprawling away from the gate to slide over the cobbles. It thrashed and writhed, but it was terribly wounded. Its bulbous pink flesh was riddled with arrows, covered in blisters, and ripped with a hundred gashes. Its eyes had been boiled out of its head, and great gouts of red-black blood pumped from the stump Victor had just made. "You're big, but you're no titan!"

He wanted to taunt it more, to cut pieces from its monstrous form, but another was already emerging from the tunnel, and this one wasn't nearly as badly hurt. It lowered one of its monstrous lumpy shoulders, revealing a row of strange black horn-like spines, and charged at him. Victor loved to grapple, and having something bigger than he was for a change was a rare treat. He lowered his center of gravity, caught hold of one of the longer horns, gripping it with a hand that could crush stone, and easily turned the monster's charge, giving it five rapid hacks with Lifedrinker as he threw it past.

Lifedrinker screamed with fury and excitement, reveling in the action, sending sparks of golden Energy flying in her wake and showering forth from each impact. She tore massive gashes through flesh and bone alike, and when Victor flung the monstrosity aside, it tumbled to the ground. As it rolled, the cobbles were splashed with blood and dark slippery things that were meant to be on the inside of the monster but had been freed by Lifedrinker's wicked blade.

Victor stepped to the side of the tunnel and peered around the stone, red fury obscuring details but making it easy to pick out the thrashing piles of undead in the passageway. The murder holes were doing their job, and the third giant struggled to push past the mounds of dead zombies and shamblers. Victor took the respite to dispatch the two downed flesh giants, hacking through their spines, splitting their skulls, and dashing their brains onto the cobbles. They were weak, in his opinion. "Not even a challenge! The soldiers could handle these stupid things." For some reason, the ease of his victories made him angry, and he could feel the rage in his heart begin to boil, beating through his blood and darkening his vision further.

He stared into the tunnel, saw the third giant was still only a third of the way through, and decided he'd had enough. Focusing on the thing, he lowered his heavy helmet and cast Energy Charge, fueling it with his most plentiful Energy—fear. In a streak of screaming shadows, he tore through the mounds of corpses and collided with the great fleshy monster, smashing it like a Mack truck T-boning a school bus. The explosion resounded through the stones of the gatehouse, but the fleshy giant came apart before the stones did, and it exploded out of the tunnel in a shower of blood, bones, viscera, and sagging empty skin.

Drenched in hot red fluids, Victor ran forward, screaming his fury. He began to curse his weak enemies as the undead massed outside the gate, waiting to come through and charge him. Some of his curses were out of character, things he'd never think of to insult someone in a rational state of mind,

"Weaklings! Worms! Dare you challenge me? Feed the soil, then, pathetic things!" Other curses were more in character, more like the old Victor dialed to the max. "Fucking die! Eat shit! I'll rip your shit-eating faces off!" Meanwhile, he tore a swath through the undead, aiming for the fourth and fifth of the lumpy misshapen flesh giants.

He hacked the zombies and shamblers apart with his axe, grabbed them with his left hand, and threw them about like playthings. He was surrounded by undead, too stupid to care that they weren't hurting him, that he was ripping them to shreds, and they kept filing in, hindering his progress toward the two giants. The big monsters were working their way around him toward the gate, and Victor had had enough. Again, he flooded his channels with fear-attuned Energy and cast Energy Charge. He obliterated scores of undead as he exploded with dark Energy, streaking through the miniature horde and slamming into the first of the giants. Just like the last one, this one came apart in a shower of blood and gore.

Victor roared and began to lay into the second one, shrugging off its tree-trunk-sized arms as they rained return blows upon him. Those big, two-hundred-pound fists crashed into his Juggernaut helm, slid off his shoulders, or were knocked aside by Victor's left hand as he went to work with Lifedrinker, carving terrible wounds into the gigantic, roaring monster. The fleshy giants were ugly as sin up close. Folds of pink flesh surrounded bright burning red eyes over huge noseless nostrils from which blood and slime sprayed forth. Beneath those sickening orifices was a round mouth filled with rows of yellow angular teeth. It tried to employ that sucker-shaped bite a few times, but Victor just threw it off, smashing it with Lifedrinker's edge for its efforts.

When the final giant was dead, torn to bits at his feet, Victor's chest heaved as he looked around. Some of the undead were still charging toward him, but most had streamed into the tunnel now that it was clear of giant bodies. There couldn't have been more than five hundred, and Victor wasn't worried about them. The soldiers could finish their work on those stupid mindless things; they had the walls to their advantage. No, he had other fish to fry. Where was that last giant? Where was the general who commanded this little horde? Where was the one who'd summoned that magical evil rain?

Drenched in blood and gore, Victor stood tall, smacking the occasional undead that strayed near, and he scanned the rocky shelf, looking toward the road. "Where are you? Come and fight!" He started forward, kicking zombies like footballs and splitting shamblers like cordwood as he walked away from the keep. He'd made it halfway to the road, a trail of ruined undead marking his progress when the giant stepped forward. His great helmeted head was the first to appear as it made its way up the last stretch of the sloping road. The helmet was black, the metal thick, and the angular eye slits shone with baleful red Energy. Then his enormous shoulders and chest rose into view, similarly clad in heavy black plates, held together by links of black chain.

While Victor watched, the giant continued forward, and the rest of him came into view—thighs like mighty oaks, fists in gauntlets that could have doubled for engine blocks, and finally, hanging from the giant's right hand, dragging a furrow in the ground behind him, an axe that made Lifedrinker look like a toy. "Glad you came out to play with old Karl, little one. I'd worried there wouldn't be any glory in this victory," the giant rumbled.

46

BATTLE ON THE BLUFF

Victor watched Karl, or Karl the Crimson if this was the guy Victoria had told him about, continue to stride closer, and as he crested the rise, Victor took his measure. He was a true giant of a man, easily as large as the monstrosities he'd sent against the keep but not misshapen and lumpy. His gigantic plates of flat black armor made him even more impressive to behold. Victor felt a wave of excitement at the prospect of a good battle, and felt his annoyance at the weakling undead begin to fade to background noise as he twisted his fist on Lifedrinker's haft. He didn't reply to the giant's taunt, but his teeth were bared in a hungry grin as he stalked toward his new opponent.

"I thought you'd moved on, taking your little army toward Hector and your inevitable destruction. I'm pleased I'll have a big fat head to mount on my next creation." With a grinding clatter, Karl dragged his giant axe over the stony ground and swung it with a *whoosh* up to his shoulder, gripping the haft with both hands. Victor didn't answer, but a low growl began to rumble through his chest as he thought about the flimsy giants this man had just claimed credit for.

"Come," Victor growled, and then he danced forward. He moved like a bear, power evident in every step, every flex of his wrist as he wove Lifedrinker left and right. He wasn't impressed by the giant axe; when did making something big make it better? True, as a titan, he wasn't known for being small, and much of his dominating power came from his size, but he wasn't a giant, overfilled sack of bones like those creatures he'd just slain; he was

Quinametzin, and he was hard as steel. The cords of muscle standing out on his forearms, shoulders, and back were powerful, ready to snap into action like pressure-driven pistons. Karl might have more bulk than he, especially with all that plate armor, but Victor saw him as a concrete wall, and he was the sledgehammer.

Karl waited for him to get near, then, like a spring snapping a bear trap closed, he ripped his great axe in an overhead smash, aiming to split Victor in half. The axe fell like a lightning-charged guillotine, slicing the air and crashing into the stony ground, showering the vicinity with shards of gray rock and hundreds of brilliant sparks. Victor wasn't there to appreciate the mighty blow, however; he'd darted to the left, and as he skirted around the black-clad giant, he hacked Lifedrinker not once but three times into his armor-covered side, taking advantage of Karl's arms being extended, swinging that giant axe.

Lifedrinker had cooled during the lull between Victor's slaughter of the undead and this new contest. As he swung her, though, she burst into molten fury, her inner heat adding to the power of his enchantment. She still shed brilliant sparks of glory-attuned Energy, but they were hot and sizzled the air as they fell, scoring the stony ground with black burn marks. Her gleaming edge shimmered hotly, heating the air to the point that even getting near her edge was a dangerous proposition. Karl's armor screeched as she split it, carving deep grooves in the dense material, so hot that she liquified the metal where her blade touched it.

When Karl regained his momentum and hacked his gigantic axe in a wide flat arc, hoping to catch Victor still on his flank, his face beneath the black metal visor of his helm was crimson with fury and pain as blood sizzled against the torn hot metal plates on his side. Victor wasn't there to receive the blow; he'd continued to circle the giant, and this time, he darted forward and delivered one mighty hack to the side of Karl's right knee. Lifedrinker didn't have to cut through any inch-thick metal plates; he struck the gap between the jointed round cap over Karl's knee and his thigh plate. Lifedrinker screamed her excitement and lust for violence as she split the air, slicing through the chain armor as though it wasn't there and burying herself deep in the giant's flesh, biting into his bone.

Karl roared in agony and swept his axe around, kicking out with his other leg, trying to get at Victor. Victor ducked the whooshing blade and yanked on Lifedrinker, using her grip on Karl's bone to pull his leg out from under him. The armor-plated giant's sweeping kick turned into a pirouette as he toppled and crashed to the ground with a tremendous thud and the rattle and clank of metal. Victor stepped on Karl's outflung forearm, holding it to the ground, then he lifted Lifedrinker high, her blade smoking as it scorched the very air, and chopped her at the giant's face with enough force to split stone.

Lifedrinker's eager high-pitched war cry echoed and bounced off the stone as she fell toward the giant, a lightning-fast streak of burning metal, but just as she was about to deliver her fatal blow, Karl exploded with cold death-attuned Energy twisted with something else, something familiar to Victor from his duels with Valla—iron. The Energy billowed out of Karl like an expanding shell, and Lifedrinker smashed into it. The defensive ability or spell was effective in that it slowed her descent, but it wasn't enough to stop her; Lifedrinker struck that shell with such burning deadly force that its blue-gray surface turned white at the point of impact and instantly began to shatter and come apart.

Though Lifedrinker broke through the barrier, she'd been slowed enough for Karl to lift an armored forearm and deflect her deadly blow. Still, Victor ground down on Karl's other arm, keeping him in place as he lifted Lifedrinker for another hack. Karl wasn't out of surprises, though; his right hand was pinned, and he hugged his left arm in front of his face, yet somehow his giant axe smashed into Victor's back, splitting his wyrm-scale armor and gouging deep into his tough Quinametzin flesh.

Victor stumbled at the unexpected blow, growling in fury as he spun, expecting to see that some undead remnants of Karl's army had interfered with their contest. Instead, he saw the enormous axe wielded by a ghostly translucent replica of Karl sans his armor. Karl's spirit form glowed with a deathly blue Energy, and Victor knew this was some kind of Death Caster magic. He instantly poured a torrent of fear-attuned Energy into his pathways and summoned his bear totem—if Karl wanted to bring friends into the fight, Victor would oblige.

As he stepped back, lifting Lifedrinker, warily circling the spectral copy of Karl, a dark roiling mound of shadows rose from the ground, and deep angry roars echoed out of it. Victor grinned as he heard his bear brother's fury. The giant axe-wielding spirit dove at him, whipping the enormous axe in a great cleave, and Victor backed away, tapping the clumsy strike with a quick thrust of Lifedrinker's head, adding to its momentum and then stepping into the blow as it *whooshed* past him. Meanwhile, with a bone-rattling roar, his great, dark shadow-clad bear erupted from the pile of darkness and fixed its furious purple-lit eyes upon Karl as he struggled to rise.

While Victor went to work on the spirit, his bear pounced on the giant. Even big as it was, the bear looked more like a dog as it slammed into him, but Karl's knee wasn't working right, and he wasn't armed. They both tumbled to the ground in a furious grappling melee as Victor's totem swiped its dark eight-inch claws in a frenzy, snapping its great maw against Karl's arms as he tried to throw the bear off him. Victor hacked Lifedrinker, one-handed like a killer with a hatchet, to great effect on the spirit-like copy, cleaving off big hunks of its essence, which splattered to the stone ground in steaming gel-like puddles.

The spirit opened its mouth in silent screams as Victor whittled it down, easily dodging the clumsy swings of the massive axe, a weapon ill-suited for up close, dirty fighting. The spirit seemed to know what it was doing, constantly backpedaling to get some room to swing the weapon. Even so, it was trivial for Victor, an epic-ranked axe fighter, to press his advantage, to stay inside the big axe's arc, and continue to deliver blow after devastating blow to the spirit's form. It grew paler and paler, and after a final powerful hack that seemed to shatter its essence, it exploded into a cold, damp, softly glowing mist and faded away.

As Karl's axe fell to the stone with a cacophonous clatter, he turned to the giant only to see him finally on his feet, lifting his bear above his head, ready to throw Victor's brave totem down the rocky slope toward the ocean. Victor growled in fury, released his bear to return to the spirit plane, and then, as Karl stumbled, suddenly holding nothing but air, he cast Energy Charge, powering it with glory-attuned Energy.

In a shower of golden sparks and a streak of bright light, he ripped over the rocky ground to slam into Karl's exposed flank. The giant wasn't ready. How could he be? Victor hit him like a battering ram, the concussion so deafening that boulders broke free of their centuries-long resting places and tumbled from the heights, crashing their way down the mountain slopes, many bouncing and cracking all the way to the sea. Victor nearly drained his glory-attuned pool of Energy as the spell worked to deflect the force of the impact. Karl wasn't so lucky.

As Victor smashed into Karl's back, a ripple of energy tore through the giant that exploded blood vessels, ruptured organs, and sent fluids bursting out of Karl's every orifice. Many of his armor plates ripped free of the chains holding them, flying out over the rocky slope, and then Karl's body followed them, tumbling as he cried out in a final gasp of surprise and agony. He soared past the winding gravel road to land with a great *thump*, flopping like a broken toy from one rocky shelf to the next until he came to rest on the edge of the beach.

Victor watched Karl's descent with a wild grin, and even before Karl's body came to a rest, he leapt down after him. He wouldn't leave the giant any room for some *pinché* undead recovery. In two Titanic Leaps, he stood on the beach and approached the broken giant with Lifedrinker buzzing in his hand, hungry for her due. As Victor's heavy footprints shook the ground and the giant, amazingly not yet dead, opened his blood-soaked eyes, he wheezed, "What are you?"

Victor regarded the giant. Much of his armor had fallen away as he'd bounced his way down the rocky slope. His exposed flesh was pale and deathly, and Victor knew he was undead. His arms were twisted and broken, his knee that Lifedrinker had chopped was utterly ruined, and that foot rested near his shoulder, so badly bent was the leg. His helmet had broken free, and his thick head of orange-red hair lay spread on the sand, almost like a pool of blood. Victor's anger was cooling quickly; he felt only contempt for this unnatural giant. He lifted Lifedrinker high, her smoldering blade dripping hot sparks on Karl's broken chest. "I'm a titan!"

"But," Karl wheezed, "you're smaller than I . . ."

"You're a giant of a man, Karl, but a giant next to a titan is like wood before steel. Make your peace." With that, Victor brought Lifedrinker down in a devastating chop, planting her gleaming white-hot edge directly through the center of Karl's breastplate. She split the metal like a sheet of paper-thin tin, burying herself to the wood of her haft into Karl's chest. Karl's bloody eyes widened almost comically, and he opened his beard-covered mouth in a silent O of pain and dismay. Then, the light faded from his eyes as Lifedrinker earned her name.

As Victor's rage cooled further and he lost his Iron Berserk, he stood beside the gigantic corpse and waited until Lifedrinker had finished. After he'd yanked her free and hung her in her harness, he pulled the rings from Karl's giant fingers, three of them the size of bracelets. That done, he cast Honor the Spirits, watching as the brilliant white ghostly fire consumed the massive corpse. As the flames died away, the ethereal smoke vanishing into nothing, he turned and began trudging up the slope to the keep.

He was glad to have won, glad there hadn't been any terrible surprises with the army's attack, but he also felt uneasy, as though he were wasting time. The giant had claimed not to know Victor was there, but the whole thing almost felt like a distraction. He supposed it would be strange for Karl to throw his life away for a distraction. Victor shook his head, continuing up the ramp, ears peeled, listening for the sounds of battle from the keep. They were still there, clashes of metal on metal, men and women shouting, but they were infrequent, and nothing sounded desperate. He figured the undead were struggling to do anything against the walls now that the giants were gone and their commander was dead. The soldiers were probably whittling them down from safety.

When he reached the top of the slope and paused by the scene of his battle, he stooped to pick up the gigantic axe. Now that he was back to his normal size, the weapon seemed more monstrous, even absurd. It was a dark, gleaming gray-black, singular piece of metal molded into a haft and an axe-head, utilitarian and plain. The blade was shaped like a gigantic wedge, a simple shape for an axe, but large and heavy and clearly designed to cut through anything with that deadly sharp blade. Victor lifted it, his muscles straining from the weight, and laughed at the absurdity; the weapon was bigger than he was. "Are you alive?"

No answer was forthcoming, so he lowered the weapon and continued toward the gate, dragging it behind him, digging a trail in the blood-spattered gravel. He walked past hundreds of dead zombies and shamblers with only a vague recollection of slaying them all. There'd been more than he thought. He had to force his way through piles of the undead in the gate tunnel, and when he finally emerged, he paused to watch as the soldiers continued their slaughter. They'd come out of the gatehouse and their shelter in the higher inner courtyard walls to surround the bailey, raining death upon the shambling, lurching monsters.

The rain had ceased when Victor engaged Karl, and the clouds that had obscured the moon were gone. Fiery bolts, arrows streaking with Energy, lightning, frost, and even stone projectiles fell from the heights. Only a few dozen of the undead, already battered and broken, still stumbled about on the cobbles, listless and undirected in their failed assault. Victor leaned against the giant axe, propping the cold metal haft against his shoulder as he watched the slaughter. It was only minutes before the battle was over, and golden motes began to gather around the mounds of corpses.

Victor chuckled, turning to look through the tunnel, but couldn't see anything through the massive clouds of golden stuff. "Here we go," he laughed, then let the massive axe haft fall to the ground with a clang as he braced himself. Seconds later, he was struck with a torrent of Energy; his conscious thoughts were dashed away as he spun on a wave of euphoria, drifting through rainbow-colored hallucinations of ecstasy. He swore he saw Valla dancing through his visions, laughing and smiling like he'd rarely seen her in reality. Tingles of pleasure danced through his skin as his muscles spasmed, and the reward for his efforts washed through him. The influx recharged and renewed him, leaving him gasping on his hands and knees minutes later.

Victor grinned, still debilitated by the afterglow of the infusion, when he saw the System message before his eyes:

Congratulations! You have achieved level 57 Battlemaster and gained 10 strength, 9 vitality, 4 agility, 4 dexterity, 3 will, and 3 intelligence.

"Huh. Nothing more? I guess it wasn't that hard a fight." Victor stood, lifting the big axe again, and walked across the bailey, dragging the giant weapon. He could hear the soldiers cheering and celebrating all around him, and when he reached the inner gate, Rano was there, bloody but happy, snapping a perfect salute.

"Sir! Well fought! You slaughtered those giants!"

"Good fight to you, Rano. You and your soldiers didn't give an inch. Do me a favor and secure that outer gate, then write a message in the command book."

"What's the message, sir?"

"Tell Borrius to quit twiddling his thumbs and attack High Keep; I just killed Karl the Crimson, and it should be easy pickings."

"That was one of the barons? I was on the outer wall when you threw him from the ledge! You smashed him like a training dummy!"

"Heh. Well, let's hope whatever's holding the citadels dies as easily, huh? All right, get to it. Oh, one more thing. Get some men together and take this axe into the great hall. Hang it above the biggest fireplace."

"Yes, sir!" Rano saluted again, then hurried toward the outer gates, hollering for some soldiers on the wall to join him.

A few minutes later, Victor sat on the floor at the foot of his bed, watching the weird colorful steam swirling around Valla. "Well, you missed a good one, Valla. Eh, not really. It was just a bit of a workout. You probably wouldn't have liked it—no chance for fancy sword work." Of course, she didn't stir, so Victor looked at his Core and saw his Energies throbbing with potential, ready for anything. He'd run a little low on rage during the battle and almost burned up his glory-attuned Energy once, but he'd never really been in danger of running dry. It would take a much longer battle to do that.

Looking at his Core, though, studying his different Energies, a thought occurred to him: Why hadn't he tried to build any new Energy attunements?

He'd learned to make courage and justice, but many more combinations were possible now that he had his glory affinity. What would glory and fear create? Glory and rage? What about glory and inspiration? "Then there's the triple combos like justice. What if I replaced inspiration in the justice weave with glory? What about glory, inspiration, and fear or rage? What if I could weave them all together?"

He was just thinking out loud, but he pitched his voice as though he were speaking to Valla. When she didn't respond, he sighed and pulled out a stack of paper sheets and some differently colored pens. "I think I'll start working on some ideas while you're resting, *amor mío*." He felt Lifedrinker vibrate slightly in her harness and chuckled. "Don't be jealous, *chica*. I love you differently." With no further protest from the axe, Victor smiled and settled down to his work.

47

RIHVEN

Over the next couple of days, Victor spent less time than he wanted working on his new Energy weaves. The soldiers on garrison duty were still members of the ninth cohort, and they'd gotten an infusion of excitement and enthusiasm when they'd witnessed Victor's fights with the giants and then from their flawless destruction of the undead swarm. He couldn't hold it against them when they asked for more training. After their extended bouts, Victor felt guilty going inside while they marched out to the roadway and began constructing barricades and rebuilding the watch tower on the beach. The only solution he could think of was to spend some of his free time helping with that endeavor.

So he spent most of his days working with the soldiers, and then in the evenings, while he sat with Valla, he took time to visit with Khul Bach and worked on his cultivation drill, which he felt was very close to advancing out of the "basic" category. Finally, after cooking up a large meal and checking his Far Scribe books and pages for correspondence, he would sit with his notes and ponder the complex patterns of Energy that he hoped to weave. He was making progress, but it was slower than he'd anticipated.

When he'd created courage and justice, he'd had help from Gorz and Old Mother. Sure, he'd learned a lot since then, even made some spells of his own, but weaving Energies was different from building spell patterns. At first, he thought he'd do something simple by replacing the inspiration in his justice weave with glory. He'd thought it was a no-brainer—a complex weave, sure, but all the hard work had been done. It turned out that different affinities weren't exactly plug-and-play. When he tried to build the weave in his pathway, the glory-attuned Energy didn't hold the pattern where inspiration did; it kept slipping and drifting. He tried to force it with the power of his will, and though he could do so, keeping it where he wanted it, the pattern never "snapped" together; it never flashed and became a new attunement.

He wasted two days trying to modify the pattern to make the glory-attuned Energy work with it, but, in the end, he decided it was like trying to force a spring into a mechanism that wanted something more like a cog wheel. What he needed was to craft a mechanism meant for the spring from the ground up. What it boiled down to was that Victor's idea of tackling what he'd thought would be the easiest new weave turned out to be one of the more complicated ones, so after two days of struggling, he decided to try working with something a little simpler. Rather than trying to put together another weave involving three Energies, he chose two—rage and glory.

On the fourth night after Karl's ill-fated attack on the keep, after a hard day sparring and working on the watch tower, Victor sat down to eat a plate of sliced meats, cheeses, and fruits. He quietly munched as he flipped through the pages he was sharing with Edeya, turning to her latest missive:

Victor,

I received word from Rellia today. The legion has captured High Keep and, leaving a sizeable garrison behind, will begin the march to reinforce us at the citadels. She said Borrius plans to split the legion; half will march north along the western edge of Hector's current territory, and the other half will march along the eastern perimeter. Along the way, they plan to split off support units to add to each keep's garrison. They know we've called for the reserve cohort at the pass to join us, so they plan to take their time, ensuring they haven't missed any other "surprise" armies like the one that assaulted you at the Sea Keep.

As for us, we finally have eyes on the citadels. I thought we'd see one, have to deal with it, and then the other, but they truly are twin structures, and they're connected via a great marble span that crosses a wide raging river. We've learned that the river flows from the east, originating in the mountains beyond Rust Keep. The legion crossed it on their way south to High Keep, but it was much more docile on the plains. Here among the hills surrounding Hector's mountain, the river is a formidable barrier, rushing with white waters over boulders and falls. We've crossed it farther west and now make our way up through the hills toward the first citadel.

The castles are intimidating, each guarding a side of the massive arch. Their walls must be a hundred feet high, built from the same white stone as the bridge. Only a narrow approach is possible because of the steep slope, and there's no room to stage an army before the enormous gates. For now, Sarl and Kethelket have judged our best course of action will be to lay siege, holding ground out of range of the defenders and preventing any more of Hector's forces from leaving the mountain. Sarl intends to build siege weapons, hoping to soften the defense and perhaps destroy the gate before our eventual charge.

It's good that we got here ahead of the army; it'll take weeks to properly prepare for what looks to be a difficult assault. I hope you and Valla are well and that we'll see you soon.

With affection,

Lieutenant Edeya

Victor frowned, staring at the page with unseeing eyes; he was busy picturing the scene, imagining the two tall keeps and the bridge between them. He was glad the army would hold off, dig in, and prepare for a real siege. He wanted to be there when they attacked. If they couldn't breach the gates with siege equipment, then Victor would be the one to assault them. In days past, he'd determined that Karl's axe was not conscious. However, it seemed to be made of incredibly dense enchanted metal, and he had an idea that it would be better at smashing defensive structures than Lifedrinker. "Which is good, lovely," he said, resting a hand on Lifedrinker's haft. "You're meant for better things than chopping wood."

He wasn't surprised when she didn't answer but simply hummed with pleasure. She wasn't the talkative sort. "Unless you count screaming in battle." Amusement rippled forth from the axe, and his grin widened. Victor stuffed the last slice of peppery cured meat into his mouth and stood. "Okay, let's go check on Valla, then get to work on that Energy weave." With a final pat to Lifedrinker's haft, he walked down the stairs through the long hallway to his bedroom. On some level, he knew something had changed the second he opened the door; he'd grown used to the layer of magical fog hanging in the air near the ceiling, and when it wasn't present, he jerked his eyes to the bed, only to find it empty.

"Valla?" He frantically scanned the room, eyes settling on the door to the bathroom.

"Don't come in here!" her voice cried from behind it. Of course, Victor immediately started for the door.

"What's wrong?" He rested a palm on the warm wood, his need to see she was all right warring with his desire to respect her request.

"I'm . . . I think I made a mistake, Victor! I'm not me anymore!"

Victor touched his hand to the handle, and the house, recognizing him as the owner, unlocked the door with a click. Still, he didn't open it. "Take a breath, Valla. Can I come in?" He tried to keep his voice steady, tried to slow his pounding heart.

"No! Ancestors! Oh, Victor! Just wait until night, close your eyes, and let me slip away in the shadows. Let me hide among the other outcasts in the world!"

"You're freaking me out, Valla. I'm opening the door."

"No!" A thud accompanied her objection, and he knew she was leaning against the other side of the door, pressing it closed.

"Okay, then tell me what happened."

"One of my ancestors spoke to me. Somehow. Ugh! I don't know how it's even possible. Is she in my blood? Did I meet her spirit? No, she said it was just a fraction of herself . . ."

"Valla, slow down! Take a breath. What actually happened?"

"She wasn't Ardeni, she was Ordeni." Her words stirred a faint memory in Victor's mind, and he tried to pin it down. It was something Chandri had told him . . . a story about the world forming.

"Oh! Aren't they the people who got destroyed when the world was new? Didn't they all gather to build a new city, using what they learned when the System arrived? Like, weren't they really talented with Energy?"

"And the Yovashi called down a piece of the yet-unformed moons to annihilate them."

"Oh, yeah. Well, that part sucks, but it's neat that you have a piece of them in your ancestry."

"A piece? Ha!" Soft thuds accompanied her words, and Victor could tell she was bouncing her forehead against the wood.

"Come on, Valla, just tell me."

"My ancestor had the Rihven bloodline. She asked me to take it up."

"Okay . . ."

"I thought it was the noble thing to do. I thought I should rise to the occasion, to bring forth this lost bloodline, to 'share it with the world,' or some other nonsense she spouted."

"That's exciting, right?" Silence. "Valla?" She didn't answer for several long seconds, and Victor pressed, "Talk to me."

"I just, well, I just didn't expect such changes. I should have known better; the Rihven were compared to the Ridonne. Why don't I remember any art depicting them? Did the Ridonne purge them from history? I didn't know I'd look like this, damn it!" As she swore, Victor had to fight to push his amusement down; the woman he loved was in despair—this was the time to be serious.

"I don't give a shit if you've sprouted tentacles and grown a dozen eyes. I love you, Valla. Come on! I'm a titan, not a chickenshit boy. Let me see what my lovely, beautiful, sweet, brave, powerful woman looks like." In response, Victor felt the doorknob twist, and he let go of the handle as it slowly swung open, revealing her. "Holy fucking shit, you dummy! You're gorgeous!"

"I am?" Tears streamed from her eyes, and Victor reached out to wipe them with a thumb as he looked at her, really taking in the changes. He could see why she'd be upset, even though she was totally wrong. Yeah, she'd changed a lot, but she was still Valla; she was still amazingly beautiful by any standard. Even so, if he'd changed that much with his first dose of the Quinametzin bloodline, he might have been freaked out at first, too. Valla was a good foot taller than she'd been, and though his house was built with high ceilings and accommodating doors, she was as tall as he was in his slightly reduced form. Her skin, while still retaining a hint of blue, was much paler, and strangely, Victor thought he saw a shimmer of silver in it as he rubbed her tear away with his thumb.

If the changes had ended there, with her added height and different skin, he imagined she would've taken them in stride. Those were the most minor of changes, however. Her hair, too, was different. Only hints of its seafoam color remained, largely replaced by shimmering metallic silver tresses. Her eyes, once pure glittering teal, were flecked with swaths of silver. Even her facial structure was different; he felt as if he were looking at Valla's long-lost older sister; her cheeks were higher, her jaw more defined, and her brow more angular. She looked more . . . regal was the only word Victor could think of.

Despite all those changes, Victor thought the last was the one she was really struggling with. Valla had grown wings, and they weren't little fairy wings like a Ghelli's. They were full-on, massive, feather-covered wings. They twitched, expanding and contracting awkwardly, one at a time, clearly throwing Valla off balance. He could see her struggling to control them as he regarded her. Even so, the wings, while big and maybe cumbersome, were beautiful. The feathers were silver with teal highlights, just like her hair. "Yeah, silly. If you were a ten before, now you're a fucking twenty."

"What?"

"Nothing, just trust me, okay? You look amazing. You're the prettiest person I've ever seen, and I've seen some knockouts, as you know . . ."

Valla punched him, blurting out a noise that was half sob, half laugh. "Stop it! These wings are terrible! I don't know how to keep them still! Look at the bathroom; I destroyed it!" Victor looked over her shoulder to see the towels, knickknacks, and toiletries they'd accumulated on the counters were spilled and scattered all over the floor.

"You just got 'em, silly. It's going to take a little getting used to. Why do you think I was so obsessed with learning to make myself smaller when I first started to look a little like a Quinametzin? It's hard to change your mental image of yourself. You need to practice with those wings, but think about it, Valla! You're going to fly!" He watched her eyes, watched the tears still pooling, but saw something light up in them, a glimmer of excitement. "Yeah, I'm jealous of that, damn it! Hey! If I make myself small enough, you could fly me around . . ."

"I'm not carrying my lover around like a baby!" she growled, and Victor noticed another change; her sharp catlike teeth were mostly gone—her dentition looked very human now. Was that a result of her embracing her Ordeni ancestry? Was that one of the differences between them and the Ardeni?

"Okay, forget all this physical stuff. How do you *feel*? Did anything else change?"

"Yes!" She started to cry again, tears bursting out of her eyes and streaming down her cheeks. Victor pulled her close, still standing in the doorway, holding her against his chest and stroking her head, smoothing his fingers over her light, surprisingly fluffy, silvery hair. "I . . . I'm not crying from being sad! When I looked at my status sheet, I got hung up staring at my race; it says I'm Ordeni now with a Rihven bloodline." She sniffed and, pressing her face into his chest, kept speaking. "But when I finally looked further, I saw the biggest change of all. I worked so *hard* to get my affinities up over six using the techniques I'd learned from Tes. So *hard*!"

"Yeah?" Victor was waiting for the other shoe to drop. Had she lost her affinity?

"Now my air affinity is over eight. Just like that, without any work!" She pushed away from him, scowling, and boy, could she scowl with those angular silver brows. "I feel like I cheated!"

"Shit, Valla, are you kidding?" Victor shook his head, bemused. "You worked hard to get it up to six, and now it's eight. If you hadn't worked hard, it might not have risen as high. You're not a damn cheater. Anyone who can advance their race will do so. You know that!"

"Not everyone does . . ."

"Well, they aren't our peers. We need to be strong, and this is how you do it. Fucking A, Valla! Your affinity is awesome! This is going to help so much!"

Valla sniffed, the waterworks drying up. She looked into Victor's eyes, and he savored it, enjoying a little dive into those beautiful silver-teal orbs. After a moment, she let go of his arms and took another step back, shaking her head ruefully. "I can't even put my armor on."

"Ah, shit." Victor glanced at her new, huge appendages sprouting from between her shoulders and frowned. "We gotta think of a way to fix that." He frowned, shaking his head, putting the thought away for another time. "We'll figure it out. On another note, though, how many racial ranks did you get? I got three . . ."

"Ten!"

"Damn! I'm glad I gave you one of those apples, then."

"Well, you're the one talking about how we need to get stronger, but that's a good example of how you don't follow through with your own advice."

"Not true! If I ate another apple, I might get two ranks out of it. You think two more racial ranks for me is as valuable as having an ally as strong as you? How about having to worry less about the woman I love? How much is that worth?"

"A lot, because this woman isn't going to let the man she loves do all the heavy lifting anymore."

"Right." Victor nodded. "Heavy lifting. Like when you fly me around . . ." Again, Valla punched him, and he took a step back, laughing. "Hey! Careful! I think your knuckles are bigger." With that, she chased him out of the bathroom, and as she ran behind him into the bedroom, her wings unfurled, and she laughed, leaping after him. Soon they were entangled, wrestling on the bed, and their horseplay transitioned from laughter to kisses, and not much sleep was had in Victor's house that night.

When he woke in the morning, he lay with his face in the pillow, listening to the odd sounds of Valla muttering and cursing to herself, accompanied by the repeated sound of her wings folding and unfolding, sometimes slowly and sometimes with an audible *crack* as they snapped to their full span. He slowly turned to his side and peeked through one half-open eyelid to see her pacing back and forth through the room in nothing but her underwear as she fought to gain control over her new appendages. "We'll stop early each day so you can practice on the way, too," he muttered.

"We're supposed to . . . how did you put it? 'Haul ass on Guapo,' not dilly around so I can learn to control my gods-damned body!"

"Gods, huh?"

"Well, how do I know? Sure, we have ancestors, but your grandmother believed in a god. Tes mentioned old gods. Who knows what's out there?" She snapped her response at him, and when she turned to regard his sleepy smile, her angry, furrowed brow softened, and she laughed and flopped to the ground, sitting on the carpet beside the bed. "I'm ridiculous!"

"Nah, you're great." Victor sat up and stretched, yawning. "Anyway, it's okay if we take a little extra time; the Ninth is just sieging the road leading up to the first citadel while they wait for the reinforcements. Come on! Let's get breakfast, and then we'll get on the road. Have you got an old breastplate or something you can wear till we find an armorer qualified to mess with Tes's wyrm scale?"

"Of course. In any case, I'll need you to help me cut some holes in the backs of my shirts."

"I dunno, I kinda like you like that." As Valla's cheeks bloomed red and her eyebrows drew together, Victor laughed and rolled to his side, burying his head under a pillow, bracing for her retaliatory attack.

48

WINGS

Rano and a few of his sergeants hung around in the courtyard while Victor prepared to leave. He'd summoned Guapo, and Uvu prowled around the courtyard, well aware that something was going on. He kept sniffing the air, chuffing, and pacing near the stairs leading into Victor's travel home. Victor figured the big cat knew Valla was awake and would emerge soon, probably alerted through their bond. While he waited for her, Victor took some time to go through the big storage rings he'd taken from Karl.

One was full of supplies—barrels of lamp oil, timbers, iron brackets, bolts, and pins, along with the tools that would be used to put them together. When Victor showed Rano, he suggested they were for building siege equipment. Victor shook his head, bewildered. "Why wouldn't the idiot use some of this stuff?"

Rano shrugged. "Perhaps he was overconfident in the power of his giants. Perhaps he didn't realize you laid in wait."

Another of the rings was filled with more disturbing things. There were dozens of sealed casks within, and when Victor took one out and hammered it open, he found it full of blood. There were huge crates stuffed with body parts, from human limbs and skin to organs. Victor grew disgusted in his perusal and handed the ring off to Rano. "Build bonfires near the sea and burn these things."

"Aye, sir."

In the last of the storage rings, Victor found more personal things—clothes, armor, notebooks, weapons, and myriad disgusting things that could only have been trophies or mementos. The latter ranged from fingers in velvet-lined jewelry boxes to large portions of human skin mounted on frames meant for hanging on a wall. Scanning through them, Victor didn't find anything that interested him other than some sacks of beads numbering in the hundreds of thousands. He took those and again handed the ring to Rano. "You can distribute the weapons and armor as awards to those who need them, but I'd like you to destroy the disgusting trophies."

"Trophies?"

"Yeah, I think that sick asshole kept parts of, I dunno, victims or maybe friends to display. You'll see what I mean."

"I'll see it's done, sir." Rano was mid-salute when he suddenly gasped and took a step back, eyes on something over Victor's shoulder. Uvu made a funny rumbling, yawning sound, and Victor knew Valla had emerged. He turned to her, face lighting up with affection. He caught his breath, much like Rano, when he saw her standing there on the stoop of his travel home, her wings partially extended, catching the morning sunlight in a spectacular shimmer of silver and soft green-blue iridescence. She was tall, powerful, and sharp-looking in her snug black uniform pants, well-shined boots, and white tucked-in uniform shirt.

Victor had helped her to trim some holes in the backs of her shirts for her wings, and they seemed to have worked well. Midnight hung from her waist on her sword belt, and Valla had donned a shiny silver breastplate that covered her chest and matched her helmet. To him, she looked like a Valkyrie or angel, girded for war. When she met his eyes with those spectacular silver and teal irises awash with the rich warm sunlight, he felt he could forget everything in the world and simply stare at her. Then she smiled, and he wanted nothing more than to rush over to her, hold her, and kiss her.

Of course, Victor knew none of that would be cool with Valla, not with the soldiers gathering in the courtyard and on the ramparts to stare. Silence had fallen over the keep like a blanket; everyone was still, stunned by the appearance of a creature only vague legends alluded to. Valla wasn't one to speak much in the best of times; she didn't like attention focused on her, and Victor could tell this was a struggle for her. Nonetheless, she squared her shoulders and spoke into the courtyard. Her voice, while still hers, was loud and powerful, and it carried well—she'd been trained to address troops, after all.

"Soldiers, I thank you for guarding me well while I went through my bloodline evolution! As you can see, I've brought forth the aspect of one of my more distant ancestors—she was an Ordeni and, more than that, a proud carrier of the Rihven bloodline. Look upon me and behold the last of a people who once walked among the Shadeni and Ardeni—a people who stood up to the Ridonne and were exterminated for their trouble. Now, enough gawking! Back to your work! Guard this keep well in our absence!"

It became apparent that the soldiers weren't sure how to react. Some cheered, some clapped, some did as she said—stopped gawking and got back to work—and some kept staring, unable to wipe the stupefaction from their faces. Victor broke the spell on Rano by walking between him and Valla, holding out his hand to take hers. "You look great."

"Thank you, love." She took his hand and stepped down to the cobbles where Uvu paced, rubbing his long furry body against her as he circled with repeated rumbling chuffs vibrating his chest. "Hi, Uvu, sweet boy," she cooed, rubbing his head and massaging his fuzzy ears. Looking at her with the cat, Victor wasn't so sure he'd serve very well as a mount. Valla had sort of out-grown him. He wondered if that mattered now that she had wings. Would she be able to fly farther than the Ghelli? Her wings were undoubtedly much larger. He wondered how that would work—didn't birds have hollow bones and a skeletal structure designed to support flight? He knew for a fact that Valla was no lighter than before. In fact, she was heavier . . .

"Anything else, sir?" Rano asked, finally having found his voice, interrupting Victor's musing.

"No, I don't think so. We'll be off shortly."

"In that case, I'll make my rounds. It's wonderful to see you, Tribune Primus."

"Thank you, Lieutenant." Valla smiled, looking up from the affections she was pouring onto Uvu.

As Rano saluted and walked away, Victor asked, "What will you do about this big boy? I suppose you can still ride him, but your feet might touch the ground."

"He'll follow at his own pace. If not a mount, he's a boon companion." She hugged the giant cat around his neck. "Aren't you, big soft boy?" The great cat yawned hugely, exposing six-inch fangs by way of reply.

Victor clicked his tongue, and Guapo, golden and proud in his glory-attuned form, walked closer to the small group. "I'll pack up the house—you're done in there?"

"For now, aye." Valla's words were muffled, her face still buried in the fur of Uvu's neck. Victor chuckled, rested a hand on the travel home's front stoop rail, and mentally issued the command to compress. A few minutes later, home securely fastened to his belt, he hopped onto Guapo's back and held his hand down for Valla, swinging her up behind him. As they trotted out of the courtyard and through the bailey, Victor was surprised and a little embarrassed to see Rano and all of his soldiers lined up to watch them depart.

He sat up straight and, not wanting to look like some kind of dopey nobleman or something, didn't wave. He just locked eyes with as many soldiers as possible, nodding his appreciation. He wasn't sure how Valla responded to the attention, but he felt her shifting behind him and figured she might be waving or saluting. When they exited the outer gate, Victor urged Guapo to pick up the pace, and soon they were trotting down the steep winding road toward the beach. "Hey," he called over his shoulder, "when are you going to try flying?"

"When no one else can see me!" Valla laughed, squeezing his ribs as she leaned into him. Victor chuckled, then leaned forward, urging Guapo to go as fast as he could over the rough, curving road. They made the beach in no time, and then they really started to move as Guapo understood Victor wanted to follow in the tracks left behind by the Ninth. Despite a couple of weeks having passed, the passage of six hundred soldiers was still quite evident, especially as they got into the shrub-covered, loosely wooded hills. The turf was well-torn, and bushes were trampled in a wide swath. The cohort had chosen a route traversable on foot, and Guapo had no trouble pounding over the same path.

After an hour or so, Victor knew poor Uvu was well behind them, and he shifted so he could look back at Valla. At some point, she'd removed her helmet, and though she still held his sides, she was leaning back, face in the wind, her hair streaming behind her. Her wings weren't unfurled, but they weren't tight to her back, either. Her eyes were closed, and she wore a contented smile. It looked as if she was really enjoying the air coursing through her hair and feathers. Victor had intended to ask her if she worried about Uvu but didn't want to interrupt her joy with a worry she'd clearly put out of her mind. Instead, he turned back to the front and enjoyed the ride himself.

When he ran like this, Victor had no doubt that Guapo was twenty or more times as fast as the cohort. He figured they could reach their destination in less than two days if they tried, but he didn't intend to hurry. He planned to let Guapo run until noon, and then he and Valla would make camp, and he'd give her some time to practice with her wings. Victor didn't want to bring her into combat if she'd never even sparred with those new appendages; what if she couldn't find her balance?

When he pulled Guapo to a halt on a broad grassy hill, it wasn't even noon, but he liked the spot so much that he'd decided to stop early. A single tree, young and green, sat atop the hill next to a burned broken stump of a much larger one. Victor liked to imagine the sapling was growing from a seed left behind by the dead tree. When his big spirit horse stopped beside the tree, and Victor scanned the horizon, he could clearly see the wall of gray mist that made up the border of Hector's lands. It was still quite distant, beyond hills and canyons, but from that height, he could imagine the route and figured Guapo could get there in less than a day.

Of course, their route wasn't straight to Hector's mountain—they had to turn north, skirt those foothills, and find the river that led up to the dormant volcano and the roadway the citadels guarded. Even so, he knew if they left early the next day, they'd make it; Guapo had hardly slowed from his fastest gallop all day as he followed the cohort's trail. "Let's stop here."

"For lunch?"

"Nah, for the day. We can finish the journey tomorrow, so let's take some time for you to practice with those wings."

"Ugh! I was hoping to be alone. It's going to be embarrassing!"

Victor laughed, sliding off Guapo. "Don't be like that. You know I'm not going to tease you! Much." He reached up to help her dismount, but she ignored his hand, sliding off on her own.

"Think you're funny?" She stretched her back, slowly turning in a circle, admiring the view from the hilltop. "A nice spot, at least!" She turned to look back the way they'd come over rolling hills covered in a mostly green carpet of grass that faded into the horizon. "I hope Uvu enjoys himself and does some hunting and exploring on his way."

"I'm sure he's loving it." Victor began pulling chairs and camping equipment from his storage rings, setting up a picnic area in the grass. "How about I cook us up something for lunch while you stretch those wings out?"

"Well, I can see you're not going to let the matter rest, hmm? All right. I *am* curious, but please, don't watch me at first."

"Cross my heart." Victor laughed at her puzzled expression, then got to work, lighting up his camp stove and boiling some water. He could hear her steps as she moved down the hill a short way, then the flutter of wind through her wings as she spread them out. His hearing had improved along with the rest of his senses as he'd grown more powerful and his body had evolved, so it wasn't hard to pick up her soft exhalation and the ruffle of feathers as she tried flying for the first time. He was surprised, though, when the sound rapidly faded. Had she taken flight so quickly? He broke his promise and turned to look for her.

He immediately saw her, higher than the hilltop, yet hundreds of yards distant. She jerked from left to right as though trying to find her balance, but it looked awkward and difficult, as if she was at the mercy of the wind. Then her feet, trailing beneath her, straightened out behind her, and he could see her pull her heels together. Almost like magic, her flight evened out, and she banked to the left, exposing the full expanse of her massive wings. They glittered in the sunlight, and a distant laugh came to him on the breeze. Victor sat down on one of the comfortable chairs he'd set out, envy gripping his heart as he watched her flap those wings, gaining altitude and truly soaring like a bird.

"There must be magic involved," he said to Guapo, who stood near the green sapling, idly chewing on grass. "Her body isn't like a bird's, so magic must be buoying her flight, making those wings work so well." He stared at the proud spirit mustang for a long second. "Why are you eating grass, you goofball?" Of course, no answer was forthcoming, so Victor chuckled and returned to cooking. He didn't have a vast repertoire of dishes, and in fact, he wasn't really cooking at all. He was just heating some soup he'd bought in Coloss and adding some fresh ingredients. It was a brothy vegetable soup, and he pulled the meat from a whole roast bird he had from his time with the Shadeni, adding it to the pot. Guapo wandered closer, and Victor laughed. "I know it's a warm day, but I was in the mood for soup. Don't get any ideas; it's not for mustangs."

As he stirred the pot, the thud of feet hitting the ground and rapid steps told him Valla had landed, so he turned to regard her. Her hair was wild, her cheeks were flushed, and a huge smile told him things had gone fine. "Victor! I wish you could fly!"

"Ha! Me too! It went well?"

"Yes! It was like . . . well, it was like my body knew what to do as soon as I got some wind in my feathers!" She came closer to his camp stove, sniffing the air. "Smells great!"

"Chicken vegetable soup!"

Valla folded her wings tight to her back and tried to sit on the chair, but they hung below her butt, and she couldn't make it work. "This is absurd! How am I supposed to sit?"

"Maybe open them partially? So they hang to the sides of the chair?" He watched her frown with concentration, trying different positions and finally settling on something like what he'd suggested. "It'll take some getting used to, huh?"

"Yes, but it's all worth it! I never imagined the feeling I had up there! I was so free and fast! I wager I can travel as quickly as Guapo!"

"Faster, I'll bet, once you get used to it. If you get really high and just soar on the wind, you won't have to worry about obstacles like he does."

"True! And they're different from Ghelli and Naghelli wings, at least at the level we've seen. I know I can go higher and faster than any of them."

"Yeah, those wings of yours are serious business. Lam and Edeya have pretty wings, but there's no way they could keep up with you."

"You watched me?" Valla scowled in mock outrage.

"I waited for a little while . . . well, until you were in the air, at least!"

Valla's laugh trilled again, and Victor couldn't help joining her. It was good to see her so happy; he could probably count on his ten fingers the times she'd really laughed in the past. The two of them sat together, enjoying each other's company, eating soup and salty wafer-like bread for a good hour. After lunch, Valla took another flight. Then, when she returned, flushed and excited, full of tales of the things she'd seen, they sat together, just taking in the fresh air and warm sunshine. Toward mid-afternoon, Victor suggested they spar for a while so Valla could get used to her wings in such an activity.

They started off slow, moving at half intensity, practicing their forms, their attacks, and counters. They had to stop and repeat things several times as Valla kept throwing herself off balance with her wings. After a while, Victor stopped and suggested, "Why don't you try using your wings more rather than trying to control them? Go ahead and extend them and use them like the limbs they are."

"I've just been trying to hold them tight so they don't throw me off . . ."

"Yeah, but have you ever seen birds fight? They have their wings out and use them as much as their talons or beaks."

"Where have you watched birds fight?"

"Ha, I don't know. Probably some internet videos." He laughed and shook his head. "Never mind—it's a thing from my world."

"You'll have to explain it to me sometime. I'd like to hear more about your world." When Victor nodded, Valla spread her wings with a crack, and they began again. This time, she kept her wings out, flapping them to aid in her movement, and Victor found it a lot harder to close with her and deliver his attacks. Her wings were very strong, and she could use the hard bony edge to knock him or his arm aside when she spun. He wondered at the metallic sheen to her feathers; would they continue to harden as she advanced her bloodline? Would they eventually be as good as armor?

When they decided to break for dinner, she laughed and charged him with a violent, exuberant hug. "You were right! I did much better when I stopped trying to control them, when I stopped trying to move like I did before I had them."

Victor hugged her back, smiling. She'd been slower and a little awkward, but he could tell she was going to get stronger and stronger—her ceiling had, literally, been vastly expanded. She would be very formidable when she grew used to those wings and their movement became second nature. "It's good, beautiful. You're going to be great." As he hugged her, he set his eyes on the distant wall of eerie green-tinted mist. Hector was waiting for him. He wondered what the *pendejo* was even like. "When we catch up to the cohort, let's talk to Victoria about Hector. I want to end this *pinché* invasion."

She laughed and squeezed him harder. "We will. Who could stop us now?" Victor chuckled at her confidence; she was sounding almost Quinametzin. It was good, but something in him wanted to look for a piece of wood to knock his knuckles against.

49

STAGING

It was near sunset the next day when Guapo powered up a steep hillside, providing an unobstructed view of the mountain approach, the cascading falls, and the citadels that sat like whitewashed chess pieces on either side of the raging river. They were still too distant for Victor to pick out details; he couldn't see any people on the ramparts or crossing the impressive stone span of the bridge between them. He could see the snakelike road that led up through the foothills to the first citadel, and not far from where he and Valla sat atop Guapo's back, he could see his army encamped, guarding the approach to that road.

He frowned as he looked away from the army, up the hill, back to the two massive keeps guarding the road to Hector's base, the town at the top of the mountain. He still couldn't see anything of the actual volcano or plateau or whatever it was. Just past the second citadel, the curtain of green-tinted fog grew too thick. It was like a sickly cloud had come down to the ground, obscuring all observation. Even the air around the citadels was hazy, and Victor had a feeling that if they weren't so high on open hilltops, so exposed to the air currents and the flow of that raging river, they'd also be near impossible to see.

Valla shifted behind him and pointed. "It looks like the reserves from the pass are here." It was true; the encampment was far too large just to be the ninth cohort. They'd set up a perimeter fortification and even constructed a stone watchtower farther out, directly on the curve of the gravel-strewn mountain road leading toward those two final fortifications guarding the approach to Hector's base.

"Yeah. Looks like they noticed us." Victor pointed to movement down the slope, about halfway to the encampment. A rider on a roladii was galloping toward the camp.

"Well, I suppose we'll need to get this over with." Valla didn't sound excited, and Victor knew she was nervous. It would be the first time people who really knew her, other than Victor, would see how she'd changed.

He clicked his tongue, getting Guapo moving again, then reached back and found Valla's hand, squeezing it in his. "You'll be fine. Are you sure you don't want to fly into the camp? Really give them something to talk about?"

"No!" She snaked her other arm up around his chest, pulling herself close to his back. "Could you maybe make yourself a little bigger so I don't look so tall?"

"Hmm?" Victor had been reducing his size the same amount as usual, which happened to be just about the same height Valla now stood. "Seriously?"

"At least at first?"

"I mean, we're tall right now, too tall for comfort in some houses. You want me to add another couple of feet to myself? 'Cause that's what'll happen if I cancel my spell."

"Don't cancel it! Just relax it a little. Give yourself another six inches. Just for now, Victor!" She squeezed him again, and he sighed, chuckling. His protest was more about teasing her than him actually caring. He extended his will and pulled back the flow of Energy to his Alter Self spell, and he and Guapo both expanded in size. "Better!" Valla laughed.

Victor tapped his heels against Guapo's sides, and the mustang leapt into a gallop, tearing down the hillside and thundering over the grass and scrub-covered ground toward the encampment. No one could mistake the massive horse for anything other than Victor's mount, so he wasn't worried about alarming the sentries. As they pounded over the cleared area outside the camp's fortifications, Victor urged Guapo to slow, and they trotted through the wooden palisade gate. The soldiers atop the ramparts saluted, and some shouted excited greetings. Victor waved and turned back to wink at Valla. She smiled, encouraged, and partly extended her beautiful silver-teal wings, allowing her feathers to ripple in the breeze of their passage.

When they'd ridden past the latrines, the stockyards, a few hundred tents, and the cook pavilion, Victor caught sight of Lam and Edeya, their wings glittering blue and gold in the early twilight, and turned Guapo toward them. Just as they arrived and slid down from the horse's back, so too did Kethelket and Sarl, one fluttering in from the east on dark silent wings and the other walking briskly attended by a small retinue of junior officers.

"Valla! Roots!" Lam cried, the first to find her voice as Victor and Valla, smiling and waving, stepped toward the group.

"Rihven?" Kethelket asked, his voice hushed and his eyes distant with some ancient memory.

"Rihven?" Edeya asked, looking around the group, clearly puzzled by the word.

Valla wasn't one to enjoy the spotlight, and she spoke up, probably to put the mystery to rest so they'd stop talking about her, "That's right. I've awakened the Rihven bloodline from an Ordeni ancestor. Now, forget about that, will you? Tell us what news you have of your siege efforts."

"Oh, no!" Lam laughed. "We won't be put off quite that easily! I've never even heard of the Rihven bloodline, but Valla, your wings! They're just as spectacular as the Ridonne's! But you're far more beautiful than any Ridonne could hope . . ."

Valla frowned and folded her arms. "The Ridonne killed my ancestors. They drove them to extinction. Well, I suppose that's not wholly true, or I wouldn't exist. There are likely others among the Shadeni and Ardeni with traces of their bloodline, but . . . well, let's say I'd rather you didn't compare me to one of them."

"I'm sorry . . ." Lam seemed to be having trouble finding the right words, and Victor was about to step in, but Edeya beat him to it.

"Valla, Tribune, we Ghelli aren't always cognizant of the histories of the peoples from your homeworld. Tribune Lam didn't mean any offense."

"Right, I didn't . . ."

Valla took a deep breath, and Victor noticed her clench and unclench her fists. "Oh, relax, you two," she said. "I know you didn't mean anything by it. I have a newfound animosity for the Ridonne, finding myself disliking them even more now that I've learned how they've doctored history to erase entire species of people. I don't hold it against you." Valla turned to Kethelket. "You recognized my bloodline?"

"Oh, aye. During the joining, when the world was new, I saw more than one Rihven among the Ordeni. I visited their settlement, the great garden city they'd constructed at the heart of the continent."

"Starfall Sea," Sarl said softly.

"Aye. From a hundred leagues distant, I witnessed their destruction. It was cataclysmic. A single act that wiped out one people and sealed the doom of another."

"What other?" Edeya's eyes were wide with fascination at the impromptu history lesson.

"The Yovashi, of course. When they called down the mountain-sized piece of moon to smash the Ordeni city, the disaster shook the ground and darkened the sky over the entire continent for months. It was the one thing that could unite all the other peoples from all four worlds; they made a pact to wipe out the Yovashi, and that's what they've done. Largely."

As the little group grew quiet, Victor glanced over their heads, noting the crowds gathering nearby—soldiers were curious, wondering what their arrival might herald. He was thinking about whether or not he should address everyone when Sarl spoke up. "It's wonderful to see you both. Shall we go to the command tent and review what we've learned and how our preparations have gone?"

Victor nodded. "Lead the way." As the group followed Sarl further into the camp, Edeya moved to walk beside Victor.

"You can see the reinforcements from the pass have arrived." Victor could tell she had more to add, so he just nodded. "Um, it seems one of your old companions came along with them. I know this because she came to me asking where you were and when you might arrive in camp. Her name is Chandri, and I know I wasn't supposed to read the note Thayla sent you, but I'm a fast reader, and I noticed that name in the text, so . . ."

"Ahh! She's here?" Victor looked around, twisting his neck left and right, wondering if he'd catch a glimpse of her watching them among the other soldiers. When he didn't spy her, he looked back toward Edeya and caught Valla grinning, shaking her head. "Thanks for letting me know, but I'll have to think of an appropriate punishment for reading my personal messages."

Edeya's cheeks bloomed, and she sputtered, "I didn't read . . ."

"He's teasing you, Edeya." Valla squeezed the much smaller woman's shoulder, *tsk*ing her tongue. "You know him better than that."

"True!" Edeya laughed. "When he's this large, though, it's a little hard to remember that he's the same friend I had back in the mines."

"All right, all right." Victor held up his hand, shaking his head. "I can see where this is going. Let's stay serious for a minute, okay? We have a war to win."

"That's rich coming from you." Valla wasn't letting him off that easily, but Victor was rescued by the group's arrival at the command tent.

"Here we are. I can go over the lay of the land on this map." Sarl gestured to a big square table where a large colorful map had been drawn, complete with handcrafted, painted wooden models representing troops, hills, and structures.

Victor stepped up to the table, and behind him, Valla cleared her throat. "Where's your prisoner?"

Kethelket answered, "Victoria? She's under guard in a nearby tent."

Victor was glad she'd asked. He had more questions for the woman and was happy to see Kethelket was taking his duty as her warden seriously. "I'll want to meet with her after this."

"Of course." Kethelket moved around the table to stand near Sarl. Victor approached on the near side, studying the table, already resenting his height; it felt as if he were looking down at a child's play table. Still, when Valla stood beside him, he remembered why he was so large and pushed the selfish complaint out of his mind, concentrating.

"I see you have some of the road past the citadel mapped out."

"My scouts flew into the death fog in the darkness of night. The road follows a switchback pattern for approximately three miles before descending into the caldera."

Valla leaned forward and ran her finger along the curved road to a blank space on the map. "And what's that like? The caldera?"

"My scouts couldn't go within. Hector's magic is too thick in the air there. He has ward stones set up around the entire mountaintop." He paused, frowned, and stroked his chin. "I have some soldiers who wanted to try anyway, to push past the wards, but I forbade it. I'm sure they'll be caught."

Victor felt a growl rumbling in his chest. "Good. I won't feed that bastard any easy victories." He tapped his big thick finger on the map near the white-painted models of the citadels. "What about here? What kind of resistance are we going to face?"

Sarl fielded the question. "We've estimated the troops in the first citadel at something more than a thousand, but we don't know much about them. They wear armor similar to the reavers we slew near Old Keep. Victoria claims ignorance about the lords of these keeps."

"Any plan for attack yet? Are we waiting for the main army?"

Lam cleared her throat. "That's one option. We've constructed six trebuchets designed to be used by our Earth Casters. I believe we can destroy that gate."

While Victor stared at the map and tried to picture the assault, Valla asked, "And can they return fire? Are there no siege weapons atop those walls?"

"There are, but we can spread out, whereas those gates are stationary. We've also only seen catapults and ballistae. Our Energy-driven trebuchets have a much greater range." Sarl reached forward to the map and tapped the area where their camp was drawn. "We can set up the trebuchets in a wide area." He drew a semicircular line with his finger. "They can hit the gate from every angle, and it will take the engineers in the castle a long time and great luck before they'll return any damage to our fire teams. We can also reposition as they lock in a target. Time is on our side in a siege like this."

Victor finally spoke. "Have you seen any troop reinforcements come down the mountain?"

"None per se," Sarl replied, "though our scouts and watchers have seen things flying in the mist. I'm of the opinion that we don't have a good grasp on the forces Hector may yet bring to bear."

"How far out is my mother?" Valla asked.

"A week or more," Edeya replied. "The same with Borrius. They've both encountered remnants of the armies Hector had patrolling his former territories, though they've made short work of them."

"Huh." Victor rubbed his chin, and his scowl must have been heavier than he'd intended because everyone grew quiet, until finally Sarl asked what everyone was wondering.

"Something's bothering you?"

"Yeah. Everything's going too damn well. I can see we caught Hector by surprise. I can believe that much; we caught him with his pants down and picked apart his armies one by one by keeping our momentum in the face of some lucky initial encounters. I don't believe that we're going to wrap this up so easily, however. It feels too . . . neat. I think he's biding his time—he saw we were wiping out his far-flung armies, and rather than throw his reinforcements at us piece by piece, he's consolidating. I think this mountain is going to be a bitch to invade."

Kethelket nodded. "As troubling as those words are, I fear you're correct. From my understanding, this man was a prince in a world where war and competition are fierce. He won't be a pushover."

Edeya surprised Victor by speaking up without prompting. "So what do we do?"

He looked at her and grinned, and his Quinametzin heritage gave the expression a savage aspect. "We take it one bite at a time. We take the first citadel, and then we'll have a much stronger foothold on this mountain from which to advance. If we play it right, we might be able to lure more and more of his forces down to defend it and the bridge. Rellia and Borrius are setting up watch stations all around the mountain; we'll know if he does something unexpected. So, as Sarl said, we take our time, wear down this first citadel, then storm it. From there, we'll reassess."

When everyone was quiet, some nodding, some frowning, but everyone staring at the map, Victor continued, "I'll go and speak with Victoria now. Let's begin our bombardment at dawn. Can you be ready by then, Sarl?"

"Yes, sir! I'll have the trebuchets moved into position tonight."

Lam cleared her throat. "Be sure they have strong fire teams with elementalists to guard against ranged responses."

Sarl chuckled. "Standard Legion protocol, aye?"

"Aye." Lam smiled and clapped him on the shoulder.

Victor turned to the tent flap. "Right. I'm off to speak with Victoria. Valla?"

"Not this time. Hand me your house, and I'll get it set up. I want to meet with Edeya and compose some messages to Borrius and Rellia."

"All right." Victor pulled his jade travel home from the pouch at his belt and handed it to her. Her fingers lingered on his for a moment, and it looked as though she wanted to say more, but she didn't. She nodded quickly and turned to leave the tent ahead of him, Edeya hot on her heels.

Kethelket stepped forward. "I'll show you the prisoner's tent." He led the way out, and Victor followed him just a few dozen yards to a dark tent with a single amber glow lamp posted outside. One of Kethelket's masked Naghelli stood outside. He saluted, and Kethelket nodded to him. "The legate will see the prisoner."

"Sir!" The guard hurried to lift the tent flap.

"I'll meet you later, Victor. Shall we spar tomorrow, time permitting?"

"Maybe. Let's see how the bombardment goes."

"Of course. I didn't say it before, but I hope you know how glad we all are to have you here with us. The troops don't show it, but being in the shadow of that mist-shrouded mountain comes with a burden that can be felt in lost sleep. Shadows within shadows awaken fears most men and women haven't felt since childhood."

Victor stared into his dark eyes for a minute, thinking about what he'd said, then nodded solemnly. "We'll shed some light on things around here, Kethelket. Starting tomorrow, the creatures on that mountain will be the ones losing sleep." Kethelket smiled grimly, then snapped a sharp salute, something he'd obviously been working on, and turned to walk briskly into the night.

Victor stooped to enter the tent, glad that the post at the center was a tall one, vaulting the fabric ceiling. When the second Naghelli guard saw him enter, she slipped out behind him. Victoria sat in a comfortable chair, a thick book in her lap. The only other furnishings in the room were a plush red carpet and another amber-tinted glow lamp. She'd closed the book when he entered, but her fingers were inside, holding her place. Victor summoned a chair from his storage ring and sat before her. "Reading something good?"

"It's a book of folktales from this world. Fascinating stories, honestly."

"Who gave you that?"

"The tall winged woman with the golden hair. Lam, I think, is her name." Victor frowned at her, something about that answer rubbing him the wrong way. Victoria knew Victor spoke to Lam often. She knew her name. Why did she put on this show of being unsure about it? Why did she describe her as though she wasn't sure?

"Been spending a lot of time speaking to Lam? Anyone else?"

"I . . . you didn't tell me I couldn't speak to anyone. Not since you first put me in the tower."

"That's not an answer."

"I've spoken to anyone who would take the time to do so, Victor! I'm alone, lonely, bored. Having people to speak to, things to read"—she held up the book—"keeps me from thinking about the uncertainty of my future. I still fear Hector's reprisal. I fear a change in heart among you and your allies. I count every dawn I wake, still alive, as a small victory."

"Are you? Alive?"

"I'm more alive than dead. Might we agree to that, at least?"

Victor waved his hand, dismissing the subject. "Let's turn our attention to something a little more important. Who commands these citadels? Why haven't you told us about them as you did the other barons in the outposts? More importantly, talk to me about Hector. What kind of creature is he? Don't spare any details."

50

BLOWING OFF STEAM

Hector? He's a Death Caster, as pure of one as I've ever known; he doesn't dabble in blood magic, nor does he feast on the life force of the living. He takes his power from beyond the veil, from the creatures he summons, and the dark pacts he makes. As for who he's put in charge of the citadels, I couldn't tell you. He didn't share that information with me."

Victor stared at Victoria as she spoke, unblinking, looking for any hint of subterfuge. He wasn't good at reading lies, though, and he briefly wished Rellia was there with him. If anyone could read a liar, it was her, perhaps because of her life navigating the dishonest politics of the Ridonne Empire. He shifted in his chair, rubbed the stubble on his chin, and asked, "Isn't it a little strange that you knew the other barons in the outposts but not the lords of these great castles?"

"I don't know. Is it? Hector gathered us barons to talk about his strategy for expansion on many occasions, but never was any lord or lady of the citadels announced to us. He has his sycophants, his hangers-on. He has powerful guardians that follow him everywhere. It's possible he's given one of those people command of citadels as they're quite close to his base, all things considered. Perhaps he simply has armies stationed within, led by one of his apprentices."

"He has apprentices?"

"Of course! While you are a master of your Spirit Core, weaving spells with anger, fear, and glory, he is a master of death-attuned Energy. Many come to him for tutelage. Even some of the great lords of Dark Ember send their young his way. Why do you think he was chosen to lead this invasion?"

Victor frowned, something bothering him. It took a minute for him to realize it was how she'd spoken about his Energy affinities. "What do you know of my Spirit Core?"

"Hmm?" She leaned back, raising an eyebrow. "Well, you nearly killed me with it . . ."

"Wasn't it strange to list off my affinities like that?" Victor leaned forward. Like an adult sitting before a child, he dwarfed her with his presence.

"I didn't list them all . . ."

"You didn't?"

"No! Is there a point to these questions, Victor? You're making me uneasy."

"Who's been talking to you about my affinities?"

"Victor." She swallowed nervously, running her tongue over her pale, dry lips. "You are the most powerful man I've ever met. Your soldiers and followers talk about you all the time; all I do is listen. You hold my fate in your hands, so of course, I listen."

Victor glanced around the tent, straining his ears. "I can hear murmured voices here and there, but no conversations taking place nearby. Are your ears better than mine?"

"No! Lord Victor." She paused, shaking her head, and Victor noticed the return of the honorific in her address. "I think I must have said something to upset you, and that wasn't my intention. I traveled for weeks with this army from Black Keep to the Sea Keep and then to this encampment. I'm sorry if I should have ignored the men talking as they marched. I'm sorry if I grew too comfortable chatting with the army's leaders. I didn't intend to cause any trouble . . ."

"Forget it." Victor had grown tired of the topic. He wasn't even sure why he'd been bothered. Perhaps he simply didn't like someone who'd been an enemy talking about his affinities like that. Her explanation made sense, though, and he supposed it was a strange thing to complain about. It wasn't as if he'd tried to hide his power when they'd fought, and he'd nearly killed her. "Tell me something useful, then. How many soldiers can Hector bring through his gateway? Is there a limit?"

"I don't know the exact—"

Victor growled, interrupting her. "Make an educated guess."

"He raised funds and soldiers by holding lotteries for the barons he'd take with him in the invasion. Karl and Eric were the first to claim their places;

they led the initial invading armies, conquering most of the territory." She sneered in contempt, her voice twisting into a snarl. "Small feat that it was—nothing was here to resist them!"

"Don't get sidetracked." Victor rolled his hand for her to continue.

"Dunstan, Faust, and I were part of Hector's second wave. We were chosen to hold three of the keeps that Eric and Karl uncovered."

"Faust?"

"The lord stationed in the keep your people have dubbed 'Rust.' He was of middling power—something of a savage. An upjumped ghoul, if you want me to get to the meat of the matter."

"Huh. I guess I missed that detail from Borrius and Rellia."

"Likely they didn't know they'd slain a baron; as I said, he was a savage, barely capable of speech."

"So, was there a third 'wave' of invaders?"

"Not that I'm aware of. Hector made it known from the early days that he'd be awarding five slots for other nobles to join in his invasion. I believe the System put limits on how many from our world could pass through the portal. He's not helpless, though; he's a powerful Death Caster, and his personal army is—was—enormous. The great horde you burned up in the forest was part of it, but he keeps his strongest soldiers close to hand."

Victor leaned back in his chair and thought for a minute, mulling over her words. He didn't see how lying to him would help her at this point, but he still felt like she was holding something back. It seemed strange that Hector would appoint barons to command the outposts but not the citadels. Could it be that Victoria simply didn't know? It was apparent these death-worshipping invaders didn't trust each other overly much, so perhaps Hector had kept her in the dark on purpose. Hadn't he sent an assassin to Black Keep to try to dispatch her after Victor severed their tether? "How do I destroy that veil star?" He jerked his thumb in the direction of the mist-shrouded mountain.

"If you slay Hector, it will be easy enough. If you try to extinguish it before his demise, you'll have to battle with it on the spirit plane."

"How about that? If I spirit walk now and make my way up that mountain, will I find Hector on that plane? Could I end this invasion that way?"

"I wouldn't advise it, Lord Victor. I fought you on the spirit plane, and you are, indeed, mighty in that realm. Hector is, too, and the veil star gives him great strength. If you ventured into its light and faced Hector with all of his apprentices, I think you'd lose." She held up her hands as Victor's scowl deepened, and his Quinametzin pride allowed a trickle of rage to slip into his pathways. "I mean no offense, Lord. In a fair fight, I'm sure you could beat Hector on this plane or any other."

Victor forced himself to calm down, pushing that bristling part of himself back. Had that been his problem when she'd mentioned his affinities? Had his Quinametzin nature been offended to have someone he viewed as a prisoner talking about him? Was he simply going to have to keep a tighter grip on his pride and watch himself for inexplicable frustration with others? "All right. Tell me about Hector's base. What's inside that caldera?"

"I was last there months ago." When Victor scowled, she hurriedly continued, "I'll describe what I saw—a wide low wall and dozens of stone buildings built from basalt quarried in the depths of the ancient lava flows. He has a castle there, but it was built hastily by vassals. It's no ancient keep with mighty walls. If you can bring your army past the citadels and into the caldera, I think you will be able to crush him."

"This army?"

"Oh." She licked her lips again. "I meant your entire army. I don't doubt you may win with just this force, but I've heard talk of a much larger army en route; was I mistaken?"

"Does he have innocent people working or living up there? People who aren't in his army?"

"With the restrictions on the portal, I don't think he brought his slaves with him. I heard Eric and Dunstan talking about how Hector had promised them the first choice of natives to replace their thralls."

"Uh-huh." Victor stood and sent his chair back into his storage ring. "We'll talk more later."

"Thank you, Victor. By the way, I appreciate you allowing me to have this back." She touched the silver bracelet on her wrist. It was set with a large, nearly pink pearl.

"I did?"

"Your lieutenant. The one with the blue wings? She said you gave her permission . . ."

"Oh yeah. I think I told her you could have any non-magical items back. You said they were heirlooms, yeah?"

"Yes! This was my mother's." She looked a little pathetic as she gently touched the bracelet, and Victor could appreciate wanting something to remember your mother by. As he felt his heart softening, he scowled and allowed some more rage into his pathways.

"You're welcome." He turned and left before she could say anything more. "Keep a close eye on her," he said to the guards as he walked by. Standing outside the tent, he scanned the area, wondering where Sarl was. He didn't see him, but he saw Kethelket speaking to some Naghelli not too far away, so he approached the ancient prince.

When he saw him coming, Kethelket waved to Victor, dismissing his scouts. "Well, how was your meeting with the prisoner?"

"Not too enlightening, to be honest. More unsettling. I wish we had eyes on Hector's town and his troops. Don't take that the wrong way; I'm not hinting that I want to send your scouts in there. We can't afford to throw lives away."

"I'm not so sure it would be a death sentence . . ."

"No, Kethelket. If someone's going to try to get eyes on that place, it'll be me. Victoria gave me an idea, but I don't think she meant to. If I could spirit walk up there . . ."

"Into the heart of a Death Caster's territory? Victor, you've said yourself that Belikot was far weaker than even Hector's barons. How strong do you think he is? It feels like an opportunity to spring a trap to me."

Victor nodded, rubbing his chin and looking back at the tent where Victoria was being held. "You know, it really does, doesn't it? She's cunning, that one; do you think she mentioned something offhand like that only to tempt my ego? Gah!" Victor shook his head and spat, a foul taste in his mouth. "I can't wrap my head around it. Why would she try to trick me at this point? I had to break Hector's tether on her and kill an assassin he sent her way. She's seen us take one keep after another. Would she try to sabotage me somehow after all that? Still, I get a feeling . . ."

"Did she try to convince you to go up there via the spirit plane?"

"No. That's the thing, she said what you said—told me not to go, that Hector would be too strong. My Quinametzin pride, though, it doesn't like to back down from a challenge . . ."

"And you think she knows that? I think you give her too much credit. Take her words at face value and don't go up there, Victor. We'll start our assault at dawn, yes? Let's see how things go before we start taking drastic action." He turned and gestured further into the camp. "If you're wondering, I saw Valla setting your home up that way, just past the command tent."

"Ha! Now I know what you're doing—get me to speak to Valla, and she'll surely talk me out of it, eh?" Victor clapped a massive hand on Kethelket's shoulder, and the much older man chuckled.

"You give me too much credit! I was hoping thoughts of your lady love would send your blood pumping a different way . . ."

"Shit! You dirty dog!" Victor laughed. "Forget that, though. Let's spar, huh? That'll get my mind off these irritating thoughts."

"How can I deny such a request?" Kethelket pointed to the western edge of the encampment. "We have some cleared space for drills over there. Shall we?"

Victor nodded, and the two men walked that way. He knew there were probably a dozen things he should do before taking the time to practice with his axe, but Victor had some pent-up frustration that he wanted to work out. He wanted to clear his head and try to see things in a new light, and the best way he knew how to do that was to exercise. He felt he had to take advantage of the old sword master while he still could; who knew when they'd be parting ways again?

Victor felt that this campaign was drawing near the end, which meant he'd be moving on. He supposed he didn't have to do so immediately. It might be nice to hang around in the Marches for a while to see how things shaped up. He could spend some weeks or months training with Kethelket and helping some of his other friends to make some gains before he left. The more he thought about it, the more he liked the idea. Wouldn't it be interesting to see how Rellia and Borrius grew the colony? He, too, had lands to claim. Shouldn't he build a house or something? He had the storage container holding the plans and materials for the hermitage. He could set that up before he left, maybe. Then there was Olivia to consider and the rest of the humans from their colony . . .

"How does this look?" Kethelket interrupted his thoughts, and Victor saw they stood in a wide open gravel and dirt field outside the camp's fortifications. Several other soldiers were scattered around the space, sparring or working on maneuvers, but he and the onetime prince stood in a large empty area.

"Perfect." Victor slipped Lifedrinker out of her harness and stretched his back and neck, limbering up.

"Are you going to stay that size?"

"You want me smaller?" He grinned. "Or bigger?"

"If you're going to go big, perhaps I'll need some teammates." Kethelket let his eyes drift over the soldiers on the practice grounds. Victor shrugged, watching and waiting to see what the old sword master would decide. Kethelket lifted his fingers to his lips and let out a shrill whistle, waving to a group of four soldiers. When they stopped their sparring and looked up, he gestured for them to come over. They hurried to comply, all four jogging toward them and saluting Kethelket and Victor as they slid to a halt in the dusty gravel. Kethelket nodded to them and jerked his thumb at Victor. "We'll practice fighting a much stronger opponent as a team today. Victor, sir, will you do us the honor?"

"Yeah, of course." Victor smiled, then severed the connection to his Alter Self spell, sighing with pleasure as his full potential unlocked. He stretched to his near ten-foot height, and his muscles rippled with renewed energy.

"Is that all?" a familiar voice called from behind him. Victor turned to see Chandri dropping down from the stone perimeter wall, crunching over the gravel with her long spear in her hands. She was painted for war, as usual, but she was also dressed for it, wearing a shiny steel helmet and breastplate that Victor hadn't ever seen on her before. "I remember you being bigger when you went berserk!"

"Oh? You want me to berserk?"

"Seems only fair if six of us are going to fight you." She circled Victor as she approached, moving near Kethelket. "You don't mind if I help, sir?"

"Oh? Do you want to spar? I'm not sure we've met, yet you speak as though I should know you . . ."

"Kethelket, this is my old friend Chandri." Victor sighed and shook his head at her. "What are you doing? You don't know the drills or formations the soldiers—"

"I've been practicing with the troops back at the pass. I know the maneuvers and formations. I won't get in the way, sir." She directed the last to Kethelket, and Victor frowned again. Was she trying to prove some kind of point?

"Chandri, are you . . ."

This time, she did speak to him. "I'm just trying to get better, sir. I'm officially enrolled in the ninth cohort. I joined up with the reserves. Captain Sarl placed me with the Red Boyii Unit."

"That's true, sir," one of the other soldiers said, a tall Ardeni woman wearing brown chitinous armor. "She's in my brother's unit."

"Huh. Well." Victor shrugged. "Enough standing around wasting time. I need some exercise." With that, he reached into his Core and summoned a thick rope of rage-attuned Energy, casting Iron Berserk. As he exploded in size, he swapped Lifedrinker to his left hand and lunged forward, swiping at Chandri's with his open right hand, sending her sprawling, tumbling through the gravel and dirt. He turned to the other soldiers and Kethelket, and he roared, his voice like a peal of thunder. Two of them nearly dropped their weapons in surprise. Not Kethelket, though; the old sword master burst into motion, moving like a gust of windblown smoke as he circled behind Victor, slashing at his hamstrings with his two named blades.

Victor laughed and rolled forward over one shoulder, shaking the earth and sending more soldiers stumbling. When he bounded to his feet, he saw Chandri was back up, wiping bloody dust from under her nose and off her chin. She scowled darkly, but he saw an eager gleam in her eyes as she charged at him with her spear. Victor laughed again, beckoning her and two other soldiers as they leapt forward, weapons lifted high.

He kept fighting with his open hand, using Lifedrinker only to defend himself, knocking away weapons or waving her about to give himself space. He laughed and laughed, slapping soldiers and friends left and right. It wasn't a mean-spirited laugh, more one of pleasure and genuine joy seeing his much smaller allies get up again and again to come at him. When Kethelket landed a brutal cut to his calf and Victor stumbled, the soldiers cheered and renewed their efforts. Victor felt his cheeks stretch with joy as he tossed Lifedrinker aside and fell to his knees, grappling with them all.

He didn't try to hurt anyone but wasn't gentle either. He sent them flying, tumbling, rolling, and flopping through dirt and gravel. He smacked them with his open palm, stunning them, bloodying them, but always showed it when they got a hit in, cutting him or saving one another with a heroic parry or attack. They carried on like that for at least an hour, and Kethelket gave Victor a dozen good cuts in the process. Victor didn't care; his body was so sturdy and his healing so rapid that he hardly bled.

Some of the other soldiers landed hits on his armor or helm, mostly because Victor didn't try to defend against those blows, and once Chandri capitalized on Victor's distraction as he dodged away from a lightning combination by Kethelket and managed to drive her spear nearly four inches into his thigh. He wailed in mock agony, and Chandri laughed as the soldiers cheered. After everyone was scraped, bloodied, and filthy from repeated tumbles through the gravel, Victor held up his hand and shouted, "Enough, enough!"

"What?" Chandri cried, utterly covered in blood-caked dust. "We're just starting to get the knack of it . . ."

"Hold on," Victor said, rising from his knees to stand at his full, absurd height. He severed the connection to his Iron Berserk, then cast Alter Self, reducing himself to something more like seven feet tall. He stepped over and picked up Lifedrinker, then summoned his Globe of Inspiration. "That was a good warmup, but now I'd like to get in some weapon practice. I won't use any abilities, and your team can attack me two at a time. Anytime one of you needs a rest, you must tap one of the onlookers' shoulders, and then they can take your place." He grinned and held Lifedrinker before himself in two hands. "Who's first?"

51

MOTIVATIONS

Victor sat beside Chandri on the stone wall Sarl's engineers had built around the encampment. They were facing the mountain where, in the darkness, Victor could make out the dim lights of the twin keeps guarding the road up to Hector's base of operations. After their lengthy sparring, when everyone, including Victor, had let off a good amount of steam and the soldiers moved off to perform their evening duties, Victor had pulled Chandri aside and asked if he could speak with her. Now they sat, looking into the darkness, Chandri quiet, perhaps uncomfortable, and Victor unsure of what he'd wanted to say.

After a few moments, he cleared his throat and pointed toward the dim lights up on the mountain. "Can you hear it? The river roaring down the falls?"

"Of course. It's a big river, but not so big as the Rill Catcher. I've seen bigger falls west of Gelica, toward the frontier."

"Yeah. I guess you're right. I've seen that river, too, but not the falls. Where I grew up, there weren't any big rivers; I lived in a desert. Sometimes when it rained really hard, the washes, as we called them, would flood and pour through the desert like rivers, but they usually dried up in a day or two."

"Do you miss it? Home?"

"Yeah, of course. Mostly, I miss people. My grandmother especially. I've learned a lot about spirits and my ancestry, though. I know she's in here." Victor thumped his fist against his chest. "And out there." He gestured toward the distant, twinkling stars. "I'm sure we'll meet again someday, though probably not in this life."

"I remember you asking me questions about how we Shadeni are always talking to our ancestors. It's interesting to see you take it even further. I've heard about your sacrifices and how your ancestors take action through you. For weeks, everyone at the pass talked about how you fought off an entire army, breathing fire and shouting for your ancestors' glory."

Victor turned away from the stars to look at her face, her magenta eyes dark in the shadows. "Is that why you came here? The stories of our victories?"

"Well . . ." She frowned and folded her arms, covered in bloody, dusty scrapes. Victor felt a twinge of guilt at how rough he'd been with her and the other soldiers, but they'd seemed to enjoy it at the time. Besides, it was good for them to feel how a giant opponent might toss them about, wasn't it? "To be honest, I'm not sure. I felt like . . . I felt like I was missing something. I was spending my days watching children and teaching them to hunt. I know it's an important task, but Chala knows as much as I do, and she's matured a lot lately. I think having Deyni look up to her has helped in that regard. Anyway, I've felt angry, and I don't know why, but I knew I wanted to see you, and I wanted to help somehow."

"Hmm." Victor nodded and rubbed his chin, feeling a little nervous. If they'd heard the tales of his exploits back at the pass, had they also heard that he and Valla were together? She wouldn't be here to try to rekindle any sort of . . .

Chandri interrupted his racing thoughts. "I don't think I regret rejecting you back when you stayed with us, Victor. I think I regret deciding I wanted a simple life, though. How could so much change in a few months? I'd been sure I wanted to continue our old way of life, following the same hunting migration my father and his fathers had followed for a hundred years. Now we're in a new land, fighting wars, joining with people I'd never imagined would be so close. Everything highlights how simple I'd been, how short-sighted." She paused, *tsk*ing and shaking her head, but before Victor could respond, she kept talking.

"I was angry with you initially, and I know how irrational that is. Was it your fault you were born with such potential? Was it your fault you were molded from a lump of iron into a blade by the crucible of your hardships? Those are Tellen's words—he and I had a good long talk before I left to join this army. I think a part of my heart was angry with myself for limiting my future with simple dreams, for not at least entertaining the idea that my future wasn't with the clan, living as a huntress. Still, it's hard to see so much change and not feel some heartache. Where will we hang our midwinter ribbons this year? What trees will fill that role? The Blue Deep is too far. What about in spring? Will we still have a feast to welcome the spirits of the small creatures? Many of our old ones have died, and I worry that traditions will be lost."

"I get that . . ."

"I know you've suffered loss, too. I also know that I'm not making sense! In one breath, I talk about how I'm angry that I limited myself, and in another, I lament the loss of tradition."

"There aren't easy answers, Chandri. I can't promise that things will be better here, but that's what I'm working for. Once we drive out these invaders, your people will have a part of this new land to call their own. You won't have to look over your shoulders any longer. The animals you hunt and the land you nurture will be your own. Your traditions will survive, especially if there are more like you who value them."

"I know that's your dream, Victor. I hope you're right, and I think it will bring me joy to see my father, Thayla, and the others build something permanent. I hope it will make things easier for me as I leave to know they've done so, that they'll be here."

"Ah!" Victor was beginning to understand. "You've decided to leave?"

"Yes. I want to help the effort to claim this land, and then I intend to travel and adventure. There are lands beyond these marches, beyond the mountains and the sea. I'm going to explore, Victor! I know there are other continents and other unclaimed lands. I want to return to the town my father settles with maps and tales of places and people that no one in the Ridonne Empire has seen or heard of in hundreds of years."

"A lot of history has been lost because of those guys, the Ridonne. Have you seen Valla?" Victor intended to talk about the Ordeni and Rihven, but Chandri's eyes told him he'd misstepped.

"Your lady love?" She chuckled, but Victor detected a bitter note in the laugh. "How could I not? She's a goddess walking among primitives."

"Hey!" Victor couldn't help himself. He reached out and grabbed her chin, turning her face to his. He stared into her eyes as he spoke. "Don't be stupid, all right? If your face wasn't smeared with dusty bloody war paint, you wouldn't look half so scary . . ." He grinned, flinching back, hoping she'd take a swipe at him because of his stupid joke, but she shook her head, and he saw tears forming in her eyes. "Come on! That was a joke! I'm trying to lighten the mood here. You know she's had a lot of racial enhancements, right? You could . . ."

"I could what? Do you know how many racial enhancements our entire clan has come across in my lifetime? One. One that Tellen tried to get Old Mother to consume, but she refused, saying it was better used on a hunter. So we had a festival with contests to choose the recipient, and my cousin Rorrin won. Guess where he is now."

"I don't—"

"Dead. Killed by a boyii alpha while he sought a vision from the spirits." She sighed and slapped her hands on her leather-clad thighs, stirring up a cloud of dust. "Forget it, Victor. I appreciate you talking with me. I know you have a good heart, and I want you to know I'm not angry with you. I'm just angry. I need to do something meaningful, and that starts with helping to finish this war. Will you let me be? Will you let me seek my own destiny?"

"Of course, I . . ."

She hopped to her feet with a grunt. "That's all I want. Thank you for taking the time to speak, Legate." She snapped a perfect salute, her fist sending another puff of dust off her chest, and then she turned and hopped off the wall, leaving Victor sitting there feeling dumbfounded. After a while, he stood up and wandered around the camp, observing soldiers performing evening tasks, sitting around cookfires, or rushing to and fro, likely working on tasks vital to Sarl's planned bombardment of the citadel gates in the morning. Eventually, he made his way to his travel home, and when he went inside, he wasn't surprised to find Valla still talking with Lam and Edeya. They sat near each other around one end of his dining table.

"There he is! Were your ears itching?" Lam smiled when she saw him coming in from the foyer.

"You were talking about me?"

"We were wondering how serious you were about the assault in the morning," Valla said, standing up and walking to meet him.

"What do you mean?" He held open his arms so she could hug him more easily.

Lam provided the response. "If the trebuchets work and break the gates, will you attack?"

"And if they don't, will you break them yourself?" Edeya added.

"You guys think I can?"

Valla pulled away and looked up into his face. "Is that a question meant to confound us? If we say yes, are we encouraging you? If we say no, will you take it as a challenge?" She winked at him and turned back to the table, pulling his hand to bring him along.

"I don't know. It's been a while since I've had a good fight, and I'm getting antsy. The more time we give someone like Hector, if he's anything like Belikot, the longer he'll have to prepare something surprising. I feel like we should take the citadels so he can't stage some kind of surprise. If we hold them, or at least the first one, it will be a much stronger position. Also, I don't like Hector in charge of that bridge; what if he broke it?"

"I told you," Lam said, nodding. "Sarl, though he prepares his bombardment for the morning, is of the opinion that you mean to wait for Rellia and Borrius to bring the full legion here."

"I do intend to wait for them, but I'd rather wait from within one of those fortresses."

Lam nodded, pounding her fist on the table. "And then we could launch a full-scale assault on the mountain!"

Victor smiled at her enthusiasm, but it was half-hearted. He pulled out a chair, and Edeya poured a glass of some kind of chilled wine for him. He sat there sipping it while Valla and Lam began a conversation about siege engines, their effectiveness against warded structures, and the different times they'd seen them put to use. He nodded, made encouraging sounds, and tried to follow the conversation, but he kept thinking about Chandri charging that wall with the other soldiers. He kept thinking about how quiet Hector had been. He felt he was missing something.

It was still relatively early when he pushed his chair back and said, "I think I'm going to turn in. Maybe I'll do some cultivating and try to clear my head. I'd hoped some exercise would do it, but my brain is still pretty damn busy. Don't mind me."

"I'll come with you . . ." Valla started to stand, but Victor shook his head.

"Nah, I won't be good company. You should invite Kethelket over for his opinion on the siege. He has a couple hundred flying troops, after all."

Lam chuckled. "Well, of course, we were going to talk to him. I'm surprised he's not here already—did you hurt him on the practice field?"

"Nah." Victor smiled a little ruefully. "In fact, I think he got more solid hits in than I did. Anyway, tell me how it goes when you finish up." He leaned forward and kissed Valla's forehead.

"You're sure you don't want company?" Valla stood and took his hand, following him as he walked toward the dimly lit staircase.

"No, I have some things tickling my brain that I need to figure out. Some quiet is all I'm after." He squeezed her fingers and started down the steps, happy to hear her turn and call for Edeya to "go find Kethelket." Something was bothering him, but the problem was that he couldn't tell if it was all in his head. Maybe he was being paranoid. Still, he kept replaying his conversation with Victoria over in his mind; who had mentioned spirit walking first? She had, right? Something about him having to battle the veil star on the spirit plane if he wanted to be rid of it. "Then she said I shouldn't try . . ." Victor growled as he opened the door to his bedroom.

No matter how hard he tried to stop, he kept thinking back to Belikot. He kept remembering how everyone said not to mess with him on the spirit plane, to build a troop of heroes to dig out his lair and face him that way. Victor had ended the matter by ignoring them, by using his prodigious gift with spirit-attuned Energies to crush him in the spirit plane. Hadn't Old Mother encouraged him to do so? Growling, Victor sat down on the rug in the empty area beside his bed. How much time and how many lives had he saved by handling Belikot in such a way? Was he irritated because his pride had been questioned or because he felt that Victoria was scheming somehow? Why did he feel that way?

Victor unstrapped Lifedrinker and held her on his lap. "She doesn't want me in there. She doesn't want me to see what Hector is doing up there on that mountain."

"We should hunt! Let your enemies quake, knowing you are on the prowl!"

"Yeah," Victor growled to Lifedrinker. "I think we should." He reached into his Core and severed the connection to his Alter Self spell. The stone flags under the rug didn't complain as his mass surged and he expanded, occupying a much more significant portion of his bedroom. He took long, deep breaths and tried to calm his mind. He wasn't sure he was doing something clever, but it felt right—how could he ask his troops to begin an assault at dawn when they had no idea what to expect from Hector? What if he had another massive horde of undead up there, just waiting for his army to become entrenched in a battle?

They needed intel, and he couldn't risk more Naghelli, not when he was perfectly capable of taking a look around. Hadn't he already proven he was powerful enough to match Hector's Death Casters? Hadn't he slaughtered Victoria's ghostly guardians and thrashed her into submission? "Yeah. I think it's time I got my eyes on Hector and gave him something to worry about."

Victor reached into his Core and pulled out a strand of inspiration-attuned Energy, pulling it into the pattern for Spirit Walk.

Victoria's eyes snapped open, and she smiled, unable to contain her glee. She'd glimpsed Victor's spirit, blooming into being on the spirit plane like a bonfire among candles. She'd immediately fled, long before he might have taken note of her presence. As she continued to grin, wringing her hands in excitement, her guard scowled at her from within the dark folds of his cowl, but she ignored him. He might have a solid resistance to her charms, but he was utterly blind where her spirit walking was concerned. It hardly took a trickle of Energy for her to send part of herself into that realm; her phylactery kept her partially anchored to it at all times.

Her little ruse with the tether she'd had Victor sever had done a good job of building trust, showing a false animosity between her and the dark prince. That and the "assassination attempt" had served to convince all of these fools to lower their guard, at least enough so she could work around their watchful attention. Meanwhile, her connection to her phylactery and, through it, to Hector had been her saving grace. Just a tiny trickle of Energy was all it took to contact him. To convey news of Victor's armies and warn him about the champions who sought to slay him and halt his imminent dominion over this rich world.

What a simple matter it had been to ensconce herself among these mortals! When Eric's man, Porter, came running, weak and near death, a bloody stump where his powerful arm had once been, Hector had made the plan, and Victor had fallen for it every step of the way. Hector's idea to place her in the Obsidian Keep, the next obvious target of Victor's assault, had only been the first step. Oh, Victor was strong and a cunning fighter, but not cunning enough. She chuckled, ignoring the glare of the guardian standing near the tent's exit. She'd learned so much about Victor, first from battling with him, then from listening to the tales spun by his followers. They worshiped him like a god among men, and in that worship, she'd found his downfall.

His rage, glory, and fear were apparent; she'd felt them for herself. The tales from his lieutenants and even the soldiers' gossip had filled in the rest of the story—justice to hunt down the wicked, inspiration to help his allies learn, and courage to bolster them in the face of even the most awful and terrifying of foes. It was a potent mix of attunements, but nothing that couldn't be prepared for. She'd whispered her news to her lord; she'd told him all she'd learned, and now Victor was on the spirit plane, and she knew what he was doing there.

"What a fool." She chuckled, grinning at the guard as he stepped forward, hand on his sword hilt.

"Silence!"

Victoria smirked and settled back in her chair. All it had taken was a hint, a mere mention of the spirit plane, and then feigned concern. "No, no! You mustn't go there! Hector is too strong under the veil star!" She almost laughed again as she remembered how the titan-blood had bristled. That was another thing his worshipful troops loved to speak about—Victor's pride. It wouldn't matter if they never mentioned it; she'd tasted it herself. Still, she'd heard the story of Belikot and played Victor like a harp, strumming the chords of his downfall.

"Well," she said, standing from her chair, "I think it's time I introduce myself . . ."

"Silence!" the guard yelled, and the tent flap opened, admitting the other two, each with an exposed blade.

"No, I think not. My name is Catalina, consort and confidant of Prince Hector, the rightful monarch of these lands, and I'm afraid my patience has expired." She unstoppered the flow of her death Energy, and as the guards burst into lightning motion, slashing her with their wickedly sharp blades, she exploded into cool mist, wrapping herself around them, pulling them close, draining the heat and life force from their bodies.

52

DESPAIR

Catalina floated above the bodies of her guards, full to bursting on their life Energy. They'd certainly provided much needed nourishment! What a toil it had been to remain pleasant and demure all these weeks while existing on the dregs of a months-old meal! She allowed a tendril of her misty form to seep under the tent flap, scanning the area. As she'd hoped, it was well dark, and mist had begun to encroach on the army's encampment despite their glow lamps and fires. Victor would need to claim one of the citadels if he meant to keep Hector's mist at bay, and there was little hope of that now.

She could feel it, the mounting pressure of Hector's will. Soon, his crypt ghouls would pour down that mountain road, over the ridgelines, down the slopes, and over the walls that poor pitiful Sarl had worked so hard to construct. She almost laughed aloud, thinking of his surprise as this little camp was overrun and their great hero was brought low by the Prince of Heart Rot. "Now, to find that blue-winged simpleton of a girl." Catalina allowed her misty form to flow and merge with the tainted tendrils of fog clinging to the cold soil outside her tent. She drifted through the camp, picking up snatches of conversation as she peered into clusters of soldiers and drifted toward the command tents.

". . . first thing in the morning."

"Then we'll get old Troff to carry it, 'cause my back's had enough . . ."

". . . this mist, it gives me . . ."

". . . the legate will show 'em . . ."

"Makes me wonder about them lights . . ."

Catalina swept past the last cluster of soldiers stationed near the inner perimeter of the camp, and as she flowed between two large, vaulted tents, she paused in the shadows, her form nearly invisible as she clung to the cold grassy soil, observing the green jade house where Victor had once imprisoned her. She was sure she'd heard passersby mention the commanders were meeting there tonight. Had they already left, or was this a good place to wait for the girl?

She didn't have to wonder long. Not fifteen minutes after she'd arrived, the two "Ghelli" women who kept Victor's counsel stepped out of the home. The taller, older one with golden wings led the way, while the younger one, Catalina's target, followed close behind, her slender hand gripping the taller one's elbow. They laughed and spoke loudly as they departed the home, moving toward a cluster of narrow but high-ceilinged red tents. Catalina silently followed.

"Wonder what's gotten into Victor. He seemed kind of morose," the one with the pale blonde hair said.

"He's probably trying to think of a way to justify charging alone up that mountain," the blue-winged one said with a trill of high-pitched laughter.

"You don't give him enough credit! Look at all he's done for our efforts here!" Lam *tsk*ed, but she also chuckled, signaling at least tacit agreement with Edeya's teasing.

They paused before one of the tents, and Edeya asked, "Will you sleep?"

"Aye. We should get rest if we're to be of use when the bombardment starts. Who knows what insects might stir when we begin kicking that mound."

"Okay." Edeya leaned into the slightly taller woman, and as though she'd expected it, Lam pulled her into an embrace. She kissed the top of Edeya's head and then pushed her back so their eyes could meet.

"I was proud of you tonight. Your smiles toward Kethelket seemed genuine."

"My ancestor begins to learn, I think. It was hard at first, but I think her nature is deferring more and more to me."

"As Victor said it would!" Lam laughed.

"Yes, yes; I need to give him more credit." Edeya smiled and added, "Tomorrow, then."

"Tomorrow." With one more gentle squeeze of her shoulders, Lam released Edeya and turned to meander toward a campfire where several lieutenants stood drinking steamy liquid from mugs. Catalina shivered with anticipation as she watched Edeya lift the tent flap and step inside. She flowed over the ground toward the shadow-decked rear of the tent and pushed a tendril under the heavy canvas, peering with her magic sight inside. She saw the beautiful girl standing beside a comfortable pillow-bedecked bed, removing her armor piece by piece and placing it upon a wooden stand.

She was half finished, down to an undershirt and her silvery greaves, when she spun, peering into the shadows at the deep folds of her tent where it touched the ground, as though she could feel Catalina's presence. "Ugh, that mist!" She turned to a flickering lamp near her bed, an actual lamp with a flame, not a glowing Energy stone, and turned the knob. The fire dancing on the fuel-soaked wick jumped, and Catalina had to withdraw further to keep her misty form from being revealed. "Better," Edeya said, returning to her task, unbuckling the straps holding her armor to her thighs.

Many of the soldiers had procured fire-based lamps. Catalina had heard them speaking of their effectiveness against the clinging, death-tainted mist. It was true; a fire was far more a hindrance to the death fog than glowing Energy. Nevertheless, the little fiery lamp wouldn't save this wretch. Catalina surged under the canvas, bringing her entire form into the tent. Then, while Edeya was still bent, loosening her greaves, she expanded into the center of the tent, sending a thick tendril of nearly corporeal mist around Edeya's face and neck, squeezing tight, jerking her back, fully into her cold embrace. At the same time, she pinched the flame of her lamp, throwing the tent into darkness.

"Well, girl," she hissed, a whisper of death itself, "where have you put my necklace? The one with the beautiful lady?" Edeya tried to speak, tried to claw the mist away from her face and neck, but her fingers passed through Catalina harmlessly. She summoned a torrent of stormy Energy, but Catalina wrapped around her tighter, folding her cold, wet, misty form around the girl, pulling her Energy out of her before she could form it into an attack. She wasn't a weakling, this beautiful girl, but she was no match for Catalina. Dozens of levels separated them.

She peeled back a bit of her grip on the girl's mouth and neck, still holding the rest of her tightly, wrapped up like a warm pulsing meal. Her glowing flesh and ruddy cheeks had turned ashen. Her brightly sparkling blue dragonfly wings were dull and lusterless. Catalina hissed a graveyard breath into the girl's ear. "Fading so quickly? No, no, love, not before I have my answer."

Poor Edeya could barely utter a whispered, "Wha . . . what?"

"The amulet, girl. The one that gave you shivers. The beautiful woman?" She could see it in her memories, could see her cringe from it, could feel her fear, even now. An image came to her of a pearl-inlaid box. Catalina jerked her gaze toward the bed and the bureau beside it. There! Still holding the girl tightly, she sent a tendril of her misty form flowing toward the beautifully crafted chest of drawers and the delicate box atop it. As she threw the lid back, she felt it, felt *her*, pulsing and throbbing within, waiting for Catalina's touch to release her.

"Thank you for keeping her safe, girl." Catalina shifted to support her head, forcing her eyes upon the figurine as she lifted it from the box. "She's one of my patrons and hungers for release. I promised her a feast, and she's unhappy with the wait. Watch now! You can be the first to feel her kiss!" Catalina's whispery voice purred as she caressed the limp girl's neck with a tendril of her ethereal form. She pulled a thick coil of death-attuned Energy out of her Core and sent it through her into the effigy, summoning her malevolent mistress for a night of slaughter. It was time for chaos to ensue amid these hapless natives.

Victor climbed the volcano as it rose, magnificent and smoldering, into the twilight sky of the spirit plane. There were no keeps, bridges, or roads here, only the rough creviced slope and the eerie green light high above, tinting everything with its malignant glow. The mountain was more prominent on this plane, more alive, and definitely angry. Victor could feel its wrath bubbling deep beneath his feet.

At first, as he strode toward the foothills and lesser slopes, he'd made good time, but now, as the incline grew steep and the smoldering peak seemed farther and farther away, he began to wonder if some dark magic was at work, much as it had been in Black Keep when he'd tried to climb the walls. He'd learned his lesson there, so he didn't waste time—he focused his mind on his destination and concentrated on putting one foot in front of the other, willing himself to traverse the spirit lands as he always had, devouring the distance between himself and his goal.

It wasn't with any surprise when, in hardly any time at all, he found his steps on more level ground, and he saw the stony crags that bordered the volcano's ancient caldera. He turned and looked out on the twilight lands, unable to move or even breathe when he beheld the glorious vista behind him. Everything shimmered with that strange ethereal twilight nature that seemed to infuse the spirit plane. The stars and moons above were bright and impossibly close, and as Victor's eyes tracked the enormous glittering starscape toward the distant horizon, it seemed as if the planet's surface merged with space.

He could see plains and forests and seas shimmering in the reflection of the starlight. He could see ribbons of sparkling rivers and glistening clouds of moisture, rich with the essential Energy of the planet, laid out like thick fluffy carpets here and there over the valleys and woodlands. He stared for a long time, then he noticed the flickering green light on the nearby slopes, tinting the rocks—Fanwath's very bones—and his anger and pride began to stir anew. With a low growl, he turned back to the caldera and the sickly mist clouding the interior. He reached into his Core, summoned a rope of glory-attuned Energy, and brought his banner into being, bathing the area in its glittering golden light.

He stepped toward the volcano's rocky crown, and by the time he'd taken three strides, he was the size of a titan, simmering with and radiating rage. The green tint was gone; now he saw things in a haze of red rage, lit brightly by the powerful shine of his banner. The spiked rocky ridge had seemed daunting before, but now it was child's play to traverse. He hopped over boulders larger than vehicles or even homes. He vaulted ridges an ordinary man would need to climb with ropes, and in no time at all, he was over the top, sliding down a steep rocky slope into the dense, roiling, death-attuned mist.

His banner drove it back for a hundred yards, and Victor, encouraged by his easy progress, leapt and slid down the slope. He held Lifedrinker's spirit form in one mighty fist, ready to visit his rage upon the Death Casters and their creations that must surely lurk within. Soon, the slope leveled off to rough stone, the leavings of ancient eruptions, no doubt, and Victor increased his pace, jogging deeper and deeper into the caldera, frustrated by the mist that hugged the limits of his light, making it impossible to gain any perspective on distance or see any sign of what lurked further ahead.

That eerie green glow suffused the mist around and above him; his banner created a ball of light that pushed it away, but it hung so heavy in the air that it was like he was traversing the inside of a massive sickly cloud. Where was the veil star? Shouldn't he be able to see a brighter spot? He made the mistake of turning in a circle, hoping to see some sign of the star, a hint of the center of the caldera, but as the mist swirled and writhed around his light, he lost his sense of direction; the ground was the same rough basalt, pumice, and other dark stones in every direction. He saw shards of obsidian and a few larger clumps of rocks, but he hadn't memorized them before turning, and now his senses were frustrated.

Growling, Victor bunched his legs and leapt straight upward, soaring into the air, his bright banner ripping through the fog above him. Even at the apex of his jump, though, he was surrounded by the mist, and when he came down, the ground was different, and he was further disoriented. Closing his eyes and cursing briefly, Victor racked his brain for a clue. He gathered up a thick band of inspiration and summoned his coyotes; if he couldn't find his way through the mist, perhaps they could. They came into being, bursting out of pools of white-gold light, yipping, howling, and immediately pacing in circles around him.

"Find me that *pinché* green star, *hermanos*!"

His coyotes howled and yipped, crying their weird nervous sounds as they launched into action, charging into the mist. Victor twisted his hand on Lifedrinker's haft, waiting to sense something from them, closing his eyes to maintain his connection better. He felt them, clouded by the death Energy, but still there, as they ran in ever widening circles, trying to find what he sought. He might have stood there like that for five minutes, or it could have been five hours. The spirit plane was strange in that regard, and the mist and his disorientation made it worse.

Eventually, though, it came, a feeling of excitement and encouragement, and Victor felt his successful coyote like a beacon in the dark, a lighthouse guiding him on. He leapt into action, charging toward the coyote, sprinting headlong into the mist, blasting it away in a wide cone as his banner's light preceded him. In just minutes, he burst through the last wall of the fog, and there was his coyote, sitting atop a mound of frozen magma, staring at the veil star where it hung over the empty center of the volcano's basin. Victor could see dark openings in the ground, leading down into volcano—ancient lava tubes that still steamed and smoldered here on the spirit plane.

"Good boy," Victor said, brushing his hand over the coyote's furry neck and head as he strode past it, staring at the veil star, scanning the ground around it for any sign of Hector or his apprentices. Not a soul stirred, and the light pulsed balefully as though daring him to approach. It was massive, hanging at least a hundred yards over the top of the caldera, smoldering like a green bonfire rolled into a ball and sent aloft to blaze its deathly glory into the night. It was bright, too bright to stare at comfortably, so Victor looked down as he approached, wondering how he was supposed to destroy the thing, for if Hector wasn't here to challenge him, Victor intended to do so.

As he strode toward the center, to the smooth spot under the veil star, Victor began to notice formations of shaped stones—pillars, carved round stones, and half-moon shapes arranged in a circular pattern beneath the star. He hurried toward the nearest one, and as he drew close, the cruel sickly light became burdensome, even for him. He found himself shielding his eyes as he slid to a halt near the first cluster of weird artifacts, his rage waning and his strength fading under that harsh baleful gaze. Standing there, he began to note runes and sigils carved into the shaped rocks.

Determined to do some damage and perhaps banish the foul star before retreating to regather his strength, Victor grabbed up one of the rune-covered stones and threw it over his shoulder, putting all his titanic might into the act. The stone was heavy, heavier than it should have been, and cold blue Energy flashed and smoked through the air as he threw it. "Ha!" he roared, kicking one of the rune-covered pillars over, watching as it fell to the hard rocky ground and split in half with another flash of death-attuned Energy.

The caldera began to vibrate, shaking beneath Victor's feet, and he held Lifedrinker high, roaring his fury and determination. Had he ruined the spell? Was it so easy to bring that numbing, ghostly light out of the sky? Something didn't feel right. Something in the pit of his stomach began to ache, and he felt a deep horrid surge of ennui, a kind of sickness of the spirit that made him want simply to sit down and rest. He looked up at the star, squinting to see what he'd done, but it looked the same. Then he felt his coyotes' spirits wink out, one by one, their manifestations banished by something.

Victor felt slow and sluggish, not just physically but mentally. It took him far too long to realize his coyotes had faded due to his low Energy. His Berserk was gone, his banner too, and now the cold sickly mist was closing in on him even more tightly. When he turned and started to try to walk away from the veil star, he saw what had caused the ground to rumble. In a loose circle around him, a dozen more pillars had risen from the ground, and atop each, a smaller version of the veil star burned, though each modulated its pulsing light differently. They hurt to look at; their weird pulses seemed tuned to wring him of strength, to wrack his mind with torturous patterns.

Victor looked into his Core and saw his powerful, blazing orbs of attuned Energies, now shrunken cold balls, just tiny flickers of smoky Energy tendrils keeping them alive. It seemed that as soon as Victor's Core generated more Energy, it was pulled off and dispersed. He was devoid of power, brought low by this sickly star and its echoes that surrounded him. Despair began to claim him as weakness found its way into every muscle of his body. He wanted to sit, wanted to collapse into a heap and pull his knees to his chest as the waves of nausea and fatigue continued to wrack him. "What have I done?" he groaned, though even that was almost too much work, just a frail whimper slipping past his lips.

53

HOPE AND ITS ABSENCE

Lam spied a group of soldiers standing around a camp stove, warm mugs steaming in their hands, and feeling a little cozy in her heart from Edeya's parting hug, she thought she'd stop by to have a sip with the troops. Grinning, she walked that way and already had her favorite mug in hand when she stepped up. "Something good in the kettle?"

"Tribune!" the first to notice her sputtered, trying to salute while still holding a hot drink.

"Relax! At ease, everyone. It's a chilly night, and the warm drink looked appealing. We've a big day tomorrow, so I thought I'd have a drink before sleep. Do you mind?"

"Of course, Tribune." A young Ardeni woman bent to pick up the steaming kettle and poured it into Lam's mug. She had interesting tattoos on the back of her hand and wrist, visible because she'd rolled up the sleeves of her uniform.

Lam smiled, blowing on the warm liquid to cool it, catching a whiff of hot cider and something spicy. "What's the significance of that tattoo, the one with the broken wall?"

"Oh, that's one our unit got after the Ridonne attacked our encampment!" a different soldier said, this one a burly Shadeni man. He pulled aside his unbuttoned uniform shirt to display the same tattoo on his chest.

"Ah, I've quite a few commemorating battles myself." Lam took a sip of the cider, enjoying the sweet and spicy mix. "Carry on! What were you all talking about?"

Another man chuckled, a wiry bald-headed Ardeni with a long jagged scar running the length of his forehead. "Well, it's a little embarrassing, ma'am, but they were all teasing me about how one of the new recruits beat me to a pulp with a quarterstaff this afternoon."

"New recruits?" Lam raised an eyebrow.

"Well, not so new anymore—them the legate recruited back at the Sea Keep."

"Oh, aye, I've heard good things about them, watched 'em drilling with you all. Seems they're fitting in nicely." Her words opened the floodgates as the unit started sharing their experiences working with the humans from Dark Ember, and Lam listened with a smile, enjoying her stolen camaraderie. She was about half done with her cider when a shiver ran up her spine, so sharp and cold that she almost dropped her mug. She turned to look behind her, sure some shadowy nightmare had come for her, but saw nothing except an empty path and, a couple of dozen paces down it, Edeya's dark tent.

"Ancestors! Did you feel that chill? I hope a storm's not coming," the young woman with the tattooed wrist said. Lam didn't turn to respond; she was still staring at Edeya's tent. Something about the shadows and mist clinging to the ground nearby bothered her. The fool girl should have a lamp burning—all the soldiers had been admonished to sleep with a flame nearby while this close to Hector's territory. She tilted her mug, draining the rest of her cider onto the ground, and then sent it into her storage ring.

"Thanks, soldiers," she said, still facing away. They all hurried to wish her a good night and thank her for her company, but the words fell on deaf ears; Lam was focusing on Edeya's tent, a dark feeling gripping her heart. Was she seeing things? Was she jumping at shadows? Perhaps, but Edeya wouldn't mind her poking her head in to check on her. As she approached the tent, the chill in the air seemed to intensify, and Lam felt an irrational panic, a fear that something terrible was happening. She looked to the sky and glanced at the mountainside cloaked in darkness, but nothing save the chill in the air supported her mounting dread.

Nevertheless, almost unbidden, her heavy hammer appeared in her hands, and she began to pull Energy out of her Core into her pathways. Her wings shed more motes, sparkling in the dark, banishing the fog that tried to cling to her ankles as she drew near the tent. Her breath plumed in the air, and realizing that, she knew her perception of the chill wasn't in her head. Lam heard something, then a dark sibilant whisper that lifted the fine hairs on the back of her neck. With doubt driven from her mind, she leapt the last few feet to the tent and yanked the flap to the side. "Damned roots!" she cried when she took in the scene.

Edeya hung in the air, gripped by thick ropes of sickly mist. Her eyes were white, the color drained from her irises, her face ashen, her mouth agape as a horrible rattling breath choked out through the constricting tendrils. Lam was so shocked by the sight of her distress that she almost missed the horror that hunched in the darkness at the back of the tent. A slender figure with ropes of shadowy hair falling around a pale face with blood-red eyes. As her eyes adjusted and her shimmering wings pushed back some of the darkness, Lam took in the creature and found that she was a woman. She stood in the darkness, pale breasts wreathed in that dark hair, fingers tipped in long black claws like knives, fangs dripping blood on her chin as she grinned wickedly and ran her tongue over her lower lip.

Lam's fear fled from her as fury boiled in her heart. She screamed in outraged anger and sent a torrent of Energy into her hammer. Lifting it high, she brought it down, smashing the shadows with the weapon's projection—a golden maul the size of a draft roladii that crashed into the ground, ripping the mist to shreds. The hammer's impact rolled through the tent with a shockwave that upended furniture and sent rugs, splintered wood, and Edeya's many little treasures flying. The explosive Energy of the spell disrupted whatever held Edeya aloft, and she fell, flopping to the ground, utterly still.

The darkness-clad woman stood tall and cackled as Lam's shockwave rolled harmlessly over her feet, past her long naked legs, and tore through the back of the tent. Lam was already furious, but the laughter drove her to further madness. Her wings hummed as they sent her flying forward, hammer high, a deathblow aimed at the woman's smiling face. She hurtled through the air, closing the distance to the center of the tent in a fraction of a second, but there her momentum halted; those thick mists that had held Edeya wrapped around her, stopping her like a butterfly in a net.

"Fool," a hissing whisper said into her ear, and then Lam realized her error; the tall naked woman wasn't alone. The prisoner, Victoria, was in the mist—no, she *was* the mist.

Victor slumped to the ground, dropping his axe, but not before he desperately tried to sever his connection to the spirit plane. Just as he'd held Victoria there, however, something held him. Was it the veil star? The smaller pulsing echoes of it? Was it Hector flexing his will upon a weakened opponent?

Victor couldn't tell, and that knowledge deepened his despair. A sensation unlike anything he'd felt in a very long time began to seep through him, chilling him to the bone—hopelessness. Weakness and a loss of drive pervaded his being.

It happened so suddenly and with such finality that Victor was stunned by his new frailty. How long had it been since he'd felt weak? How long since he'd felt the world was closing in on him, that he was doomed and alone? The suddenness of it was the worst thing; he hadn't had a chance to mount a defense, to rally his will, to fight back with his prodigious rage and lust for glory. Where was that lust now? Where was the anger? He was bereft, stripped bare, a hollow husk of himself. What had he thought he'd do, charging into the seat of a Death Caster's power? What had he expected would happen when he confronted that baleful star of death-attuned Energy? Was he a god? Was he even a true hero? "No," he spat.

Victor buried his face in his hands. What could he do? Bathed in the sickly terrible light of the veil star, he racked his mind, feeble as it felt, for an answer. He had trouble thinking about who he was, let alone what he could do in this predicament. He was just a stupid kid. How could he think he could face a powerful necromantic lord from a distant world? Was he a match for a being who'd gathered his power over centuries? He was in a trap, a trap he'd walked into like the idiot he was. Still, angry as he knew he should be, he had trouble stirring up the emotion. Naturally—the trap was draining his anger. Was that how it worked? Victor struggled to bring his mind back to the point he'd almost made.

"How . . . what worked?" Even his voice was weak, soft, and hoarse, a bare whisper that struggled to emerge from his lips.

Despite the frailty of his voice, an answering whisper came to him on the wind, "Child. Soak in the light of my star. Reflect on your worthlessness. As I slay those you love, remember that you are the cause. In a decade or century, perhaps I'll pull you forth from your prison and make you a thrall, and we can reflect together on your failings."

Something cold and wet tickled Victor's cheek as he absorbed the words. It took his sluggish mind several seconds to realize he was crying. How strange, he thought, that he could feel such horrible despair and loss but not any anger or fear. Something tickled his mind again, and he knew he'd almost had a brilliant thought. Another wave of despair ran through him, though, pushing the idea away. What had the voice said to bring the moisture to his eyes? "Oh," Victor moaned as he remembered the words; Hector was going to kill everyone he loved. "Valla," he sighed, unable to muster the strength to vibrate his vocal cords.

"Victor!" Valla cried, leaping out of the bed. When she'd come to the room and found Victor in his meditation pose, unresponsive to her words, she'd figured he was conducting a spirit walk. He'd done it many times in her presence, so she knew the look of it. His face was always the same, serene and untroubled, and he never responded to words or even jostling shakes. When he'd moved against Black Keep, she'd learned all too well that he wouldn't wake from any stimulus she could provide. Still, it didn't worry her; his many spirit trips had dulled her to any risk involved. So with a kiss on his forehead, she'd gotten ready for bed and climbed under the covers. That was when she'd felt the change.

The air had grown cold, and Valla had felt something almost like a vacuum or void tugging at her Core, pulling at her Energy. As she leapt out of her covers, she saw that Victor had turned ashen and wan, the color gone from his vibrant flesh. Moreover, he was the center of the chill, and the ever-present throbbing furnace of his Core had faded. His powerful spirit-attuned Energies had fled, and their sudden absence was still pulling at her own. "Victor!" she cried again, running to him, grasping the sides of his head, jostling him, trying to get him to open his eyes.

He didn't respond, of course, and Valla felt herself being pulled as though she could be drawn through whatever void had taken his spirit. Crying with despair and fear, she let go of him and took a step back. "Victor! Wake up!" Desperately, she looked around the room. Where were his companions, his steadfast coyotes? Where was his great bear? Where was the heat of his dominating spirit? Something terrible was happening, and she had no answers. Would a healing draught work? With flickering hope, she dug one out of her ring and rushed forward again, tipping it into his mouth. It dribbled from the corners of his lips, and she clapped her hand over them, trying to tilt his head so the precious fluid would roll down his throat.

As he reflexively swallowed, she backed up, still feeling that horrible pulling sensation. She watched and watched for two long painful minutes, and when he didn't move or react, she snatched up Midnight and sprinted past him, running through the house toward the front door. She didn't know who could help her, but she had Kethelket in her mind; he was old and had seen many horrible things. Perhaps he would know what to do. When she burst through the door into the night air, she wasn't prepared for what she found.

Chaos reigned around her. Pale naked creatures ran amok, hunched figures bereft of hair with long faces bearing glowing red and yellow eyes. They opened their yawning mouths filled with fangs as they leapt upon soldiers who desperately battled for their lives and the ground the ninth cohort had claimed. Shrieks, screams, and bellows filled the air. Fires burned as spells thrown by the defenders ignited enemies and tents alike. Smoke added to the sickly fog to make Valla's eyes water as she stared, mouth agape. Her hopes of finding help for Victor were dashed as she realized the camp was being overrun.

Scowling grimly, she drew Midnight from her sheath and felt a spark of hope ignite in her chest as her blade sang her song into the darkness. Wearing nothing but her nightgown, Valla lifted her glorious sword, spread her wings, and launched herself into the air. Victor was a hero, and he'd have to look after himself for now. The Glorious Ninth was under attack, and they needed her.

Once she was aloft, the cold wind tickling her feathers, she saw the scene more clearly. Dark shadows rushed down the hillsides, pouring out of the citadel, swarming the wall with their mad leaps and frenzied battle lust. They weren't ghouls like she'd seen before, but something worse. She focused on a clump of the creatures overwhelming the defenders at the center of the wall and called down a lightning strike, pouring a good fraction of her air-attuned Energy into it. With a crack of thunder, blue Energy exploded in the pack, sending a dozen creatures flying and giving the defenders a chance to press the attack.

Valla scanned the air and saw the orange and ochre glow of Naghelli wings all over, doing their best to aid from the air, fighting the horde of undead savages. Were they ghouls? Were they lesser vampires? Whatever they were, the Ninth was struggling, failing to hold the line at the wall, and packs of the creatures were rampaging through the camp. Valla summoned her helmet from her ring, pressed it onto her head, and trailing the silky layers of her gown, she lifted Midnight and dove for the largest group.

Gradually, Victor's mind turned back to the despair he felt, to his depression at the thought of losing Valla, Edeya, Chandri, Lam, Kethelket, Sarl, and all the soldiers he'd come to appreciate. With the study of that despair, he wondered again why he wasn't afraid. Hadn't he always feared being alone? Why wasn't he angry? Shouldn't he be furious at himself, at Hector? Finally, his sluggish mind held onto the thought long enough for him to make the connection. Naturally, he couldn't feel those things when this trap was dragging his Energy from his Spirit Core—his Spirit Core that fed on those emotions.

After he realized that, he shook his head. Didn't he already know that? What was the point? Why did it matter? Finally, after going over the thought ten or more times, he realized what he'd been trying to bring into his conscious thought—he could still feel despair and love, but not his attuned emotions. His glory was gone, his inspiration, his fear, his anger—all gone. Briefly, despite the dullness of his mind, he managed to contemplate forming a different Energy—justice or courage—but how could he? He needed Energy to weave, and he had none. As soon as some formed in his Core, it was gone.

Again, he fell into a wallowing well of self-loathing. He thought about his stupid mistakes, his lifetime of failing in one way or another, and he capped it all off with a reaffirming whisper, "Without my Energy, I'm nothing." When he heard the words aloud, however, something stirred in his heart, something related to glory but different, something that had been held down by his loss of that bright, wonderful Energy but not wholly banished—his pride. "I'm not nothing," he whispered, and then, mustering everything he had in him, he managed to make his vocal cords rumble in a faint growl. "I'm Quinametzin."

At the words, the thing in his heart grew hotter, and then he realized it wasn't in his heart but in his chest. His despair and the weakness he'd felt as his mighty Core was depleted had been so overwhelming that he'd forgotten his Breath Core. Even so, shouldn't he have felt it? Shouldn't he have realized he still had Energy within him? As the heat grew, his mind became less sluggish, and Victor realized something: the trap had depleted his Breath Core, too, but it couldn't stop it from replenishing. "But how," he breathed, and then the ball of magma in his chest flared again.

Victor closed his eyes and focused his inner eye upon his magma Breath Core, and though it was dim, smoldering weakly, it burned. He exhaled and took his first truly deep breath since he'd fallen into despair. Sure enough, hot tendrils of roiling red-orange Energy, carried by his breath, flowed into his Magma Core, charging it further, brightening the furnace in his chest like a bellows in a forge. Victor took another deep breath and followed the trails of those ribbons of fiery Energy, and now that he'd identified them, he could see their long wispy tails leading away into the magma tubes that opened beyond the ring of his veil star prison.

As the heat spread through him and the chill of his Energy-deprived titanic form faded, he found his thoughts coming more quickly and sharply.

The emotions tied to his Spirit Core might have faded and might be eluding him, but his Breath Core held a different kind of smoldering rage, and he could feel it echoed in the mountain beneath him. The veil star prison was keeping him in, was blocking his regeneration of Energies, but it couldn't block the furious wrath of the mountain beneath it. It was like trying to put a wine cork on a fire hydrant.

Now that he could think again, Victor put his mind to work—what could he do with his Breath Core? Could he pull its Energy into his pathways and into his Spirit Core, changing it into rage-attuned Energy? What if he could? What would being enraged do for him? If he could recover enough, perhaps he could force his way out of his trap. Maybe he could battle this prison with his will. He shook his head, doubtful. He'd had a full Core when he came in and lost it so quickly that he'd never had a chance to fight. If he converted his magma-attuned Energy to rage or any other attunement, he'd just lose it again.

Could he force the magma-attuned Energy into his pathways and then use it to cast a spell? Could he berserk with it? Was that a thing? Could elemental Energy be used to alter one's state? He'd never seen any "fire ber-serkers" or anything like that. He glanced at his status sheet, and doubt grew heavy in his heart. Even if he could manage the spell, it would be a shadow of his normal Iron Berserk—his magma Energy had a maximum value of five hundred, whereas his Spirit Core topped twenty-one thousand.

Growling and inhaling, savoring the hot magma-attuned Energy as it entered his lungs, Victor grabbed hold of Lifedrinker and stood up. If he could do that much, could he fight back? Could he break this trap? Victor stepped toward the veil star and started gathering his breath, preparing to exhale, sending his magma Energy out with his breath. He stopped, though, noticing something different. The fog around him had thinned. When he looked past the smaller veil stars, shielding his eyes from their painful pulsing patterns, he saw thick hot vapors rising around the nearby magma tubes, and the deathly mist was retreating from the heat.

"Oh?" Victor looked at his feet, imagining the roiling lake of magma in the center of the mountain. He closed his eyes, and with all his might, he sucked in an enormous breath, willing his lungs to keep filling, willing the magma in the depths to come to him, to fill his Core and expand it. With an explosion of heat and warmth, he felt his Core expand and stretch, and then, as if he'd broken bands strapping it tight, it surged to new heights, and more Energy came into him.

*****Congratulations! You have learned a new skill: Breath Core Cultivation Drill, Basic.*****

*****Congratulations! Your Breath Core has advanced: Base 6.*****

Victor looked at his status sheet, saw his Breath Core Energy had risen to six hundred, then lifted his head to the baleful pulsing star and roared. As his voice faded, sucked into the misty air high above his head, he felt an echoing rumble from beneath his feet, and Victor began to breathe, returning to his new cultivation drill with a savage purpose. "Time to wake up, big brother."

54

TESTS OF HEART

Lam felt the icy numbing grip of Victoria's misty tendril begin to pull the Energy from her Core, and she raged against it. She fought the pull with everything in her, desperately struggling to keep the Death Caster from overwhelming her with her insidious will. She pulled and thrashed, willing her Energy to stay in her pathways, knowing the mist would pull it from her if she cast a spell. In her struggles, she caught a glimpse of Edeya lying insensate, devoid of color, by her feet. Even her wings had lost their azure luster, and there were no beautiful motes of blue Energy anywhere in their transparent, fragile membranes.

The tent was in shambles, half collapsed, many of the furnishings blown out, through or under the fabric by her explosive attack. She might have gotten herself caught, but at least she'd knocked Edeya from that vile bitch's misty clutches. The other one, the tall demonic woman, regarded her thrashing, watching as Victoria worked to subdue her. "You waste time, Catalina," she hissed in a voice that sounded like a chorus of shrieking children. "Shall I take my due?" She reached a long arm, tipped in needle-sharp black claws, toward Lam. Her voice brought tears to Lam's eyes, and she thrashed and struggled more, fighting with everything she had to keep her Energy in her Core, resisting the insidious pull of the mist.

"She's mine!" Victoria hissed. Lam fought hard, barely able to wonder if she'd heard the demon right—was her name really Catalina? Where had she heard it before? "Long have I lusted for her golden Energy. Long has she tormented me with her vibrance. Come, sweet, relax, and succumb to my embrace. I'll always keep a part of you alive within me."

"Foolish child," the beautiful, horrible woman said. "Do you not hear the commotion? Finish your meal quickly, then I will begin my own feast." She stood tall, lifting her skeletally thin arm high, pushing the lopsided canvas of the tent away from her as she turned away and began to work free from the failing structure. Lam grunted, sweat streaming down her brow, dripping from her chin, as she was held motionless. Her sweat was proof of her efforts, for it was frigidly cold in the tent surrounded by the Death Caster's mist. The tall demonic woman only took two steps before, in a gust of cleansing air, the entire tent was ripped away from the ground, lifted into the air by the fluttering ochre wings of several Naghelli.

Like a snake striking from its hole, the naked woman leapt into the air, wrapping her long arms around one of the Naghelli, bearing her to the ground, and biting into her neck. The Naghelli didn't even have time to cry out as the demon drank her life force and Energy. A crowd of soldiers and other Naghelli fell on her, but Lam lost sight of the mad melee that ensued as Catalina redoubled her efforts, squeezing with her mist and jerking her left and right. "Succumb, fairy woman! Succumb!"

"And why should she, witch?" Suddenly, Kethelket was there, dancing through the freezing tendrils that made up Catalina's misty body, slashing his two named swords left and right, shredding the misty arms, eliciting screams of pain and outrage from the Death Caster. Lam felt the grip on her neck loosen and fall away, felt herself falling to the ground, and she caught herself, dropping into a squat. She snatched up her fallen hammer, spared Edeya's insensate form a single worrying glance, and then leapt into action, bright, golden Energy exploding through her pathways.

Kethelket had driven Catalina back, forcing her to pull her misty tendrils in, solidifying herself further so she might have a chance to parry those wicked twin blades. She moved with unbelievable speed, surging left and right, forward and back, up and down. Kethelket was more than a match with his shadowy Energy. He drove her back, farther and farther away. Lam followed their duel, and seeing a pattern, she brought down a hammer strike directly where Catalina next retreated. The Energy poured out of her Core as she gave it everything she had, and a massive dense hammer-shaped construct fell from the heavens, spinning as a thrown war hammer might, and smashing into Catalina, driving her to the turf in a ground-shaking impact.

Kethelket, in a blur of shadows, darted into the spray of dirt, fog, and shattered camp equipment, his blades flashing in brilliant arcs, ripping the now physical form of the Death Caster to shreds. Lam heard her wails, ear-piercing, horrible sounds that threatened to render anyone nearby deaf. She clapped her hands to her ears, her hammer falling to the ground, and stumbled over to Edeya. Chaos had erupted around her—soldiers screamed, magical attacks exploded everywhere, wild rainbow lights flashed in the night sky, and the thunder of thousands of feet pounding the ground rumbled under her knees as she fell beside her friend's pitiful figure.

"Edeya!" she cried. "Edeya!" She gripped her face, shivering at the chill of the flesh. Was she too late? Was she dead? Tears burst from her eyes, running down her cheeks as a sob of impotent rage and despair constricted her throat. Why hadn't she checked on her just a little sooner? Desperately, she summoned a healing draught from her ring and tipped it into Edeya's colorless lips. The liquid pooled against her teeth, running from the corners of her mouth. Lam pulled at her chin, letting the potion into her mouth, but nothing seemed to happen.

Suddenly, a shadow loomed over her, and she looked up to see the dark Naghelli prince. "The witch didn't die. With my third eye, I saw her tether pulsing with her death Energy. She must have a phylactery up on yonder mount."

Lam was too stupefied by her grief, too stunned with guilt to register his words. She hugged Edeya's cold body to her chest, lifting her limp, too-light form from the soil and hugging her tightly. Had she really loved the girl so much? The answer was in the stuttering skips of her heart and her desire to stop breathing. If Edeya had fled this world, then what was the point of anything? What was the point of all the wealth she'd built, all the battles she'd won? What was the point of founding a new country away from the Ridonne nobility when she had no one to love, no one with whom to share it?

Through the blur of her tears, she saw the shadow, Kethelket, loom closer, and he said with an urgent note in his voice. "Her wings!" Lam sniffed and blinked her eyes, clearing them enough to look down at Edeya's limp, colorless wings, and, as fresh waves of despair threatened to constrict her throat further, she saw briefly a tiny flicker of sapphire light. It was so dim and fleeting that she doubted herself, wondering if it had been a trick of the light. As she stared, though, another flickered in a different spot, gone before she could focus on it. Kethelket straightened, already turning away. "She yet lives, though barely. Get her to a safe place—I must face the demon that wreaks havoc among the troops. Make haste! Enemy soldiers assault the walls. See if Victor has yet emerged from his home!"

Lesh sat in his hiding spot among the hills, watching the camp below. Many nights had he followed Victor's army through the fair soft lands they sought to conquer. Many nights had he contemplated showing himself, asking about their giant hero, about his uncanny ability to breathe fire and his unstoppable physical might. He'd seen him conquer enemy after enemy, seen him descend into depths swarming with powerful undead, only to come up days later, unscathed. Lesh had abandoned his quest from the System and, along with it, any thoughts of returning home. How could he face the War Council in Garspire? How could he face his father? How could he face Yassa?

That last hurt the most. While the others pained his pride, the loss of Yassa crushed his heart. Nevertheless, his decision had been made. On that fateful night when he'd seen the titan-blood breathe fire that would be the envy of an elder drake, he'd known—Victor was not a man he would kill but a man he would follow. Was it fear? Was it inspiration? Lesh wasn't sure, and to claim one or the other would be dishonest. Regardless, he refused to entertain the idea of challenging that man who'd done nothing to impugn his honor, threaten his home, or lay claim to his freedom—he wouldn't let the System twist his hunger for power into something dishonorable. So he'd bided his time, watching, waiting, seeking the right opportunity to approach.

He wanted to speak, to sound out his thoughts as he often did while alone. He was quiet, though, knowing the titan's dark-winged watchers were out there, seeking any danger to their camp. It seemed they were preparing to begin their assault on the undead stronghold. Shouldn't he approach before then? Shouldn't he give his aid here before it was too late, before it was over, and he came scrounging around like a carrion hound to the slaughter? Not in the dark, however. No, he'd approach with the dawn's light, offering his services to break the defenses of those high keeps.

Would the titan even want him? He'd grown more and more powerful, and so had his mate. Elder wyrms! Lesh shook his head, remembering her shimmering wings and impressive figure as he'd watched the two ride into camp. She was no Yassa, but she was something special. Well, Lesh might not be ready or willing to challenge Victor, but he was mighty in his own right. He'd make a good case for himself, and when the time came to assault those walls, he and Belagog would make a name for themselves among these people.

Lesh's inner dialogue grew silent as he saw something strange on the hillside. His yellow-tinted sight made short work of the darkness, piercing even the dense layers of life-draining mist clinging to the hills. He looked for the dark-winged watchers sent by Victor's general into the slopes. Their wings had patterns of Energy that stood out like beacons, burning silver-white in his enhanced vision. It made them easy for him to avoid, and Lesh made it a habit to mark their locations each night, drawing a mental map of his surroundings. Something new had happened just now, though. Those watchers in the hills had disappeared; the glow of their wings winking out had drawn his attention.

He stood, still hooded in his obscuring cloak, and peered, sending a touch of Energy into his pathways, enhancing his vision further, into the distant hills, staring at the spot where he'd last seen the scouts. He almost missed it, taking the movement as mist shifting on the wind, but then he looked closer and saw that, clinging to the shadows and fog, a line of pale feral undead creatures were creeping down from the heights. He followed their line upward, catching glimpses of their column in gaps between hills, slipping through groves of gnarled trees and dropping down sheer rock faces. When his eyes finally came to rest on their source, a bend in the high cliffside above which roared the mighty falls, Lesh knew the truth—there was a tunnel behind those waters, and it was spilling forth thousands of the creatures.

Lesh threw back his hood and picked up Belagog. "It's time we made an appearance, brother."

Victor could feel the fury of the volcano beneath him. The ground rumbled, the air grew warm, and Hector's deathly mist had been almost wholly cooked out of the caldera. All he'd been doing was pulling on that hot magma-attuned Energy, drawing it into his Breath Core, compressing and packing it in until it grew too full to contain, and *boom*, his Breath Core expanded, gaining a new rank, making room for more and more Energy. He could tell he was on the brink of another gain, another expansion of his Breath Core as his lungs filled to bursting with air, and he sucked in those hot, potent vapors, driving them into the swirling ball of magma in his chest with every ounce of his will.

Like a dam breaking, his Core expanded, and he felt a flare of heat course through his body—he was veritably glowing with the Energy by now.

*****Congratulations! You have learned a new skill: Breath Core Cultivation Drill, Improved.*****

*****Congratulations! Your Breath Core has advanced: Base 9.*****

He couldn't believe how quickly he was making gains. It felt as if he'd only been at it for minutes, but he knew it had to be longer than that. As he started another cycle, impressed by how much more Energy he could pull using the improved cultivation drill, he wondered if he was doing the right thing. Was there a faster way out of the caldera? Could he destroy this trap with the flames in his Core? He'd seen how quickly the trap had drained him; it might not be able to contain the Energy coming from the volcano, but wouldn't it be able to suck away his measly nine hundred points of breath Energy?

And then what? If he drained himself again and left his body with no Energy, how long would he wallow before he began to recover? How much time would he lose trying to fight for a simple thought or to move his Energy-starved body? No, his Breath Core was fueling him, a titanic form grown powerful and accustomed to twenty times that much Energy. He was thinking; he was doing something; he couldn't risk that by blowing off his painstakingly gained progress.

He funneled another deep breath of hot Energy into his Core and heard and felt the burning magma furnace beneath him ever more intimately. It was waking. Its anger was stoking. Victor didn't know what would happen if he could get the magma to start flowing or even go so far as to make the volcano erupt. If it happened here, on the spirit plane, would it be echoed on the material plane? Would he destroy Hector's army? Would he kill the Glorious Ninth? Victor shook the worry from his mind—he had to do something, or he'd be trapped here forever, and right now, waking the magma beneath him felt right.

"Come on! One more!" he growled, pulling in another massive lungful of hot smoky air. He didn't know what would happen when he pushed his Breath Core out of the base levels, but he hoped it would be more than a simple hundred-point boost. He didn't have an attribute that improved his breath Energy like will and intelligence did for his Spirit Core, so he did the only thing he knew how—he gathered the rich, powerful magma-attuned Energy from the volcano and he packed it in, folding, layering, compressing it with his will, building that Breath Core up. He watched as the red-orange fury of it grew brighter, orange-yellow, yellow, yellow-white—pulsing, throbbing, straining. "Just a little more!" he growled, inhaling, compressing, expanding his lungs until they hurt.

He was making a draft, a vacuum almost, prodding the hot Energy to flow quicker and quicker up from the depths. The veil stars were still there, throbbing their green light at him, but he felt them less and less. The volcano's Energy was overwhelming them. Could that bastard, Hector, feel what he was doing? Was he worried? "Or is that *pendejo* too busy killing my friends?"

The thought came to him on a wave of red fury, and Victor realized his vision was tinted slightly red as he pulled another massive breath of magma-attuned hot air into his lungs. As he packed the Energy into his Breath Core, he turned his gaze to his Spirit Core, hoping to see his rage recovering, but it was still dim, still flickering with wisps of Energy that faded as soon as they formed. Where was this rage coming from? The ground rumbled beneath him, and his chest answered with a rumbled growl of his own. "You're pissed off, eh, *hermano*? Me too!"

As he finished compressing the last of his current magma Energy haul, Victor leapt to his feet and shouted into the smoky green-tinted darkness, "Come on, brother! Wake up and fuck this shit up!" Victor could feel it in his bones, in his blood, in his flesh—the heat of his Magma Core was boiling over, ready to burst, and it had deep echoes of rage in it. Could he use it like rage? Could he turn his Breath Core inward? As he contemplated, he automatically started another cycle of his Breath Core cultivation drill. He pumped his lungs like a bellows, expanding, contracting, expanding, siphoning the magma-attuned Energy from the hot air he brought in and exhaling vast plumes of smoke.

The heat in his chest intensified. His Core, a ball of white-hot compressed magma, was ready to blow, the pressure so intense that it dwarfed the last few expansions he'd managed. He was certain something momentous was going to happen when he broke through. It felt as though it could destroy him. If his other Core was full, rich with Energy, he might not feel the expansion of his Magma Core so acutely, but as it was, it felt as if he were building a bomb in his chest.

With each cycle of his drill, the Energy in the air grew thicker. The heat grew more sweltering. The smoke obscured more and more of the sickly green light. He felt the ground rumbling, felt the torrents of magma-attuned Energy swirling up out of the lava tubes. "Come on!" he screamed and began another cycle. The Energy flew into him, almost more fire than air as he sucked it in. It was so thick and dense with power that it took him longer to pack it into his Core than it did to process the breath.

As he compressed the air in his lungs, bearing down with all his might, forcing the Energy into his Core, he stood there red-faced, body clenched in a mad tight-fisted pose. When he finally broke through, advancing his Core to the next tier, he exhaled with a ground-shaking roar, and a plume of fire exploded out of his mouth.

Valla found her rhythm fighting among the hairless, naked, savage ghouls. She danced among them cloaked in lightning-laced wind, her wings adding a new dimension to her fighting that made her death incarnate to the feral creatures. She whirled, dashed, and leapt, her wings cracking the air to grant her more speed, manipulating the elemental magic of her Core, lashing out with lightning and iron-charged Energy, knocking aside slashing claws and ripping through pale flesh.

Midnight was like a bolt of lightning held tight in her fist, exploding through the air, shattering pale bodies, cracking against skulls, claws, and bones with claps of thunder that stunned her opponents. When she felt they were crowding too thickly, she'd flex her mighty wings and jump, soaring above their heads, only to come down riding the wind like an angelic avalanche of lightning and metal. Her silky white gown was torn, soaked in blood, but not her own. It flowed on the wind, presenting itself as a target for claws, but as the foolish undead sought to swipe at it, Valla cut them apart with her deadly blade.

She was fighting outside the northern gate, serving as a magnet for the hordes of monsters making their way out of the hills. There were thousands of them, maybe tens of thousands, but she couldn't be bothered to count, couldn't be bothered to care. She was busy dancing and killing, slaughtering them by the hundreds. Her distraction had given the defenders on the ramparts time to retake their ground, to hurl the vicious undead out of the camp. Now, they were raining death upon the incoming horde. Lightning, fireballs, arrows, stones—any kind of missile you could imagine—fell from the air, slaughtering the monsters wholesale.

In the back of her mind, Valla wondered where Victor was, where Kethelket was. Why was she the lone hero, holding back the horde, giving the army time to mount their defense? She shook her head at the thought, angry with herself—she wasn't alone. The heroes of the Ninth were all over the wall, performing feats that would humble the decorated champions of the Ridonne Empire. She was doing fine; the mountains of dead around here were a testament to that. They could win, they could . . .

A horrible shriek shook the night, echoing through the darkness, stunning everyone, even the undead, into stillness for a heartbeat. Valla tracked the sound, looking into the sky, and that glimmer of hope, that flicker of confidence, began to fall apart in her heart. A skeletal nightmare soared through the darkness, descending toward the encampment. It looked like a wyrm, a hundred times the size of Guapo, with skeletal wings pumping the air, catching the wind with membranes of sickly green magic. Worse, atop its head, perched between two massive horns, rode a black-robed demon of a man wielding an enormous spear and wearing a crown of red lightning.

55

VICTORIES AND DEFEATS

Kethelket followed the trail of bodies farther into the camp. He could hear the rallying cries at the walls, the horns bleating their frantic alarms. He knew the camp was under attack from the outside as well as within, but he couldn't turn from his quarry. He'd shouted for his people to take flight, to aid from the safety of the black fog-filled sky. Already, he'd lost too many—poor Divinia, snatched and drained by the creature he now pursued, Velnar, Brosk, and Evedelia, the guardians slain by Victoria, and who knew how many others Kethelket had yet to find. As he pushed his way through the wreckage and chaos, he saw evidence of plenty of slaughter, though none of the victims bore the dark wings of his kind.

The creature, demon, evil woman—he didn't know what to call it—seemed to prefer disembowelment as a means of quick murder. Kethelket ran down a bloody path strewn with entrails and pale bodies. He could see clusters of defenders here and there, torn, broken, ripped apart like caricatures at a child's party. Whatever the thing was, it was strong. His pursuit brought him toward the north wall, and he could guess the thing was heading for the gates. Did it hope to open them? He supposed it made sense. The camp had sturdy fortifications. They were well dug in. A flash of shadow in the corner of his eye sent a jolt of adrenaline through him, and Kethelket exploded into shadow, streaking away from flashing claws as they ripped the air where he'd been.

"A quick plaything?" the creature's voice grated on his ears like nails over bone. A dozen voices vied for control of those vocal cords, and the chorus was mind-racking. Kethelket didn't wait for an invitation. He streaked through the air, his vision gray and white from the expansion of shadow-attuned Energy through his pathways. Gevel and Uthac were angry, hungry for the blood of this slayer of Kethelket's kin. They lashed out, quicker than thought, and carved twin gashes along the demon's naked ribs. An answering rake of claws caught Kethelket's shoulder, and he burned some more Energy, streaking through the shadowscape to lessen their bite.

He moved, in a semi-incorporeal blur, around the tall gangly creature, aiming to assault her from behind. Up close, he was disturbed by the incongruous nature of the monster—her face was beautiful and bore a pleasant smile, while her body was all sharp angles and claws, too-long limbs, corpse-like flesh, and hair that hung in long damp strands, heavy with the blood of those she'd already slain. Kethelket drove Gevel into the woman's lower back and hacked Uthac into her knee. Gevel bit deeply, and a spurt of dark blood followed as Kethelket pulled him out, but Uthac rebounded from bone, the impact painfully jarring.

Kethelket expected a quick response; he'd see how the creature could move. He'd already shifted to shadow and was streaking away when the nightmare whirled and clawed. Her movement was fast enough to catch the tail end of his passage, and Kethelket cried out as his concentration was shattered by pain. Somehow, she'd torn those long black claws through his shadow form and broken his spell. He tumbled into the side of a tent, collapsing the canvas and rolling through it. Though fiery aches told him he'd been badly cut from his lower back down to his left knee, he leapt into motion again, ripping Gevel in a slashing upward parry, knocking aside the creature's follow-up attack.

With everything he had, he launched a masterful combination of hacks, stabs, feints, and parries, driving forward into the frenzied flurry of claws and insane multivoiced laughter. They battled that way for mere seconds, but those seconds stretched into hours, days, and weeks in Kethelket's mind. Every slash, every parry, every riposte became the focus of his lifetime, the pinnacle of everything he'd studied for. A hundred years of swordsmanship, three times that many studying combat with other weapons, building his Core, learning to use the shadow Energy instinctually—everything came down to that moment, that furious exchange that was over before most people would realize it had happened.

When Kethelket stepped back, the demonic woman fell at his feet, her heart punctured, her throat cut to the bone, and her entrails drooping from a gaping wound. Kethelket stood over her, victorious, then he fell to a knee, planting his two swords in the cold damp soil to prop himself up. He'd felt her claws part the soft flesh of his neck, felt them puncture his side, driving six inches into his vulnerable organs. He knew he'd choke if he breathed, so he didn't. He held his breath and watched the darkness closing in on his vision. He willed it away, furious that his body would give in before he'd seen the foul light go out of his enemy's eyes.

As the darkness shrank away from his furious will, he refocused on the woman's face, watching those lips spew blood as she tried to breathe, watching as she heaved and shuddered, fitfully scrabbling at the cold earth with her long fingers, trying to pull her failing body closer to him. Kethelket couldn't breathe, but he refused to stay on his knees before her. Holding on to the hilts of his swords, he slowly, shakily, regained his feet, staring down at the creature, watching its struggles fade. Only then, when it shuddered its last breath, did Kethelket pull a healing draught from his storage ring and tip it into his mouth.

*****Congratulations! Your Breath Core has advanced: Improved 1.*****

As the smoke and waves of hot air washed over him, as the release of Energy flowing hotly through his lungs and igniting in the air just past his mouth began to fade, Victor read the System notification and then looked at his Energy status:

Breath Core:	Elder Class: Improved 1		
Core:	Spirit Class: Advanced 8		
Breath Core Affinity:	Magma: 9	**Breath Core Energy:**	2000/2000
Energy Affinity:	Fear 9.4, Rage 9.1, Glory 8.6, Inspiration 7.4, Unattuned 3.1	Energy:	15/21864

When his Breath Core had been Base 9, he'd had 900 Energy. Did that mean he'd simply gained 1,100 from the level up, or had he gained the usual 100, and then his total had doubled? He shook his head—no way to tell until he did it again. "I don't have time for this." Victor twisted his hands around Lifedrinker's ghostly spirit plane projection, but the axe was silent, just as she had been since the trap had been sprung. Was it draining her, too? Was it cutting her off somehow?

Victor looked up at the veil star, pleased to see it obscured by waves of hot stinging smoke. The lava tubes looked like giant incense burners, the black smoke pouring out of them laced with tiny flickering motes of fiery ash. He was doing something. That much was certain. Something under his feet was waking up—the magma-attuned Energy was so heavy and thick in the air that he barely had to breathe to pull it into his Core. The more prevalent it became, the more Victor felt its secondary effects; he found it easier and easier to find the anger in his heart, the fury he knew he should be feeling toward Hector. Before, the thought of Valla and the others in danger brought him only despair. Now, anger surged within him. He felt his teeth grind, his vision tint red, and a deep-seated desire to find Hector and put an end to him.

If the anger in the air could do that for him and allow him to feel the emotion the veil star trap was blocking from his Core, could he use that? He'd built up his Breath Core significantly; could he use that Energy to kick-start his rage? To summon enough into his pathways to cast Berserk again? If he did that, would it be enough to break the hold on him? Could he break free of his prison? The idea felt good, but as soon as he looked more closely at it, he knew it would fail. He'd *been* berserk when the trap was sprung, and he'd had a hell of a lot more than two thousand Energy. As soon as he managed to cast the spell, his Spirit Core would be drained, and the spell would fade.

No, if he wanted any spell to last, it had to be fueled by his magma-attuned Energy. "But my *pinché* spells are meant for spirit Energies!" Victor growled, thumping his clenched fist against his forehead. As he stood there, anger grinding his teeth, frustration making him pound his head over and over again, something of a lightbulb went off in his brain. There had to be more to this magma-attuned Energy than the elemental aspect. He could feel it, the fury of the mountain beneath him, the smoldering anger in the air. More than that, he could *use* it. His brain was working because of it. Thanks to that Energy, his back was straight, and he wasn't wallowing in the dirt. Rather than self-pitying defeat, he felt angry.

"Okay, *hermano,* if you're pissed off and your anger is thick in the air and in my Breath Core, then why the hell can't I use that?" Victor closed his eyes again, turning his gaze inward to the smoldering, throbbing heart of his Breath Core. It was apparent that the volcano's Energy was spewing forth much faster than the veil star and its smaller twins could siphon it off. Hector's trap had meant to deprive Victor, a single person, of his magma-attuned

Energy. But it wasn't a match for the mighty, angry spirit under his feet. That idea got Victor thinking. Was it a spirit? Was the mountain alive, or was it just a natural generator for the kind of Energy he could feel? Victor felt it was more than that. Something was angry under him.

Looking closely at his Breath Core, he focused his will and pulled a tendril of that Energy out, studying its smoldering, pulsing flow as he pushed it around in the pathways of his lungs. Just as he'd instinctively known, he could see the Energy was multifaceted. Entwined with the amber glow of the fiery Energy was a tendril of deep crimson. It echoed the appearance of his rage-attuned Energy so closely that Victor couldn't help but recognize it. He supposed some might think it was just another brand of fiery Energy, a complexity to the magma that separated it from other, purer forms of elemental fire Energy. Victor knew better.

Victor slowly began to inhale, pulling a steady stream of the volcano's magma-attuned Energy into his lungs, sending it into his Breath Core. At the same time, as the Core swirled and pulsed, he pulled that tiny thread of red furious Energy out of it, separating it from his magma-attuned Core and slipping it into his pathway, out of his lungs, and down, into his Spirit Core. Once that thin thread of Energy felt the tug of his rage-attuned Core, it began to siphon, and he didn't have to try any longer.

Grinning madly, he continued to pull the mountain's Energy into his lungs, feeding it to his Breath Core and watching as the ribbon of red furious Energy rippled down through his pathways into his Spirit Core. His dim cold Rage Core began to smolder like an ember given a breath of wind. He saw the Energy sucked away, like crimson smoke, into the trap Hector had created, but as he continued to pull Energy into his lungs, that ribbon kept flowing, and it was slowly gaining ground—the Core was getting brighter.

If he weren't busy inhaling, following the cultivation drill he'd figured out for his Breath Core, Victor would have howled with bloodthirsty excitement. He could feel the heat of his rage truly begin to take shape. He'd only been at it for a few moments when suddenly, System messages flashed in his vision:

*****Congratulations! You have learned a new skill: Breath Core Cultivation Drill, Advanced.*****

*****Congratulations! You have learned a new skill: Spirit Core Cultivation Drill, Advanced.*****

Victor's insane grin spread wider, and his immense, rhythmic, chest-expanding inhalations took on a maniacal frenzied pace as the messages encouraged him. He'd been on the brink of improving his Spirit Core cultivation drill for months but never broken through. Now he'd skipped "improved" and gone straight to "advanced." Was this what he'd been meant to do? To see the reflections of his spirit Energies in the elements around him? He'd always cultivated from his own emotions, but apparently, that was only part of the equation.

Victor continued to watch his Cores with his inner eye. His Breath Core was full, growing slowly brighter, his input of magma-attuned Energy faster than the outlet of red angry Energy he was sending into his Spirit Core. His Rage Core continued to grow, continued to get brighter and brighter. What was his goal? What would he do? If he stopped cultivating the magma Energy in the air, his Rage Core would just be drained again. Could he berserk and still cultivate? Could he . . . Victor frowned as an idea came to him, something that he should have seen the moment he realized he could harvest rage from the magma Energy.

If he could pull rage out of his Breath Core into his pathways and down into his Spirit Core, why couldn't he pull that rage into a spell? He could do it. He could cast Berserk with his Breath Core. He wasn't sure it would work the same, but it was better than doing nothing. Nodding to himself, still sucking Energy out of the air, he took that thread of red furious Energy and rather than stopping it from flowing into his Spirit Core, he pulled it back out into his pathway and wound it into the pattern for Berserk, just as he'd done hundreds of other times.

As the spell took shape, snapping into place, he felt the pull on his Breath Core intensify. The spell was compensating for his depleted Spirit Core, pulling on that long thread running through his pathways. Iron Berserk was a hungry spell, brutal in its demands for instant Energy, and that thin thread of angry red Energy wasn't enough. As it pulled, a thick rope of orange-red magma-attuned Energy flowed out of his Breath Core, into his pathways, into the spell, and then Victor erupted with mad, fiery Energy.

Lam burst into Victor's home, charging down the short hallway to the dining area with Edeya in her arms. "Victor!" she screamed. "Valla!" She gently laid Edeya on the table and put her ear to her lips, confirming she was still breathing, though her wispy puffs were hardly breaths. "Victor!" she screamed again, desperate fear and frail hope adding a note of panic to her voice. She charged down the steps, down the hallway to Victor's wide open bedroom door. "They must be out fighting." Nevertheless, she went through the door, wanting to be sure, and then she saw him.

Victor sat on the rug, huge and pale as ash, the air cold around him. His eyes were closed but jumping around behind the lids. He breathed fitfully, strangely, and Lam thought she could hear some weird muttered unformed words in his throat. "Victor! Wake up! Victor!" She ran to him, grasped his massive shoulders, and shook him. He was stiff and so bound with muscle, it felt like trying to shake a tree. She moved around to face him and, winding back her arm, slapped him full across the face. He hardly moved. "Rotten roots!" she cried and ran from the room, returning to check on Edeya.

The frail pale Ghelli was the same. The only hints she was alive were the occasional tiny motes of color in her wings and the faint wispy shallow breaths puffing between her colorless lips. "Why won't the healing draught work?" Lam knew the answer: Her body wasn't hurt. It was her spirit, and the one person she hoped might be able to help her was similarly lifeless. Something was happening elsewhere. Something was happening in that place of spirits Victor often spoke about. If he was under assault there, if Edeya had been taken there, then Lam could only do her best to give them time to finish their fights. She had to help protect the encampment.

Valla crashed and tumbled over the ground, tucking her wings, charging them with air-attuned Energy to protect them and herself. Gusts of wind sheathed her, made her light, and added a great distance to her tumbling, sliding progress. The skeletal dragon, for that was what Valla had decided the terrible monstrous mount had to be, had smashed her with its tremendous spiny tail, knocking her aside as she might do to a rodent. Hector had brought the beast down onto the wall. The thing had gripped the ramparts with its roladii-sized talons and ripped them apart. Men and women had been smashed, sent flying, or torn to pieces by the horrific show of power.

Valla had tried to attack, had leapt into the air, streaking toward Hector, aiming Midnight like a lightning-charged headsman's blade at his neck, only to be smashed by the dragon's tail as Hector spun the creature. He'd laughed and roared, firing bolts or red lightning at defenders while the great dead dragon snapped up soldiers and crunched them into a paste in its fleshless jaws. Valla finally came to rest against a gnarled tree trunk, and she unfolded her battered wings and wearily climbed to her feet. She was a hundred yards from the wall and could see the battle clearly.

Hector and his pet were too much. They'd leveled most of the northern wall, allowing the ghouls easy ingress. The dragon shrugged off the feeble-looking ranged attacks of the defenders—arrows did nothing, and fire-balls failed to ignite. Lightning might hurt it, but not the tiny bolts thrown by the beleaguered defenders. She saw stinging ice shards, hurled earthen balls, and even freezing rains—none harmed the gigantic green-glowing skeletal mount. Its wings tore through entire units, sending broken men and women flying. Its jaws and claws were instant death, and though some Naghelli tried to attack Hector directly, he blasted them from the air with those horrible red lightning bolts.

"We have to flee," Valla muttered, with little hope of making it happen. How could you run away from a creature like that? What about the thousands of savage ghouls? They were too fast. "Some might live." Valla didn't voice her unspoken cowardly thought—she could escape. Scowling, angry that the notion had even entered her mind, she gripped Midnight's hilt and stalked toward the horrible melee. She breathed deeply, steeling her mind, finding her focus, staring at Hector, carefully timing the lurching momentum of the giant mount. When she was sure of herself, she channeled most of her remaining air-attuned Energy into a mighty Lightning Strike, seeking to reduce the damned Death Caster to ash.

Just as Hector threw a red bolt of lightning into the air, sending yet another Naghelli hurtling to the ground trailing black smoke, Valla's bolt of blue lightning exploded out of the dark sky, poleaxing him. His arms flew wide, and he vibrated for a long second with the surge of powerful Energy. A ragged cheer broke out from the entrenched soldiers as the Death Caster slumped and the bone dragon's animating green Energy faded. Just as Valla felt herself begin to breathe, just as she felt there might yet be some hope for them, Hector jerked his head up, his red lightning-bound crown flared to life, and the dragon whirled, suddenly full of life again.

Valla spread her wings, lifted Midnight, and in her shredded bloody nightgown, she screamed, "Come on then!" The bone dragon bunched its legs and leapt, snapping its tremendous wings hard enough to send soldiers and ghouls flying. Hector and his mount soared through the air, ready to flatten Valla with those enormous talons. She didn't plan to stand still, however. Valla cracked her own wings, launching into the air.

If she couldn't kill Hector, she could perhaps give the Ninth some room. She could lead him on a chase. Maybe, just maybe, she could keep him busy until Victor finally woke, finally came to help. With those thoughts in her mind, she pumped her wings as she never had before, streaking upward, urging the Energy in her pathways to aid her flight. That's when she realized her miscalculation; her air-attuned Energy was nearly depleted. More, the dragon was faster than she'd thought. She felt it closing on her almost immediately. Valla cried out with effort as she furiously worked her wings. Her weary body tried to obey her, but all too quickly, she heard Hector's high screeching laughter and then felt the bony talons of his mount closing around her.

56

VOLCANIC FURY

Valla thrashed and struggled in the terrible grip of the skeletal dragon. Its talons were hard and unyielding, and her arms were pinned uncomfortably by its grasp. She could feel the rough texture of the bones, and her racing mind took a moment to wonder how old they were. Where had Hector dug up this ancient construct? Panic and despair made her thoughts erratic as she struggled to get free. She still gripped Midnight, though the blade was awkwardly pinned to her side by the grip of the massive bones. She tried everything she could, even burning most of her remaining Energy to summon her Steel Tempest, hoping the whirling winds and slashing, razor-sharp bits of metal would aggravate the dragon, making it loosen its hold.

Her efforts were for naught. Drained, weak, struggling to breathe, she wondered if this was the end. Would Hector, still madly cackling above her, command his undead beast to crunch her in its great toothy maw? Would she never see Victor again? Her stomach lurched as the dragon plummeted toward the ground, and Valla still had the presence of mind to wonder if it took a great effort to keep the monstrous mount aloft. Tears streaming from her eyes, pulled out by the whistling wind, Valla watched the ground rapidly approach, bracing for the beast to smash her against it with a forceful landing.

Though her descent ended in a spine-thrashing wrench, she didn't get pulverized into the ground; it seemed Hector wasn't done with her yet. The dragon took a lurching step, holding her above the ground, and Valla had just enough time to wonder what she could do to break free before a colossal deafening crack resounded through the bony claw grasping her, and the dragon spastically released her to tumble onto the ground. Valla knew an opportunity when she felt one and exploded into motion, pushing the dregs of her wind-attuned Energy into her pathways, then into her wings. She jerked them with a *snap* and leapt up, streaking into the air.

She had time to hear a deep bellowing voice roar, "You dare to ride my ancestor's bones?" Then, another cracking impact echoed through the night, and Hector's red lightning flared in Valla's peripheral vision. She spun and pumped her wings, gaining distance, sure she was being pursued, but after a moment, when no grasping talons or snapping jaws came for her, she turned to look back and down at what had saved her. She saw a figure, small now that she was high in the air, but even the dragon looked small from there. No, the dark, hulking man had to be big and strong, for she watched as he smashed away a grasping skeletal talon with a huge, strangely pulsating cudgel.

Hector's skeletal mount reared back and then lunged forward with its great fang-filled maw, aiming to snap Valla's rescuer in half, but the nimble black-clad figure leapt backward, smashing that cudgel with its weird throbbing, resonating Energy against the dragon's bony chin. He used the giant skeleton's momentum to drive himself back, away from the deafening *clack* of those snapping jaws.

Valla didn't know who the man was or where he'd come from, but she wasn't about to let his distraction go to waste. Her little flight and the dragon's pursuit had brought Hector more than a mile away from the encampment into the wilderness, and that meant the Ninth might have a chance to regroup and throw out the undead, especially if Victor snapped out of his trance and helped them rally.

"So let's help this stranger and keep Hector busy." Valla lifted Midnight high and dove, using the pull of gravity and her uncanny ability to ride the wind to streak down. She bared her teeth, eyes narrowed against the wind, and though she was silent, Midnight began to howl, eager to clash with Valla's black-robed tormentor. The stranger continued to harass the dragon, and Valla saw him shrug aside not one or two but several of Hector's lightning strikes. The red bolts of blasting, cacophonous Energy slid off him like drops of hot oil on a stone. Hector failed to notice Valla until she was almost upon him, but, at the last second, he threw up his left arm, and a dome of blistering red Energy snapped into place between them.

Valla barely altered her course enough to avoid smashing into the dome, but she managed, and as she streaked by, she hammered that shield of sizzling

Energy with Midnight. The blade struck with such force that, though she refused to let go of her hilt, the bones in her hand and wrist vibrated painfully together. Still, the impact had an effect on Hector as well. The shield flared like a miniature nova, and Valla knew she'd cost him dearly in terms of Energy usage. She continued her glide, aiming for a low hill a few hundred yards beyond the dragon. Exhausted, arm aching, Core nearly drained, she came to a running, stumbling halt.

Turning back, she saw the colossal stranger more clearly now that she was on the ground. He was unlike anyone she'd ever seen. He was similar in size to Victor now that he'd awoken so much of his titanic bloodline—probably nine or ten feet tall. What she'd taken for dark armor turned out to be scales grown on black flesh; he looked like a man who was half drake or wyrm. He wore clothes, but not many—dark leather leggings that ended just below his knees, no boots, for his feet were big and bore heavy talons, no shirt, and no armor other than his natural scales. A dark, weirdly shadowy, light-shifting cloak hung from his shoulders, whipped to and fro by the wind of his and the dragon's movements.

The stranger continued to growl insults and challenges at Hector, swinging his pulsating cudgel in powerful arcing parries, batting away the dragon's repeated attempts to grasp him in its claws or maw. "Put those bones to rest, undead scum! Face me on the firm soil!" Though a massive man, he was still too small to stand firmly and pound away at the dragon; its swiping blows sent him sliding or scrabbling every time he knocked them aside. Nevertheless, he was impressively resilient, shrugging off Hector's magical attacks and confounding the bony dragon's attacks.

Valla looked to her Core, saw it very slowly recovering, and growling with frustration, she lifted Midnight, snapping her wings. If she could only harry Hector with her sword, then that was what she would do. This time, she didn't spend the effort gaining altitude; she pumped her wings and flew straight at Hector, hoping his Energy was running low. If it was, she didn't find out—Hector saw her coming and pointed one pale long-fingered hand her way, and a bolt of red lightning struck her full in the chest. Valla screamed and flew off course, stunned by the jolt of electricity, her white bloody gown charred black and trailing smoke as she crashed to the ground.

Some instinct or reflexive contraction of her wings saved her from breaking her limbs; she wrapped those massive shimmering appendages around herself and tumbled like a lopsided ball over the ground, flattening shrubs, sliding over loose gravel and dirt, and rolling down into a gully. She lay there, stunned, for several long seconds, and then she felt the ground shake and knew the skeletal dragon was coming for her. She was exhausted, burned, and bloody. Her Energy was spent, but still she lifted her sword, arm shaking, and tried to sit up. The ground rumbled and shook again, and she braced herself; the dragon must be close, about to slide down the slope and smash her.

When she heard the stranger shouting and cursing distantly and heard the similarly distant *clack* of the dragon's jaws, she frowned. Had she imagined the ground shaking? Could the giant skeleton make the stones jump from such a distance? Valla struggled to her knees, using Midnight to brace herself. Then the ground lurched, and she fell onto her face. Distantly, she heard a different noise, like low rumbling thunder that went on and on. Valla stood, shaky, bloody knees struggling to support her as she wondered what new nightmare was about to be unleashed.

As the pattern for Iron Berserk absorbed the potent, furious magma-attuned Energy, combined with the thread of rage coming from his Spirit Core, Victor's vision tinted crimson, and fury boiled in his blood as it hadn't in a very long time. If he'd had the presence of mind to think about it, he would have compared his blind, thoughtless anger to the way he'd felt in the early days of his Rage Core, back when he'd fought for the Wagon Wheel. The absolute dominance of the emotion was so overwhelming that every thought fled his mind. As his body expanded and hot red-orange flames ignited along his shoulders and arms, he lifted his fire-filled eyes to the sky, opened his mouth, and roared.

His voice was the fury of the boiling, hidden depths of the world, his breath the smoky fire of the mountain's heart. When he stomped toward the green light that had tormented him, the ground cracked under his feet, and orange flames licked the stones where he stepped. He felt something in his hand and lifted it high—a burning brand topped with white-hot metal shaped like a crescent moon, screaming her fury, a match for his own. Victor wanted to kill that green light, wanted to smash it in his hands, bite it, rip it, grind it into nothing. It was out of his reach, but he wasn't beyond trying to leap for it.

He stomped closer, but then an answering fury echoed beneath his feet. The ground lurched, and hot volatile Energy poured out of the round tunnels all over the mountaintop. Victor breathed it in, sending it into his Core without conscious thought. His transformation used it, fueled itself with that Energy. Again, he roared into the green-tinted smoky night, and this time, his black cinder-filled breath caught fire, bursting upward in a cloud of rolling crimson flames. As he stared, something like squiggly worms danced across his blood-red vision, but he snarled and slapped at his face until they no longer bothered him.

He was power incarnate, destruction given form, and he wanted to fulfill his purpose. Rather than focus on the big floating green light, he turned to the smaller ones. Roaring, cloaked in flames and black smoke, he charged the nearest one. His shoulder smashed into the enormous stone pillar upon which it sat, and he exploded through it as if it were made of matchsticks. The green pulsating veil star winked out as the rune-inscribed stone pillar crumbled and shattered into dust and fragments. The destruction felt good, and Victor whirled to the next pillar, charging it, smashing it, and howling as the ground rumbled again and another hot surge of magma-infused Energy pumped into the air.

Victor knew only fury, only the mad need for destruction, and he took it out on the only things within reach. He smashed the other pillars, one after another, and when he finished, the ground lurched, the mountain roared, and explosive steamy smoke blasted out of the lava tubes. At one with the volcano's fury, Victor, nimble beyond reason, rode the rumbling, tilting ground as if he was born to it. He stood at the center of the caldera, eyes focused on the hated veil star, and he screamed his fury. He could feel the mountain wanting to answer him. He could feel the furious thick Energy in the air, and he sucked it in with each breath. With each exhalation, plumes of smoke and sparks flew.

Staring at that green pulsing orb in the sky, Victor began to pump his lungs like a bellows, sucking in breath after breath, holding the Energy he harvested on those hot winds until he thought he'd burst. His body swelled with it, and his veins burned with it, standing out on his red flesh like yellow-white rivers of lava. His eyes burned incandescent with the heat of the Energy in his pathways, turning the world a brighter shade of crimson, blotting out the green of the veil star, making it a wispy pale light that he needed to extinguish. When he couldn't bear it any longer, when he felt his flesh would crack and his bones explode, Victor roared out that pent-up Energy, sending it forth on a plume of black smoky breath. It ignited with a *whoosh* that sucked the oxygen out of the air for a hundred yards around him.

Bright yellow magma exploded from Victor's breath, straight up in a fanning plume that fully engulfed the veil star. Victor's rage dimmed markedly as that tremendous burst of magma-attuned Energy was ejected from his body, and he leaned forward, gasping for breath, Lifedrinker loose in his grip. He felt the ground bucking under him, rolling up and down like rocky, earthen waves. The volcano had felt his outburst, and it wanted to answer him. Victor looked up and saw the veil star was dim, sputtering, and weak.

He was still furious, still felt the anger in the air influencing him, but he'd lost that single-minded madness for destruction with the expenditure of magma-attuned Energy. He glanced inward and saw his Spirit Core recovering—every one of his attuned orbs of Energy was growing brighter or, in the case of his fear, darker. The stink of death-attuned Energy was gone; nothing but smoke and heat filled the air around him. The volcano would destroy whatever shreds of the veil star might survive his attack.

Victor took one more look around his onetime prison, and then, before something might happen to stop him, he focused his will and ended his spirit walk. With a gasp, he returned to himself, falling forward onto his hands. It was disorienting at first to find himself gripping the thick pile of his bedroom rug. As his senses recovered, he lifted his face and blinked. "Valla?" He leapt to his feet, glanced around the room, and saw it was empty. Victor turned to the door but paused to clear the System messages hovering in front of his eyes, dismissing them one by one as he glanced over them.

*****Congratulations! Your Breath Core has advanced: Improved 2.*****

*****Congratulations! You have learned a new spell: Volcanic Fury, Basic.*****

*****Volcanic Fury, Basic. Prerequisites: Rage, Fury, or Hatred Affinity; Magma Affinity. You channel the fury of the fiery depths. While affected by this transformation, you are immune to fire-based attacks, your magma-based abilities double in effectiveness, and you benefit from the effects of Berserk: double strength and speed, increased resilience, and powerful regenerative capabilities. Be cautious, for the fury of the volcano knows no bounds—reason and compassion will flee before its heat. Energy Cost: Minimum 1000, scalable. Cooldown: Long.*****

The notifications were good news, and he wanted to read them and savor his accomplishment, but he had yet to learn the costs of his imprisonment. He didn't even know how long he'd been held on the spirit plane. Had Hector's taunting whisper been just that, a taunt? "Come on, *chica*." Victor picked up Lifedrinker and started walking up the hallway, dreading what he was about to find. As he climbed the steps, he summoned his helmet from his storage ring and placed the heavy dense armor on his head. When he stepped onto the upper landing, his eyes fell on a still pale form lying on his dining table.

"Edeya?" He hurried to her, gripped her tiny wrist in his overlarge, warm hand, and leaned close to her face. She looked dead, and the thought of it nearly stopped his heart. He felt his fear begin to bleed out of his Core into his pathways, but then, like a tiny fluttering vibration, he felt her pulse. It was slow and soft, but it was there. "Edeya!" He pressed his big palm over her forehead, cupping her entire skull in his hand. Closing his eyes, he said, "Come on, *hermanita*. Come back to me. Wake up."

Eyes closed, Victor turned his gaze inward, starting at his Core. It burned brightly with Energy as it rapidly recovered from his ordeal. He followed his pathways outward, and when he looked away from his body into Edeya, he saw the answer: A sickly blue tether stretched away from her into darkness. "Those *pinché* motherfuckers did something to you, huh? I'll fix it, little sister. Hang in there." Victor let go of her and turned, and growling with renewed fury, he twisted his hands on Lifedrinker's haft as he stalked toward the door of his home.

As soon as he stepped out, his senses were nearly overwhelmed. He smelled smoke, blood, guts, and the rotten, unmistakable stench of the undead. He saw flashes of light—fire, Energy bolts, lightning. He heard shrieks, roars, screams, sobbing, growling. Under it all, he felt the ground shifting and rumbling as, just as he'd feared, the volcano began to wake. Victor summoned his Banner of the Champion, and he cast Iron Berserk. He wanted to explore the strengths and benefits of his new transformation, but right now, he needed control, and he needed to be able to think.

As his banner's light burst into fiery glory and he expanded in size and potency, he looked around, wondering why the noise seemed so distant. His answer came to his ears with the sounds of horns blowing—the command to charge. He turned to the north, and there he saw a concentration of spell Energy flying through the black night. Nodding, he lifted Lifedrinker and ran that way, intent on helping the troops. He'd covered half the distance when a terrible gut-wrenching shriek shook the night off to his left, and in the light of a massive red lightning bolt, he saw the nightmare form of a gigantic undead dragon.

Victor altered his path, aiming for the dragon. Perhaps it was simply the size of it that awoke some desire in his Quinametzin heart to fight the strongest opponent. Perhaps it was something else in his heart, sensing that Valla was there and that she needed him. Perhaps it was the red lightning and the distant echoes of unnatural laughter that reminded his subconscious of the voice that had taunted him on the spirit plane. Whatever the reason, Victor knew his battle lay there with that gigantic undead beast.

57

TO WAKE THE MOUNTAIN

As Victor raced through the camp, building up momentum, planning to leap the fortification between himself and the distant gigantic form of the skeletal dragon, he berated himself for being a fool. It was obvious the camp had been overrun at one point, obvious the soldiers had managed to rally, but not without cost—bodies were everywhere, scattered among the piles of pale naked ghoulish undead. How much of this assault had been due to his entrapment? Would Hector have sprung this assault if Victor hadn't spirit walked into the caldera? As if it could hear him thinking about it, the volcano rumbled again, sending him sliding into an overturned wagon.

The stumble brought his thoughts back to the present, and he growled, shaking his head. "Focus!" He sprinted several steps, bunched his legs, and leapt over the rough stone wall the soldiers had spent the last week building. When he landed, sliding over the hard-packed gravel-strewn ground outside, he caught his first full view of the gigantic draconic skeleton and the battle it waged. In a flash of red lightning, his sharp eyes caught sight of Valla's silhouette, flying in an arcing dive, trying to hit the cloaked figure atop the dragon's horn-crowned head. She was rebuffed by a curved shield of red Energy, sent spiraling to the ground and tumbling into a nearby gully.

The sight of her going down cleared Victor's mind, driving out all thoughts, leaving behind only a hunger for battle, a thirst for vengeance, and a deep pulsating fury at the idea that this worm would dare to harm the woman he loved. As he burst into motion, his gigantic powerful legs driving him into a mad sprint, he was sure Hector would turn his mount to pursue Valla, to finish her while she was down. He jumped a narrow scrub-filled gully, and when he mounted the last hilltop between himself and his foe, he realized another combatant was on the field. A huge, powerfully built man was standing toe to toe with the giant skeleton, smashing aside its swiping claws and snapping maw with a rod-like cudgel, its impacts resounding with thunderous *cracks*.

The dragon skeleton wasn't as big as the elder wyrm Victor had helped to slay on Zaafor. It wasn't even half as large, but it was massive. Even in his full titanic aspect, Victor doubted he could manhandle it, but if that man, big as he was, could stand against those swipes, Victor knew he could do better. "Come on, beautiful!" he growled, lifting Lifedrinker high and furiously pumping his legs into a sprint. He was channeling Sovereign Will into his strength and agility. He wanted to move quickly and powerfully and had a target in mind.

As he closed the last hundred yards, his opponent utterly oblivious to his approach, Victor focused on the joint where one of the dragon's wings met with its spine. Victor was fast when he sprinted. His strides devoured the distance, covering half a dozen yards at a time. As soon as he felt close enough, he channeled rage into an Energy Charge and exploded through the air, ripping a furrow in the rough scrub and grass. He and Lifedrinker impacted the skeletal dragon with such a thunderous crash that it rumbled over the countryside like a bomb going off.

He'd kept his focus on his target, and when he hit, Lifedrinker sank into that joint, cleaving into the bone, sending fragments flying like razor-edged daggers. Victor felt the Energy being sucked out of his Core, summoned by the spell to protect him from the horrific forces generated by his violent impact into the airliner-sized pile of animated bones. His Core was ready for it; brilliant furious Energy expanded in a ball around him, and he felt none of the devastating concussion. The same couldn't be said for the skeleton or its rider.

Lifedrinker's edge served as a focal point for the ruinous energies unleashed by Victor's charge. They entered that gap and, having found purchase, expanded between the bones into the cavity of the skeleton's animated ribs, blasting them apart. The dragon's wing burst into thousands of its component pieces, flying in every direction. Its spine rippled with the impact, dozens of gigantic vertebrae ripping through the air and riding the shockwave of Victor's freight train charge. The entire skeleton tumbled sideways down the hillside, the sickly green Energy animating its wings and bones flickering, fading, and winking out as Hector fell, bouncing onto the ground.

"Well timed, titan!" the hulking club-wielding stranger hollered, though Victor hardly registered the words; he had eyes only for his tumbling enemy. Lifting Lifedrinker, exulting in her furious war cry, he leapt after him. Hector didn't lie still, waiting for him. More of the bright red lightning-like Energy Victor had seen him flinging about burst into existence around him. It shimmered and flashed, a tremendous whirling maelstrom of destruction that spun around Hector's darkly cloaked form for a dozen feet in every direction. Victor didn't care, and neither did Lifedrinker. She erupted into molten fury at the proximity of their foe, and Victor ran straight into that maelstrom of lightning.

If he'd been expecting to shrug it off, Victor might have learned a lesson. He hadn't been, however. That would have required thought, and Victor wasn't thinking about anything other than reducing Hector to a pile of bloody chunks. When he entered that red whirlwind, the lightning surrounding Hector seemed to pause in its flickering random discharges. The lightning hung in the air for a fraction of a second, brightening to the point of painful brilliance, and then, in unison, a hundred different bolts exploded into Victor's chest.

Victor had yet to see Hector's face, but he dimly heard his echoing, maniacal laughter as his vision went black, his body went numb, and he lost all sense of direction, tumbling through the air. He didn't even feel it when he crashed to the ground, sliding through the dirt, his helmet and armor scraping over rocks and prickly rough scrub brush. Victor lay insensate for several long seconds, and Hector's laughter grew increasingly mad as he recloaked himself in red sparkling Energy, lifting himself into the air and hovering as easily as a person might float in placid water.

If he'd thought Victor vanquished, he must have been disappointed when, with a *thump* that resounded through the ground beneath him, Victor's heart began to pump, no longer stunned by the electrical burst of Energy. As light flooded his eyes, Victor was immediately cognizant of the heat around his waist, the furious ticking of his dragonsteel belt—it had absorbed its fill. Still flat on his back, Victor looked up, saw Hector floating toward him, and then heard the crunch of gravel as heavy feet stepped close. He glanced to his left and saw the tall hulking stranger, noticing for the first time that he was covered in dark scales and that his face was reptilian with a short snout and bright yellow-green eyes.

Victor noticed how horns swooped back along the sides of the stranger's head as he glanced down at him. "Get up, titan. This isn't over."

"No shit," Victor growled. He flexed his core muscles and lurched to his feet, staggering a little. The lightning blast had broken his concentration, extinguishing his banner and his Berserk, but he felt fine, if a little numb. Hector still hovered twenty feet in the air, maybe three times that distant, facing the two large men. He'd stopped short at the reptilian man's approach, and when Victor regained his feet, his laughter died down.

"So you broke free of your prison, hmm?" His voice reverberated in the air, hollow and grating, as if it echoed out of a metal pipe. "No matter. I can still feel the veil star, so you failed in that regard. You'll learn you're no match for a true Death Caster, pitiful Berserker."

"He dares to mock you? After you freed the spirit of my ancestor with a single blow?" The stranger's words rumbled, deep and powerful, and Victor could hear the fury beneath them. He thought about what he'd said—did he mean the dragon skeleton? Was he related to dragons? He eyed Hector and his cloak of lightning. Would it strike so powerfully a second time? How big were his reserves of Energy? Surely he must be running low on that caustic lightning. Victor glanced at his Core and saw that most of his Energies were full, that his rage was recovering quickly, perhaps fueled by his frustration.

Movement caught his eye behind Hector, and he saw Valla limping up the slope, Midnight gripped in one hand. One of her wings was held askew, and he thought it looked injured. The sight of her like that, dressed in bloody white rags, limping, injured, clearly on her last dregs of Energy, Victor felt his fury stoking to new heights, and he began to channel it into his pathways, ready to cast Iron Berserk again. Hector, too, had noticed Valla and turned toward her, lifting a hand high. Victor bunched his legs, ready to leap at him, ready to interrupt whatever attack he meant to deliver, but then the ground shook more violently than ever, and Victor stumbled, falling to a knee.

The stranger completely lost his footing, sliding and tumbling for several feet, and Valla, too, fell, slipping out of view back down the slope she'd just mounted. Hector might have pursued her, might have turned his lightning on Victor or the stranger, but along with the rumbling of the ground, a plume of orange fiery magma erupted from the high slope of the volcano. It sparked into the night like a fiery geyser, showering down, backlighting the high citadels. The magma flew through the air, falling to the slope, gathering in clump-like pools not yet thick enough to flow. "You can kiss your veil star goodbye, asshole!" Victor shouted, gripping Lifedrinker and stalking toward the death-wielding wizard.

Hector had frozen at the eruption, but he whirled at Victor's taunt, turning to face him as he stomped forward. "Fool!" he screamed, and for the first time, Victor saw his face through the shadows of his robes and the glare of his red-lightning crown—he looked like a human man, pale with sunken black eyes and flesh so thin and stretched that Victor could see the contours of his skull and the rictus grin of his exposed black-gummed teeth. His death mask said it all—he wanted Victor dead, and he intended to kill him, but he had to deal with an emergency.

When he felt Hector gathering a massive torrent of Energy, Victor lifted Lifedrinker and pulled her back, ready to throw her, but Hector's flight was more abrupt and quicker than he'd expected. He streaked through the air in a flash of red sparks, flying like a bottle rocket straight toward the top of the waking volcano. "*Pinché* motherfucker!" Victor roared, then sprinted to where he'd seen Valla fall. He found her at the bottom of the slope, tilting a healing draught to her lips. Blood, soot, and tears streaked her face, but she smiled when she saw him approaching.

"I knew you'd come."

Heavy footfalls told him the stranger was approaching. He turned to him just in time to see his draconic fang-filled mouth snarl out a curse. "Shit-eating undead. He fears the volcano will demolish his portal and his source of strength, that green star."

Valla clambered to her feet while Victor regarded the stranger, turning to follow his gaze toward that venting tendril of lava on the side of the volcano. "Thank you for your help, stranger. I might have been in dire trouble if not for you and that mighty weapon."

"Belagog enjoys a good challenge." The man lifted his rough metallic cudgel, and Victor could see how it throbbed with Energy.

"I have to go up there. I can't let him recover. I can't let him calm the volcano. I can finish waking it."

"No! Victor . . ."

"I have to, Valla. This attack is my fault. I got stuck in the spirit plane by that fucker. Please help the troops rally, gather the survivors, and get away from here."

"We can help you, titan," the stranger said.

Victor shook his head. "No. No one can help me with this. I'm going to be mad with rage. Nothing will be safe near me."

"But you can control your rage . . ."

"No, Valla, this is different. I'll explain later, but I have to hurry. It's going to take me a few minutes to climb that slope, and I don't want that asshole to have any more time. Please! Get the troops to safety. Trust me." Victor turned to the big draconic warrior. "Thank you . . ."

"Lesh'ro'zellan. Lesh."

Victor felt a wave of gratitude for the giant fighter. Had he really saved Valla? He held out his hand, and the man took it in his rough callused grip. His hand was nearly a match for Victor's in size, and the two men nodded, locking eyes for a minute while they squeezed against each other's might.

"Victor, is there no other . . ."

"I have to do this, Valla. Get Edeya out of the house before you pack it. Please! Go now!" He turned and started walking, getting ready to cast Volcanic Fury. He didn't know exactly how it would work, but he knew that if he wanted to encourage the volcano, if he wanted to keep Hector from somehow stopping it from waking, he had to let it feel his answering fury. He'd taken two steps before he felt Valla grab his elbow and pull, forcing him to turn toward her if he didn't want to send her sprawling.

Her eyes were pooled with tears, and she practically screamed at him, "I don't know what happened, where you were, but I need you to know that I was desperate to help you. I . . . I didn't want to leave you, but the others . . ." She shook her head, grimacing at her struggle to find the right words. "I want to help!"

"I'm sorry, Valla, but the best help you can give me is to save these people. I care about them, and if I know you're saving them, I can focus on stopping Hector!" He started walking again, and she kept hold of his arm, running beside him.

"How will you get free if you wake that volcano? How will . . ."

"Valla!" Victor stopped, grabbed her shoulders, and looked into her eyes. "The volcano is not going to harm me. I promise you that much. Let me get up there and fuck this asshole up, please!"

"I love you!" she said, almost like pleading, and Victor couldn't help his hardened angry heart from melting a little. He grabbed her into a hug and squeezed her tight, his arms enveloping even her wings. She sobbed, "I want you to return. You have to survive!"

"I'm not planning to die!" Victor kissed the top of her head, still smashing her into a hug, then he let go and began to jog up the slope, and this time Valla didn't follow. When he'd made a dozen long strides away from her, he formed the pattern for Volcanic Fury and let it pull the Energy out of his Cores.

Valla stood, watching Victor run up the slope toward the gravel-and-dirt road leading up to the first citadel. He'd just reached the crest of the first low hill when she felt a surge of Energy, felt his aura break loose of his constant hold, and, as she reeled from the weight of it, she saw him expand, growing into his titan-sized form, but something was different. As his mass more than doubled, as his corded muscles bunched and piled atop each other, his body exploded with red-orange flames. He stood limned in fire, drops of magma falling to the ground around him, scorching the rocks, burning the grass and scrub.

Victor lifted Lifedrinker high, and her metallic head burst into answering red-hot brilliance. He arched his back, arms wide, and screamed a furious, horrible challenge at the mountain. His voice rumbled and echoed over the hillsides, crashing off the high rocky slopes and cliffs. Valla was distracted at first by the war cry, but then she saw that Victor had turned back toward her. He stared at her for a long terrifying moment, his eyes burning like white-hot flames, smoke flowing out of his nostrils as his chest heaved and pumped. The worst part of that gaze, of those blazing orbs, was that she saw not a single hint of recognition in them. She didn't dare move, fearing that he'd change course and fly down that hill, intent on ripping her to shreds.

As he seethed and stared, fire dripping off his hands, the ground burning under his feet, a distant rumble shook the hillside, and the magma flow high on the mountain erupted again, showering the night with its orange glow. Victor turned away from Valla and, on seeing the eruption, roared his fury again and began running up the slope, loping over the near vertical climb as if it were nothing. "That was scary," Valla hissed, her voice shaking.

"He's awe-inspiring. I haven't felt that cold bite of fear in my heart since I was a hatchling." The stranger's deep voice rumbled beside her, and Valla turned quickly, startled by the stranger's—Lesh's—proximity.

"Thank you again." She turned to the encampment. "I have to do what Victor asked."

"And I will aid you." Lesh turned, looking over Valla's head toward the distant signs of battle. "The dark-winged warrior, the one with twin blades, has led the soldiers in an offensive, driving back and crushing most of the remaining undead."

"You can see so far?"

"Aye. I fear you've lost many soldiers this night, but if the titan can destroy the undead base, their lives will have been well spent."

Valla frowned, not liking the gigantic fighter's pragmatism. "I'll fly ahead. I have to get my friend out of our travel home before we hurry away from here."

"Yes. I'll run quickly behind. Best if I stay with you so the soldiers know not to attack me." He nodded, his dark eyes bright in the darkness. Then he turned back to the slope where Victor still climbed, a bright humanoid torch leaving a trail of fire, and he added, "We have enough time to flee. He'll be a few minutes making that climb, and then we don't know how long it will take him to succeed in his task. Even so, I've seen many a volcano in my day, and this one is old and sluggish. We'll get free of danger. Go now! I will hurry behind."

Valla nodded, stretching her wings, relieved to feel only a slight stiffness; the healing potion had done its work. She snapped them downward, sending Energy into her pathways, and soon she was soaring upward and then almost immediately angling down to glide toward the glimmering jade travel home. She'd just begun to descend when another rumble shook the night, and a new plume of lava erupted from the side of the mountain, this one higher, nearly at the caldera. Seeing it, Valla realized most of the green-tinted fog was gone.

She could see clearly all the way to the summit of the high volcanic mountain, and much more easily, she could see the citadels outlined in orange light from the rapidly gathering lava high on the slopes. As her eyes fell on the first, closest of the keeps, she saw its gates were burning, smashed open. Victor had already broken through. "Go, love. Go with speed and vengeance and destroy them all," she breathed, spiraling down to land outside the travel home. "Destroy them all and hurry back to me."

58

CALDERA OF MADNESS

Through the hazy red fire of his fury, Victor could see figures on the long arching span that crossed the raging waters. He didn't care what they were doing. The idea that they might be planning something nefarious to break the bridge or send him tumbling into the waters didn't enter his mind. He had a singular goal—find the *pendejo* who flew away from him, who fled their fight, and smash him to a pulp. He ran, loping on long powerful legs, leaving a trail of smoking, burning footsteps. Fire flickered in his wake whether he traversed grass, dirt, or stone. Lifedrinker buzzed with anticipation, hunger, and glee; she was ablaze, a partner in his fiery rage.

When Victor mounted the bridge and began to sprint toward the distant figures, an Energy Charge might have been an apt choice, the right thing to close that gap in a hurry and put an end to whatever they were doing. Unfortunately, Victor's singular mindset, driven by the rage boiling through his pathways, didn't leave room for other spells. When the stone beneath his feet lurched and gunshot-loud cracks erupted in the stone, he didn't panic, didn't react other than to pump his legs harder. When the arch shattered ahead of him, the stone crumbling down into the abyss, falling to the white-capped river, he watched the group of robed figures plummet to their doom, a sacrifice for their undead master.

Maybe if he weren't so enraged, Victor would have reacted differently. Maybe he would have turned and tried to outrun the crumbling stone. Victor didn't slow, however. Engorged by rage and fire, he pushed harder, and when the falling curtain of stones was right before him, he bunched his legs and leapt for the far side of the gap. Whatever mad strength powered his burning titanic form pushed his Titanic Leap to new levels, and he soared through the air, a smoking comet hell-bent on destruction. He crashed onto the intact portion of the bridge near the far edge. Showers of sparks, droplets of magma, and black smoke burst into the air with his impact. In two heartbeats, Victor was pounding up the ramp away from the fallen span toward the second gateway citadel.

Just as he had when he charged the first tall keep, Victor focused on the gates and ignored all else. Arrows burst into flame as they touched his form. Firebolts and lightning glanced off him, insignificant as the thrall-like subordinates who threw them. By the time he smashed into the high stone gates, he must have been running more than sixty miles per hour, and with a lowered shoulder, he impacted them with the ferocity of a hurtling granite boulder. As he shattered the Energy-enhanced crossbeam, the crack was so loud that it echoed up and down the mountain like a bomb blast.

Victor hardly slowed as the gates slammed open, and dense fragments of timber and stone exploded away from him, ripping through the puny defenders crowding the gatehouse tunnel. He steamrolled through them, moving too fast, his form too large, his Energy too hot and caustic for them to withstand. They burst into flames as he approached, screaming their silent screams. Victor barely acknowledged their existence—some kind of skeletal warriors in ragged armor lined up with zombies, shamblers, and ghouls. They were nothing more than a minor impediment, like brambles on a path, something to stumble on before he found sound footing and exploded forth again.

In moments, Victor had cleared the second citadel and was racing up the road, climbing toward the top of the mountain, his giant grumbling brother. He knew his prey was up there. He knew the Death Caster was doing something Victor wanted to stop, but he didn't care. The only thing he really wanted was to see him ripped apart, reduced to several hunks of smoldering ash. He rounded a corner in the road, and a wall of ice sheeted up from the ground before him. Dense frozen Energy radiated from it, and Victor didn't have time to slow, didn't have time to jump. He lowered his shoulder and pushed on.

He felt the cold sapping his heat, felt it pulling the hot magma-rich Energy out of his pathways. He felt the fire limning his form dim and the white-hot flames in his eyes fading, but then he hit the ice. It resisted him for a fraction of a second, but Victor bunched his legs and drove forward, a rage-fueled locomotive hell-bent on ripping up the track. The ice began to crack, and then it was all over—Victor burst through it in a shower of spraying shards, and his heat flared back to life. His vision brightened, his form burst into flame anew, and he powered on. He caught sight of a blue-robed figure kneeling on the side of the road, his skeletal hands gripping his head in agony. With a mad laugh, Victor swiped his blazing axe through the undead elementalist, cleaving his skull in twain.

He saw a curve ahead, realized the road switched back and forth, and impatient to get to his quarry, he faced the mountainside and jumped, clearing twenty yards of slope to land higher up the road. Victor was too mad with battle lust, too engorged by fire and fury to think about his Energy reserves, but if he hadn't been, he would have noted that his rage-attuned Energy was slowly burning down, and his magma-fueled Breath Core was more than half empty. He didn't, though; it wasn't even a flicker of concern in his mind.

Victor continued apace, leaping to avoid long switchbacks several more times, and soon he was nearing the mountain's top, the volcanic caldera. Luck was with him that night, for when he rounded that last bend, he came close to the lava flow that had erupted from the mountain's side. When he grew near, he felt the fury in the air. He felt the kindred heat and anger of the mountain beneath him, but sharper, richer, thick enough to breathe, thick enough to channel almost passively into his Breath Core. As he felt that decadent power flowing into him, as he felt the rumble under his feet and heard the mountain's anger, Victor paused to lift his head to the sky and howl madly into the night.

His voice, deep at first, then rising into a wild ululation, echoed off the stones, reverberating back and forth through the many canyons surrounding the tall, high-sloped mountain. Smoke and cinders escaped his mouth as he screamed his madness, and the mountain heard him. It bucked wildly, but Victor moved with the motion instinctually, not bothered in the least. The lava flows that had already burst from the mountain's ancient shoulders geysered forth again, and Victor heard the distant sounds of more destruction above him. The mountain was waking, and those in the caldera were feeling its wrath.

He pulled back his lips, revealing a hungry savage grin limned in black smoke as he leapt into motion, pounding up the slope, aiming for that rough stony rampart behind which he knew the caldera valley opened up. He saw fortifications around the road, battlements, gates, and even siege equipment, but it was all scattered and abandoned. He didn't bother smashing the gates.

Instead, he kept running and leapt over the wall, only twenty feet high. At the apex of his flight, he saw a glorious view of the caldera valley, and what he saw brought more mad laughter out of him.

Unlike the version on the spirit plane, this material version of the caldera was packed with structures—towers, walls, and buildings of all shapes and sizes. He didn't laugh because he saw them; he laughed because they were crumbling, and fires were everywhere. He saw crowds fleeing through broken cobbled roads, scrabbling around collapsed stone buildings, and hordes of undead furiously working to dig rubble out from around the wreckage. What spurred his madness the most, though, was the scene at the center of the caldera.

Hundreds of robed figures knelt in a circle around the high, flickering, dim veil star. Beneath it, on a stone platform, sat a dark rip in the fabric of reality. Victor wasn't in a state of mind to contemplate the meaning of the weird rent in space, but something told him that his quarry might try to escape through it. Even in his madness, he knew the kneeling magic users were working to keep the green light ablaze and that it was somehow connected to that shimmering doorway to another world. As he crashed to the ground, sliding down the gravel and dirt of the roadway, he bunched his legs and sprinted toward the distant scene.

Thousands of undead and living thralls were between him and his target, but he paid them no heed. If they got in his way, they would die like those in the citadels. If they fled before his approach, they might live long enough to feel the volcano's wrath. Either way, Victor didn't care. He was tall, more than eighteen feet in his titanic form, and he saw over the buildings to the caldera's center.

He saw a long line of figures forming, many carrying heavy bags and some bearing children in their arms. His eyes were good, superhuman in their fiery glory. He could see through the darkness as though it were noon with a bright sun in the sky. He could pick out faces among those distant figures and see that they weren't undead, not all of them, but Victor didn't care in his state. Enemies were trying to flee him, servants of the bastard who'd tried to kill people he cared about. Dim visions of Valla's face floated through his mind, snatches of memory when they'd been in bed together, fought together, laughed together.

The images were almost abstract in their vagueness, but they were enough to stoke his rage, to remind him that these people and creatures ahead of him had tried to kill someone he cared about. Moreover, the air in the caldera was so thick with magma-fueled Energy, so heavy with the volcano's fury, that he felt he was swimming through it. He could feel it flowing over him, brushing his skin, fanning the flames that flickered and lashed out behind him. He could taste it in every breath. He could feel it pour into his Breath Core, stream into his pathways, and ignite, joining his rage-attuned Energy to power his Volcanic Fury.

He grew hotter and hotter, more and more furious as he charged into the caldera. He began to lose focus even on chasing Hector, began to look for things near at hand to destroy. When he jumped over a fallen tower, and the volcano shuddered again, sending an arcing spray of magma into the air on the far side of the caldera, he paused and screamed again, his mouth forming mangled, nearly inarticulate words. "Come on, *hermano!*" He glimpsed a crowd of undead digging away at some rubble and couldn't help himself from charging into them, laying about with Lifedrinker.

He was so large, his furious heat so potent that they withered before him, falling back, scrabbling to get away, but he pursued, hacking, kicking, grabbing, and throwing them until all were dead or scattered out of his sight. The green veil star pulsed, catching his attention, and when he looked at it and saw it was brighter than before, his eyes burned so intensely that anyone watching him would have looked away in pain. Victor began to rant as he charged toward the veil star, words that made no sense, noises that probably wouldn't have been considered words to anyone listening.

He didn't know what he was saying; he didn't care. He was trying to vent some of the fury that boiled in his veins and pathways. He was trying to release some of the pressure. He indiscriminately swung Lifedrinker left and right, sometimes chopping her into wood, sometimes into stone, and sometimes into a foe. She screamed and screamed, just as furious as he. She was white hot with fiery fury, and when Victor burst into the clearing around the veil star, he lifted her high and threw her at it. It wasn't a planned attack. It wasn't something he'd ever have done if he were himself, but he wanted that thing dead, and so did Lifedrinker.

The idea of "killing" the veil star wasn't a rational one. It wasn't something Victor would think to try if he had a shred of reason in his mind. Still, Lifedrinker didn't object, and his throw was true—she flew like a smoking white-hot comet, ripping the air in concussive shockwaves that thundered over the flat stone clearing, sending the more frail of Hector's wizards sprawling. When she hit the veil star, Victor saw, in his red-tinted madness, the green glow shrink to a tiny point, eclipsed by the blazing heat of Lifedrinker's flames, and then it expanded, rolling out like an inflating ball of dense green energy.

The globe of green and fiery Energy expanded to something that looked to be a good fifty feet in diameter, seeming to suck the noise and light out of the caldera. As the green Energy shifted more and more to yellow-white, as it became more and more a roiling ball of fire, everything was still. Everyone was quiet for a pregnant heartbeat, and then the massive ball of roiling Energy exploded, washing the center of the caldera in fiery white-hot flames. Victor arched his back and roared, watching the fire roll toward him, stomping toward it, hungry for its touch.

As the flames engulfed him, he felt Lifedrinker in them and knew she'd won her battle with the veil star. Whatever it was, whatever had hung in the air up there, she'd pierced it, and she'd overcome it. Of course, the explosion and the fire did nothing to quench the furnace in his heart nor in that of the volcano. Victor rushed forward through the flames, hands clenching and unclenching, eyes mad with the lust for violence. The volcano bucked and shook, more lava flows erupting out of the stony ground, and some part of Victor knew it was done—the volcano was waking, and nothing would stop it.

He charged among the hundreds of robed Death Casters, snatching up those who still moved, those who'd shielded themselves from the veil star's destruction. He threw them, used them as weapons, smashing them about, ripping them limb from limb. He shrugged off magical attacks, nothing fazing him. None of Hector's apprentices, at least those still gathered there at the center of the volcano, had anything near enough power to penetrate Victor's furious constitution or to leave a wound that his magma-filled blood wouldn't instantly heal. All they did was further infuriate him, further drive him into a berserker frenzy as he sought the true target of his wrath.

As he ripped the arms from a screaming, ashen-faced mage, he looked through the mist of blood toward the central platform where the rip in space still hung. He saw Hector's people wildly charging through, saw tall powerful figures trying to hold some of them back, and though he couldn't contemplate their intentions, Victor saw them as a better outlet for his frustrated rage. He leapt toward them, coming down among a crowd of fleeing people. Victor snatched a woman up and, as she burst into flame, threw her at the front of the line, smashing her smoldering corpse into one of the tall guardians of the gateway.

The man, dressed in black plate that might have been familiar to a rational Victor, might have reminded him of the reavers he'd slain weeks earlier, tumbled backward, bouncing over the stone dais. At the same time, his companion slammed the visor down on his helmet, lifted a massive black-bladed two-handed sword, and charged straight at Victor. The people fleeing screamed and cried, running to and fro in a panic, trying to get away from Victor, but having nowhere to go—madness had overcome the caldera, geysers of flame were exploding everywhere, the ground was rumbling and shaking, and the air was thick with ash and smoke.

When the sword-wielding giant, a good four feet shy of Victor's height, reached him, hacking down with that mighty blade, Victor caught it in his left hand and squeezed. The blade bit his flesh and opened an outlet for his fiery blood. It ran down the blade, turning the black metal orange with heat, and the warrior cried out inside his helmet, letting go as the leather-wrapped hilt burst into flame. Victor pounded his right fist down on that helmet, smashing his head with a sickening series of wet crunches. When the warrior collapsed, Victor stepped forward, resting his foot on his chest.

He eyed the rip in space as the corpse began to smoke, and the metal armor began to glow with heat. Had his quarry gone through already? The only thing stopping Victor from madly charging through was a feeling in his gut that his foe was still here, a deep-seated desire not to be fooled into going somewhere where he'd lose track of him. Absent Hector to fight, he had to find an outlet for his rage, so he furiously scanned the platform for a target, and that's when he saw, just beyond the portal to another world, a floating, spinning stone, dimly glowing with gold and silver runes.

Victor stalked forward, crunching the corpse, now ash inside hot metal, and angled himself around the rift, getting a better look at the floating stone. Something deep in the back of his mind said, "System." Was this the source of the portal? Was it something else? Victor pulled back his lips, exposing his insane grin as he took a deep breath, inhaling until he felt his lungs would burst. If Hector wanted to hide, he'd take out his frustration on this thing. Maybe if he could break it, the portal would close. Just as he was about to exhale, to bathe the floating stone in the magma fury of his breath, a tremendous crack of thunder shook the air, and a massive bolt of red lightning hit him in the shoulder, sending him stumbling toward the rift.

The ground lurched as the volcano continued to wake, and Victor might have fallen, might have rolled right into that gap through time and space, but he was awash with Volcanic Fury. He was brother to the mountain, and he walked along the bucking ground as though it were placid and flat. He avoided the rift and turned to see where his enemy was. His shoulder was sore, but he could feel it rapidly healing; Hector's lightning was powerful, but a single bolt wasn't enough to stop him, or really to even give him pause.

Hector rode on a cloud of charged air. It crackled with red electricity, and as he swooped by, firing another bolt of lightning at him, Victor saw Hector's pale rictus face beneath his blazing red crown. The sight renewed his fury and reminded him of why he was there. Something deep in him woke up at the proximity of his foe—something with a stiff back and pride that wouldn't be quenched by fury alone. Who was this worm floating around, daring to taunt him with tickles of lightning? Who was this man who'd threatened the friends and loved ones of a mighty Quinametzin?

Victor took two steps away from the rift and stooped to pick up Lifedrinker from where she'd fallen, her blade buried in the stone. As soon as he pulled her free, she burst into flames again, and he heard her seething whisper in his mind.

"Come, love! Let us lay waste to this fool and bask in the glory of the volcano's fury!"

The words were sharp and spoke straight to his soul—the only way he heard them, for Victor's ears buzzed with fury. His mind could focus only on his hatred of the man floating about above him. He stood before the rift, staring at Hector, clenching and unclenching his fist on Lifedrinker's haft. He could feel his rage building, could feel his bones and flesh igniting with it. How much could he take? How much of the mountain's horrible temper could he absorb before he burst?

Hector swooped toward him, streaking like a Roman candle, and Victor swiped at him, forcing him to veer away. Had he been trying to get past him? Trying to enter the rift? The idea of his foe running away, disappearing through that hole, was so upsetting that Victor felt his rage cool slightly as his mind raced for a way to keep him here. Could he close the rift by breaking the stone? *Could* he break the stone? Lifedrinker was a powerful weapon, but Victor knew she was nothing to the System. Would he risk her by smashing her against that System Stone? He felt his rage cool further as his thoughts raced, and then Hector hit him with another red thunderbolt.

The burning shock shook him enough to knock the thoughts out of his head. Hector raced forward again, clearly trying to swoop past him to the rift, but Victor wasn't stunned, just refocused. He squared off with the Death Caster and lifted his axe. Hector jerked away, streaking off into the caldera at the last instant, clearly afraid of Lifedrinker's bite.

"Throw me again, love!"

Lifedrinker's hungry plea rang through Victor's mind, and he almost did it, almost listened to her, but he had another action in mind and was too stubborn with rage to turn away from it. He stared at Hector, watching him, inhaling, breathing deep into his belly, pulling Energy into his Breath Core just as he'd done on the spirit plane. He pumped his lungs in and out, gathering the Volcano's furious magma-fueled Energy, packing his pathways with it, and letting it seep into his blood, flesh, and bones. As Hector swooped around, ready for another pass, gathering red crackling lightning on the tip of a dark scepter, Victor's grin grew, and the madness overtook him again. He laughed, and yellow flames licked his lips, sending black smoke into the air with the sounds of his insanity.

59

ESCAPE

Rather than attack or try to charge past him, Hector stymied Victor's desire to fight by hovering a good twenty yards away and shouting, "Fool! You've conjured ruin upon us all! Let me leave, and you can rule over this wasted land!" Victor didn't reply but shifted, putting himself squarely before the portal. His grin widened, and as he exhaled, black smoke tendrils drifted out of his nostrils. The message was clear—if Hector wanted to flee this world, he'd need to remove Victor. In wild frustration, Hector jerked back his head and screamed, his crown of red lightning sparking and dancing with Energy, creating an arcing feedback loop with the black scepter that Hector raised aloft. With a grimace of desperate determination, he raced forward, blasting Victor with a torrent of arcing, writhing crimson electricity.

Victor was full to bursting with magma-attuned Energy. His Core was overflowing, on the verge of another expansion. He'd stretched it to its limit with his lungs, inhaling the heavy thick Energy of the volcano, cultivating as he stood there, waiting for Hector's next attack. As that blast of arcane thunderous Energy arced out of Hector's dark scepter, he took it full in the center of his chest. It burned and pulsed and would probably have stunned or killed a lesser foe, someone not so maddened with his own fury and the echoing, long-slumbering rage of a mountain. As it was, the powerful blast only served to contract Victor's lungs further as he exhaled a plume of hot air so thick with Energy that it misted the air more like a liquid than a gas before igniting with a *whoosh*.

The jet of superheated magma-infused fire sucked the oxygen out of the air as it engulfed Hector, cooking through his cloud of charged red Energy. The Death Caster screamed and gathered up all his reserves to save himself, cloaking himself in a red crackling shield and girding his flesh and bones with cold blue death-attuned Energy, clearly something he'd been holding back. Victor tracked him as he descended to the ground, still spraying forth a plume of magma. The Energy coming from his mouth was dense and thick and hot, but it wasn't aflame; it didn't burn until it was several inches from his lips. From there, it streamed like a demon's fire hose, bright with destructive power, unrelenting as it coated his foe, slowly burning through his defenses.

Victor had made incredible gains with his Breath Core in a brief span of time, all thanks to the Volcano's radiated Energy. It was that heat, that magma-fueled rage in the air, that allowed Victor to send forth a plume of destructive force that would otherwise be beyond his young Magma Core. More than that, his Volcanic Fury doubled his potential, extending his breath and increasing its potency. All that said, he only had so much; he couldn't maintain his Volcanic Fury with an empty Breath Core, and some instinctive self-preservation wouldn't allow him to breathe it dry. After blasting Hector for several seconds with fiery destruction, Victor stopped and, heaving with the effort, began to suck air into his lungs again, restarting the cycle that would send Energy into his Core and then into his pathways, extending his Volcanic Fury's duration.

Hector was crouched low, his arms above his head. Victor had watched his magma-based fire destroy Hector's crimson shield of electricity, and he'd watched as Hector fought to sustain himself by expending a massive amount of cold, grave-scented, death-attuned power. Though he was hell-bent on destruction, his enraged mind incapable of clever quips or convoluted planning, he understood that Hector was spent, that he'd nearly exhausted himself. He wouldn't be flying out of reach anytime soon. Victor lifted Life-drinker and, on long powerful titan-sized legs, he stalked toward his prey. He grinned, a burning fiery smile that spread from ear to ear, exposing flame-licked teeth as a low, rumbling growl built in his gut.

Hector stood, backing rapidly away from the much larger titan, his arms high, sputtering blue wisps of smoky Energy tendrils gathering on his fingertips. He couldn't go far. Behind him, the mountain had shaken open a rift in the ground, and hot billows of black smoky air drifted up from it. Victor's growl intensified as his mouth began to salivate, dripping from his toothy grin in orange fiery droplets to sizzle on the rough blackened stone. He was savoring the moment, his fury hot and smoldering, ready to feel the satisfaction as Lifedrinker split the Death Caster from neck to crotch.

As though she could see the images playing through Victor's mind, Lifedrinker began to hum in anticipation, vibrating and bucking in his hand as he lifted her high. When he was just two titan-sized strides away, Hector lashed out with spectral blue misty claws. They flickered and faded in the hot air, hardly scratching Victor's neck and groin. Hector had aimed for his softest, least armored body parts and failed to make an impact; the Death Caster was truly spent, and his remaining Energy affinity was ineffectual in the magma-thick air. Victor lifted Lifedrinker, and too mad to form any words, he grunted savagely, swiping her downward.

His blow should surely have destroyed his enemy; Lifedrinker's smoldering edge was wide enough, and with Victor's strength behind her, she would have cleaved him in half lengthwise. Something strange happened, however. Billowing steam rose from the ground and materialized out of the hot air, clouding Victor's view. A high-pitched screech resounded, echoing weirdly through the vaporous air, but not before Victor ripped Lifedrinker downward, aiming to destroy Hector utterly. She rippled through the steam, sending it whirling away on superheated winds, and before he could stop the downward chop short, she bit into the stony ground with a tremendous crash and an explosion of basalt shards. Hector was gone.

Victor whirled in time to see a familiar ghostly form. Victoria hovered near the rift, and before her, condensing into flesh from the hot moist air, was Hector; somehow she'd transported him in her foggy tendrils away from Victor's destructive blow. Victor's fury soared to new heights. His vision darkened to murderous crimson so dense that he felt he was swimming in blood. He roared his frustration, fire erupting from his mouth, the flames limning his shoulders and arms torching upward in white-hot tendrils. He focused on Hector and ran, lifting Lifedrinker high again.

Victoria didn't stick around to watch; she spun and, trailing a cackling laugh, soared through the portal. Hector wasn't a fool; he could see his destruction written on Victor's face. Only two steps from the rift, he leapt for it, and despite Victor's explosive speed, his mad surge of muscular rage-driven power, he was just shy of catching the Death Caster before he hit the weird tear in the universe. Victor screamed in wild frustrated fury, continuing with his diving charge, hacking Lifedrinker at Hector's leaping form despite knowing he would come up short.

Hector wore a desperate grin, almost as if he couldn't believe he was still alive, that he would escape. As his outstretched arms hit the rift, though, they were rebuffed. He came up against the tear in space and stopped short as if he'd hit a solid wall. Victor, unable to comprehend what had just happened, didn't care—he finished his diving chop, and Lifedrinker buried herself in the center of Hector's spine, splitting through his torso and pinning him to the stone platform as she bit into it. Victor slammed into the stony ground beside Hector's much smaller form, still gripping Lifedrinker. He twisted her left and right, growling in savage pleasure as Hector screamed and wailed, thrashing his arms and legs.

Hector's lips twisted into a grimace, and he wheezed a defeated curse: "Goddamned System." Then Lifedrinker's ministrations rendered him incapable of speech, and Victor was too furious for words. The only sounds beyond the bubbling of lava, the rumble of the mountain, and the weird hissing crackle of the rift above them were Victor's growls and Hector's desperate mewling gasps. Lifedrinker bucked and throbbed, pulling the dregs out of Hector's Core. Victor watched through a deep crimson haze as the Death Caster's pale drawn flesh began to blacken and crumble from his bones in a fine powdery ash.

The anger in Victor's heart throbbed with each beat, and as he watched his nemesis crumble into dust, he felt a deep, profound satisfaction. He'd destroyed his enemy, answered the challenge to his bloodline, avenged himself against the man who'd trapped him, and redeemed his failure, his mistake that had enabled this man's foul attack on his friends and soldiers. When nothing was left of Hector other than a pile of black ash, a hissing, sizzling *pop* resounded through the air, and Victor looked up in time to see the rip in the air disappear in a brilliant flash of white light.

As the mountain bucked and throbbed, he stood to his feet, and still engorged by furious magma, he was barely able to comprehend the System messages blinking before his eyes, one of which had been there for several minutes already:

*****Transport Refused: A System invasion commander may not flee the field during combat.*****

*****Congratulations! Challenge of Conquest Completed! You have put an end to the invasion from the world of Dark Ember. Prince Hector of Heart Rot is no more. The enemy stronghold will suffer imminent destruction. Should you survive, claim your reward at any other outpost System Stone. Rewards due: Colony Stone and a Chest of Conquest.*****

Victor glanced at the text, flicking the messages away in his rage-addled state. He turned to look around the caldera. Nothing in sight lived. He saw flowing magma, jets of superheated black smoke and steam, and trembling, lurching stone in every direction. The air was dark with smoke, though he thought he could glimpse some brighter light in one direction. He wasn't sure why, but he began to laugh as he loped that way, fearlessly stepping into magma, riding the roiling, heaving ground as though he was born to it. He could hear the angry rumble of the mountain beneath him, could feel it ready to burst.

"Yes!" he roared, his voice thick with wild, mad laughter. "Yes! Shout your fury to the world, *hermano*!"

"Gather the dead as we run! Put them in your storage containers," Valla screamed, looking up to the billowing clouds of black smoke and thick orange lava flows beginning to pour from the distant volcano. The sky had grown light with the dawn, illuminating the destruction all around the remnants of the ninth cohort. She'd never seen a volcano before, didn't know what it would be like if it erupted, but something in her knew they had to get farther away. She led by example, dashing from body to body, throwing them into her storage rings. The soldiers did the same, and she could see Kethelket's people flitting on their dark wings up and down around the scattered battle-field and broken encampment.

When she'd picked up at least a dozen corpses and didn't see any others nearby, she gathered Edeya's still unconscious form into her arms and chan-neled Energy into her wings, flapping them to bring her aloft. "To the west! Rally to the west!" she screamed, and though she wanted to streak away, rid-ing the wind to a distant hilltop far from the volcano, she held herself back, watching the poor beleaguered soldiers still afoot, trying to hurry away from the enraged mountain. She couldn't get an accurate count in the messy spo-radic line, but she didn't think there were more than a few hundred.

Less than half of the cohort and the reserves had survived the night, but judging from the System message she'd just seen, at least the battle was won. She hoped Rellia and Borrius would be smart enough to heed their instinct, that deep-seated primal desire to live, and get away from the rumbling, angry mountain. Surely, they'd already put many miles between themselves and its smoldering slopes. Spiraling slowly, using the wind to keep herself aloft with-out straining her muscles, she looked down at Edeya, still wan, still hardly alive, and she wondered what it would take to wake her. The conquest was over—Hector was dead. Why hadn't she recovered?

Occasionally, she'd swoop low and shout encouragement to the fleeing soldiers. They were exhausted, but they were Energy users, and the Glorious Ninth had plenty of troops in the fourth and fifth tiers. With a grimace, Valla acknowledged the cold truth that most of the deaths had probably come from the lower-tier ranks. These survivors, bloody, filthy, and exhausted though they were, flew over the ground on powerful legs, gaining strength and momentum despite their hard labor—their Cores were recovering.

As their flight lengthened into dozens of minutes, they received another boost as streams of thick potent yellow Energy began to flow toward them from the distant battlefield. The System had finally agreed that the fight was won and was delivering their reward. Valla knew what was coming and didn't want to be airborne when the surge hit her. She watched as the Naghelli and a handful of Ghelli flyers came to the same conclusion, hurrying to the ground ahead of the rushing yellow ribbons.

She'd just landed when Lam fluttered down beside her. "I was looking for her! Thank you for bringing her out!"

Valla held Edeya close, offering Lam a fierce smile. "Victor told me to get her."

"Thank the roots he awoke. Whatever he did up in that volcano, it won the day. Do you think . . ." Lam let her words trail away, but Valla knew what she was going to ask—did she think Victor had lived?

"I don't feel like he's dead, but I suppose I can't really know. I hope he can get away before . . ."

Her words were cut off as a river of Energy smashed into her, and a similar one hit Lam. They both cried out in ecstasy, and though she tried not to, Valla dropped Edeya to the hilltop as her arms flew wide, and she lost herself in the euphoria.

Congratulations! You have achieved level 60 Sword Dancer, gained 20 agility and 20 dexterity, and have 16 attribute points to allocate.

Level 60 Class refinement is available. Class refinement is permanent. Ordeni Energy cultivators will next be offered a Class refinement selection at level 70. To view your options and make your selection, access the menu through your status page.

The message awaited her when she fell to her feet and regained her mental faculties. "Two levels," she said to Lam as the other woman staggered to her feet.

"Three!" Lam replied, stooping to pick up Edeya. Valla grasped her shoulder, stopping her short.

"Let me carry her. My wings can ride the wind." She'd seen how the Ghelli flew; they had to flap their little sets of wings rapidly, and she knew it was tiring. Lam herself had told her she couldn't fly very far, even when rested.

"Ah. Thank you, then."

Valla stooped to pick up Edeya, and that's when the mountain exploded. Even where she stood, some six leagues away, Valla was thrown to the ground. The air boomed with a continuous thunderclap sound that temporarily deafened her. As she struggled to her hands and knees, eyes on the distant peak, the ground bucking and shaking underneath her, she felt the flow of hot furious Energy rippling through the air, dwarfing the Energies in her Core like grains of sand whipped aloft by a hurricane.

The mountain was ejecting a plume of ash and smoke high into the sky, towering toward the firmament, flashing and rippling with menacing colors—grays, blacks, and lower down, reds and oranges. The sky darkened as the ash cloud spread, and Valla finally regained her feet. Orange rivers ran down from the mountain's peak, and she wondered how far they'd reach before the volcano's fury was spent.

"It feels like Victor!" Lam screamed, and Valla knew what she meant—the fury and hatred in the air reminded her of Victor's aura when she'd first felt its full weight, though it was a thousand times heavier.

"We need to keep moving!" She bent to pick up Edeya, and as she and Lam retook the air, she could see the surviving members of the ninth cohort had similar ideas; they raced pell-mell away from the mountain toward the distant clear sky in the west.

When Victor came back to himself, he was utterly disoriented. He sat up, blinking rapidly, staring at his environment for several long minutes before blurry memories began to fill the gaps in his mind. He sat on a warm ash-covered stone, and looking around, he realized it was a boulder the size of a small house. All around him was a dim smoky wasteland. Leafless, blackened trees dotted a nearby hillside, but most vegetation was gone entirely, with nothing on the ground but ash, as far as he could see. A ticking, steaming river of half-hardened lava filled a gulley to his left, and the sky was dark gray, barely lit by the faint white orb of the sun overhead.

"Volcano," he muttered, his throat dry and his voice hoarse. In a series of images and feelings, he remembered what had happened, though it was like looking at a slideshow in his memory, not a movie. Flashes of the roiling caldera, the rift to Dark Ember, Victoria escaping, Hector dying to Life-drinker's bite . . . "Lifedrinker!" Victor furiously scrabbled at her harness, only to find it gone; all of his belongings were gone save his helmet, his wyrm-scale vest, his dragonsteel belt, his bracer with Khul Bach's shard, and his various storage rings. Panic sending his heart racing, he leapt to his feet. Like a cold shower, relief washed over him when he saw Lifedrinker lying on the boulder behind where he'd been sitting.

"Thank God, *chica*." He breathed a deep sigh of relief, running his hands through his hair. He looked down at himself, half-naked as he was, and chuckled, pulling some new pants and boots out of his ring. "Shit!" He patted at his waist, realizing that his older dimensional pouches hadn't survived. It had been so long since he'd organized his things that he didn't even know what items he'd lost. Regardless, he knew his most precious belongings were in his rings; he hardly touched the pouches anymore.

Once he'd put on a new pair of self-sizing and repairing leather pants and a pair of sturdy boots, he scooped up Lifedrinker and turned his attention to the System messages that at some point during his madness, he'd shoved to the side of his vision.

He vaguely remembered the first one:

*****Transport Refused: A System invasion commander may not flee the field during combat.*****

Victor laughed when he read it. He laughed and laughed, slapping his hands together as he imagined Hector's thoughts when he'd realized he wasn't going to escape. "That poor *pendejo!* First, he thought I'd kill him, then he thought Victoria had saved him, then the System yanked it away!" Shaking his head in amusement, Victor looked at the next message:

*****Congratulations! Challenge of Conquest Completed! You have put an end to the invasion from the world of Dark Ember. Prince Hector of Heart Rot is no more. The enemy stronghold will suffer imminent destruction. Should you survive, claim your reward at any other outpost System Stone. Rewards due: Colony Stone and a Chest of Conquest.*****

"Right." He turned in a slow circle, looking through the dim smoky air. He could see the volcano's slope a dozen miles or more behind him. It no longer shook, and only a half-hearted plume of smoke continued to rise from its peak. The lava flows were still orange near the top but faded as they descended the slopes. "You were pissed, but you shouted out your rage all at once, eh, *hermano?*" He turned back to the System messages:

*****Congratulations! You have achieved level 59 Battlemaster and gained 20 strength, 18 vitality, 8 agility, 8 dexterity, 6 will, and 6 intelligence.*****

*****Congratulations! Your Breath Core has advanced: Improved 3.*****

"Two levels and a Breath Core rank, huh?" Victor nodded, looking up at the top of the smoking mountain. "Thanks, Hector." His amusement was short-lived when he thought back further than his victory over the Death Caster. What damage had been done? How many lives had been lost because of Hector's ambush, because Victor had let himself get trapped? He turned and looked over the ash-covered wasteland, wondering how many of his friends had escaped.

"Valla . . ." He reached into his Core and used some inspiration-attuned Energy to summon Guapo. As he swung onto his back, the mustang knew where he wanted to go—the System said to collect his reward at an outpost, and the closest one was the Sea Keep, west of the mountain. Valla had been on the same side of the mountain. It stood to reason that she and the surviving members of the Ninth would go that way. "Let's go, buddy." He slapped Guapo's shoulder and leaned forward, urging the horse to pick up the pace. Hope and dread battled in his heart as he raced toward the distant sliver of blue sky.

60

COMING TO GRIPS

Riding on Guapo, it only took a few hours before Victor cleared the area covered in soot by the volcano's eruption. Even so, the sky remained dark, the sun obscured by the ash in the air, so much so that it felt as if he was riding under heavy cloud cover. He might have thought that was the case if not for the gritty, stinging nature of the breeze that blew into his face as the mustang charged over hills, raced through meadows, and splashed through streams and rivers.

Essentially, Victor retraced his journey from the Sea Keep with Valla, though he veered to follow signs of the Ninth's passage. On many occasions, he spotted their tracks and even passed by more than one campsite, which made him wonder—how long had he been mad with the volcano's rage? How long had it been since it erupted?

To Victor, it felt as if he'd awoken the day after his battle with Hector, but if that were the case, he would have passed the fleeing soldiers by now; Guapo was far faster than they. So in contrast to his relaxing journey from the sea with Valla, Victor urged Guapo to hurry, and he didn't stop to rest. The spirit mustang tore through the countryside, and despite his thundering passage, he hardly left a trail in his wake. Where other mounts might need Victor to skirt a rocky slope, Guapo pounded up it without slowing. While some creatures might need to hunt for hours to find a ford, Guapo tore through placid rivers, even leaping and swimming when shallow water couldn't be found.

So, it was only midway through the second day of his journey when Victor caught his first glimpse of the sea, and with it the tail end of the column of soldiers, the straggling remnants of the Glorious Ninth. They were in a staggered, disorderly line, wending their way up the curving gravel-and-dirt road to the keep. This far from the mountain, the sky was hazy but not heavy with the ash that had blotted the sun, making it a glowering orange ball. Looking east toward the distant volcano, it seemed as if a great cataclysmic storm hung in the air, and he wondered how long it would take for the ash to finish falling.

In no time, Guapo was pounding over the sandy beach toward the road, and some of the soldiers noted the sounds of his thundering hooves. He could see them stop and turn, then shout and wave their arms. Before he knew it, the entire line of rough-looking, beleaguered troops watched his approach. Victor hoped this was only a part of the surviving cohort—it looked like a much smaller group than when he'd last seen them marching.

Guapo rapidly climbed the steep road, approaching the rear of the ragged column, and slowed. As the thunder of the spirit horse's steps faded, he heard a cheer rise up from the soldiers, and it twisted something in his gut. It took him a moment to realize he was scowling, that he'd let his inner disappointment and guilt show on his face. When the cheer faded, and some of the soldiers stepped back, uncertainty on their dirty haggard faces, Victor forced his brows to even out and spread his lips into something like a smile. He nodded to the cluster of men and women to his right and called out, "Are you just arriving?"

"Aye, Legate, sir!" one of the bigger, bolder soldiers shouted. He looked familiar, and Victor chased the memory in his mind, trying to remember if he knew the soldier's name. After a moment of staring, it clicked; he was one of the adventurers who'd approached him outside the Granite Pass just before any of this had started. Victor had sent him with his friends to join the ninth cohort. His frown returned when he wondered if the man regretted approaching him that day.

Reaching deep into his memory, he surprised himself when he asked, "Thed, right?"

"You remember me, sir?"

"Yeah, I do. Glad to see you made it."

"Yes, sir!" He pounded his chest. "Gave them undead a right thrashing. Shame we lost so many, but none went easy! We made them scum pay dearly!" Scattered cheers broke out among the disordered line of soldiers, and Victor took the clue; this wasn't the time to be morose. These men and women were celebrating being alive. Yet again, the Glorious Ninth had come through hell.

"Well fought, soldiers. Thanks to you"—Victor turned and gestured expansively, from the sea all the way around and back to the keep—"all of this land is ours. The invaders are dead or home licking their wounds, millions of miles away." Another cheer met his words, much louder this time. "Is your captain above?"

Thed frowned and shielded his eyes, looking up at Victor on his massive horse. "I, uh, I'm sorry, sir, but Captain Sarl didn't make it through the fight. Lieutenant ap'Lissa has taken command." He turned and squinted up the hill. "She's at the head of the line, near the gate." The words hit Victor in the gut like swallowing a mouthful of cold stones. Sarl, his oldest friend in the world, the only man who might remember Victor the way he'd been when he came to Fanwath, was gone. He couldn't fake pleasantries after that. He nodded, lips pressed together, eyes distant, unfocused, and urged Guapo back into a canter.

Hearing Sarl was dead had sobered him immensely, and he began to wonder about others. Why hadn't Valla flown out to meet him? Was she dead? Injured? What about Kethelket? He heard soldiers shouting things at him. It sounded mostly like cheers, and Victor wanted to stop and scream at them. He wanted to let them know that he'd caused their losses, that if he hadn't gotten himself trapped, Hector's ambush wouldn't have been half as effective. If he'd been able to meet him and his bone dragon from the start, if he'd been bolstering the troops with his banner, they might have only lost a handful of soldiers in that battle.

He saw Lieutenant ap'Lissa standing before the gate, nodding to her troops as they went by, speaking quietly to other officers, one of whom was writing in a command book. When Victor jumped off Guapo with a massive *thud* and dismissed his trusty mount back to the spirit plane, she stopped what she was doing and snapped a smart salute. All of them did. Victor wanted to ignore her and rush inside, but he couldn't bring himself to do it. It wasn't her fault that all of this had happened. Instead, he nodded to her and barked, "At ease." He stepped up to her, cutting off the flow of soldiers who all stopped, staring openly at their giant commander. "Lieutenant, I've been unconscious, it seems, after my battle with Hector. How much time has passed since the mountain blew?"

"Nine days, sir!"

"And our losses?"

"There are currently four hundred and sixty-three members of the ninth cohort, including the reserves we pulled in from the pass, and not counting those we left behind as garrison troops."

Victor wanted to exclaim, wanted to cuss, but he wouldn't let the soldiers think he was disappointed in them. How many had they had before the battle? A thousand? He knew the number had swelled far past six hundred with the reserves. "A tragic loss, but you should all be proud." He spoke loudly, ensuring the soldiers gathering behind him could hear. "And the Naghelli?"

"I haven't seen an official report, but we unofficially counted more than seventy flying ahead of us. Groups of them flew past a few times, too, picking up wounded and slower troops."

Victor dreaded the answer, wanted to slip past her and seek out the truth of his worry himself, but steeled himself and asked, "Tribune ap'Yensha?"

"She's been here since the first day! She flew back to scout out stragglers and check on us daily, too, sir." Relief washed over him, and it must have shown because the lieutenant added, "She seems quite hale, sir."

"And Captain Kethelket?"

"I haven't seen him, but at camp last night, some soldiers said they saw him flying with the other Naghelli."

Victor had heard enough. "All right. Back to your work; I'll head in." As they all saluted again, Victor stomped into the long gate tunnel and across the bailey to the inner gate. He'd only made it halfway through the yard before, in a flash of silvery shimmering feathers, Valla hurtled over the inner wall and landed in front of him, smashing into his stomach with a furious hug. He wanted to laugh, joke about her crushing his ribs, but he couldn't find the humor in him. Despite his relief, he felt dour and depressed, and underlying those emotions was his guilt. Sarl was dead because of him. In a sudden wave of panic, other faces ran through his mind—Chandri, Lam, Edeya. He pushed Valla's shoulders, separating her from him so he could look her in the face.

Tears flowed down her cheeks as she spoke. "I knew you'd return. Some feared the mountain took you. Some speculated you'd chased Hector through his portal. I could feel you, though. I knew you'd show up soon." Her smile was dazzling, her beauty something unearthly, and Victor's angry, sullen heart lightened. Even so, he couldn't stop the words that slipped from his lips.

"I killed them."

"The invaders? Hector? Catalina?" Valla's eyes narrowed, and her broad smile faded when she saw the look on Victor's face and heard the dour tone in his voice.

"No." Victor glanced around at the straggling soldiers working their way into the inner gate, giving him and Valla a wide berth. "No. I killed Sarl and the Ninth. I got myself trapped, Valla. That ambush was my fault."

Valla's left hand darted up to stroke his jawline, and she spoke instantly, without hesitation. "Hush! Don't you dare say that. Without you, how many soldiers would have died in this war? Sarl died a hero, Victor. Don't take that from him."

Before he could stop himself, he blurted out, "What about Chandri? Edeya?"

Valla took a steadying breath and then said, "I haven't seen Chandri yet. Edeya is alive, but there's something wrong with her. She was frail, hardly breathing, and we feared she'd die if something weren't done soon, so I carried one of the surviving healers here. He's a Blood Caster and an Artificer; he's stabilized her and ensured her body won't waste away while we try to figure out the rest. Lam's with her in your house."

Victor started walking, and Valla hurried to keep pace, her long fingers gripping his wrist, almost as if she feared he'd disappear or leave her. When he stepped into the inner courtyard, he saw a queue of soldiers lined up before the main doors of the keep. "What are they lining up for?"

"Their System reward. Everyone gets a conquest chest if they interact with the stone inside."

Thinking of the soldiers getting rewarded brought to mind the others who'd gotten the conquest challenge but hadn't been at the final battle. "Any word from Rellia? Borrius?"

"They're both fine. Rellia took her half of the cohort to Old Keep, and Borrius retreated to High Keep ahead of the ashfall."

"Are they all getting awarded, too?"

"Yes! Everyone with the quest! Even those at the pass."

"Shit, that's good." Victor set his sights on his jade travel home and hurried toward it.

"It's proportionate to your contribution. I received a purple chest, and so did Kethelket. Some of the garrison troops only got green or blue chests."

"Green?"

"Seems to be lower than blue." Valla hopped up the steps ahead of him because Victor had paused. He was too big to enter the home comfortably. With a moment's concentration, he reduced his height to be closer to Valla's, which was still incredibly tall by any human standard. He followed her into the home, but a dark thought had entered his mind. He'd ridden past the surviving soldiers; Valla had been in the keep. If neither he nor she had seen Chandri, didn't that mean she was dead? The idea brought a sick, fluttering lump into his throat, and he found himself holding his breath when he entered his foyer.

Valla tugged on his wrist, but he resisted, and she looked into his eyes again. "What is it?"

"I think Chandri's dead. I passed the soldiers. You . . . you would have known if she was here." He balled up his left fist and pounded it on his forehead. "Damn it! She was so full of life, Valla! She had dreams! I know that's stupid—everyone has dreams, but she'd just sat down with me and told me about them." Victor leaned forward, hands on his knees, and Valla gently stroked the back of his neck. "What am I going to tell Thayla and Tellen?"

"You'll tell them the truth. Wait, though, Victor. I didn't study every face, and some of the first to arrive were the worst wounded, carried by the Naghelli. I haven't seen to them because the healers shoo us away. Kethelket and his people have made several trips to pick up stragglers. I didn't recognize every face, especially covered in ash and blood! She could be here. We'll check after you see Edeya, okay?"

"Is that Victor?" Lam called from off to the right. Victor straightened up, nodded to Valla, and walked into the short hallway leading to his library.

"You in there?"

"Yes!" Lam rushed into the hallway, and Victor immediately noticed something different about her. She was maybe a little taller, but her wings were much larger than before. All four of the shimmering gossamer wings, though folded and hanging downward, were easily four feet long, and they shimmered with densely packed motes of golden Energy, far more than he'd noticed before. Moreover, it appeared that many of Lam's tattoos had faded. Only a few with bright shining azure ink remained on her forearms. Her eyes were brighter than ever, like backlit emeralds, and seeing her so glorious brought a smile to Victor's lips, banishing some of the storm clouds that had been following him.

"You advanced your race?" he asked, unconsciously touching his shoulder with his left hand, thinking about the tattoo Chandri had given him. It was still there, somehow surviving all of his racial advancements.

"I did! My award in the conquest chest was a 'cake of heritage.' It gave me five ranks. Victor, we can speak about happy news anytime. Please, come and look at Edeya! I'm so worried about her." She turned, and he and Valla followed her into the library. He immediately saw his young friend sitting in one of the puffy comfortable chairs, staring straight ahead, breathing slowly, hands folded in her lap. She looked pale and fragile, more so than when he'd last seen her, fresh and strong from her racial advancement. She wore a set of silky blue robes, and his eyes were drawn to a silver rune-etched metal band about an inch thick around her forehead.

"Edeya!" he said, hurrying toward her. He took one of her hands in his and found it warm but limp. She didn't react to him at all. "The hell's going on with her?"

"She was catatonic, barely breathing. We struggled to get her to eat or drink anything, and the healer was afraid her body would wither and die. He crafted this crown that gives her some vitality, allows her blood to flow better, and gives her caretaker some control over her body—I can get her to walk beside me, eat, drink, and sleep. I can bring her to the bathroom . . ."

"Ah, sheesh." Victor ran a hand through his hair, frowning at the blank-eyed woman. "She's like a robot now? A living robot?"

"Robot?"

"I mean, she doesn't do anything on her own? What did the healer say? What's actually wrong with her? Brain damage?"

"We don't know. When that traitorous bitch escaped . . ."

"Victoria did this?" Victor growled, scowling.

"Catalina. She was lying the whole time—she was Hector's lover." At Valla's words, Victor felt his blood begin to boil, felt both his Cores begin to roil, and it wasn't until he noticed Lam and Valla had taken a step back that he realized he was radiating hot, furious Energy. With a great effort of will, he dragged his Energy back into his Core and tamped down on his fury. With a deep cleansing breath, he gently let go of Edeya's hand and looked at Lam.

"Tell me what happened."

"I found her in Vict . . . Catalina's grasp, wrapped up in her mist, pale and dead-looking. When Kethelket drove Catalina off, destroyed her body, he said she didn't seem to die, that she might have a . . . a, uh . . ."

Valla provided the word she was struggling to find. "Phylactery."

"Right. When she was gone, I carried Edeya to your home, and she's been like this ever since. She wasn't injured physically, not that I could see. I even got her to drink a healing draught, but it did nothing."

Victor felt a sinking sensation in his stomach as he heard the tale. Closing his eyes, he turned his gaze inward to his Core and followed his pathways into his hand that still grasped Edeya's. He had no trouble finding her pathway in her palm and sending a tendril of Energy into it. He knew it should have been difficult to do so; he should have felt some resistance. There was nothing there, though, nothing in her pathways to contend with his thin tendril of inspiration-attuned Energy.

He guided it further into her, seeking out her Core. Her pathways were laid out similarly to his, though with more loops and swirls, and it took him a minute to find his way to the cool, pulsing blue heart of her Energy. It was there, alive and full of shimmering Energy, but it wasn't animated. Nothing moved it. He'd hoped to see the problem there, that maybe Catalina had cut off her flow of Energy. Finding nothing amiss, he opened his eyes and pulled back his Energy with a growl of frustration.

"Do you see anything?" Lam asked, breathless hope in her voice.

"Not yet. Watch me a minute; I'm going into the spirit plane." Victor knelt on the floor, and taking Edeya's hands in his, he cast Spirit Walk. He stood up immediately, surrounded by pristine blue-tinted grass. When he looked around, he saw the smooth slope of the hillside falling away to the glittering frothy waves of the sea. The water shone with the expansive infinite dome of stars that seemed close enough to touch. He looked down at the grass in front of his feet, frowning at the spot where Edeya would be if she'd come through with him into the spirit plane.

At first, he saw nothing and almost canceled his spell in frustration, but then he caught a glimpse of a faint shimmering tendril of wispy, smoky air. Like a streamer of the Energy he sent to his ancestors when he cast Honor the Spirits. When Victor knelt to study the weird wispy ribbon, it brought Belikot and what he'd learned about spirit shards and phylacteries to mind. Gently, he ran his translucent fingers through that ribbon, and he felt, fainter than the gentle brush of a butterfly's wing, a wisp of emotion, of personality distinctly reminiscent of Edeya. Like a jolt of electricity, understanding hit him, and Victor ended his spirit walk and leapt to his feet. "I know what's wrong with her."

61

NO TIME FOR BLAME

You do?" Lam leaned forward, hope in her eyes. Victor wanted to comfort her, to give her good news, but he felt such an overwhelming sense of frustration and defeat that he had a hard time keeping it out of his voice.

"Yeah. Victoria or Catalina—whatever the *bruja's* name is—I'm pretty sure she was capturing Edeya's spirit when you and Kethelket interrupted her."

"What does that mean?" Lam pressed, kneeling before Edeya, grasping her hand between hers.

"She took it with her—well, most of it. There's a sliver of her spirit still in here, a shard." Victor gently stroked Edeya's pale hair, pushing a loose tendril away from her face. "It's what's keeping her alive."

"Took it where?" Valla's voice was hard, hinting at pent-up violence.

Victor groaned and stood up, looking away from Edeya. He felt frustrated and angry, but worse, he felt the warm painful heat of shame flushing the blood up the back of his neck. He squeezed his eyes shut and, while he spoke, thumped a clenched fist against his forehead. "She slipped past me. Through the portal. She's back on Dark Ember, I guess."

"Dark Ember?" Lam frowned and continued to massage Edeya's hand. "Can't we call her back? She's still alive; there's still part of her spirit here! You said so yourself! Will she recover? Can this fragment be strengthened?"

"I don't know," Victor groaned. "Goddamn it! I should have chased that lying . . ." Victor frowned from Lam to Valla, saw the anger and frustration in their eyes, and knew he couldn't be the one to act out right now. As much as he cared about Edeya, Lam cared more. As much as he wanted to blame himself for everything, that wouldn't get her spirit back. "She interrupted me fighting with Hector. She almost helped him escape, too, but he couldn't go through the portal. I don't know why, but his last breath was spent cursing the System. Maybe it was something to do with the quest, the conquest challenge."

"Is the portal gone?" Lam asked, her eyes drifting to the exit as though she'd charge away, up into the volcano, right that second.

"Yeah, it's gone. Nothing would last through that eruption, but it was closed before the mountain blew. Screw this." Victor took Lam's shoulders in his hands, turning the woman he'd once idolized to face him. "I'll get her spirit back, Lam, or I'll die trying." She stared at him with those glittering jewel-like eyes. She was a woman so beautiful he'd struggled to breathe in her presence when he'd first arrived as a slave to Greatbone Mine. Where once she'd looked at him with pity, kindness, and encouragement, she now looked at him with hope, a kind of beseeching, searching look in those eyes as she stared into his.

"I believe you, and I'll help."

"As will I, Lam!" Valla reached out to grasp Victor's shoulder with one hand and the back of Lam's neck with the other. They stared at each other, and it was evident in their eyes what they were saying, even without words: They would do whatever they could to get Edeya's spirit away from Victoria, no matter what. "Victor, claim your reward from the System. I don't know how it works, but we've yet to get the promised Colony Stone. I think, if we plant it, whatever settlement we build around it will be our capital."

"And if we have a capital stone, it might open up options for world travel," Lam said, finishing Valla's point. "Rellia will be angry if we plant it without consulting her . . ."

"I don't care." Victor let go of Lam's shoulders and turned toward the exit. "If you want, send her a message. Tell her what's going on. If she has another idea, I'll listen." He took two steps, then paused. "Valla, can you show me where the wounded are? I'd like to see if Chandri . . ."

"Of course!" Once again, she took his hand and started walking, tugging him toward the exit.

"I'll stay with Edeya." Victor glanced back at Lam when she spoke and saw her sitting in the seat she'd pulled close to Edeya's. She held the girl's hand and stared at her face, whispering something clearly meant for her alone. He wondered if it was a prayer or a promise.

When they stepped outside into the courtyard, Victor came face to face with Kethelket and, beside him, the gigantic stranger who'd intervened in the battle with Hector and his dragon skeleton. In the light of day, the man was no less impressive. If Victor had never seen the people of Zaafor, the giant Degh, the animalistic Vesh, and the snake-like Yazzians, he might have been more taken aback by the newcomer's massive draconic form. With his size currently reduced, even Victor had to look up to meet the man's gaze. After staring for a half second, Victor reached out and took the hand Kethelket held out. "I'm glad you made it."

"As am I, Victor. Your victory and survival won the day, however. Ancestors! I would have loved to see that battle!"

"I as well," the big stranger rumbled. Victor let go of Kethelket's hand and looked at the scaled man, frowning with suspicion. He knew he didn't have a right to accuse him of anything, but after Victoria's lies, after learning she was really Catalina and had been playing him all along, he felt it would be stupid to trust anyone blindly.

"I'm sorry, but your name . . . did you tell it to me during the fight? I was enraged . . ."

"I am Lesh'ro'zellan, and I hail from the world of Ashenshoal. Simply call me Lesh." His voice was deep with a kind of guttural edge, especially when he pronounced the Z in his name.

"I know you helped Valla against Hector, so you have my thanks, but tell me, what brings you to Fanwath? Why were we so lucky to have your aid?"

The big, darkly scaled man's mouth was surprisingly expressive as it twisted into a snarl. He practically spat as he growled, "The System." Victor watched his taloned hand twist on the heavy black metal haft of his huge staff-like cudgel.

"Can you elaborate?"

Kethelket's nervous fidget and sour expression weren't lost on Victor as he said, "Perhaps now isn't the time for that tale, Legate. It's a lengthy one."

"Just a quick summary, maybe?" Victor stared hard into the draconic man's darkly gleaming green eyes. Victor might have expected an answer or a polite refusal, but he didn't expect Lesh to fall to a knee before him, holding his enormous cudgel lengthwise on his open palms.

"I offer you my service, Lord Victor. As such, I cannot build upon a foundation of lies or deceit. I came here, to this world, to slay you."

Victor felt something in him break free, something he subconsciously always held in check. Without thought, he severed his connection to his

Alter Self spell, surging in size while he ripped Lifedrinker from the temporary loop at his belt. His aura fell around him, heavy and dense with murderous intent. As his muscles bunched and coiled, as Valla stumbled away from
him, he loomed over Lesh and growled, eyes red with rage and smoldering
heat, "You *what?*"

To his credit, Lesh didn't flinch. "I answered a System quest, months and
months ago, to come to this world and slay the one known as Victor."

"You dare to challenge me?" If he thought about it, Victor would have
recognized his Quinametzin pride asserting itself. As it was, he was barely
cognizant of his ancestral need to be respected and dominate his surroundings. Victor twisted his hands on Lifedrinker and felt her vibrate with eagerness. Was this a worthy foe at last? He could smell something in the man
kneeling before him, something ancient that echoed in his blood memories.
"Kneeling . . ." his voice rumbled. Again, something deep in him recognized
the respect Lesh was showing, and that recognition gave Victor just enough
control to stay his hand.

"Yes, I kneel. Months ago, the thought of it would have broken me.
Months ago, I would have sooner dug out my own heart than bend the knee
to anyone. That was before I met you, Victor, before I watched you battle a
thousand powerful undead. It was before I saw you breathe fire that would
have shamed every dragonkin on Ashenshoal. It was before I followed you
through these lands and saw the respect your actions demanded. When I
measured myself against you, I found myself wanting. Lord Victor, I stood
tall on Ashenshoal because strength is what earns respect there, and I was
stronger than any in my clan. I believed myself stronger than those in the
capital, Garspire. When I witnessed your might, I knew I must follow you
rather than attempt to slay you by underhanded means."

"And I should believe you?"

"Victor!" Valla tried to interject, but he ignored her, staring at the kneeling dragonkin as he had labeled himself.

"I have rejected the System's quest, forfeiting my reward. To return to
Ashenshoal would be shameful, for I will not lie. Nothing matters more to
me than my honor, and so I give up my life, my love, my people, and my
home. I will follow you, or I will die by your hand." He lifted his huge staff-
like cudgel higher as though offering it to Victor, and that angry voice in
Victor's heart subsided, appeased by the man's obeisance.

"Keep your weapon," he growled, pushing his rage back into his Core and
straining to pull in his aura.

Lesh didn't move as he spoke again. "Will you accept me into your service?"

His instinct was to say yes, but Victor had newfound doubts about his instincts. Hadn't he decided Victoria wasn't a threat? Hadn't he nearly trusted her to go free on more than one occasion? Hadn't he refused to let Sarl collar her? Wasn't Sarl dead now because of his sentimentality and desire to see the good in everyone? Rather than say yes or no, Victor looked down at Kethelket, and the heroic dark-eyed prince nodded to him. He trusted Kethelket's judgment, even if he couldn't trust his own right then. Still, he had questions. "Why the hell did the System give you a quest to kill me?"

"I have no idea." Lesh didn't offer anything more, but his words rang true to Victor.

"It's not unheard of," Valla said, "for the System to take an interest in a person. There are stories of heroes, champions of the Ridonne . . ."

Victor didn't want to speculate right then. He had a million things on his mind, and the System's apparent vendetta against him wasn't something he could spare the mental bandwidth on. "I accept your service, Lesh, but we need to talk about what that means. Later, though; this isn't the time."

The man's draconic face split into a grin that exposed fangs that would've given a Bengal tiger a run for its money as he leapt to his feet. "Thank you, Lord . . ."

"Just Victor."

"Thank you, Victor! What task shall I busy myself with?"

"I'm going to visit the wounded. Can you and Kethelket meet me by the System Stone?" Victor turned to Kethelket as he spoke.

"We can," the onetime prince said with a salute.

"Kethelket. Lesh." Victor held up a hand, forestalling their departure. "Thank you for fighting with me against Hector and his people. Thank you for saving the lives of people I care about. It's not lost on me that if it weren't for you, I'd be mourning a great deal more today. I'm grateful."

Kethelket didn't object, nor did he belabor the issue. He nodded and turned, and Lesh followed suit. Victor watched them march up the steps and into the keep, a giant leather-clad, scale-covered hulk and a much smaller, slender man with mothlike wings glimmering with bright ochre patterns. He couldn't imagine a more dissimilar pair, but they seemed easy in each other's company. "They've made friends quickly."

Once again, Valla's fingers entwined with his. "After you chased Hector up the mountain, the two of them laid waste to the undead, rallying the soldiers and driving them away from the encampment. I believe a strong bond was forged that night."

"And you?"

"Oh, I slew my fair share." She squeezed his hand. "Come, make yourself smaller again, and let's see if Chandri's in the barracks."

Victor took her advice, recasting Alter Self, and followed her into a different keep entrance and down a short hallway that opened into a much longer one lined with doors. A soldier sat at a desk in the hallway, and she jumped up, face flushed, saluting Victor and Valla. She stood, straight as a board, staring into the wall opposite her desk until Valla said, "At ease, Sergeant. Do you have a list of the wounded?"

"Yes, ma'am!" She turned to the desk and lifted a clipboard, dense with script. "Who are you looking for, ma'am?"

"A soldier named Chandri. I don't recall what unit . . ." Victor started to say, but the young sergeant perked up and lowered the clipboard.

"She's here, sir! Healer Breeva just approved and administered one of the regeneration draughts for her. She's in the first room on the left." She might have kept speaking, but Victor didn't hear her; his blood had rushed to his ears, throbbing and pounding as he hurried to the door and yanked it open. He didn't know what he'd expected, but it wasn't a room filled with six beds, most occupied by sleeping soldiers. He barely got hold of the door, halting it before it slammed into the wall. When he, more calmly, peered through the doorway, scrutinizing the beds, his eyes finally found her on the third bed to the left. She was lying on her back, eyes closed, tightly swathed in blankets. Thick bandages covered her forehead and right eye, but the unbandaged side of her face was visible, and Victor recognized her immediately.

When he felt Valla next to him, also peering through the door, he asked softly, so as not to wake the sleeping soldiers, "Regeneration draught?"

"We've won quite a few from the System chests. I just looked at her patient notes—Chandri lost an eye, and her right arm was badly smashed. She was on the wall when Hector's dragon skeleton tore it apart." She wound her cool fingers around his wrist and added, "We should let her rest. The regeneration magic is powerful but works slowly."

"Shouldn't I sit with her?" Victor kept his voice hushed. He knew he should be worried about Chandri, upset that she'd been hurt so badly, but the fact that she was alive overwhelmed those feelings, filling him with relief that was so tangible he could taste it.

"Give it a little time; there's still much for you to do today, yes? We can sit with her after we have some answers and plans regarding . . ."

"Edeya. The stone. Right." Victor slowly closed the door. Then it was he who led Valla out to the courtyard and up into the central hall where straggling soldiers were still lined up, waiting for their turn with the System Stone. Victor stood at the entrance, taking in the scene, amazed by how much the hall had changed since he and Valla had left. The garrison soldiers had been hard at work, it seemed.

Long tables lined both sides of the hall, three on each side, leaving a long central aisle strewn with colorful but mismatched rugs, likely taken from personal storage rings or those looted from the dead wampyrs. Warm light shone down from two Energy chandeliers hanging on the high rafters, and the smell of cooked food wafted from the plates and bowls in front of the many soldiers who'd gathered to eat. The mood was festive, and Victor could see why—these people were celebrating being alive, celebrating victory and a bright future despite their loss of comrades. More than that, every couple of minutes, another soldier received a magical chest delivered in clouds of green, blue, or even golden steamy Energy.

"There's Kethelket." Valla pointed to the Naghelli leader sitting on a bench near the far end of the hall, watching the soldiers interacting with the System Stone. Lesh was beside him, though he sat on the hard floor, his legs folded before him, studying a text of some sort. Victor walked toward them, nodding to the soldiers who grew quiet and stared as he and Valla passed. Her wings were folded tightly against her back, and Victor draped an arm over her shoulders, too happy to be near her to care what others thought about propriety.

"I can see from the lack of gloom that your friend lives." Kethelket held up a mug of something steamy and asked, "Would you like some cider? It's not something I pulled from my ring; the soldiers found an apple orchard in the hills to the east."

"Ah! I knew it smelled good in here, but I hadn't placed the scent." Victor's mouth had begun to salivate at the idea. "I'll go to the kitchen in a while. Maybe after I clean up."

"Will you claim your prize, Victor?" Lesh asked, looking up from his thick book.

"I'll wait for the soldiers to finish. Looks like only a dozen or so still in line." Victor studied the dragonkin momentarily, then asked, "How'd you get here, Lesh? A portal?"

"I used the System Stone in our capital."

"I know there are ways to open portals to worlds without using the System Stones, but it's not easy, is it? We had a powerful friend help us travel here from Zaafor."

"No, not easy at all. None in my clan have the knowledge."

Valla sat beside Kethelket and interjected, "Didn't your cousin say she knew how to open portals? Or was that her powerful friend?"

"I . . . don't remember. We talked about a lot in a short time. Even if she can make portals, do you think she can open one to anywhere?"

"What's all this about?" Kethelket asked. "Portal to where?"

Valla turned to him and bluntly summarized, "Catalina has Edeya's spirit, or most of it. We're trying to figure out how we can get to her."

"That's the girl with the pretty blue wings?" Lesh asked, closing his book and, perhaps unintentionally, growling deep in his chest.

"Yeah." Victor sighed and scratched his head, running his fingers through his stiff hair, for a moment wondering why it was so stiff and clumpy before he realized his sweat had soaked up the ash in the air.

Kethelket took a sip of his cider. "Can you not summon her spirit? Rip it from that Death Caster's clutches?"

"I don't know. If so, it's beyond what I know how to do."

"Why not go to a hub world?" Lesh asked, his frown deepening.

Valla saved Victor from embarrassment by asking, "Hub world?"

Lesh looked at her with narrow eyes, then he turned to Kethelket and Victor, and when he saw no understanding in either of their faces, he said, "You've not traveled to a hub world?"

Kethelket shrugged. "I've been locked in a dimensional dungeon for the last few hundred years."

Victor shook his head, and Valla said, "The rulers of this world have restricted access to the System Stone in the capital. We can reach certain worlds from the other City Stones, but I've never heard of a hub world."

The draconic man took a deep breath and began a lengthy explanation in his rumbling, rather pleasant baritone. "Aha. Well, if the System gives you a Colony or Settlement Stone, you'll probably have limited world travel options at first, but I'm sure one of the options will be a hub world. A hub world is like a crossroads, a world where the people have worked hard to meet the System's requirements to open more and more world connections. They do it in the hopes that their singular focus will facilitate trade and the flow of travelers and wealth, offsetting their neglect of other System options."

"What other options?" Kethelket had grown very still, clearly intrigued by Lesh's words.

"Hmm, let me see." As he paused, Victor saw, for the first time, a tendril of greenish-gray vapor drift up out of Lesh's snout. "On my homeworld, the rulers have concentrated their efforts on opening more and more dungeons to challenge us. The central goal of my people is always to improve individual strength and advancement. Every dragonkin lives with the ultimate desire to achieve evolution into a true dragon or, failing that, to have a clutch of strong children starting further along than their parents."

"So a hub world concentrates on world connections rather than dungeons?" Valla clarified, nodding her head.

"Yes, though there are myriad other ways to spend Energy at a Colony Stone."

"No wonder those bastards have held onto power so long," Victor growled, and he knew Kethelket and Valla would understand who he meant—the Ridonne.

"Uh, yes, well." Lesh held up his thick book. "You can find knowledge about nearly any topic in a hub world."

"All right." Victor nodded, rubbing his chin. He turned back to the stone and saw that only three more soldiers were in the queue to interact. "It's time I find out what the System decided I deserve as my award."

<h1 style="text-align:center">62</h1>

VICTORIOUS

Victor waited until all of the soldiers who'd been lined up at the stone had collected their prizes and moved away. He'd hoped to be able to interact with the relatively small, slowly spinning System artifact without making too much of a scene, but his hopes were in vain. As soon as he strode forward, the hall grew quiet. People stopped eating, and their conversations lowered to hushed whispers. As he lifted his palm toward the stone, it stopped moving, but he hesitated, looking toward Valla. He wasn't sure why; he needed to do this, had to find out if he'd be awarded the Colony Stone, but for some reason, he was nervous.

Valla sat on the bench near Kethelket, both looking small next to Lesh's hulking figure despite the dragonkin sitting on the floor. She looked him right in the eye and nodded, and something relaxed in his chest. Part of him was annoyed by the reaction. He was Quinametzin; why should he care what anyone thought? Was it not his right to claim his award for his contributions during the campaign? Victor growled, driving that voice down, and turned away from Valla, focusing on the weirdly shifting golden and silver runes that seemed to be buried just under the stone's surface. "Okay, System. You want me dead, huh? Well, tough shit, 'cause it ain't happening today. What you got for me?"

When his large wide palm rested on the cool surface of the stone, the runes all flared for a fraction of a second, and then System messages flooded his field of view.

*****Congratulations! You are victorious! Your exceptional bravery and skill have earned you the apex position in the campaign against the invaders from Dark Ember. Your pivotal role in vanquishing the enemy forces, defeating their commanders, and sealing the invasion portal stands unparalleled. For your heroic deeds, you will be awarded a legendary conquest chest, guaranteed to contain a Colony Stone, allowing you to establish a third System-recognized capital on the world of Fanwath. Do you wish to claim your prize at this time?*****

"Third?" Victor narrowed his eyes in confusion. Was there another capital on Fanwath? He'd thought Tharcray was the only one. Perhaps his confusion showed on his face because the whispers of anticipation became speculative murmurs, and Victor thought he saw movement to his left where Valla sat. Was she coming over? He shook the feeling off; it didn't matter if there was another capital somewhere. What mattered was that he needed this stone to set up the capital he and everyone else had fought for. There wasn't a menu or anything that he could interact with, so he just said, "Yes."

Nothing happened for a few seconds, and Victor began to reread the System message, wondering if he'd missed something. He'd just gotten to the part about his "heroic deeds" when, with little sizzling crackles, sparks began to pop into existence above the faded blue carpet at his feet. He stepped back and watched as more and more sparks sprang into existence, flashing and crackling. With each spark, a brilliant, shimmering golden cloud of smoke or mist or steam began to take shape. Before he knew it, the cloud had grown large enough to engulf him up to the waist. Excited chatter broke out in the hall as people leapt up from their seats and crowded closer.

Victor stood still, waving his hands through the cloud, unable to feel or smell it; he decided it was simply a visual artifact of whatever summoning magic the System used to conjure up his award. He'd wondered before, but the thought reoccurred to him that he had no idea if the awards the System granted were crafted on the spot from the System's tremendous stores of Energy or if it had awards in some magical dimension, a repository of sorts, and simply sent them forth with a kind of dimensional magic. He added the question to the list of things he didn't know and probably never would.

The sizzling, crackling flashes were new to him. He'd seen the System deliver items in colorful gasses, but never with all those sparks. They sort of reminded him of his glory-attuned Energy, and he began to get excited; was the System tailoring a prize for his particular affinity? It took longer than usual for the golden steam or smoke to fade away, but when it did, the crowd erupted in excited chatter and a smattering of applause—a large golden metallic chest sat at Victor's feet. "If size is any measure, you've won quite a prize," Kethelket said. Victor turned to the man, surprised by his nearness, only to find Lesh, Valla, and a dozen others had crowded close.

"Yeah." Victor felt he should say more, but he didn't have the words, and he still didn't feel like himself. He still had that nagging worry about Edeya hanging over him and the lingering guilt that hundreds had died because of his foolishness. With that thought, he clenched his jaw and tried to shake off the gloom—what good was he doing anyone by moping with self-doubt? Rather than saying more or worrying about what everyone around him was thinking, he lifted the metallic clasp on the chest and flung the heavy lid wide, sending it to crash against the back of the chest, straining the ornate hinges.

A cloud of golden steam rushed into the air, and Victor waved it away, peering inside the big red-velvet-lined container. He leaned forward to look within, and behind him, he heard Valla sternly caution the crowding soldiers, "Stand back. Your legate will share with you what he wills." Victor heard more chatter, questions, exclamations, and further warnings, but he tuned them out as his eyes fell on the objects within. He reached down and picked up the first reward, a folded pile of what seemed to be supple, silky-smooth, black leather. A card embossed with golden curly elaborate lettering told him what it was.

He decided he'd put on a show for the soldiers; they'd been through hell, and he owed them at least that much. He turned and held the supple leather aloft and read the card, "Master-artisan-grade hide of a lava king."

All sorts of comments, questions, and exclamations resulted from his pronouncement, such as, "What's a lava king?" "Master artisan grade? Is that the highest?" "It must be magical!" "Is it because of the volcano?"

Victor laughed, sent the hide into his ring, and turned back to the chest. He purposefully ignored the object at the center and reached in to lift out a shimmering red-orange gem. As soon as he touched it, he felt the deep wells of Energy within it, and his Magma Core flared and roiled. He held it aloft, turning so all could see it clearly, and read the card: "A legendary-tier magma-attunement gem. Use to enchant a suitably powerful artifact."

"What will you enchant, Legate?"

"Amazing!"

"Ancestors!"

"It has to be the volcano!" The same soldier piped up about the volcano again, and Victor couldn't help the smile that tugged his cheeks toward his ears. The hype was getting to him. He sent the gem into his ring and reached into the chest again. He tried to grab a shimmering ball of golden Energy, but it wouldn't move, and as soon as he touched it, he felt the power within trying to flow into his pathway. He pushed his will against it and quickly pulled his hand away. It seemed the System would award him with an infusion of Energy, but he didn't want to do that yet. There was something else to examine first. He moved his hand to the right and lifted the next item and its card.

It was a black pouch the size of his fist, and when he read the card, the soldiers erupted in a clamor of disbelief and rowdy excitement: "One million magma-attuned Energy beads." Victor laughed, watched, and listened as the soldiers cheered, joked, and speculated about the amount, comparing it to their much smaller prizes. None seemed bitter, and the smiling faces told him they were happy. Their good humor and excitement made it seem as if they were winning the prizes alongside him, and Victor was glad he hadn't taken his awards in private.

"Two more!" Victor shouted, his deep powerful voice booming over the noise. The soldiers grew quiet with anticipation, and he reached into the chest and touched the ball of golden Energy, this time allowing it to flow into his pathways. Victor had won Energy in System chests before and earned plenty of infusions after battles. This one was large, but nothing like he'd gotten after slaying the reaver army. It flowed into his Core, swelling each of his attunements to bursting before flooding into his body, lifting him off the ground. A golden shimmering halo exploded around him, eclipsing the glow lamps in the hall.

The soldiers exclaimed, some of them shielding their eyes and stumbling back. Victor spread his arms and arched his back, enjoying the infusion, and not for the first time, he noted the euphoria that came with it. Perhaps it was because of his underlying guilt, his worry about Edeya, but this time, he really noticed how his outlook changed—how, when the euphoria passed, he felt better, less troubled than before. It struck him how he always seemed to bounce back after traumatic, horrific ordeals, and he wondered how much of that was due to the Energy healing his mind as much as it did his weary body. Whatever the cause, Victor felt better, and it was with a wide grin that he read the new System messages floating before his eyes.

Congratulations! You have achieved level 60 Battlemaster and gained 10 strength, 9 vitality, 4 agility, 4 dexterity, 3 will, and 3 intelligence.

***Level 60 Class refinement is available. Class refinement is permanent. Quinametzin Energy cultivators will next be offered a Class

refinement selection at level 70. To view your options and make your selection, access the menu through your status page.***

Victor lifted his hands in the air, turned in a slow circle, and roared, "Level Sixty!" The crowd's reaction was thunderous, and Victor laughed when he heard them cheering, stomping, and howling. They slapped each other's backs, summoned drinks from dimensional containers, downed them, and shook each other, faces flushed with excitement. Looking over their heads, Victor saw the crowd had grown, that most of the ninth cohort's survivors were now gathered in the great hall, and he nodded at them, proud and pleased that he could give them something more to celebrate. After a while, he shouted, "One more!"

When the noise died down, he reached into the chest and lifted the impossibly heavy, pint-glass-sized, oblong stone. It had six facets, each etched with the now familiar gold and silver runes of the System. He held it aloft and shouted, "Our Colony Stone!" It probably weighed a hundred pounds, which was a lot for such a small item, but really nothing to Victor. He held it up for a long time as the crowd went wild again, and the chest disappeared in a cloud of golden steam.

After a while, Valla pushed closer to him and wrapped one arm around his waist, pressing herself against him. When he looked down at her, she smiled, and nothing but happiness could find a grip on his heart at that moment. Even when he looked around the hall, over the heads of the cheering soldiers, and saw a large group of Naghelli sitting at one of the now-empty tables with Kethelket, he didn't let dour guilt invade his mind. They weren't celebrating as raucously as the soldiers, but they wore friendly expressions, and he could see drinks in their hands. They'd lost many and suffered, but their long exile was over. They had a home. Plenty of people would think that was worth dying for—Victor certainly did.

A long time later, after much drinking, feasting, and storytelling, Victor and Valla left the celebration and moved Chandri to one of the empty rooms in his home, furnishing it for her with items taken from plundered storage containers. She was still out of it, her body working hard to regenerate her damaged and missing tissue. The process required Energy, and her Core had to slowly recuperate it, constantly being drained to feed the elixir she'd been given. While they were making Chandri comfortable, Lam spent time with Edeya, sending messages back and forth to Rellia; they were trying to figure out where Victor should plant the Colony Stone.

"How urgent do you think it is?" Valla asked. They'd put a comfortable blue-upholstered couch next to Edeya's bed and sat on it together, watching her sleep.

"It?" Victor looked at Chandri and frowned. "Her healing?"

"No, I'm sorry. I was talking about Edeya."

"I don't know. I know I'm not an expert, but, well, forget that; I think I know more about Death Casters than a lot of people. I've certainly dealt with some real bastards in that regard." Victor chuckled at himself and scratched his head. "What I'm trying to say is that it seems to me that Death Casters don't do things quickly. They have big plans that take years, decades, and centuries to put together. I think if Catalina were going to try to destroy Edeya's spirit, we'd have seen it by now. The attack she used on her, the way she snatched her spirit out of her, wasn't something she could do to me. Maybe not to you, either; she took Edeya because she's much weaker. I mean, in comparison to Catalina."

"That's not exactly good, though . . ."

"Well, it kind of is. What can she do with a single spirit that's so many Energy tiers beneath her? Not much. She probably has rituals she performs, a way of gaining power from her victims, but I bet she gathers a lot of them. I bet she locks them away in a phylactery, something like the skull Belikot was inhabiting with his spirit shard. So, she has a big part of Edeya's spirit, but we have part of it, too. I don't think she can do a lot with that. I think we'll have time to figure out a way to help her. I have to think that, Valla, or I'm going to go crazy with worry and do something rash."

"Something rash? I like it when you talk that way." Valla snuggled closer into his side, and Victor couldn't tell if she was being serious or teasing him. He decided he didn't care. He'd already decided he wanted to enjoy good things while he could, and, despite his mistakes, as long as he wasn't actually trying to harm the people he cared about, he wasn't going to wallow in grief and guilt.

"What do you think about Lesh?" She sounded almost sleepy, and he wondered why she was bringing the dragonkin up if she was so tired.

"What? I guess I think he's pretty cool. I mean, he helped a lot during the battle. I'm not sure I'm cool about him wanting to follow me or whatever, though. He's pretty . . . intense."

"He's very strong. He reminded me of you when he faced off against Hector and his dragon skeleton. That weapon of his is conscious, I'm sure.

He calls it Belagog. I asked him about it, and he offered to let me hold it, so I tried, and it fell to the ground, pulling me with it. I couldn't budge it! Oh, he laughed raucously!"

"You think he was testing me when he held it out? You think I should have tried to take it?"

"Oh, that's an interesting question! I hadn't thought of that. It puts his supposed fealty in a new light."

"Well, the System chose him to come after me for a reason. I figure we're both kind of . . ." Victor frowned, trying to pick the right word without sounding like an ass. Finally, he sighed and just said what he'd been thinking. "I guess the System views us as overpowered for our level. Well, I think—what level is he?"

"I don't know. Use your little scope thing on him!"

"My scope thing? Am I getting more articulate while you become less so?"

Her eyes narrowed mischievously. "Hush, *pendejo*."

"Hey!" Victor's outburst broke the spell of their whispered conversation, and Chandri groaned and turned to her side. Her unbandaged magenta eye opened a bare slit, and she stared at Victor and Valla for several seconds before recognition illuminated it, and she croaked out a question.

"What's going on?"

Valla jumped up and gently smoothed Chandri's hair, whispering softly, "Nothing, sorry we woke you. You were injured in the battle, but you'll be fine. You need to rest."

"Mm." Chandri murmured something else, but Victor couldn't make sense of it. Then she fell back asleep.

When Valla sat back down, he pulled her close, squeezing her into his side, and whispered, "So are we going to talk about our class refinements?"

"I already made my selection. I'm sorry, but I did it while you were missing, hoping it would somehow make it easier to find you."

Victor's eyes opened wide, and he stared at her for a long minute. How could she be so cool about something like that? She'd been fifth tier for longer than he'd known her. She had to have been bursting with excitement about the refinement. "Well?"

"Well, I chose something I thought Tes would approve of." She grinned, leaning back, closing her eyes, and generally taking her sweet time. Victor reached toward her neck, pretending to choke her, lifting his upper lip in a snarl.

"If you make me choke it out of you . . ."

She clapped a hand over his mouth. "Hush! Okay, okay. My new class is Storm Dancer, which, based on the description, will help me gain more offensive magic and skills to use while in flight. It's an epic class, and the prerequisites were interesting. I had to have the 'power of flight,' affinity with air-attuned Energy, and a previous 'dancer' class."

"That's awesome, Valla! You were a Sword Dancer before, yeah?"

"That's right." She smiled, clearly pleased with herself. Victor pulled her tight again, and they snuggled side by side for a few minutes before she said, "Well? What about you?"

63

THE FREE MARCHES

You mean my refinement?" Victor whispered, leaning close and resting his cheek against Valla's head as she leaned into him. "I haven't looked yet. I'm nervous about it, and, well, we've been busy."

"Nervous?"

"Yeah, the whole reason I took this Battlemaster Class instead of a legendary option was because it's supposed to open up better classes or something. What if it didn't?"

"I wouldn't worry. Even if you were stuck with keeping Battlemaster, it's not as if it's weak. My new class isn't legendary. Should I be ashamed?"

Victor could tell from her tone that she wasn't upset; she was teasing. Nevertheless, he felt bad for his choice of words. "I didn't mean that. I just—"

"Hush; I know what you meant." She pulled away from him and gestured to Chandri. "She'll probably sleep through the night. Why don't we go someplace we can talk." Victor let her pull him up from the couch and followed her into the hallway, then down to their bedroom. They had a table and chairs in the corner to the left of the door, but he walked past and sat on the thick red rug beside the bed. Valla sat down in front of him and waited expectantly.

"All right. Let me pull up the options." He activated his status page, gave his attributes a quick once-over, then mentally selected the blinking "Class Refinement" tab. The first option filled his view:

*****Class refinement option 1: Quinametzin Foe Slayer, Legendary. Prerequisites: 1. Sufficiently advanced Quinametzin bloodline. 2. Epic-level**

Berserk or Berserk-like ability. 3. Epic-level strength or vitality. You have unlocked the secrets of one of your primogenitors' Classes. Accepting this new Class will grant you abilities based upon those buried deep in the history of your blood. Class attributes: strength, vitality.***

"Do you remember the Quinametzin Foe Slayer I was offered last time?"

"The name is familiar . . ."

"It's my first choice this time. Um, it's legendary, and basically, all it says is, 'Accepting this new Class will grant you abilities based upon those buried deep in the history of your blood.' The Class attributes are strength and vitality."

"It doesn't sound bad. I imagine if it's only granting you increases to two attributes, they'll be significant."

"Yeah, I bet." Victor shrugged. "Let's see what option two is." He mentally selected "Next," and his eyes widened as he read the description.

Class refinement option 2: Warlord, Legendary. Prerequisites: 1. Prior Class levels in Battlemaster, Martial Sage, or Combat Savant. 2. Sufficiently advanced bloodline. 3. Sufficiently advanced weapon skills. 4. Sufficiently advanced attributes. 5. A sufficiently advanced Core with appropriate affinities. 6. A history of leading followers into large-scale conflicts and achieving victory. Class attributes: vitality, intelligence.

"Well, shit. I guess Khul Bach knew what he was talking about."

"Warlord?" Valla's voice was hushed as she leaned toward him, clenching her fists excitedly.

"Yep! It lists Battlemaster as a prerequisite, but also some other Classes I haven't heard of, Martial Sage and Combat Savant."

"Really? It makes you wonder if other worlds have more knowledge of Classes and their refinements."

"Wonder? Nah, I'm certain they do. I bet, for example, whatever world Tes was operating out of, the one with the guild she was a member of, has entire libraries dedicated to the subject."

"You think so? Do you think the 'hub worlds' Lesh mentioned will have something like that?"

"I mean, they must. Don't you think? Imagine how much money people could make offering access to their secret class tomes. On the other hand, I guess there are probably sects that don't let anyone know their secrets." Victor shrugged. "Something we can try to find out, huh?"

"Yes! Do you have other options?"

"Let's see." Victor could see that another option awaited because of the still-blinking "Next" floating on his System interface, but he didn't know if it was simply the old "keep your current class" option. He selected it:

*****Class refinement option 3: Herald of the Mountain's Wrath, Legendary. Prerequisites: 1. Titan, giantkin, leviathan, behemoth, or colossus bloodline. 2. Rage or rage-derived affinity. 3. Magma, or magma-derived affinity. 4. Berserk or berserk-like ability. 5. Marked by the mountain's fury. You have discovered the depthless anger of a mountain's heart, and the furious spirit of that mountain has marked you as kindred. Accepting this new Class will further mark you as a herald of the angry, sleeping gods of the earth, reminding the waking world of the smoldering anger that rests in their hearts. Class attributes: strength, vitality, will.*****

"Holy . . ." Victor struggled for words, so many questions springing into his mind that he couldn't get his tongue to form them one at a time. As Valla stared at him, he finally blurted out, "Have you ever heard the System describe anything as a god or gods?"

"The System? Never."

"I can't tell if it's being, like, figurative or literal, but it seems to be calling volcanos sleeping gods."

Valla's eyes widened. "Back up, Victor. What's the class?"

"Herald of the Mountain's Wrath. It's also legendary, and it has some pretty wild prerequisites. I think the fifth one is the hardest—a person has to have been 'marked as kindred' by the 'furious spirit' of a mountain. Also, it requires specific bloodlines, rage, and magma affinities. Like, I can't imagine those combinations are common."

"Does it interest you more than the Warlord Class?"

Victor thought about her question. He'd taken the Battlemaster Class specifically to try to get the Warlord Class offered to him. Now he had it before him and found himself less than enthused. Something in him was vibrating with excitement about the Herald Class, though, and he didn't have to try very hard to see the root of his enthusiasm. He knew it was his Quinametzin nature. He knew it was his memory of the volcano's power, the heat of its fury in the air. The volcano had saved him. More than that, it had saved the people he most cared about.

Victor had truly felt the hand of something unimaginably powerful. He'd bathed in its Energy, incorporated it into himself, and turned it against his enemies. He'd met a Warlord, one who'd come to dominate his world with that class, but what was he next to a volcano? Sure, Warlord Thoargh was strong; he'd intimidated Victor and chased him out of his world, but would he be able to stand in a volcano's fury unscathed? Victor didn't think so. This class, this Herald of the Mountain's Wrath, seemed to be offering him the chance to take what he'd experienced inside the volcano and carry it out into the world. "Worlds," he corrected himself.

"Hmm?"

"Will you be angry if I don't take the Warlord Class?"

"What? Why would I be angry? It's Khul Bach you might have a problem with."

"Tough. I'm Quinametzin, not Degh, and everything in my blood is screaming for me to take this class." It was true. He felt it in his bones, in his blood, and in his spirit, a deep reverberating sureness. He'd speak to Khul Bach about it eventually, but he didn't need the old giant's advice right then. If Khul Bach had never heard of the class, he might argue, might try to change his mind, and Victor didn't want to deal with that. Khul Bach didn't know what he'd felt when he'd stood in that caldera, steeped in the Energy of the volcano. There was something there, a connection that couldn't be described with words.

"The, um, Mountain Herald one?" Valla was smiling, looking at him in a way that he'd come to recognize as loving acquiescence; she knew he'd made up his mind. "Shouldn't you at least see if there are more choices?"

"Yeah, good call." Victor advanced the selection screen and was strangely relieved when he read:

*****Class refinement option 4: No Refinement. You are pleased with the path on which you find yourself and choose to continue until your next refinement option.*****

"No other options."

"So you're sure?"

"Yeah, more sure than I've felt about anything for a long time."

"Well, the Warlord Class will probably be available at seventy if you change your mind." Valla laughed and shook her head. "Imagine! I never thought I'd be talking so blithely about reaching Level Seventy!"

Victor struggled to find any trace of his earlier gloom as he leaned forward to kiss her. She gently returned the affection, reaching up to lightly scratch the short stiff hair on the sides of his head with her nails. Victor felt like melting into her embrace, but he chuckled, pulling himself away. "All right, I'm doing it." Before any doubt could find its way into his heart, Victor scrolled back to the third refinement option and selected it. Warmth rushed through his body as System messages scrolled before his eyes.

Congratulations! You have refined your Class: Herald of the Mountain's Wrath.

Congratulations! World-first Herald of the Mountain's Wrath! Feat awarded: Mountain's Resilience.

Congratulations! You have earned a Class spell: Wake the Earth, Basic.

Mountain's Resilience: The strength of the mountain infuses your very bones. Like the mighty rocky slopes of a slumbering god, you are resilient against the elemental Energies. You will take 80% less damage from earth, 80% less damage from fire, 50% less damage from air, and 25% less damage from water. These resistances will stack with other sources of protection.

Wake the Earth, Basic: Remind the earth under your feet of the fury that lies dormant in its depths. When you cast this spell, you will cause a violent upheaval by transferring some of your Energy into the ground beneath your feet. The size and magnitude of the upheaval will depend on the Energy you unleash. Energy Cost: Minimum 2500, scalable. Cooldown: Medium.

"Uh, this is awesome." Victor swiped the last message away, and as he refocused on his surroundings, he saw that Valla had moved away from him, standing by the door. It was only then that he realized the air was full of smoke.

"You're going to burn up the furniture!" Valla cried. Victor looked down and saw the carpet turning to ash in a circle around him and his body outlined in smoldering flames.

"Oh, shit!" Victor turned his gaze inward, saw that his pathways were absolutely flooded with magma-attuned Energy, and laboriously forced it back into his lungs and then into his Breath Core. As he did so, the flames flickered and winked out, and the heat radiating from his flesh faded to a much more tolerable level. He looked at Valla sheepishly. "Sorry about that."

She arched an eyebrow and stepped closer to him. "Are you pleased with your choice?"

"Yes! I got a title and feat for being the 'world-first' in my new Class. That's never happened before!"

"Hmm." She nodded, tapping a nail thoughtfully on her chin. "I've heard of that. Obviously, it happens less frequently nowadays, but when Fanwath was new, many such titles were handed out."

She walked in a circle around him, stomping on the still smoldering carpet. "Well? Tell me about what you gained."

Victor joined her, stomping on the ruined carpet with his much larger feet. "All right, I'll give you the details, but then I want to hear more about your new class."

"I'll make that bargain, but let's go sit upstairs while this room airs out."

"Will it?" The bottom level of Victor's home was devoid of windows, his one big complaint about it.

"I'll get a wind gust circulating, just a moment." While Valla concentrated, a soft gentle breeze flowing from her outstretched hand, Victor pulled up his status sheet and perused the details. He wanted to get the numbers right when he and Valla compared their gains:

Status				
Name:	**Victor Sandoval**			
Race:	**Quinametzin Bloodline: Epic 1**			
Class:	**Herald of the Mountain's Wrath: Legendary**			
Level:	**60**			
Breath Core:	**Elder Class: Improved 3**			
Core:	**Spirit Class: Advanced 8**			
Breath Core Affinity:	**Magma: 9**	**Breath Core Energy:**	**2200/2200**	
Energy Affinity:	**Fear 9.4, Rage 9.1, Glory 8.6, Inspiration 7.4, Unattuned 3.1**	**Energy:**	**23243/23243**	
Strength:	**370**	**Vitality:**	**475 (523)**	
Dexterity:	**190**	**Agility:**	**213**	
Intelligence:	**172**	**Will:**	**553**	
Points Available:	**0**			

Titles & Feats:	Titanic Rage, Ancestral Bond, Flame-Touched, Greater Titanic Constitution, Titanic Presence, Desperate Grace, Challenger, Elder Magic, Born of Terror, Battlefield Awareness, Battlefield Presence, Aura of Command, Epic Quinametzin, Mountain's Resilience

Skills:	
System Language Integration	Not Upgradeable
Spirit Core Cultivation Drill	Advanced
Breath Core Cultivation Drill	Advanced
Cooking	Basic
Animal Taming	Basic
Unarmed Combat	Basic
Knife Mastery	Basic
Spear Mastery	Basic
Bludgeon Mastery	Improved
Axe Mastery	Epic
Grappling	Advanced
Sovereign Will	Advanced
Titanic Leap	Improved
Spells:	
Iron Berserk	Epic
Inspiration of the Quinametzin	Epic
Channel Spirit	Improved
Enraging Orb	Basic
Globe of Insight	Improved
Project Spirit	Improved
Dauntless Radiance	Basic
Heroic Heart	Basic
Spirit Walk	Basic

Tether Spirit	**Basic**
Harsh Light of Justice	**Improved**
The Inevitable Huntsman	**Improved**
Aspect of Terror	**Advanced**
Imbue Spirit	**Basic**
Honor the Spirits	**Improved**
Titanic Aspect	**Basic**
Alter Self	**Basic**
Energy Charge	**Basic**
Banner of the Champion	**Basic**
Wild Totem	**Advanced**
Impart Nightmare	**Basic**
Guard Ally	**Basic**
Volcanic Fury	**Basic**
Wake the Earth	**Basic**

The next day, Victor found himself arguing with Rellia; she'd ridden ahead of her portion of the legion, pushing her vidanii to its limits to get to the Sea Keep in time to personally help Victor and Lam decide what to do with the Colony Stone. They sat at his dining table with Valla, Kethelket, and Edeya, though the latter simply stared blankly, sipping from a cup of lukewarm tea Lam had given her. Victor had watched Lam touch a thin matching silver rod to Edeya's crown and tell her to drink. It was creepy, and he hated seeing Edeya that way, which was the root of his argument with Rellia. "I don't want to waste another week gathering everyone to plant the stone. We need to get Edeya help, like, starting today."

Rellia looked at Edeya, and though her eyes betrayed her sympathy, she frowned. "I understand, but consider the fact that she's already been stable like this for more than ten days. Consider also that we'll need time to build up the System stone once it's planted. It won't have the options for world travel right away. We'll need the legion members to claim their citizenship. We'll need to set up portal stones to Gelica and Persi Gables to bring our families over, and then they'll need to claim citizenship. The options for growth are dependent on citizens. Once we've done that, we'll need to sink millions of Energy beads into the stone to open up construction and development avenues in the System menu and—"

"I get it! Shit!" Victor growled, staring at Edeya, scratching his stubble angrily. "How much time are we talking?"

"Weeks, perhaps. I hope not months. We can't jump straight to world travel; we have to go through certain growth phases. The System does things in a methodical way, and, no, I'm not sure why. I'm going off books written by some of the people who were around when Fanwath was formed. They weren't easy to come by, you know; the Ridonne have done much to destroy the history of those times. Nevertheless, I think it's your best option of quickly finding reliable passage off-world unless you want to go to Persi Gables or Gelica and travel to one of the backwater worlds the Ridonne have opened up in those cities."

"What about Tharcray?"

Rellia chuckled. "By all means. Go and ask the Ridonne to allow you to use their Colony Stone. Never mind the months-long journey to get there."

Lam interrupted the speculation with some of her own, "Didn't you say Catalina probably won't do anything with Edeya's spirit right away, that she might have plans that spanned decades or centuries?"

"Lam, I don't know, though! I was just guessing, thinking aloud, trying to make people feel better. Regardless, we should hurry. I thought you'd be the first to agree with me on that point."

Lam's eyes narrowed, and Victor could see she was getting angry. She held Edeya's free hand, and her thumb outlined little circles on the young woman's palm. "I agree with you. I do. It's just that she has a good point; thousands have sacrificed for this endeavor. Should we really plant the Colony Stone here, ahead of their arrival? Is this the best place for it?"

Kethelket cleared his throat. "The central location, the one Hector held, is not an option."

"Yeah, I will recommend that you all do not build anything on that volcano." Victor couldn't keep the amusement out of his voice.

"This isn't a time for jokes," Lam growled.

"I'm not joking. Do you think I'm the only one who might be able to wake that volcano?" He didn't wait for an answer. Gesturing to Kethelket, he added, "He has a point. The central location is a no-go. We don't want the capital at the pass; what if Ridonne invades? We don't know what's south of these lands, so why build it south? We're on the western edge of the Marches, and there's a sea here. On the eastern edge, you've got more mountains. I think this *is* the best spot! Wouldn't it be smart for the capital to have a port?"

"I agree." Kethelket nodded. He and Victor had spoken at length that morning, and Victor had spent a good part of that conversation trying to apologize for the losses the Naghelli had suffered. Kethelket wouldn't hear it; he insisted that Victor was responsible for a swift victory with relatively minor losses, all told. No matter how Victor described his foolish mistake of venturing into the caldera alone and becoming trapped, Kethelket continued to point out their crushing victories over much greater numbers. More than that, he insisted that they all shared in the blame; they could have done more to hobble Victoria—Catalina. All in all, there were still more than two hundred Naghelli, and they were eager to live among the Ghelli again, no longer outcasts.

Rellia surprised him by nodding, clearing her throat, and pushing her chair back. Victor hadn't seen her in weeks, and though she looked much the same, she also looked different. It took him a while when she first arrived to realize what it was, but after he'd figured it out, it was obvious—she'd advanced her race at some point. She was taller than before, leaner with brighter eyes and more pronounced canines. He couldn't help noting how her ears curved upward through her thick lustrous red hair. He wondered if she'd unlocked the same bloodline as that catlike Ardeni he'd killed near Fainhallow after they'd attacked his airship. She stood up and rested a hand on Lam's shoulder. "I agree. We'll find a suitable site here, near the sea. Better to get the stone in the ground and start working on it."

Victor climbed to the top of the grassy hill. He could hear Lesh's steps close on his heels, but his long powerful legs devoured the slope, leaving most of the others behind. When he reached the broad flat hilltop and stood at the center, he turned in a slow circle, taking in the view. To the south, small in the distance, he saw the Sea Keep butting up to a range of rocky cliffs and hills. To the west, maybe a mile distant, the Silver Sea stretched to the horizon, glittering in the sun's light. To the north, more rolling hills fell away, and distantly on the horizon, he saw the green-blue smear of grasslands. He knew that beyond those grasslands was the burnt-out forest of Black Keep. Turning to the east, he saw the ash-dark sky hanging over more hills and valleys and, just a purple smear in the gray sky, the slope of the mighty volcano.

"A good site," Lesh rumbled. Victor turned to him and saw that many others had mounted the hill—Rellia, Valla, Kethelket, Lam, dozens of soldiers, and most of the Naghelli. He watched them continue to climb up the slope, coming into view, and that's when he picked out Chandri. She was much recovered from her injuries. Her hair was short, cut that way to keep it out of her wounds before she'd gotten the regeneration potion, but otherwise, she looked like her old self. She was even laughing at something the soldier beside her had said.

"I think so too. From here, the city will have space to grow out toward the sea and in every other direction. And this hilltop is the highest around—a good place to defend." Victor watched as Valla approached, and she smiled brightly, waving. She could have flown up ahead of everyone, but she kept Lam company, holding one of Edeya's hands while Lam held the other. As he stared at her, his eyes wandered to Lam, Rellia, and even Edeya; they all looked stunningly beautiful in the bright sunlight, their clothing clean and colorful, their eyes glittering like jewels as they flashed smiles, talking excitedly. Victor hoped their good mood wasn't misplaced; he hoped he was right and they'd still be able to help Edeya. It made him nervous that Lam was acting as though it was a sure thing. He figured that might be how she coped with the stress.

He waited a few more minutes until almost everyone had assembled, forming a big loose semicircle around him at the center of the hilltop. Lesh stepped back and sat in the grass near Kethelket, and Victor raised his voice. "Everyone! Give your attention to Legate ap'Yensha!" He locked eyes with Rellia, and she smiled and nodded.

"Soldiers! Fellow citizens of these new lands! Our time has come to make our claim! I rushed to get here, but many other worthy comrades are also hurrying to join us, so let's keep them in our hearts on this momentous day! Today, we found our colony. Today, we claim our freedom! Today, we begin building toward something great, leaving our mark on this world so that our children's children will remember us and be grateful for the freedom we fought for, for their lives unburdened by the yoke of Ridonne oppression!" She smiled and nodded as her words were drowned in cheers and applause. The soldiers were happy for her praise, but everyone knew the situation. Everyone knew that Edeya, standing there with a blank expression, desperately needed help, and that the Colony Stone was the fastest way to get it for her.

When it didn't seem that Rellia would say more, Victor hollered, "Glorious Ninth! We're here because of your bravery!" Again, the soldiers went wild with cheers, and Victor saw Agnes and some of the other former thralls shaking their fists in the air, howling with excitement. They'd fit in well with the cohort, and it looked as though they'd made many friends, judging by how close the others crowded around, exchanging slaps on the shoulders. "I don't have much more to say other than I'm proud of you all. We're going to build something amazing here."

Victor smiled and turned away as the crowd continued to applaud. He looked questioningly at Rellia, then Lam and Valla. When they all nodded, he hefted the heavy System-created Colony Stone and knelt in the grass, twisting it with the slightly broader end until it was stuck in the grass, standing upright. Nothing happened, and Victor chuckled; what had he expected? He had to activate it. "Channel some Energy . . ." Lam called, but Victor lifted a hand and waved her off. He knew how to kick-start a magical item. He pulled a thread of inspiration-attuned Energy out of his Core and sent it out through his palm into the stone.

*****Colony Stone, activate at the present location?*****

Victor smiled and turned to nod at the largest part of the crowd behind him. "Yes."

*****Who is the leader of this settlement?*****

Rellia had prepared Victor for this. As soon as she'd realized they were going to go through with the colony founding that day, she'd walked Victor through a ten-page dissertation about the Colony Stone and what he should do to set it up properly. As he sat there, contemplating the question from the System, Victor knew he could be selfish and claim the colony for himself. He could even make himself a dictator like the Warlord in Coloss. "I'm not that kind of *pendejo*, though." He spoke aloud, low so only he could hear himself, but he almost had a heart attack when the prompt flashed in his vision:

*****Who is the leader of this settlement?*****

Seeing it was the same question, his racing heart slowed, and Victor carefully said what Rellia had written, "Rellia ap'Yensha, Victor Sandoval, Lam, daughter of Fellis from Twilight Home. A temporary triumvirate with equal voting authority and weight." Lam and Rellia had some sort of landholder republic in mind, and Victor didn't know enough about the subject to want to argue. He just wanted his share of the lands they'd conquered. The temporary triumvirate would serve until they'd opened more options up in the stone, and she could change things around.

*****What is the name of your settlement?*****

Victor smiled and loudly proclaimed, "The Free Marches." Of course, cheers broke out around him as the prompt disappeared, and he heard the sound of thousands of tiny cracks splitting the stone. Heat and steam burst forth from the seams, and Victor grinned, inhaling the hot gasses, utterly unfazed.

"What's happening?" someone cried, and he realized he was leaning over the stone, watching, and blocking almost everyone's view with his bulk. He stood up and backed away, watching as in seemingly random order, segments of the stone split apart, stretched, and then re-fused with the whole. This occurred over and over, hundreds or thousands of times; all the while, steam lit with golden highlights burst forth from the splits in the stone. With each cracking and fusing, the obelisk grew, and Victor continued to back up until he was standing beside Valla.

The crowd became quiet, watching, mouths agape, as the stone grew to immense proportions; after a minute or two, there was so much steam flowing down the sides of the hilltop that it rose to even Victor's hips, and some people had to cough and wave it away from their faces. The stone continued to grow, cracking, fusing, and emitting gouts of dense steam the whole time. After what must have been fifteen or twenty minutes, it finally started to slow and gradually settled into its final solid shape. The little obelisk-shaped stone was now a true monolith, towering forty feet into the air, each of its six facets measuring four feet wide at the base.

The enormous monolithic stone had planted itself in the ground, and its dark gray surface ticked as it settled. Victor watched as the golden runes seemed to float up from the depths, hovering and shimmering just beneath the stony surface. As the steam blew away on the wind, a System message appeared in front of his eyes:

*****Colony: The Free Marches, established. Initial area of influence: The lands granted in the System-generated conquest challenge—66 million acres south of the mountains known as the Granite Gates, east of the body of water known as the Silver Sea, and bordered on the south and east by as-yet-unnamed mountain ranges. Current population: 3. Colony Stone level: 1.*****

ABOUT THE AUTHOR

Plum Parrot is the pen name of author Miles Gallup, who grew up in Southern Arizona and spent much of his youth wandering around the Sonoran Desert, hunting imaginary monsters and building forts. He studied creative writing at the University of Arizona and, for a number of years, attempted to teach middle schoolers to love literature and write their own stories. If he's not spending time with his dog, you can find Gallup writing, reading his favorite authors, or playing *D&D* with friends and family.